Sagamore Gold

– W J CRITCHLEY –

An environmentally friendly book printed and bound in England by
www.printondemand-worldwide.com

Mixed Sources
Product group from well-managed
forests, and other controlled sources
www.fsc.org Cert no. TT-COC-002641
© 1996 Forest Stewardship Council
FSC

PEFC Certified
This product is
from sustainably
managed forests
and controlled
sources
PEFC
PEFC/16-33-415
www.pefc.org

www.fast-print.net/store.php

SAGAMORE GOLD
Copyright © W J Critchley 2011

All characters are fictional.
Any similarity to any actual person is purely coincidental.

ISBN 978-178035-040-0

First published 2011 by
FASTPRINT PUBLISHING
Peterborough, England.

Acknowledgements

The author wishes to thank his daughter, Carole, for her encouragement over the years that it has taken to create this story. I also want to thank my long-time friend, and editor of this novel, Daren Johnson, for his suggestions and great knowledge of America.

Introduction

This novel is a family biography of a miner's family, in the North of England during the pre-war years. England during this time was beginning to slip from the shackles of a class system of hereditary aristocracy, the origins of which dated back long before the Victorian era.

There existed, and remains, a constitutional monarchy. A similar change evolved among the titled nobility in that nation. Whatever the causes and catalysts, from and after the Second World War in Great Britain the lines delineating social rank and economic privilege have dimmed to where they are no longer predominant. The historical, social and economic chasms have narrowed between those who derived their social and economic status from an accident of birth and those who filled the ranks of merchants, miners and the so-called working classes in that once great Empire.

Sagamore Gold is a story of a family who lived through this transition. Although the story is told in the medium of fiction, it is based on many true facts witnessed by the author. WJ Critchley has undertaken to depict the more engrossing and significant events of those whose story is told.

Our novel is not intended to tell the story of the Second World War, as such, but rather to trace the effects of that historic event on the lives of our principal characters.

Part One
Before the War

Chapter One

It was a cool and misty morning in October of 1926. James Roberts, thirty-six, was a born and bred a Lancashire man, and a miner. He dragged himself from his bed in what was called a 'row' house in the small village of Gateley, population 206. James had to get up to go to work, regardless of how good that nice warm bed felt.

Damn this damp cold that ruins decent living in the North, he thought. Goddammit! as the Americans say.

Surrendering all further mental protests, he sat up and turned to his left, as his bare feet reached the cold slate floor. Another day. He stood and changed into his work clothes.

Actually, this drill for James Roberts was not much different from any other morning, save possibly that this day was exceptionally damp, cold and overcast.

Winter was obviously imminent.

James drew a wash pan of water and washed his arms, hands and face in the sink. His wife, Celia, had got up as soon James was out of their bed. She prepared hot tea for them both and a bowl of oatmeal for James. She then made a sandwich, consisting of two thick slices of bread. It dripped with fried bacon grease. This would be James's lunch at the mine.

This sandwich was expected to sustain James's energy and alertness from noon through the rest of the day, most of which he would spend 3,800 feet below the earth's surface in a mine whose breathing air churned endlessly with the father of black lung disease, coal dust.

Celia was a frail woman, and looked much older than her thirty-one years. The hard life common to all miners' families had taken its toll. After the ritual goodbye peck, James left the house promptly at 6.15. His job in the mine started at 7 a.m. but he had to walk two miles, crossing fields, to the pithead.

He was a driller on the coalface. Drilling was very hard work, at least at the hard coal seam where James worked. The prodigious pollution of air nearly saturated with coal dust was in stark contrast with the wages. James's pay was never more than barely enough to support his wife and their two children.

James had worked in the mines since he was twelve years of age. His father had suffered the same fate, except he died at age thirty-two from non-survivable injuries he received in a roof fall; a roof 3,600 feet underground. Such hazards were lamely accepted as part of the job.

It was now 7.30, and time for Celia to rouse the children for school. The boy, Adam, was twelve years old. He was a solid, well-built lad, and very bright. His sister, Mary, was two years younger. She was a very pretty girl, with even features and blonde hair. Mary was always smiling and singing funny little songs she seemed to make up as she went along. Adam used to tease her all the time. They both liked going to school and got on very well with the teacher, Amos Cooper. The school was the only one in the village. It was a one-room affair furnished with small joined but movable desks that were moved to the sidewalls on Sundays. On the Sabbath, the school became the only church in Gateley where Anglican services were regularly conducted by a vicar from Lancaster, or sometimes Preston.

Between the two great wars, most of the North of England was bereft of anything resembling prosperity, at least among the working classes. This unfortunate reality was well reflected in the Roberts family. As Adam turned twelve in 1926, his school attendance was reduced to three days per week, thereby permitting him to seek odd jobs along the Lancaster canal where it ran by Gateley.

Directly or indirectly, the patchwork of lesser canals in the North of England all fed into the 'master' waterway known since its inception in 1773 as the Leeds and Liverpool canal. This historic canal, spanning England from Leeds in Yorkshire to Liverpool on the west edge of Lancashire, was a major transportation artery in the massive canal system that criss-crossed Britain. It was the main eastbound highway on which imported raw materials of every description made their way from the great port of Liverpool to the hundreds of mills, mines, and factories in the North of England. The profusion of those facilities reflected the industrial demands of the Great War and the economic binge that followed, the Roaring Twenties. Leeds and Liverpool was also the main westbound 'highway' for the output of those same mills, mines and factories.

Chapter Two

When young Adam Roberts started doing odd jobs along the nearby canal, he was usually just running errands. Then he talked an elderly liveryman into teaching him how to harness horses. In 1926, horse-power was still the principal propellant of barges in the North of England. The gregarious young Adam soon was getting farthings, then halfpennies, to help weary boatmen remove the harness from their weary horses at the local livery. As he endeared himself to more and more of the passing boatmen, sometimes he was allowed to take the tiller, steering the barges for a short time. This was his favourite job, even though it produced no earnings.

Adam was well liked by the barge operators. Their satisfaction with him showed in the few extra pence they would slip him. He was bigger and stronger than all the other lads who were also adding to their families' tiny incomes by doing odd jobs along the canal.

The captain on most barges was usually the man of a family who lived on the barge. Often the wife or one of their children would lead the horse that pulled their barge. Sometimes, of course, a barge would be manned by a couple of partners, who shared the chores of leading the horse and manning the tiller. Sometimes a lone boatman would man the tiller, and keep his horse's attention off the tasty sweet grass along the canal path by using a catapult, which was a sling shot for firing stones at the horse's rump, if necessary.

When barges approached a village, such as Gateley, the local kids for hire would gather along the side of the canal in hopes of getting a signal from a passing boatman indicating he wanted the youngster to open and close a lock, lead his horse for a while or run the odd errand.

Most of these odd jobs for village kids came from the smaller crews of passing barges; typically a man and his wife, both of whom often needed a respite from leading their pull-horse.

Whether the job involved opening or closing the locks, leading the horses or running errands, Adam increasingly became the lad of choice among the passing boatmen. He was bigger, stronger, smarter and faster than his peers. As this fact became better known, the passing boatmen wanting some local help at Gateley increasingly scanned the cuts for that 'biggest kid'. That was Adam Roberts.

If the job involved leading the horse, Adam had a way of perking up the animal's enthusiasm for his bestial job. He talked to the horse. The boatmen could hear talking, and see their animal's favourable response. However, they could never hear what it was that Adam was saying. Trade secret.

During the next two years, Adam Roberts learned many new skills that were all exciting new adventures to him.

As the 1920s got nearer to the 1930s, a visible transition occurred that ultimately displaced horses entirely from the work of pulling barges. The advent of the diesel engine changed everything. Diesel oil was cheap. Diesel engines didn't take up much barge space. They didn't have to be led along a canal path. They weren't distracted by sweet grass. They didn't require hay, rests or veterinarians, and they never fell into the canal or caused the calamity those unusual events always brought about.

In a more positive vein, the diesel engine was more than adequate to provide for the propulsion needs of even the largest and fully loaded barge.

Before the worldwide stock-market crashes in 1929, the needs and production of the mines, mills and factories in the North created an eternally expanding need for barges. The ever-increasing number of barges in use was exemplified by the common sight of long lines of barges at Wigan Pier being loaded, or unloading their cargoes of timber, cotton, industrial and farm equipment, linen, calico, cloth, coal, limestone, and so on. The railroads provided some competition, but barges transported the great bulk of all commerce.

Both the canals and the railroads were under the strict control of Parliament. Accordingly, the larger barging enterprises, such as the Leeds and Liverpool Canal Company, maintained an effective staff of solicitors, accountants and other professionals in London whose jobs were to impede the spread of the railroads whenever possible. In the end, the five-mile-per-hour barges lost out to the many-more-miles-per-hour trains. But that end came decades after the Roaring Twenties.

In terms of cause and effect, the enormous expansion of barging between the two wars was reflected by the increasing barge traffic on the maze of connecting canals, particularly in the North of England.

Chapter Three

Walter and Lil White were in their late forties. They were only in their late teens when they married. By 1926 they had the largest privately owned barge operating on the Lancaster and the Leeds and Liverpool canals. It was a sixty-footer, with a wide beam and was painted bright yellow with red trim. They had excellent living quarters specially built in the bow, below deck, which enabled them to enjoy their lifestyle thoroughly.

Walter and Lil had a special affection for Adam, which was a testament to his own winning good nature. Undoubtedly, their feelings were influenced by the fact that they had no children of their own. They had first come to know Adam when Walter worked with Adam's father in the mines. The Whites, however, saw only a grim future in working coal mines. After much thought, many discussions and much saving they made the very wise decision to make a great change in where they lived and how they made their living. They invested practically their life savings to buy the barge they now called home. Walter had urged James to make a similar change. But James declined, feeling the security of his family was his first priority. He stayed in the mines.

Although young Adam worked doing odd jobs along the Lancaster canal as it wended its way past Gateley, he always preferred helping Walter White. The Whites operated mainly from the Albert Dock in the Port of Liverpool, where Walter's long-time friend Bob Harrison was the chief dock foreman. Such men were in charge of everything that happened at the Albert Dock, one of the preeminent docks in the Port of Liverpool. Thus Walter was to virtually have his pick of barging cargoes from that great port to and from the mills and factories in Lancashire. Being frequently in that area, the Whites were able to maintain their lifelong friendships with the numerous acquaintances in Gateley, Wigan and its environs. Walter refused to haul coal or limestone, and his clean, well-kept barge openly reflected this wise decision. This gave him an edge in attracting the hauling business of the higher-quality mill owners who didn't want their cargoes of linens and silks sullied by the dusts that stayed on barges long after their ore deliveries were completed – or not infrequently 'lightened' a bit by the likes which operated the grimy scows that lined up at the hoppers.

As Adam approached his thirteenth birthday, Walter started teaching him to work the tiller in steering a barge. Adam was ecstatic. It had long been Adam's ambition to own his own barge; when he was older, of course.

At the end of every day he worked, Adam would race home and proudly hand over to his mother the money he had earned. Very ceremoniously they would count it, and Celia would put it in the small tin box that Adam kept under his bed. As he was returning this treasure to the dark place of safety under his bed, Celia would always smile, embrace him, and feel grateful to have such wonderful son.

Adam and his younger sister, Mary, were very close and fond of each other. Adam was born in 1914; Mary in 1916. The contrast in their relative physical size was striking. Almost since infancy, Adam had been big for his age, raw-boned and tall. Mary, on the other hand, was fine-boned, and quite petite. By the time Adam was twelve, he was a head taller than his sister. Somehow, this difference seemed to induce a very protective sense in the lad. In the evenings, Mary always looked forward to hearing everything Adam had done that day on the canal. He would then let Mary help him count the money in his tin box. As James and Celia heard their children counting, they both hoped their offspring would grow up with a sensible perspective on money.

Each week the amount in the tin box grew a little. Just enough to give the lad the feeling he was really making progress. Not infrequently during 1926, the immediate food or clothing needs of the family compelled Celia to withdraw some of that money. All this would be explained to Adam whenever such necessity arose. Rather than harbouring any sense of losing his money, Adam would always feel his importance in supporting the family had just increased a mite.

Adam liked to tell Mary that when he grew up, he was going to own several barges, and earn a lot of money. Today, such castles in the air would be described as fantasy. But Adam and Mary took it all very seriously; especially when Adam promised he would look after his 'little sister always'.

Between 1926 and 1928, practically everything with the Roberts family went well. In those two years, Adam gained three inches in height, and he was visibly filling out in his chest and arms. When he turned fourteen in 1928, the small family could afford a small birthday celebration party in their small home, Row House Number 28.

One particularly favourable turn was that James was moved to work at a different part of the mine, which had a much softer seam of coal. It was a lot easier for James to drill the holes in the softer coalface, which markedly reduced the time between the dynamite blasts that freed the coal. Happily, this turn of events resulted in almost doubling James's earnings, which eased the Roberts family living conditions considerably. Not enough, unfortunately, to permit Adam to spend time at school and work less on the canal.

Because of the descending local landscape, about a third of a mile west of

Gateley a lock had been built into the Lancaster canal. This lock could accommodate two regular-size barges at a time. Gateley could not, or at least did not, afford a lock-keeper until 1937. Before then, closing and opening the lock was done by the boatmen themselves, or by a strong young local lad whom a boatman was willing to pay threepence.

With Adam's increasing growth and maturity, he was ever-proving he could handle the more difficult jobs, such as opening and closing the lock, and, under Walter's tutelage, positioning barges under the coal hopper. As with most callings, time is money. Thus it was in a boatman's interest to spend his time getting better hauling orders from dock foremen, while a capable young man would steer his barge about a pier after it was unloaded and moved to where its next cargo would be taken on.

When Adam acquired the proficiency of steering barges about in their turnaround, his daily trips to the tin box at day's end became increasingly more enjoyable.

In 1928, Celia and Mary had been making lots of little improvements to the cottage. Between James's good fortune in his job assignments and Adam's increased earning capacity, they had a little more money for such purposes. Although it was only August, all the family was looking forward to Christmas, and both the parents and the children began to generate increasing enthusiasm over the anticipated Yuletide. A new attitude within the Roberts family must have been quite apparent; at least it was the subject of comments exchanged between others living in Gateley.

On the second Sunday in August of that year, following the church services but before the children's Sunday School adjourned, Amos Cooper told James and Celia how impressed he was with the school work being performed by both Adam and Mary. That, and his comments about how good they both looked, made James and Celia feel very proud. They thanked Mr Cooper for his kind words. Just after this exchange, Adam and Mary came bursting out of the Sunday schoolroom of the little village church, and the family departed for the usual long way back to their cottage.

Every Sunday they would take this long way home, which was back down the lane, across the bridge, and through the woods to a pub named the Navigation Inn. The inn was a very popular meeting place for most of the villagers, particularly after church services on Sunday. Behind the inn was a large field which was ideal for the children to play their games and to drink endless glasses of homemade lemonade. The recipe for the lemonade had been left at the inn by a grateful traveller, who had lost his way and been given shelter at the inn. The local myth was that if you drank three such glasses before sunset you would have good luck which would last until the following

Sunday. Then, of course, you would have to buy three more glasses for the children next Sunday. Naturally, all the villagers knew it was a good story to boost the sales, made up by the present innkeeper. But the children believed every word, as they consumed the beverage in prodigious amounts.

Another pub attraction was Edward the donkey, whom the pub owner kept for the children's entertainment in a small paddock in the field behind the pub. Edward wasn't particularly clever or anything else, but he never ceased to fascinate the kids.

Mrs Barker was believed to be the oldest person in the village, although no one knew for certain just how old she was. She said he had 'always' been there. Mrs Barker was well known and well regarded throughout the area. She assisted in childbirths, in laying people out for their burial, and she was respected for her herbal remedies.

All these subjects and countless others were discussed regularly among the villagers who gathered at the Navigation Inn on Sundays. Between the chinning and the children larking about in the field hosted by Edward the donkey, everyone always seemed to have a good time.

Chapter Four

By the time he reached his sixteenth birthday in 1930, Adam was almost six feet tall. His body had become that of a man. In fact, he was often taken as a grown man by strangers who had seen him only from behind. His facial features remained quite youthful until he was in his mid-thirties. By that time, of course, the worldwide depression was visiting all manner of hardship everywhere. Lancashire in the North of England was no exception. Somehow the mine where James Roberts worked stayed open, and the Roberts family was spared some of the grimmer hardships that often became commonplace among the working classes.

Walter White maintained his working relationships with the upmarket mills and factories he had been serving for almost ten years. While those enterprises had to cut back production because of diminished worldwide demand, for the most part the better-capitalised business remained afloat. It was the more marginal operations and the already-not-so-prosperous people who took the full brunt of the depression.

Walter had kept a close eye on Adam's growing up, and he very much liked what he saw. Adam was able to get enough schooling from Amos Cooper to enable him to write well and to read very well. His natural aptitude for mathematics and grasp of the fundamentals of bookkeeping were nothing short of remarkable. As the worldwide depression that began in 1929 played out, the Roberts family was indeed often strapped for cash. Those hard times forced them to live very frugal lives, very similar to their peers in England's working classes. The Roberts' advantage over their peers lay in their upbeat attitude and their strong belief that a better life was out there for those willing to do the work necessary to get there. The poor attitudes of the many became self-fulfilling prophesies. Those who were convinced that everything was going to the dogs seemed to have an uncanny knack of proving how right they were – individually.

Like his parents, Adam would have none of the pessimism which he often heard from his peers. They're just making excuses for why they always come in second, if they come in at all, he thought. Just exactly what his father had been telling him all along.

When Adam got a job, he did it as promptly and as perfectly as he could. His zeal and his increasing capabilities were not lost on the dock foremen or the more capable boatmen, and particularly, not on Walter White.

Two days before his eighteenth birthday in 1932, Walter summoned Adam aboard his barge and told him that he had just concluded several new hauling deals with a number of people, mainly in the Liverpool area, and that he'd saved enough to get a second barge, which would be required to handle the new business. Then Walter made the speech that changed Adam's life.

'I put this deal to you, Adam,' said Walter, just as if he was talking to a grown man. 'You come to work for me full-time operating a second barge. You work for wages for two years. If things go right – and, listen now, it'll be up to you and me to be sure they do go right – I won't want you working for wages after that. I'll make you a partner and, together, we'll succeed while all these griping sods you always hear whining about this and that, well, eh, they can all go to the devil. We'll succeed while they whimper. How does all this sound to you?'

Needless to say, Adam was thrilled and dazzled at what he had just heard. All of Walter's words were a little beyond him, but he knew Walter didn't deal in codswallop. To signal his concurrence, Adam's face broke into a broad smile, and his right hand shot out to seal the deal by shaking hands.

Walter shook his hand vigorously and almost triumphantly uttered one word: 'Done.' Then he called to Lil to bring in the teapot. 'We've got something to toast,' he said.

Adam had no idea what Walter would pay him for full-time. He just knew that Walter was the finest man, next to his father, he'd ever known, and he was certain that Walter would treat him right.

At his age, Adam just assumed that 'partners' in a business were always fifty-fifty. Aside from the reality that this is not usually the case, as between Walter White and Adam Roberts, that's exactly how it all turned out.

Walter did get work where others failed to do so. Adam did prove to be the best man Walter could have joined with in business. And at the party held in the Roberts' small cottage on Adam's eighteenth birthday, Walter joyously announced that during the next two weeks, the new barging company of White and Roberts would register with the Liverpool Port Authority, and wherever else it was necessary.

Both James and Celia were bursting with pride. Mary was also happy, but she was simply too young to realise how her big brother had just positioned himself for a much more rewarding life than his parents had ever known.

The year 1932 was no record-setter in terms of prosperity generally, but in ways far too numerous to count, it was the greatest year that had ever happened to Adam Roberts, eighteen, of No. 28, Cottage Row, Gateley, Lancashire.

Chapter Five

Walter anticipated correctly that Adam would accept his offer of working for him as the route to a future partnership. He had already had some serious discussions with an ageing barge operator named Richards in Liverpool about buying his barge. It was a fifty-footer that had, admittedly, seen better days. Nevertheless, if was far from being worn out, and best of all, it was equipped with a fairly new diesel engine. Richards was ready to retire, and he had told the Liverpool dock foreman of his intentions. That was like putting a notice on a bulletin board. Within the week, several boatmen had approached him about buying the barge. Their problem was that Richards wanted cash, so he could 'toss it all in' and go to Cornwall. He planned to spend his last years with his unmarried sister, who was a schoolteacher and was also about to retire. God love her, she owned a small cottage on the edge of Newquay that had two bedrooms.

Few boatmen had the cash it took to buy the Richards barge. Walter White did. He and Lil had long known how to live well but frugally. They also knew how to set aside small amounts of money regularly, which they deposited safely in the most unlikely cranny, right there on their own barge. By the time Walter wanted to buy Richards' barge, he had the necessary cash. He closed the Richards deal within the week after his serious conversation with Adam.

The Roberts family understood that Adam's going to work for Walter meant he would begin living on the barge that Walter would provide for him. Celia packed his clothes as she sadly prepared for her wonderful young son's imminent departure. At the Roberts cottage, there were moist eyes all around as the close-knit Roberts family had their last meal together before Adam's departure. It was an early meal because the coach Adam would be taking left Gateley for Preston well before noon. Adam repeatedly said he would write regularly and stay in touch, and made all the usual promises one would expect in a close family wedded to the work ethic.

It was agreed that Mary would be the one to walk Adam to the coach stop in Gateley. Both James and Celia knew that if they went they wouldn't be able to hold back the tears, and they didn't want Adam leaving with that sight in his memory. Mary was too young to appreciate the big change in family life that was about to occur. She was delighted that she would the one to see Adam to the coach. In Preston he would board another coach bound for Liverpool direct.

Shortly before 2 p.m., Adam came walking up to Walter's barge at the Albert Dock in Liverpool, exactly as he had promised. The Richards barge was tied three berths to the north. By then it had been thoroughly scrubbed, partially repainted and put in fit condition for Adam to start working right away. Lil made sure that the living quarters were both clean and properly furnished.

Adam had arrived at the coach station nearest the Liverpool dock. Inside the station he saw a man seated at a desk by a large sign that read, 'Traveller's Information Desk'. The man gave him directions to the Albert Dock.

'About a twenty-minute walk. Out that door, bear right, up the High Street to the Golden Crown, bear left, straight on. You can't miss it.'

Thus informed and assured, the husky young lad from the small village of Gateley set out in England's third largest city, trying desperately to remember just what that friendly fellow at the information desk had said. Nevertheless, exactly twenty-one minutes later, Adam walked on to Walter's barge and rapped at the door to the living quarters.

Lil opened the door and there was an immediate joyful reunion. Lil poured the tea and served the biscuits. A jabbering session ensued in which Adam answered all their questions about his family and the coach trip to Liverpool. Walter told him about finalising the barge deal with Richards, and how delighted they all were to be getting underway.

To get his young charge off on the right foot, Walter decided to join him on his first assignment. This part of getting underway began during the mid-afternoon of Adam's day of arrival. Walter walked him to the little office of the Albert Dock foreman, Bob Harrison.

The Albert Dock was one of the larger docks built along the east side of the Mersey estuary that made up the Port of Liverpool. Its volume of operations was so great that it was partitioned into separate loading and unloading zones, which were built at the water's edge next to great warehouses where most cargoes were stored and sorted before proceeding on to large merchant ships or the not-so-large barges, depending on their destinations. At the Albert Dock, Bob Harrison had a separate loading foreman and unloading foreman. By 1934, Harrison had his pick of the most capable men to fill these jobs, and he truly ran a superbly efficient operation. The computerised complexes of today operate unquestionably a great deal faster, but not a whit more accurately than the receipt–store–dispatch operation which Bob Harrison brought to the Albert Dock in the early thirties.

Bob Harrison was seated at his desk when Walter and Adam walked in. Walter made the introductions. Which were followed by the traditional shaking of hands. Bob eyed Walter's new, albeit quite young, man and was pleased at what he saw. Walter said a few words about how optimistic he was about how fast Adam would 'fit in' to the operations. Then he asked Bob Harrison whether he had a cargo for, say, Wigan, that he could take the next day, 'By way of showing Adam how we do this sort of thing from Liverpool.'

The dock foreman sorted through a stack of bill of ladings stored in an open wooden box with 'Wigan' printed on the side, and withdrew two sets, each joined with a metal paperclip.

As he was sorting, Adam's attention swept the open faced honeycomb of wooden boxes on the wall behind the foreman's desk. His eyes flared with delight when he spotted the box along whose top he read, 'White and Roberts'.

'It's to and from Wigan,' Bob announced. 'Cotton up. Linen back. Alton Mills is the customer, both ways.'

Alton Mills was a big and busy linen mill in Wigan, big enough to have reserved space at both Wigan Pier and at the Albert Dock.

Walter thanked Bob, who handed him a number of carbon copies of the bill of ladings, saying, by way of explanation to Adam, standing at Walter's side, 'One for each of our local loading and unloading foremen, one for the dock foreman in Wigan and, of course, one of each for 'White and Roberts'.

Walter turned to Adam, saying, 'I'll go over these with you outside.'

Walter and Adam bade Bob Harrison goodbye, and walked towards Adam's barge.

As they strolled along the dock, Walter pointed out the loading sections and the unloading sections and told him the names of the foremen in charge of each.

'Those are the men you have to get your berth assignments from before you load and when you arrive with a load. They also have to sign the bill of ladings marked "Company's Copy", so we can get paid.'

Adam paid rapt attention.

They stopped at the entrance of a wire-fenced area, over which the sign read, 'Albert Dock – Loading'.

'Let's stop in here and get our loading berth assignment,' said Walter, handing the "To Wigan" bill of ladings to Adam, and pointing towards the small loading foreman's shack just inside the open gate.

Walter introduced Adam to the loading foreman, a much older man, whose enthusiasm for mere lads was something less than obvious. Adam handed him the invoice, which the older man studied briefly. Then he looked at a map on his wall, and uttered two words, 'Berth nineteen.'

With that utterance he turned his head to study something on his desk. Both Walter and Adam had the distinct impression the meeting was over. Walter gestured towards the open door, and they walked out of the loading zone. The proceeded on to where the Richards barge was tied down.

'This is it, Adam,' said Walter, pointing to the new barge. 'Let's go below.'

Adam contained his excitement at having his barge, but his eyes swept every inch of her he could take in as they proceeded down the short ladder-type stairs that led to the living quarters.

Once they were below, Walter opened a built-in cabinet, from which he withdrew a new hardbound Activity Log. The two sat at a tiny table, where Walter explained the procedure which Adam would have to follow in keeping this log for each day he worked. Using the invoices he had just received from Bob Harrison, he showed Adam where and how he would enter each day's bill of lading numbers, and the dates, times and places of all of his departures, and the arrivals of his trips. If he were to take on diesel fuel, the date, time, place and quantity of that would be recorded also.

'Just think of it this way, Adam,' Walter explained. 'If you were off, say, making a short visit to your family, and I needed to know every place you'd been with this barge, and anything about anything you'd handled en route, I could come down here and read this activity log you've kept, and I'd have the information immediately.

'This doesn't have anything to do with checking on you – Lord knows if that were involved we wouldn't be sitting here talking now,' he continued. 'But understand, all the time I get all kinds of questions from dock foremen, shippers, receivers and so on, and I have to have a record I can rely on to give them right answers. I keep the same kind of log for that very purpose. As to any trip you've made or cargoes you've handled, all I'd have to do is check your activity log and I'd have all the necessary answers, even if you were away. Believe me, Adam, you'll get into the habit of keeping this record routinely. Just think of it as like keeping a kind of diary.'

'Oh, I understand, Mr White.'

'Adam,' interrupted Walter, smiling, 'from now on, it will be "Walter", not Mr White. Understood?'

Walter's words and mood caused Adam to feel more relaxed and a smile crossed his face.

'Understood.'

At the end of this conference, Walter handed Adam the bill of ladings and said, 'Take her to our loading berth.'

Walter watched closely as Adam made his pre-trip check of the barge before starting the diesel engine. He was pleased to see that Adam first checked the oil level in the crank case, and then the fuel tank. All being well, Adam started the diesel engine and neatly manoeuvred the barge to their assigned loading berth.

Under Walter's watchful eye, Adam gave a copy of the bill of lading to the loading dock foreman, who had come to confirm that the young man who had tied the barge to the pier had done so securely.

Walter then told Adam the location of a shop nearby where he would be able to get groceries for his meals for a week.

The cotton bales were being wheeled on board when Adam returned with his food supplies. He had declined Walter's offer to have his supper with the Whites. He wanted to get on with learning to 'do for himself'. For his supper that night he heated scouse sold at the small grocery in quart jars. Scouse is a stew well known for decades in Liverpool.

That night was the first time in his life that Adam Roberts, eighteen, ever slept on a barge. It would not be the last.

The next morning, Walter watched as Adam followed the required preliminary pre-starting procedures, then started his engine and made no mistakes in steering the barge along the Leeds and Liverpool canal, and right to the designated place for delivering the Alton Mills loads at Wigan Pier. After the cotton was removed, Adam did all the right things to move the barge to the Alton Mills assigned area of the Wigan loading dock. Then he took the bill of lading copy marked 'Company Copy' and another copy to the Wigan Dock foreman, Matt Shepherd.

Walter, of course, was ever the watchful onlooker. He was in no way surprised, but he was positively delighted at how Adam performed every aspect of his job to perfection.

Chapter Six

After Walter and Adam had their midday meal at a little pub just off Wigan Pier, they walked back to the barge, now loaded and ready for the return trip to Liverpool. As they approached the barge, a really attractive young girl with rather long silky black hair walked up to them, and spoke to Walter. She was holding a large canvas bag in one hand and a leash that led to a Jack Russell terrier in the other.

'Are you Mr White?' she asked very courteously.

'I am,' replied Walter very graciously.

The young lady went on to say that she had obtained Walter's name from the loading foreman as the man who owned the next barge most likely to leave for Liverpool, and could she ride as far as Rufford. Of course, Walter and the actual operator of this barge, Adam Roberts, would be delighted to have the company of the young lady and her cute little dog, and would both of them please be careful in stepping on board, as they were just about to leave. By the way, what was her name?

'Rose Birchall,' was the reply.

The village of Rufford was a few miles north of the Leeds and Liverpool canal. It was on a branch canal that connected the Leeds and Liverpool with the important Lancashire towns of Preston and Burscough. Neither Adam nor Walter had any intention of leaving this beautiful young lady and her cute Jack Russell dog at the junction. The extra time to take her to Rufford was no trouble at all. The scenery on board alone was well worth it.

Although learning how to handle a barge had been Adam's first love for some time, as he passed through puberty he certainly found himself increasingly liking girls, and his eye was always spotting the prettiest one around. But nothing in his girl-watching to date compared with how dumbstruck he was at the sight of Rose Birchall. She was absolutely stunning! What a beautiful girl!

As soon as she said her name, an involuntary thought crossed Adam's mind. She is just what the doctor ordered. He wanted to get to know this girl, and he wanted to make an impression on her.

'That's it,' Adam burst out.

'That's what?' asked a surprised Walter White.

'Rose,' said Adam. 'The name, Rose. Add that to Mary –' he turned quickly to face Rose – 'Mary, that's my sister's name.' He turned back to Walter. 'You asked me what I wanted to name this barge, and now I have the name. *Mary Rose*, that's just perfect. When we get to Liverpool, that's the name I want to register, and that's the name I want that ship signpainter right off the dock to pain on the bow of this barge.

'You agree, don't you Walter?' asked Adam, his eyes almost pleading.

'Yes, uh, yes, of course, Adam,' said Walter. '*Mary Rose*. Although we're going to have to spruce the old girl up a bit to live up to a classy name like that.'

All three of them then had a little laugh. Rose was taken completely by surprise with this dialogue, but she couldn't help but feel very flattered. Her face reddened slightly.

I don't know who Adam is, she thought, but I find myself certainly liking this fine young man. I wonder how my brothers would like him, or my parents. Whoa, she thought, that's getting things a bit piled up ahead, isn't it? He's never even met my family, or asked to, for that matter. Anyway, let's just see how it all plays out.

The Wigan-to-Rufford leg of this trip took about two hours. Rose sat on the deck in a little chair a few feet from Walter, who had brought up two chairs from the living quarters. Her little dog sat nearby, turning his head frequently to observe anything that moved. His leash was tied to the leg of Rose's chair. Adam stood at the stern, manning the tiller.

When they approached the Rufford lock, Rose pointed to the man standing by the lock gates. She announced rather loudly, 'That's my father. He's the regular Rufford lock-keeper.' As she intended, Adam heard every word. She waved.

Albert Birchall recognised his daughter on the deck of the approaching barge. She was hollering something and waving at him. He waved back. Then he signalled the young man at the tiller to steer his barge into the left side of the lock.

As Adam complied, he felt disappointment creep over him. He realised that feasting his eyes on this gorgeous girl was about to end.

Oh well, he thought, I'll be back through here in a few days, and with the new name *Mary Rose* painted on the bow I'll have the perfect reason for stopping by. Then I'll get to see her again, and meet the rest of her family, I hope.

As the barge neared the forward end of the lock, Adam shifted the diesel engine's gear into reverse briefly to stop the forward movement. He heard Rose call out to the lock-keeper, 'Daddy, I want you to meet my two new friends: Adam, I mean, Mr Walter White and his assistant Mr Adam Roberts.'

My, that was formal, thought Adam, but I liked it.

The lock-keeper leaned from the bank and extended an arm to shake hands first with Walter and then with Adam, who had lost no time getting from the stern up to meet the man who might someday be his father-in-law, or so he thought impetuously.

Albert then grasped his daughter's hand to assist her off the barge. The Jack Russell jumped ashore with ease.

'And guess what?' she exclaimed to her father. 'They're going to name this barge after me. Well, partly after me, and Mr Roberts' sister, Mary. They're going to register it in Liverpool as the *Mary Rose*.'

'That's right,' affirmed Walter. 'Adam's barge. Adam's idea. And I think it's a good one.'

'Tomorrow morning. First thing,' chimed in Adam. 'I'll be back by in a few days, and show you.'

Everyone was all smiles.

It was time for Albert to close the rear lock gates and begin releasing the water to lower the barge to the level of the canal to the west.

And these fine gentlemen can be on their way, thought Albert.

Farewells were expressed and Albert went about his tasks. As he did so, it occurred to him that the eager young man who had steered this barge so artfully to a proper stop in the lock appeared more than slightly interested in his attractive young daughter.

She is so very young, Albert thought, but not too young for a handsome lad like this to get interested in her. At least he's a clean-cut young man. And he seems bright enough, unlike a lot of unwashed young scum I see go through this lock every day.

When the barge had descended to the lower canal level, the forward lock gates opened fully. Adam engaged the forward gear, and the barge proceeded west at the customary five-miles-per-hour.

When they had travelled about a hundred yards, Adam turned back to see if Rose was still watching them. She was. They exchanged waves.

Adam quickly returned his attention ahead to steer the barge. He just wondered, what if.

Rose gave her father an affectionate peck on the cheek and proceeded to the lock-keeper's cottage. She just wondered, too. Her wondering came to an abrupt end when her mother called out, 'Is that you, Rose?'

•

Chapter Seven

Going with the canal current, Walter and Adam arrived at their Liverpool Pier a little over four hours later. Walter took his leave, assured that Adam would take care of the details. As soon as Adam tied the barge at the Alton Mills-designated section of the unloading dock, he handed over a copy of the second bill of lading and hastened to the painter's shack near the far end of the pier.

After getting the painter's promise to paint the names on his barge first thing the next morning, Adam went to Dock Foreman Harrison's office where he received three hauling jobs.

'Tomorrow lumber to Chester, and boxed goods back. Next day, cotton to Wigan.'

Adam received the copies of the bill of ladings gratefully.

By the time the timber was loaded on his barge the next morning, the painter had completed his work. In gilt-tinted paint, the words 'Mary Rose' glittered in the morning sun along the forward port bow. Across the stern, a considerably less expensive paint read:

Mary Rose
Liverpool

Adam's trip to Chester took him north-west from Liverpool, then about eight miles west by south-west, just beyond the English side of the Irish Sea, and then south into the canal to Chester. The entire trip was a little over thirty miles and took almost seven hours each way. Add to that an hour for unloading and to take on a shipment of boxed goods to be brought back to Liverpool, and Adam's working day was over. He arrived back at the Liverpool Pier after dark and tied down at the unloading dock. He made a small meal in his living quarters. After washing his dishes, he walked up to the Whites' barge, which was tied several berths to the north. He dropped in on Walter and Lil for a short chat and a cup of tea. Then he returned to his own barge and promptly went to bed.

All the while he had been thinking about his job for the next day: the load of cotton to Wigan. That would just compel his going through the Rufford lock, and who knows, that gorgeous girl with the black silky hair might just be at home. Anticipation hardly describes his growing zeal for his work.

Chapter Eight

The next morning, Adam was awake long before he could have his barge unloaded. He had gone promptly to the loading dock, where sixty bales of cotton from India were deposited on his barge's deck. He could hardly wait for his clearance to Wigan. First stop: Rufford. What a life!

After almost five hours, the Rufford lock came into view. Lock-keeper Albert Birchall saw the barge approaching from the west. As it got nearer, he could read the gold-painted words 'Mary Rose' along the forward port bow. He called out to his daughter, who was in the lock-keeper's cottage. That was the family's living facility that came with the job. Rose heard her father's call and sprinted to the lock to meet her company.

When the *Mary Rose* was advanced to about 200 feet from the west gate of the Rufford lock, Albert swung the entrance gate open and waved Adam into the lock. Adam slowed as he entered the lock, and did a very neat job of arresting the barge's forward motion to allow Albert to open the east gates to admit the canal flow to float the *Mary Rose* to the higher water level that prevailed from Rufford to Wigan. Rose had arrived at the lock to view the entire proceedings.

Adam tied the *Mary Rose* just beyond the lock, as Mary stood by taking in the gilt glittering name on the forward bow, 'Mary Rose'. Needless to say, Rose was bursting with pride, and Adam was simply about to burst on his own.

He could not turn this stop into any social event. He still had to reach Wigan in time to have the cotton unloaded on board, and get his return load of whatever the Wigan dock foreman decreed, so he could leave for Liverpool at first light. And when all these things occurred, he had to enter them in that activity log. Walter had told him they had to use both barges for a special job of timber to go to Oxford. He had contracted this job as 'Priority Cargo', which upped the shipping rate by thirty per cent. Lengthy social calls along the way were nothing Adam could consider seriously.

For the twenty minutes he could spend, Adam advanced his acquaintance with the Birchall family a good deal. He got to meet Rose's mother, Doris, and her two older brothers, Tim and John. They were in their late teens, and the best-natured chaps Adam had met since he had begun working for Walter. And for a lot longer than that, when he thought about it. John was nearly twenty and reflected his rural upbringing in dress, manner, and speech. Tim, who was two years younger, was not as talkative as John, but he always had a twinkle in his eyes and seemed to see the humorous side of about everything discussed. Mary had already alerted her brothers about having met this handsome young man 'from someplace north of here', who seemed a bit young to be operating such a big barge, but 'he and his boss get along like a couple of pals' and she expected he would be 'dropping by' in a few days, wanted them 'to see what his barge is named'.

All of these thoughts were going back and forth in Adam's mind as he steered the *Mary Rose* eastward to Wigan. My God, she is even more beautiful than I first thought. What a pity she's going to be visiting some relative when I come back through tomorrow. I don't know about absence making hearts grow fonder, but I sure hope she finds out that's true – at least I hope it's true.

The *Mary Rose* continued on to Wigan, and her smitten captain stood at her stern skilfully manning the tiller, monitoring the sound from his diesel engine, and totally absorbed in recounting the exciting events of the past seventy-two hours.

Chapter Nine

The next twelve months saw many changes in the life of Adam Roberts. His becoming acquainted with Rose Birchall and her family matured into first a warm friendship, and an inevitable romance. Rose was just as much taken by Adam as he was with her. He began to see her regularly on weekends, and as often during the week as his work demands would allow, which wasn't very often. More on the reoccurring side, he would make it to Rufford on Saturdays by coach. There were two pubs in the village where they often went to eat out.

Rose was unsuccessful in her efforts to get Adam to the only local dance hall, the Tango. Adam had never learned to dance, and he didn't want to be embarrassed trying to learn how in such a public establishment. He would usually 'sleep over' on Saturday nights on the couch in the small living room of the lock-keeper's cottage. All the while, he developed real friendships with Rose's mother, father and her two brothers. There was something about Adam that engendered a trust in each of them that he was an honest and hard-working young man who had no wrong designs on this young girl. His eyes were on her a seeming inordinate part of the time, but the looks were those of a decent young man, not those of a lecher.

Work for Walter involved some quite long trips, which at five miles per hour were not all that exciting. Nevertheless, Adam was keenly aware of the responsibility for the safe transporting of very valuable property. Besides, he had a lot to occupy his thoughts as his barge took him on many, many trips to many, many places to and from the Albert Dock.

During all this time, his friendship with Walter and Lil continued to grow in depth and warmness. More often than not, when they were all tied down in Liverpool, Lil would insist that Adam have supper with them and Adam was glad to do so, both for the food and the good company.

Chapter Ten

As the first year of Adam's working for Walter ended, Walter informed him that he was 'ready to discuss that partnership of White and Roberts'.

During that first year they had worked well together and made good money, for the depressed times. Walter was of a mind to be generous, but, of course, not foolish. He had worked hard in the mines to buy his first barge, and had worked not as hard but much longer hours to earn and save the money to buy the barge that Adam was operating.

Walter and Adam sat in the living quarters on Adam's barge. Walter began by explaining 'the equities' to him. 'That means "ownership interest", Adam,' he went on to explain that in order to work, a partnership must be meaningful and rewarding for all of the partners.

'I propose,' said Walter, 'that we consider this a fifty-fifty partnership. If we had both put in the same money, we would both be taking out one-half of what we earned after we paid all our operating expenses.

'I'll forget the fact,' he went on, 'that I started all this out as my business, and I'll let you buy your equity – that is your ownership – as I said, by paying me for the barge I bought for you to run when you started out with me.'

'How would I do that?' asked Adam.

'Well, as partners, we each take a monthly draw from what we've earned after paying all our operating costs, diesel fuel and the like. Each month you get credit for one-half of what we earned, but you only take out the same amount you've been taking as wages. The rest of your half goes to me until I've been repaid what I paid Richards for your barge. I figure that doing it like that, you'll have me paid off in maybe less than a year – year and a half at most, I guarantee that – then you'll have your fifty, that is your half, paid for. From then on our "fifty-fifty" means we divide equally the money we take in after paying our operating costs.

'Incidentally, Adam,' Walter went on, 'the jobs are coming in so fast that very soon we'll have to add another barge and that also means hiring a good barge man to run it. He'll be our employee.'

'Like I was your employee?' asked Adam.

'Exactly,' said Walter. 'Once we get his barge paid for, we've made our investment. From then on we start getting not only what we earn but also what we have left over after paying that employee. That's called a "return on investment", and that's when you really start to make money in a partnership.

Do you get the picture?'

Adam had done practically none of the talking in this discussion, but he had listened very carefully to everything Walter had said. It all sounded very fair to Adam. When he considered how his nineteen-year-old peers back in Gateley were probably doing, it sounded like a fantastic opportunity. Adam did not hesitate.

'Walter,' said Adam, 'you've always treated me fair to say the least, and I'll show you by how hard I work how much I appreciate what you're offering me now.'

Walter smiled and extended his right hand. 'Put her there, partner!'

Adam shook his hand vigorously, and the White and Roberts partnership became a fact that would change a good many lives in the years to come.

The next person on this scene was the first employee hired by the officially registered partnership, White and Roberts. The man's name was Norman Nelson, twenty-seven. He'd been working as a boatman on barges for eight years. The Liverpool dock foreman told Walter he thought Norman was ready to make a change, and that he was an all-round good boatman. Walter located Norman and told him what he and his nineteen-year-old partner were doing, and what they would like to do in offering him a job.

'I think I might like that,' replied Norman.

'Think you'd have any problem occasionally taking orders from my young partner?'

'Not if he's the man you describe.'

'He is. Every bit. And very bright. He's good natured, works hard. Handles a barge at least as well as I can. His activity log is accurate to the minute – I've checked on that – and I know you'll like him. I'm sure you two will get along well.'

Norman extended his right hand, which Walter shook vigorously.

White and Roberts had just hired their first employee.

Chapter Eleven

Norman joined White and Roberts in early May of 1933, exactly twenty-two days after he gave notice at his former job. During that time, Walter and Adam bought a two-year-old sixty-foot diesel-powered Kingston barge. Before closing the deal, Walter insisted the broker have the barge completely checked by the diesel-engine mechanic who regularly did the maintenance on White and Roberts barges at the Crown Bargeworks at Burscough, a small town on the Leeds and Liverpool canal about twenty miles north-east of Liverpool.

The mechanic reported that, 'This barge may be two years old, but whoever owned it must not have had much business. The original paint is barely scuffed and the engine tests like it just left the factory.'

When Norman reported for work at Walter's barge at the Albert Dock, Adam was also there to welcome him aboard. After a short tea, Adam and Walter walked Norman to his barge, which was tied down three berths away.

'This will be your regular barge,' said Walter, 'so you get to pick the name we'll register.'

Norman was quite flattered at this.

Almost gleefully, he responded, 'Why not name her *White and Roberts Three*?'

'*White and Roberts Three* it is,' said Walter as he handed him the barge keys.

Norman seemed eager to receive them.

I read that people don't work so hard for money as they do recognition, thought Walter. I think our new man is going to prove there's something to that.

During the next year, business remained very good, at least for White and Roberts. Walter was almost like a nagging housewife in repeatedly impressing on Adam and Norman the importance of making their pick-ups and deliveries 'on time – as scheduled!' He regularly checked their activity logs. He would congratulate them for all 'on-time' performance, and invariably asked about the reasons for any late arrivals or departures.

For several months after Norman joined White and Roberts, Walter quietly confirmed the logged timeliness of his colleagues by checking with the various dock foremen who had their own records of all barges' arrival and departure times. He was very pleased that the accuracy of what Adam and Norman reported was always verified.

In a sense, Walter had anticipated an historic remark by an American president years later who proclaimed that in serious matters, it was important to 'trust but verify'. The greater dividend of such performance and the head man's verifying interest was that White and Roberts generated a special reputation for reliability among dock foremen throughout Lancashire. And who did the transport agents at the mills and factories ask about getting such reliable service? The local dock foremen, of course.

Walter, being a good deal older than his two colleagues, and also the founder of the business, naturally fell into the multiple roles of billing customers, keeping the business books and scheduling all shipments, as well as operating one of the transporting barges. While Adam and Norman did their cavorting about after their day's sailing was complete, Walter and Lil poured over the books or the new bill of ladings to work out who would haul which cargoes to which destinations. Doing all of these jobs created a good deal of stress on Walter.

The evil of that unhappy fact was compounded by the additional fact that Walter was largely confined to a sixty-foot barge, which didn't afford him much opportunity for any real physical exercise.

Unfortunately the White and Roberts barging operation was just getting into full swing when Walter first began to experience aching pains that started in his left upper chest and radiated into his left upper arm. Today such symptoms would be generally recognised as angina pectoris, which is now well known as the likely precursor of a heart attack. Walter noticed that these symptoms usually occurred after he'd done some physical exertion, such as walking fast or getting into a strenuous positions in checking his diesel engine. If he rested for about five minutes, the pains went away. After three weeks of experiencing these symptoms Walter admitted to himself that something was wrong, so as the Whites were westbound on the Leeds and Liverpool approaching Burscough, he told Lil all about it.

Although she had no experience in such matters, her womanly instincts immediately signalled danger. She insisted that they tie down at Burscough so Walter could see a local doctor. Walter agreed.

Lil insisted on doing the tie-down, and that Walter remain comfortably seated in a small sofa in the living quarters. Then she walked briskly to the nearby small office of the local dock foreman. The man was seated at his desk transcribing invoice numbers as Lil entered.

'My husband, Walter White,' Lil said, when the dock foreman interrupted.

'I know him,' he said, and seeing her worried look asked, 'What's the problem?'

'I don't know,' she replied, 'but I think he's about to have a heart attack. Where's the nearest doctor?'

'Well, none here in Burscough for anything that serious,' said the dock foreman. 'Nearest doctor for anything like that would be in Southport. You're welcome to use my car,' he said, pointing toward the little Austin parked close by.

'The nearest place I know of for something like that,' he continued, 'would be Dr Barton's surgery in Southport.' He paused for a second to think. 'It's on the Scarisbrick Road, on the corner. I think the cross street is Linaker. Its about twelve miles, but it shouldn't take you long to get there at this time of day.'

He handed Lil the car keys. She thanked him and returned to Walter in the barge.

Within five minutes, the tiny Austin was speeding west on the Scarisbrick Road. Lil drove as fast as she thought she could go without causing an accident. Walter was seated in the front passenger seat. His face was quite red, and he looked very concerned. In her peripheral vision, Lil saw Walter wince. She glanced to her left and saw sweat on his upper lip. Manfully, he did not complain. Lil increased the Austin's speed by ten miles per hour, and hoped a policeman would pull them over, so she could persuade him to lead the way even faster.

Twenty-five minutes after the Whites left the Burscough dock, the single-storey brick building at the corner of Scarisbrick Road and Linaker Street came into view. Lil stopped the Austin directly in front of the entrance, over which a sign read: 'Surgery – Dr Roland Barton MRCGP'.

As the car came to a stop, Walter said, 'Lil, I feel like someone just turned a light bulb on in the front of my chest.'

She noticed that as he spoke, he was taking short, rapid breaths.

'Wait here,' she said, 'don't move. I'll get the doctor.'

She sprang from the tiny car and virtually ran into the surgery.

An hour later, Walter was resting comfortably on Dr Barton's examination table and feeling a good deal better. Once the doctor saw how things were improving, he had walked to the waiting room and invited Lil to join her husband.

Dr Barton had no doubt that his new patient had just had a heart attack. He had given Walter an experimental drug that contained nitroglycerin, which, he told them, was known to dilate the blood vessels.

'According to theory, that means the heart doesn't have to work so hard. All heart attacks inflict some injury on the heart muscle. How much depends on how bad the attack was. But the nitro's opening up the blood vessels eases the heart's work of pumping blood. That supposedly promotes its recovery.

'Looking at you now, I think you probably had a fairly mild attack, but even that is going to keep you off work for at least four to six months.'

'Six months!' boomed Walter; his face getting slightly red. 'Why, I have a business to run! I can't take off for any six months, or even four months, for that matter.'

Dr Barton gave him a friendly, ingratiating smile.

'My dear fellow,' he said. 'Of course, the choice is yours. But it is my duty to tell you what that choice is. It's between a good deal of time resting in bed or a full-time permanent rest in the graveyard. Now, knowing that, which do you choose?'

That took all the wind out of Walter's sails. He slumped in resigned defeat.

'For goodness' sake, Walter,' said Lil, trying to sound a bit cheerful, 'don't forget, we've got Adam and Norman, and with all the boatmen who are out of work, we've got our pick on who fills in for you till you get back to work. I'll manage the books, and Adam and I can work out the scheduling, even if we have to do it by phone. And, best of all, remember my sister Susan and her house in Chester that's been much too big for one person ever since Edward died and that ingrate of son of theirs left for America.

'I can tell from her letters,' Lil added, 'Susan is very lonely – poor thing. I'm sure she'll be glad to have us.'

'Well,' replied Walter, 'I guess we could switch Norman to our barge for a short while, and hire a new man to operate Norman's barge. Lord knows the devil himself couldn't pry Adam from the *Mary Rose*, which he fairly itches to take to Rufford at every opportunity.'

Chester is a small town with a colourful past. It lies at the head of the estuary of the River Dee. It was founded by the Romans as a 'headquarters city' and was later abandoned. It was revived as a commercial centre by the advent of railroads in the nineteenth century. Chester is in the county of Cheshire, which is bordered by Lancashire to the north, and Wales to the south. For a crow, the distance from the Liverpool docks to Chester is nineteen miles. By train, the distance is twenty-eight miles. By barge, it is thirty-eight miles, as a barge has to go by way of the Irish Sea. In 1935 Chester's population was just under 10,000, including Lil White's sister, the widow Susan Wooten, whose two-storey house had all of the modern conveniences, but only one occupant.

Within three weeks of Walter's heart attack, he and Lil were ensconced in the Wooten home in Chester to the absolute delight of the head of the house. When her sister and brother-in-law arrived, the dear soul felt she had been retrieved from the jaws of infinite boredom. She truly hoped the Whites would stay indefinitely. It was the widow Wooten's idea to have a second telephone installed in a back bedroom, which she converted into 'an office for Walter'. With that telephone in 'his office', after a few weeks, Walter was able to control the dispatching of the White and Roberts fleet at least as well as he had before.

After all, the White's almost opulent barge did not have a telephone. In Liverpool, he had to walk to the nearest phone to communicate with Adam and Norman, or leave messages for them with dock foremen if that was required. Norman, of course, had no objection whatever to his temporary transfer to the most comfortable barge he had ever boarded.

Norman also put Walter in contact with a twenty-four-year-old boatman who was glad to get a job. He originally came from Bristol and had five years' experience in operating barges on the canals in Oxfordshire and Lancashire. Best of all, in Walter's view, he was teetotaller, who understood and carried out his assignments. He worked out so well that when Walter did get back to work, Walter and Adam expanded the fleet to four barges. The man from Bristol remained with White and Roberts until he was drafted into the army in November of 1939.

During his convalescence, Walter tried to remain as vigorous and active as his limitations would permit. He and Lil frequently took long walks, as his strength returned. He was determined that his temporary 'lay by' was not going to spoil his building a highly profitable first-rate barging business, 'depression or no depression'. Nevertheless, that 'lay by' rendered White and Roberts highly dependent on Adam's continued good performance in the face-to-face dealing with the regular customers. Adam did not disappoint him.

Walter remained in Chester for almost a year, getting over his 'lay by.' Practically every Saturday morning, Adam would board a train for Chester, where he and Walter would spend as long as required on scheduling, discussing any new problems and deciding anything else the two had to resolve. When these weekly conferences were concluded, Adam would dash to the Chester train station to board the next train for Liverpool, where he would board a coach to Rufford. While business had chief priority over everything else, Adam's romance with Rose Birchall was the most important thing in his life. He was truly smitten.

Chapter Twelve

About 1 p.m. on the third Friday in January of 1935, Adam was piloting the *Mary Rose* south from Preston, which lies about fifteen miles north of Wigan, and twelve miles by canal from Rufford. White and Roberts' barge scheduling tried to avoid deadhead trips, but getting a return load wasn't always possible. Preston often presented this problem, as it did that Friday. The *Mary Rose* had no cargo. Her captain was en route to the lock-keeper's cottage at Rufford, where he planned to spend the evening with Rose and stay overnight, which had become something of a pattern whenever possible. Had everything proceeded according to pattern, Adam would have stayed the night and left early for Liverpool, where he would have boarded a train for Chester after tying down at the Albert Dock. Perhaps everything didn't follow that pattern because Adam decided to think through a few things that were bothering him as he passed through the quiet peaceful countryside.

I've got some things to decide and this is as good a time as any, he thought. Now, I have already decided to ask Rose to marry me, but, admit it, I haven't had the courage to ask her. Maybe I'm afraid she'll say no.

Then his thoughts took the form of a resolve.

Even if she does turn me down, I'm going to, uh, how did that guy in the movie put it? Ah yes, 'Pop the question'. I'm going to pop the question! Oh, God, she's just got to say yes.

Now, about visiting Mum and Dad and Mary. I haven't seen 'em since last August. And that's just too long. I'm not enough of a letter-writer to make up for that.

Then Adam almost felt like a light turned on in his brain.

That's what I'll do, I'll ask Rose 'the question', and when she says yes, we'll plan a short trip to Gateley for her to meet everybody, and we'll decide when we'll get married.

That'd be overnight, maybe two nights. What would her parents say about that? Well, they know I'm no spiv. I'll ask them. They're about the best people outside my family and Walter and Lil that I ever knew. I think they'll agree.

Of course, going to Gateley has to be worked out with Walter. Business before pleasure! But going to Gateley shouldn't be such a problem. I'll only be gone for a weekend, and maybe one extra day. I'll ask Lil to check for a Friday delivery to Preston or some place north of here.

Come to think of it, Walter looked really good last Saturday. But he's still not back to work, so till then about everything else comes second, I guess.

Resolving to pop the question and to rectify his family relations seemed to put Adam's mind at rest. He felt a slight thrill of anticipation as his thoughts turned to his impending arrival at the Birchall cottage at Rufford.

Three hours later Adam was steering the *Mary Rose* along the stretch of canal just north of the Rufford locks. Rose came into view. She was waiting for him, standing near the cut bank. As the *Mary Rose* drew nearer, the gold words on her port bow glinted in the descending sun. Mary knew it was Adam, and began waving to him. The sight quickened his heartbeat, and he waved back vigorously. His youthful excitement seemed to grow as he brought the *Mary Rose* to the side of canal, just short of the Rufford lock, and cut the engine. He was tying the mooring rope as Rose walked up. Her pretty young face simply radiated her love and happiness. Adam stood, and the two embraced spontaneously. It was apparent they were both smitten, and they made an awfully good-looking young couple.

This amorous sight was not lost on Rose's mother, who had a clear view from inside her cottage. She watched closely as they broke their embrace, and started walking toward the cottage, hand in hand.

After about ten steps, Adam decided it was time to pop the question. With his voice betraying a bit of nervousness, he almost blurted out, 'Rose, I'm very serious. Will you marry me and be my wife?'

Rose stopped dead. She turned to face him. For an instant she was truly nonplussed. As the full comprehension of what he had just said dawned, her face broke into a great smile. She threw her arms around his neck, looked up into his serious countenance and gleefully said, 'Why Adam Roberts, you rake, I thought you would never ask me!'

This tender moment was briefly shattered when Rose's mother called out very audibly, 'Are you two coming in for tea? We're all ready.'

Rose waved one hand toward the cottage, as if to say, 'Don't bother us,' and the two embraced again. This time, their embrace was unmistakably a very hard kiss.

Rose and Adam entered the cottage just as the family was about to sit down at the table. After the exchange of greetings, they all sat and enjoyed a nice afternoon tea featuring very tasty homemade bread, scones and cakes. After tea, John and Tim, got up to leave. Rose, suddenly said, 'All of you, stay sitting. Adam wants to say something to everyone.'

John and Tim sat back, and everyone turned expectantly towards Adam. His face went quite red. His throat suddenly became very dry. After a few seconds, which seemed like hours, Rose's father, Albert, said, 'Adam, what is it you want to say?'

Adam started by saying, 'I would like to tell you…' Then he started to stutter. Obviously, public speaking wasn't his strong suit.

Rose could not contain herself and burst out laughing. She stood up, radiating sheer exuberance, and almost shouted out, 'Adam has asked me to marry him, and I have accepted.'

There were warm smiles all around the table. It was either Tim or John who uttered the word 'Congratulations'. The news clearly set well with all of the family.

Although the marriage proposal and the announcement to Rose's family hadn't gone exactly as Adam had planned, at least as the 'planned' scenario had been running through his mind en route to Rufford, regardless, he felt very relieved. Rose had said yes. The family had been told. And everyone seemed quite pleased. What more could he ask?

John and Tim rose from their chairs and walked over to Adam. Both told him how glad they were he was going to be their brother-in-law. Rose's mother stood, walked over to Adam and kissed him on the cheek. She, too, said how pleased she was that her little girl would be marrying such a nice young man. Understandably, Adam felt on top of the world.

Rose's father went into the little parlour. He returned shortly with a bottle of wine and a corkscrew and announced. 'I think a celebration drink is in order.'

Chapter Thirteen

As the family sat enjoying the wine and engaging in small talk, a thought flashed across Adam's mind. He asked to use the telephone, as thought turned into action at an unprecedented speed.

He called Walter in Chester and told him where he was, that Rose and he had just became engaged and that since she hadn't met his family, he wanted to take her this weekend to Gateley to meet them. He explained they could go by coach and be back Sunday afternoon, but that he far better preferred to go on the *Mary Rose*, so his family could both meet Rose and get to see his barge.

'Problem is,' he continued, 'that would mean I couldn't get to Liverpool before late Monday afternoon deadhead, unless we've got a shipment to be picked up in, say, Preston or Wigan.'

'Well,' responded Walter, 'this is a bundle of news! Congratulations on landing Rose. Lil and I were betting you would. I've not seen her much since we first met, but the minute I first laid eyes on her I knew she was what my father called a peach – blue eyes, black hair, pretty face, and all.'

Realising he had strayed a bit from the business at hand, Walter got quickly got back to the subject.

'Uh, well, never mind that. Give Rose our love and tell her we're very happy for the both of you.'

Lil handed Walter a bill of lading, which she had located in the 'new invoice' pile. He scanned it briefly and returned to his phone conversation.

'I see we've got a full cargo shipment on Tuesday from Wigan to Liverpool for Talbott Furniture. The invoice lists twelve boxed items. "Large" and "heavy" are checked for all items. If you're back to Rufford by Monday evening, you can pick up that shipment at Wigan Pier early on Tuesday. That should help you to earn your way,' he concluded lightly.

'That's great,' replied Adam, 'Matt Shepherd can make out a lost invoice if he doesn't have a copy. If he has to, I'll have him call you.'

'He's got a copy,' Walter said, sounding very sure of himself. 'Probably more than one. I see this cargo is insured for £500.'

'So my being off Monday won't make any big problems?' asked Adam very earnestly.

'I don't think so. Assuming, as I do, that you won't make a habit of taking such lavish holidays at such short notice.'

Adam heard Lil laugh as Walter finished that last statement. 'Don't worry,

Adam. If we get into any binds, we'll figure it out. And give your folks and Mary our best regards.'

All that said, the phone conversation was over. Adam returned to the parlour to tell the Birchalls what he had just arranged. Then he turned to face Rose's parents with a rather serious face and asked, 'You've got no problem with Rose being gone two nights, have you? Mary – that's my sister – Mary's bedroom is plenty big enough for the both of them.'

'Well,' said Albert, obviously feigning seriousness, 'we might have to talk this over.' He paused shortly, then said rather rapidly, 'But I suppose we don't.'

Smiles broke out on everyone in the room. The relieved Adam's smile was the broadest, as he realised his father-in-law to be had just given his consent.

Then Adam called his father to tell him of his engagement and his immediate plans to visit so everyone could met Rose.

In both Gateley and Rufford that evening, in at least one house, everyone there was delighted, if not in a state of exuberance.

It was decided that everyone would retire a bit early so Adam and Rose could get an early start in the morning. Adam hardly slept that night, reclining, as usual, on the bed that was made by pulling out from underneath on the Birchall's living-room sofa. He could have slept on his barge, but he much preferred accepting the Birchall's hospitality to be nearer them all.

Chapter Fourteen

Came the dawn and everyone was up early. Rose prepared a quick breakfast of porridge, and the young couple prepared to depart. Because he made such good company, they decided to take Skipper along. His eternal good nature seemed to be signalled by his eternally wagging tail.

Shortly after 6 a.m. that morning, the *Mary Rose* started north with her three happy occupants on board. North of Garstang, they would turn on to the Lancaster canal to reach Gateley.

Neither Adam nor Rose talked a lot during most of the trip. Each seemed absorbed in their own thoughts about their future. Adam steered the tiller at the stern. Rose sat peacefully in the small wicker chair on the aft deck, content just to be with the love of her life. Skipper stood staring beyond the port rail, as if guarding against the occasional grazing sheep and a few horses in the fields they passed by.

The *Mary Rose* moved cleanly through the water under the steady power of its diesel engine that puffed its sooty black exhaust into the pristine blue sky. On one occasion during the trip, Adam and Rose were all quite surprised when they were passed by another north-bound barge loaded with forty tonnes of coal and being pulled by a very spirited horse. Adam called out to Rose, 'Oh, how the Leeds and Liverpool Canal Company could use more nags like that!'

As they approached Gateley, Adam pointed out to Rose various places along the canal where he used to work. Skipper dutifully checked every place Adam pointed for possible movement.

There was plenty room to tie up at the Gateley Pier when they arrived just before 5.00 p.m. Adam thought the whole place looked on the sleepy side, which wasn't unusual for a weekend. He didn't recognise any of the few people who were about the small pier. He selected a spot, and steered the *Mary Rose* alongside.

Chapter Fifteen

Life at the Roberts home in Gateley had not changed a great deal since Adam joined Walter. James and Celia still ran their fresh vegetable stall in Gateley on the market days, Thursdays and Saturdays. James had rented a half-acre garden plot near his allotment on which he grew more vegetables and built a small shed for his gardening tools. He and Celia now transported their own produce to market days, their youthful helpers having gone on to the tasks of growing up.

Mary had been at grammar school when Adam left for Liverpool. When she was sixteen, still a year from graduation, Amos Cooper informed her that Gateley's only doctor, Roger Tate, would like to speak to her about a job doing office work. Dr Tate's decision to hire an office assistant stemmed from a stern letter he'd received from an irate specialist in Lancaster to whom he had referred a patient. The specialist's letter informed him to refer patients elsewhere in future 'if their charts are as illegible as the one you sent with Mrs Ethyl Jones'. Dr Tate knew the specialist was actually a fine fellow, so his letter was obviously written in a fit of temper; but equally obviously, he realised that his handwriting was getting difficult even for him to read after a few hours. At his next encounter with Amos Cooper, Gateley's only doctor confided his problem. Did Amos know of any bright eager student who would have the time and wit to transcribe his visitation notes into his patients' charts, 'and maybe learn how to handle the business books, too?'

'I know just the young lady you're looking for,' assured the amiable Cooper. Mary had her first job. Salary: £1-10 per week.

Mary quickly learned to decipher Dr Tate's awful handwriting which she would neatly transcribe into his patients' charts. After her third week in this job, she no longer had to bother the doctor for any 'translations'. Once he saw she was competent in her first job, he added the job of getting out patients' bills and doing the books when the payments came in.

When Mary was about to graduate from grammar school, Amos Cooper told her he just bet she would be accepted at the Regis College in Lancaster if she were to apply. She was. Just as Adam had found the canals so intriguing, Mary found formal education one grand thrill of discovery. Her top grades accurately reflected both her high intelligence and her absorption with learning. She attended classes at St Regis fifteen hours per week, which were distributed between Mondays, Wednesdays and Fridays. She commuted to

Lancaster by coach. The financial burden in obtaining her higher education was eased by a scholarship she was given in recognition of her high grammar school grades, and the not-so-high income of her family.

Mary was able to continue her job with Dr Tate after she began college, often using her commuting time on the coach to translate his visitation notes. Neither the six-hours of riding coaches nor working an average of twenty hours a week at Dr Tate's office prevented her from being always at the top of her class at St Regis College. Without any doubt, James and Celia had produced two highly intelligent siblings.

When Adam, Mary and Skipper arrived at the Gateley pier, James was pulling a small four-wheel cart containing his scales and other light equipment from their market stall to the shed he had built on his allotment.

Celia had left the stall at noon to return home to prepare the best supper she could for everyone that evening. She prepared a meal of Yorkshire pudding and beef dripping, along with some choice vegetables she selected that afternoon from the allotment. This meal will surely delight them all, she thought. It did.

As soon as Adam had his barge securely tied to the dock, he, Rose and Skipper (now on a short lead) set off. Adam led the way. They walked first along the towpath to the village, over the old bridge near the Lune estuary, through the woods, and then through the middle of the village. Ironically, at one point they walked by the closed Tate surgery, oblivious to the fact that Mary was in the back office. There she was, dutifully transcribing the doctor's 'awful' notes into the patients' charts. She would work until 6 p.m. and then walk the identical route home as had her big brother, his bride-to-be and chief canine, Skipper, had taken almost two hours before.

James heard Adam and Rose talking as they approached the house. He flung the door open to behold his wonderful son and the bride-to-be. As they exchanged hugs, Celia ran to join the embrace.

Adam said, 'Mum and Dad, I want you to meet Rose, who, like I said on the phone, is, that is, we're gonna be married. This is her.'

The senior Roberts beamed at the beautiful young brunette standing by Adam's side. Although she was blushing a bit, Rose's very pretty smiling face and lovely clear blue eyes were a sight that thrilled her future in-laws.

Well, my boy can sure pick 'em, thought James.

Oh, she's lovely. I know she will make Adam a wonderful wife, thought Celia.

James shook Rose's right hand, while his left hand squeezed her right elbow.

'I can't say how glad we are to meet you, Rose,' he said, and leaned forward planting a light kiss on her left cheek.

Celia stepped forward, gently placed her hands on Rose's shoulders, and gently kissed her right cheek. She stepped back, her face aglow.

'I know you will both be very happy, and we can't tell you how thrilled we are.'

'Mary ought to be home shortly,' said James, as he stepped back, and gestured Adam and Rose to enter the small house. He nodded towards the sofa, and they were seated.

'Let's have a cup of tea,' suggested Celia, and immediately produced the cups and saucers from the small kitchen cabinet. 'We want to hear all about everything, and get to know you, Rose. Oh my, you're such a pretty girl,' she could not help adding. 'Adam must have had to fight the lads off to get close enough to get to know you.'

Rose laughed. 'No, in fact,' she answered, 'I met Adam when I asked his boss, or, I should say, now, his partner, Mr White, for a lift on their barge at Wigan Pier. I was trying to get home to Rufford.'

'I know all about it,' said James. 'Adam wrote to us all about it the next day, as I recall. He said he'd decided to name his barge after his sister and you. I'll always remember first tossing those two first names around in my mind, Mary and Rose. I told Celia at the time it sounded like Adam was getting serious about a girl named Rose.'

Adam blushed.

Celia poured the tea and the four of them sat busy in small talk for the next half hour. Celia excused herself and walked to her small kitchen to make the final preparations for the dinner.

James had just begun to tell them what about his 'new' garden plot when Mary opened the front door, home from work.

Adam stood, gave his sister a peck on the cheek, and proceeded to introduce Rose. Both Rose and Mary took an immediate liking for each other, and throughout the remainder of the visit, conversation between them was affable and came easily. Rose was quite impressed with the many jobs Mary was carrying on, and said she envied Mary's going to college.

'What are we having for supper?' asked Adam.

'Yorkshire pud and beef dripping,' replied his mother from the kitchen.

'I don't mean to interrupt you two,' said Adam, directing his attention to Rose and Mary, 'but...' He hesitated. 'Now, Rose, don't take this wrong, I think your mother is a wonderful cook, but you're about to find out there are some things about making Yorkshire pud she's yet to learn. I just say that to suggest maybe you might want to go in the kitchen and see how my mother does it.'

Celia, of course, heard this and felt quite pleased.

Rose was not the least bit offended and hastened to the kitchen.

Seeing Rose was interested, Celia opened an upper drawer in the cabinet next to her stove and withdrew a somewhat tattered old cook book, whose face read *Yorkshires* by Celia's mother-in-law, Lucy Roberts. She proceeded to articulate how she had assembled the recipe ingredients, that went into the popular dish. Rose listened attentively, and then asked if she might copy the recipe.

'Sure,' called Mary out from the front room. 'Here's a sheet of paper and a pencil.'

Rose took these materials, and quickly copied Lucy Roberts' special recipe out, and saved the sheet on which she had written in her handbag.

'Everything's ready,' Celia called out just as Rose was stowing the copied recipe.

Celia had already set the table. As everyone was being seated, Celia placed the Yorkshire pud, the beef dripping, and the lovely vegetables on the table.

The delicious smells that accompanied these servings could only be known to someone who has had such a feast. The food was so good that conversation visibly lagged until the meal was over. Dessert consisted of apple pie and Jersey cream. She had baked the pie that afternoon, and had bought the Jersey cream at a farmer's stall just before she leaving the market.

I don't remember my mother being such a cook, thought Adam as he consumed the best meal he could remember ever eating. My gawd, this is delicious, Adam thought, almost salivating.

When everyone had finished eating, the dishes were removed to the kitchen and the group settled in the Roberts' small, but comfortable front room. The conversation flowed like wine, but, wine was the one thing that didn't flow at all. The Roberts family had no compunction against a glass of spirits. Those were indulgences which this family simply hadn't felt able to afford over their earlier years; wine was not part of their regular food fare. Neither James nor Celia even thought of getting some wine; an oversight that would never have occurred at the Birchall cottage.

As they sat chatting, Mary said to Rose, 'I've got a bit of homework you might enjoy seeing.' She had brought a little 'homework' from the Tate surgery. She showed Rose a page of Dr Tate's 'medical hieroglyphics'.

Rose's face fell into an uncomprehending frown as she scanned the page that Mary held in her hand.

'What language is that?' Rose asked.

'Oh, it's not from St Regis,' said Mary, 'It's one of the visitation notes of my employer, Dr Tate. That's part of my job,' she went on. 'I have to translate this scribbling into English, and then write it in the patient's medical chart.'

'However in the world can you read it?' asked Rose.

'Believe me, it took some time before I learned to,' replied Mary. 'I don't know what all they teach doctors at medical school, but I know it isn't penmanship.'

They all had a good laugh, at the unknowing expense of Gateley's finest, if only, doctor, Roger Tate.

'I don't mean to be critical,' said Mary. 'He's probably the hardest-working man in Gateley, and he is a lovely person. Who knows? If his handwriting were not so awful, I might not even have a job.'

Everyone saw the humour in that sage observation.

After another hour or so of small talk, the ladies repaired to the kitchen to do the dishes. Adam and his father remained in the front room, where Adam told his father how it was 'to be in the barge business.

By 10 p.m. it was bedtime. Adam slept in his old bed. Mary's bed was fully wide enough to accommodate her and Rose.

Before it was lamp lights out, everyone agreed that tomorrow, Sunday, they would go to the regular church service, then to the Navigation Pub for lunch and frolics and end up at the Gateley pier, where Adam would show the family the *Mary Rose*.

Chapter Sixteen

The next morning, Celia made short work of preparing a tasty breakfast, after which the Roberts family and Rose attended the Anglican service at the small church in Gateley. Skipper was tied to a rope lead at the back of the Roberts' house, with firm instructions to bark and growl with life-threatening resolve should he detect any intruders before the family got back from church.

Depression or no depression, Gateley had managed to build a small church since the old days when the only school was 'converted' on Sundays. Rose and her family did not customarily attend church, but she thought that might be different if the atmosphere in Rufford was as congenial as she found among the amiable folk who arrived for services on this Sunday. Everyone seemed to know everyone else.

Although Rose was not looking for any feelings of ill will, she could not help noting how friendly and amiable were these obviously not-so-prosperous people. They showed a friendly, outgoing attitude in spite of the hard times of the period. To Rose, the absent signs of prosperity were the same as she sensed in Wigan. The people's clothing was obviously far from new, but she saw no one in rags or tatters. No unmended holes. Consistently neat and clean. Well-worn, but far from worn out. Rose was also impressed by the general atmosphere which seemed entirely devoid of ill will or of anyone seeming to try to avoid anyone else.

The vicar conducted a typical Anglican service, in which his mercifully short sermon was unswerving in terms of Christian doctrine, but delivered in the usual unruffled English attitude that became recognised worldwide during the Second World War by BBC announcers regularly beginning their broadcasts with a perfunctory 'This is the news', and proceeded to describe wartime events, sometimes of disastrous import, with that same unruffled matter-of-fact tone of voice. As expected, such subdued eloquence did not noticeably elevate the blood pressure of any parishioner.

After the service finished, there was the usual mixing and gabbing in front of the church. One of those in attendance was the visibly greying schoolmaster, Amos Cooper. Amos had spotted the Roberts family and Rose shortly after he had entered the church. Once the service was over, his first order of socialising was to seek out the Robertses, mainly to greet Adam and meet the attractive young lady who had sat next to him and who had 'fiancée' written all over her pretty face.

Of course the most cordial of greetings were exchanged when Amos joined the Roberts party. His natural amiability was at its best. Rose was quite impressed with him. Mary had already told her that Amos Cooper was the nearest thing to a patron saint as she ever expected to have. Their chatting in getting acquainted went on for nearly a half-hour.

Amos had to decline James's invitation to join them at the Navigation Inn. He had a prior commitment to meet with school officials who were coming all the way from Manchester. James declined to ask him what that was all about. If Amos wanted him to know, he would tell him, or so the unprying James thought.

Alternating, both Adam and Mary introduced Rose to various others before the midday tolling of the church bell signalled the end of the customary post-service socialising. When the church bell rang out at exactly 12, the parishioners began to disperse in almost a knee-jerk response. Fourteen in all of the faithful, including the Roberts party, began walking in a rather loose formation in the direction of the Navigation Inn, Gateley's vaunted afternoon social centre, especially on Sundays.

When the 'church crowd' arrived at the inn, all but Rose was a bit surprised to see that only a few tables that were not occupied. James and Adam pulled two small tables together, then the chairs, permitting all five to sit together. James and Celia walked to the pub's bar and placed their order for the midday snack. Adam excused himself briefly to make the rounds to greet some of his old chums from his Gateley canal days whom he had spotted in the crowd. In five minutes he returned with three of his oldest friends to introduce them to his fiancée. Rose was very gracious during all these proceedings. One of Adam's old friends, a solidly built young man with coal-black hair and rather piercing blue eyes, was unusually struck by Rose's radiant good looks. He seemed unable to take his eyes off of her. During the introductions, his consuming look left no doubt, at least, in Rose's mind, that his utterance of being 'very glad to meet you' was entirely heartfelt. His professed state of mind was certainly affirmed by the firmness of his handshake; at least Rose wasn't left with any doubts.

The Gateley Pier was about a ten-minute walk from the Navigation Inn. James was eager to see his son's barge, but agreed that all that could be left to the next morning when Rose, Adam and Skipper were to leave on their return trip to Rufford. Actually, James was almost relieved to defer that inspection tour because he had about two hours of work at his allotment that was badly overdue.

After a couple of hours of this-and-that socialising at the Navigation Inn, it was agreed that Mary and her parents would walk on home so James could tend to his chores and Mary could do her college homework. Adam would show Rose about the area, and they would plan to be back at the Roberts house later in the afternoon.

As soon as James, Celia and Mary had departed through the pub's entrance, Adam took Rose's hand and led her to the side door near the rear of the pub.

'I want you to meet Edward. He's retired,' said Adam as they neared the door.

Rose replied with something about Edward being a fairly common name, and then she asked, 'Which one is Edward?'

Adam did not reply. He led her through the door and then to the paddock at the back of the pub. It was a small field, an acre at most. In the centre area was a small triangular coral, which was formed by three parallel logs bolted to fence posts on each side, with a small stable built within the enclosure. Inside this coral stood a donkey. Pub owners, having the space, often kept such animals as pets to entertain children, while their parents socialised in the pub. Even when youngsters were permitted inside where food was served, they invariably chose the freedom of being outside the smoky pubs, playing their games, or if the pub had a paddock, then climbing on the wooden fence rails talking to the pet donkey, or trying to lure him close enough to scratch his ears.

As they approached, Adam picked an apple from a nearby tree, and shouted, 'Edward!' The donkey's ears pointed skyward. He turned in the direction of the sound. He recognised Adam. His ears lay back, and he trotted up to them and pushed his head through the rails. Adam stroked his nose and fed him the apple. There was sheer delight on both sides of the fence. Rose thought Edward was so very cute she wanted to take him home.

Adam related to Rose a short biography of Edward pulling barges in his youth, and becoming the pet property of the Navigation Inn owner after old age began to catch up with him. Adam recalled when they were building the coral and Edward becoming its first occupant. That event happened when Adam was about ten or eleven years old. He and Edward had become great friends. This enduring friendship was apparently based on their unspoken agreement that feeding Edward apples and scratching his large pointed ears were both excellent ideas.

After spending almost half an hour by the coral, Adam took Rose on a walking tour of Gateley and environs, during which he recited childhood memories about most everything they passed by. Gateley did not bear any resemblance to Rufford in terms of people, structures or landscape. Rose was delighted at the whole day. The sky was a cloudless ceiling of beautiful blue. The temperature was just right. One of their sorties led through the woods, where they took advantage of the privacy of their surroundings to engage in several long-lasting embraces. When Rose became aware that she was beginning to feel somewhat aroused by it all, she stepped back from Adam to communicate that it was time to go. No exchange of words was necessary. They simply joined hands, and walked innocently out of the woods in the direction of the Roberts house.

They arrived back around 5.30 p.m. James had just returned from his allotment and Mary was deeply engrossed in her homework. Celia had prepared what would be a light supper, as they all felt they had been eating more than usual.

After the supper was over and the girls had assisted Celia with the dishes, Adam took both of the young ladies by the arm and announced he was going to show them the garden, which was a beautiful flowered area nearby the Row, which was kept up through the volunteer efforts of everyone in the Row.

They walked outside, to the back of the cottage. There they saw a very large garden and several apple trees. Beyond was a little stream at the bottom of the path. Mary led the way to the stream, where they proceeded to sit on an old wooden seat.

'This is where Adam and I played when we were very small. Adam would read to me, and it was here that he taught me how to write.'

Rose listened closely as Mary continued explaining how much she and Adam had enjoyed their childhood.

'I must have had the best brother in the world,' Mary concluded.

This made Adam feel a bit awkward, but he decided to just sit out a short unheralded silence. No sense in denying the gospel truth, he thought.

'Have you got a boyfriend?' asked Rose.

'Oh no!' said Mary, blushing, 'I haven't met one yet that meets my fancy, I suppose.'

Adam turned to his sister, and said, 'Well, wait until you meet Rose's brothers.'

Now, Mary really blushed, but not knowing what to say, she said nothing.

The conversation got a bit lighter as they strolled around the garden area and then returned to the Roberts house.

The rest of the evening was pleasant and uneventful. Best of all, the Roberts family and Rose were getting to know each other, and each seemed well pleased with the other. They went to bed early, knowing that tomorrow was going to be a very full day for everyone.

Celia arose before anyone else the next morning, and made it a point not to wake the others while she assembled what she would be serving for breakfast. After the morning meal, everyone plus Skipper took the twenty-minute stroll to the Gateley pier, where the *Mary Rose* lay safely tied to the north edge of the Lancaster canal.

When they arrived at the mooring they saw the name 'Mary Rose' painted in gold letters at the bow and also across the stern. It was too much for Mary. The thought of her brother leaving, and that he had put her name on his boat. She couldn't hold back the tears of emotion. Celia had the same feelings and reaction. Adam felt a bit embarrassed and went studiously about taking them all on a short tour of the boat below deck.

James looked over Adam's modern barge carefully and was particularly impressed that it was motor-powered, no less!

'You've done well, my son,' said James admiringly.

After James looked over the barge, and inspected the engine he said to Adam. 'This must be forty feet long.'

Adam smiled, and replied, 'It's fifty-five feet stem to stern, twenty foot in the beam, and can carry one hundred tonnes.' James was duly impressed. Adam could read the delight on his father's face.

It was, however, time to leave. They all said their farewells and briefly embraced.

James, Celia and Mary stepped off the *Mary Rose*. Adam started the diesel engine, and skilfully steered his barge around to the south.

During the farewell waving, Rose shouted to Mary that she must visit soon.

She added, 'And I want you to meet my brothers.'

In the parting, Adam also promised his mother that he would name the next barge he bought the *Celia*.

As the *Mary Rose* settled on its southerly course, the remaining members of the Roberts family began their stroll back to their cottage.

Thanks to a south-flowing current of the canal and a southerly breeze, they arrived back at the Birchall cottage in better time than had been possible on their trip to Gateley. Nevertheless, they arrived well after the Birchalls had had their supper.

Doris prepared a hasty late supper for Adam and Rose, then it was time to retire. Adam had to be at the Wigan pier by 8 a.m. the next morning.

Chapter Seventeen

It was in the late afternoon on Tuesday, 8 November 1934 when Adam tied the *Mary Rose* down at his assigned berth at the Albert Dock in Liverpool. At least two underwriters at Lloyds of London would have drawn a noticeable sigh of relief had they been able to see the insured cargo from Talbott Furniture safely and securely tied on the barge's deck. It never crossed Adam's mind that the day would come when all Lloyd's underwriters providing haulage insurance to Lancashire factories would offer a five per cent reduction in premium to those who used White and Roberts to haul the cargoes they saw fit to insure. After Adam had the particulars of his arrival in his activity log, he tended to the paperwork with the unloading dock foreman, and sought out Norman. He'd seen Norman's barge – that is, Walter's barge – in Walter's usual tie-down berth. Norman had come from Chester with a load of heavy timber that was unloaded shortly before Adam arrived. He had left word with the unloading dock foremen that if Adam arrived before he got back, he'd be having a late lunch at the Sleeping Dragon, a so-so pub just off the Albert Dock.

Adam entered the Sleeping Dragon, spotted Norman, gave him an 'I'll be right there' wave, and got a pint of bitter. Then he walked to the small table where Norman was savouring his shepherd's pie.

Before leaving Chester, Norman had met with Walter in his back-bedroom office. Knowing Adam and Norman would meet up in Liverpool, Walter had asked him to tell Adam that he wanted to see him right away.

Norman described this meeting to Adam, at which he had noticed Walter's revived energy. After relaying Walter's instructions, Norman added that, 'Walter's colour is coming back good, too.'

If Walter needs to see me right away, it's got to be about something more important than anything we could've worked out over the phone, thought Adam.

'How can we work that?' asked Adam. 'Bob's holding an invoice for me for a morning trip to Wigan.'

'Walter mentioned that,' said Norman, 'he said we should switch loads. In the morning, I'm due to a take a shipment of Canadian lumber to Chester.'

'That should work,' said Adam. 'Let's get over to Harrison's office before this all starts getting complicated.'

Norman quickly devoured the two remaining bites of his shepherd's pie, and the two set off for the Albert Dock foreman's office.

Shortly after 3 p.m. on the following day, Adam arrived in Chester. He promptly got the Chester dock foreman's signature on his delivery invoice, and made the arrangements for his return load. Then he set off on the fifteen-minute walk to the Wooten house.

Lil spotted Adam coming up the front walk. She signalled Walter. As Adam was about to knock on the door, it opened. Adam's repressed concerns vanished as he saw the welcoming looks on the smiling faces of the two people who had come to mean to him almost as much as his parents. Walter and Lil greeted him warmly with an affectionate embrace. Adam was introduced to Lil's sister, Susan, who stood several feet behind the Whites with a building anticipation in meeting the young man whose praises she had almost wearied of hearing. Lil suggested Adam bring them 'up to date about his trip to Gateley, his family, Rose, and everything that's being planed.'

'Wonderful idea!' chimed in Lil's sister, 'and, it's time for tea. It's all prepared.'

As the four gathered around the dining room table, Adam eyed Walter in particular. Norman was right about his colour coming back.

Adam related the recent family events, concluding, 'Rose and I haven't picked a date yet. She wants to discuss it with her mum. Once we're married, of course, Rose will be moving out, and she wants to assure her mum how safe it all is, and that we don't expect it'll be for all that long.'

Walter then told the ladies they would have to excuse him and Adam, as they had 'some business matters to discuss back in my office'.

Walter rose, and Adam dutifully followed him to his office, the former back bedroom, which now held a nicely made bed moved against one wall, a bona fide roll desk, on which sat a telephone, Walter's sway-back chair facing the desk and a small sofa.

Once in the room, Walter closed the door and signalled Adam to be seated on the sofa.

As Walter seated himself at his desk, Adam noticed his face had a serious but not concerned appearance, reminiscent of how he looked at their talk on Adam's eighteenth birthday.

'Adam,' Walter began, 'some time ago I read an article in a business magazine about the life blood of every business being new business, and I believe it.'

Adam sort of blinked at him, as if to say, 'So?'

'Now you know, Adam, I didn't ask you to come all the way from Liverpool just to hear a speech. What I just said fits in very neatly with some telephone talks I've been having with the man who heads up the Leeds and

Liverpool Canal Company's office in Manchester. Chap named Everett Jennings. I've never met him, but on the phone he sounds like a real straightforward well-educated man.' He paused, then added, 'In fact, he called me.'

'What about?' asked Adam, anticipating that Walter was about to tell him something important. He did.

'Well,' said Walter, 'it seems like Leeds and Liverpool is setting up a new programme which Mr Jennings describes as one that's going to skin the arse off the railroads when it comes to anything that can be hauled by a barge; anything but coal or limestone. And, that's a quote,' Walter added, 'I wrote it down.' He held up the writing tablet on which he'd scrawled notes during his last telephone talk with Everett Jennings.

'Well,' interjected Adam, 'how would little us fit in any programme like that with a big company like Leeds and Liverpool?'

'Leeds and Liverpool,' replied Walter, 'plans to contract with most of the upmarket mills and factories from the Pennines to Burscough to handle all their transportation needs that can be done by barges. Those will be Leeds and Liverpool's customers. They also plan to contract that barge service out to what Mr Jennings called "choice barge operators" who will each have a specific list of those customers they're agreeing to provide all that service for. Mr Jennings called these "Term Contracts".

'Leeds and Liverpool,' continued Walter, 'is clearly out to push the railroads back to hauling passengers only, and all the coal and limestone they care to. Maybe they will. Maybe they won't. Who knows? Regardless, that's their plan, and,' he added with considerable emphasis in his voice, 'they're looking for the right kind of people to do the barging. People who can operate as if it was their own business.

'The people,' he continued, 'they make these "term contracts" with will receive thirty-five per cent of the haulage fees that Leeds and Liverpool charges, and will be paid their running costs to boot. Mr Jennings told me he wasn't at liberty to tell me what those charges are, but he did say words to the effect that they were a good deal more than we regularly charge. I remember his exact words when we were discussing this. He said, "Trust me, Mr White, you'll make a great deal more money performing our service contracts than you would in the market you're working." I asked him how he knew what we were charging. He just said, "As I said, Mr White, trust me. No one ever went wrong doing that." Then he changed the subject.

'Mr Jennings said they estimate servicing the Leeds and Liverpool customers on any of their lists will require a minimum of seven barges, and that ten to twelve barges would be much closer to the mark, on average. And, this thing he made very clear. I wrote it down.' Walter read from his tablet.

'Barges used to service Leeds and Liverpool customers must be diesel-powered and kept in first-rate condition.'

Again he held up the tablet to show Adam where he had written down the words just recited.

Then he continued, 'They're going to limit each operator to one list of their customers who will be located within about a ten-square-mile area. The contracts will be for three-year terms, renewable at the company's option.

'Mr Jennings said Leeds and Liverpool reckon they can compete successfully if their customers know their raw materials coming in and their products going out are being carried in first-rate, well-maintained barges being run by responsible people who make the words "on time" their Eleventh Commandment.'

This time, Walter held the tablet in one hand, and pointed to where he had written the words 'On Time Eleventh Commandment'.

'I've told Mr Jennings all about our operation, including my recent problems, and how you had stepped in and the kind of job you've been doing. He didn't say as much, but I got the idea I wasn't telling him anything he didn't already know along those lines.

'My impression, Adam, is that he was favourably impressed, but our last talk ended with him saying that before we get into any more detail about a contract, he wants to meet both of us.'

'In short, Adam,' Walter now spoke more emphatically, 'I mean we may very well be on the verge of a true win–win situation: the Leeds and Liverpool Canal Company using us to service its customers, and we use Leeds and Liverpool to acquire a real fleet of good-quality barges while building our standing and reputation. By the end of the first three-year contract, the name White and Roberts won't just be well known among Lancashire dock foremen and a handful of good clients. This whole thing will give us the opportunity to have a top name in barging sought out by the upmarket lot we'll be serving as Leeds and Liverpool customers. And believe me, Adam, these people don't live their lives in a vacuum. They move in their own circles, and common sense tells me they let each other know who best provides the services they need. And these people are running the companies that are surviving this damnable depression. Just being on Leeds and Liverpool's list means two big things: One, they need the kind of service we can provide. Two, they can pay for such service, and are willing to do so. Now, Adam, that is a plan, and now is the time!

'Am I making contact inside of your mind?'

Walter leaned back in his chair to observe Adam's reaction.

'Tell me, what do you think of all this?' he asked.

As Walter had spoken, several visions had flashed across Adam's mind.

Visions of his forthcoming wedding. Him and Rose living on a barge, as modern as that of Walter and Lil. Ah, but we'll have kids, and canals are no place for raising kids. Then he visualised a beautiful home nestled in a grove of ash trees, and a fair-sized town in the background within easy driving distance. Then his attention returned to reality, as he picked up on Walter's last statement, 'What do you think of all this?'

'It sounds so grand I feel like pinching myself to be sure I'm not dreaming,' Adam's replied.

Walter smiled in delight at this response. This young man is every bit as solid and ambitious as I'd figured, he thought.

'Wonderful,' said Walter. 'Well, since Mr Jennings wants to meet the both of us, now's the time to set that up.' A quick phone call to Jennings's office wrapped up those arrangements. As Walter was concluding this call, he said out loud the words he was writing on his tablet: 'Mister Jennings's office. Tuesday, 16 November 1.30 p.m.'

Walter replaced the phone in its cradle and turned to Adam.

'Nine days hence, my boy,' he said, 'I think we should plan to meet at the news-stand on platform nine of the Piccadilly train station in Manchester. I'd think we should plan to be there as near to noon as possible. I can't say for certain where you'll be coming from, but wherever it is, I'm sure they've got a train station.'

Before Adam could concur, Walter added, 'And, Adam, for this meeting, there's also a little matter of wardrobe.'

'Road what?' asked Adam, with a look of sheer incomprehension of his face.

'Now, don't misunderstand,' said Walter, half apologetically, 'wardrobe means how you're dressed. First, let me say I think you wear just the right clothes for your job, but you'll have to get some dressier clothes for our meeting with Mr Jennings. Nothing extra special or extra expensive, I'd think, but, uh, tell you what, you'll be in Wigan before the week's out. Why don't you go to the Harris Tweed store on the high street in Standish Gate? Their prices are always sensible. What you need to get are a white linen shirt with extra collars, studs, a dark blue sports jacket, grey flannel trousers and a nice red tie. That ought to give you the right look.'

Walter's eyes involuntarily roamed to view Adam's high-top leather work shoes, both of which showed stains of diesel fuel.

'Oh yes,' he continued, 'and shoes. Right over the road from Harris's there's a Kimpsons, where you can buy a pair of black brogues.' He pointed to Adam's shoes, saying, 'Lord knows we wouldn't want any of those petrol stains rubbing off on any of the fine furniture I think we'll see when we get to Mr Jennings's office.'

Both Adam and Walter had to laugh briefly at the vision of Adam walking into the supposed fancy office wearing the shoes they were both looking at. Nothing hilarious. But amusing.

Adam nodded his full concurrence with Walter's ideas – and asked his mentor to please write down 'those wardrobe specifics'. Walter complied and handed Adam the list. Then he directed their attention to a related subject.

'I'm getting my energy back, and I've no doubt I can handle the management parts of what we work out with Mr Jennings. If, of course, we work it out,' he added, briefly staring into space. Then he turned to face Adam very directly.

'If all this comes off, and somehow I feel certain it will, your first expanded role will be to get together with Norman to work out hiring the right kind of men for White and Roberts' soon-to-be-expanded fleet of barges. I don't know how Norman knows so many boatmen, but there's no denying he's proven more useful than just another barge driver. I think we ought to give Norman a special bonus for Christmas – coming up, you know. You think that over.

'Anyway, about your expanded role. As I foresee it, once we get good control of things in a bigger operation, it'll have to be your job to make sure our boatmen are meeting their assignments and I mean meeting them on time,' he emphasised. 'I can get the arrival/departure numbers from dock foremen by phone, but charging up our boatmen to do it all on time always, well, that takes someone on the scene with clout that knows how to act like a cheerleader. That will have to be you, Adam.'

Adam nodded his understanding of what Walter was saying.

'Your getting married,' Walter went on, 'means you'll need a barge fit for the likes of Rose to live on. The *Mary Rose* has served us well, and we've got plenty of work for her, Leeds and Liverpool or no Leeds and Liverpool, but no one in his right mind would expect a real lady like Rose to live on her.'

Adam felt quite relieved at these remarks. He'd have to decide on the way back to Chester just how much of all this he'd tell Rose for the present. The thought crossed his mind, nevertheless, that Adam Roberts would get the first new barge that White and Roberts bought.

The remainder of their conference covered the kind of detail items that could have been handled by telephone. Regardless, it is always better when partners discuss their mutual business face to face.

Walter at last stood, signifying the meeting was over. Adam rose from the sofa and followed him back to the living room. They had been conferring for nearly an hour.

Adam graciously declined the invitation to stay for supper. He had to get back to the Chester Pier to check his load, which, by now, should be chained to the deck of the *Mary Rose*. The patch of the Irish Sea he would have to pass through getting back to Liverpool could get very dicey, and the young lads who loaded cargoes at the Chester Pier did not enjoy a good reputation when it came to lashing loads to barge decks. Also, he had to check his diesel engine that had sounded a bit strange on three separate occasions during the last mile of his approach to the Chester Pier. If repairs or replacements were needed, he would have to get them done by nightfall. He planned to start north on the River Dee at first light. Meeting that schedule simply didn't include any time for further socialising. He also wanted to avoid the risk of waking everyone up before dawn by his early departure.

Walter and Lil readily understood Adam's time constrictions. Sara Wooten understood them after Lil filled her in on the details following Adam's goodbyes.

When he returned to the Chester Pier, Adam saw about forty tonnes of oak timber chained tightly to his deck. True to his earlier suspicions, however, there was a problem with his diesel engine. He readily discovered it required replacement of a gasket, which he was able to buy from Chester Marine Engines, a small boat-oriented shop near the pier. By 9.30 that evening, he had replaced the gasket. Feeling both hope and fear, he started the engine. To his great relief, it purred like a kitten. He cleaned himself up, prepared a light supper, and got to his bunk in his living quarters shortly after 10. He wound his clock and set its alarm for 5.30.

He crawled into his bunk, anticipating he would go right to sleep. Instead, his mind roamed, turning over all manner of subjects and possibilities. Rose. What was she doing right now? The wedding. The date had to be set and all the arrangements made. The honeymoon. Ought to be in the Lake District. Leeds and Liverpool. How did this Mr Everett Jennings look? Tall? Fat? Skinny? How old is he? Forgot to ask Walter what he thought about that. How would he react to someone Adam's age?

Just as the mental meandering list was about to go on and on, Adam thought, No, I'll do like counting sheep. I'll just try to remember everything I was just thinking about. That worked. He drifted off to sleep before he was halfway through trying to recall the questions he had just asked himself.

By first light the next morning, Adam was heading north on the River Dee. Destination: Liverpool. That return trip took the usual seven hours' barge time. The Irish Sea part of the journey got a bit rough, but the secure chains held his cargo neatly in place. En route, Adam tried to think through just how much he should tell Rose about White and Roberts' blossoming business prospects. After nearly half an hour of mulling the subject over in his mind, the conclusions simply flowed in.

I'll just tell her we've got some talks going on but I won't know anything for sure until Walter and I have been to Manchester next week. No details until we have a signed deal with Leeds and Liverpool. Till then, I'd only be raising her hopes. No sense in getting anyone's hopes up just to have to explain later why something didn't work out. It all sounds good, but so do lots of things. When I have something real to tell Rose, I'll tell her. Not until! His mind was well made up.

Chapter Eighteen

The plan for Thursday was that Adam and Walter would meet up at the news-stand on platform eight of Manchester's Piccadilly station at noon. Walter arrived with about ten minutes to spare. He was all decked out in the only suit he owned, a dark green hard worsted he'd bought years ago at England's posh chainstore for men's clothing, Burton's. The Burton's outlet in Liverpool was on the high street. While Burton's continued into the next century, in 1935 it had stores in Liverpool, and on the high streets of twenty-eight other cities and towns throughout the country.

Walter was standing by the news-stand, looking very smart, when up walked Adam Roberts in the new clothes he had just bought in Standish Gate. My, what an impression they both made! No one would have guessed the true occupation of either of them, going by appearance alone. Walter's greying temples would fit him into a dozen callings. Adam looked like a newly appointed junior professor at a public school. Walter could hardly believe his eyes at the fine cut of man his partner presented. His red tie was not too red, but it was an eye-catcher. The two shook hands in greeting and hastened to the small café right next to the train station where their lunch was promptly served. Walter paid the bill, and the they walked to the line of taxis that perpetually formed up in front of this train station.

Upon entering the 'nex' up' taxi, Walter told the driver Mr Jennings's office address.

'Right, guv'nor,' replied the driver, who promptly started his engine and pulled into the traffic.

They arrived at the offices of the Leeds and Liverpool Canal Company five minutes before their 1.30 appointment. Perfect timing. Their promptness was not lost on Everett Jennings, who ushered them into his office, and asked his secretary to bring tea as he waved his guests to chairs before his large oak desk.

Mr Jennings then seated himself behind the deck and turned his gaze to Adam.

'I assume Mr White has informed you about our conversations during these last few weeks,' he said to Adam.

'He has, sir,' said Adam, showing a very serious demeanour.

'Fine,' said Jennings. 'Without undue repetition, I want to note a few additional points.'

He briefly described Leeds and Liverpool's expansion plans, and then got down to specifics. 'I know you currently run a three-barge operation, and that Mr White is just coming back from a heart condition. I made it clear to Mr White last week that if we sign a deal, the volume you'll have to handle as a result will require a minimum of seven to eight barges within the initial three months and ultimately could involve up to twelve barges, and possibly more.

'We've got a selling job, Mr Roberts,' he continued, 'which is to convince our customers and our future customers by deeds that all of their property entrusted to us to be transported by barges will be on first-rate, diesel-powered barges that are being operated by responsible, capable people whom they can trust to pick their property up on time, and deliver it on time, and that it will be properly taken care of while in their custody.'

He paused to observe the apparent effect of his words on his guests.

Adam and Walter nodded their understanding and agreement.

'Ordinarily we wouldn't consider contracting with – let me say with all respect – small operators. But, I'm frank to tell you, we check out the people we plan to deal with. And over the past year, dock foreman after dock foreman has repeatedly told us that no barge operator on the Leeds and Liverpool canal equals your record for on-time arrivals and departures, and there is never a complaint by any customers about how their property was handled. That's the quality of service we intend to provide to every factory and mill, and every other customer that does business with us.'

In a concluding but friendly tone of voice, Everett Jennings said, 'Your reputation, gentlemen, is why we've come to you. You've earned a reputation that can't be bought. Now, I have the feeling you are about to begin reaping the rewards of your efforts.'

Quite a speech! thought Walter and no small part of the record he's talking about was made while I was flat on my back. Lil couldn't have been more accurate when she said, 'I know Adam can do it.'

Adam squirmed a little in his chair as he sat listening to the sage Mr Jennings, but he was clearly pleased with what he was hearing.

'Mr Roberts,' said Everett Jennings, staring directly into Adam's eyes, 'you're quite young for assuming such responsibilities as we're discussing. On the other hand, we at Leeds and Liverpool have seen any number of older men who weren't so reliable, and some younger men who were. Given the record we know you have made, we've decided you are one younger man we believe we can rely on.

'Therefore,' concluded the spokesman for the Leeds and Liverpool Canal Company, as he returned his gaze to both of his guests, 'we are prepared to offer White and Roberts a three-year contract, plus the collateral financing I've discussed with you, Mr White.'

Everett Jennings pulled open the desk drawer on his right and withdrew three sets of identical papers. The face sheet of one was stamped 'original'; the face sheets on the other two were stamped 'duplicate original'. He pushed them across the desk.

'While I want you to study these documents alone in a few minutes, I would like to explain that the first four pages are standard term contracts Leeds and Liverpool Canal Company is using for this programme. The fifth page contains the provisions Mr White and I have discussed by phone regarding this company's co-signing the paper under which you will be buying additional barges. The sixth page is the list of Leeds and Liverpool customers whose every barge needs you will be assuming. Each of them are within twenty miles of Wigan Pier. Most shipments will be between the customer's facility and Liverpool. There will be the occasional haul to Birmingham or Bristol or Manchester. In most cases, you will be able to haul the cargoes of three to five customers on most trips to and from Liverpool. That will vary, of course, but we know it can be done. Any time you've got a situation where you need our help, you know my phone number. Always remember, the one thing our customers don't expect are reasons why their shipments weren't picked up or delivered as scheduled. They're all paying premium shipping prices, and, rightfully, they expect premium service.'

There was a brief silence in the room.

'I am really a bit flabbergasted, Mr Jennings,' volunteered Adam, 'but I'm absolutely sure we will meet all your expectations, and then some.'

'Right as rain!' chimed in Walter.

Jennings pulled open the desk drawer on the right side of his desk and withdrew three identically worded sets of a contract. The face sheet on the top set was again stamped 'original'; the face sheets of the two sets below were stamped 'duplicate original'.

He pushed the lot across the desk in front of Walter.

'I think you'll find this a very straightforward contract,' he announced. 'Before we get around to signing it, however, I want you and Mr Roberts to take these into the little room to the right of my office and read them over carefully. Miss Dobbins will show you the way,' he added as he pressed a signal button on the left side of his desk top.

Miss Dobbins, his secretary, appeared almost immediately.

'When you've read the contract over, let Miss Dobbins know you're ready to come back in here. Oh yes,' he added, 'write down any questions you may have, and we'll address them when you return.'

With that, Walter picked up the contract documents. He and Adam stood and followed Miss Dobbins to the adjacent small conference room.

Once seated in the small room, Walter handed Adam one copy of the proposed contract and they both sat down to read. After five minutes, each had completed his reading of the entire contract.

'As I read it, it says just what you told me back in Chester,' said Adam.

'It does indeed,' said Walter. 'You know, Adam, I have a good feeling about Mr Jennings. I think he's an honest man. The kind we want to do business with. I suggest we sign on.'

Adam nodded his concurrence.

Within a few minutes they were back in Everett Jennings' office and seated before his large oak desk.

'We're both satisfied these papers set out exactly what you've told us your company is proposing,' said Walter, 'and we're prepared to sign.'

A very pleased look came over Everett Jennings's face as he said a single word, 'Splendid.'

The signing ceremonies were quickly completed. After Walter and Adam had signed all three sets of the contract, Everett Jennings signed for the Leeds and Liverpool Canal Company Ltd. He waved the two duplicate originals briefly to dry the ink, and then handed one each to Walter and Adam.

'Now,' he said, 'let's talk a bit about logistics.'

Logistics, thought Adam. I never heard that word before, but I have the feeling I'm about to find out what it means.

'Three items,' said Everett Jennings. 'Ordering your barges, getting the paperwork signed at the bank, and, number three, introducing you to our customers you'll be serving.

'Barges,' he continued. 'Of course just whose barges you buy will be your decision, but in making it, we'd be pleased if you consider the seventy-footers made by Kingston Marine Barges Ltd at Bradford. Their size pretty much assures you can carry the cargoes for at least three customers at the same time. They're reasonably priced. And, well, Kingston's barges have a touch of class. They help us project a quality image to our customers, and that's quite important, isn't it?'

Walter both nodded slightly in concurrence, but said nothing.

'Well, here,' said Everett Jennings, as he withdrew several colour brochures from his desk drawer. 'Here's a few descriptive brochures they put out. You'll be the ones to decide, and all we ask is that you look them over and give them some serious thought.'

Walter took the brochures, and noted Adam eyeing one in particular on which the words were prominently printed: 'Living quarters you can live in.'

Walter promptly handed the brochures to Adam, saying, 'Here Adam. You're the one who will want to study these carefully with Rose.'

'Rose?' said Everett Jennings. 'Am I missing something here?'

'Well, indirectly, I suppose,' said Walter. 'Our young Mr Roberts here is on the verge of becoming a married man, and I was just suggesting his bride-to-be might be particularly interested in the living quarters they'll be occupying, at least during their first year of marriage.'

Ah, thought Everett Jennings. That's capital. Sheer capital! An ambitious young man wanting to impress his new wife with how successful he can become. It's the ideal backdrop for this programme.

As the 'jewel in the crown' import of this new aspect formed in the ever-calculating mind of Everett Jennings, he rose from his desk, put out his right hand to Adam and extended his heartiest congratulations. Adam responded by also standing, and, blushing slightly, shook the older man's hand.

During the next half-hour, the specifics were resolved as to Walter and Adam's being introduced to the customers by one of Leeds and Liverpool's representatives during the next three months. Then the hauling would begin.

'After those initial contacts,' said Everett Jennings, 'you and the customers can work out the protocols for meeting their needs.'

Protocol, thought Adam. There's another new word. I've got to look that one up. It sounds pretty important to all this.

As the hour neared 4 p.m., the men agreed that Walter and Adam would return at the same time one week hence. 'All the papers for the credit line should be drawn up and in order by then,' said Everett Jennings, as the meeting drew to a close.

Walter and Adam left Mr Jennings's office with each feeling like he had been reborn. When their taxi brought them back to Piccadilly station, both of them were still feeling quite elated, and agreed the day's events called for a small celebration. So they diverted to the Black Horse pub for a pint of bitter. Without either uttering the words, each man was experiencing the same emotions. The world was a wonderful place, indeed, depression or no depression.

As they were savouring their frothy pints, Walter declared, 'We are going to make a lot of money, my boy, I sense it in every bone in my body.'

Coming from an older, more experienced man whom he respected, these words only added to Adam's delight.

'Let's get the a train to Chester so we can both give Lil the good news.'

And that's exactly what they did.

Within the hour they were comfortably seated in the passenger coach of the last London & Northwestern train whose second stop would be Chester.

When Walter and Adam arrived back at the Wooten cottage in Chester, they both tried to tell Lil all that had happened, but they were so excited each of them started talking at the same time. Lil's sister stood back smiling, not quite able to comprehend just what everyone was so elated about.

'Calm down! Calm down!' Lil cried. 'I can't understand both of you. Now just sit down and one of you tell me what happened.'

That brought some order to the occasion. They all sat down.

Walter then told her, as Adam sat gleefully nodding in agreement.

'Proud' could hardly describe what both men felt as Walter ended his narration and laid the signed contract on the table before his equally proud wife.

Lil was exuberantly happy for them all. It crossed her mind that, not so long ago, she had briefly envisioned herself as a not-so-prosperous and very lonely widow, sharing a rather bleak future with her widowed sister. There must be something to the old saw, 'It's always darkest just before the dawn,' she mused.

'Adam,' Lil said, 'why don't you ring up your parents? I'd love to be there when they hear about all this.'

Adam was very grateful for her suggestion. He turned to Walter. 'I want you to listen to what I tell them, and be sure and correct me on the spot if I make any mistakes.'

And then I'm going to call Rose and tell her, he thought, and I'm also going to tell her we want to get married before I start on these new contracts. And somehow I've got to arrange for our families to meet. After all, they're all about to become relatives to one another.

Adam got his telephone call through to his parents. His mother answered and Adam started talking with a flourish.

'Adam! Adam! Stop!' cried his mother. 'I want you to tell all this to your father. I can't I follow it all, and he can tell me later.'

She handed the phone to James.

'Yes, Adam,' said his father as he placed the receiver to his ear. As Adam's story poured out James's face melted into a broad smile.

'I've got to sign off,' said Adam, 'I have to call Rose. I'll call you back in a few days with some more news about the wedding just as soon as I've worked out the details with her.'

When he had ended the call to his parents, Adam said he would call Rose 'later', implying he didn't want to be running up anyone else's phone bill.

Lil, of course, was well aware of Adam's marriage plans by this time.

'I've got an idea,' she announced. 'There's a lot to celebrate around here, and I just wish Rose was here to share it with us. But,' she said, ever such a slight bit wistfully, 'we'll just have to do our best in her absence.'

At that point she marched to the nearby cabinet from which she removed a decanter half filled with port wine, and five crystal snifters.

Walter poured a spot of port in each little glass, handing one to each of the others. Then he hoisted his own to propose a toast:

'Here's to the future Mr and Mrs Adam Roberts and to the future transport champion of the Leeds and Liverpool canal, White and Roberts! And environs,' added Lil.

'Here, here!' said everyone, as they drank to the toast.

Environs, thought Adam. I wonder what that is. I'd look dumb asking, so I'll see if it's in that little dictionary Lil gave me. I saw it just yesterday. Oh yes, in the little stand by my bunk on the *Mary Rose*. But that's tied down at Wigan Pier.

Then an artful thought crossed Adam's mind on how to find out now without admitting he didn't know what it meant.

'Lil,' said Adam in a voice so disarming that Lil knew intuitively she was about to hear something interesting.

'Why, yes, Adam, what is it?'

'This word "environs", I'm not too familiar with it and I don't want to forget to tell Rose all about our toast. How do you spell it?

Lil understood exactly how tactfully their beloved Adam was learning a word. One he'd probably never heard before.

'It's spelled "e-n-v-i-r-o-n-s",' she said, 'and it means "surrounding area". In other words, White and Roberts is going to be the transport champion of the Leeds and Liverpool canal and all those canals around it too, isn't it?' she concluded, intoning a question at the end of her reply.

'It will if Walter and I have anything to say about it,' replied Adam to the amusement and delight of all those present.

After another few minutes of small talk about how the depression wasn't hanging any clouds 'over the likes of us', Adam took his leave. He had to catch the last train to Liverpool. From there he would take the coach to Wigan where the *Mary Rose* was surely loaded with his next cargo. That trip would bring him back to Liverpool – but not without a much anticipated stopover at the Birchall cottage in Rufford. As he walked toward the Chester train station, many, many thoughts ran through his mind.

Oh, how proud he was going to be to tell Rose and her family what White and Roberts had just done. But I've got to say it just right, he thought. I don't want them thinking I got any swelled head over all this. After all, we haven't really done anything yet. We've just signed up to do some things that might get us rich! No, can't say that. I'll just say how happy I am knowing when Rose and me are married we'll be living on a brand-new barge that's really fitted out right. I mean, the living quarters are fitted out like that. The Birchalls are all very intelligent. They'll get the idea, and all that'll make Rose and her family happy, I'd think. It sure ought to.

Adam walked into the Chester train station about ten minutes before the train for Liverpool was due to depart. He bought his ticket, and proceeded to the public phone booth just outside the station. Rose picked up on the first ring, actually two rings in England. During the next three minutes he told her the highlights of the 'big contract' he and Walter had signed with the Leeds and Liverpool Canal Company, assuring her he would fill her and her family in on all the details when got to Rufford the next afternoon. Would she and her mother think out how soon they could have the wedding? Yes, the church in Standish would be fine. Yes, they would work out the families' getting acquainted before the wedding date. And yes, he loved her with all his heart, but, unfortunately there was no more time to talk because his train to Liverpool was about to leave.

As Adam settled in his chair in the passenger coach, he realised that he had become totally exhausted. In many ways it had been the most eventful day of his life.

The train jerked and started moving forward, and quickly began to pick up speed. The hypnotic click of the iron wheels crossing the rail joints caused Adam to become drowsy. He sat back and placed his right arm on the arm rest, with his ticket sticking up between his right index and middle fingers. *Just in case I happen to nod off before the conductor comes by collecting tickets. But I won't. I'm just relaxing. All I need is a little rest.*

His eyes closed. The repetitive click of the whirring wheels continued. In less than a minute he was fast asleep.

The next thing Adam knew, he was being awakened by the conductor's bellowing 'Liverpool!' as he walked through the centre aisle. 'Liverpool! Everybody off, Liverpool!'

Adam opened his eyes, just as the overhead lights in the Liverpool freight yard flashed by. He sat up with a bolt. Instinctively, his right hand shot to the left front of his jacket, where he felt his copy of that precious contract in the inside pocket. Thus reassured, he relaxed. Then he stretched his arms and neck to get the kinks out. The conductor's bellowing was drowned out by the screeching sounds of the train's metal-on-metal braking system.

Unpleasant acoustics aside, the train came to a smooth stop facing platform three of the Liverpool train station.

As the train came to rest, Adam checked the time on his wristwatch. The trip from Chester had taken forty-seven minutes. *Well, that's a lot faster than I could have made it in the Mary Rose*, he thought.

Adam followed other passengers across the platform, by the news-stand, and through the exit. Time for a cup of tea to wake him up, and then a five-minute walk to where he would board the coach for Wigan.

This was a far different Adam Roberts that the village lad who had arrived in England's third largest city shortly after his eighteenth birthday. Although he was totally unaware of it, anyone observing him walking toward the coach station would have perceived a sublime hue of confidence in both his walk and manner. Particularly the last few months had produced a blossoming maturity in Adam Roberts. He was becoming not only a man, but a man among men.

Chapter Nineteen

At 10 a.m. the motor coach arrived at the coach station in Wigan and discharged Adam along with eighteen other passengers. As he stepped from the coach, he realised he was hungry. He walked to a small nearby restaurant and ordered beans on toast, and tea. While waiting for his order, he gazed idly about at the other five customers having their first meal of the day. It was beans on toast and tea all around.

After finishing his light breakfast, Adam took the ten-minute walk to Wigan Pier.

He found the *Mary Rose* neatly tied at berth eighteen, with a small mountain of wooden packing boxes securely lashed to her deck. One glance at the port bow waterline marker told him his cargo weighed slightly over forty tonnes.

He went on board and headed for his living quarters. He found an envelope jammed in at the edge of the entry door, just above the handle. On the face of the envelope was scrawled 'Adam R'. He recognised the handwriting of Wigan Dock foreman Matt Shepherd. He removed the single sheet in the envelope and read:

Walter wants you to call him – Matt.

Adam walked directly to the red telephone box at the entrance to Wigan Pier. Walter picked up on the second ring.

During the next five minutes, Walter told Adam about a call he had received earlier in the day from Jim Essex, the managing shipping agent at Alton Mills, who had abruptly asked him whether they should start looking for a new barge service as he had heard rumours that White and Roberts was being acquired by Leeds and Liverpool, 'or some such business'.

Adam was dumbstruck.

'How on earth could he have heard anything so soon?' asked Adam 'We haven't said anything except to Lil and her sister, and they sure haven't said anything that Jim Essex would hear about!'

'I know. You're no more surprised than I was. Maybe someone at Leeds and Liverpool following up on that line of credit said something to someone that knows we haul for Alton Mills. I don't know. But I do know I just had my faith restored in the old saw about men being bigger gossips than women.'

Aside from his concern, Adam couldn't help smiling in amusement at

Walter's last remark. Walter seemed to be just full of those 'old saws'. Wonder where he hears them, he thought.

'Look, Adam,' Walter continued, 'there's nothing in our contract that says we can haul only for Leeds and Liverpool customers. I don't see any reason why we should stop hauling for any of our customers. Our business isn't changing. It's just expanding. There's plenty of good boatmen around we can hire. All we – that is, you and Norman – have to do is find such men and hire 'em. We've got, or at least we're about to get, the means to get all the barges we need.'

Walter decided to get to the point. 'I left things with Jim Essex kind of unresolved, at least as far as telling him what we're doing. I didn't want to tell him about our Leeds and Liverpool contract, and I wasn't about to deny it. So I just gave him some soft soap about us never ending our excellent business relation with Alton Mills. But by the time we were about to ring off, I was sounding like a politician answering a question. And that's no good for anyone. So I told him I'd ask you to drop around and discuss it all with him. I know you and Essex are on good terms. He never fails to say something good about you. So what I want you to do, Adam, before you leave Wigan today is to meet with him. As soon as we're through, ring him up and tell him I asked you to stop by to discuss some things that are strictly confidential. Yes, use those very words, Adam, say "strictly confidential". That way, after you two have talked, he won't be making our business the business of everyone on the street. And, I fancy we won't have any more doubts about keeping the Alton Mills business.'

'What should I tell him?' asked Adam.

'Just tell him the truth, except don't get into any details about what we'll be getting paid for hauling for Leeds and Liverpool customers. He wouldn't expect that kind of information anyway. Just tell him we're going to be hauling also for a bunch of Leeds and Liverpool customers, as will several other barge operators – we don't know just who – and that Leeds and Liverpool is going to help us expand our fleet so we can do the added work. Make it clear to him this won't make any difference in our work for our customers, and should a matter of priorities ever get involved – which we don't figure ever will, but if it did tell him, our customers will always come first! He knows our word is good. That ought to clear the air.'

'This sure sounds to me like the right way to get all this behind us.'

Walter was immensely pleased at Adam's reaction.

'I know,' added Walter a bit sheepishly, 'why didn't I tell him all those soothing answers when he called me?'

'I didn't say that!' exclaimed Adam defensively.

'Well, you sure could have said that. I should have. Truth is, I was so surprised at his call, the right answers just didn't occur to me.'

Adam assured his partner and mentor that he would not leave Wigan until he had all this attended to.

After ringing off with Walter, Adam paused briefly to think about 'all this' before calling Jim Essex.

What Walter wants me to do is exactly the right way to handle this, regardless of what he didn't say when Mr Essex called, he thought. Besides, this doesn't strike me as the kind of thing to talk about with a customer over the telephone anyway. Talking on the telephone isn't all that 'strictly confidential'. Leastwise, I don't think it is.

True to form, Adam followed through with the success Walter had expected. Adam promptly located the shipping agent by phone, and met him in his office at 1.30 p.m. Mr Essex responded to what Adam told him by expressing his delight at how 'his predictions' of White and Roberts' blossoming success were coming to pass. Of course, he wouldn't say a word to anyone about this 'strictly confidential' information. And, except to reassure his managing director that all was well, he didn't.

After leaving Jim Essex's office, Adam returned to Wigan Pier. He stopped by Matt Shepherd's office to thank him for Walter's message and to pay for the diesel that now filled his tanks. Then he returned to his barge. Within a matter of minutes, the hearty little diesel engine was powering the *Mary Rose* west under the skilful hand of twenty-one-year-old Adam Roberts, who was just about to pop out of his skin as he anticipated the remainder of the day.

Two hours later, the top of the Rufford lock gates came in to view. Then Adam recognised the profile of Albert Birchall standing near the lock gates. He flicked his barge's headlight on and off three times in rapid succession to get Albert's attention. Albert recognised the signal, and called out to Rose, the only one in the cottage, 'Adam's arriving!'

Rose was the only one to hear this news. Her mother was in Standish visiting her sister, Auntie Elizabeth. Her brothers, Tim and John, were totally absorbed in repairing their tractor in back of the barn.

Rose dashed from the cottage and was waiting at the tie-down when Adam eased the *Mary Rose* to her mooring, 200 feet east of the Rufford locks. The tie-down was a rusted iron hook which had been screwed into a canal-side tree stump that was two feet in diameter.

Adam hopped to the ground, quickly secured his barge and turned to embrace this gorgeous creature he was about to marry. Knowing that Albert was watching from the lock, the young lovers embraced meaningfully, but not passionately. Then (for Albert's benefit) Adam conspicuously gestured towards the barge's stern, as if he wanted to show Rose something in the living quarters.

'Why don't we go below,' he said, 'so we can really say hello?'

Rose smiled at his boyish ploy and conspicuously nodded her head forward and backwards to indicate her concurrence. Then the two stepped on board the *Mary Rose*, and proceeded to the living quarters.

By this time, the romance in this young love was nearing crescendo. Both Adam and Rose were aware that each embrace triggered arousal, and heightened their physical yearnings. After three prolonged and passionate embraces, their very human instincts were promptly tempered by their mutual restraint. Following their third sensuous embrace, without a word being said, each stepped back and they promptly departed for the cottage to work out their big plans coming up.

Albert Birchall hadn't timed anything, but idly, he estimated that Adam and Rose reappeared about three minutes after they had disappeared below deck.

Now that seemed like an appropriate non-involved period of time, thought Albert, as he opened the lock gates in preparation for a barge he saw approaching from the west.

Once seated on the living-room couch inside the cottage, Adam led off the conversation by profiling the Leeds and Liverpool deal to Rose. He had intentionally left his 'duplicate original' of the contract in a cabinet drawer in his living quarters. No need in complicating anyone's life with a bunch of contract talk, he had thought as he had tucked the papers far back in the drawer. In his discourse with Rose, Adam avoided any mention of how much the new barges were going to cost, or how long it would take to pay for them. No need to get anyone worried about the subject of money. Work, not worry, solves those problems, and Rose's worrying along those lines would only age her, he thought to himself – with all the fathomless fearless confidence of youth.

In fact, as soon as Adam said that he and Walter were going to buy several new barges, Rose realised that big debt was going to be assumed. Her confidence in Adam was such, however, that she quickly decided if he didn't want to discuss it, then it didn't need discussing.

Adam showed Rose the brochure on the Kingston barge which touted the model with 'Living quarters you can live in'. The brochure included six professional photographs of different parts of the living quarters. Although the actual quarters were a good deal smaller than the pictures implied, they were, indeed, quarters you could live in. Rose was thrilled.

Doris Birchall had told her daughter that having the wedding on 25 June would allow enough time for making all the necessary arrangements. Now Rose told Adam. This gave them just over three weeks. By this time he was so eager to tie the wedding knot, he would have agreed to three days. The wedding date of 25 June 1935 was thereupon set. That decision was sealed with a loving tender kiss that was as devoid of passion as these two smitten young couple could manage.

Rose gently pushed Adam back from the embrace and suggested that he find Tim and John 'somewhere near the barn, I think,' and talk with them while she prepared supper. Paradoxically, at the very moment she made this suggestion, her mother had started helping Auntie Elizabeth in Standish with exactly the same task.

Adam smiled his concurrence and gave Rose a light kiss on her forehead.

'I'll join the lads in a moment,' he said, 'but first I want to call Walter, and make sure that tomorrow I'll be hauling to Wigan.'

Tomorrow was to be their first big day in making actual wedding preparations, and a good deal depended on Adam going on to Liverpool after supper and having a cargo for Wigan the next day. He worked all that out with Walter over the phone in a matter of minutes. Walter was especially pleased to hear that the Alton Mills business was 'All worked out, just like you said'.

At supper that evening, Adam told the Birchalls generally what Walter and he were up to with the Leeds and Liverpool Canal Company. It all sounded very promising, particularly Adam's reassurances about the first-class living quarters he and Rose would have on a Kingston seventy-footer they were going to name the *Mary Rose II*.

The Birchalls were all very familiar with the sight of families living on barges. That sight usually involved a collection of unwashed and uneducated young children scampering about, often unruly and up to no good.

'How long do you think you'll both be living on your barge?' asked John, in a tone of disarming innocence.

'Well, I really don't know. But if you were wondering if we're going to raise any kids on a barge, you'll be pleased to know the answer is a big *no*. We've been all through that,' he continued, glancing toward Rose, 'and we've both seen too much to do anything like that.'

Everyone felt reassured and relieved.

After supper, they moved to the small living room where Rose announced their specific wedding plans, including the date. On that occasion, John and Tim flipped a coin to determine who would be Adam's best man. Tim won the toss.

Beyond doubt, a most amiable atmosphere prevailed that evening at the Rufford lock-keeper's cottage.

At 9.30 p.m. Adam made his late departure for Liverpool. Goodbyes were exchanged at the cottage, after which Albert accompanied Adam to the lock. It was still filled, which shaved at least twenty minutes off his trip to Liverpool. Adam freed the *Mary Rose* from her tie-down, started his diesel engine and entered the lock. Albert closed the lock's rear gates behind the cargo-laden barge. Then he opened the westerly gates to release the water in the lock. The *Mary Rose* slowly descended to the level of the westbound canal. Adam's only remaining lock involvement that night would be in Liverpool when he transferred to the Mersey estuary in order to reach the Albert Dock.

Albert and Adam exchanged waves as Adam engaged the gears to power the *Mary Rose* forward. Within a few minutes he heard the diesel engine slow slightly; the engine's governor had just decided the *Mary Rose* had reached the legal speed limit of five miles per hour. At that steady rate, she proceeded westerly, puffing small bursts of black exhaust into the cloudless starlit sky. Albert remained by the lock a few minutes to watch the *Mary Rose*'s running lights fade into the night. Standing there all alone, he found himself experiencing great pride at how his only daughter's life was turning out.

Who knows, he mused, what kind of a future she would have? Although Albert couldn't know with any certainty, he felt certain she had met the right man and would have a wonderful future.

Chapter Twenty

Adam tied down at the Albert Dock shortly before midnight. From the empty berth he selected, his barge would be unloaded when the dock operations began the next morning at 6 a.m. Before that was concluded, he would have the bill of lading from Bob Harrison for taking on a cargo of sixty tonnes of Indian cotton to be hauled to Wigan. Apart from unexpected delays, he hoped to arrive at the Birchall cottage by 9.30. Rose was to be ready to join him on the remaining trip to Wigan Pier.

Between no unexpected delays, a mild westerly current and a bit of good luck, the Rufford lock gates and the Birchall cottage come into Adam's view at 9 a.m.

Rose had the breakfast dishes all washed and put away when her father's voice rang out the now familiar, 'Adam's arriving!'

She grabbed her handbag and a small carrying bag, and dashed from the cottage. She was standing by the lock when Adam entered. Her father secured the west gates and opened the east gates, admitting the water that raised the *Mary Rose* to ground level. As he was rising in the lock, Adam greeted his father-in-law-to-be and his bride-to-be with a jaunty smile as he stood by the tiller. When Albert Birchall waved him on, Adam engaged the gear and proceeded to the tree-stump tie-down. Rose walked along side the barge and hopped aboard as Adam steered close to the cut. They both waved goodbye to Albert, and the *Mary Rose* resumed her easterly trek toward Wigan.

Rose went below briefly and then joined Adam at the tiller with a cup of tea in either hand. They chatted amiably as they approached Wigan. Along the way, Adam had the spontaneous thought that it would be appropriate to plant a light kiss on Rose's lips. Just as thought was followed by action, they were both startled by the joyous screeching of two unwashed teenage Cockney urchins who were standing on the starboard bow of a passing coal barge, moving in the opposite direction.

'Look at 'im,' cried the larger of the two.

'An' ain't she luvly!' added the smaller one.

'Quite so. Quite so,' replied the larger urchin, effecting a haughty tone. Then they both burst out in uncontrollable laughter, totally consumed by their combined sense of humour.

For an instant, Adam and Rose were stunned in surprise. Then the comedy of the whole scene became apparent and they too broke into hysterical laughter. To an observer on the bank, it would appear the young couple had chimed in with the teenage urchins who had so cleverly exploited their discovery of such a tender moment.

The distance between the two barges lengthened quickly, leaving highly amused occupants going in both directions on the canal.

Adam steered the *Mary Rose* neatly into vacant berth eight in the unloading section of Wigan Pier. As soon as he had his barge secured at tie, he went to the tiny shack on the pier that was the office of the unloading foreman. After the bill-of-lading exchange, Adam returned to his barge, and joined Rose in the living quarters.

Spontaneously, he gave her a very passionate embrace and she melted into his arms. Remarkably, as most young lovers get ever closer to their wedding, their emotional make-up puts them in lockstep with Mother Nature's artful plans, which will have them eagerly donning the yoke of parental responsibilities. The paradox in all this is that before the love bug bites them, most young folk daydream at length about getting old enough to really have some fun. The more adventurous often mull a good deal about travelling and seeing the world. But put a wedding in their agenda, and the vast majority readily change course towards just what Mother Nature had in mind all along: propagate the human race. Life must go on!

Well, until their love has the imprimatur of marriage, the likes of Rose Birchall and Adam Roberts are impelled to don the yoke of parental responsibility almost. By now it had become their pattern to recognise the dangers of sweet surrender, and to back off, when those danger bells began to ring. Although unspoken, neither of them wanted any shadow of compulsion to cloud their impending marriage. It just wasn't worth it. And after they were married, there would be all the time in the world, they, like many of those at the life-goes-on-for-ever stage assumed.

After this passionate encounter, Adam and Rose sat in separate chairs to review their plans for the rest of the day. Those plans covered a good deal of important territory.

From the coach-stop just off Wigan Pier, Rose would take the coach to Standish, where she would join her mother at Auntie Elizabeth's house. She and her mother would call at the nearby church to make the wedding arrangements with the local vicar. They would also do what shopping they could in the small shops in Standish. Then, before taking the coach to Wigan, they hoped to spend some time together with Auntie Elizabeth. Rose was due at 2.30 that afternoon to be measured for her wedding dress at Berman's Bridal Gowns, just off the high street. After that, Rose and her mother would walk to Wigan Pier and find the *Mary Rose*.

Adam's agenda was a good deal different. After handling the necessary paperwork with Matt Shepherd, he would go to Bailey's Café near the Old Wigan Pier to make reservations for the wedding reception. Then he would walk to the Ribble Coach booking office to make the arrangements for a chartered coach on 25 June to take the wedding guests from a selected meeting place in Wigan to the church in Standish. After the ceremony, the coach was to take the guests from the church to Bailey's for the reception. After those arrangements were made, Adam was to get measured at Burton's for his wedding suit, which, as with most Englishmen in those days, would be his dress suit for years to come.

After Adam had completed the reception and charter-coach arrangements, he was thinking to himself as he walked along the high street towards the fifty-bob tailor, Burton's. Harris Tweeds was a fine store, but not fine enough for this. He also felt some personal pleasure in being able to afford a Burton's suit.

Yes, he thought, it's just grand to have enough lolly for all this, and to have Mr Everett Jennings thinking I'm qualified to cast off on a sea of debt. He smiled slightly as these thoughts involuntarily crossed his mind. He straightened up slightly as the next thought occurred.

Now I just wonder how many of me mates back in Gateley could be doing all this? None of 'em, I'm sure. Then the inborn humility that was to be one of Adam Roberts' lifelong major assets took charge. Of course, none of them had the good luck to have people like Walter and Lil take an interest in 'em either, I suppose.

Adam walked into the fifty-bob tailors outlet in Wigan. He was immediately spotted by an alert young salesman who approached him without hesitation.

'And what can we do for you today, sir?' purred the alert young salesman. Adam told him.

A middle-aged, rather heavy-set tailor was promptly summoned, and the trio proceeded to the pole holding hard worsted suits that would fit both Adam's needs and his pocketbook. Twenty-five minutes later, the subjects of suit selection, alterations to be made and payment were all settled. Adam's new Burton's suit would be ready and waiting 'any time after next Tuesday'.

Adam returned to Wigan Pier just before 3 p.m. The *Mary Rose* was tied in berth sixteen near the end of the pier. Six enormous wooden boxes were stacked on her deck. They did not require any securing by ropes or chains. The port-bow waterline marker showed the cargo weighed fifty-eight tonnes.

My gawd, thought Adam. If those boxes were a bit bigger, I'd suspect they held small tractors.

Actually, Adam was quite pleased when he deduced the cargo's weight from the waterline marker. The heavier the load, the more it cost to ship. Walter had, indeed, given him a full informal education on the economic aspects of commercial barging.

Now Adam had only to await the arrival of Rose and her mother. He had had a most eventful day and several hours at the tiller remained. It was time to relax.

When Rose and her mother arrived forty minutes later, Adam was fast asleep half in his bunk and half out.

In short order, the revived Adam Roberts did the necessary to have the *Mary Rose* under way for Rufford. A brisk breeze from the west didn't make the trip any shorter, but it certainly kept the helmsman wide awake all the way. Rose made tea on Adam's tiny stove. She poured three cups: one for her mother, and the other two she walked to the stern, where she joined Adam at the tiller. Adam steered with one hand and managed his cup of tea with the other. For most of the two-hour trip, Doris Birchall relaxed below. Rose spent most of that time exchanging details of the day with Adam. The rest of the day was uneventful, except in one respect: the Birchall family had a very late and entirely forgettable supper.

Adam stayed over, sleeping on the living-room couch.

My, he thought just before dropping off to sleep, it's getting to be more like family all the time.

Chapter Twenty-one

The remainder of the three weeks before the wedding were eventful, to put it mildly. The most pleasant of those events, to Adam and Rose at least, was the day Rose picked up her wedding dress at Berman's Bridal Gowns, and Adam picked up his wedding suit at Burton's. Doris Birchall accompanied her daughter on this mission. The customary trying on for size went perfectly. The tailors in both shops were obviously highly skilled.

Fortunately, picking up the clothes was all that was involved. Even that had to be accomplished within the span of ninety minutes.

The urgency of the occasion stemmed from a priority hauling schedule of an enormous shipment from Alton Mills that had to be on board a certain German freighter that was sailing from Liverpool for New York at 5 p.m. on the dot. On-time arrivals and departures were a well-known obsession with virtually every *Kapitän* in Germany's merchant marine. Those who sailed in and out of Liverpool were no exception.

Adam's job, of course, did not bring him into direct contact with the officers or crews of seagoing merchant ships. From time to time, nevertheless, he saw any number of German seamen around the Albert Dock and the nearby pubs. There was something very unappealing about their all-knowing arrogance or smugness. Adam didn't know which.

After he had let Rose and her mother off at their cottage, he continued toward Liverpool. Once he was travelling alone, he caught himself repeatedly checking the time on his wristwatch against his location. This gave him the unpleasant feeling that he was skipping rope to keep time set by the German. Damn those pompous Germans, raced across his mind. Like most Englishmen in 1935, Adam had not the slightest inkling of how that decade would end vis-à-vis the Germans.

Regardless, Alton Mills's precious cargo bound for New York was safely in the hold of the *Seewolf - Hamburg* well before 5 p.m.

On Thursday, one week to the day after Walter and Adam had first met with Everett Jennings, they met again at noon at the news-stand on platform eight of Manchester's Piccadilly station. Each was wearing the same dress clothes he had worn the week before, except Adam was wearing a mint-green tie, which nicely matched his Reed's tweeds. Walter suspected Rose had done the matching, but said nothing about the tie.

Walter told Adam of a call he'd received from Everett Jennings just before leaving the house in Chester. All of the necessary papers were drawn up, and would be at Mr Jennings' office at 1.30 p.m.

'So,' added Walter, 'we've got time now to get a bite and discuss which barges we want to order.'

Adam was delighted on Walter's every point. He particularly wanted to discuss with Walter the possibilities of ordering the Kingston seventy-footer, which, at least the brochure still in his inside suit pocket professed, had 'Living quarters you can live in'.

Being well aware of the poor-tasting food served at train stations, Walter and Adam walked to a small restaurant across the road. While waiting for their order, Adam withdrew the now-tattered Kingston brochure, and handed it to Walter.

'Do you think we could afford this one for me, and Rose too, of course?' he asked a bit wistfully.

Walter took the brochure from Adam and studied the photographs carefully. He pondered.

'It is reaching a bit right now but, all things considered, that's probably the very class of barge our head man on the canals should have, as far as image goes. Adam Roberts at the tiller of that barge should really project the up-market image that Everett Jennings was talking about last week.

'Well, Adam,' Walter drawled, pausing slightly for dramatic effect. 'Uh,' he seemed to stutter slightly, and then spoke very positively, 'I think I'm looking at the *Mary Rose II*.'

Adam's face broke into a broad smile. I can hardly wait to tell this news to Rose, he thought.

After completing their lunch, Walter and Adam walked to the perpetual line of taxis in front of the train station. They boarded the next-up for the fifteen-minute drive to Leeds and Liverpool House. They arrived at Everett Jennings's office exactly on time.

'Please show them in.' Everett Jennings's voice came out of the little speaker in the intercom on Miss Dobbins's desk.

This was in response to her having pressed some magic button on the intercom and uttering, 'Mr White and Mr Roberts are here, sir.'

What will they come up with next? Adam asked himself, as he looked at the strange-appearing little apparatus on Miss Dobbins's desk. Part radio, and part, uh, I dunno what.

Everett Jennings met them at the door and greeted them warmly. The warmth of this reception was surely enhanced by a final report which Everett Jennings had just read on White and Roberts from the intelligence-gathering apparatus of his employer. He had dropped that report into a desk drawer when Miss Dobbins informed him Walter and Adam had arrived. The conclusion in that report stated:

Our investigation of White and Roberts is now complete. Inland Revenue records confirm those of the Trustee Bank in Liverpool, where they have banked since filing their articles of partnership in 1932. White and Roberts has maintained a steady increase in business. Collections have been prompt. They have had no bad-debt write-offs. This operation meets or exceeds all prescribed criteria for participation in your programme.

We were provided with a list of sixteen-barge hauling operations you are considering for the programme. Our investigation is now complete on fourteen of those on your list. Only White and Roberts and two others meet or exceed all your criteria. This is quite exceptional, considering Walter White's heart attack in 1934. We have determined he has essentially made a full recovery. He manages all operations from a residence in Chester. Telephone exchange billings indicate he is very active.

After the customary greetings the three got right down to business. Everett Jennings began the conference by producing a number of documents from his desk drawer. Those consisted of a promissory note made payable to the Trustee bank, Manchester, 'in a sum not to exceed £38,000' in progressively increasing monthly instalments over a five-year term. Next to the promissory note lay a deposit receipt clipped to a small bank book that had been issued to 'White and Roberts, a partnership' on account number 44564. The only entry in the bank book was date-stamped '9/6/35'. It consisted of some totally illegible initials next to a perfectly legible entry in the column captioned 'deposits'. The entry read: £20,000.

Next to the bank book lay a thick-paper card bearing the bold printed title: 'depositors' authorised signature card'. Below that title was printed some legal-sounding language which, at least on second reading, would inform anyone that the account to which it pertained was that of 'William White Esq. and Adam Roberts Esq., partners, doing business as White and Roberts.' The signatures below were those of those persons who were authorised to sign cheques drawn on that account. Next to these documents was a cheque book containing twenty blank cheques, which could be drawn on account number 44564.

Lastly, there was an executed letter of credit which authorised either of the White and Roberts partners to instruct the Trustee Bank to deposit additional monies into the numbered account 'from the £38,000 line of credit'.

Everett Jennings asked Walter and Adam to sign the promissory note. After they had done so, he signed it on behalf of the Leeds and Liverpool Canal Company Ltd as guarantor. Then Walter and Adam each signed the depositors' authorised signature card.

Once the signing ceremonies were complete, Everett Jennings took the original promissory note and signature card for transmittal to the Trustee Bank. He pushed the bank book, the blank cheques and the original letter of credit across the desk to Walter, along with the White and Roberts copy of the promissory note.

The whole affair took less than twenty minutes.

Everett Jennings rose to indicate the conference was over and walked from behind his desk to escort his guests to the door.

'In my experience,' he said, as the party moved towards the door, 'doing business is only truly successful when it works to the benefit of everyone engaged. I am convinced, gentlemen, we have just ended the beginning of a true business success.'

My, but he does have a way with words, thought Adam, who was trying to contain his glee at what had just been concluded.

At the door, the three shook hands and their meeting was over.

Walter and Adam walked out of Leeds and Liverpool House and into the warm afternoon sunlight. Walter hadn't felt better in years, and Adam wasn't sure his feet were reaching the pavement.

Walter hailed an approaching taxi. Within minutes, the two were standing in front of Piccadilly station. The plan was that Walter would take the next train to Bradford, where he would make the barge selections and sign the purchase order with Kingston Marine Barges. Hopefully he would be back in Chester for supper. He had promised to call Lil in all events. Adam would return to the *Mary Rose* at Wigan Pier, which should be loaded and ready with a cargo to be barged to Liverpool. He expected to stay overnight at Rufford and be in Liverpool by noon the next day.

Walter's train for Bradford was being called when the two entered the train station. Accordingly, their farewell was quick, but the parting handshakes were firm and heartfelt. Walter and Adam had developed a genuine man-to-man rapport.

Adam had to wait almost an hour before leaving on the train for Wigan. This didn't bother him. He had a myriad of things to think about, each one of them turning out great or heading in that direction. As he ambled toward platform seven, he passed the news-stand. He scanned the headline of the latest edition of the *Manchester Guardian*:

HAWKER TO TEST NEW HURRICANE FIGHTER AT BROOKLANDS

Like most Britons of the day, Adam was totally unaware of the clouds of war that were forming.

Now, I wonder where Brooklands is, he mused. He went back to visualising telling Rose and her family about the new Kingston barge now on order, or so he hoped it would be.

Adam was so absorbed in his thoughts he didn't even notice the empty train that would carry him to Wigan move into position by platform nine. He was jarred back to reality by a deep voice coming out of the station's loudspeaker: 'Wigan. Train for Wigan. Platform nine. Leaving at 4.07.'

There it was, right before him.

Now thoroughly back among the conscious living, he walked on to the nearest passenger coach, and took the first empty seat he came to.

At 4.07 p.m. the train lurched forward as the engineer sounded the steam engine's whistle. Next stop: Wigan.

Once back in Wigan, Adam walked briskly to the pier, where he found the *Mary Rose* tied in berth seven. Twenty large wooden boxes were stacked neatly on her deck. Per the port-bow waterline, they weighed thirty-five tonnes. The business logo of Lancashire Iron & Foundry Ltd appeared on two sides of each box. Adam walked to Matt Shepherd's office, where he was given the bills of lading, which recited that his cargo consisted of automotive parts bound for Singapore in a proper British merchant ship. That's more like it, he thought, with almost a patriotic satisfaction. He would take them as far as Liverpool.

He quickly changed to his working clothes in the living quarters, and then joined forces with his trusty diesel engine to get him and his cargo as far as Rufford. Liverpool could wait until the next morning.

As soon as Adam could make out the top of the Rufford lock gates and their tender standing nearby, he flicked his forward deck light on and off twice and began waving his arms back and forth in front of his body, hoping Albert Birchall would understand that he wanted to surprise Rose, and that he shouldn't call out that he was arriving. He wanted to surprise her.

Even though he and Albert had never discussed or tried this signal, Albert got it and carried on as if he didn't see any barge traffic approaching whatever.

Adam cut his diesel engine almost a hundred yards short of his tie-down. He let the current carry the *Mary Rose* in utter silence to where her port bow came alongside the rusted iron hook protruding from canal-side tree stump. He jumped from the deck and quickly tied his barge to this mooring. Then he waved at Albert and ran like a lovesick boy to the Birchall cottage.

To Adam's delight and surprise, who should be awaiting him along with Rose and her mother inside the Birchall cottage but his sister Mary. She and Rose had worked out these arrangements earlier in the week by phone. Rose had met Mary at the Rufford coach stop earlier the day before. They had walked to the Birchall cottage, where Rose introduced her to all the family.

Mary and Tim were about the same age and immediately seemed to find each other's company somewhat fascinating. Mary's eyes had fairly sparkled when Tim asked her to go to the farmer's dance in Rufford the night before. As usual, this dance was well attended by almost every young person living in the area. Tim had introduced Mary to his many friends at the dance. He was obviously a very popular fellow. The lads had almost lined up to dance with Mary. Before the evening was out, however, she had lost count of how many. By 10 p.m., she was truly beginning to tire.

As she and Tim walked home from the dance, he had asked her how many of the lads she had danced with.

'I don't really remember,' she had said, 'I'm probably just too tired.'

'Well,' Tim had said, 'there was supposed to be fourteen dances, and only four of them were with me.'

Mary had sensed the slight pique in his tone.

'Then it had to be thirteen, since you were the only one I danced with more than once.'

She was ever so slightly pleased that Tim was apparently a tad jealous. She was really pleased when the Birchall cottage came into view. She never had a better night's sleep in her life.

When Adam knocked and entered, he was obviously surprised to see Mary there and embraced the ladies all around.

At supper he proudly announced that everything in Manchester had gone according to plan and he imagined Walter was 'probably on the train from Bradford right now with a signed order from Kingston Marine for a brand new one of these.' He handed Mary the tattered brochure that depicted the seventy-foot barge with 'Living quarters you can live in'.

Everyone at the supper table felt joy and satisfaction in contemplating the described events, and in anticipation of those about to unfold. The wedding was just over a week away.

After supper, the ladies cleared the table. Rose and Mary helped Doris do the dishes and then joined the men in the Birchall living room. There followed a back-and-forth discussion that touched the very subjects one would expect. Where would they go for their honeymoon? How long would they be gone? When was the new barge you could live in expected? When were the Roberts family expected? Who was this Amos Cooper that would be coming with the Robertses? Where was the reception going to be? And on and on.

Tim joined in the conversation with gusto, although he could hardly keep his eyes off Mary. She was well aware of his attention, and occasionally cast a half-flirtatious glance in his direction.

Ah, the artfulness with which we women are born, thought the observant Doris Birchall.

Adam and Rose provided a good many estimates and best guesses. As the hour grew late, involuntary yawning became almost contagious. It had become time to go to bed.

Given the space limitations of the Birchall cottage, and his expected early departure, Adam kissed his sister, his bride-to-be and his future mother-in-law all goodnight and slept on the *Mary Rose*.

At first light next morning, without waking a soul, Adam managed the lock gates to let himself through, and proceeded on to Liverpool. At 10.30 a.m., Rose walked Mary to the Rufford motor coach stop. She returned to Gateley by way of Preston.

Rose and her mother got the last wedding invitation in the pillar box in Rufford on Friday, the eighth day before the wedding.

Until the following Friday, everyone carried on with their usual daily involvements. During that time, Adam was moving on the canals an average of fifteen hours a day. For the most part, he slept in open county, with the *Mary Rose* tethered to his steel tie-down rod with its two-foot shaft driven deep into the cuts.

Chapter Twenty-two

On Tuesday before the wedding Mary phoned Rose to tell her that she, her parents and Amos Cooper expected to arrive at the Rufford motor coach stop on Friday at 11.15 a.m. Adam had already told Rose he expected to arrive on Friday, 'late in the day, probably around dusk.' After Mary's call, Rose and her mother sat in the living room to work out the Friday-night accommodations logistics.

'It seems pretty simple to me,' said Doris.

Rose was glad to hear that was going to be the case, but gave her a mother an inquiring look as if to ask 'Just how?'

'The Roberts and Birchall ladies will take the 2.20 p.m. motor coach to Wigan, and on to Auntie Elizabeth's. The men can have the house to themselves,' said Doris.

'The wedding isn't until 2 p.m. on Saturday,' she added, 'so we can work out the detail of getting together by phone in the forenoon.'

Now why didn't all that occur to me? Rose asked herself. Her mind promptly provided the answer. I was just too busy with a hundred other things.

When they finished their tea, Doris walked to the lock gates to tell her husband how 'all this is going to work out'.

After Doris had told Albert the plans for Friday, she concluded, 'Now, Albert, this means you're going to be the host, so you ought to be thinking about that.' He did.

Actually, Albert demonstrated extraordinary foresight in planning for this all-male enclave. He would surely need something in the way of a social catalyst. 'Group warmer' was the specific description he had muttered to himself as he entered Rufford's only off-licence early the next evening. After discussing the matter with the proprietor, he had purchased two bottles of dry sherry. He had managed to hide this purchase in a small cupboard, while Rose and her mother busied themselves preparing supper in the kitchen.

The Friday before the Saturday wedding involved a host of memorable events beginning with the arrival at the Rufford motor coach stop of Adam's family, accompanied by the affable Amos Cooper. Rose was waiting. Amos was particularly chatty as the group walked to the Birchall cottage. Amos had never been to Rufford and remarked that he found it quite lovely and interesting.

Barge traffic was light that day, so Albert was able to be with his wife and sons when the Roberts party and Rose arrived. Affability is the only word to describe the next two hours, during which a light lunch was served along with the inveterate elixir of England, a good cup of tea.

The mothers and their daughters departed on time for Standish. John and Tim carried their luggage until it was safely aboard the Wigan-bound motor coach. Before Adam arrived around six that evening, Albert operated the lock to pass three westbound and two eastbound barges. John and Tim showed James and Amos around their farm amid a never-ending flow of conversation.

By the time Adam arrived, his father, Amos and the Birchalls were chatting away like old friends.

After Adam had the *Mary Rose* tied down and his clothes changed, he joined the others in the Birchall cottage. Seeing that all were present, 'host' Albert Birchall decided it was time to have a little toast.

'After all, we've got a lot to toast,' said Albert as he headed for small cupboard, from which he withdrew one full-litre flagon of dry sherry. Next he brought five crystal snifters from a kitchen cupboard and placed them on the table. He poured the sherry, half-filling each little glass. He picked up one of the snifters and waved his sons and guests to pick up theirs, which they promptly did.

'To Adam, Rose, and the wedding,' announced Albert, as he raised his drink to eye level.

'Here, here.' said the others, as each raised his glass to his lips.

Oddly enough, only Albert emptied his glass on the first swig.

James and Amos were simply not used to drinking spirits, and each decided to have only a sip, thus limiting their exposure to possible adverse effects. John, Tim and Adam felt similarly restrained, but not because of any imagined effects. Only once or twice had any of them tasted any drinks stronger than beer. Now each of them was a bit leery of the dark amber fluid in the full-litre flagon.

After thoroughly enjoying the toast 'to Adam, Rose and the wedding', Albert was inspired to propose a second toast 'to friends today and family tomorrow'. The same pattern of ingestion was repeated. In fact, the pattern continued for as long as Albert could think up someone or someplace to toast, or when the supply of dry sherry was exhausted. The next day, he couldn't specifically recall which occurred first. Amos Cooper wasn't quite sure how he fitted into the 'friends today and family tomorrow' equation, but as the evening drew on, he was increasingly amused at the host's growing sense of humour.

Albert awoke around seven the next morning, face down, turned cross-wise on his own bed. He was still in his regular clothes. His first thoughts were to try to remember last night.

He recalled quite clearly the initial toast, but after that they all seemed to run together. He believed the last toast had been 'to that upstanding honourable gentleman, the Prince of Wales!' Wonder how *he* got into it?

Involuntarily, his concentration swiftly shifted from the Prince of Wales to wondering how long this splitting headache would last. Just think, he mused, if we'd had a proper supper, maybe everything wouldn't have turned out so painful.

Over the evening, Albert's sons and guests did drink enough of the dry sherry to prove its merits as a group warmer. Tim, in particular, had laughed himself silly on two occasions – not so much because of anything he drank, but at his father. Until this night Tim had never thought his dad was funny or had much of a sense of humour, for that matter.

Only Albert proved a victim of the Friday evening proceedings. Had he been more familiar with the recoil effects of ingesting prodigious amounts of dry sherry, he would undoubtedly have been more moderate in his role as a host. All the rest awoke the next morning without noticeable after effects.

John and Tim were preparing a breakfast when Albert wandered in from his bedroom. Tim saw him flinch a bit when the two empty flagons on the dining table came into focus. He saw him flinch even more when the telephone emitted two short rings. It was Doris, wanting to be sure that everything was all right. Tim answered the call and assured his mother that everything just couldn't be better. Yes, he would have his dad give her a call just as soon as he got up, which Tim imagined 'will be very soon'.

Albert settled in a sofa chair and nodded his thanks to his youngest son.

Events in Wigan on that busy Friday were quite different.

The Whites had booked their room at the Chadwick Inn on Mesne Street, easy walking distance to the motor coach stop by Wigan Pier, where the Ribble Coach was to pick everyone up the next morning. After they had checked into the Chadwick, Lil went shopping in search of an appropriate wedding gift. Walter stayed in their room, where he studied a lengthy letter he had received from Everett Jennings about getting to know the key people of the Leeds and Liverpool customers whom 'White and Roberts will be servicing'. The letter provided the name and office phone number of the Leeds and Liverpool customer representative, whom Walter was to contact to set up the introductory meetings. The letter made it clear that Everett Jennings had no preferences as to whether Walter or Adam was the White and Roberts representative who attended any of these meetings.

Walter had had offered to book a room for Norman Nelson, but Norman had to decline. That Friday, after getting back to Liverpool around 4.30 p.m., he had to go through the unloading and reloading process, and then depart for Preston, where he arrived at 7.30 p.m. At Preston, Norman's barge would not be unloaded until 9 a.m. the next day, the morning of the wedding. No trains or buses ran on Friday evening from Preston to Wigan after 8.30 p.m., so, Norman's only means to attend the wedding was to spend the night in Preston on his barge, and catch the early bus to Wigan on Saturday morning.

Lil found just what she was looking for at Pendlebury's, the town's leading general merchandise store. She bought a neatly packaged set of silverware, a service for six.

Adam and Rose won't ever feed even six people on their barge, she thought, and I know a thing or two about the endless search for storage space in a barge cabin. This set is just right.

She completed her purchase, paid tuppence to have it gift-wrapped, and returned to the Chadwick inn. Later, she and Walter walked to the inn's carvery for an early supper.

Chapter Twenty-three

The wedding on Saturday played out like a well-directed symphony, in spite of the hustle and bustle and last-minute items that somehow all got done. Albert, John, Tim, James, Amos and Adam all arrived in a timely fashion at the church. Adam looked splendid in his dark-green hard-worsted Burton's suit. Albert, John and Tim Birchall would hardly have been recognised by their neighbours when they arrived in Standish in their nice-fitting rented wedding suits. Albert's suit was charcoal grey. Those of John and Tim were much lighter, more befitting younger men. If there was a down side, it was poor Albert. He mournfully wondered which looked the worse, his bloodshot eyes or his flush-red face. Those visible vestiges of his ill-spent night before were accompanied by a splitting headache and hypersensitive eardrums. Albert realised he couldn't undo anything. He would just have to hope that people at the wedding either wouldn't notice his residuals, or that, if they did, they would fail to guess their origin. He also swore off dry sherry for life, or so he vowed.

Around 1.30 p.m. the guests began arriving at the church in Standish. Friends and family of the groom were seated in the pews on the right of the centre aisle; those of the bride were seated on the left. After the Ribble coach arrived from Wigan, most of the seats in the church were taken.

James and Celia Roberts and Amos Cooper, in that order, were seated in the front pew on the right of the aisle. After seeing that all was well with Rose in the small waiting room near the back of the church, Doris Birchall and Auntie Elizabeth were escorted by one of the church's wedding volunteers to the front pew on the left. They sat, leaving a place by the aisle for Albert, after he had escorted his daughter down the aisle to the alter.

At exactly 1.40 p.m. the newly appointed church organist seated herself at the large reed organ by the north wall that faced toward an empty choir box on the opposite side. While the organ bore no date of manufacture, without doubt it had been in the church before any other person in attendance ever saw the inside of this church. The new organist was a lean and frumpy spinster whose bouncy light brown ringlets looked like the curlers had been removed within the hour. She had a plain but friendly face and was obviously in her mid-forties. She had long ago convinced herself that her only love was her music. Being the most recent addition to the church's staff, today she intended to impress one and all with her considerable musical skills. She began creating the wedding atmosphere by playing a number of traditional wedding pieces. The vicar, standing near the raised podium, was duly impressed with the resonant wedding songs coming from the organ. At 1.50 p.m. Albert Birchall stood well off the aisle at the back of the church waiting for his daughter to emerge from the little waiting room. In spite of his splitting headache, Albert enjoyed the organist's rendition of 'Because I Love Thee'.

At 1.55 p.m. while the sonorous wedding refrains continued to fill the air, another wedding volunteer signalled Adam, best-man Tim and John Birchall to stand just to the right of the altar. Mary Roberts and one of Rose's school chums were the bridesmaids. As instructed, they stood to the left of the altar dressed in attractive yellow flowered dresses, which each had made just for the wedding.

As the hour neared 2 p.m., still another wedding volunteer tapped on Rose's door, signalling to her that it was time to join her father at the head of the aisle. Rose complied, but she was too nervous to notice Albert's condition.

When the vicar, now standing at the altar, saw the bride and her father were ready at the back of the church, he signalled to the new organist. Her nimble fingers pounced on the ageing organ's ivory keyboard to produce a very audible rendition of Richard Wagner's 'Here Comes the Bride'. That spirited classic was revised only by the clipped cadence interjected by the performing artist at the keyboard. The vicar had never heard such vibrant sounds out of the organ, which, he made a mental note, was far from new when he became the 'new vicar' here and that was eighteen years ago!

Albert winced as 'Here Comes the Bride' crashed against his tender eardrums. But with stiff-upper-lip British resolve he continued to escort his daughter down the aisle at a measured pace. As they advanced down the aisle, Albert fervently hoped his frail condition would not be noticed. He needn't have worried. All eyes were on Rose, except those of the more worldly Norman Nelson, who was satisfied he was definitely looking at a hangover as he watched Albert walk by in the nearby aisle.

The beautiful bride was another matter. Between Rose's pretty face, her black silken hair and her gorgeous white satin wedding dress, she looked like a princess out of a fairy tale. (Two years later, when the American film *Snow White and the Seven Dwarfs* played in the pictures in England, the striking resemblance between the animated heroine and Rose Birchall at her wedding was noted by more than a dozen of the ladies who had been in attendance.) Except for one brief glance at her mother, Rose followed the wedding volunteer's instruction to look straight ahead as she walked down the aisle.

After handing Rose off to her handsome groom, Albert turned to his left and sat next to his wife. He had no suspicion that the couple sitting directly behind had keenly viewed his flush-red complexion, bloodshot eyes and strained facial expression. The pair exchanged knowing glances and brief smiles. At least two more guests had accurately diagnosed Albert's symptoms.

On cue, Adam and Rose turned to face the vicar directly. In a very serious voice he proclaimed, 'In the presence of God, Father, Son and Holy Spirit, we have come together to witness the marriage of Adam and Rose.'

There followed the wedding ceremony, as prescribed by the Church of England. After the exchange of vows, the vicar pronounced the young couple to be man and wife, and gestured for the best man to hand Adam the wedding ring. Adam promptly placed the gold band on Rose's left hand and eagerly followed the vicar's instruction, 'You may kiss the bride.'

The vicar took one step back and glanced toward the organist, nodding slightly. The bride and groom turned to face the back of the church and started walking up the aisle, arm in arm. At their first step, Mendelssohn's famous 'Wedding March' thundered from the ancient reed organ. As the newlyweds proceeded forward, the organist's skinny legs churned furiously, like pistons, as if she were racing the newlyweds up the aisle. The vicar continued to be amazed at the ageing organ's sheer volume. Our new organist must have found a hitherto undiscovered fortissimo stop, he thought, erroneously.

By this time, having already been buffeted by 'Here Comes the Bride', Albert Birchall had become numb to further acoustic assault. Despite the impressive decibels, Mendelssohn's 'Wedding March' rolled by him with no more effect that a strong breeze would have on a tombstone. When Doris nudged him, Albert stood and stepped into the aisle. The senior Robertses and Birchalls then led the exodus of guests to the cement enclave in front of the church.

As soon as Adam and Rose emerged from the church, they were spotted by the official church bell-ringer, George Morely, and his son, who were standing in the belfry, forty feet above ground level. Each of them held a pull rope which extended around the grooved circumference of the wheels affixed to the left side of two suspended but enormous brass bells. Hanging inside each bell was a cast-iron clapper, whose impact against the sides of the bells, when rotating back and forth, cascaded thunderclaps of vibrant ringing noise across the country side. After weddings, the sounding of these bells was an age-old tradition of welcoming newlyweds into a new life together.

Local people often joined the jubilant wedding guests in front of the church in throwing of rice over the newlyweds. Today, a total of seventy loud and cheering celebrants launched a monsoon of rice over the joyous Adam and Rose. George and son were swept up in the festive atmosphere as they hauled tirelessly on their ropes, oblivious to the invisible risk of deafness from the thunderous pressure levels they were producing.

Rose's mother had hired Wigan's most prominent photographer, Graham

Scott, to be the official wedding photographer. His stock-in-trade consisted of a medium-format Leica camera and a sturdy wooden tripod. He also had a messy flashgun, which provided artificial light for indoor photographs. Use of this device often led to photographs showing the shock and surprise of the subjects at being briefly blinded by the brilliant flash. The vicar in Standish would not permit this fiendish demon to be 'exploded' inside the church. Knowing this was a 'Standish ground rule', Graham had left his flashgun in his Vauxhall for possible later use at the reception.

Graham's first picture was of the bride and groom, whom he asked to pause briefly when they emerged from the church. Subsequently he took many additional pictures in front of the church. Most of his photographs were of the Birchall and Roberts family members posing in various combinations. Many years later, the print of a photograph Graham took that day of Tim and Mary would accompany both of them virtually all over the world.

Graham Scott was an affable fellow who was well liked generally. He had one pet peeve, however, which only surfaced after weddings, such as the Roberts–Birchall wedding in Standish on 25 June 1935. The objects of his scorn were the increasing number of dolts showing up at such occasions with a cheap little American invention called a Kodak Box Brownie. In callous disregard of the obvious fact that a qualified wedding photographer was present and doing a professional job, these confounding amateurs milled about, asking his subjects to pose so they could take wedding pictures!

'Those twits can take a wedding picture with that piece of junk and I'm the King of England!' he complained.

He scowled at these dolts, but he was too much the good businessman to suggest where they might stick their little tin-pot cameras.

A good friend of Auntie Elizabeth was also the proud owner of a 1930 jet-black Vauxhall saloon. He had agreed to drive the bride and groom to the reception in Wigan. At the appointed time, the proud Vauxhall owner drove up in his highly polished automobile in front of the church. Blue and red ribbons streamed from the bonnet. Adam and Rose stepped into the Vauxhall and departed amid the cacophony of jubilant cheering and peeling church bells.

Shortly thereafter, the newlyweds' parents were whisked off to Wigan in another, less splendid, vehicle, a Morris Eight that had been volunteered by Auntie Elizabeth's next-door neighbour. She also prevailed on another neighbour to loan his Ford Y to Adam and Rose for their honeymoon. That neighbour actually volunteered his car, which 'needed driving'. He had been unable to drive the car for over a month because of his diminishing eyesight, and a short hop to the Lake District would do just fine. Before being told of this good fortune, Adam had very limited experience in driving automobiles. During the last two weeks before the wedding, he had prevailed on a very casual friend to give him driving lessons on four separate occasions when his evening layover was in Liverpool.

Chapter Twenty-four

After delivering the wedding guests who came by Ribble coach at the church, Harry Cunliffe, the driver, had parked his coach behind the church.

While everything was going on inside the church, he enjoyed a little snooze. He always delighted in such napping, as it involved getting paid for his time while sleeping. To Harry, this seemed like a fun trick that had the zestful little frisson of petty larceny. Today he enjoyed the added dividend of being able to remove his new dentures while he napped.

Harry was rapidly returned to the land of the living when George and son began shaking the countryside with their thundering church bells. He bolted upright in his seat. His personal antennas were equally responsive. At first, he moved only his eyes to peer about for snoopers who might be cruising about, hoping to discover something that might be of value to his employer; something like eyewitness proof that coach driver Harry Cunliffe was seen sleeping on the job, thus jeopardising the good name and reputation of Ribble Coaches Ltd.

After moving only his eyes to check, Harry moved his head, neck and shoulders, looking out for the snoopers. So far, so good; at least from what could be seen from his position. Then he got out of the coach to scan the whole area, using the disarming ploy of appearing to be checking the coach's tires. Well, if there were any snoopers about, they missed the boat by miles today! he thought triumphantly.

Once Harry was completely satisfied that he and the coach had been all alone behind the church, he breathed a sigh of relief and re-entered the vehicle. To assure his continued privacy, he pulled the handle that closed the door from the inside. Then he seated himself behind his large steering wheel. He tilted the rear-view mirror downward so he could see his reflection as he combed his hair and replaced his dentures. Yes indeed, if any snoopers were peeking now, they could report that Harry Cunliffe was very keen when it came, to personal grooming. Right there in the mirror he was looking at a splendid example of the Ribble standard for coach drivers. 'All's well,' he said to himself, almost joyously.

Harry straightened his back for a little more formal approach to the task at hand, and started the mighty diesel engine that was located in the rear end of the coach.

Clutch in. Gearshift into first. He eased out the clutch and pulled the coach around to the front of the church, where he parked to await the goings-on there.

Through the din of church bells and jumbled conversations, Harry could occasionally hear Graham Scott calling out, 'Yes, madam, your lovely handbag will be in the picture. That's fine, now everyone smile. In a bit closer together.' And so on.

Harry saw the beaming bride and groom depart in the Vauxhall. A short time later he saw two older couples leave in a Morris Eight.

Harry's instructions were to 'have 'em loaded and headed for Wigan no later than 3.30'. As the minute hand of his watch approached the designated departure time, he decided it was time to get them moving.

Just as Harry stepped out of the coach, mercifully, the church bells stopped ringing. He faced the crowd. 'All right, ladies and gentlemen,' he said in a very stentorian tone of voice, 'it's time for everyone going to the reception at Bailey's by coach to get on board.'

As the guests walked up, Harry signalled to them to form a line in single file, beginning at the open entrance door. In less than ten minutes, forty-eight reception-bound wedding guests were seated on board. Harry always did have a knack for crowd control, or so he frequently thought.

Norman had got in the line and boarded when it was his turn. He ended up in an aisle seat, near the middle of the coach. Wanting to be sociable, he turned to introduce himself to the older gentleman sitting on his right. Extending his hand, he said, 'I'm Norman Nelson. I operate a barge for Adam, that is, for Mr Roberts and Mr White.'

The older gentleman's face broke into a friendly smile. He reached to shake Norman's hand.

'My name is Amos Cooper,' he said. 'I'm a retired schoolmaster and I taught both Adam and his sister Mary at grammar school.'

Norman was quite familiar with the name Amos Cooper.

'I've heard your name several times,' said Norman, showing real interest. 'Adam has often mentioned you. You're the one who taught him to read and write, and how to keep a set of books.'

From then on these two chatted affably all the way to Wigan.

At the back of the coach, Tim managed to get the seat next to Mary, and was secretly wishing the passengers wouldn't talk so loud. All that separated him and Mary from the roaring diesel engine was some kind of partition that had no resemblance to a sound barrier. Between the noise from the crowd and the diesel, Tim and Mary realised they couldn't converse until the coach ride was over. Once we get to the reception, it will be a different story, each one of them quietly thought. The seeds of mutual attraction were clearly beginning to take root. The coach ride to Bailey's took about twenty minutes.

Fifteen minutes after discharging the last passenger, Henry Cunliffe returned the coach to the Ribble car park and turned in his time card at the company's nearby booking office. Naturally, he included the time during when he had just been relaxing.

Why not? he thought. I was protecting their property, wasn't I?

Chapter Twenty-five

The reception at Bailey's was an exciting, exuberant and expensive affair. There was an open bar, which seemed to be well appreciated by all but the bride's father.

Shortly after Albert arrived at Bailey's, he was approached by an old friend, whose name his poor aching brain could not recall. The friend had spotted him right off and could tell at a glance that Albert had either overindulged the night before, 'Or,' he joked with the ailing lock-keeper, 'you've been sitting far too near to someone who had.'

Albert was in no condition to appreciate any humour from his nameless friend. He just muttered something inaudible as he shook the man's hand rather limply.

'Albert,' his nameless friend pressed on, 'I've had a good deal of experience in coping with the after-effects of strong drink, and you'd be well advised to follow the good advice I'm about to give you.'

'I think I'd dance with the Devil,' said Albert, 'if it would get rid of this splitting headache.'

But having conceded the origin of his painful condition, Albert continued to ramble. 'Oh yes! If anyone asks, I no longer like organ music. I swear that woman pumping that organ at the church saw right through me, and I know she set out to make me pay for my sins. She's probably some kind of fanatic in the Temperance Movement. She ought to go to America, where they take that sort of thing seriously.'

'Well,' said No-name, 'the organ music was a bit loud, but compared to those church bells it was almost hard to hear.'

'You've got a point,' said Albert, 'but I don't see how those bell-ringers would have any such intentions. They were somewhere up in the tower. They couldn't even see me, up close, that is. But that frothy frump at the organ was staring right at me when Rose and I got down to the front. She just glared. I'm surprised Doris didn't catch the crone giving me the evil eye. But she didn't say a thing. Matter of fact, Doris didn't say much of anything all the way to Wigan. Rather surprises me, that. She usually picks right up on about everything that happens.'

No-name smiled knowingly, but thought it best not to get into what women do and don't pick up on.

'I'm not talking about organ music or bell-ringers, or even wives,' said

Albert's anonymous friend. 'I'm talking about a remedy! Something that will end your misery and lift your spirits.'

'I'll try anything,' said Albert. 'Just name it.'

'A shandy,' said No-name. 'It's what the Americans call "hair of the dog".'

'A shandy?' asked Albert incredulously. 'Alcohol?'

'Ah,' said his unrecalled friend, 'alcohol, yes – but only that within the contents of less than a half-pint of bitter, and all that is watered down with lemonade. It's in the nature of fighting fire with fire, Albert. I absolutely guarantee you will feel immediate relief.'

The argument was compelling.

Albert hailed the first passing waiter and asked him to bring a mild shandy.

The results were phenomenal. Within a half-hour, Albert's headache was almost gone and he was chinning affably about mostly nothing with his brilliant friend, name or no name. True, Albert's reddened eyes suggested that bleeding to death might still be a hazard, but a small one. For most intents and purposes, Albert Birchall had been recalled to life.

The reception featured all of the regular events that occur at such events. The vicar from Standish had arrived at Bailey's just as the Roberts and Birchall parents were getting out of the Morris Eight. He was in his street clothes, having changed from his ceremonial religious garb. He was truly a congenial fellow, who enjoyed good company as well as good spirits – if not 'too strong'.

The chatty and affable vicar fitted in very well at the reception, and ended up as the master of ceremonies after all the guests had been fed. When the serving dishes were removed, it was time for some customary formalities. The vicar led off with a short speech in which he purported to speak for all present in wishing Mr and Mrs Adam Roberts a wonderful marriage. He concluded these remarks by proposing the first toast.

One after another, various guests stood, intending to make some kind of congratulatory speech. As at most wedding receptions, the majority of these spontaneous toastmasters end up proving that speech making was not their forté, and a few always betray that, perhaps, they had spent a might too much time at the open bar.

In all events, the speech-making didn't last long. Then two chaps in their thirties emerged from the kitchen in white chefs' uniforms, pushing a trolley about three feet high. Atop this rolling platform rode a large and absolutely magnificent three-tiered wedding cake. Whether or not, the reception guests all believed they were now in the presence of Bailey's head pastry chefs, the two men pushed the delicious sight to the head table, where they stopped just opposite Rose. Then the taller of the two ceremoniously handed Rose a long, large and shiny cake knife. The time had come.

All of the food served by Bailey's fully lived up the establishment's reputation. The wedding cake just turned out to be the best-tasting food served that evening. Rose cut the top tier of the wedding cake into several slices, which were served to the bride, the groom and their parents. Then the pastry chefs took over, and everyone there savoured an awesome piece of wedding cake. After allowing time for everyone to enjoy their scrumptious repast, Bailey's wedding man signalled the four hired musicians to begin the music.

The dancing began with Rose's dancing first with her new husband, then with her father-in-law, and then with her father. As soon as Rose and Adam had started dancing, other couples began to join in. In a short time, the small dance floor was full, if not a bit jammed.

Tim and Mary were among the first to join in. As the dancers became more compressed due to their own increasing numbers, Tim decided that the dear and close young lady he was holding in his arms was just about the most gorgeous creature on earth. Mary was, indeed, a pretty young girl, but Tim's magnanimous appraisal went well beyond, say, a calm reasoned conclusion. For that matter, anyone would likely search Tim and his contemporaries of the day in vain looking for calm reasoned conclusions; a least those involving the opposite sex.

Also among those having a very good time were Albert and Doris Birchall; he, a bit more than she. For medicinal purposes only, Albert had drunk two additional shandies. They proved to have both a therapeutic effect on Albert's debilities, and elevated his general mood to fit the gaiety of the occasion. Of course, Doris had deduced what had happened the night before when she first laid eyes on Albert as he and the others arrived in Standish. She was a very sensible lady, however, and kept her own counsel. No reason to let him think I'm exactly pleased, she thought. But no cause to spoil a wedding, either. By the time the wedding-day festivities were concluded, Albert and Doris were back on the best of terms.

In fact, it can accurately be reported that except for a little temporary 'down time' for Albert, a very good time was had by everyone who attended the wedding and the reception.

Chapter Twenty-six

At 10.10 p.m. Adam and Rose took their leave, and left for the Lake District in the borrowed Ford Y. The crowd gathered in front of Bailey's to say their farewells. Adam helped Rose into the car. He got behind the wheel. The canvas top was down. Adam started the engine and waved a grand goodbye to all. After a few traffic turns, Adam was on the Windermere Road. They arrived at their hotel about two hours later. Newlyweds were no novelty at that hotel. The small staff expected that Mr and Mrs Adam Roberts would arrive a bit late. No one that night was disappointed.

Doris Birchall had made the reservations for Adam and Rose for one-week at the small hotel. The back of this hotel faced on to Lake Windermere. On three of the seven nights Adam and Rose spent there, a full moon made a picture postcard view of the historic lake, when viewed from the Roberts' rooms.

As one would expect after a day such as Adam and Rose had spent on 25 June 1935, they were a bit tired when they arrived at their hotel. Fatigue, however, is not to be confused with exhaustion on such occasions. Neither Adam nor Rose was exhausted. Life and each other were about the grandest things that either of them had ever discovered. And, for topping on that cake, now they had this whole coming week for a wonderful honeymoon.

This honeymoon in the Lake District was everything such an occasion should be. Mr and Mrs Adam Roberts stayed up late, slept late, and came to know each other as a husband and wife should. They toured the scenic areas, and tasted its best cuisine in its finest restaurants. A few times Adam even did a tolerable job of trying to dance to late-night romantic music.

By the end of the week, however, they were both spent. Each of them was quite ready to get back to their roots, and to begin life together aboard a barge. Kingston Marine Barges Ltd had refused to guarantee that the barge they could live in would be waiting at Wigan Pier when the newlyweds returned, but had assured Walter they would make every effort to have it there.

The entire delicious, but unreal atmosphere of the honeymoon was marred by only one incident which happened while Adam and Rose were on their way home. About twenty minutes after leaving the Lake District, they heard a loud 'pop', and the Ford Y begin to swerve as Adam brought it to a stop on the verge.

The Ford Y was equipped with both a spare tyre and a jack. Thank goodness! Unfortunately, Adam was not experienced in changing tyres on cars. He withdrew the jack from where it was stored, freed the spare tyre, and went about the task of learning how to change tyres as he went along. His inexperience overlooked the fact that he had not stopped the car on a very flat area. Not to worry. He worked the jack into position under the car's A-frame. He inserted the jack handle and began to work it up and down. The car began to rise. When the wheel holding the flat tyre rose free, Adam used the wrench he found in the boot to remove the bolts. Now he was ready to switch the spare tyre for the one that had failed. He pulled on the tyre to be removed, but it didn't respond. Adam braced his left foot against the jack and gave the reluctant wheel a mighty tug. The Ford swayed. The jack tipped sideways. The A-frame slid off the jack; and, the car came crashing down on Adam's extended leg, fracturing Adam's left tibia, or shin bone, just above the ankle. Although it is difficult to find a good side to such events, at least in Adam's case the fracture was only a crack in the bone.

A passing motorist saw the Ford fall off the jack and heard Adam cry out in pain. He promptly stopped to render aid. He ran to Adam who was writhing in pain. Then he ran back to his own car and returned quickly with his own jack. Within a few minutes, he managed to re-lift the Ford, and pulled Adam clear.

By that time, poor Rose was near-frantic. She helped to support Adam into the Good Samaritan's car, and the three were off to the nearest doctor's surgery. That surgery was found about ten miles to the west.

After developing his X-ray of Adam's left shinbone, the doctor put the film in a viewing light box, as Adam and Rose looked on. He pointed out a whitish line about mid-shaft.

'This is what we call an undisplaced tibial fracture,' he said, 'and that means I have to apply a cast that will assure no stress and no movement so the bone can heel.'

The pain in Adam's left leg had lessened, but was still too intense to raise any arguments as to what had to be done.

The doctor built a plaster-of-Paris cast that encased Adam's left lower leg from just below the knee to and including the left foot.

As the doctor was making ready by mixing the plaster of Paris, Rose obtained his permission to use the telephone on the vacant receptionist's desk to call home. She had no more than walked out of the treating room when Adam posed an important question to the doctor.

'How long is all this going to keep me down?' he asked.

'Well, it won't keep you down at all,' answered the doctor. 'You'll be on crutches for about four to five weeks. Then your doctor at home will X-ray this again, and if it shows normal healing – and at your age and apparent health, it surely will – then he'll probably replace this cast with a walking cast you'll probably have to wear for another, say, three weeks.

'A little piece of rubber tyre is built into a walking cast. By that time, you can bear your weight on that leg, but you'll want to do that on a limited basis for the first few days.

'So,' the doctor concluded, 'my prognosis is that this will all be behind you in about seven weeks.'

The doctor could easily read the saddened look on Adam's face.

It was time to cheer the poor chap up a bit.

'I know all this is a great inconvenience,' the doctor said, 'but let me assure you that having a vehicle weighing over a tonne fall on you can cause a great deal more injury and fracturing than you've experienced.'

Adam still stared into space with a dejected look on his face.

'Take heart, lad,' the doctor encouraged. 'You're young. You're healthy. These things happen. If you were twenty or thirty years older, the break would have been far worse, and the outlook wouldn't be half as promising.'

'Are you going to tell me I'm lucky?' Adam asked, half-quizzically.

'Not really,' replied the doctor. 'I'm just telling you that you'll feel a lot better physically and mentally if you keep in mind that as bad as they seem, the consequences could have been a great deal worse, and within a couple of months your leg will be as good as new, and all this will just be a bad memory.'

Regardless, Adam just wasn't in a condition to appreciate the good fortune being described by the doctor.

Oh well, thought Adam. I remember when I thought the earth was going to cave in when Walter had his heart attack. Some way, somehow, I know we'll all survive it.

While the doctor was putting the cast on Adam and trying to cheer him up, Rose placed a telephone call to her brother John in Rufford. John thought he would be able to borrow the Ford car owned by their neighbour, the widow Drayton, and would call Rose back if there were any problems. John told Rose that if she didn't get a call back in the next half hour, she could expect him and Tim to be at the surgery in about two and a half hours.

There was no problem. Although the Drayton Ford Y was a relatively new model Ford in England, the one in a large shed on the Drayton property had only stood in one place and gathered dust since the demise of the late Miles Drayton. The rotter had never seen any reason to teach his wife how to drive it. The widow Drayton told Jim she was delighted to loan the vehicle 'for this serious occasion'. Actually, she was cunningly hoping the Birchall boys would become so enamoured with driving the car that they would want to buy it from her.

Because this Ford had been just standing for several months, getting it started was not all that easy. John and Tim had to prime the engine five times.

To prime the engine, the spark control had to be full on, the choke had to be pulled about an inch from the dashboard, the crank that came with the car had to be inserted into the front of the engine's driveshaft via a circular hole just below the radiator, and the bonnet raised. Tim would stand at the front of the car, grasping the crank handle in his right hand. John would pour about a half-cup of raw petrol into the carburettor. On seeing John do this, Tim would turn the crank furiously in a circular motion.

The lads' first and second attempts to get the Ford's engine started by priming it drew no response. On the third go, the engine emitted a slight but encouraging cough. On the fourth go, it almost took. On the fifth go, the thirty-five-horsepower engine started with a fury, causing the still-engaged crank to spin rapidly until it fell out of engagement with the driveshaft. Tim's hand was wisely out of the way. He had learned the prudence of swiftly removing his hand from a crank in a near-miss that happened when he and John were performing similar procedures on their stubborn tractor. When the Ford Y's engine started of the fifth priming, it raced ferociously for several seconds as it exploded the overabundance of petrol that had accumulated in the cylinders. Both John and Tim were jolted a bit by the engine's initial ferocity and both were silently happy that the gearshift was in neutral, another dividend from their tractor experience.

On their way to the surgery, the Birchall boys found that driving the borrowed Ford was such great fun that they took turns. There were very few cars on the road that day. So in spite of the small delays from their trading off, John and Tim arrived two and a half hours after Rose had called.

By the time Tim and John arrived, the plaster of Paris in Adam's cast was sufficiently set to permit their immediate departure. By that time, Adam could walk, after a fashion, by using two crutches and keeping his left knee bent to keep the cast slightly elevated.

When they all arrived back at the scene of the blow out, Adam and Rose stayed in the Drayton Ford while Jim and Tim got the other Ford back on its own tyre jack, and the spare tyre mounted. When all was ready, Tim and Adam started west in the Drayton Ford. John and Rose followed in the other Ford, new spare tyre on the ground and all. Shortly after they all got underway, Tim told Adam how and from whom he and John had borrowed the Ford. No sooner did Adam learn those details when an idea swooped into his mind.

'Tim,' said Adam, 'if you aren't going to be too busy during the next week, or maybe a little bit longer, I'm sure I can talk Walter, our partnership – White and Roberts, that is – into hiring you and this Ford for some much needed transporting.'

'I don't think me being too busy is any problem, but what needs transporting,' said Tim, adding, 'and I'm sure the widow Drayton would be glad to get some money from this car. Lord knows it's not doing her any good just sitting in that shed. I think I mentioned that her husband, Miles, never taught her how to drive.

'Fact is,' continued Tim, 'Jim and I are saving up, and when we figure she's really fed up with having a useless car, we're planning to make her an offer to buy it – a reasonable offer, of course. Lord knows we wouldn't take advantage of a woman 'cause she is a widow and maybe needs money.'

'I know that thought would never cross your minds,' replied Adam, in a reassuring but good-natured tone of voice. 'I'm even surprised it ever even occurred to you as something to make sure didn't happen.'

They both broke out in short laughter. Then Adam told him what he had in mind.

'Fact is,' said Adam, 'I'm hoping that new barge is tied up at Wigan Pier, and if it is, me and Rose have some hauling to do to get us moved in. Maybe I'll have to hobble around your place for a few days, but sooner rather than later we've got to get on our own. Use of a car would come in mighty handy along that line. Course, I wouldn't be calling Walter about that. What I've mainly got in mind for this car is something else.

'In our new deal with Leeds and Liverpool,' Adam continued, 'we're going to do all the barge-hauling for sixteen or seventeen businesses – mills, factories, that sort of thing – in the Wigan area, and we've got to meet those people and learn just what their hauling needs are and then work out how we're going to be scheduling barges and how many barges we're gonna need. Walter says, and I agree, this whole deal is just expanding our business. We intend to keep on working for the customers we're already working for. Now we've got to add some boatmen and some barges. Getting around to meet these new people and figuring out how we're gonna meet their needs has to come first. Since I'm gonna be sort of laid up for a few weeks with this bloody cast,' Adam said, pointing to the very white case that encased his left lower leg and foot, 'I can do this meeting with new customers business that'll leave Walter free to keep things going and do some hiring and maybe order more new barges, if we figure we need 'em. As I said, this Ford could be a great asset to me getting around to meet these people.'

'Sure makes sense to me,' said Tim, 'but I've got a curiosity question that's got nothin' to do with butting into anybody else's business.'

'What is it?' asked Adam.

'Why are you getting new barges?' said Tim. 'I know for you and Rose it seems like the right thing to do, but I just don't understand why you'd get new barges for the rest. I don't claim to know anything about the barge business or barge prices, but I do know new things are much dearer than used ones. I seem to remember that when you started in that work, the *Mary Rose* was not any new barge.'

'Well,' said Adam, 'the main reason, I think, is that Leeds and Liverpool seems to reckon these customers they've lined up are kind of toffee-nosed, and expect to have their goods hauled in pretty spiffy barges. I won't go into shipping rates, since Walter says they aren't things to be discussed generally, but I do know that those so-called Leeds and Liverpool customers are willing to pay to get their stuff hauled in spiffy barges. Doesn't matter to me and Walter. We figure that we'll end up owning a bunch of fairly new barges when the Leeds and Liverpool contract runs out. Who knows, maybe some of those toffee-nosed businesses might run out at the same time, and want to be White and Roberts customers.'

'You mentioned a three-year contract right after you and Walter signed up for all this. Is it all over in three years?' asked Tim.

'Not necessarily,' answered Adam. 'Leeds and Liverpool has what they call an option to renew. I guess that means if they like us and are making the kind of money on the deal they had in mind, then they can renew our contract for another three years. But we're only guaranteed three years. Either way three, six, or even nine – it doesn't make any difference to Walter and me. We figure we'll do OK as long as we do good work, and keep the boatmen we hire doing good work, too.'

Adam completed this remark just as Tim drove into the driveway at the Birchall cottage. A minute later John stopped the other Ford directly behind them. It was 2.15 p.m.

When they went into the Birchall cottage, Doris made a big fuss about 'poor Adam', how the couple had been missed, and insisted everyone get seated while she prepared tea. After embracing his new mother-in-law, Adam placed a call to Matt Shepherd at Wigan Pier. No, the new barge had not arrived, but Matt had earlier received a call from someone with Kingston Marine Barges who said the new Kingston barge for White/Adams would be at Wigan Pier by 11 a.m. the next day.

By day's end, the Ford Y belonging to Auntie Elizabeth's generous neighbour was safely back with its owner. Walter had agreed by phone to Adam's proposal of him visiting with 'our new customers' and left entirely up to Adam what would be paid for the use of the neighbour's Ford and 'to your brother-in-law who'll be driving you around'.

Adam smiled at Walter's decisions and half-winced when he looked back at his crutches. What a day!

Chapter Twenty-seven

With Adam's new barge on order from Kingston Marine Barges, a replacement was needed to man the *Mary Rose*. When Norman called for his dispatch orders several days before the wedding, Walter had brought this subject up and asked him to 'do some looking around' for a reliable replacement.

'You know, Norman, the kind of man we're looking for. Experienced. Sober. No rolling stones. Be sure and find out how long any man you consider held his last job. And don't consider anyone you think would be shy about calling his wife to tell her some unexpected trip come up and he won't be home for a few days.'

'I'll do some inquiring,' Norman had replied. 'Wigan is probably the best place to look. As we're talking, one man comes to mind I've seen lately hanging around Wigan Pier who used to work for a small operator in Preston. Just a couple of days ago I saw him there with a sort of half-worried, half-expectant look on his face. If he's still around there when I get to Wigan tomorrow, I'll check him out and let you know.'

'That's fine, Norman!' replied Walter, injecting a distinctly friendly tone in his voice. 'And by the way,' he added, 'don't think your good work and help in us hiring boatmen aren't noticed. Adam and I were discussing you just yesterday. Hope your ears weren't burning. Anyway, you'll see our appreciation in your year-end bonus. Naturally, I can't tell you now what's supposed to be a surprise –' he paused a full second to let that sink in – 'but if you decide to buy your dear old mum a Christmas present that costs about £20 I'm sure you'll be able to afford it.'

Norman was, naturally, delighted.

Recognition, Walter said to himself, that's the key with this man. Now watch him come pluck a real jewel for us out of the army of the unemployed.

He did.

The next day Norman arrived at Wigan Pier in the late afternoon. While his barge was being unloaded, he dropped by the foreman's shack, where he found Matt Shepherd pouring over a boring stack of bills of lading.

'White and Roberts may be hiring a new boatman,' said Norman, 'and that brings up the subject of that man out there,' pointing to the fellow standing at the edge of the pier some hundred feet distant.

As expected, Matt was a treasure trove of information. During the next few minutes Norman learned that the man was Ted Watson. True to his appearance, he was looking for work. For the past three years he'd worked for Ed Whitney, a small operator, based in Preston. Whitney had two barges. One he was buying; the other he leased. As the descending clouds of the depression took their toll, things got to where Ed Whitney couldn't afford the payments on his barges or wages for Ted Watson.

'Kind of sad when I think about it,' said the dock foreman, holding up a clipboard holding his record on every commercial barge that had arrived at or left Wigan Pier during the last eighteen months. Matt's record reflected actual time of arrival or departure compared with the scheduled time, per the bill of lading. If the two matched within ten minutes, only the date was scribbled in the column captioned 'On Time'. He directed Norman's attention to Ted Watson's perfect record for timely arrivals and departures totalling 208 entries during the past year and a half.

'Until three weeks ago, that is. He's a good man,' said the dock foreman. 'I don't know where you'll find a better one.'

Norman took this last comment with a grain of salt. If he's so perfect as all that, why hasn't someone snapped him up by now? Obviously Matt feels sorry for the man. Still and all, he seems to be what Walter had in mind. Well, we'll just see.

In the next half-hour, Norman cornered two other boatmen on the pier of his acquaintance who knew Ted Watson. Both spoke well of him. At 4.15 p.m. Norman approached the downcast man and introduced himself.

'I'm Norman Nelson,' he said, extending his right hand, 'and you're Ted Watson, I know. I'm with White and Roberts, and they may be thinking of adding a new man. I understand you're sort of available.'

'You've got that right,' said Ted Watson, as he shook Norman's hand very firmly.

Norman invited the man to have a cup of tea at the nearby Yellow Canary Café. 'So we can discuss maybe your joining the ranks of the gainfully employed.'

Ted was elated and promptly followed Norman into the small café.

As the two sipped their tea and talked, Norman confirmed what he had learned about Ted Watson, and a bit more in the process. Ted lived with his wife and two small children in a rented house in Appley Bridge. Everything had been going fine ('That is, we were able to make ends meet') until Ed Whitney had to shut down almost a month ago. Since then he'd been looking for work, and doing a few odd jobs he'd obtained at Wigan's labour exchange. As for drinking, he couldn't afford it. And, as a youngster he'd been brainwashed by his pious mother about the 'evils of drink', so he didn't miss it either.

Ah, Walter will sure go for this man, thought Norman. It's obvious. He'll fit in with us just perfect.

Walter walked Ted Watson to the Wigan train station. There he bought him two tickets: one from Wigan to Chester to Liverpool by train; the other from Liverpool to Appley Bridge by coach. Walter also gave him simple directions to the widow Wooten's two-storey house once he got to Chester.

Before boarding the train, Ted called one of his more prosperous neighbours who had a telephone. He asked the man to get word to his wife that he'd be home late because he was 'going by train to Chester to see a man about a new job'. As Ted's train left the platform, Norman walked to the phone box by the news-stand and called Walter. When their short phone conversation ended, Walter knew a good deal about the man he could expect to be knocking on the door in about two hours.

Later that same day, Ted Watson became a White and Roberts employee. The job lasted from that day until he retired in 1966.

While the wedding was going on in Standish, Ted Watson stepped on board the *Mary Rose*, tied down just east of the Rufford locks. He found the barge's keys hidden exactly where Walter had described. Two hours later he steered the *Mary Rose* to the loading dock at Wigan Pier. The venerable barge was back in service. Matt Shepherd signalled Ted to a berth at the loading dock.

As it came to pass, the personal characteristics of virtually every White and Roberts boatman over the years seemed pretty much the same. Near the end of the war in 1945, Walter mentioned that to Lil. 'Starting with Adam, they've all been on the sober side. Responsible men who did their jobs on time. In two words: reliable men.'

This reflection recalled to Walter a conversation he'd once overheard between two men who owned a blocks of flats. One had warned the other about being extra careful in hiring managers because 'in about five years, most of your tenants will look just like 'em.' In this meditative moment, Walter glanced into a nearby mirror. Could be.

Walter and Adam had planned the new barge, *Mary Rose II*, would join the White and Roberts fleet right after Adam's honeymoon. Obviously, those plans had to be changed. On the day the new barge was due to arrive in Wigan, Adam and Walter had a long phone conversation about their immediate plans.

'I don't see the sense of us having this barge doing nothing but being a home for Rose and me till my fracture heals,' Adam had said. 'It can be earning us good money, and I think we should figure out how. Besides, for this next month, I'll be out calling on our new customers.'

'I know. I know, Adam,' responded Walter, 'but it's still not right that your new home be a barge some boatman has been living on either.'

Adam had no answer to that statement.

'I can't disagree, Walter,' he said, 'but, uh, I don't know. What I do know is this damn fracture creates a lot of awkward problems. Too awkward for me. You say how we're going to work all this out.'

Walter had already thought the situation through.

'All right, here's how I see it. First thing, it's not the money. Of course, we could use the money another barge can make, a specially a new one, but that's not the point or the problem. We'll always be able to use more money. I never met anyone who had enough money. But Adam, we're talking about yours and Rose's new home, at least for a year or so.

'I'm sure,' he continued, 'we can handle all our work with the barges we're using now until we start hauling for Leeds and Liverpool. By that time, you'll probably be able to run a barge, even if you have to hop around a bit on that walking cast the doctor is going to put on you.'

'You're right, Walter,' said Adam warming to what Walter was proposing. 'I'm due to get the walking cast in four weeks, and we don't start hauling for Leeds and Liverpool for six weeks.'

'All right,' said Walter, 'that settles that. Now let's talk about the next few weeks. Since your new brother-in-law is going be driving you around in that neighbour's Ford, I imagine you'll want to tie down near your in-laws at Rufford. That's for you to decide. If you do that, at least the phone in their cottage will come in very handy.

'Everett Jennings is mailing you a letter of introduction for when you call on our, or rather Leeds and Liverpool's, new customers. Like we've discussed, we need to meet the men we'll be dealing with and we need to know what they're shipping and their shipping and receiving routines. So once you start these meetings, it's important you give me a call at the end of every day while all that kind of information is fresh in mind. Lil and I will be fitting it all together so when we start this expanded service we'll have the schedules all worked out for dispatching our barges. Just as important, that information will tell us just how many barges we're going to need.'

'I've already bought a thick tablet for taking notes,' said Adam.

'Getting a bit ahead of present needs,' Walter continued, 'you have mentioned you're planning to buy or build a house. How long do you and Rose plan to live on the barge?'

'About a year,' answered Adam. 'Two at most. The main thing is we don't plan to raise any kids on a barge, and I imagine we'll start having a family fairly soon.'

'I agree,' replied Walter, 'both of you are being sensible about that. The reason I asked,' he continued, 'is that now's the time for us to set some guidelines for getting these new barges paid for as soon as we can. Within reason, of course.'

'I couldn't agree more,' said Adam, 'but you're the one who has to figure out how we go about that. I've learned a lot of things since we started, but that's all been about running our business – not paying for what we use to do it with. What do you have in mind?'

'Well, it all gets back to how a partnership operates,' said Walter. 'You remember how I explained that partners don't get wages. We only get paid from what's left after all wages and the other costs of doing business are paid. Like I said before, "No risk. No money," but we've been all through that.'

'I remember,' replied Adam. 'Partners just divide up what's left, if anything is left, after everyone else gets paid.'

'Right you are,' said Walter. 'We run the risk of being like old mother Hubbard and her empty cupboard – but with that risk comes the potential to be dividing up some real money – "profits", I believe they call them.'

Adam was unaware of it, but a distinct smile came over his face.

'So, I suppose,' said Adam, 'it gets down to figuring out how to make all the ends meet.'

'Exactly,' replied Walter, 'and here's what I've figured out. Incidentally, so any surprises are good news not bad news, I did my figuring on the assumption that White and Roberts' gross revenues will be ten per cent less than what Everett Jennings predicted. Don't misunderstand, I think Everett Jennings is a very honest man, and his figures will probably prove correct. But we want to be conservative in all this. None of that pie-in-the-sky nonsense.'

'And what have you figured out, partner?'

'Well,' Walter said, 'first let's talk about partners' draws. Lil and I are very comfortable on my present draw of £120 a month. Up to now, your monthly draw has been £80, so your ownership interest has been going up £40 more than mine each month. But now there's two of you, and there's no good reason why your draw shouldn't be same as mine. So, effective about right now, your draw is £120 a month.'

Needless to say, Adam was pleased at that.

'And,' Walter continued, 'by holding our draws at that level and paying everything else over operating expenses to the bank, we'll get way ahead of the payments called for by our promissory note. I'm estimating we'll have ordered six or seven new barges to fulfil our contract. By paying all we can while we go – and I mean "go" comfortably – we should get them all paid for within five years. And that adds up to a company that can generate some real profits for its owners. If Everett Jennings's estimates are the right ones, it'll be much closer to four years.

'And,' Walter was quick to continue, 'that projection takes into account that during this time you'll buy or build a home, and you'll be taking an overdraw to finance that.'

'What exactly is an overdraw?' asked Adam, whose head was beginning to swirl.

'It means that, for some special reason, a partner takes more money out of the business than he would normally take in his draw. As long as everyone is taking out enough to be comfortable, the overdraw is adjusted out painlessly over the long term so each partner ends up owning, or getting, just what his percentage of the business is. It's not a loan. It's in the nature of an advance that gets adjusted out over time.'

This explanation brought unexpected relief to Adam's mind. He and Rose had often talked about when they would get a house to raise their kids in. But they had never come to grips with exactly how they were going to afford that goal. Now the shrewdest man he'd ever known just explained it, and told him how achievable it was at the same time. Momentarily, Adam mentally pictured Row House No. 28, Gateley. Then he envisioned the stately home he had thought of during his daydreaming with Rose. Maybe life isn't any bowl of cherries, but what Adam had just heard made him wonder a bit about that.

Then, spontaneously, Adam posed the question that just flashed across his mind.

'Walter, what's your idea of things to come if Leeds and Liverpool doesn't renew us after three years?' Adam asked.

'Let them!' Walter replied without the slightest hesitation. 'If they don't want to renew our contract after our first three years, sod 'em! By that time I think most of those so-called Leeds and Liverpool customers will decide they need us more than they need Leeds and Liverpool. If we handle this thing right, after our first three years we'll be in so tight with those customers they won't go for any change, except where they pay their barging fees, if necessary.'

He's absolutely right, Adam thought. By then we're sure to be closer with those people than a sitting duck on hatching eggs.

'Walter,' said Adam, 'you're a wonderful man and I hope you know how much Rose and I appreciate your kindness. I promise you I'll never let you down. On these hauling protocols you'll be working out, I suggest our motto should be: Never less than the goods of at least three customers on every trip. That will give us, what was the word you used? Yes, leverage.'

'Duly noted,' said Walter. 'Now get that Ford-driving brother-in-law to get you and Rose over to Wigan. Odds are your new home has arrived by now.'

Two hours later, Adam and Rose first stepped on board the brand spanking new Kingston Marine seventy-foot-long barge on whose port bow gold paint read *Mary Rose II*.

In jet-black letters across the stern was painted:

Mary Rose II
Liverpool

Adam and Rose went directly to the living quarters below deck. It was immediately obvious these were the 'living quarters you can live in'. The furniture was a bit smaller than standard, but otherwise of the quality that was usually found in upmarket homes. There was a handsome white enamelled cook stove whose top featured four burners. It was an American product made by the Tappan Stove Company. There was also a no-moving-parts Servel refrigerator. Both appliances were fuelled by propane gas from a concealed twenty-pound cylinder. Rose was emotionally overwhelmed. She turned to her new husband and pulled him to her in a passionate embrace. It seemed inconceivable she could ever be happier.

After exchanging a few affable words with Matt Shepherd, Adam and Rose returned to the *Mary Rose II*, and Adam made ready to leave. Using her new propane stove, Rose prepared tea, which she and Adam enjoyed by the tiller as their new barge made its way west towards the old rusted hook just east of the Rufford Locks. It was time to start setting up the meetings with the new customers.

Soon after Adam began his introductory visits with the new Leeds and Liverpool customers, he had an idea that turned out to add a whole new dimension to the business of barging. It also advanced the fortunes of White and Roberts beyond all expectation. The *Mary Rose II* was tied to the rusted hook on a Sunday. Everett Jennings's letter of introduction arrived for Adam in the Birchalls' mail the next day. On that Monday morning Adam mounted his crutches and made his way to the Birchall cottage. He started making his calls to the shipping and receiving agents of the Leeds and Liverpool customers on his list.

Starting well before the 1930s, the county of Lancashire was virtually dotted with mines, mills and factories. The mills and factories with whom the Leeds and Liverpool Canal Company had contracted for 'total barge service' were the better, bigger and longer-established businesses. They were the survivors of the seismic reverberations in world trade set off by the stock market crashes that closed the Roaring Twenties. Most of these larger companies had capital backing from a good deal of old money. That enabled them to withstand the adversities far better than most enterprises. By the mid-Thirties, the aftershocks were occurring less frequently, and things were beginning to ease slightly; more so in Europe than elsewhere.

Using the Birchalls' telephone, Adam began scheduling his visits with the men in charge of shipping and receiving at each of their thirty-two Leeds and Liverpool customers. At the end of his first day of calling, Adam was struck by the fact that at every place he had called, one man was solely responsible for the company's shipping and receiving. He also got the impression that this lot were much better organised than most of White and Roberts' current customers. The reality of those impressions started the next day when Tim drove him to his first meetings.

These customers were cotton, linen and woollen mills, factories turning out endless machinery parts or appliances. At every one of these new customers' premises, Adam sensed something dynamic in the atmosphere, always pervaded with meaningful activity. Most people Adam met at these places seemed better educated and more capable than he was used to. Most of the shipping and receiving agents didn't have to refer to any records or books before answering his questions about the size, weight and scheduling of everything they sent and received by barge.

Although the representative of their new barging service was temporarily hobbled a bit with his crutches and the cast on one leg, he was obviously a friendly, capable, and knowledgeable young man. Adam had that magic quality of instilling confidence in those with whom he dealt. Yes, it was becoming increasingly apparent: things were turning for the better.

On the third day of customer calls, Adam and Tim were in Chorley, Lancashire, population 9,086, thirteen barging miles north of Wigan Pier. Adam had crutched his way back to the Ford after completing his meeting with Edgar Rutgers, shipping and receiving manager of Brendan Mills on Euxton Lane. Adam and Tim had developed a routine following such conferences, in which Tim would not start the Ford's engine until Adam had checked the notes on the conference. The wait permitted him to return briefly to the customer's office, if needs be.

After scanning through his notes, Adam signalled Tim by moving his right hand back and forth, as if to say, 'Drive on, my man.' He closed his tablet as Tim drove from the parking area by Brendan Mills. As the Ford proceeded east on Euxton Lane, Adam's silence suggested he was deep in thought. Tim respected the silence. As they were about to pass by a smaller mill near the next crossroads, Adam read out loud the painted sign that nearly covered the entire south side-wall of the mill.

'Ferry Road Cotton Mill, Chorley, Lancs.'

'Tim,' said Adam, 'I just had an idea. Would you bear left at this next road? I want to spend a few minutes at –' he read from the sign – 'Ferry Road Cotton Mill.'

Tim stopped the Ford by some other cars that had all seen better days. This was just opposite the only door on the east side of the mill. A small sign just over the door read 'Office'. Adam got himself and his crutches out of the Ford and told Tim he would just be a minute. He grasped a crutch in either hand and made his way to the office.

Ferry Road Cotton Mill wasn't large enough to have a separate shipping and receiving manager. It had a manager, who oversaw all of the operations. He was a fifty-year-old and very short Welshman with sea-blue eyes and jet-black hair. He exhibited something less than excitement on seeing the towering but friendly young man on crutches make his way into the office, which contained three desks and five wooden filing cabinets. The manager's desk was on the far right. On the left sat a slight, very lean, bookish-appearing man in his early thirties. Adam noted the man was squinting in his effort to read from a large hardbound ledger lying on his desk. A maiden lady in her mid-forties sat at the desk in the middle. She was totally preoccupied staring at her notepad while her fingers stabbed swiftly at the keys of an LC Smith typewriter.

Now this must be the boss, his secretary and the company's bookkeeper, thought Adam.

Behind this trio was a wall consisting of glass windows that provided a full view of the mill's looms in action on the other side. Adam could see ten or fifteen people walking back and forth between the looms. Each of them was staring at different parts of the moving equipment as they moved about. Adam had not the slightest idea what they were tracking, but whatever it was it had to be totally engrossing.

'And what can we do for you?' asked the Welshman in a friendly tone of voice as he rose from his chair.

'Give me about five minutes of your valuable time,' said Adam, smiling, 'if that won't upset anything too much.'

The Welshman liked Adam right off and signalled him into a small conference room a few feet from his desk.

At the manager's gesture, Adam ambled forward, and the two introduced themselves. They shook hands. Now it was Mr Jones and Mr Roberts, as the two walked into the conference room and sat at a small table.

Adam began the conversation. At first the Welshman showed no emotion or reaction whatever. His face lit up, however, when the young man informed him that starting in about three weeks his barging company, Something or Other Roberts, was going to start transporting 'dry goods' for his big neighbour Brendan Mills between Liverpool and Chorley, and could offer their services to smaller companies such as his at well below the regular rates, with the understanding, of course, that his big neighbour would only see the fairness of such lesser prices if it was agreed that shipments for the smaller enterprise were on a 'space available only' basis.

'Would that really make a difference?' the young man had asked.

'Not really, I'm sure,' the Welshman had answered, thinking all the while, Except possibly in the size of the freight bills we've been paying.

Actually Mr Jones was quite entertained by the double talk about what would and would not make a difference.

'And what does "well below the regular rates" translate in to?' asked Mr Jones.

'Well,' replied Mr Roberts, 'I'd imagine you're now paying at least £2 6/- per tonne mile.'

'Close, but too low,' said Mr Jones. 'We're paying £3 6/- per tonne mile and seven shillings per hundred weight of excess whenever the scales at Liverpool read more than twenty pounds over the weight shown on our bills of lading.'

At that point Adam Roberts made the spontaneous speech of his life.

'Well,' he said, 'our only charge is for the freighting, that is "freight-on-board". Since the dock scales at Liverpool are watched like a hawk by the Port Authority, we, like everyone else, go by them if there's any conflict with the shipper's bill of lading. To answer your question direct, Mr Jones, while I'll have to confirm this quote with my partner, Mr Walter White, I think White and Roberts can quote you a flat rate of £1 6/- per tonne mile, weight as determined by dock scales. No penalties. All shipments are freight-on-board, Chorley and Liverpool. Space available only. Aside from what you're now paying for hundredweight penalties, I calculate that shipping with White and Roberts would mean at least a forty per cent reduction over what you're now paying. How does that sound?'

'Actually,' said Mr Jones, smiling because he was unable to contain his delight, 'I've heard of your company before. Good reputation. And to answer your question directly, Mr Roberts, it sounds damn good. You have your Mr White mail us a quote and I'll take it up with the owners. Personally, I think such a quote couldn't be beat, but of course, I don't make those decisions.'

Adam left Ferry Road Cotton Mill thinking he had made a new friend, and that he had hit upon a great idea. Both proved to be the case.

That evening Adam made his regular call to Walter. After he had related the usual data about the Leeds and Liverpool customers that day, he told Walter about the idea that came to him out of the blue and what had happened at Ferry Road Cotton Mill.

Walter was absolutely delighted.

'Adam, this is a winner! With a space-available-only contract, we won't be making any trips we wouldn't be making anyway, and our added cost is just the gallon or so of diesel it takes to move a few more tonnes. We won't be involved with the costs of loading or unloading. I'll have the solicitor I know here in Chester prepare a simple contract which I want to start out at the top of the page reading: "Space-Available-Only Contract of Hire". Mr Jones and Ferry Road Cotton Mill will have their quote in two days.

'And Adam,' added Walter, his voice scintillating with delight, 'your idea of £1 6/- per tonne mile is just right. High enough to make it worth our while, and not so low as to end up in the "too good to be true" dust bin.'

This telephone conversation ended with sheer exultation at both ends of the line. Time would prove that was wholly justified.

Adam followed through in like manner with every small mill or factory in the vicinity of their Leeds and Liverpool customers. Then he backtracked to the areas he had visited before having this inspired idea.

By the end of 1935 White and Roberts was hauling large cargoes for thirty-two of Leeds and Liverpool's large customers. On the same trips they hauled smaller cargoes for forty-six new White and Roberts customers.

Such a good idea wasn't about to be any secret. In a matter of months, the smaller mills and factories were routinely working out reduced-rate barging deals with the operators of barges who regularly hauled for their larger neighbours.

White and Roberts carried off this little coup of multi-rates during the entire twelve years they hauled for Leeds and Liverpool customers. Their 'large' customers could not have cared less. They were only paying market rates and accommodating the small fry in the neighbourhood didn't affect their service whatever. After all, the goods of the lesser lights were only being hauled if there was space available.

Chapter Twenty-eight

Adam and Rose lived on the *Mary Rose II* for a total of ten months. Thus began the family life of two bright young people whose backgrounds were similar in that both were from the working class, but in many ways vastly different.

Like most young people from working class families, Rose had had a grammar-school education in the customary pattern in England since the industrial revolution in the latter part of the nineteenth century. For them, going to school started when they were six and ended when they were fifteen, with their attending that last daily assembly at grammar school, where the schoolmaster expressed the school's best wishes to 'those who will be leaving today'. That unceremonious event ended their adolescence. It was now time to find jobs and become part of the family economy until they married and started having families of their own.

As the Birchall family economy was adequately fuelled by the work of Rose's father and her two older brothers, since leaving grammar school she had been mainly occupied in learning the 1,001 things that go into a woman's being the centre of the family home. Happily, she inherited her mother's love of reading books, which surely contributed to her personality and more worldly outlook. Throughout her life, Rose was an interesting person whose company was always sought out by others.

As we've seen, Adam's earlier life was much different. The harsh realities of sheer poverty had denied him much of the usual schooling, however minimal that might be considered by later standards. Nevertheless, unlike most of his peers, Adam was spared the conventional life sentence to mediocre accomplishments. Truth be told, he avoided that fate by the interplay of numerous factors. His course out of working-class poverty was clearly begun by his father's repeated sermonising about 'aiming high and working hard'. Equally significant to Adam's having avoided the usual trip to nowhere was the indisputable fact that he had applied himself so as to become the very embodiment of what his father had proclaimed over and over and over again. His pursuits in all this were surely enhanced by Adam's inborn intelligence, depth of character, some good friends and some downright good luck.

From these historic ingredients, the marriage of Adam and Rose proved to be a very prosperous union that was never marred by boredom, rifts or unhappiness. It was also blessed with children.

After Adam and Rose settled into living on the *Mary Rose II*, their lives fell into a routine of being almost constantly on the move, a good deal of which was at that sizzling five miles per hour speed limit. Rose spent many hours by the tiller, just talking with her handsome husband. She also spent a good deal of time below in her modern kitchen and reading, in both of which she found much pleasure. For all the shortages that became commonplace in England during the 1930s, the availability of good books at public libraries wasn't one of them.

During the ten months that Adam and Rose lived on a barge, the one thing that did truly change in their lives was going to the pictures. They went to the pictures two to three times a week in whatever town they happened to tie down for the night. Cinemas had become common in practically all towns in England. The larger towns offered even larger varieties of entertainment, which was appropriately priced for the times. With rare exception, cinemas in those days showed films made in England and America. Wigan alone had eight cinemas as well as the Wigan Hippodrome, which featured live variety shows and pantomime. The Court Cinema at the upper end of Market Street was immensely popular with the younger set. It offered both the motion pictures and, thanks to its much lowered houselights, a splendid darkened privacy in which to enjoy them.

Of course, Adam and Rose were well beyond any temptations along those lines by the time their married life began on the *Mary Rose II*. On the nights they went to the pictures, they would usually dress up like they were going on a date. If the town where the cinema was located had a good restaurant, they would eat out, too. During their first ten months, and long after, their cinema of choice in Wigan was the Pavilion.

In a sense, the marriage of Adam and Rose was the fruition of a romance, whose origins were no big bang; rather, a mere spark that occurred when Walter and Adam gave that silky black-haired girl a lift on their barge, all the way to Rufford.

During the weeks Tim was driving Adam around meeting with new customers, he spent a good deal of time waiting in the widow Drayton's Ford Y parked by the mills and factories which Adam visited. This gave Tim a lot of time to daydream. His idle thoughts often turned to Mary Roberts. Mentally he relived every moment he had spent with her several times over and over. As thinking of Mary seemed to grow in Tim's mind, a perfectly brilliant idea formed.

When Tim had conveyed Adam's offer to pay the widow Drayton twelve shillings per day for the use of her car, she had tried to conceal her delight when she accepted. During the four weeks this went on, Tim would always return the Ford on Friday late afternoons. On the first Friday, the lady seemed so pleased as Tim handed her the car keys and the agreed £3, he was tempted to ask her for the free loan of the car that weekend.

No, I don't know what plans Mary might have, or even if she'd be at home. Better to set everything up, say, for next weekend. And that clever little assessment worked in all particulars.

On the following Saturday, shortly before noon he arrived in the Ford at the Roberts' row house in Gateley to whisk Mary Roberts off on a real date at Blackpool, where they truly took in the sights. They travelled via the Blackpool Road. Tim had parked in Central Drive, close to the famed Blackpool Tower. They had ridden the fearsome Big Dipper roller coaster, and also the new Grand National woodie, whose five attached carriages, called a 'train,' dived down from sixty-two feet in the air, then shot up and down while rounding tight curves as its daredevil riders screamed in delight as they trundled up to fifty miles an hour along its 3,302 feet of wooden track. Mary clung to Tim for dear life as she tried to get over the shock of leaving her stomach at the top and then at the bottom along the way.

They toured the Tussaud wax works, went onto the Promenade, and rode the tram to the Pleasure Beach. Halfway back, Tim bought two ice-cream cornets, which they ate while sitting on a bench, laughing uncontrollably as they watched two very large ladies tying not to fall off two very small donkeys. Back in the centre, they went on the Central Pier, where they had a good meal. As late evening drew nigh, they danced at the Winter Gardens to the refrains of Billy Cotton's Dance Band until after 11 p.m.

They arrived back in Gateley just before midnight. James and Celia had gone to bed. It was the end of a vibrant day, the likes of which neither Tim nor Mary had ever spent. Because it was so late and Tim was so exhausted, he slept in Adam's old tiny room. He left for Rufford the next morning after a short breakfast. During the next week he could hardly stop recalling to Adam one thing or another that had happened as they were back travelling between the new customers. Tim was as entranced as Adam became slightly bored. Mary did not recover physically until nearly mid-week. Ah, the follies of youth.

Thanks to the widow Drayton's generosity over Adam's rental of her Ford over the next three weeks, Tim was able to have several less expensive dates with Mary over the summer. Twice he brought her to Rufford to show her off again at the farm dance.

When classes resumed at Regis College in Lancaster, however, Mary's availability for social occasions ground to a resounding halt. She and Tim were able to continue their friendship principally by telephone calls.

Chapter Twenty-nine

During the sixth months of life on a barge, Rose began to wake up in the mornings feeling quite ill for no apparent reason. Adam was alarmed and insisted that she see a doctor. He accompanied her to the surgery of a general practitioner in Preston. Thirty minutes later they were back outside, each with the mixed emotions of joy and surprise. Well, not really surprise. The doctor's diagnosis was that Rose B Roberts was two months pregnant. He readily diagnosed that his patient was merely having morning sickness due to pregnancy. With a little calculation, he informed his patient and her husband that seven months hence they could expect their first child. No, he couldn't tell for sure whether she would have a boy or a girl. Feigning some expertise on the subject, however, he ventured the guess she would have a boy. He couldn't have been more accurate in either his diagnosis or prognosis.

Seven months to the day of the doctor's prediction, the labour pains began just as the *Mary Rose II* was nearing Wigan. As soon as they docked at Wigan Pier, Adam rushed Rose to the Billinge Maternity Hospital two miles south of Wigan Pier. Five hours later Martyn Adam Roberts, six pounds and three ounces, was delivered without any complications to mother or child.

It was time to stop living on a barge.

Rose and Martin remained at the hospital for four days. By then, the doctor was certain that all was well. Mr and Mrs Adam Roberts and son Martyn promptly repaired to the living quarters on the *Mary Rose II*.

A week later Adam was strolling about Wigan Pier while waiting to be reloaded. Rose and the infant Martyn were in the barge's living quarters. Martyn was asleep. Rose was busy in her kitchen, digging through a recipe book which she discovered the first time she opened the oven door. What to prepare for supper?

Gazing idly about as he was killing time on the pier, Adam recognised a familiar face: Old Dick Stead whom he had known as a kid in Gateley. Adam had grown so much since those days that his old friend hadn't recognised him at first. The two stood chatting for almost twenty minutes. Old Dick was now a widower who was no longer working. He told Adam that he had sold his old barge for enough to buy a small property near Appley Bridge, which he described as an old farmhouse on three acres of open field surrounded by hedgerows. He lived there with his ageing horse, also retired from the canals, just living out the rest of their lives. The way Old Dick described the arrangement, he kept up the house, and the nibbling horse kept the pasture grass down.

Adam briefly outlined what he had been doing since the old days. Then he got to the part of having a wife and newborn son, and his need to find a home, as they 'Had absolutely no intention of raising any kids on a barge'. At this point, the chance encounter turned into a very fortuitous conversation. Old Dick told Adam about a 'very good property' in Wrightington (just north of Parbold) that was about to be auctioned at a probate estate sale. The estate was that of the recently deceased widow of a small linen mill owner. Her two children, a boy and a girl, had left Lancashire several years before. The son had become an officer in the Royal Navy. The daughter had married into a wealthy family in Devon. Neither had any lingering memories of the North of England, and each visited their ageing mother very infrequently. Both thought the old lady had died of loneliness, and each was probably right.

Adam eyed his old friend with considerably curiosity. For a widower living alone in the middle of nowhere with only an ageing horse for company, he seemed remarkably informed on what was going on for miles around. Adam surmised Old Dick had simply failed to mention that his lonely life got spiced up a bit now and then by dropping around to the Horse and Feathers, the only pub in Appley Bridge.

Adam got a hand signal from Matt Shepherd that the *Mary Rose II* was loaded. He shook Old Dick's hand in farewell, and promised to stay in touch.

About ten canal miles north-west of Wigan the Leeds and Liverpool canal passes about a quarter of a mile south of Parbold. As they covered this distance Adam told Rose of his conversation with Old Dick.

'Why don't we take a look?' asked Adam. 'I estimate we can tie down just south of Parbold. We can take a walk and look the place over, and we'll still get to Liverpool over an hour before the unloading dock closes.'

The thought of moving into a house was music to Rose's ears. She couldn't get into her walking shoes fast enough.

Using a steel temporary tie-down stake, Adam anchored the *Mary Rose II* just south of Parbold. With everything on the barge neatly under lock and key, and Adam carrying baby Martyn, they walked to the property Old Dick had described. In a heartbeat they could see that the widow had kept a well-maintained home. On closer inspection, it was obvious that she had never hesitated to spend good money to keep the property in first-rate condition, inside and out; at least as far as they could see inside.

Unbeknownst to Rose and Adam, and even Old Dick for that matter, the widow had made no secret of her preference of spending her money to promote her own remaining comfort, as the alternative to leaving it for the pleasure of two 'ungrateful kids'. In her oft-stated view, neither one of them ever showed any proper respect for their father, her fine husband. God rest his soul.

Adam had bought a used Vauxhall about six months after he and Rose were married. He kept it parked at the Birchalls, and let Tim drive it in payment for keeping it in good operating condition. This arrangement worked out well for the needs of all concerned. Ten days before the probate sale, Adam drove Rose again to the Wrightington house, which was being formally shown. This time they could inspect the interior of the house and outbuildings in detail.

In terms of size, condition and location, Rose thought it was just smashing. She could see a 'family home' from the first time it came into view. Adam was of the same frame of mind.

When Adam later attended the estate sale, he did not intend to be outbid.

He wasn't.

One month after Martyn was born, Adam and Rose moved their personal belongings from the *Mary Rose II* to their new home in Wrightington. Albert and Doris were especially pleased. Their only daughter and her family would be living within a few miles, and 'not on those awful canals'. The latter impression was that of Albert and Doris. Rose had had a wonderful time.

One other sort of shock occurred in 1937. John Birchall got married. He had met May Edwards at the Bailey's reception after Adam and Rose's wedding. She had accompanied a friend of a friend who had received a written invitation. For reasons best known to whoever or whatever divined how humans look, talk, act and think, there was something between John and May from the first time they danced at the reception. The chap she had come with was just plain getting tired, and saw his friend John Birchall standing just outside the dancers. He introduced John and May, and suggested they 'give it a go' while he grabbed a pint and rested a bit. After two dances, both thoroughly enjoyed by each, John asked May if she would like to rest a bit, and he would grab a pint for both of them. She was delighted and made no move to see where her original escort may have gone. She and John sort of paired up for the remainder of the evening. As they were saying their goodbyes, John had asked it he might call her so that 'Maybe we could go out, on a date, I mean.'

May was twenty-one, two years younger than John Birchall. She was quite pretty, and was being asked to go on dates by any number of young men she knew in the Wigan area. She did date quite frequently, but knew in her heart that these were just nice guys, and none she would consider getting serious about. With John Birchall, however, everything was different. He was nice-looking, but not what a girl would regard as good-looking. He was a farmer, but she didn't have to talk with him very long to detect that he knew about a lot of things not normally associated with farmers. His knowledge of tractors and automobile mechanics would have qualified him for any number of jobs that had nothing to do with farming. Like John, May had the standard grammar school education. After leaving grammar school, she had gone into nurses' training, which she found very much to her liking. Well, everything except the bedpan part, and that was for only a very brief period. She was now a full-fledged nurse, and had been employed at Wigan General for the past three years.

John and May started dating regularly, to the exclusion of all others. When John asked her to marry him, she had smiled, kissed him very meaningfully, and said, 'I was about to ask you.'

As far as the engaged John and May were concerned, 1937 was far from a prosperous year. Yet they had each saved enough to 'make a start'. Instead of an expensive wedding such as Adam and Rose had had two years earlier, these two sensibly decided it would make far more sense to go the Lake District for an extended weekend and get married there. 'Everyone' already knew they were engaged, and just hadn't set a date. When they returned from the Lake District, May had a gold band on her wedding finger, and 'happily married' was written all over their faces. Doris Birchall made a mild protest that they should have waited so 'we could have had a proper wedding', but both she and Albert knew that the newlyweds had done the sensible thing.

'I don't know what Adam spent for him and Rose's wedding,' Doris said as she and Albert were going to bed at the end of the day on which Mr and Mrs John Birchall had arrived back from the Lakes.

'I don't either,' said Albert, 'but I'm glad it wasn't me paying for it.'

Doris turned out the light. She was glad, too.

As Walter and Adam had expected, particularly after the available-space-only trade turned into pounds, they generated a much higher profit margin than was ever expected per the estimates of Walter or Everett Jennings. Adam, who was out and about much more than Walter, was perpetually struck by how odd it was to see the ascending good fortune of White and Roberts amid the same places and people which George Orwell chose in 1936 to research for his book entitled *The Road to Wigan Pier*, published in 1937. That book was intended to bring home to one and all the severity of the depression in England. Depression be damned. The increasing prosperity of White and Roberts continued, having its main redemption in the fact that it was based on providing much needed services, with appropriate cost reductions for the smaller customers.

Walter and Adam stayed with their limited draws and payment guidelines.

The promissory note held by the Trustee Bank at Manchester called for the final payment by 12 June 1946. On 21 September 1941, the manager of the Trustee Bank in Manchester stamped that note 'paid in full', and handed it over to Walter and Adam, along with twelve certificates of full title to their barges.

Of course, making that goal had sometimes involved longer hours for the boatmen operating the White and Roberts barges. Those occasional disadvantages were more than offset by the fact Walter and Adam were never greedy. They were also shrewd enough to show their appreciation for their men's extra efforts by way of performance bonuses, rather than wage increases. The one inspired even better performance. The other just added to overheads.

In their elation, Walter and Adam each carried a cloth bag to the final payment ceremony in the bank manager's office. They had also invited Everett Jennings, who was nearing retirement. Walter's cloth bag held a recently iced bottle of hard-to-find Rheims champagne; Adam's held four crystal snifters. After the paid-in-full promissory note and the certificates of title were in Walter's inside suit pocket, he signalled Adam. On cue, the champagne and snifters were produced. The precious champagne was poured. Walter lifted his glass to eye level and proposed a toast.

'To the end of this damned war and the best of health to us all.'

The four men savoured the moment and the champagne.

As Adam sipped from his glass he recalled Jennings telling him a long time ago, 'A truly good deal is when everyone involved gains from it.' Now he thought he knew just what Jennings meant.

At the second signing of a three-year contract back in June of 1938, the same affability prevailed as before on both sides of Everett Jennings's memorable big oak desk. Only this time, it was Everett Jennings who had the concealed apprehension. The reports that Leeds and Liverpool's intelligence people had sent to Manchester included the results of a poll they had conducted in May of 1938. The poll was of all of the canal company's customers who were part of its plan to put the railroads out of the freight-hauling business in Lancashire. Fourteen barge operators had been signed up when the programme was launched. Two of those had been replaced for various reasons. When the customers' responses were all in as on 22 May 1938, White and Roberts and a barging operator based in Garstang were the only ones who had received the best possible ratings: one hundred per cent as to service and handling and timeliness. Most of the other barging participants scored 'good or better'. The 'survey' also included the question:

If your Leeds and Liverpool barging service were to be switched to another quality barging company would you: (a) Renew your hauling contract with us?, or (b) Refuse to renew your hauling contract with us? Please circle your response.

As to the barge service providers other than White and Roberts, the customers' responses varied. Some even ignored the '(a)' or '(b)' options and wrote narratives on what they thought of the arrangement. To the considerable surprise of Leeds and Liverpool, however, thirty-one of the thirty-three customers served by White and Roberts list circled option '(b)'.

That was a shocker at several levels in the giant canal company. Everett Jennings regarded it as nothing more than an affirmation of his good judgment when he insisted involving the small White and Roberts concern. White and Roberts, of course, were never told about the survey. Such information might inspire some unreasonable new demands. Never mind. Both Walter and Adam knew they had a barge operation second to none.

Chapter Thirty

Things changed a good deal after White and Roberts got underway with their first Leeds and Liverpool contract. Within sixteen months, White and Roberts had nine barges in addition to the *Mary Rose II*. The staff consisted of nine boatmen plus Walter, Lil, and Adam. In April of 1937 White and Roberts hauled 16,800 tonnes of cargo. Their Leeds and Liverpool customers were averaging the receipt of three to four raw materials shipments per month, and were shipping four to six cargoes of finished product. The smaller space-available-only customers had roughly the same averages, only smaller cargoes. Hauling for White and Roberts' old customers had increased slightly since the Leeds and Liverpool three-year contract got underway. Walter and Lil were spending almost fourteen hours per day sorting out bills of lading from which they got 'past' data for making out bills and 'future' data for scheduling the partnership's barges. On the couple's fifteen-hour days, they kept the regular books of account. Adam was spending the same amount of time, or a bit more, hauling cargoes on the *Mary Rose II* and driving a Vauxhall they had bought around Lancashire. These trips involved tending to matters that ranged from barge problems to customer relations, and everything imaginable in between.

Things had reached the point where some organisational revisions just had to be made. Walter was inspired to initiate the talks along this line by a remark Adam made to him and Lil on one of his visits to Chester. Adam had noticed that both of them looked very tired, and Walter looked downright frayed at the edges. The sight caused Adam to recall Walter's heart attack. As the three of them were sitting down for a conference at Widow Wooten's dining-room table, Adam put one hand over one of Walter's hands.

'I've been thinking,' said Adam, staring directly into Walter's eyes, 'money's fine and it buys lots of things. But there's no future in being the richest man in the bloody graveyard.'

A chill went across Lil's entire body.

'You and Lil are just taking on too much! And Rose hasn't been complaining about seeing too much of me lately, for that matter.'

During the brief but awkward silence which followed, Adam's statement truly soaked in with Walter and Lil.

'You're right, Adam,' said Walter, 'we've all talked about that occasionally, but just talking doesn't solve the problem.

'I've got an idea,' Walter continued, 'before we start considering this change or that, I'd like to discuss it all with Everett Jennings, by phone of course. He's had a world of experience at sorting out big problems and I know from comments he's made in our talks he really likes us, Adam. And, especially since our success is Leeds and Liverpool's success, I've no doubt he'll be glad to consult with me – I mean us – so I'll call him tomorrow afternoon. He's usually free to talk on the phone after about 4 p.m. After we know what he's got to say, let's sit down and decide on some changes that let us get all this done without becoming slaves or corpses in the process.'

Quite a speech, thought Adam. And what could make more sense? We don't really know much about big business, and that's what our partnership is turning in to.

Walter placed his call the next afternoon and told his friend Everett Jennings he was wondering if the Leeds and Liverpool executive had any thoughts that might help White and Roberts 'to start doing it right'.

In response, Everett Jennings told Walter some little known facts about some subjects on which he had a great deal of knowledge.

Based on his broad experience in large-scale business operations, Everett Jennings knew that an able manager could only make wise decisions if he had an intimate and current knowledge of what his company's books showed about how it was doing. Such knowledge could not come from the periodic, but sterile, profit and loss statements or balance sheets that normally issue from a company's accounting department. It could only be felt if one person had the primary responsibility for both the hands-on management and the related book-keeping.

'Quite by chance, Walter,' Everett Jennings had said, 'my impression is that you have fallen into this dual role, which is one of the major explanations for how far your business has come.'

'Well,' replied Walter, 'with my background and other limitations I'm about to fall right through it. Now to avoid that catastrophe, what do you suggest?'

'I'd suggest you hire a... what should the title be? How about a "traffic and account manager"? I know, Walter, you never heard of such a company official. Neither have I. I just made that title up. But thinking about it, that's exactly what I'm talking about, at least for a growing company like yours in the barge sector of commercial transportation.'

'I see what you're saying, Mr Jennings, and I've no doubt Adam will too. Now, where do we find such a – what's the word? – "ambidextrous" – uses both hands to write with – yes, where do we find such an ambidextrous manager?'

'I think I've got just your man,' answered Everett Jennings. 'Very bright chap with Eagle Mills Ltd here in Manchester. Name's John Edwards. In his early forties. Hired there as an accountant about ten years ago. Most accountants are pretty laid back, not very interesting people. Not John Edwards. He knows everything that's going on in that place. He's also the one I always try to talk to whenever I deal with those people. He knows their business inside out, and I suspect he's dying to break out of the not-so-interesting work of just being an accountant. You give the word and I'll ring him up and schedule a very interesting lunch.'

'By all means,' said Walter. 'I know I speak for Adam when I say please proceed forthwith. Also, I'm speaking for the both of us when I say how grateful we both are for your advice and help.'

The next day, two of the midday guests in Manchester's Lyon's House were Everett Jennings and John Edwards. This meeting proved fruitful for everyone but Eagle Mills Ltd. White and Roberts had their traffic and account manager. He was introduced to Walter and Adam one week later while they were all standing in front of Everett Jennings's big oak desk. Walter took almost fifteen minutes to describe the management problems at White and Roberts. When he concluded, he observed that John Edwards was paying rapt attention.

'Still interested?' asked Walter.

'I am, sir,' said John Edwards, 'it all sounds like just what I'd like to get my teeth into.'

Walter looked at Adam, who nodded affirmatively.

'You're hired,' said Walter. 'Why don't we let Mr Jennings name your salary? He's someone we all know and trust.'

John Edwards' face broke into a broad smile.

'Somehow, I just couldn't be more delighted. Mr Jennings,' he said, turning to face the desk, 'how much am I starting to earn?'

Later that day, John Edwards, asked the managing director of Eagle Mills how much notice would be reasonable. 'Two weeks' was the disappointed managing director's reply.

Two weeks later, John Edwards moved to Wigan and within two more weeks he had things up and running in a small building which the partnership had leased...

By the following September all of the major changes were in place. Walter and Lil had moved into a small but very comfortable house they had bought in Wigan about two miles from Wigan Pier. The house was also within easy walking distance of the small building which now housed all of the partnership's books, business papers and their new traffic and account manager, John Edwards.

We'll see how Adam was reprieved very shortly.

Before leaving Chester, Walter and Lil discussed many things. One subject that came up was how wonderful the Widow Wooten had been to them. She had been reluctant about letting them share in the buying of groceries, and was adamant in refusing to accept 'anything resembling rent'.

They decided to express their appreciation by deeds of which the generous old dear would only learn if she survived both of them. Walter's heart attack had made Walter and Lil acutely aware of their own mortality. Soon after they moved to Chester they had a local solicitor draw their will. In that document each of them left their estate:

> to the other, as the survivor, except in the event testators should die within fourteen (14) days of each other. In the latter event, our entire estate shall go to Adam Roberts, whom we have come to regard as our own son.

On the day before leaving Chester, Walter and Lil slipped away from the Wooten residence to keep an appointment with the solicitor. When they left the solicitor's office later, the inside pocket of Walter's coat contained a freshly executed codicil, or addition, to their will, which provided for the 'payment of any balance of any outstanding mortgage on the residence of Priscilla Wooten in Chester which may exist at the time the last of us passes away.'

Adam's job also came to be a reasonable undertaking with one more hire. Again, Everett Jennings had recommended creating the job and the man White and Roberts hired to fill it. The man was Robert Scott, thirty-seven, who had spent nine years in a Manchester advertising firm. He had started in sales, and was later promoted in management. He, like John Edwards, was outgrowing his job, and this frustration was compounded by his dislike of being tied to a desk. But people and problem-solving were subjects in which he delighted. He was hired as White and Roberts' field representative. He had a desk in the smaller leased building, and, about five years later, an office in the building next door which White and Roberts had bought. His job did not tie him to either facility. He handled all the matters which Adam had been driving all over Lancashire to tend to except the direct contacts with customers. Everett Jennings explained that customers of the size that White and Roberts was servicing invariably preferred to deal with the top people, not just a representative. Adam kept that role, and an ever-growing number of customers in the process.

Almost five years after John Edwards became the traffic and account manager, he moved his office in to the building next door. By that time, he had a staff of six. His job performance was superb from his first day. Like Ted Watson from Appley Bridge, he was with the partnership until the day he retired in 1966. Field representative Robert Scott's future was a bit different. When Britain's so-called Phoney War with Germany became a real war in 1940, Robert Scott answered his country's call, even though he was well above draft age at that time. Unfortunately, he did not survive that war, but such is the inevitable cost of such tragic events.

Long before anyone even dreamed of the computerised business world we know today, White and Roberts became and remained a smoothly running integrated operation, starting about three weeks after John Edwards was hired. Walter and Adam had intended to set the standard in quality barging service. They never looked back. Even had they done so, there were no close competitors to be seen.

Chapter Thirty-one

In September 1937 the young Roberts family of three moved into their new home in Wrightington. The house was meticulously clean, and conspicuously empty. That situation presented only a temporary inconvenience that was quickly resolved, thanks to Adam's 'draw' of £120 per month; for the times, a princely income almost worthy of a country squire.

Except for going to the pictures, and occasionally eating out, this income made no change in the attitude or habits of Adam or Rose. Neither forgot having been raised in homes where money was in chronically short supply. Their indoctrination showed clearly when they furnished only those parts of their house in which they actually lived. That left almost half of the house bare of furniture for the next two years. Adam was glad to leave furniture-selection to Rose. She persuaded her mother to 'come along and help me decide what I ought to get'. Rose, her mother, and baby Martyn made four trips to Wigan on this mission. Rose had only one fixed opinion as to furnishings. She was going to have a propane-fuelled cooking stove and a Servel refrigerator, like those 'fantastic' conveniences she first discovered on the *Mary Rose II*. All of the furniture and furnishings which Rose ordered were delivered and installed within two weeks, even though the propane appliances had to come from Birmingham.

In 1937, Adam and Rose learned that the lady of the house was again with child. As the months passed, Rose seemed to show a good deal more than expected. Her increasingly ample profile, however, did not draw any concern or alarm. After all, it was the second time around. A more plausible explanation for Rose's prenatal profile was known two hours after her second admission to the Billinge Maternity Hospital. And the word surprise would hardly describe the look on Adam's face after Rose's doctor found him in the father's waiting room.

'Congratulations, Mr Roberts,' said the doctor, extending his right hand. 'You are now the proud father of three happy, healthy infants. Rose just had twins!'

'Oh, my God,' gulped Adam. 'Twins! Two. That's two, or three, I mean. Now we've got three?'

'That's right, Mr Roberts,' said the doctor in a tone half-amused and half-reassuring. 'One, little Martyn as I recall, and two more, who don't have names yet. One new boy and one new girl. Sure as the world, you've now got three!'

After getting the doctor's perfunctory OK, Adam ran all the way to Rose's room. There she lay in her bed, looking very tired. Each arm was wrapped around a tiny bundled infant. Amid all that security, each was fast asleep. Tired or not, the sight of her husband brought a smile to the young mother's face. Adam eyed the sleeping infants briefly, then leaned down and embraced his wonderful wife. Although countless millions of young parents had been down the same path, it is inconceivable that any of them savoured the magic of this moment more that Adam and Rose Roberts. Two days later Adam drove his family of five home to Wrightington. Rose sat in Vauxhall's rear seat holding the twins, now officially named Carole and Gary. Grandmother Doris Birchall sat in the left front seat, with little Martyn on her lap.

Chapter Thirty-two

In September 1938, Amos Cooper received a highly unusual letter on the letterhead of Educational Endowments International Ltd, Roxbury House, London. He recalled hearing of that organisation as a well-financed philanthropic concern that was somehow involved in education in general, and the learning arts in particular.

In fact, Educational Endowments tailored its numerous world-scope programmes along the lines of the expressed interests of its donors, who, after all, financed its various grants. The project referred to in the letter to Amos Cooper involved a subject which had become a consuming passion of the late Edwin Carmichael KBE, who had left a small fortune to Educational Endowments; all old money which he, too, had inherited. Sir Edwin's obsession had been how human beings learned and taught just about anything.

In the spring of 1938 the chairman of Educational Endowments new projects committee had a brainstorm that would surely impress the trustees administering Sir Edwin's handsome bequest. They would fund two very select groups of high-ranking academic scholars and teachers, one in England and one in America. Each group would spend one year in the other's collegiate domain 'to learn the other's best teaching and learning techniques', which each would take home to further the education process 'on both sides of the Atlantic'. International Endowments Ltd would pay all of each participant's travel, living and school expenses from departure to return. It would also pay £80 monthly to each participant for his or her personal use.

Admittedly such an undertaking seems odd when viewed against the backdrop of the economic depression then rampant on both sides of the Atlantic, and the darkening clouds of war descending in Europe. Such unpleasantries, however, were often not a concern of the beneficiaries of old money. Many ivory-tower habitués of that ilk frequently carried on as if such harsh realities did not exist. They were, of course, free to spend their unearned lucre as they saw fit. Educational Endowment's projected plan called for the English participants to be selected and on their way by 15 November 1938. In this letter Amos was asked to become a member of the Selection Committee. Should he accept, he was also asked to recommend any outstanding college level students and teachers in Lancashire whom he felt would be qualified and interested in such an exciting adventure.

Mary Roberts was an education major in her third year at Regis College.

She had selected that major largely because teaching was one of the few careers readily open to women at that time. Amos, of course, was well aware of all this. With her degree in education from Regis College and the exposure which Amos surmised she would gain from the programme described in his letter from Educational Endowments International Ltd, who could know? One day she might even become head of something truly big, such as the Manchester Unified School District.

Amos Cooper was about to drop a highly unusual opportunity right into the lap of Mary Roberts.

At 8 a.m. on the following Saturday Mary reported for work at the Tate surgery in Gateley. She heard a rapping at the door just as she settled behind the desk where she was about to start translating her employer's awful patient notes. The caller was none other than Amos Cooper.

What an adventure he had to outline to her. Mary could see the amused delight on Amos's face when she opened the door to let him in. During the next twenty minutes, Amos told Mary exactly what he had come to tell her. Mary's head was swimming in delight.

Would Amos please have supper with the Roberts family that night? she asked. Mary was preparing the meal, as her parents would be spending most the day tending their vegetable stall. Of course he would, he replied.

That night, after the supper dishes were cleared, Amos produced his letter from Educational Endowments, which he read to Mary, James and Celia. It sounded like a highly remarkable opportunity might well be available to their Mary. None of the Roberts family had ever been outside of England. It all seemed too good to be true. This endowments company would even be providing spending money for Mary while she was in America, providing, of course, that she be one of the student participants selected. Amos, of course, promised nothing but his vigorous support.

Amos left the Roberts' row house at 9.30 p.m. Mary hardly slept that night as her mind soared over the many-splendored things she imagined seeing if she were one of those selected. She lay awake, imagining the multitude of things she might be after a great sea voyage all the way to New York City! The biggest city in the world!

And it's all free – at least to me, she realised exultantly.

Mary tried in vain to remember something she'd seen in the pictures about New York City. Sometime before dawn, she finally dropped off to sleep.

Chapter Thirty-three

The New Projects Committee decided to name this project the Anglo-American Educational Studies Programme. It would involve four selected student and four selected professorial participants from both England and America. The student participants had to be in their third or fourth year of college, have exceptionally high academic grades and be highly recommended. The professorial participants would have the academic rank of associate professor or above, and be highly recommended. Educational Endowments would handle all visitation arrangements with selected institutions of higher learning, as well as the participants' living situations abroad. The activities of the student and professorial participants would be entirely separate. It was widely expected that this study experience would enrich the future professional careers of all participants.

When Mary arrived home from Lancaster on 30 October 1938, Celia handed her an envelope bearing the return address of Educational Endowments International Ltd, Roxbury House, London. She opened it and read a formal announcement.

The English students selected for the Anglo-American Educational Studies Programme are Laura Johnson of Yorkshire, Mary Roberts of Lancashire, Linda O'Brien of Norwich, and Tina Williams of Devon. This student contingent will be escorted by Mr Amos Cooper of Lancashire to their first school of destination. This will be Vassar University at Poughkeepsie, New York, seventy-two miles north of New York City in the Hudson Valley. The period of study at Vassar will be for three months.

These student participants will then travel to Florida Southern College near the City of Lakeland, Florida, where their period of study will be for three months. They will then travel by train to St Mary's College at Moraga, California, which is located a few miles east of Oakland, California, on the east side of San Francisco Bay. At St Mary's the student participants will study the educational methods used in conducting the summer school. Discussions are still underway with the Administration of Stanford University at Palo Alto, California, thirty-five miles south of San Francisco. It is anticipated this tour will conclude after three months of study at that prestigious institution.

Upon completion of the tour, each student participant will be awarded an official certificate of completion from Educational Endowments International Ltd.

Mary had no idea how much their certificate of completion would add to her qualifications once she graduated from college, but instinct told her it could only help. Mary read the announcement with swelling pride. Just imagine being in all those places and back home in only one year! In June of 1940, she would graduate with her bachelor of arts degree in education from Regis College. With all those credentials, she surmised that she should almost have her pick of teaching jobs. She had to pinch herself to be sure she wasn't dreaming. Everything just seemed too good to be true.

When word of Mary's unexpected opportunity to spend a year studying in America became known, all of her family and friends were delighted for her, and expressed some kind of good wish. Everyone, that is, except Tim Birchall. He was almost devastated. Without doubt, Tim had fallen deeply in love with Mary Roberts. Equally true was the fact that he hadn't told her, and the fact that her deep affection for Tim wasn't on a par with what she perceived to be love. She and Tim had engaged in some enjoyable hugging and kissing, one evening for almost an hour, for some unexplained reason. But they had known nothing akin to the almost immediate need for self-restraint which Adam and Rose had experienced.

Tim drove to Gateley in the widow Drayton's Ford Y to see Mary on the day before she was due to leave. Being naturally inarticulate when it came to talking to girls, Tim had suspected that he just wouldn't muster the courage to tell Mary how he felt. So he had written it all out in a letter which he had put in a sealed envelope, now safely tucked in his inside coat pocket.

As Tim and Mary wandered around Gateley that day, she was gaily chattering away at first one thing, and then another. Wasn't her getting to go all those places just fantastic? Wasn't it all so wonderful? She recalled once telling Rose that Amos Cooper was her patron saint. And if she ever had any doubts about that, they were history now and for ever. God must have sent Amos to her. No, her to him. Regardless. Who cared which?

'Amos has been as great a friend to me as Walter and Lil White have to Adam.'

On she rattled. When it came to having great friends, she and Adam were the luckiest people in the world.

Tim tried to keep the conversation light, as if to share in Mary's enthusiasm, but he felt a nagging sadness that simply wouldn't go away. Mary's woman's instinct told her he was distinctly unhappy about her going away, even if it was for only a year.

As they were walking through a grove of trees, the thought crossed Mary's mind that the whole atmosphere would become lighter and happier if, somehow, she could give her sad-faced boyfriend some kind of reassurance.

She stopped and pulled slightly on his left arm. Tim turned so the two were face to face and standing quite close. She put her hands on both sides of his neck, looked very tenderly into his eyes and assured him, as if she were taking an oath, that she wouldn't look at another man all the time she was gone. Then, smiling, she said, 'And when I get back, we'll pick up from here, just where we left off.'

Tim just looked back into her eyes, but he did not reciprocate her smile.

She pulled his head towards her and kissed him, not passionately, but tenderly. A very meaningful kiss, which almost made him cry.

Tim cleared his throat and said, 'I'll bet,' trying to make light of the terrible loss which he sensed was already in motion. He forced a smile, and Mary smiled back. They walked on, both silent for more than a full minute.

When Tim left Gateley in the late afternoon, he said his goodbyes to James and Celia inside their house. Mary walked him to the Ford, and they embraced, almost passionately. Then Tim produced the envelope from his inside coat pocket and handed it to her.

'Here, Mary,' he said, forcing a light tone to his voice. 'This is for you. Promise me,' he said in a more sombre voice, 'you won't open it until you're on the boat.'

'I promise,' she replied, taking the envelope. As she took it she saw her first name scrawled on the front.

'Goodbye, Tim,' she said. 'I don't know why,' she went on, 'but I think maybe I'm falling in love with you, you no-good scamp!'

The exchanged brief laughs, and Tim drove away. Neither Tim nor Mary had the slightest inkling of when they would meet again and how vastly their lives might change in the interim.

Chapter Thirty-four

On 14 November 1938, Mary Roberts and Amos Cooper took the coach from Gateley to Wigan, via Preston. From Wigan they had a four-hour train ride which ended at Victoria station in London. Mary had never been in a town larger than Blackpool. Understandably, she found London truly mind-boggling. She and Amos stayed the night in a small hotel near Roxbury House. The next morning they met the other student participants in the waiting room outside the office of Angus Edgerton, chairman of the projects committee of Educational Endowments International Ltd. Promptly at 9 a.m. the chairman's secretary asked the four girls to step into Mr Edgerton's office for a few minutes. She asked Amos to meet briefly with the chairman's assistant in the office next door.

Mr Edgerton's office was just short of lavish in its appointments. He stood to shake hands with each of the young ladies as his secretary introduced them. He asked his guests to be seated in the four chairs facing his desk. Then he delivered a mercifully short speech that covered how glad everyone was to be there and what an exciting adventure these young ladies were about to begin.

Amos had gone, as requested, to the office of the chairman's assistant, who was a lean, gaunt man in his early thirties. The assistant concentrated more on the business at hand. First he handed Amos a sealed envelope addressed to the general manager of Macy's Department Store in New York City.

'This will get everyone the necessary winter clothing after you arrive in New York,' said the assistant as he pushed the envelope toward the seated Amos.

Then he asked Amos to spend some time with his student participants during their forthcoming voyage, explaining to them that their first visit at Vassar would involve monitoring two upper-division education courses that were 'in mid-term'. He provided Amos with four identical summaries to pass out to the girls.

'These should get them up to date on the each of those courses.'

He ended this meeting with the suggestion that Amos familiarise himself with the summaries in advance, 'just in case any of the participants has any questions'.

The timing at Roxbury House seemed almost coordinated. As Amos emerged from the office next door, the smiling young ladies walked out of Chairman Edgerton's impressive domain. A typical black London taxi was waiting in front of Roxbury House, which sped this entourage of five to Paddington station for the train to Southampton. Amos sat in the front seat next to the cab driver. His exuberant four charges sat in the back, making full use of the pull-down seats common to London taxis.

Five hours and seventeen minutes after leaving Paddington station, the train bearing Amos, the four student participants and seventy-eight other passengers arrived in Southampton. The *Queen Mary* was conspicuously the largest ship in port; she was 975 feet long and 118 feet across at mid-ship. To Mary it was all becoming unreal. Was she dreaming it?

The *Queen Mary* was Cunard's newest passenger liner, having entered service in May of 1936. In August of 1938, she had seized the Blue Riband, or speed record, from the French liner *Normandy* with a sizzling average of 30.24 knots between New York and Southampton. The *Queen*'s mighty steam turbines thrust her over the oceans at thirteen feet per gallon. She provided 776 first-class accommodations referred to as cabin class, 784 second-class accommodations referred to as tourist class and 578 third-class cabins.

At 7.30 p.m. of 15 November 1938, the *Queen Mary* steamed south past the Isle of Wight, and then west to the open sea. Educational Endowments had sent the student participants and their escort in tourist class. This was second class, and very comfortable in all respects. Considering the differences in fares, it was understandably not as cushy as the velvet-lined comforts provided for the first-class passengers. On the other hand, tourist-class cabins presented a stark contrast to the austere facilities in third class, which were located on and below the third deck.

The Educational Endowments student participants were paired in two adjacent tourist-class cabins looking out to starboard on the second deck. Amos had his own cabin down the hall nearer the ship's stern. Mary Roberts and Laura Johnson shared the same cabin. They had been fast friends almost since they had met in London. Their personalities just seemed to mesh in the right way.

The passengers in each class on the *Queen Mary* had their own facilities and dining rooms. There was simply no intermixing of the classes. Aside from heading to the same destination, the only thing the three classes seemed to have in common was the view: 360 degrees of nothing but open ocean, occasionally visited by passing cloud formations in myriad shapes and sizes. Once during the crossing they saw a smoke trail that could only be coming from a ship that was too far away to be seen.

Except for some of the thirstier passengers who frequented the well-stocked bars in first class, most passengers spent their daytime reading, engaging in small talk with fellow passengers or playing cards. Bridge was the card game of choice in first class. Elsewhere on the ship, the card games were usually gin rummy when there were only two, or otherwise just plain rummy.

Amos realised that Mary and her peers would want to be principally around their own age group. He spent most of his travel time reading one of the three books he had brought for the occasion, or chatting amiably but aimlessly with a dear old widow who had the cabin next to his.

Mary resisted reading Tim's letter until the second day out. Laura was next door in a fierce game of rummy when Mary decided to read what Tim apparently had not had the courage to say. Three minutes later she was a much better-informed young lady. Tim had confessed his love and his 'wild hopes that we can get married when you get out of school'. Mary was anything but an intellectual snob. Still, she had read articles about special problems in marriages where the wife is much better educated than her husband. Tim had the typical grammar-school education, which had ended when he was fifteen years old. Even in their normal talking Mary had noticed that she had a much larger vocabulary than Tim. That difference between them refused to stop nagging at her.

Would I have to use smaller or more common words when I talked just so my husband wouldn't feel demeaned? she asked herself. What husband? Why? It's way too early to be thinking along those lines.

Mary was undeniably troubled by Tim's letter, which she read several times. However much she cared for Tim, her feelings weren't on a par with his. She hadn't led him on, and maybe, down deep she did love him. Of course, if she did, there shouldn't be any maybes about it.

It's all too much, too soon, she said to herself. I'll think about it later. I just don't know.

Mary decided to go to the next cabin to make it a foursome. She returned Tim's letter back in the envelope, which she put back where she had been keeping it; between the pages of a book she was reading. A wry smile crossed her face as she noticed her book's title: *Tomorrow*.

On the third day out, Amos met with all four girls in the second-class lounge, where he provided them with the summaries he'd been given by Chairman Edgerton's assistant. Amos sipped his coffee as the girls read their summaries. Everything was crystal clear. There were no questions.

Averaging twenty-eight knots on this voyage, the *Queen Mary* travelled from Southampton to New York in just over four days. On the third day out of Southampton, a notice was posted on the tourist-class bulletin board of an Orientation Meeting at 3 p.m. the next day in the second-class dining room. 'All passengers who have never been to America are especially urged to attend,' it read.

Almost without exception, every second-class passenger was there. The speaker was the ship's third officer, a neat-appearing, rather thin man in his early thirties who spoke as if he'd never left Yorkshire. Accent aside, in short order the fellow convinced one and all that he knew exactly what he was talking about. At first he addressed several nuances between the American and British cultures and language usage. He drew loud laughter when he gingerly explained that getting 'knocked up in the morning' in America ordinarily had nothing to do with being awakened.

He emphatically warned the passengers about New York taxi drivers.

'If you plan to take a taxi, get a little street map and brandish it like you know the city and exactly where you want to go,' he told them.

After that tip, he repeated his warning, 'For your own good, don't forget that many of those cabbies have a bad reputation for taking foreigners for a ride – and a very expensive ride at that!'

He closed with telling the passengers which personal documents to have at the ready when they went through customs in the morning, and what they could expect by way of questions during that process.

Then he asked, 'Any questions?' Not a hand was raised. 'Splendid,' the third officer announced, 'now let's all clear out of 'ere so the dining-room staff can get on with their duties.'

Ocean liners on the Atlantic bound for New York City must enter New York's lower harbour through the Verrazano Narrows, which is a 1.94-mile-wide opening through which the Hudson River pours into the ocean. The adjacent land masses are the west end of Long Island on the north and east, and Staten Island on the south and west. In 1938, arriving ships commonly passed through the Narrows and proceeded northerly to the piers on the west side of Manhattan that extended into the Hudson River. This part of the journey covered just over six miles, going first through New York's lower harbour and then the upper harbour. Before passing by the south end of vibrant Manhattan Island, on a nice sunny day ships' passengers would see Governor's Island pass by on the ship's starboard side, and the Statue of Liberty pass by on the port side, perhaps a quarter to a half-mile away.

19 November 1938 was not a nice sunny day. A cloud cover hovered over the New York part of the world about 3,000 feet above ground level, and the pesky clots of ground fog kept ship's navigators and lookouts at peak alert. At 7 a.m. the *Queen Mary* was approaching out of the Atlantic on a westerly course about ten miles off of Long Island's Atlantic Beach. A radio communication advised that the pilot would join them at approximately 7.15. The *Queen Mary*'s turbines were slowed to produce a speed of only six knots. In a matter of minutes, a well-lit little speedboat appeared off starboard. As it drew near, the passengers on deck could read its markings that identified it as a craft of the

New York Port Authority. The *Queen Mary* stopped briefly to allow the Port Authority's pilot to come aboard. He was greeted by *Queen Mary*'s first officer, who walked him to the wheelhouse located high above the forward deck.

As they sighted the Narrows, the pilot took over the ship's wheel, which he controlled until the mighty ship was gently nudged into its berth at Pier 9. A gangplank was dropped into place. It extended from the Queen Mary's portside to the West Pier on the west side of Manhattan Island.

As the Queen Mary moved through the lower harbour, passengers flocked to the forward deck to see the historic skyline. Oohs and aahs were heard all around as the new arrivals saw the outlines of the cone-shaped Chrysler Building and the Empire State Building. The latter resembled a rectangular concrete finger extending 1,456 feet into the sky. In 1938, that height conferred the distinction on the Empire State of being the world's tallest building.

As the *Queen Mary* approached the upper harbour area which extended south of Manhattan Island, Amos and the four young ladies in his charge walked to the port side of the ship in the hope of seeing the Statue of Liberty that lay hidden somewhere out there in the confounded fog. Their widely distributed little tourists' maps showed this landmark quite clearly about a mile west-south-west of Battery Park on the top of lower Manhattan in the upper harbour. It was built on a twelve-acre patch of land in the harbour. An explanatory note in the little maps recited that the statue had been engineered by Gustave Eiffel, of Eiffel Tower fame, who had insisted it be made of copper. The copper had long since turned to a light green from inevitable effects of oxidation. But where was it?

Everyone was peering through the fog, searching for the famous statue. Suddenly, it seemed to burst out of the fog. Lady Liberty was towering less than a half-mile to the west, appearing to be walking triumphantly through her broken shackles, with her torch of freedom in her right hand, and holding a tablet in her left. The tip of her torch extends skyward 965 feet above sea level. On her tablet is inscribed: 'July IV, MDCCLXXVI' – American Independence Day, 4 July 1776.

The whole process of newcomers arriving in New York by sea is an impressive experience, which most can vividly recall for years to come. The dramatic appearance of the Statue of Liberty on 19 November 1938 was the most impressive experience Mary had ever had. She never forgot it.

Once they were through customs, Amos led the four young ladies to a nearby taxi stand, where they got into the next-up taxi. Amos sat in the front passenger seat, the young ladies sat in the back, which required Laura Johnson to sit on Mary's lap. All of the girls thought Amos would ask the driver to take them to Grand Central station, although none of them had the slightest idea where that might be from where they were. Instead, Amos showed the driver his little street map of New York, on which he had made two 'X' marks.

'We're here,' said Amos pointing to the X that was marked over the words 'Westside Pier'. 'We want to go to Macy's Department Store,' he said, 'which is here,' pointing to the second X. 'If my memory serves me correctly,' he continued, 'it's at Herald Square Street and 34th.'

The driver nodded his acquiescence, and proceeded by the most direct route possible.

When Amos and his companions got out of the taxi in front of Macy's he turned to face the girls.

'I'll just bet you're all wondering what we're doing here,' he said in an amused tone of voice.

They all smiled and nodded their agreement.

'It's winter, ladies. And if the current temperature feels a bit cold, just wait until you get to Vassar College, which is seventy-five miles north of here. And,' he continued, 'one of the instructions I received while you four were in charming Mr Angus Edgerton was to be sure that none of you froze to death. Our benefactor was so fixed on avoiding any such catastrophe that I was handed a letter of introduction to this very establishment signed by Mr Edgerton himself, which I invite you to read.'

He withdrew the single sheet from an envelope in his inside coat pocket and passed it to the group. The letter was directed to the general manager of Macy's (by name, no less) and authorised the purchase of 'appropriate winter wardrobes' for each of the participants (by name, no less) and 'anything that may be appropriate by way of winter wear for Mr Amos Cooper, who will only be staying perhaps a day in Poughkeepsie, New York before returning to New York City and then to back to England.'

In the last paragraph of the letter, the Macy's general manager was asked to 'please do us the honour of posting all charges in complying with this request and authorisation to our account.'

'I must presume,' said Amos, after the girls had scanned the letter, 'that "our account" in this letter refers to an account which Educational Endowments International has with the store we are about to enter.'

The girls all smiled in amusement.

'Let's find out,' said Amos, and he led his party into the prestigious store. He encountered no difficulty whatever in locating the general manager. Two hours later, Amos and his party walked out of Macy's with some more luggage, and considerably more attire than when they had arrived. Then they proceeded to Grand Central station. While their ride from Macy's to Grand Central was much shorter than the ride from the docks, it required the use of two taxis.

Chapter Thirty-five

At Poughkeepsie, Amos Cooper and the four girls from England had been met by a small delegation from Vassar and driven to the campus. The girls were ensconced in a posh four-storey dormitory in an ornate building named Cushing House. Amos spent the night in a handsomely appointed smaller building whose exterior wall placard read 'Guest House'. Amos had left the next day and returned to England. The four English girls diligently pursued their Anglo-American educational studies programme at Vassar for the next three months, ending on 21 February 1939.

Early the next morning, on 22 February 1939, the four English girls entrained for Florida and the second school on their programme. By late afternoon they were seated in a chair car on a train of the Atlantic Coastal Railway and heading south, still about one hundred miles north of Atlanta. Destination: the little town of Lakeland, Florida, population 2,354. Identical signs were posted by the highway at both sides of the town listing their prominent organisations. The signs listed the local churches, lodges and Florida Southern College.

At Orlando, the Atlantic Coastal train would change to a south-westerly course aimed at its final destination on Florida's west coast: historic St Petersburg. The small town of Lakeland was about midway in that course.

The chair car was about half filled with passengers. It was configured in the typical American style of rows of passenger seats: four across, with two on each side of a centre aisle. In the sixth row Mary Roberts had the window seat next to Laura Johnson. Linda O'Brien and Tina Williams occupied the two seats on the opposite side. All of these girls except Mary had dozed off to sleep. Mary had closed her eyes, trying to nod off, but it just didn't happen.

Instead, she found herself taking a trip down memory lane, recalling events since she arrived in America. Her reminiscences roamed to their trip from Manhattan to Poughkeepsie, being met by the Vassar people, arriving at the college, the orientation lecture the next day, the field trips to nearby Schenectady and Troy, New York, and the 'last supper' on their last day at Vassar.

Of the seventy-one mile trip up the Hudson Valley from New York City to Poughkeepsie, she visualised the beautiful train ride. The train hugged the east side of the Hudson River. It began snowing right after they had left metropolitan New York City. The only change in weather during the next two hours was the increasing size and density of the snowfall. The train seemed to be passing through a never-ending forest of oak, hickory and chestnut trees, which proliferated on both sides of the Hudson River. The trees retained many leaves despite the passing of autumn. Ridges of snow grew on both the branches and the leaves on the towering trees. Before darkness fell, the entire valley was softly lit by the setting westerly sun. At the time Mary had thought the only thing missing were the elves and fairies.

Since that magic journey, Mary had seen a good deal more of America. In terms of scenery, however, nothing rivalled the exotic sights in the Hudson Valley.

Then her thoughts went to their arrival at Poughkeepsie where they were met by warden Helen Jackson, and her assistant warden, Miss Linda Trevor, both unmarried. They were accompanied by three husky young men who had come separately in a wooden-panelled station wagon which had 'Vassar Maintenance Dept.' painted on each side. A smile crossed her face when she recalled how amused, if not relieved, she and the others had been when Warden Jackson, standing there on the train platform, gleefully explained that a warden in the world of academia referred to a person who oversees college student matters, and not someone in charge of a prison.

Vassar was a women's college, hence they had only one warden. In a college catalogue, Mary had read that Florida Southern College, being coeducational, had two such school officials: a dean of women and a dean of men. Certainly no such thing for men or women back at Regis College.

Then her recollections focused on the orientation lecture the next day. She remembered being led into a small auditorium in a building named Blodgett Hall. She couldn't recall the name of the speaker, but could visualise the very lean woman awaiting them at the podium. She was in her mid-forties. Her body appeared almost frail, but her voice was quite strong. Must be some kind of compensatory effect, Mary thought.

The lean lady with the strong voice had begun her talk with a short biography of the school's founder, Matthew Vassar, whose family moved to America from England in 1800, 'when Mr Vassar was only a small child'. In 1861, he had founded and funded the first women's college in America, aptly named Vassar. This handsome contribution to higher learning was made after Mr Vassar had made a large fortune managing the family owned brewery which was the first 'to sell its foamy output' in every state in the Union. Mary had the impression the lady was intentionally avoiding the word 'beer'. The speaker went on to describe how Vassar had grown in size and academic importance over the seventy-seven years since it was chartered. She closed with a statement of how especially proud they were of the student living facilities 'here where more than ninety-five per cent of the students have always lived on campus'.

Mary had appreciated those closing remarks much better two days later when she was taken on a tour of the sumptuous student living facilities at Vassar. They consisted of four large four-storey brick buildings built to form a quadrangle, plus Cushing House, where the English girls had been assigned a single room on the third floor. Their room was furnished with four small study desks, a spacious walk-in closet, and four very comfortable bunks, stacked in pairs. The dormitory buildings that formed a quadrangle had been built at different times between 1912 and 1927. Cushing House had been built in 1927. Its architecture was 'old English', half-timbered style with leaded windows.

These splendid structures exemplified Vassar's catering to the educational needs of the more prosperous in America. Each dormitory had its own elevator, dining room, kitchen, laundry and hired staff. The staff consisted of maids, waitresses, cooks and general help. The general help were the less skilled, whose jobs ranged from washing and ironing clothes in the laundry to sweeping, running carpet sweepers, mopping, setting tables, washing dishes and disposing of trash.

Vassar's opulent student living facilities of 1938 were in stark contrast to the school's first dormitory. That more humble facility had occupied part of one of five floors in Vassar's first structure, the Main Building, which housed the ·entire college during the first eighteen years.

Mary also recalled the field trips to nearby Schenectady and Troy, New York. Such trips were required of all education majors taking a course designated as 'Adolescent Education 101'. Unlike England's 'grammar school' system, in America children in the first through the sixth grades are taught in what are called 'primary schools'. All subjects covered in each grade are taught by a single teacher in one classroom. On the field trips, the Vassar students would sit quietly in chairs placed at the back of a classroom to watch a teacher instruct the students in one of the primary grades. It was during these field trips that Mary first began to ponder the question of whether she truly wanted to spend her life teaching other people's children. Mulling over that question raised a second question that nagged at her: was she heading in that direction merely because teaching was open to women?

Then her reminiscing moved to the 'last supper', which was the funniest thing that had happened to her since she arrived in America.

For the English girls' last night, Vassar's president, Henry Noble McCracken, had suggested it would be a good idea for Warden Jackson and Assistant Warden Trevor to take them for a farewell dinner at the upscale restaurant in Poughkeepsie, which was in the Hotel Excelsior. The party of six attended this event in a new Studebaker sedan which had Vassar College painted on both sides. Assistant Warden Trevor drove, which meant that Warden Jackson could do something which she would never consider doing on campus: she could have a glass of wine with her evening meal. In fact, she had three glasses of wine, which, progressively, put her in such a good mood that she topped off the evening with a small glass of sherry.

As the meal drew on, Warden Jackson became increasingly talkative. In fact, as the meal drew on, she did all of the talking.

As she finished her third glass of the delicious wine, she decided to tell the girls a 'little tale out of school' in which she recounted how President McCracken had called her into his office after he had received 'a very important letter'.

'It was,' she said, 'a proposal of something or other from this big philanthropy in London. International Education, or something like that.

'Of course, you know,' she continued, 'President McCracken doesn't ordinarily discuss things like this with me, since my job is student matters. But he did anyway. He told me what it was all about. Then he asked me if I'd have any problem sort of overseeing it – that is, you four – in this study project you're on. Well, that's not the funny part, which is why I'm telling you about this. All very confidential, you know,' she said, slowly winking one eye as she compressed her lips a bit, giving her face an animated look of confiding one of those little private things, 'just between just us girls'.

'Henry – I mean President McCracken,' she rolled on, 'got one of those holier-than-thou looks on his face and informed me there would be only four students from England coming for a short time on a special studies project and he wanted to go ahead with it as Vassar's contribution to higher education. Well, he must have seen I wasn't buying that, because he quickly added that the proposal letter also said this International outfit was going to make a 5,000-pounds no-strings-attached donation to every school that participated in their Anglo-American something project.

'I must have looked kinda shocked,' she continued, 'I don't know why. I don't even know how much that many pounds are in 'merican money.'

Warden Jackson stopped talking as a waiter approached and placed a tot of sherry near her left hand. She smiled at him, as if to say thank you, and downed the contents in a single gulp as the waiter walked away.

'Anyway,' she went on, 'he said that except for what little these English students might add to what we pay for groceries, the trustees and he figured they won't cost Vassar a dime. We'd have the same costs for everyone's salaries and the living accommodations if the English girls are here or not. And he musta thought I was about to ask for a raise because then he started talking about something else he ordinarily wouldn't take up with me. He said our usual benefactors, I mean Vassar's usual benefactors, don't donate as much as they did before the Crash, and not as often either. Course, he was referring to the stock market crash. I imagine you heard about that, even in England. Then comes the part I remember best, where it was like him preaching a sermon.

' "Well, Warden Jackson," he said, all stern-faced and uprighteous sounding, "as you know, imaginative school administrators can always find a good use for an extra few thousand pounds, but that's not why I asked you to drop by. I did that to ask you to do a little extra when they –" that's you four – "come, and consider it as your part of helping us make this small contribution to international higher education." And I said, "Sure, we can handle 'em." And that's when I decided when you girls got here I was gonna put you up in Cushing House, it being all English-style, you know.'

At that point, Warden Jackson must have sensed she'd talked a bit too much. Her face suddenly changed expression, and she made a gesture that signalled the dinner was over. She hardly said another word until Assistant Warden Trevor dropped her off at Josselyn House, the dorm she lived in.

Mary was truly amused when recalling her experiences at Vassar, and thought perhaps she should write them down and send the description home with one of her weekly letters.

No, I don't think that's such a good idea, she decided. I don't think I'm a good enough writer to convey the real humour in it.

None of her letters home mentioned Warden Jackson in vino veritas.

Thinking about all of these things must have been a bit fatiguing, because after recalling Warden Jackson trudging up the steps at Josselyn House, Mary, too, dropped off to sleep.

The four English girls slept on – until they all bolted upright when the conductor, passing by in the centre aisle, boomed out, 'Atlanta. Next stop Atlanta. Fifteen minutes. Atlanta.'

Chapter Thirty-six

The Atlantic Coastal train made a brief stop at Lakeland's very modest train depot to permit four passengers to get off. The English girls had just assembled their luggage on the depot's small platform when they were greeted by a very pleasant and neatly dressed forty-year-old lady who identified herself as Martha Wainright, 'Dean of Women at Florida Southern College'.

She introduced the muscular man standing beside her as 'Jolly' Edwards, Florida Southern's assistant football coach, who had 'come along to help out'. The man looked about ten years younger that Miss Wainright. He was an ex-footballer and still a bachelor. His face fell into a natural smile; undoubtedly the source of his nickname. Jolly Edwards' active time at Florida Southern College was during the fall football season, which began in September, and the four preceding weeks in August when the coaching staff got the college athletes 'going out for football' into fit physical condition. Otherwise, he spent most of his time lifting weights in the school's gymnasium or jogging around the oval track which encircled the football field. When asked, he also regularly helped out other campus officials in non-academic pursuits, such as picking up arriving college guests. For Dean Wainright's task of getting the 'special studies' English girls from Lakeland to the campus, Jolly had volunteered to drive the school's black Ford panel truck 'to help with their luggage'. Dean Wainright had driven her own 1936 light grey Plymouth sedan, for which Florida Southern College would reimburse her at the princely rate of twelve cents per mile.

Once the English girls were onboard in Dean Wainright's Plymouth, and their luggage was onboard in the Ford panel truck, the party set out, en caravan, with Dean Wainright's Plymouth in the lead. Twenty minutes later Dean Wainright stopped in front of a three-bedroom white lap-siding house, mid-block on a tree-lined street in Lakeland, Florida. The house was that of Mr and Mrs Wayne Smithers.

During the trip, Dean Wainright had told the girls that their living quarters would be in two private homes 'right across the street from each other'. Also, that the plan was for two girls at each house, 'paired up as you all elect'. They would receive breakfasts and suppers at their new temporary homes, and have their midday meals in the college cafeteria. These private homes were a ten-minute walk to the campus, and about the same walking distance to 'downtown' Lakeland in the opposite direction. She had assured the girls they would find both of the host families delightful. Florida Southern College had engaged them on prior occasions 'and everyone said they had a wonderful time'.

Mary and Laura Johnson opted for the house that turned out to be that of Mr and Mrs Wayne Smithers. Linda O'Brien and Tina Williams were installed in the house across the street. By this time the girls had naturally paired off, but there had not been one incident of any discord between them.

At 9 a.m. the next morning, the English girls reported to Dean Wainright's office, which was on the second floor of a stately brick building whose bronze placard by the entrance read 'Edge Hall', the first building erected at this campus.

In 1856 Florida Southern College was chartered by the State of Florida as 'Southern College', in Orlando, Florida under the sponsorship of the United Methodist Church. Over the next eighty-two years, the school's campus had been moved to several Florida locations. Since 1922 it had been at Lakeland, and in 1935 the trustees changed its name to Florida Southern College. In 1938 the school's campus facilities were on a par with most private colleges in America, but its 400-acre plot of land was hardly occupied. There were six brick buildings. Edge Hall was the first building constructed at this, its final and ultimate location. It had two floors. Then three four-storey classroom buildings were added. A single-storey maintenance building was built well away from school buildings.

Unbeknownst to the English girls, also in 1938, Florida Southern College's ambitious president, Ludd Spivey, had invited master architect Frank Lloyd Wright to devise plans that would turn this modest campus into a 'great education temple in Florida'. When Mary Roberts first saw where architect Wright was asked to design that 'temple', she very accurately surmised that the £5,000 no-strings-attached donation from 'that big philanthropy in London' would be vastly more appreciated at Florida Southern College than a similar donation was at Vassar. Of course, Mary wasn't supposed to know about any such donations. [Many years later Tim Birchall happened to show Mary an aerial photograph of Florida Southern College in *Life Magazine* which was entitled 'The Campus Designed by Frank Lloyd Wright'. That was the only time Mary ever revealed Warden Jackson's 'confidential' communication.]

Florida Southern College struck Mary as austere as Vassar College had seemed ostentatious. Walking up the three wooden steps to the Smithers' front porch had no resemblance to riding the elevator to their dorm room on the third floor in Cushing House. Everything in Florida seemed a world apart from New York. Mary much preferred the world in Florida. She preferred the friendly Smithers couple and their modest home over the opulent appointments of the ornate Cushing House. At Florida Southern College people were friendlier, and you didn't have to put on a warm coat every time you went outdoors.

In fact, since they had arrived, every day was a warm, sunshiny day. Why not? They were in the centre of Florida.

Chapter Thirty-seven

During the third week at Florida Southern College, Mary was attending a class listed in the college catalogue of courses as Educational Outlook. She noticed that the good-looking boy who sat right across the aisle seemed to be staring at her. Every time she looked his way, he quickly looked towards the front of the room, as if he'd been caught peeking. When the class ended, Mary remained briefly in her lecture chair to mark up her class notes. While doing this, she became aware of someone standing by her. She looked up, and there stood the boy from across the aisle. He stood about six feet tall, had light brown curly hair and decidedly blue eyes. His light shirt and dark trousers looked on the expensive side. He appeared lean and athletic, about what one would expect in a twenty-year-old single boy from a well-to-do family in Miami.

'Hi,' he said in a very friendly voice, 'I'm Darren Henderson. I know you caught me looking at you, and I really didn't mean to be shifty-eyed.' He paused briefly, as if he was running out of words. 'I mean I heard you speak and I heard your English accent, and, well, my mother is English, I mean her parents were from England, so that makes her English here, and, well, I just wanted to introduce myself and hopefully get to know you.'

Mary took all this in the friendly spirit in which it was obviously intended. She stood, smiling pleasantly, and extended her right hand, which the young man promptly took to shake hands.

'I'm Mary Roberts,' she said, 'and you're right, I am from England.' She added, good naturedly, 'and this is the first time I was ever accused of having an English accent.'

'Well,' Darren responded, 'I meant like I'd be considered as having an American accent if I was in England.' All the while he continued to shake her hand.

'I know what you meant,' she said, still smiling, 'I wasn't taking offence.'

At this point she gently withdrew her hand from the extended handshake.

'Look,' said the boy, 'school's out for the day, why don't we drop over to the students' lounge and have a Coke. I'd really like to get to know you better, and I, well, whadda you say?'

'All right,' said Mary, adding, 'I'm here on a special studies programme. Part of last semester I – that is three other English girls and I – were at Vassar in New York – it's a women's college. No men allowed, except the president, a few professors and the lads in the maintenance department. At Vassar they have a no-fraternisation rule, so a conversation like this, say nothing of going to the students' lounge for a Coke, would have put some poor lad's job at risk.'

Darren laughed.

'No fraternisation, eh? You must feel like you just got out of a social jail,' he said as they started walking toward the lecture hall exit.

Thirty minutes and two Cokes later, Darren Henderson and Mary Roberts both realised that each had found a new friend. They had had a very enjoyable chit-chat, and found each other very agreeable.

As their second round of Cokes was coming to an end, Darren said, 'Look, I've got a room-mate. Name's Greg, Greg Richards. Good guy. You've got a room-mate, this Laura you mentioned. What I'm saying, or trying to say, is maybe we could all meet in a day or so and have some fun, like maybe going out to a movie or dinner or something. There's a lot more to do around here than just study and sit around thinking about back home.'

Mary smiled. This was the first time since she had arrived in America that anyone referred to an evening meal as 'dinner'. Everyone else knew it was 'supper'. Then she did something impulsively.

'That sounds like fun. You're right. My room-mate is Laura. Laura Johnson. Lovely girl. She's from Huddersfield, near Leeds. Ah, have you ever been to England?' she asked.

Darren nodded from side to side as he said, 'No.'

'Well, I imagine you've got a good idea where London is.'

'Generally, I'd say.'

'Well, Leeds is in Yorkshire, which is north of London, and Huddersfield is a little town near Leeds, also in Yorkshire.'

'And where in England are you from?' he asked, his eyes now showing real interest.

'Oh, I'm from a little village no one ever heard of named Gateley. I mean no one outside of England ever heard of it, and,' she added in an amused tone of voice, 'I'm not too sure many people in England ever heard of it either. It's just a little village in Lancashire in the North of England. That's west of Yorkshire.'

Mary paused briefly.

'My goodness,' she said, 'what started out with my telling you about my room-mate seems to have turned into a lesson in English geography.'

Darren smiled, showing he was very amused. A very friendly atmosphere was clearly setting in.

'Well,' said Darren, 'you're right. Back to people. My room-mate, Greg, is from Tampa, the biggest city on Florida's west coast. I'm from Miami, another big city, on the east coast, as I'm sure you already know. So why don't you tell you're room-mate that, ah, what I'm suggesting is two English girls from little villages. I've got it. Why don't you tell her you met this, uh, me, and I suggested these two English girls have dinner in Lakeland's finest with two big-city boys from Florida?'

They both laughed briefly.

This little get-together ended with the agreement that that Mary would speak with her room-mate about all this, and if everything looked promising, she would let Darren know at the phone number he wrote down on the back of her lecture tablet. It was the telephone number at the apartment in Lakeland where he and Greg Richards were sharing the rent.

After supper with the Smithers, Mary and Laura went to their room to do their homework.

'Before we start studying,' said Mary, 'I have to tell you what happened after class this afternoon.'

She proceeded to relate the details, starting with the staring incident right through to the part about the 'big-city' boys wanting to take them out.

'It would be something of a blind date for you,' Mary added, 'but if Darren's room-mate is anything like him, I think we'd have a lot of fun.'

During the telling of the tale, Mary had the impression Laura was not as enthusiastic about the idea as she had expected. When Mary completed her story, Laura's face broke into a half-smile, and she agreed to give it a go.

Mary didn't know what was bothering her, but this wasn't the happy-go-lucky Laura Johnson she had come to know and like.

'What is it, Laura? Something is bothering you, and if I can help in any way, I want you to tell me.'

Laura first assured her 'it' was nothing. Then she decided get to 'it' behind them both.

'Actually,' Laura said, 'I had a bad experience when I was just eighteen. It didn't come to anything, and I've tried to forget it. I've thought about it, and I've decided you can't let your life be ruined by one foolish incident, and you can't judge all men by one bad apple in the barrel that found you. So, let's forget it. I'd like to go, and I'm sure we'll all gave a good time.'

Mary understood what she was being told, and her only reaction was that Laura was showing a lot of good sense. Even Mary could recall a having a few thoughts her mother would have thought a bit evil when she and Tim were having such a great time at Blackpool. Those things pass like ships in the night. The past is past. Now is now. Laura's right. We'll all just have a good time.

The following Saturday night, Darren Henderson, accompanied by his friend and room-mate, Greg Richards, stopped his 1936 Oldsmobile convertible in front of the Smithers house. The canvas roof of the convertible was down, which made these dashing young bucks look dashing indeed. Mary and Laura were waiting in the Smithers' front room, and saw the boys walking towards the house, Darren in the lead. Mary answered Darren's knock on the front door. Then came the introductions, and the four walked out to the waiting Oldsmobile.

'This is a smart-looking car,' said Mary admiringly.

Darren smiled, but modestly. He was in full agreement.

'Tell her how you worked your fingers to the bone just to make the down payment,' quipped Greg, as he followed Laura into the rear seat.

'Beware the warnings of wolves,' replied Darren in a very jolly tone voice, as he looked at the girls, but pointed toward Greg.

'Believe me, girls,' quipped Darren, 'any calluses on his hands or mine are because both our fathers are too cheap to buy us better tennis rackets.'

A short laugh all around, and they drove off.

Light-hearted banter marked the chatter all the way to the Date Palm restaurant. It was almost Lakeland's finest – with outdoor dining on a deck that featured a terrific view of Lake Parker to the east. The truly class restaurant in the area wasn't in Lakeland. It was the Giant Turtle that was located on the far side of the lake. Getting there involved a long drive around the north end of the lake – as if going to go the country club on the far side.

Darren's family lived in Miami. His father was in the business of selling and servicing expensive fishing and pleasure boats to a distinct minority: wealthy people who lived mainly in New York, Boston, and Chicago; people who preferred Florida's moderate temperatures and perpetual sunshine to the climate of their home base, especially evident when the north and north-east were under the siege of winter. A smaller but indispensable source of his business came from former residents of those money Meccas who had retired and moved to Miami or Palm Beach, some sixty miles to the north. Darren's father was a good businessman blessed with a very engaging personality. Among the well-to-do, he knew just how to talk their language.

On that first date, the girls learned that Darren was planning to go into his father's business after college. He was taking business courses at Florida Southern College. He was taking the education course in which he met Mary on his father's recommendation. He and his dad had reviewed Florida Southern's catalogue of courses extensively. His dad thought the education course would add a little variety to his son's college exposure. 'Who knows,' he said, 'it might make you a better salesman.'

They learned that Greg's father was a partner in a law firm in St Petersburg. Greg planned to become a lawyer and hopefully join his father's firm. He was taking a 'pre-law' course at Florida Southern College. After graduation, he was going to law school at the University of Florida in Gainesville.

Darren and Greg were both twenty-one years old. Mary and Laura were both twenty. Mary's next birthday was coming up on 13 May. The friendship that blossomed among these four was ideal for all concerned. The all liked each other, and once they started dating it was invariably a foursome. Their dates were more laughs, dinners in good local restaurants and going to Rose's Roof, an upscale public ballroom in Lakeland, which featured a surprisingly good orchestra. For reasons understood by all and articulated by none, this dating was to be fun, and they were not to get heavily involved, physically or romantically. What started out as little pecks at the end of a double date did graduate into some more enjoyable embraces, but nothing in the way of restrained or unrestrained passion. Instead, there was what they called in America sessions of 'smooching'.

One aspect of these engagements struck Mary as a bit odd. Occasionally, when the four got back to the car, after being wherever they had gone for their date, Darren would nonchalantly trip the switch that would cause the canvas roof to race out of regular storing place, move forward, and require only a slight downward push to connect along the top edge of the windscreen. Then the convertible would be in the 'top-up' configuration. En route back to the Smithers house, he would simply turn off on a dark side street and park. This signalled an unannounced time for a little smooching. Laura and Greg would begin kissing in the rear seat. Darren would turn sideways to the steering wheel, and Mary would turn in the front seat so her back fell within his arms, and the two couples would 'smooch' for fifteen or twenty minutes each oblivious to the presence of the couple in the other seat.

These smooching 'sessions' were not all that frequent, and certainly never got 'heavy'. Suffice it to say that a good time was had by all. Indeed, in the more promiscuous years that followed 1960, they would have been regarded as just having good clean fun.

With Mary's birthday coming up in ten days, Laura discussed having a birthday party with Darren and Greg.

'Ah,' said Darren, 'just the right thing to have at the Giant Turtle.'

Laura had never heard of the Giant Turtle. Darren told her where it was, and that he'd been there twice. The second time, some family was having a birthday party and the restaurant really made it an occasion. He told her about the chef carrying a candlelit birthday cake followed by the head waiter and all the waitresses, 'all singing their heads off', as they sang 'Happy Birthday to You' and marching out to the celebrants' table on the deck that faces the lake.

'Sounds smashing!' said Laura.

Mary's birthday fell on a Sunday. In her mail during the week, she had received a dozen birthday cards from England. On the one from Tim was written: 'Remember me, Tim.'

Darren had taken the lead in scheduling just another date on Sunday. Perhaps they could get an early start and drive around the north end of Lake Parker and go to the Giant Turtle. Darren had a modest array of birthday presents stowed in the Oldsmobile's trunk which was still a boot, as far as Mary and Laura were concerned. No one mentioned any awareness of Mary's birthday as they motored along the north edge of Lake Parker in the warm Florida sunshine. The four young college students gaily chatted away. Their conversation ranged from who had been doing what to a little gossip making the rounds on campus about a certain younger associate professor, Paul Mitford, and Beverly Adkins, acknowledged as the most beautiful girl in the senior class.

'Just rumours,' said Darren. 'Never believe 'em.'

'I don't know,' replied Greg, with obvious scepticism in his voice.

'That's right,' said Darren, 'you don't know.'

Throughout the ride to the Giant Turtle, nothing was said about anyone having a birthday.

Darren had made all the arrangements at the restaurant. The four were shown to a table on the deck overlooking Lake Parker. Dinner was ordered. As they were concluding their meal, Darren got the head waiter's eye, and signalled that the time had come. Then he excused himself, as if he were going to the restroom, and made haste to the Oldsmobile to get the presents. Just as he was arriving back at the table, the air filled with the singing of the traditional 'Happy Birthday' song.

Mary turned in the direction of the sound and saw the chef wearing a classic white chef's hat. He was followed by the head waiter and all the waitresses gaily singing as they approached the table. They appeared to be enjoying all this tremendously. The chef was holding a birthday cake covered with white icing and topped with twenty-one small birthday cake candles, all lit. Everyone at the table and all of the customers joined in the singing.

When the chef placed the cake before Mary, she blushed as shouts of 'Happy Birthday' filled the air. It was the most momentous thing that had happened to Mary since she left England.

Chapter Thirty-eight

On the way back to Lakeland, Darren invited the other three to a big party at his family's home in Miami on the Memorial three-day weekend coming up in two weeks.

'It's a real party that lasts over the whole weekend that my father throws every year. Some come for one day, some for two days, a few stay all three. Dad throws it mainly for business friends, but social friends, too. Lotta local people and from New York, Palm Beach, and sometimes from the West Coast.' He described the party as 'having everything'. Great food. Dancing. Swimming. Tennis. Fishing. The works. 'There's even a boat ride down to the Keys.'

Where would they all stay? Mary wondered.

'No problem,' said Darren. 'The place is big. Actually, too big for me. But there's room for everyone. I never remember anyone coming to this party that had to stay at a hotel. You girls could have one of the guest rooms, and Greg can bunk in my room.'

Now, this I would like to see, thought Mary.

Mary and Laura both said they would like to go, but would have to check their study schedule to determine if they could. Their term at Florida Southern College was drawing to a close, and their courses seemed to require much more of their time than when they first arrived.

During the following week Mary received a letter from her sister-in-law, Rose Roberts, with an extra page written by her big brother Adam. Rose's letter was one of those 'we're fine, how are you?' types, with some details about the children. The twins were both growing faster than Martyn had grown, which Rose found amazing, considering that both had weighed almost two pounds less than Martyn at birth.

Adam wrote about how everyone missed her, and then added something that surprised her:

> I don't know if Tim wrote you about it, but in January I bought 200 acres of good farmland with a good solid farmhouse about midway between Burscough and Parbold. John and Tim set everything up and planted hay. They get half of what the crop brings. They also did a super job of fixing up the house. It's a lot better than before. I was so pleased I told Tim he could live in it free if he would tend the crop – it don't take much tending. Tim has a full-time job with the biggest contractor in Wigan. He is learning construction. Bet he never told you.

Love, Adam.

Indeed, Tim had not told her. He had written several letters since Mary left for America. They were all quite short and usually reported little more than how he missed her and that he 'still feels the same way'. Mary suspected the brevity of his letters was possibly because didn't want to show his lack of schooling. Who knows?

Mary still felt a deep affection for Tim, but somehow she didn't miss him as much as she had expected.

Whether I miss him or not isn't important. He's still one of the finest, kindest persons I know. Even if he was afraid to tell me in person how he felt about me, she told herself.

The next day Laura and Mary discussed their school workload, and decided they could get all the bases covered and still spend the three-day weekend which Darren had proposed.

' "All the bases covered." My, my, aren't we beginning to sound like Americans?' said Mary.

Chapter Thirty-nine

The driving time from Lakeland to Darren's home in north Miami took almost four hours. Darren and Greg picked the girls up from the Smithers house at mid-morning. The girls' suitcases fitted neatly into the convertible's trunk. This was a holiday weekend, for four fun-loving young single college students without a care in the world.

They had no sooner got out of town when Darren started the singing. He led off with 'On Moccasins', the most popular school song at Florida Southern College, at least the most popular when the students were cheering on their team at football games. Since Mary and Laura hadn't been at the school during the football season, their 'joining in' was more in the nature of following along – at least for the first round of that inspiring fight-fight-fight song. The rest of the trip was a mixture of idle chatter and more singing. Greg reported on the latest rumour about Associate Professor Paul Mitford and student beauty queen Beverly Adkins, cautioning those in whom he confided, 'Now keep in mind this is only rumour, unconfirmed by any reliable source.'

The high-spirited merrymakers were just concluding their second rendition of 'On Moccasins' when Darren stopped for lunch at a small restaurant in a small town. It was noon.

The party-bound foursome in the Oldsmobile convertible, top down, arrived in late afternoon at the Henderson home on the north side of Miami. This establishment was an upscale estate in an upscale neighbourhood which had been built for the upper-income businessman who felt the need to entertain and to impress, as well as wanting all the comforts of home. It was built in 1924, and bought by the Hendersons in 1927. Its entire four acres were surrounded by a five-foot high stonewall fence, built by master masons. There was a U-shaped concrete driveway in front of the house. The 'legs' of the 'U' ended at two decorative iron-gated entrances from the street. The house itself was a large, two-storey structure with exterior flagstone walls, also built by master masons. A three-car garage adjoined the south side of the house. At various points just inside the wall were a dozen or so princess palm trees that stood twenty to thirty feet high. Just inside the rear of the enclosure, coconut palm trees extended skyward from fifty to sixty feet. Eighteen majesty palm trees formed a line that crossed the middle of the property. A large circular concrete patio abutted the rear of the house.

From the rear of the patio, a narrow brick walkway extended through a centre gap in the majesty palms and led to a beautiful flower garden beyond. To the left of the garden there was a fenced-in tennis court; to the right, a half-Olympic-size liver-shaped swimming pool. The pool was surrounded by a large sand-coloured cement patio on which there were various chaises longues, small wooden tables, and deck chairs. On the far side of the pool was a small green wooden building which housed a dozen clothes-lockers, two dressing rooms and a restroom. To the rear of this 'changing shed' was a magnificent twenty-five-foot-high southern magnolia tree, whose fragrant spring blossoms were already ten inches wide.

Beneath the patio was a subterranean complex of eight guest rooms, whose entrance doors faced on to a well-lit centre hallway. Although the underground guest rooms could not provide any outside view, their appointments were nothing short of sublime. Each room had a few small paintings hung on the walls, as well as two beds, a bathroom and shower, walk-in closet, chest of drawers, and a full-sized vanity table with mirror. Every vanity table was well stocked with cosmetics and the artefacts commonly used for enhancing feminine beauty.

Darren parked in front of the garage and led his little group through the garage to patio at the back of the house. As they walked on to the patio they saw a good deal of activity. Various technicians and other workers were adding the finishing touches to the party preparations. Darren spotted his parents on the far side of the patio.

Mary's eyes swept the scene in awe. In terms of square footage alone, the patio was at least three times the size of Row House Number 28, Gateley, Lancashire. Directly before the back of the house she saw a temporary bandstand, complete with music stands in front of eight musician's chairs, and a standing microphone, front and centre. Temporary floodlights were mounted which would be operated to roam among the dancing guests later in the evening. A smooth-talking party equipment salesman had convinced the hosts that such illumination was 'great for creating atmosphere'.

A temporary 'wet bar' was set up about twenty feet to the right of the bandstand. To the right of that were two long tables which had been set up for serving buffet dinners. To the right of those were four long picnic-style tables, complete with bench seats on either side. A young black girl wearing a maid's uniform was placing napkins and silverware which designated sitting places at the picnic tables. At the back of the patio were eight small wooden tables, each neatly covered with a red and white chequered tablecloth. Four chairs faced each table. The open area of the patio would be a social centre before dinner and a dance floor after. As Mary tried to take this all in, she blinked her eyes, wondering if she ought to distrust them.

Darren led his guests across the centre of the patio to meet his parents. As they crossed, Mary caught sight of the fenced-in tennis court through the centre break in the majesty palms.

The introductions were quite routine. Darren's father and mother impressed Mary as a very normal couple in their mid to late forties.

Greg, Mary and Laura enjoyed meeting the parents, who showed no signs of self-importance or condescension. Darren's parents, in turn, were pleased at the apparent quality of the young people their son had for friends at college.

Darren clearly resembled his father; both were tall, slender, and athletic-looking, and had dark brown curly hair. The senior Henderson had a salesman's ready smile and a way of putting people immediately at ease. Mary noticed he was just as affable when talking to them as he was when he excused himself briefly and she could hear him speaking with one of the workers connecting some loud-speakers.

Of course, Darren's mother picked up on the girls' English accents immediately, which led to a few moments of explanation.

After the introductions, from out of nowhere, Darren produced a sheet of paper whose caption read 'Party Program Menu'.

He handed it to Mary, saying, 'Here, Mary, this is more or less what's scheduled, but we always make it a point not to follow it too closely. You and Laura can look it over while you're freshening up and getting all decked out in those fabulous dinner dresses Laura said you went out and bought.'

Mary was a bit nonplussed by this, as they had not bought any special dinner dresses.

'Well,' she said jocularly, 'I hope Laura got an extra one for me, because she didn't even tell me she was going shopping.'

'I'm kidding,' said Darren, in a sort of can't-you-take-a-joke tone of voice.

'Actually,' he continued in a slightly more serious tone, 'don't be taken in by all this. It's not a formal dress party. Except for the musicians and the temporary waiters, you probably won't see a man wearing a tie all evening.

'Not to say,' he added, in more of a now-hear-this tone of voice, 'that all of the ladies present will be so informal.'

'I'm sorry,' said Mary, 'I don't quite follow what you're saying.'

'Well, as sure as God made little apples, some of Dad's better healed clients, that is their wives, some of them, will show up like they were on parade. They always do. Every year, a few of them show up sparkling with diamonds and dressed to the nines.'

What, pray tell, thought Mary, is being 'dressed to the nines'?

'Not many,' Darren continued. 'One year I counted four. They're not hard to spot. They gotta know they look out of place, but I guess they get such a big kick out of showing off how rich they must be, they don't care.'

'Not so loud,' admonished Darren's mother. Then, in a much softer voice, she said, 'You never know when one of those showboats will come drifting through the palm trees.'

'Anyway,' said Darren, leaning closer to Mary, and almost whispering, 'as formal as this menu and that bandstand may make everything look, this is not a formal party. Course I don't expect anyone will walk in just wearing a loin cloth and carrying a spear, but sports jackets and comfortable dresses par for the course. I was just kidding about Laura on a spending spree.'

'I didn't mean whisper,' admonished Darren's mother. 'That last part, without the spear and loin cloth part, could have been said right out loud.'

Everyone had a good laugh. On balance, it was a very relaxed atmosphere.

'They'll start putting food on the buffet tables at about 6,' Darren's mother added. 'You girls get freshened up. Later Darren can take you on a tour of the place. I'm sure you will all have a good time.'

'Are they going on the boat ride to the Keys tomorrow afternoon?' asked Darren's father, looking directly at his son.

'I don't know,' answered Darren, and turning to the girls. 'Do either of you get seasick?'

'If we do,' replied Laura, 'it didn't happen on the *Queen Mary* coming over.'

'Well,' said Darren's father, 'the boat won't remind you of the *Queen Mary*, but the ride might get a little bouncy in a couple of places, so people prone to seasickness shouldn't get their weekend spoiled by that trip. They're too many other ways around here to have fun. Just thought I'd mention it.'

'Girls,' said Darren's mother, pointing to an open side door at the left rear side of the house, 'let me show you to your guest room.'

'Relax. Freshen up. Do whatever you want,' said Darren. 'We'll see you back up here in an hour or so. By then, this place ought to start filling up with guests. Maybe even a few, uh, what did you call 'em, mother, "showboats"?'

Mrs Henderson looked reproachfully at her son for an instant, and then smiled.

'Come along,' she said, turning to the girls, 'these men are just trying to corrupt you and irritate me.'

Mary and Laura followed Darren's mother through the side door, down a flight of stairs and the well-lit hallway to the guest room whose entrance was the second door on the left. She opened the door and led the girls into the room.

'Now, I'm sure you can get comfortable in here,' she said. 'The bathroom and shower are in there,' pointing to an inside door to the left of the vanity table.

Then she left, with the parting remark, 'Now you girls just relax and take your time.'

What utter luxury, both Mary and Laura thought, as they opened their small suitcases and began placing their contents in the chest of drawers.

By 6 p.m. Mary and Laura had had a little rest, taken their showers, and were dressed for the party. They were both still a bit overwhelmed by it all. After they were dressed, they lingered in the room to chat, while sort of getting up the nerve to walk upstairs and join the party. They agreed that their guest room seemed to make their perfectly comfortable accommodations at the Smithers' house look almost shabby. They also concurred that this fantastic place wasn't ostentatious, like most things were at Vassar. Darren's home was, what? Just plain rich? Filthy rich?

'So this is what they mean by "how the other half lives",' said Mary.

'Other half?' said Laura. 'Other two per cent, or less, from what I've seen.'

'I'd say,' said Mary in a conceding tone of voice, 'it's perfectly adequate for someone who is at least perfectly satisfied with the best of everything.'

'Well,' replied Laura, 'let's just say this humble abode is, as some Americans put it, mighty comfortable.'

They both laughed.

'And Darren is such a nice unassuming chap,' said Mary in a bewildered tone of voice.

'I know,' replied Laura, 'you'd think he'd be a real toffee-nose, wouldn't you?'

'I don't know,' said Mary, reflectively. 'I guess not. He's just Darren. Something like his father seems to be.'

'You mean friendly?' asked Laura.

'Yes! That's exactly the right word for both of them. Friendly,' Mary said. 'And not phoney-friendly. They all seem like really nice people that haven't let money go to their head.'

Having solved that paradox of wealth not defiling truly good people, the girls decided to give it a go. Darren and Greg were probably wondering what happened to them.

When Mary and Laura emerged through the side door onto the patio, Darren and Greg were close by, as if they had been walking in the area to be sure to be there when the girls came up. The eight-piece orchestra was in place, and playing soft 'atmosphere' music. The dance music would come later.

Guests were standing and milling around the patio, and a half-dozen or so tray holding servers were moving among them, handing out drinks and hors d'oeuvres. Mary estimated she saw about fifty guests, and more arriving, two to three at a time. She noted a short line of guests before the wet bar. She saw that many of the guests stood in groupings of two or three, vigorously chatting away in the small talk that is symbolic of cocktail parties. She saw one unusual gathering of nine or ten guests seemingly spellbound by one of their number in his early fifties who was recounting some hair-raising adventure. He looked so compelling that Mary wished she was close enough to hear what the spellbinder was saying. Glancing to the rear of the patio, she saw a half-dozen or so guests seated at the small tables with the red chequered tablecloths. They, too, were all chatting away with their drinks in hand.

During the next half-hour, Darren led Mary, Laura and Greg on a short tour of the inside of the house, and then through the centre-break in the majesty palms to the rear of the property. As the four of them were walking around the swimming pool, there was a sudden rise in the orchestra's volume, and the music stopped. Mary looked through the centre-break and saw a tall man dressed in white and wearing an elongated white hat who was standing by the now food laden buffet tables and waiving his right extended arm above his head. The chef was clearly signalling the buffet was ready. It was time for dinner.

Between the picnic tables and the small tables at the back, there was dinner seating for all of the guests. Mary couldn't figure out how Darren did it; he got his guests seated at one of the small tables. Mary thought the red and white chequered tablecloth looked smashing. After her trip to the buffet table, she quickly discovered the food left nothing to be desired. As the last of the guests found seating, the orchestra resumed the pleasant music – at a low volume.

A clear, star-filled sky and a full moon. A delightfully warm temperature. A mild breeze. Seventy-plus jolly jabbering guests. Lovely soft music. What more could you ask?

Mary thought it was the most impressive event she had ever attended. Just as she was arriving at this inspired assessment, Darren's left knee nudged her right knee under the small table. He nodded over his right shoulder, indicating look this way. She did, and found herself staring at an amply endowed and very attractive brunette in her early thirties, clad in a snug fitting luminescent white silk dress. The plunging neckline in front displayed a good deal of cleavage. Atop her meticulous Marcel waves was a diamond-studded silver tiara. Long pendulous earrings, resplendent with glittering diamonds, dangled from her tiny earlobes. She was seated at one of the picnic tables, avidly devouring her dinner.

'Showboat,' said Darren softly, with a devilish grin on his face.

Mary couldn't help it. She broke out laughing, and somehow managed to convey the impression she was only laughing at something her dinner companion had just said. Whatever that was.

As most guests were ending their dessert, Darren's father walked to the standing microphone at the centre of the bandstand. He welcomed the guests, thanked them for coming, and reminded them that this was a three-day party, so all of those who live locally were expected back during the next two days.

As Darren's father was speaking, Mary leaned close to Darren and whispered, 'How many are locals?'

'At least ninety per cent,' answered Darren.

'Now I know,' she whispered, 'why you said no one attending this party ever had to stay at a hotel.'

'In closing,' Darren's father said into the microphone, 'I want to introduce some guests who haven't been to one of these shindigs before. I hope you regulars will all make them feel welcome, and get acquainted during the next two days.'

He proceeded to call out the names of five couples and the cities they came from. As each couple's name was called, they were asked to raise their hands. A spotlight promptly found them and there was a short round of applause.

At least the applause factor changed considerably when Darren's father made the last introduction.

'The last guest I want to introduce who is new to our annual gathering is Colin Johnson, a lawyer from San Francisco. I've known Colin since he saved Henderson Marine's bacon last year on the coast. That lawsuit, I might add, was the only one ever brought against us. Last week I read in the papers that Colin was in Washington on the now celebrated case of Cemtex vs Harold Ickes and his Department of the Interior. I reached Colin by phone and invited him to join us this weekend and he graciously accepted. Considering what the Supreme Court just did to our friends Harold Ickes and company, Colin really has something to celebrate.

'I'm sure Colin's name is familiar to those of you who have been following the Cemtex case in the papers. I hope during this party you'll all get acquainted with this outstanding lawyer.'

The host then scanned the crowd and called out, 'Colin, where are you?'

A hand shot up at the picnic table just four sitting places from the showboat in the stunning white dress. There was a thundering outburst of applause when the spotlight found the unassuming lawyer. Once the spotlight found the lawyer, the spotlight technician couldn't resist turning the beam slightly to illuminate the lovely diamonds and the lovely bust of the showboat. When the spotlight found this buxom bourgeois beauty, there was a noticeable rise in the volume of the applauding. The beaming smiles that immediately graced the pretty face of this adorable symbol of sex and wealth strongly suggested she didn't mind being singled out one tiny little bit.

The Cemtex case had been well reported nationally. The *Wall Street Journal* and the *Miami Herald* had been running current accounts of its progress through the federal courts. Most of the male guests present were avid readers of the *Wall Street Journal* and the *Miami Herald*. The Supreme Court's decision two days ago had reversed a Ninth Circuit Court ruling against Cemtex Inc., and remanded the case directly back to the US District Court in San Francisco with instructions to enter judgment in favour of Colin Johnson's client Cemtex 'and against Defendant Department of Interior in the sum of three-million dollars and court costs'. Even before the decision was announced, the *Wall Street Journal* had reported Colin Johnson's recent argument before the Supreme Court as 'the most eloquent and compelling presentation by this thirty-eight-year-old attorney that anyone around here can remember'.

Without doubt, the men attending this party were quite familiar with the name of Attorney Colin Johnson of San Francisco.

Mary looked back over Darren's right shoulder, and her eyes poured over this modest guest. She had never heard of the Cemtex case, and didn't read the *Wall Street Journal* or the *Miami Herald*. She was curious, however, about the intensity of the applause when the lawyer was introduced. She might have suspected, had she known of the $3,000,000 judgment, and that it was the equivalent of £750,000.

The host's welcoming 'speech' and the individual introductions had taken less than ten minutes. Then George Henderson turned the microphone over to the smiling orchestra leader, who promptly turned the party into a dance.

Chapter Forty

Mary danced the first two dances with Darren, and the third dance with Greg. The eight-piece orchestra didn't play the dance music exactly fast, but keeping pace did tire many of the guests. Even youthful Mary and Laura became a bit fatigued, and chose to sit out the fourth dance at their table. Darren and Greg walked across the patio to talk with a couple that Greg recognised from St Petersburg. As Mary and Laura sat chatting away, Mary saw the lawyer Colin Johnson crossing the patio alone and obviously heading for the wet bar.

While Mary Roberts was anything but a 'forward' person, some inexplicable impulse inspired her to do something she could never recall doing before. Without saying a word to Laura about her intentions, she rose from her chair and caught up with the lawyer, who was walking in the opposite direction.

'Hi,' she said to the surprised lawyer. 'I'm Mary Roberts. I know who you are from the introductions.'

'And?' said the lawyer, smiling very pleasantly.

'My friend over there and I,' said Mary, pointing toward Laura, 'were wondering why you got such loud applause when Mr Henderson introduced you to a patio full of strangers.'

Before Colin Johnson could make any reply, she continued, 'We'd be pleased if you would add a couple of Coca-Colas to whatever you're on your way to get, and come over and explain it to us.'

Johnson picked up on the English accent immediately, and was both amused and pleased at this unexpected invitation. It also crossed his mind that he was looking at a lot of woman.

'Well,' he replied, assuming a half-serious demeanour, 'I might if it won't involve violating any attorney–client confidential communications.'

That reply stuck even him as a bit strained, so he quickly added, 'Are you sure you wouldn't like something a little stronger than Cokes?'

Mary had no answer. She didn't know that much about drinks.

'Well, uh, I don't know,' she replied. 'If they have shandies, I guess they would be all right.'

'No,' he said, trying to sound serious, 'if you're not used to the hard stuff, you should stay with your original order.'

'It wasn't an order,' protested Mary. 'I just—'

'I know it wasn't,' he interrupted, very congenially. 'Just relax. I'll bring the Cokes.'

Mary felt a bit awkward, but she smiled back, and said, 'OK.'

The lawyer turned to proceed to the wet bar, and Mary returned to the small table with the red and white tablecloth.

The only thing she had told Laura was that the lawyer agreed to bring them some Coca-Colas, because she had asked him to.

A few minutes later, Mary saw the lawyer weaving his way between some couples on the dance floor as he came in their direction. He was holding two filled glasses in one hand, and third glass in the other.

Having already met Mary, upon arriving at the small table he introduced himself, very charmingly, to Laura and sat down.

Just as I thought, they're both English, he mused.

'I've only got one answer,' he said in a very good-natured voice.

Laura hadn't the slightest idea what he was talking about.

'I'll bite,' said Laura, 'what is it?'

'Honest injun,' said Colin, facetiously crossing his heart with his right hand, 'I don't know.'

Now this is insane, thought Laura. I don't know what an 'honest injun' is, or even what a 'dishonest injun' is for that matter, and I also haven't the slightest idea what he doesn't know. Nothing is going nowhere!

'Why don't we start over?' said Laura. 'Aside from what an "honest injun" might be, what is it you don't know?'

Mary burst out laughing, and then all three of them were laughing.

Mary recovered her speech. 'I asked him why these people he doesn't even know applauded so loud when he was introduced and he said he would get the drinks and tell us, as long as it didn't involve some confidential something or other.'

This 'recap' was the finishing touch on a silly situation which the lawyer had never seen blossom so far, so fast or so wide in his life. He erupted in very audible laughter.

These English girls are something else, he was thinking, as he crossed his arms, clutching his sides. But he managed to stop laughing.

'Oh my God,' the lawyer said, 'maybe I'm the one who should drink the Cokes. You girls are too much.'

He quickly perceived that the English girls weren't enjoying the joke nearly as much as he was, and he didn't want to spoil his new acquaintanceship.

'I'll tell you,' he said, in confessing tone of voice. 'Why the applause from a bunch of strangers? It is true, I don't know for sure because I can't read minds. I'll tell you my best guess. I just got a judgment of three million dollars against the federal government for a corporation that is already rich. Now the government has to pay that judgment to my client and the government is going to get the money to pay that judgment from the taxpayers, many of whom are at this party. Those far-sighted souls must think paying those taxes will be some kind of fun, so they applaud the lawyer they think made that possible. It's sort of like a group knowing they've been condemned to be shot applauding their prosecutor, isn't it?' With a perfectly straight face, he added, 'That makes perfectly good sense, doesn't it?'

Colin's 'best guess' was quite a bit to digest over the din of the party, but both of these girls had excellent hearing, and excellent brains between their good ears. Of course, what he had just said made perfectly bad sense. But the gross inconsistency of the applauding taxpayers was funny; particularly the part about 'those far-sighted souls'. Both Mary and Laura quickly got it, and started laughing. The lawyer saw he had saved the day – well, at least the evening – with these two pretty young English girls, so he laughed too.

Darren and Greg came up to the table just at the end of the lawyer's 'best guess'. They were both delighted to find him at the table, and were eager to have Mary introduce them. They pulled up two more chairs, and so it became five people sitting at the small table.

Colin Johnson fit in with this younger group with remarkable ease. The enormous gap between him and these undergraduate college students was vast in all dimensions of comparative age, education, wealth, and professional experience. But the man had a pure genius for bridging those gaps in a friendly and forthright attitude and manner. He obviously wasn't humble but, equally apparent, he wasn't self-important, overbearing, or patronising to anyone.

Mary was the one to note this congeniality. She had found something intriguing about the man from the instant of their first meeting, maybe since the spotlight found him.

The men did most of the talking at this extended tête-à-tête. Colin asked as many questions about Florida Southern and what everyone was studying as Darren and Greg asked him about what it was like to practice law, and how would someone know if he was cut out to be a lawyer.

While Mary sat following the lively back-and-forth conversation, she thought of how surprised she was at herself, walking out there and sweetly, but unmistakably, forcing her company on this man. She had never done anything like that before. It was all beginning to intrigue her.

Before the first day of the party wound down that night, Mary danced two dances with Colin. Whatever the chemistry between them was, it certainly wasn't fading. During their second dance Mary had remarked that in four weeks, she and Laura were moving to St Mary's College at Moraga, California, for the summer school. After that she and Laura were then scheduled to go to 'our last school', Stanford University.

'Stanford!' exulted Colin so loud that several couples dancing nearby glanced over at him. 'That's where I was an undergraduate, and I liked it so much I stayed an additional three years for law school. You'll love it!'

'Are you staying over here at the Hendersons'?' asked Mary.

'Yes,' replied Colin, 'at least for tomorrow. I won't be here for Monday's proceedings, unfortunately. Duty calls. I have an early flight on American Airlines booked Monday morning from Miami to Denver. After a couple of hours' layover, I'm on another flight to San Francisco.'

'You are booked in at the Henderson Sub-Patio Hotel for tonight?' Mary asked.

This man has the bluest eyes I have ever seen! she thought. They're almost hypnotic. I just hope he doesn't think I'm staring at him.

'I am indeed,' answered Colin. 'As we speak, my entire travel wardrobe is on hangers in the fourth guest room on the right.' He released Mary's right hand briefly to point downward at the patio.

'Do you play tennis?' asked Colin, resuming his gentle but firm hold of her right hand.

'No,' answered Mary, 'but I love to swim, and earlier this evening I had a guided tour of a fantastic swimming pool just behind those palm trees.' This time, Mary released her right hand, and pointed to the line of majesty palms beyond the patio.

'It's a date,' said Colin. 'I bought a new pair of swimming trunks just before I left DC, and I'm dying to show them off.'

'DC?' Mary asked, quite perplexed.

'I'm sorry,' said Colin, 'I'm referring to Washington DC, where I've been all week.'

Mary got one of those 'stupid me' looks on her face.

'I'm the one who should be sorry,' she said. 'Now that much I do know. I just wasn't thinking. Oh, uh, yes,' she went on. 'It's a date. Somehow I know I'm going to enjoy that pool. I'll reserve judgment on the new swimming trunks until I see them.'

Colin gave a little squeeze of their joined hands, and with his arm around her waist. To her own amazement, Mary squeezed back. Very lightly.

When their second dance was over, someone working a master switch blinked every light in the place on and off several times. This was correctly interpreted as signalling that party time for the day was at an end. The musicians all stood, similarly signalling the end of the music. The leader of the small orchestra spoke into the standing microphone, thanking everyone and expressing the hope that everyone had had a good time. The guests responded with a short round of applause. Then the orchestra leader concluded by assuring one and all that his group would be back tomorrow with a whole new set of music 'designed to aid your digestion at dinner and inspire your dancing later.' Some guests gave a little courtesy laugh at this promising rhetoric, and the crowd began to disperse. Most guests went to their parked cars to return to their own homes in Miami. Seven of the guest rooms under the patio had been taken.

Laura, Darren and Greg walked from their small table to join Mary and Colin amid those who had been dancing. Then the group ambled toward the open door to the stairway leading to the guest rooms. It was nearing midnight. Everyone was getting tired, and glad it was time to turn in.

Tired or not, when Mary and Laura got to their guest room they still felt half-intoxicated by the wonderful time they had just enjoyed. Within minutes they were in their pyjamas, and it was lights out.

The last thing Mary thought about before dropping off to sleep was her dancing with Colin and hoping he didn't think she had been too forward. He didn't.

Although Mary had come to this extended party as Darren's date, few would have suspected that who saw the twosome of Mary and Colin the next afternoon at the swimming pool. The phenomenon is difficult to describe. They did not associate to the exclusion of others. They joined with the others in the swimming, the jabbering and the socialising. Several of the male guests came up and introduced themselves to Colin, and congratulated him on pasting that 'SOB Harold Ickes'. Yet, most of their conversation and attention were with each other. Darren certainly had no doubt that something had shifted. Fortunately, his reaction was more bewilderment that resentment. He liked the lawyer, too. He just couldn't understand how Mary seemed to be taken by a man so much older than she was.

While Darren Henderson was pondering what was happening to the jolly fun-filled relations he had always had with Mary, she was discussing the specifics of getting together with Colin once she and Laura got to St Mary's College, just across the bay from San Francisco. Darren knew the girls would be leaving in a few weeks. He decided to carry on as if he hadn't noticed a thing. Under the circumstance, this was a perfect decision.

The second night of the party came off as well as before. The eighteen guests who had taken the boat ride to the Keys came trooping onto the patio while the other guests were in the middle of another superb buffet dinner. More of the guests danced than on the first night. The orchestra played a total of twelve dances. Mary danced two of those with Darren, one with Greg, and six with Colin.

Actually, Mary was almost as mystified by her changing emotions and increasing interest in Colin as was Darren. In fact, neither of them truly understood what was happening. The only thing Mary knew for certain was that she could hardly wait to get to the West Coast.

Early Monday morning, Colin left for the Miami airport and caught his American Airline flight to Denver. Before leaving the Henderson's, however, he and Mary took a brief walk in the flower garden beyond the majestic palms. By this time, Colin, too, was aware that his interest and feelings towards this wholesome, attractive young English girl were like nothing he had ever experienced. His mind was trained in legal analysis, not introspection or subjective personal analysis. He was just as perplexed as Mary in trying to understand the 'chemistry' going on. He was only certain that he could hardly wait for Mary to get to the West Coast.

In saying his goodbyes in the flower garden, Colin took Mary in his arms and the two embraced tenderly, but firmly. Mary was beginning to experience demonic emotions very similar to those that had so perplexed her older brother when he first met Rose Birchall.

After a second heartfelt embrace, Colin held Mary by the shoulders and stepped back.

'Promise you'll call me as soon as you get installed over at St Mary's?' he asked.

'I promise,' Mary replied, still fixed on his deep blue eyes.

Colin planted a light kiss on her forehead, stepped back and smiled.

'I don't know where all this leads,' he said rather softly. 'For someone whose expected to be full of the right answers, I, uh...' He just ran out of words, and simply looked nonplussed.

Mary felt the need to lighten the atmosphere a tad.

'I don't either,' she said, smiling broadly, 'so we'll just see, won't we?'

'Right as rain,' said Colin, smiling back and releasing her.

They walked arm in arm to the front of the Henderson home, where the limousine was waiting that would take Colin to the airport. The driver stood, holding the right rear door of the vehicle open for his arriving fare. Colin gave Mary's hand a little farewell squeeze and entered the vehicle. She just stood by the street and watched the limousine speed away.

On Monday afternoon Darren and his three college friends all returned to Lakeland in the same Oldsmobile convertible. The ride back was entirely affable. The four were all still good friends and the conversation was light, focusing on various things recalled over the past few days. Darren even got some laughs when he described the piercing light that almost blinded him when the spotlight found that diamond shop hanging from the ears of the 'showboat'. Try as they did to maintain a jocular atmosphere, there is no denying that the carefree fun-loving spirit that marked their trip three days before just wasn't there. Maybe they were all just tired. Maybe not.

Chapter Forty-one

Five weeks and three days after their return from the Henderson family's resplendent three-day Memorial Day weekend, Mary and Laura, along with Linda and Tina, made the train trip to their third school, St Mary's College. The sheer length of this trip made the trip from Poughkeepsie to Lakeland seem like a walk in the park. The four started at the small train depot in Lakeland, Florida. Four days, three railroads, and 2,881 miles later, they arrived at the Southern Pacific train depot in Oakland, California.

The Atlantic Coastal Railway transported them to Orlando, Florida, in something like ninety minutes in the same type of chair car as before. From Orlando to the West Coast, however, their accommodations were quite different from anything any of the girls had known or seen before. On each of the railroads they rode coming west from Orlando, they had sleeping accommodations in what were called Pullman Cars. They took their meals in a dining car, and spent most daylight hours in chair cars, looking out at a changing countryside unlike anything to be seen in all of Britain.

Until they got to the state of Texas, they were in a South that seemed filled with dense green forests and even denser humidity. East Texas was more of the same until the train got to central Texas, which begins around the city of Amarillo. From there until the traveller gets to west Texas, the state appeared to be what Americans usually refer to as farm country: some fields, some fences, some forests, occasional small rivers and an occasional lake. West Texas was a barren wasteland; flat sand dunes, aptly characterised by one of the passengers whom Mary overheard describing it as 'miles and miles of nothing but miles and miles'. For the most part, west Texas impressed as a vast, flat, sand-laden emptiness.

As their train laboured through west Texas, by mere chance, Mary overheard a conversation between two middle-aged men sitting in the row ahead of her. One was a neatly dressed man in a grey business suit. He could have been a merchant, lawyer, or even a doctor. The other was a tall, lanky man with a pronounced Texan accent. The Texan was wearing an expensive brown western-style suit, cowboy boots, and had a cowboy hat resting on his lap.

'Why,' said Grey-suit, pointing out the window, 'would anyone live in a place like this?'

'Well,' said Brown-suit, 'I live yonder not far from the lill' ol' town of

Odessa, that ain't more'n a wide spot in the road, an' no one says it's perty. But ever' time I stand on my porch and look out at them ten oil wells on my land, just pumpin' away day and night, seven days a week, I jus' kain't he'p thinkin': it ain't all that bad!'

Grey-suit had no answer. He just rotated his head slightly from side to side in resignation.

Mary interpreted Grey-suit's response as if to say 'no' or 'no accounting for taste'. She couldn't avoid smiling in amusement. She glanced to Laura sitting to her right, and saw was smiling too.

Two hours later the train made a brief stop at a little town where a sign by the train tracks read 'Odessa'. As the train halted, Mary looked out and saw a dozen or so small single-storey buildings clustered along a gravel road leading to the train tracks. Beyond, she saw a vast forest of blackened wooden oil well derricks, which were spaced out about a hundred yards a part. Each derrick looked like every other derrick. Each was about fifty feet tall, with an enclosed platform at the base. On each platform sat a pump with a large vertical wheel that rotated endlessly. A thick steel rocker arm that swivelled at the middle was attached at one end to the outside rim of the turning wheel; the other end was attached to a plunging rod running into the ground. As the wheel turned, it raised and then lowered one end of the rocker arm. The other end pushed the plunging rod down, and then pulled it up, thus sucking up the crude oil in the ground below. The basic method of this pumping was the same as that used since the invention of the centrifugal pump in the 1600s.

Oil wells, thought Mary. They are as ugly as this 'town'. I've read they make their owners very rich. I'd like to be rich, but not if the price was looking at something like that most of my life.

Mary was glad to leave desolate west Texas, oil wells or no oil wells.

Then came New Mexico, of which Mary's principal memories were the stony-faced Indians that sat on the ground staring at the hissing steam locomotive at each of the three brief stops the train made at towns called Tucumcari, Albuquerque, and Gallup. Mary had read some very strange sounding names of towns in Florida, such as 'Tallahassee', but no stranger than 'Tucumcari', 'Albuquerque' and 'Gallup'.

The scenery in northern Arizona was much more interesting. In crossing that state, they passed through long stretches of desert that featured numerous tall cactus trees bearing brilliant red and yellow flowers. Such scenery is unique to America's south-west. Arizona had reddish soil, similar to parts of Devon. At brief stops at Phoenix and Quartzsite sat the ground-hugging stony-faced Indians, apparently as transfixed by the mighty steaming locomotive as their counterparts in New Mexico.

They entered California through a dank small town named Blythe. The eastern part of California was also a desert. It impressed Mary as being like west Texas, only with hills and without oil wells.

They changed trains when they reached a small town in southern California whose signs identified it as San Bernardino, which was located sixty miles east of Los Angeles. At this stop, the girls boarded an Oakland-bound train of the Southern Pacific Railroad. Walking along the depot platform to their new train, Mary saw any number of the usual middle-aged poorly clad people who had nothing better to do than hang around train depots and gawk at train passengers. Unlike their counterparts in New Mexico and Arizona, however, the train depot habitués sat on the hard wooden public benches and chatted rapidly with each other, but only in Spanish. Quite accurately, Mary concluded they were Mexicans.

The ride on the Southern Pacific train would be the last leg of the girls' transcontinental journey, a total of 2,836 miles. From San Bernardino, the train headed north-west. Almost immediately the scenery improved. Within twenty minutes the train plunged through a range of rugged and heavily forested mountains. Ninety minutes later it came out into the flat Mojave desert, which is referred to as 'high desert' because of its three-thousand-foot elevation. The dull desert expanse of the Mojave was just as unexciting as west Texas, its only redeeming feature being the rising mountains that border its south and west edges. After two uneventful hours of bearing north-west across the Mojave, the train made a precipitous descent to the vast San Joaquin Valley, which makes up the centre of California. This descent was made through an ingeniously designed elongated and descending spiral built into the southeast side of the Tehachapi Mountains, the Tehachapi Loop.

Mary was quite taken by the beauty of the San Joaquin Valley, which impressed her with its endless groves of fruit trees interspersed among endless verdant fields growing of every kind of vegetable. Equally impressive was the snow-capped Sierra Nevada mountain range that forms the east side of the enormous valley. After almost four hours of passing through this veritable Garden of Eden, the train broke through some grassy hill country on to the land bordering the east side of San Francisco Bay. It was 4 p.m. on a crystal-clear sunlit day. Mary wished she could paint a picture to preserve the gorgeous sight that was suddenly unfolding as the train chugged north along the East Bay.

First they passed to the east of the multi-segmented Hayward Bridge, which mainly distinguished by its twelve-mile length crossing the San Francisco Bay from east to west. To the north Mary could see the longest bridge in the world: the 'double decker' twelve-mile long San Francisco–Oakland Bay Bridge, with its four massive suspension towers rising over 200 feet out of the water. This bridge was only completed in 1937; the same year that California completed construction of the Golden Gate Bridge, the world's longest single span bridge. That scenic edifice crossed the entrance to the bay from the Pacific.

Mary found it all a bit much, and stirred inside in anticipation of getting to see all this up close in the months to come.

The train ended the journey at Oakland's Southern Pacific train depot. Passengers bound for San Francisco had to take a bus which Southern Pacific provided for just that purpose.

Chapter Forty-two

When the girls got off the train they were met by two men in black, wearing reverse collars who had come from St Mary's College in nearby Moraga, California.

The priests introduced themselves as Fathers Bronson and O'Malley. They were intelligent-looking men, appearing to be in their late thirties. They informed the girls that Fr Bronson taught English literature and Fr O'Malley taught college-level trigonometry, calculus and physics.

The priests had come for the girls in a van-like Packard car that appeared to have been modified since it was manufactured. The vehicle had three passenger seats and a good deal of open space behind the last seat. It was more than ample to transport all four girls and their luggage.

Fr Bronson asked a red cap with a trolley to haul the girls' luggage to the nearby car park where the Packard had been parked. Fr Bronson also moved into the driver's position once everyone was on board. Fr O'Malley sat in the front right seat. By now, all of the girls were used to riding in a car going down the wrong side of the street.

The trip to the St Mary's campus would involve twelve driving miles into the Oakland Hills.

'I don't know how much you ladies know about St Mary's,' started Fr O'Malley, turning sideways to face the girls in the two rear seats. 'I'm sure you know we're a Catholic school. I don't know if you're aware that we're the opposite of Vassar, where I understand you've been. We're all male – except we do invite women students to attend our summer school, which you're here to study.

'Regardless, we've made arrangements for you to stay in a private residence near campus while you're here. That's where were heading right now.

'I'm sure you wouldn't be comfortable staying in one of our dorms,' he added, trying to be funny.

The girls all smiled and gave him a little courtesy laugh.

'I've been asked to deliver your mail from Educational Endowments International,' Father O'Malley continued, handing each of the four girls an envelope, one with each girl's name handwritten on the front.

'Go ahead,' the priest said, 'go ahead and open them now. I think they contain some information that will be of interest to each of you.'

Each letter from Educational Endowments International Ltd was identical in text. Each letter also contained a cheque payable to each girl for the sum of £50. After some preliminary remarks about what fine reports had been received on each girl, the letter addressed a new aspect of the programme:

> We had anticipated that the summer session at St Mary's College would be of three months' duration. That was a mistake on our part; as you will learn from the source, their summer school lasts for only six weeks. We have finalised the arrangements with Stanford University, where you are expected on 4 September 1939.
>
> Since you will be finished at St Mary's by 12 August, there is an unanticipated hiatus in our scheduling between 13 August 1939 and 4 September 1939. You will have that interim period to spend your time as and where you wish.
>
> You may want to do some sight-seeing or otherwise to go on a short holiday. The enclosed cheque for £50 is intended to provide you with sufficient funds to pay for your food and lodgings during this unexpected twenty-two-day gap in your Anglo-American Studies Programme.

Mary made a distinct effort to appear totally nonchalant at this unexpected news. Laura and Mary turned to face each other briefly. Had anyone been looking, they would have seen a very quick lifting of the eyebrows of each girl. Certainly this news had launched the beginning of some new plans involving at least two of the visiting scholars.

When Fr O'Malley saw each of the girls had completed reading their mail, he resumed speaking.

'Now, I was saying that St Mary's is an all-male school. Well, that's true during the regular academic year from September until June, but we do admit women students to our six-week summer school, as you'll see.'

He went on to give the girls a brief history of the school, noting that it was founded in 1863 during America's Civil War. It had been at its modest campus at Moraga, California, since 1928.

What the priest didn't see any reason to include in the school's biography was that in 1935 the trustees had to seek protection under the American bankruptcy laws, and in 1937 it was rescued when Archbishop Joseph Mitty persuaded the Archdiocese of San Francisco to buy the school and assume its debts. Since the rescue, St Mary's had been faring quite well, but would certainly fare a tiny bit better when the no-strings-attached donation from Educational Endowments International Ltd arrived.

Oh, you lovely-looking English ladies just couldn't be more welcome, the good Fr O'Malley thought. His entire face and manner beamed the same attitude.

The four English girls were each given a very nice bedroom in the home of Arnold and May Bell Crowder, whose four sons, ages sixteen to twenty-two, had recently joined the US Navy. Arnold Crowder was a civilian employee of the United States Army. He had held his present job as regional warehouse manager for the past three-years at the Oakland Army Terminal in nearby Oakland, California.

In that job he had learned many things that were unknown to the public generally. He saw massive cargoes leave the terminal on ships bound for the Orient. To his personal knowledge, those cargoes contained enormous volumes of ammunition, machine guns and rifles – the tools of war. Between those inventories and numerous conversations he had overheard among army 'top brass', Arnold Crowder was convinced of two things: (1) There was going to be a war involving America, and (2) When it came, he didn't want any of his sons in the Army or, worse, in the Marine Corps.

As far as Arnold Crowder was concerned, those branches of the armed forces were for innocents who joined them, and for foolish men who fancied adventure over staying alive. His sons were at the wrong age for the times. Without disclosing any classified information (he hoped), Arnold Crowder had convinced his sons to 'get a head start' over the lot that were going to find themselves drafted to fight the coming mess. The boys had joined the Navy en masse. The 2 April 1939 edition of the *Oakland Tribune* took note of the patriotism of the Crowder family in a short article on page six captioned, 'FOUR SONS OF ARMY EXEC. JOIN NAVY'.

Thus four bedrooms became available for rent in the Arnold Crowder house. On 15 April 1939 the wanted-ad section of Moraga's *Weekly Bulletin* advertised these rooms for rent with the notation that they were within easy walking distance of St Mary's. The ad ran in three editions. It was cancelled when the Crowders signed a room and board agreement that was proffered by St Mary's Dean of Students, Fr Edgar McCarthy. The agreement provided for room and board (breakfasts and dinners) for up to four (4) students, as assigned by St Mary's College. It also obligated Arnold and Bell Crowder to provide wholesome and balanced meals to the student-tenants. Of course, 'neither alcoholic beverages nor the consumption thereof will be permitted on or in the immediate vicinity of the rented premises'. St Mary's mark-up, paid by those whom it permitted to enjoy these accommodations, was a modest ten per cent over what the school paid the Crowders.

The Crowders had known for several weeks that the English girls would be arriving on 19 June 1939. At 3.30 p.m. on that date, the St Mary's three-seater Packard was stopped at the curb in front of the Crowder home.

The priests introduced the girls to Mrs Crowder, who was particularly charmed by their English accents. She confessed she had only heard people 'talk like you do' sometimes in the movies. Fathers Bronson and O'Malley insisted on carrying the girls' luggage into the house.

Mary and Laura took two bedrooms upstairs; Tina Williams took the third. Linda O'Brien took the corner bedroom downstairs. The Crowders' telephone was on a short table in a small cove near the foot of the stairs.

The two priests left on the note that the girls should pick up certain written materials on St Mary's summer session operation at Fr Bronson's office in St Albert Hall the next morning at 9.30. The girls were told they should read these materials and have them fresh in mind for the orientation lecture they were expected to attend at 11. After that they would be served lunch in the school cafeteria, and in the afternoon there would be a tour of the campus.

Once they were settled into their third new home, each of the girls realised how tiring the last several days had been. Aside from putting their clothes in closets and chests of drawers, none of the girls did much before Arnold Crowder arrived home from work at 6.30. Mrs Crowder introduced him to the girls and shortly after that she served supper. Mary and Laura retired to their respective bedrooms, and were fast asleep before 9.30.

Chapter Forty-three

The next morning the English girls walked together to Fr Bronson's office and picked up the orientation materials, which they studied carefully in the adjacent library. Then they went to the appointed auditorium for the orientation lecture, which lasted for ninety minutes. As billed, the lecture addressed the structuring of summer school instruction, which compressed fifteen weeks of regular school year instruction into six weeks. The difference was that summer school students were only taking one or two courses; unlike the usual five courses required during a regular school year. That meant the students could spend a great deal more time doing homework on their lighter course load. In class the instructor would lecture and monitor how well the students were digesting what they were required to learn to earn the full college credit for a semester of study. The unspoken aspect of all this was that, to most summer school students, the course being taken wasn't new to them. Most of them were undertaking it to get a passing grade in a course they had failed during the regular session.

After the orientation lecture, Mary begged off attending the luncheon and campus tour scheduled to follow. She wanted to get back to the Crowder house to work out the arrangements with Mrs Crowder about placing telephone calls, particularly to San Francisco.

Mary's impression of Mrs Crowder was that she was a fine woman, who seemed continuously busy cleaning the house, making beds or preparing the morning and evening meals. When Mary arrived back from the orientation lecture, Mrs Crowder set her carpet sweeper aside, poured two cups of tea and sat with Mary at the kitchen table explaining how 'this telephone business works'. She told her that all calls to San Francisco involved toll charges, and to place them, she would have to dial zero to reach a telephone operator who would put the calls through.

'Just keep a written record of the date you place such calls and the number you called. About a week after the end of the month we get an itemised bill from the telephone company that lists the date and length of each toll call and the amount charged for it. With your record, we'll know how much of the phone bill is yours.'

Mary thanked Mrs Crowder profusely, and decided to defer placing a call to Colin until later in the afternoon. She pictured him maybe at court, or very busy doing whatever it is that lawyers do during the day. She guessed he would have time to talk with her toward the end of the afternoon. Besides, she was overdue in writing her regular letters to her parents and brother. She was also well overdue in writing to Tim. Writing to Tim had become sheer procrastination for her. She admitted that to herself, that somehow writing to him just now wasn't something she wanted to do. Tim was a wonderful fellow – too wonderful to be sending a letter that would have to avoid mentioning subjects between them she didn't want to be discussing at this time. That would be deception. Never any time for that sort of thing.

So, Mary went to her room and wrote some unusually long letters to her parents and Adam. Both letters followed the same format. After assuring them of her safe arrival and comfortable living situation, she described some of the more memorable sights on her long train trip across America, and her initial impressions of St Mary's and her new living arrangements.

Mary wrote about the stony-faced Indians she saw sitting and staring at the steam locomotives, the unimaginable barren desolation of west Texas, and on and on. She included a vivid description of the train's 3,500 descent from the Mojave high desert to the fantastic San Joaquin Valley. 'It was in and out of ten tunnels and through what they called the Tehachapi Loop which is where the Tehachapi Mountains join the southern end of an enormous range of mountains called the Sierra Nevada.' Mary wondered if she wasn't writing more of a travel brochure than a letter home.

I think not, she surmised. Considering England has few peaks over a thousand feet high, I think they'll find this pretty interesting.

She was also very conscious of the fact that she was omitting any mention of Colin Johnson in her letters.

They might even think I was getting a bit jumped up, him being a lawyer. Besides, that whole subject may turn out to be much ado about nothing. It may come to nothing after all. Maybe he was just feeling lonesome in Florida. Maybe I was too, in a way. He is a terribly good-looking chap, and he probably has women falling all over him wherever he goes. He might not even remember me.

Of course, in her heart of hearts she knew these last thoughts weren't true. Then it suddenly crossed her mind that she hadn't learned if he was married, or had been married. Well, any questions along those lines would have been out of order, or at least showing too much interest on my part.

Between her letter-writing and mental meandering, the afternoon seemed to vanish. She glanced at her alarm clock. It was 4.10 p.m. Time to call Colin's office.

Mary walked downstairs to the hallway cove that contained the Crowders' telephone. She dialled the operator and gave her the number which Colin had given her in Florida. On the second ring the call was answered by the receptionist in Suite 3106 of the Russ Building, San Francisco's tallest building.

'Colin Johnson and Associates,' answered a young-sounding woman's voice.

'My name is Mary Roberts, and I—'

'I know who you are, Miss Roberts. Mr Johnson told me to expect your call. He just got back from court. If you'll hold for just a second, I'll put you through.'

Colin's was the next voice Mary heard, and she found herself thrilled when he came on the line. After a few getting-up-to-date questions and answers, Colin suggested they have dinner together that evening at a place called Pietro's Famous Italian Restaurant.

'Actually the first time I ever heard of this "famous" restaurant was when I asked a lawyer in the building that lives in the East Bay what he could recommend that wasn't too far from Moraga. Pietro's was the name he gave me. It's in Orinda. That's a little town that's just a stone's throw from Moraga. I could pick you up at about 6.30. Sound good?'

It did indeed sound good to Mary, who hoped she didn't sound overly eager when she accepted. She gave him the address and telephone of the Crowder home.

After starting her little log of toll calls, Mary told Mrs Crowder of her plans, which meant one person fewer at supper.

At 6.20 p.m. Colin stopped his 1939 Studebaker in front of the Crowder residence in Moraga, California. Mary was dressed and peering out the Crowder's front room window when he arrived. She was too anxious to wait until he walked to the front door and knocked. From the kitchen, Mrs Crowder heard Mary call out something about being back early, and then she heard the front door being opened and closed.

Colin was just crossing the pavement when Mary came out the front door. They met midway between the pavement and the Crowder front porch. They shook hands, a bit vigorously, and Colin slipped his left arm around Mary's waist as he saw her to the car. The heart rate of both of them jumped at least ten beats per minute in no time at all.

Colin opened the front passenger door and stepped back for Mary to enter the car. After closing the door, he zealously walked around the back of the car to the driver's side. He was feeling like he was in his early twenties. In fact, both of them were feeling what writers often describe as 'the thrill of a romance'.

Once in the privacy of the car, their faces came together in a short embrace, which each felt most invigorating. Colin engaged the gear shift, and the Studebaker sped off. Except for when he had to shift the car's gears, Colin held

Mary's left hand in his right hand all the to the restaurant. The trip took less than fifteen minutes.

Colin parked 'in the back', per the sign at the side of Pietro's Famous Italian Restaurant. There was a small parking area at the rear of the building that could accommodate perhaps twenty cars; four were parked when they arrived.

Upon entering the restaurant they were greeted by a lean dark-complexioned maitre d' in his late forties. The man spoke English with a very heavy Italian accent. The restaurant had no windows to the outside. All lighting came from candlelight and wall lamps. The dining area was rimmed by electric lights spaced around the room; each had an attractive tiny red lampshade. Booths were built along two walls of the dining area. There were fifteen rather small tables in the dining area. Each table and each booth were covered with red and white chequered tablecloths. A lighted candle held in the neck of an empty wine bottle glowed from each booth and each table. Involuntarily, a vision flashed across Mary's mind of the small tables near the back of the Hendersons' great patio.

For atmosphere, continuous opera music poured from concealed wall speakers, but not loud enough to interfere with normal conversation. Four other couples were seated and dining in the restaurant when Colin and Mary arrived.

Colin told the maitre d' they would prefer to sit in a booth. As Colin and Mary were seated, the maitre' de asked if they would like to order drinks. Colin glanced at Mary, and there was immediate understanding between them.

'I'll have a half-bottle of Chianti,' said Colin, 'and the young lady would like a Coke.'

Pietro's may not have been as famous as the sign out the front proclaimed, but the food was every bit as good as Colin's lawyer friend had described. Word seemed to be getting around. Every table and booth was occupied when Colin and Mary left two hours later. Their time there seemed to pass rapidly.

Colin ordered the clam linguini. Knowing absolutely nothing about Italian cuisine, Mary ordered the same. The food was so delicious that both of them ate slowly to savour the rich flavour. That slower rate also extended their time together.

During those two hours Mary learned a great deal about Colin Johnson. By posing a battery of innocent questions, the artful woman in her intentionally steered the conversation so that Colin did most of the talking. Like most men, and particularly members in the legal profession, Colin had little reluctance to talk about himself. By the grace of God, or somebody, he had been spared the gigantic ego that often goes with becoming a highly successfully lawyer. By the time they finished their clam linguini, Mary knew a great deal about this man who had ignited a feeling of attraction and attachment she had never known before. She also found herself feeling greatly relieved to learn both that he had never been married and why that had been the case. In answering Mary's many questions, Colin found himself enjoying his life's major events from his early infancy to his current age of thirty-eight years.

Colin's family background had not been without its tragedies. His parents had been killed in 1903 in a train derailment caused by the Southern Pacific Railroad's failure to maintain its track bed properly near San Luis Obispo, California. They had left him with his Aunt Lucy in Carmel, intending to work a small vacation into a business trip his father had to make to Los Angeles. Aunt Lucy and her husband, Karl Muller, were childless, and glad to have the three-year-old Colin for company. Karl was a regional vice president of Southern Pacific, whose office was in Salinas, California. For eighteen years, Karl had commuted to his office on the narrow-gauged Monterey and Salinas Valley Railroad. It took him twenty-eight minutes to go on this train from the depot near the Monterey Pier to the Salinas Depot just over the hill.

When word came of the fatal train derailment near San Luis Obispo, no one questioned that the three-year old Colin would remain with his only living relatives in Carmel. When word came that the derailment was caused by the lax manner in which Southern Pacific's yardmen had maintained the track bed, Karl Muller hired the best lawyer in Salinas to make a wrongful death claim on behalf of his nephew. The egregious circumstances that brought about the death of Colin's parents and sixteen other passengers unquestionably put the Southern Pacific management into an almost generous frame of mind to avoid any court trials by agreeing to the best settlement the railroad lawyers could negotiate.

Southern Pacific had a bad reputation at that time for its exorbitant freight rates. Accordingly, its owners did not want to subject the company to the tender mercies of any local jury. On 12 October 1904 the Superior Court in and for the County of Monterey approved a large settlement 'of all claims, known and unknown' of Colin Johnson, a minor. The settlement money went into a trust fund that proved sufficient to pay the costs to raise and educate the Colin through 1924, when he was sworn in to become a member of the bar. He had lived with his aunt and uncle until 1918, when he left for Stanford University in Palo Alto, California, which was the better part of one hundred miles north of Carmel. During the next year, Karl Muller was fatally stricken with the Asian flu.

Colin told Mary the money was just running out when he became a licensed attorney. His first efforts to become a practising lawyer occurred in Salinas, where he remained 'just long enough to learn that the only lawyers in this state that earn good incomes practise law in San Francisco or Los Angeles'. Colin had opted for San Francisco because of its proximity to Carmel and his widowed Aunt Lucy.

Why had he never married? He told Mary he wasn't quite sure. It wasn't because of any oath of celibacy, for sure. He enjoyed the company of the fair sex as much as any man, but looking back he guessed that he had just been too absorbed with practising law and too busy meeting the demands that work imposes to get deeply involved 'emotionally' with any of the numerous girls and ladies he had known and seen, sometimes frequently, over the years. In the course of this explanation he told Mary of an old saying that the 'law is a jealous mistress'.

'Until you came along in Florida and,' he added, hesitating briefly, 'I must admit, you hit me like a tonne of bricks – I've been virtually mumbling to myself ever since.'

Mary had heard the phrase 'like a tonne of bricks' in an American movie, but didn't really understand what it meant. Now, she did.

'I know what you're talking about,' Mary said. The blush was very becoming to her pretty face in the soft candlelight. Colin could feel an increase in his pulse.

'I haven't been able to figure out exactly what happened either,' she concluded.

'I'll admit it,' said Colin, 'I'm smitten. Maybe a lot more than just smitten. And I'm frank enough to admit that our age difference is a nagging concern to me. One I've been thinking about since I left Florida.'

'Well, I'm twenty-one and you're thirty-eight. That's what? Seventeen years. It's quite a bit, but it's not ridiculous. I don't think anyone in this restaurant would look over here and think you're here with your daughter – or necessarily think anything. I don't know if I'm an "old" twenty-one, but I do know you look and act at least ten years less than thirty-eight!'

The firmness in Mary's voice made a deep impression on Colin.

'All right,' he replied, 'let's just let the so-called age factor play itself out. Any time you think I'm too old for you, promise you'll say so, and any time I think you're too young for me, I mean my likes, I promise I'll say so.'

Mary smiled and nodded her hearty concurrence.

Colin held her arm as they left Pietro's and walked to his car.

They held hands all the way back to the Crowders'. By that time it was dark. Colin parked about five car lengths short of the Crowders' driveway. In the privacy of their location they embraced several times. These were tender and loving embraces, not the steamy passionate type. Then they made plans for going out on the weekend. When Colin walked Mary to the Crowders' front door, he did indeed feel like he was in his early twenties. At the door, he gave his date a goodnight kiss, and promptly walked to his car as the lovely lady disappeared into the house.

Colin had to fly to Los Angeles on a client's legal matter, which prevented their going out the following Saturday night. On Sunday, however, Colin picked Mary up at the Crowders shortly after noon, and the two went to the Golden Gate International Exposition on the tiny man-made Treasure Island in San Francisco Bay. The Exposition was a class act by any measure. It had everything from sophisticated Egyptian, Greek and Chinese artefacts to a huge Ferris wheel and scantily clad belly dancers. It was clever coordination of rich and poor samples of European, American and Oriental cultures that seemingly offered everything from the mundane to the magnificent. There was one thing the day did not do for Mary. It did not remind her of Blackpool.

The next six weeks seemed to flash by, at least for Mary. She did the necessary to learn what she had to learn about how colleges compress full semester courses to be taught in six weeks of intensive study at summer school. Her academic performance at St Mary's, however, did not resemble the excellence she had achieved at Vassar and Florida Southern College. The difference, of course, was that at the two earlier schools there was no Colin Johnson seeing her three or four times a week, taking her out for dinners, showing her about scenic San Francisco and continually occupying her thoughts and attention.

The changes in Mary's attitude and preoccupations were as obvious to Laura as they would have been to the folk back in England, but for her intentional omission of any mention of Colin in her weekly letters home. She chose to exclude any mention of her new heartthrob for several reasons. She had no faith in her ability to conceal her deepening feelings for this man if she were to start writing about him. In her heart of hearts, she recognised that she was hoping her new-found love. She couldn't define love, but like the legislator who admitted he couldn't define pornography, but knew it when he saw it – this was the same thing. She knew it when she saw it. And she knew her feelings in ever-grander dimensions for this modest, exciting, wonderful man were just that: love. But did he really feel the same way? How would it all turn out? Mary's feared she might be confusing hope with reality. Whether or no, better to avoid the whole subject in letters home – at least for now.

The six weeks at St Mary's were coming to an end. It was time to take up a number of subjects with Laura, her very best friend. Ever.

The girls arrived back at the Crowders' house after a full day of concentrating on the summer school teaching and learning techniques at the campus. Now their study involved observing how the instructors rehashed their course subject matter to prepare the students for the upcoming final examinations.

Mary went directly to her room, where she quickly reviewed her class notes. Once satisfied they were complete, she put them in a drawer. Then she went to Laura's room. It was time to find out if Laura would come with her on the six-week break coming up.

Laura was just finalising her class notes when Mary entered.

'Mary,' she said, 'I can't read my notes here. What did Fr Eccles say about... best I can make this out... I have "comprehend" or "comprehensive"?'

Mary looked at Laura's notes and immediately wondered if she was seeing Sanskrit or some Arabian script.

'What is that?' she asked, dumbfounded.

'Pitman,' answered Laura. 'I mean Pitman shorthand.'

'I didn't know you knew shorthand,' said Mary, quite amazed.

'Oh, indeed I do,' said Laura. 'I was a bit of a poor girl when I finished grammar school, and I spent the next year at Underwood's Secretarial College in Leeds. Then my mother remarried and our family fortunes rapidly improved. So much so I was able to go to regular college. But I learned typing and shorthand at Underwood's, and I try to use the shorthand enough so I don't forget it, but what I'm looking at here makes me wonder.'

Mary recalled what Laura wanted to know, and the Pitman shorthand notes went in the drawer.

'Laura,' she said, 'I hope you don't have any big plans for the six week break before we start up again at Stanford. I hope that,' she added quickly, 'because I have some plans and I want them to include you.'

Laura was immediately interested. She had politely declined a camping trip with the American chap she had been dating on weekends. Eddie Jackson was his name. He was a regular summer-school student who made up in good looks and friendly manner what Laura strongly suspected he lacked in the way of intellect. Good company. Fun to be around. But unremarkable in every other way. The furthest west he had taken Laura was Treasure Island. One Sunday they went to the San Francisco International Exhibition. While they were stopped hundreds of feet in the air on the Ferris wheel, Laura got an excellent view of San Francisco, and strongly hinted that perhaps they might take the electric train over and have a look around. Eddie promptly declined, saying you had to know your way around over there, he had never been there and had not an inkling to go. Laura liked Eddie, but she didn't think she would miss him once they were on their way.

Mary proceeded to tell Laura that she and Colin had worked it out for her to stay during the break with his Aunt Lucy in Carmel, California, and he would come down from San Francisco on weekends.

'He said I, or hopefully we, would love the small beach at the end of Ocean avenue, love Carmel, love the seventeen-mile drive from there to Monterey, and love Monterey, which was the first capitol of California.'

Mary paused briefly, and continued, 'He also hoped I'd love him in progressively larger amounts.'

She studied Laura's face for a reaction, but saw none. Laura's womanly instincts had already informed her of the blossoming romance between Mary and Colin Johnson. She had first sensed that potential the night they all met at the Hendersons' party.

Mary fairly beamed when Laura said she would love to spend the break with her at Carmel.

'Oh, that's wonderful,' said Mary, 'I'll call Colin after supper and tell him. He has to let his aunt know too, because she'll be opening up part of her house she never uses, and she needs to know how many bedrooms to have ready.'

'She lives alone?' asked Laura.

'Oh yes,' answered Mary, 'she's been a widow since her husband died right after the war. Got the Asian flu.'

'Well, now that we're on the subject of Colin,' said Laura, 'and since Mrs Crowder won't be calling us for supper until 6.30, I'd love to hear what's been happening these past few weeks, provided of course it wouldn't mean giving away any secrets.'

Mary proceeded to tell her a good many things that had happened recently, which she had shared with no one before. She told Laura about her trip to Colin's offices, a short visit to his apartment, sight-seeing in the City, and the fantastic San Francisco restaurant on the Bay called Harpoon Louie's Saddle Rock.

'I'm sorry,' interrupted Laura, 'why do you refer to San Francisco as the City?'

'Colin told me that everyone this side of Denver, Colorado, calls it the City because it's the only metropolitan area on the West Coast that is comparable to what's regarded as a city on the East Coast. He said Los Angeles was the only other metropolitan area, but it's spread out over hundreds of square miles, and has no tall buildings because of the earthquake hazard.'

'Oh, I see,' said Laura. 'How about his office? Is it big?'

'You mentioned this chap you've been dating took you to the Exposition at Treasure Island?' asked Mary.

'Yes, but I can't say I really saw San Francisco. All I saw was a bunch of tall buildings on the other side of the Bay.'

'If you could remember the tallest one, that was the Russ Building. It's the tallest building this side of Chicago. Thirty-four floors! And Colin's offices are on the thirty-third.'

'Offices? The plural? Offices?' asked Laura.

'Well, there's Colin's individual office, and then there are offices for each one of the seven lawyers that work for him. His "associates". And there are eight legal secretaries and a receptionist. That's a young girl just out of high school who answers the phone and greets people who come into their waiting room, which they call a lobby. He took me up there one evening and showed me around after everyone had gone home. Over the double door to the suite it reads: "Law Offices of Colin P Johnson & Associates".'

'How about his apartment? I'll bet it's a mansion,' said Laura.

'No,' said Mary, 'it's not a mansion. I was only there once for a few minutes when he had forgotten something, so I didn't see all of it. It's about what you'd expect for a successful lawyer, but it's not overdone. It's on the top floor of a very swanky apartment building on Nob Hill. Oh the view is fantastic. You can stand at one corner where the windows meet in… I guess it's his living room. It's on the north-east corner of the building. Standing there, first you turn your head to the left, and you see the entire Golden Gate Bridge. Then you move only your head slowly to your right. You see what they call North Beach, Fisherman's Wharf, and north of there you see that prison island, Alcatraz, about half a mile out in the bay. As you keep turning, you see all of what they call "downtown" San Francisco, the ships and docks at the Embarcadero, then the Oakland Bay Bridge, and those enormous towers standing in the Bay that hold it. By that time you're looking east, and you can see the whole bay and the lights of Oakland and Berkeley over on this side of the bay.'

Laura felt herself beginning to resent that timid dolt Eddie Jackson.

'And that something-rock restaurant you mentioned?' asked Laura.

'Ah!' said Mary, 'Harpoon Louie's Saddle Rock. You've never seen anything like it. It's not all that big, except for the bar. That's not little. It seats maybe three dozen people. They only serve lunch and dinner. They don't even tell you what's on the menu. You just pay a cashier, who hands over your silverware wrapped in a napkin, and tells you, rather limply, you can sit in booth number so and so, or at table number so and so, or, and then his voice becomes quite vigorous as he says "you can wait for your food at the bar".

'You should have seen the "what's-wrong-with-you-dearie?" look I got when Colin told him that I was only drinking Coca-Cola. I nearly burst out laughing.

'Anyway, you can sit at the bar or tell the barman what you want, and an overworked old dear brings them to your table. Then she watches closely, and whenever your glass starts getting low, she's right there asking if you want "a refill". They really push the drinks. After about five minutes they start bringing the food. Always seafood. But it's like nothing I have ever tasted. Truly, Laura, it's almost impossible that food can be that delicious. The only word I can think of that gets even close to describing it is "awesome". Believe me, dinner at that place makes fish and chips look like dog food. I promise we'll go there. You've just got to enjoy that place.'

Then the girls got down to scheduling their departure from St Mary's and the Crowders' house.

'We're through on campus next Wednesday at noon,' said Mary.

'I gather Colin will be driving us to this place, Carmel,' said Laura.

'Yes,' answered Mary. 'I'll tell him we'll be packed and ready any time after 1 p.m.'

'I know,' she continued, 'we could make it earlier, but we never know. Fr Bronson or Fr O'Malley might get the inspiration to take us all to a farewell lunch in the cafeteria or something. Besides, Colin said it will take us less than three hours to get to Carmel, so we'll still get there before sunset.'

Laura was manifestly delighted. In fact, both girls were delighted, so much so that they were the most talkative persons that evening at the supper table. Mrs Crowder knew that something had happened, but she had the good manners not to ask.

Until 3 September 1939, everything seemed to go perfectly in the life of Mary Roberts and those around her. The drive to Carmel had been under a beautiful cloudless blue sky in perfect temperature. At Salinas, California, Colin turned south off of US Highway 101 to cross the hill beyond which lay Monterey Bay, eighteen miles distant. On that bay is the historic town of Monterey, which looks like a picture postcard of someplace in Spain, and just south of that is the quaint little hamlet of Carmel-by-the-Sea.

Once they had had passed the crest of that hill, the scenery changed dramatically. They were suddenly driving through a verdant wonderland of Monterey pine trees, native cypress trees, oak trees, California bay leaf trees, bay laurel trees. They saw prodigious and gorgeous growths of flowers, including pink lilies, ivory white calla lilies and blood-red poinsettias. Mary and Laura found the Monterey–Carmel area absolutely breathtaking. Now they were both beginning to understand why the famous English writer Robert Louis Stevenson had been so enamoured of it. By anyone's measure, this was truly a Mecca of natural and architectural beauty poised on the eastern edge of the vast Pacific Ocean.

Colin's Aunt Lucy was a cheerful lady in her seventies who showed not the slightest sign of jealously. On the contrary, she was glad to have their company, and they could not have been more welcome.

The weather was wonderful. The two fine-sand beaches in easy walking distance of Aunt Lucy's house were wonderful. The beach parties were wonderful. On one weekend Colin brought along a young lawyer who worked for him, and they had a wonderful picnic dinner on the beach with a raging fire in an open-ended fifty-gallon metal barrel. Everything was wonderful until Sunday morning, 3 September 1939, two days after the robust German

Luftwaffe and armed forces began their devastating invasion of Poland on the ludicrous claim that tiny Poland had threatened to invade the Third Reich.

About 8.30 a.m. on that Sunday, Mary sat down to breakfast at Aunt Lucy's home in Carmel. She turned on a little radio that regularly sat on a nearby shelf. After a few seconds, the vacuum tubes in the device had warmed and from its speaker Mary heard a voice she recognised immediately as that of Prime Minister Neville Chamberlain. She heard the Prime Minister announce 'a state of war exists between her majesty's government and Germany'. Her immediate response was one of numbing shock.

Mary was not politically oriented, and had never had any interest in keeping current on international events. She had a passing knowledge, at best, of the political cauldron in Europe. Now that cauldron had boiled over. The consequences would be a conflagration that would end the lives of millions, and drastically change the lives of even more millions. Very shortly, Mary learned that her life would be one of those first affected. Her repeated attempts to place an international telephone call through to her parents and to Adam were uniformly unsuccessful. All international circuits were busy. Every telephone operator who gave her that same answer invariably added, 'Please try later.'

As required, both Mary and Laura had provided Educational Endowments International with Aunt Lucy's address as the place where they could be contacted during the six-week break. On 8 September 1939 they received identical international cablegrams from the philanthropy. They were both informed that the expected danger of German submarines was such that 'until further notice' the participants in the Anglo-American Studies Programme would have to remain on whichever side of the Atlantic they now found themselves. Each cablegram also recited:

> Since we have no way currently of knowing how long you may be stranded abroad, we are attempting to work out an arrangement with Stanford University to admit you as regular students for your fourth year as an undergraduate.
>
> If this works out, you will be able to graduate next June, and receive your bachelor's degree from Stanford. Such a shift would require cancellation of our Anglo-American Studies Programme, which would be regrettable. If that occurs, we will ask you to take an equivalency examination when you return to London, and will issue your Certificate of Completion based on your passing that examination. We're sure you realise that we must all make appropriate adjustments in our lives and undertakings in light of our country's wartime situation.
>
> We expect to inform you further as to Stanford within a few days.
>
> If, as we hope, the described arrangement is worked out, Educational Endowments International Ltd will provide your tuition and remit to you monthly an amount sufficient to provide for your personal needs and lodgings until you graduate in June of 1940.

Both Mary and Laura were stunned. Mary called Colin in San Francisco and read her telegram to him over the telephone. Of course, he extended his sincere sympathy, and without hesitation added that as long as this 'war situation' continued, neither she nor Laura had a worry in the world as regards their support and accommodations 'over here'. Colin's response was reassuring, but did little to allay Mary's troubled apprehension about her parents, her brother and his family, and yes, Tim. Mary already wondered about England being bombed. Oh God!

At least I can't imagine those stupid Germans being dumb enough to waste any of their precious bombs on a little place like Gateley, she thought. Mum and Dad won't have to worry, at least about bombs. I hope.

Part Two
The War

Chapter Forty-four

On Monday, 4 September 1939, the British Government's war response began at a breath-taking pace. During the next two weeks, more emergency laws were passed than in the first twelve months of the First World War. In one day both Houses of Parliament passed, and the King signed, the Emergency Powers (Defence) Bill. It was a 'comprehensive measure' intended to avoid a repetition of the conflicts, confusion and chaos that were encountered with the series of Defence of the Realm Acts that were enacted in short succession following the outbreak of the First World War.

The sweeping measures empowered the Government to enact practically any regulations by 'Orders in Council'. It would require volumes to describe the vast and varied ways that Government authority metastasised in this delirious era. Suffice it here to note that the Government could take possession of almost any property or operation, from a horse to a hotel, from a motorboat to a railway. The state could direct farmers what crops to grow. It could regulate, or ban, 'the production, treatment, keeping, storage, movement, transport, distribution, disposal, acquisition, use or consumption of articles of any description and control the price at which such articles may be sold'.

On Thursday, 7 September 1939, Walter and Adam received identical telegraphed written orders addressed to 'White and Roberts, a partnership', from the Ministry of Transportation. They were commanded to appear before Tony Harding, director of the newly formed Internal Transport Department, Holmby House, London on 11 September 1939 at 10 a.m.

Under the Ministry of Transport, the Government was taking control of all commercial barging companies having more than a stipulated number of barges registered in their name for the duration.

On Wednesday, 10 September, Walter and Adam departed by train from Wigan. The booked into a small hotel on the Strand, and were at Holmby House on Baker Street, just off Oxford Circus by 9.30 the next morning. After the seated uniformed guard at Holmby House examined their telegraph summons and identity papers, they were seated in a waiting area and each received a bundle of papers in which the bureaucracy's principal goals for the barging industry in relation to the war effort were described. They browsed through these documents while waiting to be admitted to Mr Harding's office.

The handout materials covered subjects about how the owners were still going to operate their own organisations, but not for their 'old customers'. Petrol would be rationed, and all priorities would go into sustaining the war effort. All current private contract commitments were suspended; that meant no one could claim breach of contract against a barger whose services were being pre-empted. The country was being divided into 'sectors', and all barges would be scheduled by the Ministry of Transport's jurisdiction. All Lancashire barge operations were to be controlled out of Liverpool. Each month they would receive complete written instructions regarding all cargoes they were assigned to haul. The budding bureaucracy would issue the schedules of cargo pickups and deliveries. Needless to say, the inexperience in transport of many of those who issued such instructions created much chaos on many piers and wharves throughout Britain. Tony Harding was the newly appointed head of the newly created Internal Transport Department. He was a career civil servant about Walter's age, and very knowledgeable in the workings of bureaucracy.

By the time Walter and Adam were ushered into Mr Harding's office, they had read and re-read the newly printed handouts.

After the introductions and customary handshakes, Mr Harding asked if his involuntary guests had read the written materials just received. Walter and Adam nodded in the affirmative.

'Good,' said the bureaucrat. 'Now, other than confirming that you understand you'll be dealing principally with our Liverpool Office, do you have any questions?'

Walter quickly asked, 'How do we get paid, and how do our operations get financed?

'You're still the legal owners of your companies, which you'll run in most respects like you have in the past. Under the new regulations, your operating overhead, including the wages, will be paid by the Government. Support staff will continue at their current rate of earnings. Generally, wages will be frozen. Owner-operators are an exception. As such, you will each be paid £5,000 per year. When the war is over – assuming a favourable outcome, of course – the Government will provide you with a replacement fleet of new barges, or pay you the reasonable cost equivalent.'

Harding rose from his chair indicating the meeting was over. As he did so, he produced two envelopes from the pull drawer of his desk. He handed one to Walter and the other to Adam.

'These each contain duplicate copies of your contract. You gentlemen will find everything you'll need to know set forth in your contract, for which I'll ask you to sign this form to acknowledge you've received them, you understand them, and agree to their terms.'

Now that's what I call negotiations, Walter thought. Bloody diplomat, this one. Pity the Foreign Office didn't snag him. Walter forced a friendly look so as not to give away his thoughts.

'I'm sure we will be seeing a lot of each other. So let's all do a good job and get this bastard Hitler and his thugs out of the way.'

Adam followed Walter in signing the Receipt and Agreement form, which Tony Harding had pushed to the front of his desk. He gave them his friendly 'we're all on one team' smile. Walter and Adam smiled dutifully in response. They pocketed their envelopes, shook the bureaucrat's hand and promptly left his office.

They took the last train leaving Victoria station for Wigan.

On the way home, Adam discovered the item in their package of papers captioned 'Orders'. It read:

a duly authorised representative of White and Roberts shall report at the offices of the Ministry of Transport at Edgerton House, Liverpool, Lancs. at 10 a.m. on 18 September 1939.

Walter and Adam immediately decided that before putting themselves at the tender mercies of the Liverpool Headquarters of the Ministry of Transport, they would have a meeting with solicitor Sidney Blum of Wigan.

At 1.30 p.m. on the next afternoon, Friday, Walter and Adam walked into Solicitor Blum's office. Earlier in the day, Blum's secretary, Annie, had made the appointment. They were promptly shown into the office of the short, balding, middle-aged lawyer. The furniture and furnishings in this office were quite modest, something between austere and threadbare by London standards. Such unostentatious appointments were the lawyer's way of assuring clients that their modest fees did not finance any unnecessary overhead.

After reading the papers which Tony Harding had served on 'Walter White and Adam Roberts, doing business under the name and style of White and Roberts', the lawyer assured his clients that the Government's bureaucrats had obviously done their homework when it came to taking over the country as they deemed appropriate for waging war. He commended Walter for his foresight in getting the purchase options on nine used barges.

'No one,' said the lawyer, 'has had the time to read the mountain of regulations that are pouring out of London, and there's no way of predicting what new forms you may have to complete or what questions you'll be asked. Make sure you don't misrepresent anything about White and Roberts' assets. Any time you're in doubt, stall for time and get me on the telephone. You can read any doubtful questions to me over the phone, and we'll go from there.'

'When Annie told me you would be coming I drew up these assignments for you and your wives to sign where indicated, and then get them back to me for safe keeping.'

He handed the assignments across the desk to his clients.

'Current regulations,' he continued, 'require registration with the Ministry of Transport of all barge owners owning four or more barges. As you can see, these assignments give the right to Lil Roberts and Rose Roberts each to buy three specified barges.'

'If you can afford it,' the lawyer continued, 'as soon as these assignments are fully signed – oh, and note, by each signature the person signing is required to enter the date of his signature – as soon as all that is done, I recommend Mrs White immediately exercise her purchase option on the three barges described in her assignments, and Mrs Roberts do likewise. Before we pursue that further, tell me: can you raise the money it takes to do this?'

'Somehow we'll manage to raise the money,' replied Walter.

Walter just didn't think it wise to inform this lawyer how really well off White and Roberts was. That might distort his view of the value of his advise.

'Fine,' said the lawyer, 'to the extent the money comes from White and Roberts' bank accounts, distribute it first as income to partners, and deposit it in your personal cheque accounts. New separate cheque accounts must be opened in the individual names of your wives. The accounts should be opened in separate banks. Also make sure they're not in any bank your partnership uses. Each of you should write a cheque on your personal accounts to your wives for at least £50 or £60 more than will be paid for the used barges. That will keep the accounts open after the used barges have been paid for. These cheques will be used for each of the ladies to open individual cheque accounts. Payment for the newly acquired barges are to be made by your wives with cheques drawn on their new cheque accounts. That way, these ladies, and not White and Roberts, are the buyers and owners of these barges, and neither you nor your White and Roberts partnership will have to declare them. They're not yours. Within a day or so after you've taken over the used barges, register them at Liverpool in their lawful owners' names.

'Oh,' added solicitor Blum, 'and tie these used barges down in some nice quiet out-of-the-way place and lock them down like they were being stored. That's exactly what you'll be doing with them until you have to start using them to serve your old customers. Until then they'll just be held in reserve. Whatever you do, don't use them for White and Roberts' hauling! When it comes time use them, I'll draw a standard hauling agreement to be entered into between your wives as owners of those barges and the customers you'll be trying to keep. That will necessarily involve some new arrangements with the Leeds and Liverpool Canal Company, but we'll work all that out when it becomes necessary. I'll wager the Government will change how they operate a good deal more than will happen to White and Roberts. I only mention that by way of saying when the time comes, we'll probably find them quite flexible on working things out.'

My, he is a calculating little man, thought Walter, slightly amused. As Adam was taking this all in, he wondered whether what the solicitor was describing was legal. It was.

'Do you think all this is unpatriotic?' asked Adam.

'If I thought twelve used barges were going to make any real difference in how the Government wages this war, or how this war turns out, I might have second thoughts. But my honest opinion and answer to your question is no.'

Walter and Adam left Solicitor Blum's office with a number of legal documents. Those included applications for registration of barge, which Lil and Rose would have to sign after they obtained the titles to the used barges. Also, they had the assignments and the required notices of exercising right to purchase a total of six specific used barges. By sundown on that very same day, Lloyd's Bank in Wigan had two new cheque account holders named Lil White and Rose Roberts.

By 3 p.m. the next day, Saturday, all six notices of exercising right to purchase had been served on the sellers, who were all given cheques signed by Lil and Rose for the amounts needed to complete the sales. By sundown of the following day, Sunday, the six used barges were tied at well staggered intervals along the south side of the Leeds and Liverpool canal, just east of the Rufford Locks. One was tied to a very rusty iron hook that emerged from a venerable old tree stump, hardly a stone's throw from the lock-keeper's cottage.

Tim Birchall received two cheques signed by Lil and Rose, respectively, which totalled £60. This was the amount for which he agreed to clean and lockdown the six barges and to 'keep an eye one them'. John Birchall was paid £15 to check out the diesel engine in each barge. One of those engines emitted an ominous knocking sound when John held it at 1,500 rotations per minute; one owned by Lil, as it were. This noise was a sure sign of a loose connection of a piston rod to the engine's crankshaft. John inserted a thin metal plate, called a shim, where the rod wrapped around the crankshaft. The knocking sound was gone. Labour and materials: £5.

On Sunday afternoon, 17 September, there was a gathering of the clan at Wrightington: Adam, Rose, Albert, Doris, Tim, John, May, Walter and Lil. The Whites couldn't have been more by way of family had they been blood related. Adam's parents were also invited, but politely declined. Between their duties at their market stall and the gnawing impact of worrying about the war and their only daughter stranded in America, they just weren't up to it.

During the previous two weeks, the world seemed to have exploded. The slaughter in Poland had continued with a frenzy. England and Germany had exchanged one bombing raid each. Canada, South Africa, Iraq and Saudi Arabia had all declared war on Germany. One British submarine, the *Triton*, had mistakenly torpedoed another, the *Oxley*. German panzers had reached

Warsaw. Of course the BBC poured all this out in addition to a steady stream of bulletins, interviews and speeches which were intended to create public awareness of the dangers and sacrifices known to lie ahead.

The clan gathered in the living room, where Rose served tea.

'Everybody is talking about the war and how it will effect us all,' said Lil, adding, 'Every night we have to blackout all our windows. I don't think I will be going out at night. And last night on BBC news we heard that rationing is about to go into effect.'

Little did she know that meat rationing in England would last until 1953.

'Oh, you worry too much, dear,' Walter replied. 'We've survived worse than that Hitler can hand out,' he added in a comforting voice.

Rose told of her visit to the clinic with the twins during the week. Someone there said that very soon the Government was going to issue gas masks to everyone. 'That,' said Rose, 'really scared all the young mothers.'

Walter tried to make light of it.

'It's only a precaution the Government has to take,' he said. 'I read about it in the *Guardian*. The editor, at least, doesn't think even Hitler will break the League's rule against using poison gas. I agree. He's got too much to lose playing that game.'

Adam told the group how concerned his parents were for Mary. Her return trip from America had already been delayed, and they didn't know how long it would be until she came home.

The rest of the afternoon and evening were spent discussing this thing or that about how the war was going to change everyone's life. Not one word was said about six used barges that were then being assembled along the south side of the Leeds and Liverpool canal, just east of Rufford Locks.

No one had expected that the meeting at Adam's house involved supper. Around 5 p.m. Walter and Lil took their leave. The lot was gone within twenty minutes. Not a great deal had been accomplished, but there was an unspoken satisfaction in the atmosphere in which everyone present knew that everyone else present was a friend who could be counted on in what were sure to be trying times ahead. Promoting that atmosphere was well worth the time of all concerned.

Chapter Forty-five

On Monday 18 September, Adam, Tim and John each received letters in the mail from the Military Recruitment Department, Ministry of Labour, an official notice to appear at the old Drill Hall in Wigan on 25 September at 10 a.m. to 'register and be physically examined to determine your qualifications to serve in your country's armed forces, as provided in Para. 3 of the National Registration Act, 1939'.

Although such a communications came as no surprise, they produced some depressed attitudes in one household in Wrightington and one in Rufford.

Early on Tuesday 19 September, Walter and Adam drove to Liverpool to the still-being-set-up offices of the Ministry of Transport. They were both surprised to learn that very little had been accomplished at this location by way of setting up a Ministry of Transport office in Edgerton House. The effort had been vexed from the start, beginning with the evicted firm of accountants taking seven days more to get out than they had been officially allowed to quit the premises. The furniture allocated to this office was mistakenly shipped to Portsmouth. It finally arrived, ten days late. As Walter and Adam were walking about searching for the newly appointed regional director, they passed by small mountains of furniture still in shipping containers. The list of peccadilloes went well beyond late eviction and late arriving furniture. Seven new bureaucrats, who had been given a crash course in management in London were given orders 'to proceed forthwith to Liverpool via Edinburgh'. This wording had been composed as a joke by a young man in London who wondered just how these 'fourteen-day wonders' would react. The new bureaucrats scrupulously followed their travel orders without once questioning the specified routing. Worst of all, among the office supplies that were sent to the new office, no one could find the second most important thing for any bureaucracy: the carbon paper. Had a similar gaffe occurred with the tea-making facilities, God only knows just how chaotic things would have become.

It took twenty minutes for Walter and Adam to locate the new regional director, who was a fifty-one-year-old career bureaucrat just transferred from the Ministry of Labour. While he seemed like a rather affable sort, he didn't have the time to spend with outsiders, such as Walter and Adam, who had come in response to official directives.

'As you can see, gentlemen,' he said, gesturing towards a nearby collection of furniture still in its shipping crate, 'we're a bit behind here. I won't go into that. Just come back in two weeks. Also, just in case, be prepared to provide manned barges if we call for them.'

In the absence of such a call (which he confided he thought was 'highly unlikely') they were to carry on as usual. When Walter asked for a 'non-binding estimate' as to when operations of their size would probably get heavily involved in Ministry-directed hauling, the local director opined 'probably around mid-March'. His estimate proved prophetic.

After leaving Edgerton House, Walter and Adam registered Lil's and Rose's six used barges with the Port of Liverpool. It was time to drive back to Wigan and get to work. They did that, but on the way they yielded to the temptation to go by way of Rufford to confirm that their wives' six barges were where they were supposed to be. They found Tim hard at work cleaning the barges, preparatory to lockdown. John was busy checking out the diesel engines. All was well.

The following Friday morning all three went down to the old Drill Hall in Wigan to register. There they saw long lines of young men, all very keen to join up. John and Tim were told that because they farmers they were exempt 'at least for the time being, unless you want to volunteer'. After Adam had registered he was told to report for a medical examination the following Monday.

When they all got back to Adam's house, Rose and May were waiting.

'How did you go on?' they both asked at the same time.

'Tim and me don't have to go, for now at least. That's what they said as soon as the guy saw on our registration we were farmers.'

May was obviously pleased, but the doubtful look on Adam's face told her not to show any signs of jubilation.

Rose looked pensively at Adam, waiting for him to speak.

'I've got to go back first thing Monday morning for a physical examination. That's all they said to me.'

Rose felt devastated. She rushed into Adam's arms and started crying.

'I don't want you to go. I can't manage without you,' she lamented.

Adam put his arms around her.

'Now, now, now,' he said in a soothing tone, 'it wouldn't be all that bad, love. It would all work out.'

'Anyway,' he added resignedly, 'I do have to go for a medical next week.' Trying to lighten the atmosphere, he continued, 'I told the man I wanted to be a general, if I joined.'

Humorous? Maybe. But all round, not very funny.

Rose could not entirely hold back her tears, but she did her best to contain her emotions.

John, May and Tim were on their way shortly, and the Roberts family did their best to carry on as if the spectre of Daddy going away to war didn't loom over their otherwise happy home.

The weekend was the worst they had ever had. Adam was trying to think of how things would run if he had to go. He spoke to Walter on the telephone. Walter said he had been thinking about that possibility since the Government announced the call-up and had even called Tony Harding about it.

'You must explain your job,' said Walter, 'and get the name of the recruiting officer. If necessary, Mr Harding will send a letter.'

When Adam told this to Rose, she felt much better and gave him a big hug.

'Don't get too excited,' he cautioned, 'nothing's for certain, and even if I don't go into the Forces, I intend doing all I can by volunteering for duties here at home.'

That would be just perfect, thought Rose, since we're now living in wartime.

'Regardless,' Adam added, 'I've decided not to call my parents until we know. No use getting them all worked up.'

Early the next Monday morning, Rose left the children with May and went into Wigan with Adam. It was just before 7 a.m. when they parked on the Market Square.

Adam didn't know long he would be with his medical. They agreed to meet in the wine lodge at 10.

'That should be plenty of time,' he said.

'I'll be there,' replied Rose, and held up both hands showing her fingers were crossed.

Adam smiled and turned away, walking toward the Drill Hall.

Once inside he saw the arena had been screened off. In the first cubicle, a rather broad-faced man seated at a makeshift desk waved Adam to take the chair opposite him. He glanced over Adam's papers, and asked his preference, 'Army, Navy, or Air Force?'

'I think I would like the Navy,' Adam replied, 'because I've worked with boats all my life.'

This immediately raised the official's interest.

'Oh,' he said, 'what kind of boats?'

Adam felt a bit embarrassed answering, 'Well, as a matter of fact, only canal barges.'

The official smiled. 'I don't think you'll find the water in the North Sea quite so calm as you're used to.'

He initialled Adam's papers at the bottom, and directed him to the far cubicle whose canvas 'walls' were a dull grey.

When Adam entered, a young soldier standing just inside the cubicle told him to hang his clothes on a hanger. 'Strip to your underclothes, and then go into the next section,' he said.

As he spoke, he handed Adam a small cloth bag containing a pull-string round its top long enough to form a large loop. Large enough to be pulled over one's head.

'Put your valuables in this and keep them with you,' he added.

Of course, Adam promptly complied and was shortly walking into the cubicle marked 'Optical'.

Adam passed the eye test with flying colours.

During the general physical examination, things went a bit differently.

Adam proceeded to the canvas cubicle posted as: 'Physical Examination'.

As he entered, the standing guard gestured, indicating Adam was to go into something of a 'sub-cubicle' to his right. There he was met by a rather tall slender middle-aged doctor in Army uniform. The insignia on the doctor's shirt collar displayed his rank and branch of service. He was a major in the Medical Corps.

He'll probably determine if my body is warm and in I go, thought Adam.

After a 'well, let's see what we've got here' remark, the doctor proceeded to move his arms, legs, and trunk through a number of ranges, and then he began concentrating on Adam's slightly deformed right ankle.

'What happened here?' he asked.

Adam told him.

The doctor continued to probe about very carefully with both of his well-trained hands.

'Stand on your left foot, extend your right leg forward, and bend your great toe as far as you can toward your shin bone,' he requested.

'Now, bend your right ankle inward as far as you can.'

'Now bend it outward as far as you can.'

As Adam complied, the doctor viewed the ranges of motion through which Adam moved, and wrote down his estimates in the column captioned 'Range of Motion' on the form affixed to his clipboard.

When Adam completed his responses to the doctor's directions, he stood, looking somewhat puzzled at the doctor's rotating his head negatively from side to side as he wrote on the form.

'I think you would have great difficulty trying to climb a ladder with that right leg, and I know for certain you would never manage a twenty-mile march with full pack.'

The doctor completed the bottom of the form on his clipboard, and turned to Adam.

'I'm sorry, Mr Roberts, but I have no choice but to reject you. Your contributions to the war effort won't be in the Forces. Get dressed. You're free to go.' He removed Adam's papers from the clipboard, stapled them together, and placed them in a square basket on his makeshift desk. Without looking up, he called out, 'Next!'

As Adam was about to ask the doctor to explain his decision, but his calling for the 'next' man to examine conveyed the distinct impression that Adam's continued presence was only interfering with the many examinations yet to be done. After making an acknowledgement remark of 'I understand, sir,' Adam turned and walked back to the dressing room. He got back into his clothes and left the building.

At 10.05 Adam walked into the Wine Lodge. Rose was sitting at a table near the door. She looked at him with a worried inquiring look on her very pretty face.

The thought that this might be a bit of fun flashed across Adam's mind.

He assumed a very serious expression and walked to Rose's table.

As he came near he said, 'I've got to leave tonight for India.'

Rose was stunned. Her vision blurred briefly, and she almost fell off her chair.

Adam could see immediately his little 'joke' was the wrong thing. He quickly reached out, and held her with both arms.

'No, no, love. I was foolin'. They don't want me. They said I was too ugly.'

'Come on, Adam Roberts,' Rose said, eyeing him suspiciously, as she regained her composure. 'What did they really say?'

'Well, I'll tell you everything when we get home, but their decision was that I failed the medical examination, so you will have to put up with me for the duration.'

Rose was visibly relieved, but she knew it was certainly not the time or place to show any elation. They had a snack and a drink, and then drove towards Wrightington.

They stopped at May's to pick up the children. John had gone with Tim to Rufford. Adam told May that he had been rejected.

'He still won't tell me why,' chimed in Rose.

'OK,' said Adam, turning to face both of the girls. 'When I had that accident and the car come down on my right foot, I suppose it just didn't heal right and I've got a lot of limitation in my ankle motion. The doctor explained that it wouldn't let me keep up with the blokes who have a lot more flexibility in their feet. He as much as said I'd just be holding things up or slowing them down, something like that. I don't know. Leastways, like he was pronouncing a judgment, I'll never forget him saying, "I'm sorry, Mr Roberts, but I have no choice but to reject you".'

Adam just stood there without expression, as if he didn't know whether he'd won or lost.

After a few seconds of awkward silence, Rose started to worry.

'Does it give you any pain?'

Before Adam could answer that, she said, 'I think you should go to the doctor's tomorrow.'

'No, no, no,' insisted Adam. 'It really doesn't bother me at all, and the doctor didn't say anything about me getting any more treatment. So let's get back home. I have to call Walter.'

'Why don't you go on home and I will stay here with May and the kids?' Rose suggested. 'You can come for us later. And if you can't make it, just ring up and our John will bring us back.'

Adam was a bit relieved. He nodded his agreement, kissed Rose and shouted to Martyn who was playing outside with Jack, 'See you all later.'

Then he drove off. Business was calling.

May and Rose enjoyed some time on their own. They both felt relieved, knowing that their husbands didn't have to go off to war. May asked Rose what she would have done if Adam had been conscripted.

'I don't really know, I guess I would have managed somehow, like all the other women with kids.'

'How about you, May?'

'Well,' said May, as her face took on a sheepish look, 'I have not told John yet, but I think I'm pregnant, and I think his going in would have caused some big problems. I won't know for sure until next week when I see the doctor.'

'Oh, my God,' said Rose, as surprised as she was pleased.

'In a way,' said May, 'I hope I'm not.'

Then she started talking about all the talk about the war, and bombing and gas masks, and how it had scared her.

'I know,' said Rose, 'I'm just as scared as you. Probably more so.

'One thing,' added Rose in a reassuring tone, 'come what may, we've both got good husbands and I know they'll look after us. Knowing that comforts me when I start letting my imagination run away with me from all this war talk.'

The first thing Adam did when he arrived home was to phone his parents. He told them he'd failed his medical on account of his 'old foot injury', but not to worry; he was fine. Then he invited them to come to his house the following weekend.

'I think all the families should get together and think through some plan on how we'll deal with all this war business.'

'We'll be there,' his mother replied.

'Good,' said Adam. 'Rose is going to call her parents, and I'm sure they'll have no problem about coming, too.'

Had his mother had any news from Mary? No, not for several weeks, she said, and she just hoped Mary wasn't trying to cross the Atlantic. The memory of the *Athenia* was very much in Celia's mind, the dreaded headlines in all the newspaper *German Submarine Sinks First British Passenger Ship Cunard's 13,000-ton Athenia. Many Drowned, Including 118 Americans.*

Chapter Forty-six

When Neville Chamberlain announced on 3 September that 'a state of war exists between England and Germany', his UK audience included millions who had lost a son, a father or other relative in the Great War. His audience was generally familiar with the fact that the slaughter of humans in Britain's last war with Germany had caused no less than six and a half million combat deaths, of which no less than 600,000 were young men from England. An audience that was told after the fact that England and France had issued their guarantees of the independence of Poland. The vast majority of that audience didn't care a fig for Poland. Public feeling toward Poland, at most, was one of empathy that embraced the notion that the Poles simply did not deserve the slaughter being inflicted on them by their powerful police-state 'neighbours'.

The greater and daunting question abroad in the land was, when does the German jackal turn his invading thugs westward to settle scores with the now-weaker nations who prevailed in the Great War? In short, Neville Chamberlain's 3 September audience in the British Isles found no basis whatever for cheering their official involvement in what had all the earmarks of another Great Slaughter. But their response to his message was that of a civilised law-abiding population which was rapidly becoming aware of the impending threat that current events in Eastern Europe posed to their own freedom and way of life.

The Government presumed that Hitler would use gas in this war. By September of 1939, Germany's Geneva-Convention pledge not to use gas was on the same worthless par as Hitler's territorial pledges in the Munich Pact. Shortly after 3 September the Government embarked on the widespread distribution of gas masks for humans, horses and even some for dogs. (Reliable post-war records fail to show any serious plans by Hitler or Germany to use gas. Remarkably, they do reveal that in 1942 England, or, more accurately, Winston Churchill, was ready to unleash massive amounts of poison gas on any German invaders of the British Isles.)

Even before September 1939, the Government had sponsored distribution of kits for installing the arch-shaped Anderson Raid shelters in family gardens. The cost of an Anderson shelter was £7 for families with annual incomes above £250; below that, they were free. Altogether, 2,250,000 Anderson shelters were ultimately assembled and installed throughout Britain. While not famous for their physical comfort, they undoubtedly saved many, many lives.

Late in the last quarter of 1939, the flow of bills of lading directed to White and Roberts by the Liverpool office of the Ministry of Transport began in earnest, and grew steadily. Their first government cargoes were largely imported cotton and foodstuffs. Then came the heavy paper sacks of cement, many of which were bagged in England. The reason: the Government deemed it necessary to construct 'hardened fortifications' throughout the country.

As call-ups of manpower emerged, and unemployment disappeared, shifts in the workforce became a fact of life. In this atmosphere of change, Walter and Adam saw the need to dissuade their staff from departing for greener pastures. Walter and Adam took a cut in their partnership draws sufficient to enable them to raise every employee's wages by ten per cent from 1 January 1940. This good news was announced in small red and green envelopes attached to the last payroll in November. It is funny how money affects employee morale. After a pay rise or receipt of a bonus, every White and Roberts employee became noticeably more focused in performing their regular duties, for about three weeks.

Since these employees were not involved in the loading or unloading of their cargo-laden barges, the principal change in their work routines was providing the added skill required to manoeuvre their much heavier barges.

The bureaucrats who were involved in establishing and maintaining the supply chains paid little or no attention to jobs well done. They were far more concerned with foul-ups that often befell barge captains of lesser skills than those working for White and Roberts. Recognising that most people are inclined to do outstanding work more for recognition than for money, Walter and Adam made a point of keeping the good work of their staff well 'recognised' throughout the war. Such recognition took the form of laudatory words, bonuses and letters of praise (usually ghost-written by Sidney Blum) which could be shown to family and friends. The result was that, except for the younger bargemen who could not avoid being called up – usually into the Royal Navy – White and Roberts had essentially no staff turnover for the duration.

The cement these people transported soon changed the countryside. Concrete pillboxes were built in massive numbers and in specific models, such as the Lozenge pillbox, the Lincolnshire Three-Bay, the Dover Quad and the Somerset Defence. The one thing these 'hardened fortifications' had in common was concrete walls one foot thick. (According to a 1985 book entitled *Pillboxes: A study of UK Defences* by historian and journalist Henry Wills, in all, 28,000 pillboxes and other hardened field fortifications were constructed in the United Kingdom.) Anticipating the possibility of a German invasion from the west via the Irish Sea, thousands of these pillboxes and other hardened sites were built throughout Lancashire, and particularly along the Leeds and

Liverpool canal. Many farmers saw tank traps dug in their fields and pastures. All of these defence measures would undoubtedly have posed great difficulty for any invader. As it turned out, happily, the only use made of the pillboxes was by children, who found them very popular places in which to play. After the war, the Government filled in the tank traps in the fields and pastures. Many of the pillboxes, however, were still very much in evidence going into the twenty-first century.

The first British Expeditionary Forces reached France on 19 September 1939. This force was repeatedly supplemented and also augmented by numerous British Air squadrons in what proved to be the futile effort to stop the rampaging Germans from conquering Western Europe. By May of the following year, those forces exceeded a quarter of a million British troops.

The national identity cards required under the initial burst of new laws in September were mostly issued within three months. The information required on the applications for those cards provided the Government with a treasure trove of data regarding the skills, genders, ages and educational levels of the human assets that could be marshalled to fight the war.

The first call-ups for active duty in the Forces were limited to those who had already signed on, namely the reserves and auxiliary forces. As the data poured in from the identity-card applications, the Military Recruitment Department became increasingly more selective in their call-ups, or more accurately in deciding who not to call up. Certain classes of men were not called up as a blanket policy, such as miners and farm workers. Key individuals with key skills in such things as critical science, aircraft production, engine design and the design of other machines of war were simply not called up. Their specialised skills were deemed far greater contributions to the war effort than calling them up to become soldiers or sailors.

During the last quarter of 1939, the British civilian population was far more involved in preparing for war than in suffering any mass devastation. [Within a year that dubious balance would certainly change.] For many, the era was one of build, build, build and produce, produce, produce. Army training camps, make-do aerodromes and factories producing aircraft, tanks, cannons, ammunitions and uniforms seemed to spring up all over the British Isles. In the midst of all those accomplishments, the war news was mainly bad and depressing. The U-boat menace was horrific, and the tonnage sunk each month created all manner of difficulties.

Nevertheless, through news releases in the newspapers and those read over the BBC by those matter-of-fact, honest-sounding newsreaders, the Government issued some remarkable numbers each month of the number of U-boats sunk that month, *and* the tonnage that had gone down with them.

From 3 September through the end of 1939, the official published numbers were:

41 U-boats sunk in September (153,000 tonnes);

27 U-boats sunk in October (135000 tonnes);

21 U-boats sunk in November (52,000 tonnes); and

25 U-boats sunk in December (81,000 tonnes).

A good many in the public were sceptical of these numbers, as the Germans were widely (and correctly) believed to have numerous types of submarines, and most of those allegedly sunk were never seen or weighed before reaching the ocean floor.

'So how,' questioned many a doubting pub philosopher, 'do they know what kind of a bloody U-boat it was or how much it weighed?'

Post-war documentation from the record-fanatic Germans reveal that the Government's early pronouncements had far more to do with raising public morale than reciting historic facts. They showed that the Germans started the war with thirty ocean-going U-boats. The average number of U-boats at sea in the Atlantic during the first phase of the war was about six, and each month about two out of the six U-boats at sea were sunk. By the end of June 1940, eighteen of the original thirty U-boats had been sunk, while only fifteen new ones had been commissioned.

By 1945, however, even loftier numbers of submarines sunk per month reported by the Government became very credible. This was due mainly to the many perfections of technique and technology in waging anti-submarine warfare. These included the ever-expanding range of protective aircraft flown from bases in England, the United States and Canada; refining radar to locate U-boats on the ocean's surface; developing the ASDIC receiver amplifier which provided fantastic sensitivity in distinguishing between long- and short-range echoes; perfecting the best type of depth-charge patterns; and employing both attack planes and the 'scarecrow', which carried no bombs but sighted and reported U-boats, to made them submerge. They also perfected convoy techniques to protect the important cargoes while adding 'stragglers' to lure the U-boats to tragic ends.

By 1945 Germany had built and launched just over 1,100 U-boats in their attempt to impose a blockade on all ships in the Atlantic bound for England. Those merchants of death inflicted an awesome toll on Allied merchant ships. The ever-improving techniques of Allied anti-submarine warfare, however, sent over 700 of those U-boats to the bottom. By 1945 the bleeding German war machine could no longer afford to engage in anything resembling effective submarine warfare. The war was lost.

Notwithstanding the fearful losses inflicted by German U-boats on merchant ships bound to and from England, by 1940 the cargo volume of raw materials and manufactured goods (ranging from foodstuffs to the tools of war) arriving by sea at Liverpool Pier was growing daily. The imported raw materials were mostly barged to mills and factories in Lancashire. The other cargoes were regularly barged to inland piers for transfer to trains and lorries.

The final decisions on where these imports were to go were made at the Ministry of Transport in London, whose bureaucrats worked closely with the grand planners at 10 Downing Street. The day-to-day decisions that carried out those decisions in the North of England were made at Holmby House in Liverpool. There they produced bills of lading which were delivered daily to the dock foremen of the various docks of Liverpool Pier, where the recruited barge operators were registered.

As predicted, by the end of February of 1940, the Liverpool office of the Ministry of Transport was up and running to full capacity. Those dealing regularly with this foreboding bureau no longer referred to it by the dignified moniker of 'Ministry of Transport'. In the local idiom this prolific giver of orders was commonly referred to merely as 'Transport'. On occasion, members of the barging fraternity described their official masters with less flattering descriptions, such as 'that lot of pencil-pushing bastards', who were sometimes further said to have unusual physical attributes, such as bums ranging from fat to leaden or dead.

Normally, bills of lading issued at Holmby House listed shipments to be hauled three or more days after they were issued. In the use of White and Roberts' barges, Transport's bills of lading went to Bob Harrison's office on Albert Dock. After 4 p.m., Mondays to Saturdays, someone from White and Roberts would pick up their assigned bills of lading at Harrison's office and drive them to the partnership's offices in Wigan. There the co-ordinating staff assigned them according to barge availability, and dispatched two copies to the respective White and Roberts barge captains who would be doing the pick-ups and deliveries. By March of 1940, the Government's use of White and Roberts' barges varied from six to twelve barges daily. This, of course, required execution of 'Plan B', which was to substitute, as needed, the used barges owned by Lil White and Rose Roberts to meet the other hauling needs of White and Roberts' 'old' regular customers. That group included both Leeds and Liverpool-referred customers and many smaller mills and factories that had been signed up following Adam's 'space available' brainstorm. Those customers' barging needs remained substantial, even though many of them had also been recruited.

When it was becoming apparent that using the barges owned by Lil White and Rose Roberts was imminent, Walter had taken Sidney Blum with him to Everett Jennings's office in Manchester to work out the details of a 'modified plan to make it all work right'. Before keeping that appointment, Sidney Blum filed the charter for a new limited-liability company doing business as Lil & Rose Ltd. When the proper seal was affixed to that charter, as payment for the shares in that company, Lil White and Rose Roberts signed conveyances to it of the title to six used barges.

Times had indeed changed. A few years before, Everett Jennings would have scoffed at a small barge operator with a name like Lil & Rose Ltd. And he would have physically thrown anyone out of his office who proposed what Blum proposed the day he and Walter went to Manchester. As it was, without calling anyone up the chain of Leeds and Liverpool command, Mr Jennings gladly signed the papers tendered by the solicitor. Fittingly, one of those papers included the canal company's request that those customers provide their appropriate fuel ration books to 'either White and Roberts or Lil & Rose Ltd to assure adequate fuelling of the barges that will be transporting your goods'.

Without any vetting by the intelligence department of Leeds and Liverpool Canal Company, or other fanfare, Lil & Rose Ltd was now working for that canal company, at least as regards customers normally serviced by White and Roberts. These developments put the ever-resourceful Norman Nelson back to recruiting the best boatmen he could find to work for the new business entity, Lil & Rose Ltd. Norman's field to mine in this recruitment was far tougher than the old days, when unemployment was a chronic demon. Now there was no unemployment, and too many 'good men' had been called up. In the end, however, Norman still hired the best boatmen available. His success in this endeavour was surely aided by the fact that Lil & Rose had no history of paying wages. This enabled Norman to offer wages greater by fifteen per cent than what was regarded as 'market' for experienced bargemen.

Lil & Rose avoided being recruited by the Ministry of Transport by keeping their 'fleet' below minimums – and, even though they paid premium wages, they made a whopping good profit.

In the third week in March of 1940, two unexpected events resulted in Walter and Lil being briefly back on their original barge and, while it lasted, working out of their old berth at the Albert Dock. One of White and Roberts' regular bargemen was called up into the Royal Navy. Another of their boatmen fell ill and had to be temporarily replaced. This sudden shortage of two bargemen also put Adam back at the tiller. Adam, however, did not have the pleasure of his wife's company. She was more than occupied with her three infants at home in Wrightington.

During the late afternoon of 18 March, Adam tied down at the berth next to Walter's barge at the Albert Dock. He had just completed a run from Chester. All berths at the unloading dock area were filled. By hand signals alone, the unloading dock foreman communicated to Adam to tie down at the berth that happened to be next to Walter's barge, to leave his key on the table of his living quarters, and that his barge would be unloaded and reloaded by sunrise. That was fine by Adam, as his plans for the rest of the day were to pick up Transport's bills of lading that would now be at Dock Foreman Harrison's office, and drive them to the White and Roberts' office in Wigan. Then he planned to spend the night at home and would drive back early the next morning, to pilot his newly loaded barge to whatever destination was stated on the bill of lading that would be left in his living quarters.

Walter saw Adam's barge enter the adjacent berth. He emerged from his living quarters as Adam was tying his barge to the dock. He asked Adam to stop by after he had been to the dock foreman's office.

'We've got something we need to discuss,' he called out.

'I'll be right there,' answered Adam. 'Right after I pick up our bills of lading at Bob Harrison's office.'

When he returned, the two men sat and Lil served them both with that inimitable English panacea, 'a good cup o' tea'.

Knowing the men had to 'talk business', Lil busied herself with a magazine, which she read while continuing her endless knitting. Walter had sweaters for every weather condition imaginable.

'Adam,' said Walter, 'this morning I received word from Mark Edwards that a furniture manufacturer in London named Gordon Coleman wanted me to call him, that it was "very important"! and would I please call him collect. I called the man this afternoon and we talked for over a half-hour. I shudder to think what his telephone bill will be, but I must say we had a very interesting conversation.

'Before I get into that, proving what a small world it is, this man Coleman was someone you and I have seen before.'

'We have?' asked Adam, a bit surprised.

'Do you remember that fellow that stormed out of Tony Harding's office that day we went to the Ministry of Transport in London? The man we overheard Harding tell to use some good old British imagination on how to make desks and chairs?'

'Yes, I do,' answered Adam promptly. 'And I remember why he comes so quick to mind. I remember the odd feeling I had when we overheard Harding tell him he was far better off than the poor devils he was going to see next, which was us, and I wondered at the time what a furniture manufacturer was doing at the Ministry of Transport.'

'OK,' said Walter, in almost a congratulatory tone. 'As soon as he started telling me how his problems stemmed from the Government's refusal to reimburse him the cost of shipping materials by rail between his three factory sites, that scene all came back to me for the same reasons. So much so that I interrupted him to ask if he was the man my partner and I had seen last September coming out of Tony Harding's office at the Ministry of Transport on Baker Street. He confirmed that was him, but he didn't remember seeing anyone outside that office when he stormed out. Twice he referred to the transport director as "Helpful Harding". I think he hates the man.'

'Anyway, Adam,' Walter continued, 'because Mr Coleman was using barge transportation before the war to ship both the wood to his component parts factory in Oxfordshire, and his component parts to his assembly plant in South Lambeth, they won't reimburse him for any what they call "internal transportation costs" greater than he paid before the war.

'Since the Government has recruited Mr Coleman's company – it's called Coleman Furniture Ltd – he has had to open a second assembly plant in Reading. And, he's locked into using barges – unless he wants to finance personally the use of the more expensive trains. Now, Mr Coleman's problem is that the poor barging service he was able to hire before the war has gone from bad to worse. He never sees the same barge captain twice, and there is no such thing as arrivals and deliveries being made on time. His bills of lading are useful only to identify what's supposed to be in a cargo. Things have become so bad that it's not uncommon to see his men in all of his facilities sitting around playing cards waiting for wood to arrive in Oxford or component parts to arrive in Reading and South Lambeth.'

'Isn't South Lambeth in London?' asked Adam.

'Yes, it's on the south side of the Thames Estuary, near Vauxhall Bridge.'

'Well,' said Adam, 'Mr Coleman's story sounds very sad and unfortunate, but how do his problems involve White and Roberts here in Lancashire? The Good Lord knows all barges at our disposal are regularly overloaded without considering any of Mr Coleman's troubles.'

'I know we are, Adam,' said Walter, 'but your question brings up the next item, which is the most important thing for us to consider.'

'What's that?' asked Adam, looking a bit perplexed.

'Mr Coleman's voice clearly revealed the man at wits' end. He's been searching near and far for responsible people in the barge business. That's how he got our name. He wants to confer with us in the hope of working out an arrangement that will ease his present problems and also carry on after the war is over.'

'And no one knows when that will be,' remarked Adam.

'Of course not,' replied Walter, 'but I don't see how it can go on much longer than four or five years at most, and, for some reason, I don't think this greedy jackal Hitler is going to win it.

'What I'm saying, Adam,' said Walter, as if trying to shorten it all up, 'is that if we can work out a good permanent arrangement with this Mr Colman in his hour of need, we may have just the arrangement we need when all this war work vanishes and the countryside is overrun with lads returning from the Forces, glad to take any job available at whatever rates are available. That "availability" doesn't normally tend to the generous side, if my memory serves me correctly. Competition in barging is going to be fierce. When this country starts to respond to peacetime, everything is going to change – including the people who will be running these companies, mills and factories we've been dealing with. And that time and period will predictably be our hour of need. Mr Coleman may be presenting us with an opportunity to be positioned above the fray. Just think of it, Adam! After this war, what businesses will boom bigger than the furniture business? Not many, I'm sure. And with a good business relationship that goes back a matter of years, we could be in business with a major producer who isn't looking to see where he can find the least expensive men with barges. And sheer instinct tells me we could work out some kind of an integrated operation in which everyone prospers.'

'What do you figure we could do for Mr Coleman?' asked Adam.

'Well,' replied Walter, 'I think the first thing is, we need to know more about Mr Gordon Coleman. I told him I would discuss all this with my partner and call him back. I suggest I call him back and set up a meeting, either here in Wigan or... on second thought, I'd like to meet him at his component parts factory in Oxford, then a look-see at Reading and South Lambeth. Sort of a need-to-see-your-problem sort of thing. During that time I should get to know him well enough to get a feeling about whether he's the honest, forthright fellow he sounds like on the telephone. If he comes over as someone we would want to get involved with businesswise, I was thinking we might work out a deal in which he, or we, buy a couple of used Liverpool short boats. They're sixty feet long and fourteen feet wide, which seems like about what his needs require. Regardless of who buys the barges, they'd have to be registered in his name – and I'd prefer that to be in his personal name. Whatever we work out, we would want Sidney Blum and whatever solicitor Mr Coleman uses to reduce it all to a written agreement, guaranteed personally by Mr Coleman, you and me. If we get that far, we could have Norman search out and hire the right men to run the barges. And we could dispatch them by phone from our office in Wigan, like I used to do from Chester. As for the formalities of the boatmen's payroll, well, that's for the solicitors to work out.

'First, Adam, I need to know your thoughts about working out something with Mr Coleman. Tell me now, or sleep on it. At least let me know before you leave in the morning.'

'No need to sleep on it,' said Adam. 'It makes just as much sense to me as it does to you, and I don't doubt for a minute we can do it – if, as you say, this

Mr Coleman is the kind of man we want to get involved with. I'll gladly defer to your experience when it comes to sizing him up.'

Walter smiled slightly, and looked very pleased. Of course Lil couldn't help overhearing the whole conversation. Over Walter's shoulder, Adam could tell that she too looked very pleased.

'On the subject of hiring new men,' said Walter 'you recently mentioned a man who's not happy working for the Saloman Brothers. You described him as "sober and serious". Is he still about?'

'Yes,' answered Adam, 'we waved in passing early today just north of Chester. He was steering that same bait bucket he's been driving ever since he started with the Brothers.'

'I wonder why he hasn't been called up,' said Walter.

'I heard that a long time ago he had something bad, like malaria or tuberculosis. He recovered, but he's not fit enough for the Forces.'

Walter handed Adam a sheet of paper. 'Why don't you write his name on this? I'll find out from Bob Harrison about his on-time arrival record. If it's all right, I'll ask Bob to have him contact you or me. The sooner White and Roberts gets a permanent replacement for our last contribution to the Royal Navy, the sooner we can both get back to Wigan.'

All matters subject to agreement having been resolved, Adam took his leave and drove Transport's latest bills of lading to Wigan.

Chapter Forty-seven

By April of 1940, Charles Rainford had reached several conclusions. Foremost, he was convinced that Hitler was going to prevail, for the present at least, in overrunning and occupying France, Belgium, Holland, Denmark and Norway. These conclusions began to become facts in April and May. On 7 May 1941, Winston Churchill became England's Prime Minister, and on 10 May he delivered his famous 'blood, sweat and tears' speech. Charles took that speech as an announcement that England wasn't going to make peace with the raging Germans. Churchill's throwing down the gauntlet, or so Charles regarded the speech, was swiftly followed by German armoured divisions moving into northern France, the German occupation of Brussels, the infamous Nazi bombing of Rotterdam (600–900 dead) and Holland's surrender.

Charles also concluded that once Germany occupied France (only fifteen miles to the east) Britain would not defend its Channel Islands, as nothing had been done in preparation of their defence, and Charles could think of no reason beyond pride why England would do so.

On the other hand, Charles did not think Hitler would win the war, regardless of how swiftly he was devastating his unprepared neighbours. There was something flinty about Churchill's tone and attitude that told Charles, at least, that here was a leader who would find the wherewithal to trample this jumped-up Austrian-born guttersnipe.

Based on his own reasoning, Charles decided the time had come to get himself and his fortune out of harm's way, but still to retain his Rainford Manor, or his right to claim ownership of that property.

Charles moved swiftly once he had reached these conclusions in his self-congratulatory 'well-reasoned' manner. Through the good offices of the director of the Channel Islands Bank, Charles signed a long-term lease on a handsome eight-acre country estate near the small village of Crediton, about ten miles north-west of Exeter in the south of England. Of course there was no way Charles could have known that within a very few years most of the south of England would swarm with American soldiers undergoing intensive training for the invasion of Europe. (That part of England was selected because its beaches and off-shore land approaches were almost identical to those of Normandy.) So, on 16 May 1940, Charles made the decision and promptly executed the plans that would enable him to sit out this dreadful war amid the tranquillity he expected at the country estate near Crediton. One of his first tasks in this direction was a short walk to the basement of his manor, where he retrieved the two large trunks that had just been sitting out of the way and gathering dust since his arrival on Jersey in 1928. This time he alone filled the trunks with the rare coin treasure he had secreted within the complex of cabinets built in his basement. It took him nearly four hours to transfer the coins. That done, he locked each trunk with the keys he had wisely left inside each of them.

He planned to hire another trawler to take him to Exeter; that is, him plus trunks filled with his personal affects – the two larger and heavier trunks filled with his fortune in rare coins – and his chess-playing good friend Samuel Travers. Again, the director at the Channel Islands Bank arranged for the trawler and a lorry to transport Charles, his trunks, and his 'associate', Samuel Travers to the local pier.

Estimating he would be away for three years, Charles left £12,000 in his account at the bank. He also signed a contract with the bank which provided for a representative to call monthly at Rainford Manor and, upon satisfying himself that the entire establishment was being properly maintained, to pay Edward and Helen Travers their agreed monthly salaries. Ever a man of foresight, Charles insisted that, at the end of each twelve-month period, the Travers would receive an increase of £100 per year in their salary, provided, of course, they had performed their maintenance duties adequately during the preceding twelve months.

Charles Rainford and Samuel Travers had truly become good company for each other and good friends by this time. Their six to eight chess games each week were always thoroughly enjoyed by each man. They were also the occasion for Samuel to tell Charles of his many adventures, visiting such exciting sounding places as Cairo, Casablanca, Bombay, Singapore, Sydney and Nagasaki while he was in the Royal Navy. Intellectually, the two men had almost become equals. The class differences were such, however, that Samuel always addressed Charles as 'Mr Rainford' and Charles honoured Samuel by always addressing him as 'Mr Travers'.

Having made his decision to take temporary flight from Jersey, Charles asked Samuel if he would be agreeable to accompanying him, and to 'help out a bit'. Samuel took that as involving his becoming something of a gentleman's servant, and Samuel didn't want to do what he perceived such a servant did. He replied that he 'might be interested, provided we continue more or less on this same par'. Charles took that to mean their relationship would continue on a 'more or less equal' basis. Under the circumstances, he found that acceptable. After all, he could always hire some dolt as a servant. With this meeting of the minds, the two men shook hands, each with a perfect understanding of what their relationship beyond Jersey would involve.

The kind attentions with which the director of the Channel Islands Bank provided his valuable customer Charles Rainford even included making the arrangements for the 'Rainford party' to be met upon arriving at Exeter and transported to the leased estate near Crediton.

By 20 May 1940, Charles Rainford and Samuel Travers were ensconced in the country estate, which also had servants' quarters. Charles had the helpers that accompanied the lorry from Exeter haul his heavy trunks to the large basement in the handsome farmhouse. He did not discuss with Samuel Travers anything about the trunks except to inform him, rather formally, that 'the large trunks are strictly personal, and I want your word you shan't touch them or make any use of the basement. It's off limits. Understood?'

Samuel rightly suspected the trunks contained some kind of treasure, but he was not interested. He neither had nor savoured wealth. For Samuel, life was more a matter of getting by. And in reaching that goal, ever since he had peered over Charles's shoulder and seen the chessboard, he had been a great success.

Charles bought a used Vauxhall in Crediton, and used a small bag of rare coins to open a cheque account at the nearest Lloyd's Bank. His next undertaking was a drive to Exeter, where he inquired at the Exeter labour exchange about the availabilities of a middle-aged couple who would be prepared to move into 'most adequate servants quarters at my estate near Crediton'. That same day Charles drove his newly acquired used Vauxhall to his newly leased estate near Crediton with his newest employees, Sean and Eileen O'Toole. They were a pleasant middle-aged couple who spoke with heavy Irish accents. Charles was pleased at their apparent delight when he showed them the estate's servants' quarters.

As planned, Charles and his good friend Samuel settled into a comfortable routine for waiting out that dreadful war.

Chapter Forty-eight

During the first months of 1940, the news seemed to worsen by the day. On the Continent, the German juggernaut seemed unstoppable. By 9 April, German troops marched through tiny Denmark without resistance. The Danes promptly surrendered. In early May, Germany invaded Holland and Belgium. Both tiny nations responded with resistance much stronger than expected. But neither was a match for the combined Wehrmacht and Luftwaffe dispatched in a lethal lockstep. The sequence was becoming almost routine. First the skies filled with Luftwaffe bombers that seemed to blackout the very sun, surrounded by protective fighter planes like drones of flies. Then bombs rained down, followed by the pandemonium of ear-splitting explosions, collapsing buildings and the anguished shrieks of the fleeing, the injured and the dying. These winged messengers of death and destruction would barely depart, and the moans become whimpers of agony, when the Luftwaffe would return, filling the sky with parachutes. The young lions were thus uncaged, and the new conquerors descended on the vanquished.

The vaunted Maginot Line proved a cruel joke in the misuse of taxes. The Germans simply went around it. As they drove north and west, the French and British troops were being driven steadily westward. These allies were still reeling westward toward the sea, when the Germans occupied Paris. On 10 May, the Germans invaded Norway, and before day's end Neville Chamberlain resigned the office of Prime Minister. His Majesty promptly called on the renewed Lord of the Admiralty, Winston Churchill, to form a new government. By then, German bombers had dropped their fatal calling cards at numerous locations in Britain but, in vivid contrast to the civilian slaughter on the continent, so far they had confined their objectives in England to military targets. On three separate occasions before Mr Churchill was sworn in as Prime Minister, Adam and Rose had stood outside their house and watched the distant German bombers in the sky over Manchester to the south-east. They were too far away to hear the engines, but they could hear the retort of what must have been terrific explosions.

Adam, Rose and both of their parents sat sombrely in Adam's living room and listened to Churchill's famous first speech as Britain's new Prime Minister. 'I have nothing to offer,' he dramatically intoned, 'but blood, sweat, toil and tears.'

Adam muttered, 'His tears, and our blood and sweat.'

Rose, sitting right next to him chastised, 'Adam,' she said, 'the poor man's just telling it like it is, and I for one have faith in him!'

'Well,' replied Adam, 'so do I, but he's far from a poor man.' Those remarks caused slight smiles all around, but they were the only distraction during the sombre speech, to which the whole family paid rapt attention.

Mr Churchill's elevation was almost immediately followed by a series of events, some tragic, some heroic, and some new and different lives for the multitudes. Chief among those events occurred during the latter phases of Hitler's conquest of France and the low lands of Western Europe.

Without any doubt, things were going bad and getting worse. The Allied soldiers were being relentlessly pushed west as the German's were completing their capture of France and turning north to finish off the Low Countries of Belgium and Holland. General Guderian and his now-famed Panzer tank divisions turned sharply north, passing Boulogne and Calais, and had just crossed the so-called 'canal defence line' to eliminate the hundreds of thousands of allied soldiers now trapped on the ten miles of beach that fronted on Dunkirk. As he was about to issue his order '*Vorwärts*', he received the shock of his life. A telegram from Hitler himself ordered him to stop and await further orders. He and his fellow high-ranking officers were dumbfounded beyond belief.[1] In England the decision to attempt to evacuate these men was immediate. The Admiralty was assigned the task of getting every seaworthy craft possible into an organised evacuation.

That night while Adam and Rose were listening to the 10 p.m. BBC news, a different voice broke into the broadcast with a special bulletin.

'Important. Notice from the Admiralty.

'All owners of seaworthy boats and ships great and small and all men experienced in the operation of such craft. Over 300,000 allied soldiers are stranded on the beaches around Dunkirk, and we must evacuate them immediately. We need these boats and the men who can operate them at Folkestone immediately.

'Your King and Country are calling on you.

'Your gallant and loyal support are critical. Time is of the essence. Bring your boat and/or your boating experience to Folkestone. Immediately!'

The radio went silent for about ten seconds after this message, as if to let the message soak in. It did.

Just as the regular announcer resumed the news, Adam turned the volume

---

[1] After the war indisputable records were found in Germany which revealed that Air Marshal Göring had persuaded Hitler that his mighty Luftwaffe could eliminate the 'fish on the beach' at Dunkirk, and the Panzers could be put to better use elsewhere.

down and turned to Rose.

'I've got no choice. I must help. I'll be on the 5.30 train to London in the morning.'

Rose could tell from the look on her husband's face and the resolve in his voice that any attempt to dissuade him would be futile. She shrugged her assent, and the two retired for the night.

The next morning, the 5.30 a.m. the train departed from Wigan. All seats were filled and the corridors in the passenger carriages were filled. Adam was among the standing. Virtually all passengers were men, none of whom looked like he was any stranger to a waterfront. As the morning wore on, the seated passengers began alternating with the standing passengers for the seats.

When Martyn asked about their daddy at the breakfast table, Mary held back the tears and told them matter-of-factly that he would be 'away for a few days helping to win the war'. Happily their tender years caused them to accept the explanation without question. After all, Daddy was often away for a few days.

Given the special nature of the run, this train did not stop at all the little stations as it did usually. The train arrived at Victoria station in London in a record four hours after departure from Wigan.

When Adam walked off the train, his attention was immediately drawn to a large sign on the station platform at the end of platform nine. It read: 'Trains to Folkestone'. Adam stopped by the buffet on the platform and ordered a sticky bun and tea. The obliging lady behind the counter placed a sticky bun in a small bag, and filled a mug with tea. She handed them to Adam, who handed her tuppence.

'Take both with you,' she said. 'Just leave the mug on the train.'

Adam then noticed that the owner of the mug was clearly identified on the mug by the letters 'LMS', the London–Midlands–Scotland railway.

Now who would want to be seen with this if he wasn't right here or on the train? No one but a mug thief, I guess.

Adam boarded the train waiting at the end of platform nine. No tickets were required. Five minutes after he had found his place – standing in the aisle of a passenger car – the train pulled out of Victoria station. It was as loaded as the train on which he'd arrived, and with the same cut of men. Neither trip involved much conversation between the passengers, but from their rather common, non-smiling, determined looks, it seemed clear that everyone knew why they were where they were. A messy but necessary job was up ahead, and the men riding this train were not the least dissuaded by the inherent unpleasantries involved – even the common understanding that some of them were surely going to be killed or maimed.

At Folkestone, Adam followed the crowd to an area near the boardwalk, where several wooden desks had been placed. He got in the line before the desk containing a hand-made sign reading, 'Sign up here'.

When he became the next in line, the man seated at the desk asked him a few questions, which he answered. The man then wrote on a slip of paper, 'Adam Roberts – Barge Operator – Captain'.

'Take this to that desk over there,' said the man, pointing.

Adam walked where he was directed. Behind the desk sat an older man in his mid-fifties. Adam walked up and handed him the slip of paper, which he promptly read. As if by practice, he reached in the top desk drawer and handed Adam another smaller, but thicker piece of paper on which was printed, 'Captain'.

'Take this to the trawler in berth eleven. Your crew's waiting. Remember,' he continued, 'hold a heading of zero-eight-seven to Dunkirk, and a heading of two-six-seven back to Folkestone. You can't miss it.'

'I just hope all the hell over there misses me,' replied Adam.

'Give it your best, lad,' said the older man. 'Just stay focused on what you're about and,' he added in a bit more serious tone, 'if you don't pray a great deal usually, you might think about practicing up, say, about all the time you're at sea.'

The older man stood and extended his right hand. They shook hands quite sincerely, and Adam turned to his left and walked to berth eleven.

Introductions were short when he met his crew of three young men, all about Adam's age, and obviously deck hands of some sort. They introduced each other and then all hopped aboard. Adam entered the cockpit, faced the wheel, briefly scanned the small instrument panel and signalled the man directly aft to start the diesel.

The trawler quivered a bit when the engine caught. Adam pushed the throttle full forward, and they moved to open sea – along with about twenty other petty craft leaving at the same time.

As for the weather, it seemed almost as if divine providence had intervened on behalf of the Allies. The sky and ocean both remained clear and calm for almost a week. That spelled success for this vast undertaking.

Calm seas permitted many petty craft to be used that could not have coped with choppy seas. That clear calm air also permitted the RAF to provide the 'distraction' which the Germans never anticipated. Genuine German respect for the RAF would not come until the Battle of Britain, much later. By then, such respect was overdue, and had been overdue since Dunkirk. There, the youthful RAF pilots fought like veterans seized with a vengeance as they prevented the planes of the Luftwaffe from picking off their helpless prey on the beaches and turf below. Hatred seemed to have entered the proceedings. The RAF pilots despised the Germans. They frequently referred to them as 'bloody sods' and 'vultures' in their short conversations during refuelling stops in England.

The rescue sea craft would approach the outer breakwater off Dunkirk and turn towards the beach. The escaping soldiers, often wounded, some badly, and sometimes with the assistance of a buddy, would wade out in the surf. The ensuing, repeating chaos was maddening. Men on the rescue craft would holler and wave to the soldiers, urging them on towards their boats. Tiny sprays of seawater frequently erupted when machine gun shells from the over-flying German aircraft would strike the ocean surface. At times a soldier or one of a rescue crew would scream out as those bullets ripped through him, rather than the seawater. The Luftwaffe's interference at night involved diving German fighters firing blindly into the ocean where their pilots thought they might hit *jemand oder etwas* (someone or something). The whole wretched three-day affair was the embodiment of chaos.

As with most warlike engagements, Dunkirk was a living hell and a dying hell. On the positive side of that tragic ledger, 198,000 British and 140,000 French and Belgian soldiers were rescued in the thousands of boats that had sailed out from Britain.

Adam Roberts sustained no injuries. On his first trip, one of his original crew was shot by a strafing ME 109. He died on the deck, no more than ten feet from where Adam stood. On the third trip, a second member of the original crew took a bullet in his right shoulder as he was leaning forward to help a wounded soldier on board. The man survived, and did his best not to cry out from the pain as Adam steered the trawler back to Folkestone. The turnout of men had been such that Adam had no problem getting replacements for both men during his repeated returns to Folkestone.

Each round trip involved about seven hours to sail the forty-nine miles between Folkestone and Dunkirk, then about twenty to thirty minutes in close to the beach taking on soldiers, and about the same time discharging the evacuees and refuelling at Folkestone. Adam made a total of nine round trips during this massive rescue. He kept no written account of the exact number of the soldiers who had been rescued by 'his' trawler.

'Something over 500 is my best guess,' Adam told a *Manchester Guardian* reporter who interviewed him on the Wigan railway platform right after he stepped off the train on 3 June.

The author simply lacks the descriptive skills to verbalise the overwhelming relief and pride that surged through Rose when she saw her husband emerge from the river of passengers that poured from the London train. The children who had been at Rose's side spotted their tired but obviously proud father and ran to his arms. After those warm hugs and kisses, Adam stood before his young wife, and the two engaged in a passionate embrace. The small family was back together again and were in a small world of their own as they made their way to the parking area, all the while weaving their way through the throng of returning boatmen and their rejoicing families.

It was 10.30 that night when Adam drifted off to sleep after his not-really-triumphant train trip, returning from what became a successful retreat of historic proportions. The name 'Dunkirk' no longer conjured up the vision of some insignificant sandy beach on the Belgian coast. 'Dunkirk' became acknowledged as a miracle, where a hastily assembled massive collection of Naval and civilian ships and boats snatched 338,226 men of a beaten army from the jaws of defeat to the safety of the British Isles. Most of the civilian contribution to this massive effort were the 'little ships' that could get into the shallows of the breakwater and transport the departing soldiers to the larger naval craft offshore. Adam's trawler was large enough to be used as a transport vessel that sailed between Dunkirk and Folkestone. Had he been assigned the typical short hauls of the 'little ships,' the savage strafing by Luftwaffe fighter planes could well have changed the lives of the Roberts, Birchall and White families most dramatically. Adam knew that. Just before he dropped off to sleep on his first night home, very privately, he thanked God from the very bottom of his heart.

After his really good night's sleep, Adam arose and it was back to wartime life as usual. Right after breakfast, he called Walter, who had just got back to London himself. Word had got to him that Adam had gone to take part in the evacuation at Dunkirk. Hearing Adam's voice now on the phone was a mighty welcome relief.

Chapter Forty-nine

It was late in the afternoon of Friday, 7 June 1940. Mary was seated near the end of a long wooden table in the main library of Stanford University. She had been sitting there for almost three hours dutifully trying to study for her final examinations, which would begin at 8 a.m. on the following Tuesday. If they passed the June final written examinations, all four of the English girls who had arrived in America eighteen months before, courtesy of Educational Endowments International Ltd, would be awarded bachelor of arts degrees by a major university with true international standing. Mary Roberts' presence in that vast Stanford library was the end result of many events, most of which had been totally unforeseeable, at least through her eyes. Normally, the closer people on the rise get to their goals, the higher their anticipations. Not so with the young girl from Gateley, England. She did not envision racing from the graduation ceremony to the nearest place where the state of California gave examinations required for issuing a teaching certificate. If anything her doubts about teaching as a career had only deepened as her life had changed during the past year. Still she looked forward to the day soon to arrive when she could write letters to her proud parents and her wonderful brother, announcing that she had graduated and enclosing photographs of the bachelor's degree awarded by Stanford University to Mary Ann Roberts.

She put these thoughts out of her mind. She was here this afternoon to study, not for mental meandering. Yet her next thought was what a pleasant and peaceful place this enormous library was. Then she thought briefly of the many other students there, seated at those long wooden tables. Most were reading intently, and a few had succumbed to the tranquillity and had nodded off for a short nap. Those who spoke or walked about always did so softly.

Mary's difficulty in concentrating on her textbooks and lecture notes stemmed from her concerns about other people in other places. This was frustrating because her time to prepare for the final examinations had been shorted by her weekend plans to go to Carmel.

Still thoughts of other people and other things diverted her concentration on school work. Even the diversions were interrupted briefly when the interior lights in the library flicked on. A brief glance at the enormous wall clock confirmed it was now 4.30. But rather than glancing back at her schoolwork, Mary's mental focus involuntarily shifted to 'poor Tim' for whom she still felt the tenderest of loving thoughts. She had finally brought herself to write him the Dear John letter. But she only managed to drop the letter into a mailbox by constantly repeating to herself that it was 'Only fair. Only fair'. Yet, she could not rid herself of a nagging guilty feeling for having said to Tim on his last visit before she left that she wouldn't look at any man until she returned, and that man would be him.

What an idiotic juvenile thing for a young girl to say, she remonstrated with herself. How could I?

That was all fine and well, as pretty speeches go. But she rued ever having made that speech in light of subsequent events. She had met Colin Johnson, and the two had fallen hopelessly in love. That sequence wasn't planned or intended by either of them. If anything, it had been a surprise, bordering on shock. Colin hadn't yet asked her to marry him, but she was certain that not even his rapidly expanding law practice would long deter his proposal. Their age difference was never discussed after their understanding at the little Italian restaurant in Moraga.

With their deepening love, their physical embraces had naturally grown in intensity, but they had never crossed the line of intimacy. While neither Colin nor Mary had any particularly religious bent on the subject, they were both of a generation which knew in their heart of hearts that marriage provided abundant time and opportunities for all of the ultimates in physical pleasures. Without any discussion of the subject, both of them knew that any physical overindulgence would cast a blight on their marriage, should they go through with that. And even if that didn't happen, any such indiscretion would fracture the mutual respect that had become a real part of their relationship.

Mary's thoughts then turned back to Tim. He had never answered her last letter. Two weeks after she mailed it, she received a letter from Adam telling her how surprised everyone was that Tim had suddenly enlisted in the forces. A week later she received a second letter from Adam telling her about a conversation he had just had with John. John had told him about Mary's letter, and that Tim had taken the news very hard and Adam wrote to tell her that:

> So hard, in fact, that Tim went on a five-day bender, and when he sobered up, he found himself on a train in Somerset headed for Southampton, where he boarded a ship bound for Rangoon. Tim and all the other passengers were in uniforms identifying them as fully fledged members of the Second Brigade of the Lancashire Fusiliers, then stationed in Burma. That's where the boat they boarded took them. Seems like while he was plastered Tim found the Fusilier's recruiting station in Wigan, and they found him fully qualified to help add to their glories, after a little training, I'm sure.
>
> Rose wanted to march into the Fusilier recruiting office in Wigan and demand to know why they would sign up a man who was drunk. I talked her out that. I finally convinced her she would be wasting her time, and would probably get some smart answer like it happens all the time, or some gibberish about how it sometimes takes a little liquid courage to bring out a man's true patriotism. Personally I think Tim will take

care of himself just fine, but I sure hope I never see Rose as mad as she's been this past week.

Trust everything is going well with you. Love from all the family.

Adam.

Mary had read and re-read Adam's letter dozens of time, and sometimes she couldn't hold back the tears. Poor Tim. Now he'll probably get himself killed, and it's all because of me.

Mary had found herself getting more depressed every time she re-read Adam's letter. Fortunately, she realised that routine had nothing but downsides. Wisely, she decided to store the letter at the bottom of the one suitcase she hadn't been able to unpack because of the limited drawer space in her dormitory room.

That same day Tim was learning what to do when the drill sergeant roared, 'Right wheel, do it!'

Also on that day, the commanding general of the Lancashire Fusiliers, General Robert Leeds of Blackburn, was briefed in London by the Chief of the Imperial General Staff, General Sir Allen Brooke. The subject was his orders to keep the Fusilier's Second Brigade in Burma.

'Burma seems a bit removed from the boiling pots around the world,' observed General Leeds. 'Could I be permitted to ask a one-word question? Why?'

'Well, old boy,' replied General Brooke, 'the Empire needs some guarding in these increasingly desperate days, and the manpower we've just retrieved from Dunkirk enables us to revise our plans. Before Dunkirk, I'm told, Mr Churchill and our logistics planners felt we had no choice but to withdraw most of our forces from Singapore, India, and Burma. They were reluctant to do this because of the nasty attitude of the Japanese since their march out of the League of Nations and into China. Now, Mr Churchill and his top advisors, including my good self, have decided that the more than 200,000 trained soldiers who've recently arrived via Dunkirk will enable us to defend the British Isles and the Empire. Just where we're going to get the necessary equipment, and guns and ammunition is not entirely clear at this moment. Regardless, your piece of that puzzle is Burma.'

'Understood,' replied General Leeds. General Brooke rose to signal the end of the meeting. The two officers, long-time friends for at least two decades, shook hands firmly, and went their separate ways.

Even had Tim Birchall in far-off Burma known of these events in London, he could never have dreamed, even in the worst of nightmares, how the orders which General Leeds took from his meeting with Mr Churchill's chief military advisor would change his life during the years to come.

Mary, of course, had only heard recently on the radio that the British had achieved a miracle in rescuing 'hundreds of thousands of soldiers' from the killing sands of Dunkirk beach. Several months later she received a letter from Rose telling her how her 'brave brother' had been part of that miracle, but, 'Thank God, he didn't get a scratch.' Mary noticed that parts of Rose's letter had been literally cut out with the apparent use of scissors.

Ah! thought Mary. Censorship.

As her Friday afternoon in the library drew on, Mary firmly reminded herself that she must put these personal matters out of mind. Time was running out. She fixed her stare on her books and for the rest of the afternoon she studied. Hard.

By leaving San Francisco around mid-afternoon, Colin was to pick up Mary and Laura and the three would be off to Aunt Lucy's for a relaxing weekend at Carmel. That meant the girls had to be packed and ready by 6.30.

Just as Mary and Laura were walking down the steps from their dorm, Colin came to a stop at the nearby curb. After the greetings and stowing of small suitcases in the car's trunk, they departed for Carmel. (Mary still thought the Americans had the word 'trunk' mixed up. Trunks were what people took on trips, and boots were either footwear or the place built into cars for storing luggage.)

After Colin steered them on to US Highway 101 and headed south, he affected a sort of matter-of-fact tone as he asked Laura what she was planning to do after graduation. Both girls immediately noted he had failed to include Mary in his seemingly idle inquiry about future plans.

'Oh,' Laura replied nonchalantly, 'I haven't really given that much thought, Why? Do you need an enormously talented group leader to manage your office?'

Colin's immediate facial response gave away his absolute shock at Laura's reply.

'Well,' he almost stammered, 'you might not believe it, but my needs along that very line are taking shape, and that is exactly why I asked.'

'Really?'

'Yes, really!'

'I'm not following this,' said Mary, 'I'm not following it at all.'

'Well, ladies,' said Colin, 'I must tell you that things are changing faster than you might realise. And that includes the centre of gravity of my law practice.'

'Do go on,' urged Mary, 'this is bound to be interesting.'

'I have practically no choice but to open a second office in Southern California. I've decided to have it in Los Angeles.'

'Whatever on earth for?' asked Mary. 'I mean a second office.'

'We completed a survey this afternoon, and the results only confirmed what I thought was happening. Our client base has mushroomed. That we already knew. The head count is something else. Most of our newer clients are in the Los Angeles, Long Beach and San Diego areas. I think you know our clients are mostly businesses, mainly corporations. We got a feeler from a one-man show named Howard Hughes, but instinct tells me not to take him on. He's a playboy who's nuts about making movies, airplanes and women. I'm glad to let some other lucky firm be the legal nursemaid to the likes of him.

'Anyway, the client count has grown from eighty-five regulars a year ago to 210 as of 5 p.m. yesterday. Fifty-eight per cent of those clients are in the Los Angeles area, or south of there. They're spread out over hundreds of square miles. A good many in towns you've heard of like Santa Monica, Torrance and El Segundo. Thirty per cent of the new lot are here in the Bay Area.

'Over the past year, we've had to take more office space in our building on Montgomery, and add a flock of lawyers and support staff – that's legal secretaries, stenographers, file clerks and the like – but we could do it all much better and faster, and with fewer people, if about sixty per cent of our lawyers and support staff were in a new office about to be in Los Angeles.'

'Since it's none of my business, I've never asked,' said Mary, 'but just what is it that you – I mean your law office – do for these clients?'

'Well,' replied Colin, 'first, you have to understand that practically all of our clients are engaged in what's usually thought of as "war work". They make everything from airplanes to tanks, guns, ships and parts galore. Two of our clients just across the Bay operate factories around the clock that turn out nothing but bombs and ammunition. All but a handful of our clients are doing work that is being ordered and paid for by the War Department in Washington, DC. All this is done under contracts with the Government, or approved by the Government. For the most part, those contracts are drawn by Government lawyers. And no one beats Government lawyers when it comes to drafting complex contracts or writing wordy rules and regulations that have to be complied with by every company doing work for the Government. In turn, those companies have to have expert legal advice to understand exactly what these contracts would oblige them to do, so they can make an intelligent decision as to whether they want to get involved in the first place. Once they do sign on, they need expert legal advice to assure they're meeting their obligations. That after-the-fact part involves complying with an avalanche of bureaucratic regulations that are pouring out of Washington like a volcano erupting printed paper. Believe me, without competent legal advice, most businessmen involved with this gusher would end up broke or in jail.

'And,' Colin continued, 'the plain fact is that there aren't many lawyers around who have the experience and skills to advise these clients. Most lawyers are general practitioners. They draw a lot of wills, probate decedents' estates, obtain divorces, and the like. But counselling major businesses about averting major disasters in performing multi-million dollar contracts is just out of their league.'

'I follow that,' said Laura, 'but I don't understand how all this mind boggling subject would involve me.'

'I'm coming to that,' said Colin. 'If we could handle the work that has sprung up in Southern California by telephone and mail, believe me we would do it that way. But that just can't be done. I wish I had five dollars for every time in the last month alone that a client has said to me, "Here, I'll show you what I mean", and the next thing we're out on a factory floor where he points out something about the way they're performing their Government contract, or he's riffling through an overstuffed file cabinet looking for papers that were generated in processing work for by the Government. In the end, well over half of our work is advising clients on the legal implications of their current operations. And that has to be at the place of those operations. Clients trying to tell us their problems by phone or mail simply doesn't work.

'Currently about forty per cent of our lawyers' time is spent travelling between San Francisco and, mainly, Los Angeles, and no lawyer is generating any fees while he's soaring several thousand feet above the earth. To add insult to injury, you'd be amazed at how many lawyers are afraid of flying. This year alone four really good lawyers have left the firm because they couldn't or wouldn't continue taking the airplane rides. Regardless, the time lawyers are losing while they travel could just as well be productively spent on the ground with the clients. And that's where a second office in Los Angeles becomes indispensable.'

Colin stopped speaking abruptly for a few seconds because he had the feeling he was making a speech, and that was not his intention.

'Long story shortened, I hope,' he went on. 'To make the new office in Los Angeles work, I've got to include among those going dear old Martha Cahill, our office manager. She doesn't want to leave San Francisco, but I've convinced her that without her – talk about buttering someone up – without her unique organisational talents, the new office will implode and disgrace us all.'

'I'm sure it's a show of ignorance,' said Laura, 'but how does an office manager get to be a key player in the such a sophisticated law practice?'

'I'll tell you, and it's on a subject I never had a course on in my life. It's a matter of psychology.'

Both Mary and Laura looked dumbstruck.

'Yes,' Colin continued, 'psychology. I don't pretend to know why, but when people work in groups, whether it's at a law office, an assembly line, or any place, some one person has to be in charge. And the success of that combination turns on the person in charge having the respect of the people being supervised. It doesn't seem to matter that the person in charge can't personally do all the things the others can – but their respect is critical.

'In a law office, the lawyers have to identify the issues to be solved in every client's problem, and also come up with the solution. Turning those solutions into an effective form is another matter. Whether the solution is as simple as a letter of advice or as complex as a lengthy contract or something that has to be filed in court – that's where the support staff of secretaries, stenos and file clerks come in. They are the ones whose work has to be properly co-ordinated, combined and processed. And the person in charge for that critical phase is the one who "makes it all come together", so to speak, is the person we call the "office manager".

'Not to manage the lawyers. For the most part, they don't work as a group. They work with individual clients who have individual problems which require a lawyer to solve. Matching client problems with individual lawyers is part of my job, and I'm not concerned about having someone else in charge of the lawyers. That's me. The legal secretaries, the stenos, the file clerks and the miscellaneous are another thing. Most of those people are females, so there's no problem in having a female office manager – if you get the right one. For almost twenty years now, I've had the right one: Miss Martha Cahill. But her talents are going to be more in demand than ever if this Los Angeles office is going to be the success I know it can be. It's in the San Francisco office where there will be some eighteen or nineteen people that will make up the local support staff. Their supervision is where there's about to be a critical vacancy. And if I don't fill that spot with the right person, God help us.'

'I gather you've got me in mind,' said Laura, 'or we wouldn't be having this conversation. But assuming I was qualified – which I most certainly don't think I am – aren't you talking about a temporary thing? A job until Miss Cahill comes back? There's a war going on or none of this would be happening. Even Mary and I wouldn't be here if the war wasn't going on. But the war can't last for ever, so it seems obvious that in a few years Miss Cahill will be coming back to her beloved San Francisco. Don't you agree?'

'No,' answered Colin, in a firm voice that reflected no doubt whatever. 'I think the Los Angeles law offices of Colin Johnson & Associates will become established in Southern California, and the high calibre of lawyers I have always hired – and pay very handsomely, I might add – are the type of problem solvers that clients attach to and come to depend on. Sure, the war will go away, but the clients we're serving won't. They're making things for the war now, but when it's over, they'll be making things for a civilian population that will only get bigger.

'I know of top-flight law firms, three in New York and two in Boston, who opened second offices in Chicago, and another big East Coast law firm I know of opened a second office in Denver. Every one of those second offices was intended to be temporary – just to meet their clients' needs. This all happened several years ago. Every one of those second offices is still in action. Three of them have more lawyers and support staff than the law firm that set them up. The same thing is bound to happen with our new Los Angeles office for the same reason: substantial clients get attached to the classy lawyers who are steering them right. No, I'm confident Miss Cahill is going to be part of the Southern California scene until she retires.'

Time had seemed to pass quickly, as it always does when the conversation is absorbing. Highway 101 had taken them south to the town of Salinas, which an emerging writer named John Steinbeck was beginning to make famous. In Salinas, Colin would turn off of highway 101 and drive south over hills to Monterey and on to Carmel. As he made this turn, they had thirty to forty minutes to reach their destination.

'You've answered all my questions, Colin, but one. Why would you think that I, who have probably spent less than an hour in a law office in my entire life, and have no experience or even a rough idea of how a law office works? My goodness, just to say that seems to make the whole idea nonsensical. What makes you think I could be your office manager and "make it all come together", as you put it?'

'Ah! Now you're asking about something I've given a great deal of thought to, and I've got your answer. First, and I do literally mean first, is a quality of personality. Some people just naturally have a subtle ability to dominate a conversation, a scene, anything. And you are one of those people.

'I only mean that as a compliment, Laura,' he added quickly. 'And I don't mean "dominant" as being "bossy" in any sense of the word. It's just a quality some people I guess are born with. What shall we do? What shall we talk about? Whatever. Others expect such people to steer the way, so to speak, and they don't even think of resenting the kind of dominance I'm talking about.'

Colin glanced into his rearview mirror and saw a very perplexed look on Laura's face.

'Oh, I'm not surprised you're not aware of it. But if I weren't convinced you are one of those people, as you said, we wouldn't be having this conversation.

'Anyway, you do. Second: your college grades are straight As, which means you're able to learn new things competently. Maybe the word "comprehend" would be a better word that "learn" to say what I'm trying to say. It's the ability to comprehend a whole new subject that I'm referring to. To me that means you'd really learn the whole subject of law office procedures in a very short time. And lastly, you will have the prestige of being a Stanford University graduate. None of the people you'll be supervising have been to college. Most of the secretaries have been to a secretarial school, but that's not real college. It's my judgment that at the start, your being a Stanford graduate will make up for your youth and initial lack of experience. Once these people see how fast you learn what they're supposed to be doing to make it all come together, you will have the respect which the human "herd instinct" seems to require.

'One last thing, Laura,' added Colin as if he wanted to get all this business talk behind them, 'and that's the money. Why don't we find out what you would probably earn if you were to go into teaching? Whatever it is, your beginning salary will be exactly three times that amount – and later there'll be worthwhile raises that will reflect your growing into the job.'

'I don't know what to say,' said Laura. 'If I'd thought this all up to suggest to you, I think I'd make an appointment with a psychiatrist. At first thought it seems like sheer fantasy. Yet, the way you explain it, it all seems to make sense.'

'Good,' said Colin, 'I don't want your answer now. This is something you should decide only after you've given it a lot of thought. What I'm proposing will mean a life much different than the one you've been preparing for. Of course, if you decided to decline, I'm sure that somehow we would find a way. And if, for reasons I have no reason to think would ever happen, but if somehow it just didn't turn out as expected, your Stanford degree will still open a lot of doors for you that otherwise wouldn't be there. I mean, it's not a life sentence. From your standpoint, it's just a better way to live your life. At least, that's my honest conclusion, and, believe me, I've given all this as much thought as I'm capable of.'

They passed over the crest of the hill and the sparkling lights of Monterey came into view.

'If you want to ask any other questions, I'll try to answer them,' said Colin, 'but short of that, let's not say another word on this whole subject until we're on our way back Sunday night. After all, we didn't come all this way to talk business, but to have fun.'

They rode on in what might aptly be called meditative silence. Each of them was carefully thinking about what had been said.

Colin was thinking that for sure she would take it. Laura was mentally tracking Colin's reasons and reasoning. Mary was feeling great pride to have such a wonderful friend as Laura, and even greater pride in this man with whom she was now deeply in love. He combined intelligence and experience with genuine humility. He had convincingly asked Laura to help him.

Aunt Lucy saw the headlights turn into her drive. She flung the front door open, and ran to greet them.

Colin turned off his engine and headlights just as the dear old lady got to the driver's side of the car. Everyone was all smiles, and after the customary greetings, Aunt Lucy ushered them into the house where she had a light supper prepared. She turned a kitchen stove burner to heat the clam chowder as her welcome guests transferred the contents of their small suitcases into the chests of drawers in their bedrooms. The drive had added just enough fatigue for everyone to want to retire somewhat early. It was lights out after about twenty minutes of small talk following supper. Only Laura lay awake until the wee hours. She had a lot to think about.

Everyone arose by 7.30 the next morning, except Aunt Lucy, and she got up at 6.30. There was coffee to make and breakfast for four to be prepared. She went about these tasks with the enthusiasm and vigour of a person half her age.

Aunt Lucy commonly had a small radio on a small shelf in her kitchen. She usually had it on to listen to music. Just as her weekend guests gathered around the kitchen's breakfast nook, a voice from the radio announced, 'And now the news.'

Everyone stopped talking to hear the latest. It wasn't good. The last British and French troops had just abandoned Narvik, a small but strategic village on the Norwegian Atlantic coast, and Norway's surrender to the invading Germans was expected at any time. It occurred the next day. The German invasion of France, which had begun in earnest only four days ago, was moving like a steamroller. The BBC had announced that aerial surveillance reported a build-up of fighters and bombers at aerodromes throughout north-west Europe.

Colin noted the dejected looks this news brought on the faces of both Mary and Laura.

'Does anyone mind if I turn this off?' he asked. 'There's nothing we can do about what's going on over there right now, and we'll all feel a lot better if we concentrate on enjoying this scrumptious breakfast Aunt Lucy has made, and we then we can get ready to go to the beach.'

Hearing no dissent to his suggestion, Colin reached over and turned the radio off.

Aunt Lucy immediately picked up the breakfast conversation with a series of questions to her guests. How were things going at college? Was Colin working too hard? He did look a little frazzled. Yes, he would come down and get her to attend the graduation at Stanford. Everyone became engrossed in talking about the local things in which they were involved. The gabfest did not, however, include anything about Colin's ten- to twelve-hour working days, or his plan to open a second office, or any of a number of subjects. One of those impending subjects in the lives of Colin and Mary didn't even surface;

the little matter of becoming engaged, and how were they going to resolve the problems of their families and a wedding ceremony that certainly wasn't going to be deferred until the end of a war whose end wasn't even in sight.

After breakfast Aunt Lucy cleared away the dishes while her three guests got ready to spend most of the day at the beautiful white-sand beach that was within easy walking distance. Swimsuits were donned. Colin retrieved the long-stemmed yellow beach umbrella from the garage. He was going to surprise them all with something he had just bought and concealed in his car. A battery-operated portable radio. Such things were virtually unknown at the time. Colin had learned from a lawyer in his office that a limited supply of these new inventions had just arrived at the large Emporium department store (San Francisco's counterpart of New York's famous Macy's.) He had promptly jumped on the Market Street streetcar to go to the Emporium to get one while they lasted. In the event, he had arrived to purchase the last one in stock.

After retrieving the beach umbrella, Colin started toward his car to get the big surprise. On second thought, after that news broadcast at breakfast, he decided to defer revealing this unique product of modern science until later. He resumed course back into the house with only the beach umbrella.

With their towel and umbrella beach accoutrements in hand, the three weekend guests bid Aunt Lucy a short farewell, and began strolling toward the ocean. It was understood Aunt Lucy wouldn't be coming, as her legs were simply not steady enough to walk on the sand. Never mind. She had her usual many and varied little household tasks she normally performed to pass the time. Her trips to the beach would, as always, happen midweek, when intermittent clusters of low clouds on the horizon assured one of those beautiful sunsets for which Carmel was famous.

Chapter Fifty

The Carmel beach near Aunt Lucy's house was nearly a mile long. Colin, Mary and Laura were slightly surprised at the number of people already on the beach when they walked on to the fine white sand. Well, why not? It was a beautiful cloudless blue sky. There was a mild landward breeze of no more than two or three miles per hour. The seventy-eight-degree seawater was fairly calm, already luring in dozens of swimmers. The waves that broke at water's edge were only two to three feet high at their crest. The more adult visitors were swimming or laying on their towels sunbathing. Most of the other beachcombers were nimble kids: toddlers to teenagers. The toddlers and younger teenagers were invariably under the watchful eye of a nearby parent. Most of the older kids were either swimming, playing tag or just running about to no particular end. A few were playing hopscotch, which involved jumping through the squares of a hopscotch court they had scratched in to the firmer wet sand near the water's edge. A short stick was usually to be seen in the dry sand just beyond. Whenever a big surf breaker would sprawl over their hopscotch court promptly erasing it, one of the players would run for the stick. Within a few seconds a new hopscotch court had been scratched into the damp sand exactly where the vanished one had been.

Further down the beach a group of loud college kids were bashing a volleyball back and forth over a net strung between two wooden poles which had been forced deep into the sand. The boundaries of the volleyball court were also scratched into the sand. Loud cheers came from the small crowd of onlookers whenever players made stunning kills, which meant driving a fist into the ball, firing it over the net beyond any opponent's reach, but still landing in bounds.

Some people at the beach weren't in swimsuits. A few of those came just to walk, but most of them were walking their dogs. All of the dog tenders strictly obeyed the sign at the entrance to the beach: 'No Dogs off Leash'. A green triangular flag was flying in the mild breeze atop a small wooden building called the lifeguard shack. The green flag signalled that all was well for swimming. No sharks. No riptide. No negatives. Yellow and red flags of the same size and shape warned of hazardous conditions. On this beautiful Saturday, the warning flags were neatly tucked away inside the shack. In a chair on the flat roof of the shack sat a husky young lifeguard hired by the city of Carmel. His job mostly involved scanning the water through field glasses, looking for swimmers in distress.

Once Aunt Lucy's weekend guests found a suitable spot to lay out their towels and plant the stem of their yellow beach umbrella into the sand, they raced across the beach, through the surf and had a delightful swim for about twenty minutes. As they began to tire, Colin waved his right hand and pointed toward their beach umbrella. It was time for a rest and some sincere sunbathing. All three were quickly back on the beach.

When they walked up to where their towels were spread, Laura announced that she wanted to take a walk all on her own. The others knew she had a lot to think about, and waved her on with a chiding admonition about not getting lost or speaking to strangers. As Laura disappeared among the beachcombers, Colin followed through with a plan about which he had given a great deal of thought, and he felt sure the time and place were right. He popped the question.

Mary was elated, but not surprised. She could not have been more delighted. There was no doubt in either of their minds that they very much wanted to be husband and wife. The age difference had never come up since they discussed it at the little Italian restaurant in Moraga almost a year ago. Now it meant nothing to either of them.

When and where was the momentous wedding event to happen?

'The sooner the better, as far as I'm concerned,' said Colin, 'and I want to suggest doing it in a way I hope you'll approve of, even though it's bound to get some noses out of joint on both sides of the Atlantic.'

Mary looked at him with a quizzical but inquiring look.

'Mary, my love,' said Colin, 'obviously your family can't be there, and it's only fair that my family, which admittedly consists only of dear old Aunt Lucy, but considering your side of the family ledger, my side shouldn't be there either.'

Mary couldn't disagree with his logic, but she was slightly surprised at Colin's statement that Aunt Lucy shouldn't be there either.

'I feel you're right,' said Mary, 'but I'm not sure exactly why in the case of Aunt Lucy.'

'Now I'm doing some supposing, Mary, but consider this: I don't know your family, and haven't had any contact with any of them. But people are people, and my every instinct tells me that, deep down, they would feel cheated if only my family was invited.'

'You mean we should not invite Aunt Lucy out of consideration for my family?' she asked.

'No other reason,' said Colin. 'No one loves Aunt Lucy as much as I do, or for so long as I have. After the war I'm sure I'll be meeting your family, and I don't want what I'm satisfied they would regard as a slight to mar what I expect will be a perfect family relation.'

'Well, assuming I'm of the same mind,' said Mary, 'how do you propose to convince Aunt Lucy?'

'It involves what is called a white lie. Saying something that isn't true, but it's not told to hurt or mislead anyone. It's only told to save their feelings. Here's what I've got in mind – and this will only happen if you agree.

'We say nothing about our plans this weekend. Not even to Laura. I think she would feel awkward concealing that news from Aunt Lucy, and in the effort she might give it all away.

'On the eighteenth, I'll get an early start to Carmel and pick up Aunt Lucy to bring her to the graduation at Stanford. On the way there I'll tell her that I'm so pressed for time in my law practice that you and I are going to spend a few days in the Sierras right after the graduation, and that I've made arrangements for her to take the train back from Palo Alto, and for Old Man Ross, her next door neighbour, to meet her when the train gets to Salinas. After the graduation, we'll drop her off at the train depot in Palo Alto and then drive north to Mills Field Municipal Airport, where I've got a surprise I'll tell you about in a minute. From the airport we'll fly to Lake Tahoe, where there's a beautiful little chapel in which we will get married. It's on the Nevada side of the lake, and in Nevada there's no waiting period between getting a wedding licence and getting married. I don't know if you were aware, but in California and a number of states, the law requires anywhere from one to three days between the two. It's called a "cooling off" period. Regardless, Nevada's laws on this point fit into our plans exactly. I have a long-time client friend who has a vacation house just outside of the village, and a brand new Packard he keeps in his garage. I've prevailed on him to give us the use of both. I'll make the arrangements at the office to be away for ten days. I wish it could be longer, but that's about as long as our honeymoon is going to last. We'll have time to drive all around Tahoe, which has the most beautiful mountain scenery on earth.

'After we get back, I'll call Aunt Lucy and tell just one last white lie. Lake Tahoe was so beautiful we just seemed to get carried away and decided to get married, like it was an impulsive, spur-of-the-moment decision. Naturally she'll be disappointed at not being at the wedding, but I'm sure I'll fall back into her good graces later. Hopefully that will happen the next time she starts going over in her mind all of the reasons why I'm such a fine fellow. It may take a while but she'll understand. I know she'll approve. She's asked me several times in the past few months why I hadn't proposed. I've always answered that it was because I was afraid you'd say no, and then where'd I be? She always answers, "Well, don't know." Then I say, "There you are!" and I change the subject.

'During our ten days, we might even decide to hop up to Coeur d'Alene in Idaho, which has the second most beautiful mountain scenery on earth.'

Mary's eyebrows rose when Colin mentioned a surprise. When he talked of maybe 'even a hop' up to Idaho, she just had to interrupt.

'I agree with everything you've just proposed, but I must tell you, I'm not afraid to fly, but I've never been up in an aeroplane, and I might even get sick. I've heard of people doing that, you know.'

As she spoke, an amused smile came over Colin's face.

'Never fear, my dear,' he said, half seriously. 'With Captain Colin Johnson as the pilot in command, your travel tranquillity and safe arrival are always assured. From take-off in San Francisco to touch down at the little airport at Lake Tahoe is 130 miles, which will take us one hour and five minutes. If we decide to have a look-see at Coeur d'Alene, the flying distance is just over 600 miles, since we would have to make one stop in Boise, Idaho, to refuel. Overall, that trip would take about five and a half hours each way.'

Mary simply had to interrupt again.

'Captain Colin? Colin, I didn't know you knew how to fly or that you were a pilot!' she exclaimed in surprise.

'Only one of the many talents I've concealed out of sheer modesty,' he quipped, smiling. 'And only one of your surprises for today.'

'I'm serious,' she replied. 'All this flying back and forth to Los Angeles. Have you been flying yourself?'

'No. The firm has a standing contract for all of that with Bud Miller; that is the Miller Aviation Company. Bud is an old friend I met while taking a ground school course back in the mid-twenties, when I got the bright idea I wanted to learn to fly, in spite of Aunt Lucy's loud protests. To me it seemed like a fun thing to do, and I did. With Bud Miller it was a different matter. He wasn't going to ground school for fun. He had in mind flying for a living, which he did, and he's been very successful, in spite of the Depression. For several years he's had his own charter flight company, which he operates out of the San Francisco airport. Now he now owns seven airplanes and employs four very talented pilots that he keeps very busy. My office calls him whenever want to send lawyers to Southern California, or bring them back. The flight time between San Francisco airport and Mines Field in Los Angeles is usually two and a half hours.'

'When do you ever fly yourself?' asked Mary.

'When I can find time to steal down to Bud Miller's office and rent either his Piper Cub or his little Aeronca for an hour or so – just enough to keep my pilot's licence current. The Federal Air Regulations require that I log at least twelve hours a year in the air at the controls.

'The Aeronca and Piper are what are called puddle jumpers. They only have room for the pilot and one passenger. Bud and his pilots use them when they have to take only one passenger on a quick short hop to nearer places like Fresno or Sacramento – and to rent to his old friend Colin Johnson for a few hours every so often so he can keep his pilot's licence, and, of course, to hone his aviation skills.'

'What did you mean by "up until day before yesterday"?' asked Mary.

'Ah ha!' said Colin, with a slight tone of triumph in his voice. 'That's surprise number two. Day before yesterday I took delivery of a brand new canary-yellow two-seater airplane called the Ercoupe 415, pronounced like it was spelled "air coupe", which at this very moment is sitting safely in Bud Miller's spare hangar at the airport.'

'Is it a puddle jumper?' asked Mary, still feeling the surprise at learning that Colin flew aeroplanes.

'Technically, because it only carries two people, yes,' answered Colin. 'but I've never heard anyone refer to an Ercoupe as a puddle jumper. I'll show you some of the more visible differences when we get to the airport. Bud's puddle jumpers are tied down just back of the hangar. Aside from its luxurious upholstery and passenger comforts, a few of the best things I can say for the Ercoupe are, first and foremost, it is the safest and the easiest airplane to fly and to land of any plane in the sky. An earlier model Ercoupe won that very title in a study conducted by the Federal Bureau of Aeronautics in 1934. The Ercoupe goes faster and stays in the air longer between refuellings that any puddle jumper, and all Ercoupes come with an engine called the Continental that only stops when you turn off the ignition – or run out of gas, of course. That last problem never happens to safe pilots, and Mary, if I'm one thing, I am a safe pilot. When I say flying and landing an Ercoupe is easy, I really mean it. In fact, I don't have the slightest doubt that I could teach you to fly it solo in less than six hours – that would include takings off and landings. Not that I'm suggesting we do that. But if you ever do decide you want to learn to fly, you just tell me.'

'I'll admit it all sounds very exciting,' said Mary, 'but I don't think I'll mention it in my letters to my family. Adam might think it sounds exciting, but I know my parents would worry themselves to death.'

'Not a problem,' replied Colin. 'Actually, I've been thinking it might be a good idea, after you've told them we're engaged, for me to send your parents a letter to sort of introduce myself; say hello, sort of thing. I wasn't thinking of mentioning anything about flying. What do you think of the idea?'

'Oh, I think that's an excellent idea, Colin,' she answered. 'I'm sure you'll just charm them into liking you, even if you are about to steal my parents' only daughter and my brother's only sister.'

They laughed briefly.

'What about Laura?' asked Mary. 'When do we tell her?'

'Not until we're on our way back tomorrow evening. Like I said, there's no reason why we should ask her to feel like she was deceiving Aunt Lucy. Worse: she might not pull that off. Women can read women, and Aunt Lucy has no shortages when it comes to women's instincts.'

'What about the wedding? On the schedule you've outlined, it seems like we leave the graduation and suggest Laura make her way back to the dorm.'

'No,' said Colin, 'it won't turn out like that at all – at least if I'm right in thinking that Laura is going to accept my job offer. We'll probably learn about that on the way back tomorrow evening. If I'm right, we'll be letting Laura off at the airport to catch the regular bus that runs every half-hour to and from Union Square, which is about a quarter of a mile from my office. She'll probably want to check in to a hotel around there until she can decide on renting an apartment in the city.

'If I'm not right, well, let's cross that bridge if we get to it. Until she decides on the job, let's just say nothing about our engagement or any of this.'

As she had often found herself doing, Mary was in complete agreement with the plans Colin had outlined. They made good sense in every way she could think of. She smiled, and nodded her concurrence.

Colin smiled, and wrapped her in his arms as they kissed.

To hell with the gawkers, if there are any, each of them thought. There were. Two boys about fourteen years old were standing about fifty feet away.

'Look at the lovebirds!' one of them called out.

'Maybe they'll invite us,' the other chimed in.

The spell was broken. Colin and Mary turned toward the heckling young fry and smiled. The boys ran off like they'd been caught at something. One of them nearly ran into Laura, who was just returning from what might be aptly called a meditative walk.

At 4 p.m. the following day Colin, Mary and Laura said their goodbyes to Aunt Lucy, whose face showed she was truly sorry they had to be on their way. The whole weekend had been a great success, at least in terms of everyone enjoying themselves in a very relaxing atmosphere.

Colin and the girls had had a leisurely time of it after Laura returned from her walk. They swam, lay in the sun and engaged in small talk. Once the girls challenged Colin to get in the volleyball game, so he did. There was one unusually tall and lanky youngster already in the game who got more kills than anyone else, but Colin showed he was clearly no amateur at the game.

Come late afternoon, the three strolled back to Aunt Lucy's. On the way, Colin suggested they walk a little faster because he didn't want his aunt to start preparing supper. He wanted to drive them all down the coast a few miles to a terrific restaurant at a small resort area about twenty miles down the coast called Big Sur. They walked into Aunt Lucy's house just as she was putting a pot of water on the stove for boiling potatoes.

After taking their showers and changing to clothes a little more appropriate for going to a nice restaurant, they left for Big Sur. Colin sat in the driver's seat alongside Mary in the front; Laura and Aunt Lucy were seated in the back. Conversation flowed so freely between them they were all surprised at how fast the time passed before Colin parked near the Big Sur restaurant. Big Sur was on California's famous Highway 1 that ran along the California coast all the way from an old logging town named Eureka near the north end of California to the Mexican border. The variety of breath-taking ocean views from Highway 1 were stunning, which explained why all the traffic. The tourists loved it. When Colin and his party arrived at Big Sur they had to wait twenty minutes to be seated at that nice restaurant. In fact, it was the resort's only restaurant and it did a thriving trade.

When the waitress passed out a dinner menu, Colin spoke up.

'Aside from Aunt Lucy and me, has anyone at this table ever tasted abalone?' he asked.

When Mary and Laura both shook their heads, Colin suggested they try the abalone dinner at the top of the menu.

When the waitress returned for their order, it was simple.

'Four abalone dinners,' said Colin. Needless to say a superb dinner was everyone's reward. Abalone is a shellfish found only off the California coast, and has always been so popular that very little of it is ever shipped out of state. On the way back to Carmel, Laura could hardly stop talking about that fantastic supper.

Even with the delay in being seated at the restaurant, the four had arrived back home in time for a few hands of rummy before they turned in for the night. The next day, Sunday, it was more time at the beach and some extended small-talk time with Aunt Lucy during a late noon hour, when the three had walked back for a lunch. As mid-afternoon came around, it was time to get ready for the drive home.

Just before her company left, Aunt Lucy had written down on a piece of paper the exact date and time she was to be ready when Colin arrived to take her to the graduation at Stanford on the eighteenth!

After Colin had driven by the Monterey airport on the Monterey–Salinas leg of their return trip, Laura cleared her throat slightly, and made her speech from the back seat.

'Well, I suppose you've both just been on pins and needles wondering what I was going to decide about Colin's offer to change my career plans about 180 degrees, and be assured I have given the whole subject the most concentrated thought of which I'm capable.'

A short silence of about five seconds.

'And?' said Colin.

'I've decided to give it a go,' said Laura, voice very firm.

'I've no doubt both my mother and stepdad will think I've lost my mind, but they're not here, and they're not me. If you think I can learn and do the job you described, Colin, who am I to disagree? You've spent a lot more time studying people and sizing up their capabilities than I have. Truth be told, I'm not sure I ever spent any time like that. If you're wrong and I'm making a mistake, it won't be something that can't be straightened out. I believe with a bachelor's degree in education from Stanford, I should never have much difficulty in finding a job. But, deep down, I want more out of life than just a job. I've never assumed a lot of responsibility in my life, but any capabilities I may have along that line are about to be tested in a big way, I've got the feeling. So, Mr Lawyer, what do you say to that?'

Laura leaned back in her seat, feeling greatly relieved. She had actually made her decision the day before while she was on her meditative walk. Since then, well, she hadn't memorised her acceptance speech, but she almost had.

'I'm both delighted and relieved,' came Colin's prompt reply.

'While I've never been wrong more than a few dozen times,' he said in a lighter tone of voice, 'somehow I've got a very strong feeling I'm not wrong this time. And, as you say, in the highly unlikely event we're both wrong, it won't mean any permanent disaster for anyone.'

'Mary?' said Colin, turning briefly towards her with a don't-you-want-to-say-something look on his face.

'Yes,' said Mary, with a slightly coquettish half-smile on her pretty face.

'Well,' replied Colin, 'I've done too much of the talking this whole weekend, and I thought perhaps there's something you might like to confide in your very best friend, who will be joining my staff in the near future. Go ahead. I'll just listen in.'

Laura was following this dialogue with considerable amusement, alternating her gaze to the one in the front seat who was speaking.

Mary had then related to Laura practically all of the details of what she and Colin had discussed and agreed upon the previous day while Laura was on her walk. As Mary brought her story to a close, she ended with the question, 'And what do you say about all that?'

Laura had not been surprised at the wedding engagement. She had sensed that was in the wind before she and Laura had left Florida. Learning that Colin was a pilot and now had his own aeroplane, however, was a shocker. Laura, too, had never been up in an aeroplane. And while she admired Mary's nerve in agreeing to go on the trip that was about to happen, she wasn't quite sure she would have been as willing. Perhaps as brave is more accurate, she thought.

Everything that was planned during the weekend just described came to pass as if pre-ordained.

When Colin called Old Man Ross later in the week about picking up Aunt Lucy at Salinas, he gladly agreed, and actually enjoyed being trusted with the confidential information Colin conveyed. No, he wouldn't say a word to her about any of it. And he would have to remember not to say anything about Colin and that English girl getting married until after Aunt Lucy had learned it from Colin. Old Man Ross was delighted with all this intrigue. He was also quite flattered that Aunt Lucy's nephew, 'that smart San Francisco lawyer', would take him into his confidence like this. Must be he just trusts me on sight, the old fellow decided.

The graduation was a great success. All four of the English girls who had arrived via Educational Endowments International Ltd were awarded college degrees the likes of which none of them could ever have dreamt when they boarded the *Queen Mary* in 1939.

Mary did not get airsick on the short flight to Lake Tahoe. The views from the air on the way were awesome, and she enjoyed every minute.

Mr and Mrs Colin Johnson emerged from the little chapel in Lake Tahoe, Nevada, exactly on schedule. And they did include the hop up to Coeur d'Alene, Idaho, during their divine ten-day honeymoon.

Mary had experienced many exciting events by the time she and Colin tied down the canary-yellow Ercoupe 415 back at the San Francisco Airport. In reality, however, the only true surprise she experienced during this time in her life didn't happen until the latter part of the next month, July of 1940. One morning she woke up feeling quite sick for no apparent reason. Colin was alarmed to the extent that he insisted she be checked by a doctor friend of his who would see her on short notice. After her visit to Colin's doctor friend, it can be accurately reported that both Colin and Mary were, indeed, surprised.

Mary's letters home about getting married hadn't arrived all that long ago when her letter arrived announcing her pregnancy. Surprises from the other side of the Atlantic seemed to be coming in large doses.

On 22 March 1941, a bouncing baby boy they named Gary Colin Johnson arrived was in the maternity ward of St Francis Hospital in San Francisco.

Chapter Fifty-one

Following their arrival at the leased estate near Crediton, Devon, in the latter part of May in 1940, Charles Rainford and Samuel Travers settled into a very tolerable way of life. Charles, of course, had the large master bedroom on the upper storey of the country mansion, and Samuel had a much smaller bedroom on the ground floor. Their chess games continued with the same popularity and regularity as they had after the two became almost close friends back in Jersey. Samuel narrowed Charles's win margin slightly, thinking that might contribute in maintaining the equality which had naturally developed between them.

Neither man had any experience with government rationing in Jersey. When they arrived in Devon, however, it was another matter. Very shortly after their arrival, Charles withdrew from one of his locked heavy trunks enough gold coins to open a bank account at the Lloyds Bank in Exeter. His opening balance was £10,000, a princely sum at the time. Upon learning of his new customer who had just arrived from Jersey, the bank manager introduced himself and suggested that Charles lose no time in visiting the local office of the Ministry of Food, where 'you can all get your ration books'. The very next day, Charles and Samuel went to that office, which was just over the road from the Lloyd's Bank. After producing proper identification, both men were issued official ration books containing little tear-away stamps on which were printed numbers designated as 'points', below which words were printed, such as words as 'bacon', 'butter', 'sugar', 'meat' and 'tea'.

'Better drop by next week,' said the young man when he handed them their ration books. 'Next month rationing starts on jam, breakfast cereals, milk, eggs and tinned fruit. You won't be able to buy any of those without the right stamps.'

As Charles and Samuel walked out of the Ministry of Food office, Charles had a perfectly brilliant idea. One that was more likely to occur to a man of means, such as himself.

'Mr Travers,' said Charles, 'would you wait for me at the car? There are a couple of questions I'd like to put to that accommodating fellow I met yesterday in the bank.' He pointed across the road to the Lloyds Bank.

Charles spotted the accommodating fellow immediately on entering the bank. He approached him, and was promptly invited to have a seat at the man's desk.

'I'm sure you remember me from yesterday,' said Charles.

'Indeed I do… Rainford, Mr Charles Rainford from Jersey, of course,' said the manager in a very friendly voice.

'Well,' said Charles, 'I took your advice, and my associate who came with me from Jersey and I just left the Food Ministry office across the way where we received our ration books.'

'Yes?' replied the banker, in a tone that said he wondered where all this was leading.

'Well, I was just wondering if perhaps you might know of any place about where we might augment our purchases of some of those rationed items, should some sort of emergency arise. All very confidential, of course.'

The banker knew he was being asked if he knew of any black-market availability. And indeed he did.

'Well, not exactly,' he replied rather quietly. 'I'll bet those chaps over the road didn't tell you that rationing doesn't apply to restaurants, so there's one source you might use for unexpected needs. And, a friend of mine told me – I know nothing about any of this first hand, you understand – but a friend of mine told me that a butcher named Birket, or Burkett, something like that, might be relied on – in an emergency, of course. I believe my friend said his shop is on the A963, just north of Exeter on the right. It's just beyond the petrol station, which I'm told is operated by his brother. The brother, rumour has it, seems to have some mysterious sources of petrol that he only makes available to his close friends and customers vouched for by his brother, the butcher. You might want to drop by just to get acquainted. I don't know if mentioning my name will be of any use, but there's no harm in finding out, is there?'

After a short pause, the banker added, 'I think this sort of intelligence should remain most confidential.'

Charles thanked the gentleman for his kind advices and assured him everything would be held in strictest confidence. He added that use of these unusual sources would only occur under the most pressing circumstances.

Charles said he would stop by the butchery to introduce himself, considering it would be right along the route he would be travelling back to Crediton.

Charles returned to the car park where Samuel was seated in the Vauxhall. Samuel noted that his friend was in particularly good spirits, and even had a bit of a bounce in his step.

'Not to worry about this rationing business,' Charles announced as he seated himself in the driver's seat. 'I've just located two sources that will permit us to buy food and fuel as needed. As for the O'Tooles, well,' he added, 'they already have their ration books, and I'm sure they're both quite accustomed to living within the Government's rationing good graces by now. Lord knows I'm paying them enough, so all they have to do is get to the shops with their own stamps.'

'I think that's wonderful,' said Samuel. 'Along the line of provisions, I've been thinking of planting a vegetable garden on that flat spot at the back. The Lord knows we've got the room. And, frankly, I need the exercise.'

He's spot on with that, thought Charles. I could use the exercise, too, but I think I will start taking long walks for that. I'd surely look the fool out there shovelling earth.

While Charles and Samuel were settling in at the leased estate, other events were underway that would greatly affect everyone's future. By 24 June 1940, the French had had enough and signed the surrender documents with the truculent Hitler, who staged the signing ceremonies in the same tiny railroad coach in which the humiliated Germans had signed the Armistice of 1918. He had ordered that coach be removed from a French museum and brought to the identical spot where it had stood in 1918. In his surrender terms, the arrogant Hitler tossed something of a bone to the *grenouilles* (which was French for '*frösche*', or 'frogs', as the English called them). They were permitted to set up a friendly government at Vichy to govern a portion of their own country in the south of once-proud France.

After France's surrender, Britain stood alone as the only country actively at war with the high-riding Germans. And it was soon evident that the British weren't going to go quietly, not with the articulate, aggressive Winston Churchill replacing the gun-shy and ailing Neville Chamberlain. Hitler was well informed on Churchill's several air trips to Paris during the last weeks of May, which had to have been increasingly frantic efforts to spur the failing French to fight on.

One of Churchill's last admonitions to the wavering French government was that England would 'fight on, no matter what they decided'. Loud evidence strongly supporting those words was heard when the Royal Navy carried out Churchill's direct order to sink the French fleet, which Vichy had refused to hand over to keep out of the hands of the Germans. On 3 July 1940, HMS *Valiant*, HMS *Resolution*, HMS *Hood*, aircraft carrier HMS *Ark Royal* and a group of cruisers and battleships caught most of the French fleet by complete surprise at anchor at Mers-el-Kébir near Oran on the north coast of Algeria. All French ships were sunk or badly disabled. The death toll numbered 1,297 French sailors. The outraged Vichy government swiftly broke all diplomatic relations with Great Britain. Although British apologies for the loss of life fell on deaf ears, so too went any calls around the halls of Parliament for anything but the victory which Churchill had vowed to bring about.

The German plan was to get Britain to the peace table at which appropriately harsh terms would be imposed. Then Hitler could get on with his lifelong ambition of annihilating the hated communist Soviet Union, and in the process gain *Lebensraum* for the ever-growing German population. The fertile plains of the Ukraine seemed like the ideal place for realising that goal.

Hitler and his generals had many differences, but they were in complete agreement that fighting war on two fronts posed enormous disadvantages. Thus Hitler's frustration only increased as the arrogant English and their belligerent relatively new Prime Minister continued to confront the Reich. Hitler decided to defer his territorial ambitions in the East, in order to do the necessary to end the harassment from the West. He ordered his generals to devise a military operation to put the cantankerous English on the shelf.

The generals' solution was codenamed *Seelöwe*, or Operation Sea Lion. Now the English would suffer the same fate as had the Poles, Belgians, Dutch, Norwegians and French. The Danes had been rewarded for their passive submission with considerably less stringent treatment.

On 10 July 1940, one week after the British had sent the French fleet to the bottom Hitler unleashed the dogs of war to bring the obstinate British to heel. That date marks the beginning of the Battle of Britain.

The only precondition for launching Sea Lion was that the Luftwaffe first obtain aerial superiority over the skies of Britain. Reichsmarschal Göring assured the Führer that his mighty Luftwaffe would complete that assignment in a matter of weeks. From July to September, the Luftwaffe concentrated on frontal attacks against Fighter Command. Heavy bombing raids were also directed at aircraft factories in Bristol and Southampton, the object being to prevent the British from replacing their losses. In spite of the many vicious attacks, largely on military airfields such as Croydon, the Germans simply lost their fight for air superiority. On 20 August 1940, Churchill made his famous speech about so many owing so much to so few. His 'few', of course, were the brave young RAF pilots, many of whom bailed out once or twice in one day from their stricken, flaming aircraft, only to be picked up by some roving trawler and returned to their units to fight again, often the same day.

On 7 September 1940, the first massive German bomber formations took off from aerodromes in the north of France. Destination: London's docks and industrial facilities. Thus began the blitz phase of the Battle of Britain.

Although the Germans lost that battle in the end, it is difficult to identify the wins for the British, beyond having staved off the Nazis. During that battle the Germans bombed London for fifty-seven consecutive nights, killing over 23,000 people. During this battle, another 23,000, mainly civilians, were killed in the German bombing raids on Belfast, Birmingham, Bristol, Cardiff, Clydebank, Coventry, Greenock, Sheffield, Swansea, Liverpool, Manchester,

Portsmouth, Plymouth, Nottingham and Southampton. Paradoxically, Hitler's massive effort to break British morale only stiffened the people's resolve to fight on and survive.

While Winston Churchill provided the lion's roar that inspired the British to defeat the marauding Germans, the man who devised the actual plan that turned Operation Sea Lion into a humiliating German defeat was Air Chief Marshal Hugh Dowding, fifty-seven. That brilliant man conceived and implemented what became known as the Dowding System, in which he incorporated radar, human ground observers, air-raid plotting, and radio control of aircraft.

Dowding's young fighter pilots in their Spitfires and Hurricanes fought back with the fury of a tiger protecting her cubs. The German air fleets approaching Britain were detected by radar well before arriving. The British fighter pilots were dispatched aloft so as to be at the right altitude at the right time and place from which they inflicted enormous casualties on the slower-flying German bomber fleets and their sometime fighter escorts. While both sides suffered greatly throughout this ordeal, the Germans suffered by far the most. Hitler decided to end his ever-increasing losses of pilots and aircraft. On 12 October 1940, the German Government officially 'postponed' Operation Sea Lion until the spring of 1941. In historic fact, Sea Lion was not heard of or from for the remainder of the war.

The Prime Minister's famous speech about so many owing so much to so few was pure fact, not rhetoric. Fittingly, Dowding's success spelled the permanent fall from grace of his counterpart on the other side, the corpulent Herman Göring.

During the Battle of Britain, small outlying villages were of no interest to the Germans. They sought to crush the British will to fight by devastating large military and industrial areas. At least those appeared to be their targets until 24 August 1940 when a covey of German bombers flew a mission of bombing Thames Haven. One of these bombers piloted by one Rudolf Hallensleben broke formation and strayed over London, dropping bombs in the north-east parts of the city: Bethnal Green, Hackney, Islington, Tottenham and Finchley. The British mounted a retaliatory raid on Berlin the next night, with their bombs falling in Kreuzberg and Wedding, causing ten deaths. Hitler was furious. From that time on there were no limitations of bombing only military and industrial targets. Civilians became fair game. And civilian populations, particularly in England and Germany, were subjected to unprecedented slaughter from the air. The later fate of hundreds of thousands of Japanese civilians was even more horrible, but that is another story.

Before the Germans began sending the V-2 winged bombs on 8 September 1944, sleepy little villages off the bombers' path, such as Crediton, were not attacked from the air. As the fury of the German Blitz increased, Charles Rainford and Samuel Travers spent many hours comfortably seated in the garden, safely watching portions of the deadly 'air show' from sidelines. They saw wave after wave of Luftwaffe bombers headed for London, or beyond. Often they saw RAF fighters racing about the sky like flies attacking locusts which had been trained to fly in formation. A bomber would suddenly plunge from the formation, leaving a downward trail of smoke that traced its route to death, which frequently ended on a lovely green hillside or in a farmer's field. When the wind was right, they could hear bombs exploding, and occasionally the chug-chug-chug roar of anti-aircraft guns. Sometimes they would see parachutes blossom in the sky right after a stricken bomber or fighter began its fatal plunge.

They also witnessed (from the safe distance of more than ten miles) the bombing of Exeter, which was a result of the fuel limitations of the German bombers that were dispatched from aerodromes in the north of France to destroy choice targets in and around Plymouth on the south coast of Devon. Plymouth lay thirty miles south and forty miles to the west of peaceful Crediton. Only when the fires and explosions lit up the sky above Plymouth could Charles and Samuel see something of what was going on that far away.

How did certain events in 1940–1941 at Plymouth result in a post-war building boom in Exeter? It's an interesting story that can be told briefly.

Plymouth's large complex of docks, naval shipyards and war industries presented choice targets, which the Germans sought to destroy by precision bombing. Thus the screaming Ju 87-D Stuka dive bombers were the Luftwaffe's weapons of choice. The downside of these aircraft for those missions was the limited volume of fuel that could be stored in their two wing tanks; a total of eighty gallons when topped. Those tanks had to be topped off for the roundtrip between northern France and Plymouth. The results? Thus fuelled, the Ju 87-D could carry only one 500-pound bomb, and at the terminus of that trip, each pilot had time for only one dive at his assigned target.

The Ju 87-D could unquestionably deliver its deadly cargo where it was aimed, provided the dive was set up and made exactly as the plane's designers prescribed. If a diving German pilot's target was not in his sights at the right time, his orders were to pull up, execute a climbing turn and head back to France. Pilots who had not dropped their bombs were ordered to promptly estimate their ground speed, if possible, by timing how long it took them to travel between certain designated ground points. If the ground points weren't detected or if Stuka pilots doing the calculation concluded that easterly winds might jeopardise their making it back to base, their orders were to lighten their load by releasing their bombs.

Between the harassments of ground-based anti-aircraft fire and defending RAF pilots, a good many Stuka pilots found themselves abandoning their dive, and making the prescribed climbing turn. It is impossible to know how many disappointed Stuka pilots leaving Plymouth undertook any ground-speed calculations. But there were scores of witnesses to what most of them did to improve their chances of getting back to France. They dropped their unspent bombs while passing over little Exeter, then a small town which had no industrial or military significance whatsoever.

From their chairs in the garden, ten or so miles to the north, Charles and Samuel saw many departing Stukas darting through the beams of Klieg lights and releasing their bombs on Exeter. When the wind was right, they could even hear the explosions. Charles and Samuel were by no means the only spectators. The author has had extensive conversations with one hillside pub owner who sat night after night watching the same spectacle.

In early 1941, Charles noticed that he was winning more of the chess games than in the past, and that Samuel, rather gradually, just didn't seem like his old self. There was something odd about his complexion, too. The normal healthy look of his face was slowly replaced by a faintly yellowish-grey hue. At Charles's insistence, Samuel was examined by an older doctor in Exeter, whose diagnostic tools consisted of little more than a stethoscope and a wrap-around sleeve device for measuring blood pressure.

'Irregular heartbeat,' said the doctor, as he moved the stethoscope to different places on Samuel's bare chest, and listened. 'Every three or four beats, it makes a fast extra beat.'

Samuel was sitting on the doctor's examination table. Charles was seated a few feet away. The doctor ended his probing and reached for a volume from the ten or so medical texts on a nearby shelf. He thumbed through the book and stopped at one particular page, which he studied closely for well over a minute.

'Arrhythmia,' the doctor announced, 'that's what you've got.'

'What's that?' asked Samuel.

'Irregular heart beat,' answered the doctor. 'And there's not much anyone can do about it. It's one of those things when we don't know what causes it. It doesn't seem to run in families or happen to people who do any particular kind of work. It just pops up here and there, mostly in middle-aged people. Just don't over exert yourself, and make sure you always get a good night's sleep.'

'Is it serious?' asked Samuel.

'I think it is, but I can't truly say how serious,' answered the doctor. 'One of my patients, an older lady from Topsham, lived nearly twenty years after I diagnosed her arrhythmia. And I recall one old fellow from Exmouth who had quite a different experience.'

'Could I ask what that was?' asked Samuel.

'Of course,' replied the doctor. 'No violating any doctor–patient confidence in his case. I made the diagnosis while he was sitting about where you're sitting now, and the poor old chap hardly made it home. As I think back, however, I seem to recall he was also feeling intermittent pains in his chest. You're not having anything like that, are you?'

'No,' said Samuel, 'I don't feel all that great, but I don't feel any pains.'

'I'm pleased to hear that,' said the doctor. 'Perhaps,' he continued, 'after the war and the emphasis shifts to keeping people alive, they will come up with a way to treat arrhythmia. But I've told you all that can be told for now.'

The doctor turned to face Samuel more directly. 'Please remember: don't over-exert yourself. Don't try lifting heavy things. And get your proper sleep.'

Then with a half-smile and in a lighter tone, he added, 'So, you can get your clothes back on, and I'll see you out.'

He replaced his medical book on the shelf as Samuel began buttoning his shirt.

Charles and Samuel both appeared pretty glum as they left the doctor's surgery. Neither said more than a word or two on the drive back to Crediton. Samuel, in particular, had a very worried look on his face.

As Charles drove on to the estate, Samuel broke the silence.

'I could go to the Royal Naval Hospital at Plymouth,' he said, 'if it's still there. Free lifetime medical care is part of my retirement.'

Then in a more resigned voice, he added, 'But if it's something they don't know how to treat, I don't see any sense in that.'

'I will be happy to take you wherever you wish, Samuel,' answered Charles, 'but, in all honesty, the doctor convinced me that it's a condition for which no treatment has been discovered.

'But don't let my impression influence you,' added Charles hastily, 'It's your health and your life we're talking about. You think it over, and if you want to pop over to Plymouth, you just give the word.'

'I appreciate that,' said Samuel, in a voice reflecting his gratitude and sincerity. 'I will think it over. But at this point, I don't really feel any high hopes.'

The two men went into the house and retired early after Mrs O'Toole served their supper. No chess game tonight.

During the weeks that followed, Samuel withdrew into himself increasingly. The chess games actually came to a halt, and he finally stopped sitting in the garden with Charles to watch the 'air show'.

Charles was fearful that the atmosphere would degenerate into a death watch, and did his best to put on a cheery face. That helped, for a while.

On 10 February 1941, Mrs O'Toole signalled Charles aside to express her concern over Mr Travers.

'I know,' Charles said, 'things don't look very good. But we'll just have to see it through.'

On the morning of 15 February 1941, Mrs O'Toole almost ran into Charles as he opened his bedroom door to go to breakfast.

'It's Mr Travers,' she said excitedly, 'I fear something terrible has happened. I went to call him for breakfast, and there was no response. I opened his bedroom door to peer in. He's just lying there, staring at the ceiling.' She broke into tears.

Two days later, Samuel Travers was buried in the small graveyard at Crediton. Charles felt a great loss, but there was nothing he could do. He couldn't even send a letter to Edward Travers in Jersey to tell him that he no longer had a brother. Total sadness pervaded Charles Rainford for the next two weeks. Just being around the estate did little but remind him of the many chess games he and Samuel had enjoyed. Then he would start recounting tales that Samuel had related about some exciting shore leaves while he was in the Royal Navy. Such daydreaming would abruptly stop as Charles would visualise Samuel's coffin being lowered into his grave. He began to experience mental depression very similar to what he had experienced after his sister, Helen, passed away.

It was time to move on. Where? Charles couldn't answer that question. But move on he must. He had no worries about the O'Tooles. Decent enough people. Both fit and still young enough to make their way in the world. When he was ready to announce his decision, he would tell the O'Tooles, and give them three months' pay. That should see them through until they could make other employment arrangements. Surely jobs weren't all that hard to come by, what with the war and all those young men in the Forces.

After another week of concentrated thought, Charles Rainford decided on a plan. He would contact Derek Barnett, that bright young man who was the manager of Stein & Sons bank in Liverpool, and through him, he would make the arrangements to get away from Crediton and safely secrete his fortune in coins, which was still under lock and key in two heavy trunks in the storeroom below. Barnett would help him. Good God! Derek Barnett might be in the Forces, he thought. Even if he was beyond conscription age, he could still have volunteered.

During the next ten days, Charles learned a good deal about what had happened to Derek Barnett. Through the Lloyd's Bank manager in Exeter he learned that Derek was no longer with Stein & Sons. The bank manager's source (nameless, of course) reported that the most he could learn was that there had been some 'funny business of some kind' at the Liverpool branch of Stein & Sons, and that Mr Barnett 'had not left under the happiest of circumstances'.

'Does that mean something dishonest was involved?' Charles asked the Lloyd's manager.

'That was my first impression,' the manager answered, 'but it really doesn't say that, does it? "Funny business" is rather ambiguous. I would be inclined to give the man the benefit of the doubt, at least until I learned otherwise.'

Charles was persuaded by that logic, and set about determining Derek Barnett's present whereabouts. For a very reasonable consideration, the Lloyd's manager prevailed on a semi-retired investigator who formerly located hard to find people for Lloyd's bad debt collectors. Within a fortnight, the man sent word that Derek Barnett lived on his own barge moored near Oxford. His neighbours didn't know what he did for a living, but at times some very well dressed people came to his barge and remained for several hours.

What the investigator's informants did not relate, because they didn't know, was that Derek Barnett was a rather slippery fellow who lived by his wits, and had been sacked by Stein & Sons because of personal involvement with an individual for whom he had approved a number of dubious unsecured loans. This involvement had only come to light when one such loan went into default, and was ultimately written off as a bad debt. The neighbours also didn't know that some of Derek's well-dressed visitors were strongly suspected by some in Government of involvement in black-market operations.

Had Charles Rainford known all of these facts, most likely he would not have followed through with contacting the man who had helped him leave Liverpool back in 1928. But he did. Within another fortnight, Charles received a pre-arranged telephone call at the only pub in Crediton. Derek Barnett sounded just like Charles remembered his voice so many years ago. Firm, cheerful and confident.

On 20 March 1941, Charles Rainford and Derek Barnett met at the Rose & Crown pub on the A367 on the south edge of Bath, something of a midpoint between Crediton and Oxford. They had agreed by phone to meet at 7.30 for supper and a few drinks. The pub also offered accommodations. Charles had booked a room and planned to stay the night and return to Crediton the next day. He arrived in time to check into his room and change clothes before going downstairs to meet a man he had not seen in almost thirteen years. And one he intended to learn more about before involving him in another transfer of the Rainford family fortune.

Derek arrived right on time. Although in his early forties, he was fit and trim and appeared much closer to his mid-thirties. There was not a speck of grey in his jet-black close-cropped hair. He wore a rather expensive suit, but otherwise exhibited all of the qualities of a well-off, neatly groomed, conservative gentleman. After a couple of sherries and some small talk about how well each thought the other looked after thirteen years, Charles and Derek were shown to a small table in a corner, where they could enjoy some privacy while having their meal.

Once settled at the table, Charles was direct, without being blunt, in asking why Derek was no longer with Stein & Sons. Derek perceived Charles's apprehension, and knew he wasn't going to learn why this wealthy Rainford heir had asked for this meeting short of a convincing explanation. So Derek Barnett proceeded to tell Charles Rainford just what had happened, or about one or two per cent of what had happened.

He related how Stein & Sons had weathered the Depression quite well. Not all that surprising since they only dealt with other people's money and stayed away from the turbulent stock exchange. In 1937 or 1938, Derek had noticed one of his better customers in Liverpool, Arnold Sagmaster by name, suddenly began prospering far and away better than anyone in his peer group. The man was an investor of sorts, and his deposits at Stein & Sons began to grow steeply. As the manager, Derek was well aware of this change. He was also aware that in spite of his expanding account, the man had continued to make short-term loans ranging between £20,000 and £30,000. Excellent repayment record. No overdrafts.

Derek's curiosity had peaked to the point where he broke his own rule about not inquiring into a customer's personal business. He invited the chap to a superb four-course dinner at Hazelton's, one of Liverpool's oldest and finest upmarket eateries. Before and during their meal Derek kept refilling Sagmaster's glass with a very expensive French wine, for which he seemed to have an unquenchable thirst. As Derek had hoped, near the end of the second bottle, the old saying 'in vino veritas' was proven true once again. When Derek began to flatter his customer about his fairly recent financial success, it all started coming out. After exacting Derek's pledge of 'all this being just our little secret', he explained how he was doing it.

'Now you've got me curious,' said Charles, 'how did he do it?'

'He was trading in futures,' said Derek.

Charles confessed he had no knowledge of what 'futures' might be in the context of trading, so Derek told him. He described how there was a 'futures commodity market' in which the traders and investors didn't buy and sell equity shares, like they do in the stock exchange, but bought and sold various commodities that were going to reach the market at some future date or season.

'And how did he manage to fiddle that market?' Charles asked.

'Well,' responded Derek, 'I wouldn't put it quite that strongly, but you've got the scent. There had to be some unseen factors to buying something today and consistently coming out ahead when that something arrives at market months or even years later. By coming out ahead, I mean selling it for a great deal more than one paid for it.

'The secret is having inside information that more or less assures that the market value of the commodity being considered will be well above what he paid for it. And the secret to gaining those secrets,' beamed Derek, 'is to have the contacts with the right people working in the larger stock-brokerage firms who are privy to which commodities are going to be in short supply come market time, or what commodities are going to be in much greater demand that anyone could have guessed months and months ago.

'Believe me,' he continued, 'you would be positively amazed at what is learned in such places about future events and the big-business transactions that are going to cause the shortage or the unusually high demand. Specifically, what I'm talking about is those chaps who are often called "staff". These men don't use crystal balls, but with one unfortunate exception of which I have personal knowledge, they have good minds, excellent hearing and they use them to discreetly better their lot in life quietly and confidentially.'

'That strikes me, at least,' said Charles, 'as bordering on sharp practices. Regardless, how does all that figure in your getting sacked at Stein & Sons?'

'Well,' said Derek a bit sheepishly, 'I was thoroughly engrossed by Mr Sagmaster's story, and after checking the area for any uninvited auditors I asked him if it was possible for even a humble person like myself to get involved in futures. In a small way, at first, I premised.'

Derek proceeded to describe how his grateful guest outlined a plan along this line where everyone would make a bob.

'What we worked out,' said Derek, 'was that I started approving some fairly good-size unsecured loans to Mr Sagmaster, who would loan back a portion of the loan proceeds to me, with which I could buy in to some choice futures transactions. It all worked quite well for several months, and then it seems that the information we'd purchased from a twit that worked at a certain stock brokerage firm was – well, what the Americans refer to as a "bummer". It involved futures in rice or corn, or some such thing. Something we import a great amount of from India, as I recall. There was going to be a big shortage because of some turmoil that was supposed to happen between the Hindus and Muslims that didn't happen at all. By the time the commodity, whatever it was, reached market, its value was less than half of what we'd paid. We sold it for the best price we could, but that was still well over £20,000 less than the unsecured loan taken out from Stein & Sons to begin with. Under the bank's rules, a loan of that size should have been properly secured, but my bad debt record was so slight I never heard from London when I loaned unsecured over the limit. I guessed, wrongly as it was, that the auditors in London just didn't worry about Liverpool. Well this loan went into default.

'The same day we learned we had a problem, Mr Sagmaster withdrew all his deposits from the bank, and told me he was prepared to pay his share when I came up with my share. That was all balderdash. Sagmaster and his deposits suddenly disappeared, and I had no choice but to declare the loan in default. All £57,800 of it. That, of course, included a great deal in accrued interest and penalties.

'As soon as that smart ass Edgar Stein, the old man's youngest son, learned that such a high loan had been made unsecured, well, Mr High and Mighty got to Liverpool by overnight train. Almost before I knew he was on the premises, he was already into the books and what he didn't find he guessed. He'd been to some kind of business school and did what he called a "comparative audit", which was comparing secured and unsecured loans I'd made over the past year. It didn't take him long to tell me that it was apparent to him that I had been favouring this Sagmaster fellow to the exclusion of all others, and that had to be for a reason, but Stein & Sons weren't interested in guessing games, and he sacked me on the spot.'

'Must have been a very bad experience,' said Charles in a tone devoid of any sympathy.

'Yes and no,' replied Derek. 'Yes, in the sense of humiliation. And no, in the sense that it turned out to be what made me what I am today.'

'Oh?' asked Charles, 'and just what are you today, as you put it?'

'Well,' said Derek, 'before the problem, I had managed to put aside a few bob. Enough to carry on on my own, and to get into trading futures using insiders who might have charged a little more for their information that usual, but invariably information that was spot on. Even before the war broke out I was fairly well off financially, and still am. Today I live on a luxury barge moored in a very respectable backwater of Oxford and, granted, the war has put quite a crimp in futures trading, but I manage to live very comfortably, and have every reason to believe such will be the case until this bloody war is over and we can get back to normal.'

Studying the much less disturbed look on Charles's face, Derek thought he had succeeded in satisfying the man's apprehensions that were so evident when this conversation opened.

'Now,' said Derek, 'I've been doing all the talking, and I want to hear what's been going on with you, and why I was so honoured as to be invited to this rendezvous.'

Chapter Fifty-two

Charles felt slightly troubled at Derek's explanation of how he had become self-employed, ending up living on a luxury barge and going about so finely attired. Charles simply didn't have the natural shrewdness to detect the flaws in logic or Derek's indicative facial expressions that would have tipped a trained investigator that the former bank manager's machinations were a load of codswallop. Still Charles sensed distrust, and felt he needed time to think it all over before deciding on any full disclosure to Derek of the plans he was making.

In response to Derek's request about what he had been doing since leaving Liverpool in 1928, Charles summarised the major events, concluding with the recent death of a retired member of the Royal Navy, whom he held 'in the highest regard'.

'Sorry to hear that, old friend,' interjected Derek, with seeming sincerity. 'I've not had such an unfortunate experience, but I suppose that sort of thing is just part of life.'

Then Charles began telling some half-truths to buy some time for making up his mind about Derek Barnett.

'Now,' said Charles, 'between living in depressing surroundings and the Government's turning much of Devon into military bases, I've decided to make some changes in where I live and where I store my coin collection. Recently I was looking over a pre-war tourist guide and I somewhat fancied the area around the village of Henley-on-Thames. The countryside was described as quite pleasant and it all seems far enough away from London to be of little interest as a bombing target. Tell me, Derek, do you have any suggestions about suitable living locations where I can wait out this bloody war?'

'Indeed I do,' beamed Derek, scarcely able to believe his possible good fortune.

'Some gentlemen and I were recently inspecting farmland in the very area you mentioned. One of that lot was considering the purchase of a fee simple not far from Henley, and asked me to join his little group for a look-round. This was only three weeks ago, as I recall. Anyway, from that little tour I can tell you the availabilities of listed properties are few, and there's nothing about that's comparable to your situation back in Liverpool. But one property we looked over comes to mind that might interest you: a twenty-acre freehold of grazing land five or so miles beyond Henley. The north side of the property is on the south bank of the Thames. Two things I recall about that property that might be of special interest to you. First, it has a well built-farmhouse that's not all that ancient. We couldn't get inside, but what we could see just peering in looked comfortable and in fit condition. Second, and this would relate to storing your coin collection, within the north property line there's a very straight cut in the river bank about thirty or forty feet long. The real-estate chappie who accompanied us explained that it was part of the beginning of some sort of bridge across the Thames someone was planning to build. Seems they only got as far as dredging out for the footing for the south end of the bridge when the war broke out, and that was the end of that project. At the surface you see nothing more than the cut in the river bank, but the excavation in the riverbed below extends out some distance. I should think that would provide an ideal place for storing your coins in some type of sturdy container, at least till this bloody war is over.

'The place didn't meet the needs of the gentlemen I was with,' he continued, 'so I presume it's still listed. The asking price was £850 pounds. I'd be happy to show you about if you're interested. If you are, I should think you would want to buy the entire freehold. The farmhouse would easily meet your living needs, and you would be right there to be certain of no unusual activity in the area of the cut.

'Well,' he concluded, 'you asked for suggestions, and those are mine.'

Charles was indeed interested, but he failed in his conscious effort not to look too impressed. The perceptive Derek Barnett read his face like an open book. He was devouring Derek's 'suggestions' as if they were a good meal.

Still, Charles had that nagging feeling about Derek Barnett. What he's suggesting, thought Charles, would surely involve him knowing where my family fortune was buried. Of course he'll know that if he's involved in my moving in any event. But with me living nearby, he could never stage the effort that would be required to retrieve it without my knowing. So he wouldn't try. I don't know, he hesitated mentally, I've simply got to think all this out.

'Tell me, Charles,' asked Derek, 'are you at all familiar with the Thames Valley?'

'Not really,' answered Charles, 'but the guide book I mentioned described it as beautiful.'

'Not "beautiful",' said Derek. ' "Bloody gorgeous" is a better description. I'm sure you'd be very impressed.'

'Tell you what, old friend,' said Charles, 'it's getting a bit on, and since you didn't book in, I gather you're planning on driving back to Oxford tonight.'

'OK,' replied Derek, 'an important meeting in the morning at 10 a.m. with some investors. Potentially quite important, that.'

I'll bet, thought Charles, as he detected a rather hollow tone in Derek's voice.

'Well enough,' said Charles. 'I want to think this all over, and I do want to discuss it with you further, particularly about that place near Henley. If I might impose just a bit on your good will, would you ring me up at that pub in Crediton, tomorrow evening at, say, seven? Do you still have that number?'

'Indeed I do,' replied Derek. 'And it will be no imposition at all. As you know,' he sighed, a bit piously, 'we don't make many true friends in this life, and although our contact since you left Liverpool hasn't been all that much, I do consider you as one of my true friends, Charles, and I hope you feel the same way.'

'Oh, but of course,' replied Charles, feigning sincerity. 'If it were otherwise I would not have, well, "tracked you down" is probably the best description of all I did to locate you. And, as I'm sure you realise, Derek, I am decidedly in need of a true friend. That's why we're both sitting here now.'

Derek virtually purred at these words, even if he did detect a slight strain in Charles's voice. He extended his hand, and the two men exchanged a firm, confirming handshake, which was appropriate to the occasion. As their hands clasped, the thought crossed Derek's devious mind that someday, he and the Rainford fortune were somehow going to get together. Just a feeling.

Charles signalled for the bill, which he paid when it arrived seconds later.

The two men rose from their small table, and proceeded to the small lobby which contained only a reception desk and a short wooden bench used mainly for luggage by new visitors while booking in. After a quick departing handshake, Charles ascended the short stairway to his room, and Derek proceeded to the car park.

Derek drove on to the A367 and proceeded toward his digs in the backwater of Oxford. The convenience of making that trip in daylight was certainly not worth the cost of a night's lodgings at the Rose & Crown.

The following morning Charles left the pub and drove south on the A367 at a very moderate speed. He was providing himself time to think about Derek Barnett. Were his doubts about this bright and capable man reasonable? By the time Charles reached Crediton, he had decided to follow the suggestion of the Lloyd's bank manager: until facts compelled a different conclusion, he would give the man the benefit of what was now little more than a visceral doubt.

When Derek calls tomorrow evening, he thought, I will tell him I want him to show me that property. And I must remember to ask him to call about in Henley to rent a small rowing boat for a few hours. One we can carry on top of my car. I'll explain I want to determine how deep that 'cut' is, which we can do in a rowing boat, out a few feet from the riverbank. I'll bring a ball of twine, and we'll simply tie a stone on an end of the twine, lower it to the river bottom and then pull it up. The length of the twine that's wet is the depth of the cut. And, I must also ask Derek to locate that real-estate chappie so we can see the inside of that farmhouse.

Charles decided to continue on to the Lloyd's Bank in Exeter where he would get the necessary cash for the next phase of his plans to move; enough to cover expenses for the inspection trip coming up, and enough to open an escrow should he decide to buy the property. Derek said the owner was asking £850. That's an asking price. He'll probably take £800. Maybe not. I'll bring £425. Half down. That should be enough to open escrow. Oh yes, I must also withdraw an extra £75 for Derek. In spite of his fine talk and his fine clothes, I noticed he didn't stay over in Bath. All of that 'meeting with investors' gibberish sounded like a load of codswallop to me. I suspect he's not that well off. Regardless, his services are worth something to me, and I'm well able to pay my way.

As Charles drove down the High Street in Exeter he was pleased to see that the Lloyd's Bank had not been visited by any excess German bombs during his absence. He concluded his business at the bank in short order, and, after a short stop at his favourite petrol station, he was on his way back to the leased estate.

By the time he arrived, Charles was satisfied he had considered all aspects in making his decisions. Yet, his inborn conservative nature told him to sleep on it before telling the O'Tooles. If he awoke in the morning in the same frame of mind, he would announce his decision to leave Devon in about four to five weeks. To assure the O'Tooles' would stay on until he was ready to leave, he would also tell them that at that time he planned to give them two additional months' pay to see them through until they got settled in a new position.

The next morning Charles awoke feeling even more certain that he was making the right decisions. He carried on as usual until it was time to go to the pub to receive Derek's call. Then he told the O'Tooles of his plans. They took the news quite well, and assured him of their continuing services until he left. Mrs O'Toole added that she would have his supper prepared within ten minutes after he got back from the pub.

Charles picked up the phone in the pub on first ring, as Derek called right on time. Then he told Derek in detail what he had decided. Derek managed to contain his delight, and took written notes so he wouldn't forget exactly what his fine friend had in mind.

'Now, Derek,' asked Charles, 'would you happen to know of a pub offering accommodation in Henley?'

'To my knowledge,' answered Derek, 'there is only one pub in Henley, the Shoe & Slipper, and yes, they offer accommodation.'

'Splendid,' replied Charles, 'now there are a few things I'd like you to do in the meantime, if you have the time. For all of which I expect to pay you, of course.'

'Don't worry about paying me,' said Derek, knowing full well he was lying. 'What can I do that will assist?'

Charles proceeded to lay out his complete agenda, including Derek's hiring a moving lorry with driver to come for his worldly belongings at Crediton, and arranging for storage in Oxford until Charles could get things squared away at the farm house.

'Oh,' said Charles, 'one further important item: I'll give you the necessary funds for all this well in advance, of course.'

'Whatever works best for you, my friend,' purred Derek.

Charles went on to describe his plans for later transferring his gold coins into one larger and much sturdier trunk, one that could withstand the Thames for a number of years.

'Another thing, Derek,' said Charles, 'what do you have in mind in terms of getting the coin cargo barged from Oxford to where we want to lower it into the Thames?'

'The man I've got in mind to help us along that line,' replied Derek, 'is a furniture manufacturer named Gordon Coleman, who owns Coleman Furniture Limited. I know of two factories he operates. One in London, and the other in Oxford. I don't know if he owns the commercial barges his company uses, but I do know that for some time he's been using two and sometimes three long barges to haul wood products he makes at his factory in Oxford. Two of those barges are often tied down overnight at Oxford. In the past I've arranged some rather swift financing for him, and I've no hesitation to call on him for a favour. He's quite a decent chap, and I expect he will co-operate if he can.'

'Wonderful,' replied Charles, 'and if you think it will expedite matters, you can tell him your friend in Devon can contribute all the ration stamps that might be required to purchase diesel for the trip. I have a very generous friend near Exeter who can be relied on should fuel be a problem.

'The barge that your furniture factory friend will hopefully be providing, my question is whether it has one of those smaller lifting cranes on the deck?'

'I've seem all three barges he uses,' answered Derek, 'and each one has just such a crane.'

'Splendid!' replied Charles, 'have in mind the large trunk being inside a large sturdy wooden box, which between us I'm sure we can manage, and, I fancy that combination will better withstand the river over the next three or four years.'

'I know nothing about such things,' said Derek, 'but what you describe sounds like good sense to me. On second thought, the whole idea sounds downright perceptive.'

'How is that?' asked Charles.

'The big trunk just sitting on my deck for a few days would hardly be noticed. That same trunk sitting on the deck of a barge moving down the Thames would be so unusual I shouldn't be surprised if any number of people reported it, what with the BBC broadcasting reminders all the time for everyone to report anything unusual immediately.'

Spot on, thought Charles, now considering that as downright perspicacious.

Overall, the telephone call with Derek lasted for a full half-hour. Charles had thought through all of the tasks, purchases and details that would end with him snugly ensconced in the farmhouse east of Henley and the bulk of his family fortune safely resting at the bottom of the cut bordering his property in the River Thames.

Charles rang off feeling quite satisfied with his thoroughness and how everything was falling into in place. The progress called for a pint of bitter, which he decided to enjoy before returning to his leased estate. When he got back, Mrs O'Toole promptly served him an unusually fine supper. After that, Charles retired to the garden, not wanting to miss any 'air show' that might occur that evening.

Surprisingly, he was no sooner seated, then an unusually large number of Klieg lights were suddenly lighting up the sky to the north-east. Shortly after that he could make out greater numbers of German bombers flying to the north-west – as if heading for London or the Midlands. They were too far away to hear their engines, but he could see them moving through the Klieg lights. Because of the distance he couldn't make out any RAF fighters, but he was sure from the occasional flash of an exploding bomber that the intruders were not exactly being greeted with open arms. What he was, in fact, witnessing was the first of seventy-five consecutive nights of the bombing of London. He was witnessing the beginning of the Blitz.

Chapter Fifty-three

Derek had accurately predicted Gordon's response to his telephone call in which he requested 'a highly confidential favour' involving a one-way barge trip with a cargo consisting of one 'quite large and heavy wooden box' that could be lifted by a standard barge crane. This cargo was to be moved from the deck of Derek's barge in Oxford to a spot along the Thames east of Henley, at which Derek and his close friend from Jersey would point out to Gordon's barge man exactly where the cargo was to be lowered into the River Thames and dropped. Derek concluded his request by telling Gordon the cargo would be on his deck for hauling as of 1 September.

'And,' Derek concluded, 'while I know you'll be reasonable, I want it understood: cost is not a factor. My friend will pay cash, and he can provide petrol ration stamps too, if you wish.'

'You've been a good friend when I needed you, Derek,' Gordon had responded, 'and if I'm able to help you, I will. The only barge operator I'd trust with such a mission is a younger man named Adam Roberts who lives and works in Lancashire. I've known him for several years and, believe me, he's the soul of integrity. Seriously, I'd trust him with my life. He's a very busy man and I can't guarantee he will be available. But there's one condition that can't be waived. Both I and Mr Roberts have to know what the cargo is, and before the cargo is hoisted to my barge, you or your friend from Jersey – whoever – has to be prepared to open the box so Adam – that is, Mr Roberts – can inspect it in advance, if he wants to.'

'With respect, Gordon,' said Derek, 'I don't understand why.'

'Very simple,' replied Gordon. 'Even though you would know nothing about it, Derek, private transactions involving great secrecy can well involve objects being traded on the black market. And that mere possibility mandates such advance inspection. There is no way I would be involved without that, and without even calling him, I can assure you Mr Roberts would make the same condition, and I wouldn't ask him to do otherwise. If your friend can't agree to that, we can stop your feeding coins into that telephone in short order. I'll be surprised if you find a bargeman the Government isn't already watching that would not tell you the same thing, but you're certainly free to look around.'

'I don't want to look around,' replied Derek, 'and I personally have no objection. My friend may think I'm taking some liberties with his privacy, but taking your word to maintain the secret, and your vouching for the integrity of this Mr Adams, I'm going to tell you, and you can have your inspection. The cargo consists of rare and very valuable gold coins. They are my friend's family fortune. My friend is Charles Rainford. His father was Edward Rainford, who was a prominent coin collector in London and Liverpool years ago. I'd imagine you can read something about his father at the Royal Museum under coin collectors. I used to store this collection when I was manager of the Stein & Sons Bank in Liverpool. You can confirm that Charles Rainford lived in Jersey before the war, if you get some hold of some pre-war literature about residents of St Helier.'

Whatever misgivings Gordon had about Derek's business reputation, what he was just said had the complete ring of the truth.

'It sounds on the up and up to me,' replied Gordon, 'I'll reach Mr Adams by phone sometime today, or at least this evening. Ring me before noon tomorrow and I'll tell you if we have a deal. If we do, I'll also be able to tell you when Mr Roberts will be available. He'll have to come by train or coach from Wigan, and pick up our barge that will be moored in Oxford.'

'And,' added Gordon, 'as an afterthought, if this Mr Rainford is unhappy with your disclosures to me and wants to make other arrangements, you can let me know. If that's the case, what you've said won't go beyond Mr Roberts and me, and we'll both forget it in no time at all.'

Derek was pleased with Gordon's proposals, which on reflection were totally reasonable. If Charles Rainford wanted to throw a fit because of the secrecy has been breached a bit, and jeopardise his big opportunity, thought Derek, well, I just don't think he will.

Chapter Fifty-four

On 6 September 1941 a tired Charles Rainford and Derek Barnett descended the three short steps on Derek's luxury barge to enter the living quarters. During the past three and a half weeks, they had accomplished a good many things. On Derek's deck stood the large, sturdy wooden box containing a large, sturdy and locked metal trunk with over £700,000 worth of gold coins inside. The entire cargo weighed almost 500 pounds. The lid of the wooden box had been nailed in place to prevent any thieves or snoopers from sneaking on board and stealing the cargo, or even having a look-see at the trunk's contents, for that matter. Adam Roberts was expected to arrive the next day by 1 p.m. with a seventy-foot commercial barge named *Lil's Prize*. If Adam insisted on viewing the cargo contents before hoisting it on board the barge's deck, Derek was ready to pry the lid off the box with a small crowbar, and Charles would unlock the enclosed trunk. As soon as Adam was satisfied with what it was he'd be hauling, Derek planned to secure the wooden lid with at least a dozen iron nails.

During those three weeks, Charles and Derek had measured the depth of the cut on the north boundary line of the twenty-acre freehold using a stone tied to the twine Charles had brought for the occasion. It was forty-eight feet: twelve feet deeper than the bottom of the River Thames in the area. The two had inspected the inside of the farmhouse on the freehold, observing it had four bedrooms, a good-sized living room and dining room, and water available when the handle was worked, which was part of small pump mounted at one end of a wooden sink in the kitchen. All things considered, Charles had decided the location adequate for his needs during the next four years. He had promptly bought the property for the negotiated price of £820.

When Gordon had called Adam right after Derek's call, he explained the circumstances fully, including the fact that Derek had proven to be a good man to know when quick short-term major funding was needed.

'You can name your own price,' Gordon had told him. 'I really owe the man a favour after his last "assistance", and I'd consider it a personal favour if you can manage it.'

Adam had agreed to do the barging, but couldn't get to it until 7 September. The agreed plan was that on the seventh he would arrive around noon at Oxford by train. That was an easy walk to the pier where Coleman Furniture had the *Sycamore* tied down. Gordon told him where Derek's barge was moored in the backwater. He would fire up the *Sycamore*, and proceed to Derek's barge. He could satisfy himself as to whether he wanted to inspect the cargo contents before hoisting it on board the *Sycamore*. When all that was tended to, he would depart with the cargo and two passengers, Derek Barnett and Charles Rainford. About five miles after passing Henley-on-Thames, his passengers would show him where he was to lower the box over the side and release it to sink to the bottom of the river.

When all that was accomplished, Adam would put his passengers ashore, and proceed to the Coleman Furniture tie-down at the Lambeth Pier in the Thames Estuary. He would tie the *Sycamore* there, call Gordon to let him know exactly where the barge was, and make his way to Victoria station for the return trip to Wigan, via Manchester. Gordon had made the special effort to impress Adam with the hyper-confidential nature of the 'job', which meant he couldn't even tell Rose or Walter entirely what this unusual mission involved. Adam later told both Rose and Walter laughingly that his brief absence on the seventh and eighth would be to perform 'a highly classified mission for Gordon, who is practically owned by the Government these days'. Rose never gave the subject another thought and Walter, who was more attuned to work life, decided that discretion did not call for further inquiry.

Charles's coin collection had been hauled in the hired lorry from Crediton in the same trunks in which it had been stored. Those trunks were just part of the larger load consisting of Charles's other belongings, which were taken to a storage facility in Oxford. They would be removed from storage as he got settled in at his farmhouse. In the dead of night, Derek and Charles had transferred most of the gold coins to the large sturdy metal trunk, which had already been enclosed within the even larger sturdy wooden box on Derek's deck, the *Barnett*. Derek had spotted the wooden box sitting empty in the yard of an ironmonger's shop in Oxford. It was delivered to Derek's barge and placed on the deck that very afternoon. Then Derek found a sturdy metal trunk that was big enough to hold the Rainford gold coins, and yet small enough to fit in the wooden box. That trunk, too, was promptly bought and delivered to Derek's barge.

Before Derek and Charles started carrying heavy cloth sacks holding gold coins to the trunk on the deck, Charles had held out the number of gold coins which would provide the funds that would meet his financial needs during the next four years. He had used the coins he'd held out to open a bank account at Lloyd's Bank in Oxford. He had also made the arrangements for transferring his monies on deposit in Exeter to the Oxford branch of the same bank. Charles's opening balance was a modest £58,196 when the transferred funds from Exeter were credited to his new account.

Indeed, these tired men had accomplished a great deal during the three weeks before 7 September 1940.

Adam steered *Lil's Prize* alongside Derek's barge at 1.30 p.m. on 7 September and was promptly greeted by Derek, who introduced his friend, Mr Rainford. After the preliminary exchange of names and shaking hands, the men got right down to business. Adam had no sense of any illicit operation going on, and volunteered that he would not have to inspect the contents of the cargo. Derek promptly hammered the iron nails into the outer edge of the lid, and Adam, just as promptly, secured the large box with his small crane cable. He returned to his barge's deck, and hoisted the cargo aboard.

As they were about to start off, Adam told the others that he had to keep his barge within the five miles per hour speed limit for the entire trip, which meant it would take at least seven hours to reach Henley. Derek and Charles hastened on board and went directly to the small passenger quarters in the bow. Within twenty minutes of arriving at Derek's barge, Adam was steering through the Oxford backwater bound for the River Thames.

Chapter Fifty-five

The trip to Henley-on-Thames was quite uneventful. The noise of the diesel engine was the only sound. Derek and Charles remained in the bow, and said little to each other during the next seven hours. It had become entirely dark by the time they arrived at Henley. Although blackout regulations were strictly observed, the moonlight readily illuminated the sign of the Shoe & Slipper public house. As they passed by, Adam could see the pub's entrance door being frequently opened and closed. By that time, Adam was getting very hungry. He decided to stop for a bite.

Knowing his passengers wanted to keep their cargo's presence as little-known as possible, he stopped well beyond the village, where he came next to the south bank of the river; the barge's shielded running lights remained on. Adam made his way along the deck to the passenger compartment, where he informed Charles and Derek he was making a brief stop to eat at the pub they had just passed.

No, his passengers didn't want to go in the pub. Each denied any hunger, and Derek produced his own bottle of sherry, assuring Adam that would do him and his friend very nicely while the captain went in for a bite.

Charles peered out of the passenger quarters, and looked about.

'Could I suggest,' he said, 'that you continue on a few hundred feet before tying down?'

'I've gone beyond the village,' replied Adam.

'What I meant,' said Charles, as if explaining to a young child, 'is that if we park, or as you say "tie down" here, the next thing you know some snooping Air Raid Warden or some other roaming-around Government type comes walking by and gets interested in that unusually large wooden box on the deck, and the next thing you know we're directed to open up that box so we can all see just what is in there! No thank you!' Charles added, 'I prefer the privacy, and I'm asking you please to move on another hundred yards or so – beyond any likely foot traffic – and then you can walk back for your meal.'

'Very well,' replied Adam, 'between my long train ride earlier and the last seven hours of standing by that tiller, I'm sure I can use the exercise.'

He returned to the stern and engaged the diesel's forward gear. His next stop was several hundred yards beyond the village. Dark. Still. Virtually out in the country. Unlikely turf for any Air Raid Wardens or 'Government types'. He planted his tie-down stake at least two feet into the edge of an adjacent pasture, and headed toward the Shoe & Slipper.

As Adam walked along the south bank of the River Thames, he noted what a nice clear night it was.

On the night of 9 September 1940, Luftwaffe Oberleutnant Hans Rudolf Schmidt, twenty-one, was flying his new and longer-ranging Ju 87-D dive bomber over the Thames Valley at 6,000 feet. For the present, his seemed the only plane aloft. Had there been a flight of several aircraft in the area, their presence would have created numerous blips on surveillance radar screens, and a number of RAF pilots would undoubtedly been scrambled to meet the challenge. Oberleutnant Schmidt could see no indications of any other aircraft aloft at the time. The moonlight made the River Thames look like a silvery snake, at least from the oberleutnant's vantage. Below, he sighted a lone barge apparently moored just outside a little village. He correctly reasoned that the village could have no military significance. The barge, however, might not be so innocent. It might be stoked with war materials.

At that particular time Oberleutnant Schmidt began experiencing a problem that was common with many German pilots flying over the UK. His gauges indicated his fuel tanks were getting low. He would soon have to return to base in northern France.

The 500-pound bomb was attached to the undercarriage of the Oberleutnant Schmidt's sleek metal wings.

Better to take out that enemy barge down there now than to run out of fuel trying to identify a 'clear military target'.

Oberleutnant Schmidt lined his plane up for an attack, and pushed his control stick forward as began his dive. His sights were neatly aimed at the centre of the *Sycamore*. Adam was taking his last bite of shepherd's pie. Charles Rainford was just placing his empty sherry glass on the small compartment's table when he heard a screaming noise from the sky that grew louder by the second. Derek heard the same noise, and his face grew dark with apprehension.

Everyone in the area heard the ever louder screaming from the diving Ju 87. Just as Adam rose from a small table in the Shoe & Slipper, the screaming was replaced by the sound of a tremendous explosion, and the earth and all structures in the area jarred and shook. All structures, that is, except *Sycamore*. Neither that barge nor its unfortunate passengers exactly jarred or shook. They exploded, as the two deadly missiles from the German dive bomber found their mark just below waterline amidships.

The resulting devastation eradicated the barge fast and furiously. The bomb's explosive effect was augmented by the fuel and fumes in the barge's tank. As the hull exploded, the fractured deck rose abruptly, hurling the large wooden box first into the adjacent shoreline, from which it rapidly sank to the bottom of the Thames, as did the entire barge and every one on it. The devastation was so immediate and complete that the entire barge, its contents and occupants simply vanished in a hale of hellfire and brimstone.

Once Oberleutnant Schmidt recovered from his bombing dive, he allowed himself the luxury of turning back for an instant to see how successful he had been. By this time, there was nothing to see where his bombs had struck but that silvery snake, the River Thames. Disappointed, he turned the bomber's nose towards France, and headed home.

Adam was one of the first to emerge from the Shoe & Slipper into the moonlit night. Several people were aimlessly rushing about, apparently looking for what had been damaged in that awful explosion. Their search proved most frustrating. No damage was apparent any place.

The fading sounds of an aircraft could be heard if one listened carefully. In the moonlit sky the aircraft could also be made out moving easterly – if one looked closely. But no one listened or looked skyward. All attention was on the local scene on the ground. Where was the damage from the explosion?

Adam realised his place was back with the *Sycamore*. He had to get his barge, passengers and cargo away from this place as quickly as possible. Who knew when the investigations of whatever happened would begin, or what such investigation would encompass? All Adam knew was this was no time to be explaining to investigators why the barge was being used to haul a cargo of privately owned gold coins – and burning rationed diesel fuel in the process!

'I was just going that way anyway,' did not strike Adam as a very satisfactory explanation. As the reasons compelling his immediate departure became clearer, Adam broke into a run along the riverbank. He had to get back to that pasture and underway as fast as possible. It was right around the next bend in the river.

As the tie-down site came into view Adam blinked his eyes in disbelief. Where was the *Sycamore*? Was he in the right place? Of course he was. The pasture started at the stone wall that ended at the south bank of the River Thames. On his way to the pub he had noticed the stones in that wall were much larger than commonly seen in the North. He was assuredly in the right place, but where was his barge?

Adam walked to the exact place where he had tied the barge down. He scanned the area closely by moonlight. He was not long in discovering the residual evidence which told the whole story. The riverbank was not far from a projection of torn pasture turf where he had pounded the tie-down stake into the soil. Adam correctly deduced that his stake had been ripped from the ground so fast it had torn out the pasture turf now projecting upwards.

Adam pondered the scene. The screaming noise had to come from a dive bomber. The bugger had sent his bombs into the barge. That thundering explosion blew her up, and the lot was on the bottom. Down there. He subconsciously pointed his right index finger to where he thought his barge, his passengers and their large wooden box of gold coins were deposited on the river's bottom.

Then Adam's eyes searched both sides of the River Thames and the adjacent pasture. No one about. He was all alone.

He suddenly recalled Gordon telling him how the owner of the gold coins was obsessed with maintaining privacy. That fits right in with him wanting me to tie down way out here, he thought. That means only those two and Gordon and me knew what we were hauling. Now it's only Gordon and me! Oh, my God. I've got to call Gordon.

Adam ran back to the village. He prevailed on the owner of the Shoe & Slipper to use his telephone. Fortunately, it was in the owner's little office, which provided the privacy that Adam needed for this call.

'Gordon,' said Adam nervously but sombrely when his Gordon answered his home phone, 'you aren't going to believe what I'm about to tell you.'

'Try me,' replied Gordon in a jaunty tone of expectancy.

Adam told him what had occurred. Gordon's 'jaunty' attitude rapidly faded as the tale unfolded.

'Book a room in the pub you're calling from,' said Gordon. 'I'll meet you there in the morning. And, Adam,' Gordon continued, 'keep to yourself. Avoid conversations with anyone. At most, you're just a stranger on his way to London, passing through and staying overnight.'

'I understand,' answered Adam.

Each man rang off feeling a heavy weight from their new secret. They were the only ones in the world who knew that a small, or possibly a great, fortune in gold coins lay at the bottom of the Thames about a quarter of a mile from where Adam had placed his call.

Adam wanted to call Rose. No. I'd never fool her, and I don't even want to start trying to. She'll just have to wait till Gordon and I sort all this out.

The Shoe & Slipper's had three bedrooms for bookings. Adam rented the last one available and retired for the night. But he hardly slept as the day's events seemed to replay endlessly in his restless mind.

Gordon and Adam met in Henley early the next morning. Three weeks later 'Gordon Coleman and Adam Roberts, joint tenants' were the names on a deed recorded in the Office of Land Registration of the county of Oxfordshire. The details leading to that result are summarised for brevity.

As Gordon suspected, the pasture in which Adam had driven his tie-down stake was owned by the County of Oxfordshire, and was available for private purchase under 'conditions' specified by the Ministry of Agriculture and Fisheries, which was represented in matters by its Divisional Office for Oxfordshire County. If a private sale of government-owned farmland was approved by local authorities, those 'conditions' included, 'such buyer's agreement that grazing rights to said property will remain in the public freehold for the duration of the current war'.

With the assistance of a greying civil servant, Gordon completed the application for purchase, which he and Adam signed and filed with the county's divisional office of the Ministry of Agriculture and Fisheries. That document described 'two acres fronting on the southerly bank of the River Thames' situated as set forth in a wordy legal description of the very two acres they wanted to acquire. The reason for purchase, Gordon had given: 'Applicants intend to construct a summer home on said land for the holiday use of their respective families in future.'

The application was quickly approved. The county could certainly use the purchase money, and the 'conditions' assured that the buyers' use of the property would not interfere with cattle-grazing, which was deemed so important to the war effort.

Gordon and Adam agreed that there would be plenty of time after this bloody war to go treasure-hunting in the watery depths that fronted on the north edge of their Thames Valley property. Until the time came that would permit them to do that discreetly, they agreed to let the entire episode remain their private little secret. Adam would determine what the *Sycamore*'s market value was. He would provide one half of that amount to Gordon, who would pay it to Lil & Rose Ltd, explaining that the barge had been at the wrong place at the right time when some German bombs found it. Nothing untruthful about that. Fortunately Lil & Rose Ltd still had a barge tied down just north of the Rufford Locks that could replace the lost barge, so Gordon's hauling needs would be barely interrupted.

With this scenario, Gordon and Adam sealed their agreement with a solemn handshake. Such was the honour and the worth of the word of men of this type. Any suggestion there be a signed agreement would have been taken as questioning that honour. Out of the question!

Chapter Fifty-six

It was almost 8 a.m. on Monday 26 July 1943. Colin Johnson was driving his dark-blue 1941 Chrysler Airflow. It was one of the last automobiles manufactured for civilian use. It had 'come off the line' three weeks after America entered the war on 8 December 1941. Colin was northbound on US 101, heading for his law office on Montgomery Street in downtown San Francisco.

For Colin Johnson life had taken on a whole new meaning since he had met Mary Roberts. This morning he had kissed his wonderful wife and winsome two-year-old toddler son goodbye at their sumptuous home in Hillsborough. This was an upscale community twelve miles south of the City, and sixteen miles from Colin's office. It was also conveniently just five miles from the San Francisco Airport.

How peaceful all this looks, he thought as he peered at the bright blue and cloudless sky over San Francisco Bay. The only visible reminders that a vicious war was going on in the world were two enormous battleships Colin saw anchored inside San Francisco Bay at Hunters Point Naval Shipyard.

As he had passed Candlestick Park, the skyline of historic San Francisco came into view. No matter how many times he saw that sight, it still fascinated him. It was not big and ugly, as he considered the skyline of New York City. It was just right.

While routinely driving to work, many people reminisce over sundry events in their lives. Colin Johnson was no exception. As he proceeded toward the only real metropolis on the West Coast, he thought, with satisfaction and amusement, how he had replenished the loss of eleven of his younger lawyers who had been drafted. His Los Angeles office had lost seven lawyers; five had been called up who were in his San Francisco office. These were all highly paid and talented young professionals. Replacing them was not an option for Colin. It was a vital necessity. The firm's list of clients had risen sharply since the US entered the war nearly two years ago. Colin Johnson & Associates now employed fourteen lawyers in his Los Angeles office, and sixteen in San Francisco.

Colin had replenished his staff by raiding the two largest law firms in California: Pillsbury, Madison & Sutro of San Francisco, and O'Melveny & Myers of Los Angeles. Having decided on his sources, Colin made discreet inquiries to lawyer friends who knew who were the talented hard working lawyers in those firms, and who were the paper pushing 'wallpaper warriors'. He selected eleven of the more capable lawyers to approach; all well above draft-age.

Colin's approach was disarmingly simple. He telephoned each of his targeted lawyers, introduced himself and invited each man separately to dinner at a first-rate restaurant to 'discuss some important matters of our mutual interest'. That, of course, was legalese for a job offer. Coming from a well-known lawyer of Colin Johnson's stature, each lawyer called accepted the invitation. At the dinner Colin was very open and above board. He made his purpose known, and then made an employment offer which he thought would work. His 'package' was a beginning salary amounting to twenty-five per cent more than the 'targeted' lawyer was currently earning, and, in the event some good clients the lawyer was in tight with decided to follow him to his new firm, the lawyer would receive fifteen per cent of all future fees generated from his tag-along clients, regardless of which lawyers in the firm did the actual work that generated the fees. He also told each man that he reviewed every lawyer's salary with him on the anniversary of his joining his firm. This involved reviewing the quantity and quality of the lawyer's work as well as his production of paid fees during the past twelve months. If those factors indicated that a raise in salary or a bonus was in order, he got it. If the review revealed the man was not producing up to par, Colin undertook to help in any reasonable way to get the man back on track.

To Colin's delight, every lawyer he sought to hire came on board, and most of them brought three or four good clients with them. Colin had hoped the eighty-five per cent of the fees generated from the tag-along clients would fund another programme he knew was inevitable once he started hiring new lawyers, some of whom would start at larger salaries than he was paying some of his long-time regulars. The only way to keep peace in the family under those circumstances was a round of raises for the regulars. As it turned out, this new source of income more than funded the round of raises from the very beginning.

Colin's amusement from his 'raiding' came about a month after the eleventh lawyer joined his firm. Then, quite by chance, Colin learned that after his new hires were all comfortably ensconced in their new offices at Colin Johnson & Associates, the 'old guard' at both the Pillsbury and O'Melveny firms still could not agree about how they should go about persuading the departed lawyers not to go with this 'fly-by-night' law firm run by that 'loner' Colin Johnson.

Colin entered the City and headed for the commercial garage at California and Sansome Streets where he customarily parked. As he passed by streets and people on the pavement, his mind wandered to the great success he had derived from taking truly big risks in hiring Laura Johnson as his San Francisco office manager. At the time, several of his associates confided to him that hiring a twenty-two-year-old girl with no law office experience for such a key position was a sure sign he had gone insane. He always responded that this was probably right, but he still trusted his own judgment, which told him that this intelligent, well-educated young woman and her no-nonsense attitude could rise to the occasion and handle the job successfully. Time had proved him right.

As he was entering the parking garage, he recalled how absolutely amazed he had been at how fast and proficiently Laura had learned her job. What he did not know was that she was being coached four to five evenings a week by the lawyer that Colin regarded as his number-one man, Mark Edwards. When Laura had reported for her first day of work back in June of 1940, she was greeted by Mark. The two had previously met at Carmel. Their friendship revived on sight, and gradually grew into a very intimate relationship that led to their marriage in 1947. Their relationship had been conducted with the utmost discretion, and well outside of the office and office hours. Neither Colin nor Mary had any idea of this blossoming romance.

When Colin walked into the lobby of his offices at 9.05 a.m., Laura told him that Mr Edgerton had already called three times for him that morning.

'Samuel Edgerton?' asked Colin.

'The one and only,' Laura answered. 'The Oakland bomb-maker, as I recall.'

'Don't let him hear you say that,' Colin cautioned lightly, 'he thinks of his business as producing the means for winning freedom.'

The office switchboard opened at 8.30 a.m. Three calls during a period of thirty-five minutes clearly indicated something urgent. Colin returned Sam Edgerton's call immediately. The phone number which the munitions maker had left was his private line, which ran to a separate telephone on his desk. As soon as he heard Colin's voice, Edgerton launched into a somewhat muddled description of 'a terrible situation' from which only Colin could 'save his bacon'.

'Now, Sam,' interrupted Colin, 'just calm down, and tell me specifically about this problem and how you think I can help.'

'You're right, Colin,' agreed the President and Chief Executive Officer of Edgerton Armaments Inc. 'I did get ahead of myself there. I'll start again.'

He began by telling Colin that he had a meeting set for 'this Wednesday' with a contract officer of the War Department in Phoenix, Arizona, that was going to be an unspeakable disaster if he wasn't able to persuade Colin to accompany him.

'Now, Sam,' said Colin, 'meetings with contract officers usually precede new business, which usually isn't all that unprofitable. How could my magic presence be so critical at such an event?'

Samuel Edgerton proceeded to tell him.

'Steve Parker, that bright spark of a general counsel on my payroll, has been negotiating a government contract with this man that calls for us to build and operate a munitions factory near Phoenix, Arizona. I've looked over Parker's draft of the proposed contract and well, Colin, it is just terrible! The way it reads now, we'd end up paying the Government to be making what they're supposed to be buying from us. It doesn't even have a provision for paying us a stipulated sum, if the Government cancels the contract – which could happen, you know, any time peace breaks out. The problem is this contract officer thinks I'm about to sign what he has worked out with our house lawyer. That's a much better label for him than his lofty title of general counsel. And I need a lawyer at this Wednesday meeting who can explain to this War Department SOB what's missing and what has to go out of this ridiculous draft of a contract, and can do that without offending the man, while also providing him with some good reasons to get his superiors' OK for what will amount to a whole new deal.

'Now, Colin,' Edgerton purred, 'I know this is asking you for a big favour and with practically no notice. I would have called earlier but I didn't read this draft until last Saturday, and I've been in a state of shock ever since.

'I know,' he went on, 'with the deal being in Phoenix, any hand-holding by your office at the signing ceremonies would ordinarily be by one of your Los Angeles lawyers. And I know you're a very busy man. But Colin, I'm looking at something I simply cannot sign, and I just can't get in the position of trying to explain to my board of directors how I lost a contract that should add about a million and a half dollars annually to our balance sheet. And I'd surely look like a fool trying to blame such a lost opportunity on our house lawyer. For God sakes, I hired him!'

After a slight pause, Edgerton concluded in a plaintive tone, 'Now Colin, be the good fellow I've always known you to be, and say yes, and maybe save one of your best old friends from a coronary while you're at it.'

Colin melted. Edgerton may not be a lawyer, but he's damn persuasive, he thought. Colin would just have to postpone a couple of scheduled meetings, and have Mark Edwards re-assign a court appearance and three other matters to associates who could make themselves available. Colin agreed to meet Samuel Edgerton for breakfast in the Biltmore Hotel in Phoenix on Wednesday. His next call was to Miller Aviation at San Francisco Airport.

'You're in luck,' Bud Miller told Colin as soon he described his flight needs. 'Burbank Aviation is trying to sell me a Lockheed Lodestar, which my chief pilot, Jack Dawson, picked up yesterday at Mines Field in LA. We've got it for a week to size it up and decide. All we have to pay for is the gas we use while we're deciding. If you and your friend pay what you'd regularly pay to go in the Stinson everyone wins.' He glanced briefly at a chart on his desk. 'San Francisco to Phoenix is 1,105 miles, with a thirty minute refuelling stop in Las Vegas both ways. Your fares will cover the gas. Jack will get a better feel for the plane on the longer haul. He can even get some desert experience while you're in Phoenix tending to business. The Stinson you would normally fly in cruises at 190 miles per hour. This Lodestar cruises at 210 and, believe me, it's a whole lot more comfortable.'

Miller did some fast calculating on a notepad, and announced, 'Total trip time in the Stinson would be over six hours each way. In the Lodestar it's just over five hours. If you leave here tomorrow by noon, you'll be in Phoenix well before sun down, and you'll get back here about five hours after you leave Phoenix.

'By the way, Colin,' Miller added, 'have you ever flown in a Lodestar?'

'No,' answered Colin, 'all I know about that plane is that it's got twin radial engines, and is supposed to be an improvement over the famous Lockheed 14 Super Electra.'

'That's right,' replied Miller, 'but the improvement is mainly in the engines. It carries up to nine passengers, plus pilot, co-pilot and some luscious little dish serving Cokes and crackers to the passengers. If you and your client make this trip to Phoenix in it, I'm afraid Chief Pilot Dawson will be your only company. I know, Colin, you never liked Cokes and crackers, and such. But seriously, you'll find the comfort inside that finely upholstered cabin is absolutely first rate.'

'Book it, my friend,' said Colin, 'I'll call my client and I don't expect any objections.'

Of course, Samuel Edgerton was delighted at the shortened flight time and flying with his lawyer would allow his lawyer to get that much more familiar with the details of the 'deal' he had to bring off in Phoenix. He omitted telling Colin that he didn't really trust aeroplanes. Instead, he agreed to meet Colin at Miller Aviation the next day at 11.30 a.m.

That evening Colin explained to Mary that he had to make this unexpected trip tomorrow to Phoenix. She understood that such events were an unavoidable part of life, and assured him she would pack his overnight bag before going to bed. When Colin told her about the nervousness he had detected in his client's voice when they made the final arrangements for going in the Lodestar, Mary refrained from telling him that she wasn't all that comfortable about flying in aeroplanes either.

Strangely, Mary had no apprehensions whatever about flying in the

Ercoupe, with Colin at the controls. They had used it to visit Aunt Lucy several times since moving to Hillsborough. That jaunt involved a short flight between San Francisco Airport and a paved landing strip just north of Monterey, barely an hour each way. When they were going to take one of those trips, Colin would phone Aunt Lucy's good-natured neighbour, Sam, and sweet-talk him into meeting their plane at the landing strip. For those short flights, Mary would hold baby Gary on her lap. He usually slept for most of the way.

At 11.30 a.m. on Tuesday 27 July 1943 Samuel Edgerton parked his big black shiny Packard sedan in the public parking area of the general aviation section at San Francisco Airport. As he was removing his overnight bag from his trunk, Colin pulled alongside him in his Chrysler Airflow. It was a short walk to Miller Aviation, where Bud Miller awaited them. On the way, Colin saw the Lockheed Lodestar being fuelled from a gas truck just outside a hangar.

After Colin introduced his client, he asked, 'How does everything look?'

'Well,' replied Bud Miller, 'there is a little matter of weather I want to go over with you. The weather report from Arizona isn't good, but I can't say it's bad either. The CAA reports—'

Colin interrupted, briefly to explain to his client that 'CAA' referred to the Civil Aviation Administration, which regulated civilian flying in the US, and provided weather information 'and a whole raft of other things'.

'Sorry to interrupt, Bud,' said Colin, 'but Sam hasn't done all that much flying, and the more he understands, the better he's going to feel about it.'

'I understand,' replied Bud Miller, 'I meet lots of people with the same state of mind.

'Anyway, CAA reports there's quite a cloud build up in the north-east part of Arizona, mainly over the Grand Canyon and the Hualapai Mountains. They don't yet know what the "on tops" of the clouds are, but they shouldn't be a problem. Phoenix Airport reports clear skies, no winds, and visibility fifteen to twenty miles. So once you've cleared the clouds, getting into the Phoenix Airport will be a routine landing.'

'So?' asked Colin, with an inquiring look.

'So,' replied Bud Miller, 'they also told me that pilots flying over that part of Arizona have reported numerous lightning flashes in the clouds, which indicate scattered thunderstorms. That probably means more than likely you'll have to have your safety belts pulled pretty snug. You know, Colin, how a plane can get bounced around in moist, unstable air.

'Of course,' he continued, 'that Lodestar is a strong all-metal airplane that can easily take being tossed around. But at least Mr Edgerton should know this flight doesn't promise to be the smoothest plane ride he'll ever take.

'And I make it a practice to warn all passengers if lightning is expected. It looks a bit scary, but statistically, lightning isn't much of a problem. I'm told that's because a plane isn't grounded. Regardless, it's been well over ten years since any lightning struck an airplane – so such a thing is hardly what you'd call a substantial risk. Regardless, you should know that lightning may be encountered and that it's more in the order of a toothless tiger.'

'Well, is it safe to make this trip?' asked Samuel Edgerton, who had got a bit unnerved when Miller started talking about lightning striking airplanes.

'I think so,' answered Bud Miller, 'Jack Dawson, my chief pilot, thinks so, but that's just our opinion. Let me put it this way, Mr Edgerton...' Miller paused. 'If it was me, I'd go, knowing I might be glad I was wearing a safety belt if and when the bouncing around starts. But you two tell me whether you want to go.'

Colin, of course, had been bounced around in aeroplanes many times and had no hesitation at all.

Samuel Edgerton gained comfort from the confident look on his lawyer's face.

'I'm game if you are,' announced Samuel Edgerton, turning to face Colin.

Colin smiled, and nodded his head toward the Lodestar. Bud Miller picked up a small microphone hung next to his desk and called for his chief pilot over the new audio system he had just had installed.

The Lodestar lifted off the runway at San Francisco at 12.44 p.m., with three persons on board: the chief pilot, the ammunition manufacturer, and his lawyer.

The first leg of their trip was in clear skies, and largely uneventful. The only inconvenience for both passengers was that they had to virtually shout to be heard over the roar of the engines.

Dawson landed at the Las Vegas airport to refill the plane's wing tanks. As he approached the area, he saw the cloud formation off to the south-east in the direction of the Grand Canyon. It was high, wide, and solid. While the fixed base operator (FBO) was filling the Lodestar's wing tanks, Dawson used the phone in the FBO's shack to call the tower at the Phoenix Airport. What weather conditions could he expect between Las Vegas and Phoenix?

Aviation weather reporting in 1943 was not a patch on what such reporting became in years to come, but it was better than nothing. As soon as the controller at Phoenix came on the line, he asked his Las Vegas caller about his CAA pilot's licence and rating, his type of aircraft, its CAA registration number, navigation equipment and cruising speed. Dawson told him he was chief pilot for Miller Aviation in San Francisco, he held a commercial transport pilot's licence and had his multi-engine rating; he was flying a Lockheed

Lodestar, which cruised at 210 miles per hour, and, 'the plane has dual RDFs'.[2]

'Well,' said the controller, 'with your rating and dual RDFs, I imagine you can get here from Las Vegas without any problem. Winds are from the west, and variable. The cloud build-up is another matter. Pilots recently flying through this area report the on tops are above operating altitudes, so you can assume that at least half of your flight will be in the soup.' [i.e. in the clouds, without any view outside of the aircraft.]

'If you're ready to copy, I can give you a flight plan that should get you here in less than two hours.'

'Ready to copy,' said Jack Dawson, as he held his pencil poised to take notes.

'After lift-off at Las Vegas,' said the controller, 'fly in tight circles until you have reached an altitude of 6,000 feet. Then depart the area on a south-east magnetic compass heading of 135 degrees and maintain, repeat, maintain the cruise altitude at 6,000 feet. Before departure, tune your right RDF – that is the RDF whose dial is on the right side of the instrument panel – to Phoenix radio station KPI, which is at 980 kilocycles. That right RDF dial is the one you will be following all the way! Tune your left RDF to 640 kilocycles. That's the number for station KPA at Prescott, Arizona. You'll probably pick up the Phoenix station about the time you reach your 6,000 feet. Prescott station KPA is not as strong, so you won't be getting any needle indications from its transmitter until you're within about fifty miles of that station. Once KPA comes in, your left RDF will show it's to your left. When your left RDF points to 9.00, you'll be passing Prescott, which means you'll be one hundred miles north of Phoenix. After passing Prescott, descend to 3,500 feet at the descent rate of 200 feet per minute. Do not descend below 3,500 feet until you have broken out of the clouds and have the ground at sight, at which time you have discretion to descend to the altitude of 3,000 feet. You'll break out of the clouds fifteen to twenty miles north of the small town of Glendale, Arizona, which is just ten miles northwest of the Phoenix airport. You can confirm Glendale by a big letter 'G' the local folks built on a hill just north of the town

---

[2] The letters 'RDF' referred to an aerial navigation instrument called a radio direction finder. After turning the RDF's radio receiver on, the pilot would tune it to a known commercial radio station. On the instrument panel in the cockpit there was a glass-enclosed circular dial which might be thought of as the face of a regular clock but had only a 'big hand' containing a needle pointer that is anchored at the centre of the dial. When the nose of the aeroplane is pointed directly at the transmitter of the radio station tuned in, the needle, or 'big hand', points to the twelve o'clock position. When the station tuned to is directly abeam the plane's left wingtip, the needle points to the nine o'clock position. When the tuned-in radio station is directly abeam the plane's right wingtip, the needle points to the three o'clock position. When the tuned-in radio station's transmitter is directly behind the plane, the needle points to the six o'clock position. The RDF does not, however, indicate anything in terms of how far away the radio station tuned in is located.

with rocks painted white.

'After you've passed over Glendale, reduce your altitude to 1,750 feet and your air speed to 110 miles per hour. Look for the rotating beacon dead ahead. That's Phoenix airport, whose field elevation is 1,080 feet. Once you see the rotating beacon, contact the tower on your air to ground radio at 1,100 megacycles. The tower will provide you with the numbers on local winds, barometric pressure and give you clearance to land.'

The controller paused briefly, and said, 'Now read all that back to me so we're both sure you've got it right.'

Jack Dawson read back the instructions, letter perfect.

'Sounds good to me,' said the controller. 'You'll undoubtedly be in a lot of moist, unstable air, so be sure you've got your puke bag close by. Otherwise, just make it a nice safe flight.'

'Roger,' said Dawson to the controller, 'and thank you very much.'

Dawson emerged from the fixed base operator's shack, and double-checked his wing tanks to be certain they had been topped – that is filled to the brim. Then he conducted a walk-around inspection of the Lodestar, looking for anything unusual, such as signs of a hydraulic leak. When he was satisfied that everything was in order, he boarded the aircraft, pulled up the door and stairway and put it into the locked position, gave his two passengers a thumbs-up, 'all is well' signal, and entered the cockpit of the Lodestar. In less than a minute, Colin and his client heard the twin engines of the Lodestar roar into life. With the engines generating power for the plane's electrical system, Dawson turned on both his right and left RDFs, and tuned them as the controller had instructed. He tuned his air-to-ground radio to the Unicom frequency to broadcast customary information regarding his plane's imminent presence aloft and his intentions for the benefit of any other pilots who happened to be flying in the area. He pressed the microphone's transmit button and spoke into it.

'Lodestar seven-niner-six taxiing at Las Vegas airport for departure on runway twenty-five, climbing above the airport to 6,000 feet and then proceeding south-east on the heading 135 degrees for Phoenix.'

Dawson waved farewell to the fixed base operator as he taxied by his shack, heading towards the east end of the runway. En route he saw the red windsock which the west wind was keeping perfectly parallel with the ground.

As he taxied on to his runway, he reached again for his microphone, pressed the 'transmit' button, and announced, 'Lockheed Lodestar seven-niner-six departing Las Vegas airport on runway twenty-five.' After taxiing into position, which meant heading straight down the runway, Dawson shoved the Lodestar's dual throttle handles full forward. Both roared to 5,200 rotations per minute, pulling the plane faster and faster down runway. When the air speed indicator needle showed a speed of 110 miles per hour, Dawson hauled back on the control yoke, and the Lodestar gracefully lifted into the sky.

The fixed base operator saw the plane climbing in tight circles for almost ten minutes, and then head to the south-east.

Everything went letter perfect for the first thirty minutes of the flight. The plane entered the clouds about ten minutes after reaching the cruise altitude of 6,000 feet. Dawson's magnetic compass heading was exactly 135 degrees. His right RDF picked up the transmission signal from Phoenix station KPI five minutes after the plane entered the enormous white clouds, the soup. The right RDF needle pointed exactly to 12.00, which told the pilot that any winds were minimal. This ideal situation abruptly changed after thirty minutes into the flight, when the Lodestar flew into vicious thunderstorms, the worst Jack Dawson had ever encountered. The plane was tossed about, violently at times, and its passengers were scared witless by the frequent flashes of lightning which briefly lit up the plane's interior, and did so with increasing frequency. Dawson was having a most difficult time maintaining both his altitude and his intended heading, when a catastrophic phenomenon of nature occurred. Something that very rarely occurs, but it did. A thick and glaring bolt of lightning almost a quarter of a mile long lashed out of the clouds and hit the left wing of the Lodestar, making contact at the exact spot where the fuel cap was recessed into the top of the left wing. The impact of that powerful bolt of lightning immediately melted the tank cap causing first the fuel vapour that had been just below the cap, and then the left wing tank to explode violently.

It serves no purpose to relate the gruesome details of what swiftly followed. The remains of the Lodestar and its human cargo were strewn over the mountaintops below, where they were discovered by search aircraft on the following day. The deadly storm by then had passed eastwards into New Mexico.

The terrible news about the Lodestar was reported first to the registered owner, Burbank Aviation in Los Angeles. Within the hour, the tragedy had been reported next to Bud Miller in San Francisco, and then to Laura Johnson at the law offices of Colin Johnson. Thereupon Laura Johnson undertook the most painful task of her entire life. She called Mary.

Chapter Fifty-seven

It was Wednesday afternoon in mid-October, 1943. After a light lunch with Aunt Lucy, Mary had walked to the nearby beach, carrying her most precious possession, little Gary, in one arm and a lightweight canvas beach chair in her other hand. She had a nondescript cloth bag looped over her left shoulder, which held an oversized beach towel, a bottle of sun-tan lotion, a small bag of cookies and a novel she had been reading in spurts. Gary's toy shovels for building sandcastles were wrapped in the beach towel. He had been walking for almost a year, but his short little steps doubled the walking time it took to walk from Aunt Lucy's to the beach.

The weather could not have been better. A cloudless sky, a comfortable warm temperature and a mild breeze. As Mary and party strolled on to the beach, she faced the vast cobalt-blue ocean that extended to the western horizon. At low tide, small breakers lapped the breakwater's edge about every half-minute. There were only a few beachcombers around, mostly older people just walking about getting their exercise.

By October of 1943, Mary had been to this beach many times. It was a beautiful setting, and ideal for swimming, sunbathing, resting, relaxing, and sand-sport recreations. Its wonderful tranquillity completely belied the fact that thousands of miles beyond that western horizon, warfare was being waged that was more lethal and vicious than the world had ever known.

After she had Gary set up on the beach towel and he had become busy with his shovels, Mary reclined in her canvas chair and tried to read her book. Her mind was so unsettled from the events of the past three months, however, that she found it difficult to become absorbed in the novel. Her concentration repeatedly strayed to the series of events that began on that awful day, 26 July, Black Tuesday. At 4.45 p.m. her phone rang and she picked it up, fully expecting to hear Colin's voice telling her he had just landed in Phoenix.

Trying to shrug off these memories, Mary sat up briefly, glanced down and saw her little boy lying on the towel with his eyes closed. He still held a toy shovel in one hand. The walk must have tired him out. Mary closed her book and decided to try taking a little snooze herself.

No such luck. After closing her eyes, her mind began straying again over the recent events that had so changed her life. They passed before her mind's eye like events unfolding on a stage.

She could see herself in collapsed devastation after receiving the hardest call

Laura Johnson had ever had to make. She recalled holding little Gary close in her arms, trying to console him. The child just stared at her. He'd never seen his mother crying. She recalled Laura and Mark Edwards arriving in Hillsborough a few hours later to console her. They brought a large over-sized envelope that they had found in the safe in Colin's office. After Laura made tea, the three of them sat at the dining room table, where Mark opened the big envelope. In it were four smaller envelopes. Each had Colin's handwriting on the front: 'Mary', 'Will', 'Policies', and 'Mark'.

Mary opened her envelope first.

It contained a short note dated 12 January 1943 in which Colin wrote that while he knew he and Mary would be laughing at 'all this' in thirty years, he would enjoy those years more, knowing that everything was in order.

The envelope labelled 'Will' contained a remarkably short document leaving Colin's entire estate to 'my wife, Mary Ann Roberts Johnson'.

The envelope labelled 'Policies' contained four life-insurance policies issued by four separate life-insurance companies, each with a face value of $1,000,000. Each policy was stamped on the face page 'Paid-Up Policy', followed by someone's initials, which authenticated the status of full payment. In the envelope containing these insurance policies was also a little note in Colin's handwriting which read:

Mary,

Those damn Democrats passed an estate tax last November, which means that between the state of California and the Federal Government, you can expect they'll drain off about half of this insurance. What's left should still see you and Gary through very comfortably.

Love, Colin

Mark opened his envelope last. He started to read it aloud. It began 'Mark, all this is just in case anything happens to me – which I thoroughly don't expect to happen – but you never know.'

He had gone on to outline how Mark and four other 'heavyweight' lawyers in the firm could form a partnership and legally continue the large and lucrative law practice under the same name: 'Law Offices of Colin Johnson & Associates'.

Mark didn't want to bore the ladies with the law office details, so he scanned the letter to something that might be of mutual interest. He found it. It was in a postscript. Mary could remember what Mark read, almost word for word.

P.S. Mark

I hope that Gary grows up wanting to become a lawyer. Although I don't have a great deal to base it on, my instinct is that he would be a natural. If he does, I hope you will encourage him. And if he gets his ticket, you will bring him into the firm.

I spoke to Ed Sutro the other day, who you probably know was a Rhodes Scholar at Oxford. I asked him whether he thought a young man who got his law degree from Oxford could pass the California Bar. 'Absolutely,' he answered, adding, 'If he took a couple of cram courses in civil procedure and community property just before he took the bar examination. All the rest is on common law, and we both know where that comes from.

While I fully expect to be around to do my own encouraging of my own son, just in case I'm not, I'm asking you as my best friend to help make all this happen, if the boy is inclined to become a lawyer.

CJ

Mary recalled the other events that kept popping into her mind. Sam's bringing Aunt Lucy up to Hillsborough and staying with them through the funeral. Laura staying with her for over a week, saying the office would just have to learn how to run itself for a while. Then her mind's eye caught the friendly face of probate lawyer Maurice Greenfield, whom Colin's will had designated to be 'the lawyer who represents my estate'. Maurice had been a great source of strength to Mary when she was so devastated she had no idea of which way to turn or what to do.

In fact, Maurice had called her just before she and Gary left for the beach. He had called to tell her that he had obtained the probate court's approval of a joint tax settlement he had reached with the California Franchise Tax Board and the US Treasury.

'That will leave you with a net estate of 2.9 million dollars over and above that modest little place you've got in Hillsborough,' he said.

'That little nest egg, Mary,' Greenfield had added, 'amounts to more money that ninety per cent of the lawyers in this country could earn in two lifetimes.'

Mary had become almost numb. She was simply not accustomed to think of money in those numbers. Inexplicably, when Greenfield said those numbers, the sight of the Roberts family's house in Gateley just flashed across her mind.

'Now, Mary,' Greenfield had continued, 'you're a smart girl and I want you to do a smart thing. You've got to understand about interest income that you can generate with the right investments of most – about eighty-five per cent – of the money you'll have in the bank after we pay off the tax parasites. That interest income alone will keep you in any life style you want to maintain. The trick is to know what those investments should be in, and how wide you should spread them. Keep in mind, all investments involve some risk. What you need is to have your investments spread out in a broad portfolio. That way you could survive in grand style even a depression twice as big as the one we just came through.'

'I'll do whatever you say, Mr Greenfield,' Mary had dutifully replied.

'Good,' replied the lawyer, 'I've got to go over all this with the best investment counsellors in the country – and, I'm delighted to tell you, they are in the same building as Colin's office. Just a block up the street from my office. I'll meet with them during the next couple of weeks. I assure you it won't take that clever lot very long to identify the sound investments and know what amounts of investment money should go where. Could you be up here, say, on 28 October? My office, around 11 a.m.?'

'I'll be there,' Mary had assured him. Then she had got on with the important business of getting everything ready to go to the beach.

Mary felt downright optimistic as she and young Gary walked to the beach. Certainly whatever her concerns were, or might become, money wasn't going to be one of them.

But in her light sleep in her canvas chair at the beach, her demons made her fitfully uncomfortable. She opened her eyes briefly at the sound of an aeroplane flying over head.

That sight triggered a new psychosis that had plagued her since Black Tuesday. Every time she saw an aeroplane aloft, she began feeling very unnatural fears and trepidations. Suddenly she would picture Colin plunging helplessly to earth. She could see the terrible fear and desperation in his face as he smashed into a mountain top in northern Arizona. The sequence became so painful her mind shut it out and went blank. Then she would find herself just standing as if coming out of a trance. Then she would feel a small sweat flush over her entire body, and she would literally quiver for several seconds.

When these episodes occurred, Mary wouldn't regain her composure for eight or nine minutes. The horror of these conscious nightmares cannot be truly described, even by the few people who have experienced them. Psychiatric care might have helped, but, as intelligent and as educated as Mary was, she still held with the vast majority of thinking in those days. Only crazy people went to psychiatrists.

Mary's quivering had just receded when little Gary awoke from his short nap. He began gabbing about something. All Mary could make out was something about Auntie Lucy and she thought she heard the word 'oshun'.

It was time for a little walk. Gary needs to wake up and I need to start thinking about other things, she said to herself.

She and Gary took a little walk along the edge of the breakwater, where the mildly breaking surf flowed over their feet at about half-minute intervals. Mother and son loved it. They walked at Gary's pace for about a half a mile before ending up back at the beach chair, the big towel, and little toy shovels. Then they strolled back to Aunt Lucy's, stopping for a little chat with Good Neighbour Sam on the way.

In October of 1943 the days were getting shorter, and the evenings were beginning to get cooler in California. The pace of life in sleepy Carmel was hardly representative of the rest of America. Thousands upon thousands of factories, great and small, had been built in the past four years. And their massive output was mainly the tools of war. Enormous aeroplane factories were being worked around the clock in Seattle, Los Angeles, San Diego, Wichita, Cincinnati, Willow Run near Detroit, and in Marietta, Georgia. They were producing the fighters and bombers that were increasingly filling the skies over Europe and Asia. Great shipbuilding yards sprang up in Seattle, in Marin County (just across the Golden Gate Bridge), in Long Beach (near Los Angeles), in Port Arthur, Texas, and all along the East Coast. They were building and launching ships faster than their enemies could sink them. The momentum was surging, and the tide was turning the fortunes of war to the Allies' favour.

Among the things that changed for ever was the long-held misperception in 'main street' America that the slanted eyes of the Japanese somehow impaired their ability to aim their weapons. The Russians had been relieved of that delusion since 1905. By 1943 the Americans had become quite amazed at the skill and tenacity with which the smaller Japanese (whom many called 'little brown monkeys') aimed their bombs, fired their guns and readily sacrificed their lives in battle.

Tim Birchall would have been the first to dispute any claims that Japanese soldiers lacked anything when it came to skill or will. By October of 1943 Tim had risen to the rank of corporal, and he had become a man among men when it came to fighting the irrepressible Japanese invasion of Burma.

His big drinking spree after learning that Mary had got married in America was a very human reaction to shut out the mental pain of it all. He did a lot of sobering up and growing up on the battleship HMS *Viceroy* on which space had been found for Tim and his mates to go from Southampton, through the Mediterranean, the Suez Canal, across the Indian Ocean to Rangoon, Burma. Unfortunately, that same battleship had gone on to Singapore to join the British Far East fleet. Six months later it lay at the bottom of the Pacific, with the dubious distinction of being the first British battleship sunk in the Battle of the Coral Sea.

By the time Tim arrived in Rangoon, he was sober, and had convinced himself that he may have stumbled into this rotten war, but since he was there, he was going to make the most of it. He proved to be an outstanding soldier.

Unfortunately, the Japanese Tiger had fought with fury and determination in the air, at sea and in the jungles. By the last quarter of 1943, the flag of the Rising Sun flew over most of Burma, and the Japanese military decided to go for an invasion of eastern India.

Tim had been engaged in a valiant but losing fight in Burma. That misfortune was seemingly compounded when he was assigned to a strange mixture of soldiers who were known as the Chindits. These daring small groups of men infiltrated Japanese lines to disrupt Japanese efforts to carry off an ill-fated plan to invade eastern India.

While the Japanese were being harassed by the Chindits in October of 1943 (and, actually, within days of Mary's little jaunt with Gary to the Carmel Beach, many thousands of miles to the east), Tim was badly wounded in a jungle firefight when a Japanese mortar shell exploded within two feet of his foxhole. Tim received relatively minor head injuries, but he also sustained a terrible concussion that cost him his memory for almost three years.

He never recalled hunkering as low as he could force himself after a Scottish sergeant major four foxholes away had hollered, 'Doon, mon, doon! It's a bad one comin'.'

That particular jungle encounter was lost by the Japanese company of soldiers, as the Chindits managed to kill them. That was the only way to win. The Japs always fought to the death.

After the attacking Japanese had been annihilated, Tim's comrades thought at first that he had been killed. But his easily detected heartbeat said otherwise. There was no greater tribute to how greatly revered Tim was by his comrades when they made the heroic decision well after midnight to carry him on a stretcher through the Japanese lines to the coastal village of Sittwe, where one of the few major resistance units in Burma was still up and running.

Upon arrival at Sittwe, Tim was still barely conscious and incapable of talking. He had no identification papers, and the language barrier between the Allied soldiers at Sittwe and Tim's saviours was insurmountable. Tim had no identification, and his saviours couldn't even tell the Sittwe soldiers his nickname. It was 'Coonejaw', which was the word for 'Englishman' in some obscure dialect. The lack of papers and the impossibilities of communication however, proved not very important. Here was clearly a British soldier. His hosts simply called him 'No Name', and a clerk recorded his arrival in a rag-tag 'journal' as an 'Unidentified British Soldier.' Incomprehensible language aside, the Sittwe contingent saw the protective deference Tim's companions showed him. Anything resembling a threat to his care and safety would have set off a grisly slaughter. Somehow, this aura of respectful consideration transferred to Tim's new protectors. Two nights after, he was put aboard a submarine that was bound for Darwin, Australia. There he was transferred to an army hospital in a suburb in the north-east of the city which had been given the aboriginal name of Berrimah. By that time Tim had acquired the nickname of Pom. The identification thing was of little importance. He had already been reported as missing in action to his family.

There wasn't a great deal by way of treatment that could be prescribed for Tim at the Berrimah hospital. The trauma to his brain from the mortar explosion had obviously involved some major disruptive damage to his brain. On the positive side, his fluency in English was unimpaired, albeit a funny kind of English which one of the doctors from Bristol quickly recognised as from the North of England. Times and priorities were such, however, that that acute discovery didn't lead to any family-tree searches.

Although Tim had no paralysis, his sense of balance was also badly impaired. His memory was as clear as a bell – starting with peering out through his head bandages on the submarine and seeing a frustrated young man in whites holding a clipboard, and repeatedly saying to him, 'What is your name? What is your name?' Before then, everything was a blank.

Initially, Tim required two strong men (hospital aides) for all movement outside his wheelchair. After several months, his treatment began to include limited use of crutches. They were later replaced by a cane, and after about six months he could walk about like everyone else.

It was during the wheelchair period that a chance event occurred that cast a long shadow into Tim Birchall's future. On 15 February, Chief Nurse Lorrain Westrum assigned a volunteer, to push the English wheelchair patient, Pom, outside for some fresh air for a couple of hours. That was when Tim Birchall met Alex Wilson, who was also a patient, and would come over and chat with him. Alex told him that he lived on his parents' farm. It was 1,000 acres.

'It's outside of Darwin,' the nineteen-year-old had implored her father, James Edward Lewis, 'and there's no danger and I want to go.'

The Lewis family owned a 150-acre farm about seventy-five miles south of Darwin in the Northern Territory. Their land was split by the Adelaide River. A surprise Japanese air raid of Darwin was made on 7 February 1942. All manner of dock facilities, ships and aircraft sitting on the ground were badly damaged. The air raid had been a great shock to the Allies in general, and the Australians in particular. Ironically, the four Japanese aircraft carriers from which the first bombers of Darwin were launched in February of 1942 (the *Akaji*, the *Kaga*, the *Horuyu* and the *Soryu*) were also the four Japanese aircraft carriers that were sunk at the Battle of Midway in June of that same year. Some additional sporadic Japanese air raids in the Northern Territory had followed, but they were made entirely against military targets, and even they ceased by November.

'My head was all wrapped in gauze bandages, with two little peepholes for me to look out through. That's where my memory starts. I can still see that flush-faced twit staring down at me asking over and over again, "What is your name?" When he stopped for a second to come up for air, I blurted out, "I don't know. I can't remember." "Well try and remember." "I can't remember."

I don't know how long that went on, but it was a conversation that went nowhere.'

'So,' he added, with his naturally friendly smile, 'let's talk about you.'

Alex proceeded to tell Tim about life on the farm 'about seventy-five miles south of here'. He followed clearly everything she described. When he got to the part about 'our old tractor that my dad's named Contrary,' he told Tim about the never-ending problems they had getting it started.

'I know what that's like,' Tim interrupted, 'but if you've checked the battery, the generator and the distributor, and they're all OK, the problem's almost always with the fuel pump or the carburettor.'

All talking suddenly stopped. The two young people just stared at each other in dumb amazement.

As Tim's convalescence had shown continued improvement, he was permitted to accompany Alex on three weekend visits to his parents' farm. That involved a two-hour train ride from Berrimah to a small train station at a village named Batchelor, Northern Territories. On each occasion, they were met by Alex's parents and his two younger brothers; the brothers who hadn't gone off to war like his two older brothers had done. The amiable Tim fitted in with the amiable Lewis family to everyone's surprise and delight. No one, including Tim, knew why, but he could do farm chores like he had been raised on a farm. No one had to tell him how to milk a cow. He even got Contrary started. He quickly found a cracked rotor in the engine's distributor.

During these visits, the family decided that Pom wasn't a proper-sounding name for such a nice young man as Tim. It was agreed that until he remembered his real name, they would call him Robert.

'I like that better, too,' Tim had responded when Alex told him what they had all decided.

At 5 p.m. on 7 May 1945, a BBC announcer informed listeners that the Germans had signed the unconditional surrender documents at General Eisenhower's headquarters at Rheims, France, and that at 11 p.m. that evening 'all shooting will stop'. In Europe, the bloodiest war which that part of the world had ever known was at an end.

The next day, 8 May was officially Victory in Europe Day (VE Day), which was celebrated mightily throughout Europe, and to a lesser extent throughout the world. In England, bands played and the people marched and danced and cheered. The celebrating went on in the big cities, the not-so-big cities, the towns large and small, and in virtually every village and hamlet. The biggest blast, of course, was in London, which had the most people and the most prominent celebrities. The massive crowd that moved endlessly between

Piccadilly Circus, Trafalgar Square and Buckingham Palace found endless voice to cheer the occasion, the Royal family, and the enormously popular Prime Minister. The Royal Family and the prime minister stood for hours on the Palace balcony, and waved back at the unprecedented milling crowds.

VE Day brought less exuberant, but very visible celebrations to the streets of Darwin and the other larger cities in Australia. It even caused a certain gaiety among the patients and staff at the Berrimah hospital. The VE Day spirit in Australia, however, was restrained in comparison with Europe, and to a lesser extent in America. After all, the Japanese were still fighting, and doing so with ever-stiffening resistance as their front moved ever closer to sacred shores of the Land of the Rising Sun. The price in blood for the island of Saipan alone was 6,825 American soldiers, 8,000-plus Japanese soldiers, and 77,000 civilians – most of whom flung themselves off coastal cliffs rather than endure the humiliation and punishments their leaders in Tokyo had assured one and all would be meted out by the 'white devil' Americans.

Around Batchelor it was just another day – even though the news was good. Robert wasn't even certain where Europe was. He was, however, reasonably sure where Maria Lewis was, most of the time.

Chapter Fifty-eight

The Second World War officially ended in early August of 1945, after Emperor Hirohito prevailed over his country's more fanatical elements and accepted the Allies' terms of unconditional surrender. For most in Europe, however, it was mainly over after VE Day.

In February of 1945 Gallup polling in Britain showed Winston Churchill with an approval rating of eighty-five per cent. Tory Party leaders unanimously agreed the time was right to schedule elections while the numbers were so favourable. The election was held in July, with the shocking result that Labour won by a landslide. No one saw it coming. The worldwide impact was seismic.

In retrospect, Mr Churchill ran one of the worst elections of his career. He delighted in demeaning his opponent, Clement Atlee, as 'a modest little man with much to be modest about'. Yet Labour offered 'full employment', and a system of national health insurance. The Tories waffled on the subject of full employment, and argued that the nation could not afford the 'enormously expensive national health plan proposals'. Yet Mr Churchill's campaign speeches often sounded the expensive theme so dear to his heart: 'Advance Britannia'.

Many voters still recalled the unemployment and homelessness that greeted many soldiers returning from the Continent after the First World War. This apprehension was felt by thousands of British troops abroad. It spread. The older men in the ranks made no secret of their wariness.

Among the after-the-facts scholars (the Twenty-twenty Hindsight Brigade) who specialised in recognising previously unrecognised causes of shocking historic events, some decided that Mr Churchill lost a good deal of popularity by his numerous visits to British combat troops in Western Europe. How? He invariably appeared smoking his trademark expensive cigars. This, so theorised the Hindsight Brigade, incurred the resentment of many soldiers, most of whom hadn't had a good cigarette in months. While historians might have some jolly good debates over these mind-reading perceptions, there can be no doubt that the massive pro-Labour ballots cast by British servicemen overseas were a solid part of Labour's receiving eighty-five per cent of the popular vote. Even Mr Gallup was surprised.

Earlier Mr Churchill had taken keen measure of a number of future events that would surely erase many of those broad smiles in that sea of humanity on VE Day that beamed the public's adulation for their Royal family and their prime minister. The Honoured Ones had waved back for hours from the balcony at Buckingham Palace. While Britain still had its Empire – which included one quarter of the world's population – the Prime Minister knew the Exchequer had been spending borrowed money for most of the past three years. To say the Government was heavily in debt was a gross understatement.

In May of 1945, Mr Churchill decided it was time to start preparing the British public for the rapidly approaching day when the Government would no longer be issuing most of the pay cheques. A touchy part of all this was avoiding misapprehensions abroad that Britain was losing her zeal to defeat the hated Japanese in south-east Asia. The Prime Minister decided to have the various ministries issue the appropriate notices that massive government employment was soon to be a thing of the past.

On 7 June 1945, directives from Ten Downing Street went to each ministry instructing that individual written notices were issued to the legion of war-production contractors that the end was in sight for the wartime economy, hence they would be well advised to start making plans for turning their 'enormous talents' towards getting things back to normal. The prime minister's directive also instructed the Ministers to 'go through the contractors' solicitors whenever they are represented by counsel', adding, 'be sure to remind them there will be a twenty-day time limit for any claims over what they will be receiving as their "Close-Out Remittance".'

The letter announcing all this to Coleman Furniture Ltd came from the Ministry of Defence. It was mailed to Steven Farnsworth of Russell & Wright, Peale House, London. It arrived on 12 June 1945.

White and Roberts' letter came from the Ministry of Transport, and was received by Sidney Blum in Wigan on 16 June. After reading the letter, Solicitor Blum had a messenger take a copy to Walter White at his office in Wigan. The lawyer enclosed a handwritten note that read:

Dear Walter,

Enclosed is a letter I have just received on your behalf from the Government. I think it translates to a warning that government funding is about to dry up.

I recall your mentioning that after the war you, Adam and Mr Coleman might go into business together. If that's still your plan, perhaps you, Adam and I should meet to discuss the matter, after which we might schedule a meeting with Mr Coleman and his solicitor. Please let me know your intentions.

Sid

Part Three
After the War

Chapter Fifty-nine

As the war ended on 15 August 1945, Mary and her young son, Gary were comfortably situated in their handsome home in Hillsborough, California. The boy had passed his fourth birthday. Fortunately, the estate inheritance from Colin had left his little family in a permanently well-provided way of life.

Mary had remained close friends with Laura Johnson, who was on the verge of announcing her engagement to Mark Edwards. She was then training her replacement to be the new office manager at the Law Offices of Colin Johnson. Mark had become the managing partner. The second most capable lawyer in the firm, Jack Duncan, had moved to Southern California to head up the law firm's Los Angeles office. Dear old Miss Cahill remained as the firm's office manager there. It had always been Colin's belief that, 'strong people surround themselves with strong people. That's what makes a strong organisation.' Time had proved him right. After the shock of his death wore off, and his law firm reorganised along the lines he had recommended in his will, it turned out that the firm lost only two clients, and both of them came back within six months. Once the war was ended, the firm's lawyers had become so close with the top management in so many major corporations, the only shift in their work was to meet the broader legal needs of big companies, rather than just making sure they were properly protected in entering into contracts with the War Department.

All this was particularly heartening to Mary, as it all portended the time when, once little Gary grew up and became a licensed lawyer, he would have a great law firm in which to hone his skills and make his own mark. Although Colin had insisted that it be Gary's decision as to whether he would become a lawyer, all of his family and youthful environment pointed him only in that direction.

Things remained much the same with Aunt Lucy. She and Mary had become very close – real family – after Colin's death. Gary, of course, was the adored family link.

Mary had experienced a major psychological impact from Colin's sudden and violent death in 1942. She became exceptionally squeamish about travelling for any long distance, and was especially apprehensive about air travel. This side of her reaction was particularly apparent in her persistent finding of 'reasons' in declining her family's numerous efforts to get her to bring her little boy over for a visit until 1951. She had eagerly tried to make up for that vacuum in her family relations by her frequent long-distance phone calls and letters. The family back in England seemed to understand without her having to pour out the anxieties that had plagued her for such a long time.

'When she's ready,' Celia had often assured James, 'she'll be back – if not to stay, I'm sure for some wonderful visits. Mary hasn't changed; she's just had to find her way out of a major family tragedy, and I know she's got the character to do that.'

Celia's mother's instinct proved unerringly accurate. Before we get to that, however, we must relate two major chains of events that took place in the lives of our main characters. The first of these chains involved Adam, Walter, Lil, and the Colemans. The second involved Tim Birchall.

Chapter Sixty

Shortly after war's end, Gordon, Walter and Adam combined their business operations, which was the unusual economic marriage of a furniture manufacturer and a commercial barge-hauling business. This union simply reflected the fact that the three men liked and trusted each other, and wanted to be in business together. White and Roberts and Coleman Furniture Ltd became a new limited-liability company in which Gordon continued to manufacture furniture, and Walter and Adam continued their barging business, while also providing all of the transportation needs of the furniture side of the business. The annual division of profits was tied to the profit production of each side of the business, which avoided anyone getting the idea that anyone was 'carrying' anyone else.

Right after the war, millions of people in Britain were without homes. Many more had homes that had been badly damaged in the war, but they patched them up to make them liveable. All this set the stage for a massive demand for simple household furniture. Gordon set out to help meet that demand, and the resources and commercial transportation know-how of Walter and Adam became a big factor in that very successful effort. Gordon bought the second assembly plant the wartime Government had built for him at fire-sale prices, and enlarged it by half. He converted that and over half of his Lambeth factory facility to producing what he called 'not upmarket furniture. Walter and Adam immediately felt the drop off in the demand for commercial barging services. They cut back their staff and barge resources accordingly. Walter moaned lightly that it seemed like some of their older barges were 'going at fire sale prices, too'. As part of filling the furniture division's transportation needs, Walter and Adam bought a dozen lorries, and converted their scheduling know-how to dispatching lorries as well as barges. The new company's transportation needs were met with the careful handling and precise timing that had been White and Roberts' trademark.

All this was just getting into smooth operation when tragedy struck. 15 January 1947 was the most grievous day that Lil White and Adam Roberts ever experienced. As Walter was getting out of bed, he suddenly felt as if someone had turned a light bulb on beneath his breastbone. He clutched his chest and pitched forward. His life was snuffed out before he hit the floor. Lil heard the commotion from the kitchen, and rushed to the bedroom. 'Devastated' would hardly describe her reaction. She was crushed. She barely mustered the strength to attend the memorial service that was held for Walter. Even doing that, she was too weak to stand. Adam was as crestfallen as if his own father had died. Manfully, he avoided tears – at least when anyone was around who might see a grown man cry. For all his grief, he maintained a confident air in the attempt to assure Lil that everything was going to be all right.

Needless to say, Walter's passing had saddened Adam and all the family as they had never experienced before. After the funeral, Adam did what he knew Walter would have wanted him to do. He carried on, and conducted the business affairs with the same thoroughness as Walter would have.

Lil simply lost the will to live after Walter was buried. She avoided being morose, but it was clear to all who knew her that she was wishing her way out of what had become an intolerably lonely life. In just under a year later, she joined her beloved Walter in that great infinity beyond. Her memorial service was held in the same church where the final farewells had been made to Walter.

Shortly after Lil died, the will which she and Walter had signed before leaving Chester was found among her papers. Her estate was promptly probated. The sole heir, of course, was Adam Roberts. Once the Inland Revenue auditors completed their appraisal of the 'Estate of Lillian White, a widow', and deducted the estate duty tax, a probate decree was officially entered on 18 November 1948, which specified that the 'sole heir and beneficiary Adam Roberts shall receive the net sum of £1,875,039'.

Adam Roberts of Wrightington, Lancashire found that he had just passed from being a man who was very well off financially to a wealthy man by any measure.

Shortly after this inheritance business was all sorted out, Gordon called Adam advising he had just received the investigator's full report on this Charles Rainford business, and why didn't they scheduled a 'business meeting' in the company's offices in Oxford to discuss the whole subject. They met on 27 November 1948.

Over the years Walter had impressed on Adam the sense and importance of keeping the extent of his assets 'strictly a private affair'. The only persons who knew Adam Robert's financial worth were his public accountant and his wife, who was admonished never to reveal it. 'That's our business and ours alone,' he told her.

And, per his verbal agreement with Gordon, Adam hadn't told even Rose about the Rainford treasure that lay on the bottom of the Thames, abutting the twelve-acre parcel of land he had bought just east of Henley-on-Thames during the war. At their first meeting in Henley after the barge had been bombed, Adam and Gordon had agreed that they wouldn't even know if they could claim the sunken treasure as theirs until after the war and they could hire a competent investigator to determine if Charles Rainford had left any heirs. If so, those heirs would be the rightful owners, and they would promptly notify them of what had happened.

Gordon had retained a first-rate London private investigation agency to sort it all out. One member of that agency's staff had been assigned to get all the facts. Now he had provided indisputable documentation that Charles Rainford, formerly of Jersey, had moved to wait out the war in England. He had lived for a time in Devon at an estate he rented near the small village of Crediton, just north of Exeter.

The only persons who could be located in connection with that tenancy were a married couple named O'Toole who were downstairs servants, whom he located working at an estate near Dorchester. He had been interviewed them, and both affirmed that Mr Rainford had been very generous when he terminated them, but had said nothing as to where he was moving. There were no documents or records of where he went. He seems to have just vanished. Of course, Gordon and Adam didn't need any private investigators to fill them in on that phase of Charles Rainford's life. The investigator reported that Charles Rainford 'most definitely' was the last of the Rainford family. No heirs.

On Jersey, Charles's seven years of total absence raised a legal presumption of his death. The investigator's documentation included a copy of an official conveyance of Charles Rainford's estate on Jersey to the Island Government 'by way of escheat because there are no heirs to inherit it'. This conveyance was recorded on 23 August 1947 in the property recorder's office in St Helier, Jersey, Channel Islands.

Gordon and Adam met in the Horse & Feathers in Oxford. After reviewing the investigator's report and the documents that accompanied it, they discussed various aspects of the Charles Rainford story. They decided to let the Rainford treasure remain at the bottom of the Thames, and think of it as a 'rainy day' fund which they might have to access someday, should there be a catastrophe like the depression of the thirties. But short of facing adversity on that order, neither man nor his family had any need of that kind of money. They were both familiar with the obscene excesses which any number of the so-called upper classes had historically indulged in – invariably from the intoxicating, if not corrupting, influence of excessive unearned inherited wealth.

'You've got no kids,' said Adam, 'and mine are healthy and happy, and I don't think they'd benefit one bit from a lot of unearned money. I'm for letting things stay as they are. If we're hit with a shocker of some kind, we might have some reason to haul it up. Meanwhile, we're both well off and doing fine. If we ever need it, we know it's there, but no need to touch it short of that. What do you say?'

'Absolutely the same thing,' replied Gordon. 'I vote to keep it our little secret. We can think of it as our "Rainy Day Fund".'

The two men shook solemnly on their agreement. That was all that was required for an ironclad agreement between honest men of honour.

'On the subject of naming things,' said Adam, 'in the not too distant future I'm planning on building a nice summer holiday home on that acreage which our families can use for ever more. It ought to have a name. Tell me, if you know, are those red trees there oak?'

'They are,' answered Gordon, 'I know that for a fact.'

'I've got it,' said Adam, as a short burst of inspiration came over him. 'I was reading a book the other day that Mary sent me about American Indians, and I came across the name of a chief named Sagamore. Just for our little joke, I think I'll call the place 'Sagamore Gold', and just let everyone wonder why that name.'

'OK,' said Gordon, highly amused. 'And to anybody who asks why that name, we'll just say because those red oaks are sheer gold as far as we're concerned.'

The men had a good laugh at this little name game.

In October of 1948, a very large summer house was completed on the twelve-acre parcel just east of Henley-on-Thames, complete with a large swimming pool, special dressing rooms and a luxurious patio. In the years to come, the Adam Roberts family and their friends made increasing use of the place, usually starting in early June.

The only other major acquisitions which Adam made in the late 1940s were dozens of parcels of land at various locations in Lancashire; usually farmland. Two grand exceptions to that pattern were the purchase of a nine-acre parcel in Lancaster along the canal and also several acres of similar land in Gateley, where he had worked at odd jobs as a child. The Lancaster investment was with an eye to building a full-service marina when the time seemed right. The Gateley investment was the only sentimental investment Adam Roberts ever made in his life.

Chapter Sixty-one

Wrightington – 22 September 1950

As Adam stepped from his car in the driveway, he could hear Rose singing some song; she was obviously singing while she was working at something. He could hear nothing but joy and cheer in her voice. The singing continued as he proceeded into the house where Rose broke from the kitchen and ran to embrace him as he was removing his sports jacket.

'My God,' he proclaimed, while receiving her almost passionate kiss, 'what's the occasion? I can't remember when I last saw you so happy.'

'It's the first anniversary,' she cried, the joyous smile never leaving her face.

'Anniversary? What anniversary?'

'One year ago today. 22 September 1949. Tim landed at Manchester Airport and we all met him. Don't you recall?'

'Oh yes,' said Adam, as Rose retreated to the kitchen to pour cups of tea for toasting the occasion.

The saga of Tim Birchall was now family lore. In 1941, at age twenty-four, this still-young man threw his draft exemption to the winds, and joined the Lancashire Fusiliers in a drunken stupor that mixed booze with jealousy. Mary Roberts, the 'girl of his dreams', had married some lawyer from San Francisco in America and the emotional impact on Tim had been more than he could handle. He escaped by going off to war. In 1944 the family received a telegram from the Government saying Tim was 'missing in action, and, under the circumstances, presumed dead'.

The family waited years before they learned what 'the circumstances' had been. Years followed without any word or suggestion that this dreadful presumption was anything but deadly accurate. Then, in early August of 1949, like a bolt out of the blue, a totally unexpected telegram was delivered by messenger to the Birchall cottage at Rufford. It was from the Australian Royal Army Headquarters in Darwin, Australia:

MR/MRS A BIRCHALL. THIS HEADQUARTERS RECEIVED PHONE CALL FROM FORMER BRITISH SOLDIER TIM BIRCHALL IN KATHERINE, NORTH. TERR. REQUESTING WE INFORM YOU HE IS ALIVE & WELL & HIS MEMORY FULLY RESTORED. HE WILL CALL YOU VIA RADIO TELEPHONE FROM DARWIN ON WEDNESDAY 18 AUGUST AT 7 P.M. GMT. THIS CALL BEING SET UP IN DARWIN WITH OVERSEAS RADIO TELEPHONE SECTION, MAIN POST OFFICE IN

MANCHESTER. IMPORTANT YOU BE THERE TO RECEIVE THIS CALL. RR WINGATE, COLONEL, COMMUNICATIONS OFFICER, RAA, HQ, DARWIN, NT, AUST.

Needless to say this telegram landed like a bombshell. The whole family was electrified. Even the *Wigan Observer* carried a short article on page three captioned:

RUFFORD SOLDIER BELIEVED DEAD REGAINS MEMORY IN AUSTRALIA

At the appointed time on 18 August, all of the Birchalls plus Adam and Rose were eagerly present in the Manchester Post Office when Tim's call was put through from Darwin. The Post Office officials put the call on a speaker phone, so everyone could hear Tim during the call. He told them that he had been an amnesia victim during the war, and had only recently recovered his memory. He would fill them in with all the details when he got home, in about three weeks. He said he had a business he was going to turn over to a good friend, but that would take a few weeks. He would send a cable when he knew just when he would arrive. He planned to get from Australia to London on military aircraft and would fly from there to Manchester.

The call lasted eight minutes. Albert and Doris were overcome by the sound of their youngest son's voice. Doris could not hold back the tears. But they were tears of joy! It is virtually impossible to describe the emotional feelings of loving parents who had spent years grieving over the tragic death of their wonderful son, and while they're still adjusting to their great loss, he suddenly turns up safe, sound and fit as a fiddle. Fortunately most parents are spared that drawn-out emotional roller-coaster. Albert and Doris regained their composure when Adam remarked as they were leaving the Manchester post office, 'All's well that ends well.' He was absolutely right!

Tim arrived at Manchester Airport at exactly 3.35 p.m. in the afternoon of Friday, 17 September 1949. The only member of the Roberts and Birchall families not there was Mary, who was still in California. Adam, however, had kept her posted on the unfolding events and she was thrilled with it all.

The family greeting party had waited expectantly for the plane carrying Tim to arrive. They stood by the wire fence that kept airport visitors from venturing out where the planes were tied down and the air traffic moved on and off the runway. At first they saw almost a black speck approaching in the sky from the south. As it grew in size, the sound of its twin engines became audible. Within minutes, they could clearly make out the approach of the single wing Vickers VC1 Viking passenger liner. The plane settled gently on the runway in a perfect three-point landing. As the pilot taxied to his designated area, airport attendants rolled portable stairs and a baggage trolley to the same location. One minute after the pilot killed the engines, the plane's exit door was pushed open from the inside. Tim was the third passenger to step through the open door. He quickly spotted his family and waved at them as he descended the stairs. Once on the tarmac he ran to them, and an extended hugging session ensued.

To call this an emotional moment for all concerned would be sheer understatement. Tim was back! And he looked like he'd never had a sick day in his life. The repeated embraces were strong and heartfelt. It was a great day indeed! Now it was time to leave the airport.

After Tim retrieved his two suitcases, the party of three trailing automobiles made its way to Wrightington. Rose and her mother had already prepared what was to be served for supper, which was dispensed with in short order, and followed by a family chinfest like no other which went late into the night.

Tim, of course, was the main speaker. During the next several hours, he told them of the main events in his life since the mortar shell exploded about two feet from the edge of his foxhole in Burma. Waking up on the submarine headed for Darwin. No memory, and numerous flesh wounds that healed uneventfully. Being sent to the Berrimah Military Hospital near Darwin. Making friends with Alex Wilson, the poor sod who lost his left forearm in New Guinea. Being discharged from the hospital in 1945 before the war was over. Assuming the name of Robert Smith.

'I'll never forget my discharge meeting with the chief neurologist the day I left the hospital. My memory hadn't changed since I came to on the submarine. I had no memory problems with anything that happened after that. But before that, everything was a total blank. Now, no pity here, we've got too much to be glad about for any of that. But I'll tell you having no memory is an awful feeling. You can talk with people. Understand them. You can do a lot of things you've no idea how you learned to do. But before a certain time – nothing. I didn't even know I was English till I heard a doctor say to another doctor, "From his accent he's obviously from England. North of England, I'd say." I had no idea what all that meant, but I did notice that doctor sounded kinda funny. Later I learned he was the one with the accent. Most of the Aussies sounded just like him.'

Everyone had a laugh at that remark, but they kept it short, as they wanted Tim to continue his story of what had happened over the past nine years.

'Well,' Tim continued, 'at that discharge meeting with the chief neurosurgeon I learned more than I thought I was learning at the time. Fact is, at the time I thought he was trying to cheer me up and give me some hope. He told me that the brain is like every other part of the body. If it's injured, it tries to heal itself. And, what was that medical term he used? Oh yes, "traumatic amnesia", that's what he said I had. He said I'd had a very bad brain concussion. Probably I'd been way too close to a violent explosion that had jarred my head so violently the "memory circuits to my long term memory had simply been broken". When he gathered that I wasn't exactly following what he was saying, he told me there had been a break in the electric communication lines that connect long-term memory to my present consciousness. He also said with my good health, youth, and lack of any bad habits, he felt sure the healing process was going on, and one fine day – just when, no one could predict – the connections would be restored, and everything would come back to me. Just like that. Without warning. The electric impulses would start flowing again by way of a new route and all the lights would go on. When it happens I would remember everything the same as if I hadn't had the concussion.'

You could have heard a pin drop in the room as Tim was telling his strange story. Whenever Rose would decide to replenish the tea in everyone's cup, she'd ask him to 'hold up just a minute, Tim, while I get us all another round of tea.' When that was completed, they all turned back to Tim as if to say, 'Yes, go on. Tell us the rest.'

He told how he had gone with fellow patient Alex Wilson on several weekends to his home that was a big farm ('750 acres') near a little town named Katherine about 200 miles south of Darwin. There he'd met his friend's family. 'Lovely people, the Wilsons. Pots of money. Household staff. Field hands. Bunk house. Servant's quarters. The lot. They grew sorghum and oats as animal food, and raised beef cattle for market.'

'That wall,' he continued, 'started a series of events that changed my life. Other farmers in the area saw the wall, and they started asking me to build drystone walls on their places. It got to be such a thing that I asked Mr Wilson to cut my monthly pay in half so I could spend half my time in what I called my "stone wall business". By then, the war was over, and there wasn't such a manpower shortage, so he said OK and I was suddenly the drystone wall builder in Katherine, Northern Territory. About a year later I had saved enough money to buy a good part of the mountain where I got my limestone from, and even that started to run out and that started a chain of things that really made a big difference with me.

'I knew the time was approaching that if I was going to get more limestone out of that mountain some dynamite blasting would be needed, which was something I knew nothing about – and instinctively, I didn't much care for blasting in the first place. Since my memory came back, I think I know why. Anyway, one day when I was getting something in the dry goods store in Katherine I heard an older man who sort of hung around there talking about when he was in the mines. I stopped him and asked if he had any experience in blasting rock. He gave me a condescending smile like he was looking at a friendly idiot and said, "Well, a little, lad. A little! Like about twenty years of it!" I hired him on the spot.

'It took almost two weeks to get the dynamite from Darwin, but we got it all set up, and one Saturday we shook the countryside, blasting stone in what was by then my mountain. At least sixty acres of it. Now I know that doesn't sound too exciting, but let me tell you what happened. In what proved to be our last blasting explosion, lo and behold a sheet of limestone almost hundred feet square fell away from the side of the mountain, and there it was!'

'What was?' asked John, eagerly following the discourse.

'The most beautiful underground spring you could imagine. And flowing from an opening high up in the newly exposed wall, into a trough it had cut out of a ledge about thirty feet below. I had never seen water that blue, except maybe in the Mediterranean when I was going out to Burma early in the war. It was a beautiful blue. I didn't know that water could look like that, but I knew it was something special. The next day I asked the schoolteacher in Katherine if she could tell me who might know about this sort of thing, and she said a hydrologist. That's an expert on water and water flowing both above and below ground level. I got the name of one from a phone book they had in the dry goods store who was located in Darwin. I called him, and he came down during the next week. He seemed just as amazed as I was at that water. I remember when he first saw it, I heard him say to himself, "That's the bluest luminescence I've ever seen."

'He set a metering device in the water flow in the ledge, and left it there for a long time; over an hour. The dial stayed solidly on one number, I think it was thirty-five. "What does that tell you?" I asked. "It measures the speed the water is moving. Just how fast isn't important, but if it stays at one rate, that indicates a stable long term source of water. If the speed varies, you've got a big question mark that makes any investment in marketing the water very risky. This stream is clearly constant. I'll take some samples to analyse, and if this water is the quality of mineral water I think it is, I'm going to give you some advice that will make you forget about limestone."

'Well,' Tim said, 'long story short, the source rated as "year-round", and after testing it, this hydrologist told me it was the richest mineral water he'd ever seen. Within a week I signed what they call a licence-royalty agreement with one of the biggest mineral water companies in Australia. A company named Grave Haven Mineral Water Company. Their headquarters are at Mount Tambourine, Queensland – which is the second biggest state in Australia, and makes up the whole north-east part of the country.'

'You mean you still own the mountain with this spring in it?' asked John.

'I do,' answered Tim, 'and as long as people are buying mineral water coming from it – all being sold by the Grave Haven Mineral Water Company of course – I am paid a wee bit as royalty to the owner who licenses them to collect it on my property – very special stuff, I'm told – they bottle it, and they sell it. Before I left Australia, everything was set up for Grave Haven to send my royalties to Lloyd's Bank in Wigan.'

Everyone looked at each other and back at Tim in wonderment.

'You mean you're rich?' asked Rose.

'Oh, I wouldn't go that far,' replied Tim, smiling, 'but it is comforting to know a few quid are coming in every month, and I won't have to worry about spending a lot of time at the labour exchange.'

Tim did not want to talk about money and quickly changed the subject.

'Anyway, after Grave Haven got their facilities built in and started withdrawing water, I cut way back on building drystone walls, and I got my limestone from other locations thereabouts. That's not very exciting stuff. The real miracle happened on the day my memory returned. That was only about five weeks ago. 4 August to be exact. It was about noontime. I was sitting on my tractor, about to get off to have a couple of sandwiches, and I had a strange feeling right in the middle of my head. It wasn't a pain. It was just a feeling like something had shifted and I couldn't tell what. Then I heard myself say, "I'm not Robert Smith. I'm Tim Birchall and I'm from Rufford, Lancashire in England." And then my memories just came in gushers. I remembered everything up to where the old Scot sergeant, Rob, hollered out, "Down lads. Down. This one's a bad'n." Then I remembered waking up and I was on a submarine peeking out through the bandages that covered my entire head and neck. I just can't describe how wonderful getting back my memory was, and still is, for that matter. It happened just like that chief neurologist had described. All of a sudden the lights go on, and everything you could remember about yourself and your life is right there.

'Oh,' Tim sputtered a bit, 'there was one thing I forgot to mention. That doctor also told me that "the literature doesn't report one case where a traumatic amnesia victim who has regained his memory has lost it again." I remember asking him just what all that meant, and he translated it: "What it means is that doctors report these sort of things in articles they write in medical books and medical journals." That's what 'the literature' refers to. And from what is reported in those places it's clear that when God, or Mother Nature, or whoever does it, gets the new circuits connected between your long-term memory and your conscious memory, which is what you're aware of right now, it stays rewired. There's no record of any amnesia victim who got his memory back because nature healed his brain ever losing it again. He said, "When you're rewired, you're rewired, and that repair sticks".'

'Well, not really,' he had said, 'I don't know just who I'd go back to.'

In late September of 1945 it happened. Night had fallen, and Tim and Lillian had gone for a leisurely stroll through a grove of red gum trees located north of the Wilson farm across Giles Road. They walked hand in hand, ever deeper into the grove. When they were quite alone, they began embracing, and before long emotions and physical attraction began to dominate the scene. While neither of them had mentally planned any such thing, when reason was restored, they realised they were lying beneath a large tree, each only partially dressed, and both suddenly beginning to feel pangs of guilt. Tim didn't know why, but he knew he had gone too far. Lillian was even hasty in restoring her blouse to its proper position, and began fearing that Tim would no longer respect her.

He had pulled her close, and said, 'Let's just pretend this never happened,' and gave her a very good natured smile.

Lillian was almost grateful for his attitude, and said, 'Oh yes. That's what I want more than anything.' This agreement was sealed with a light kiss – no more displays of passion. They walked back to the Wilson place hand in hand, during which each abandoned the effort to make small talk, as if nothing had happened. Nothing more had happened in that romance. Lillian actually felt ashamed, and avoided being alone with Tim. Then, two months later she left without notice and without explanation. When Tim inquired of Mr Wilson, he replied, 'I've no idea. She didn't even say goodbye. We're still trying to figure it out. I'd contact her parents to be sure she was well and safe, but I've no idea who or where they are.'

Although the somewhat brief encounter with Lillian Foster often crossed Tim's mind, all that was long ago and far away. Certainly no business of anyone here, he thought as the evening was drawing to a bit of a late close.

'What are your plans here for now?' asked Albert.

'Well, for tonight I'd like my old room back. Then I'd like to get set up in the old farmhouse on our 200 acres between Burscough and Parbold,' answered Tim, 'assuming we still own it.' He looked directly at John. 'Oh, we do,' said John. 'And you're in luck. Our tenant moved out six weeks ago, and all we have to do is tidy the place up a bit, and you've got living quarters that make Adam's place here look like a castle.'

Everyone giggled, as humour was not John's long suit for sure.

'And,' said Tim, 'Maybe I can show John a thing or two about building drystone walls, and maybe he'll give me a job in construction.'

'Not a worry whatever,' John spoke up. 'Things went crazy right after the war, and then they slowed down badly. But for the last six months I've signed up more work than I've had since August of 1945. We'll work it out just fine.'

Tim felt a wonderful, confident glow. He had already been briefed very privately by Rose as to where Mary was, and how she lived in California with her one son. Rose had also said Adam was hopeful of luring her over for a visit in the not too distant future. After they got the telegram from the Australian

Army Headquarters that Tim was alive and would be calling, Adam called Mary within the hour. Later he said she was thrilled at the news, and that's when he said he felt sure he'd lure her back for a visit soon.

It had been a long day for everyone, particularly Tim. The party broke up. James and Celia stayed over at Adam's. John, May and their son, Little Jack, left for their home, and Tim accompanied his parents back to Rufford. That night he slept in his old bed for the first time in nearly ten years. It was nearly dawn before he nodded off to sleep.

Chapter Sixty-two

The year was 1951. Mary Roberts had been in America for thirteen years. As she lay on the sun lounger, by the pool, in her beautiful home in California, letting her mind go back over the last nine years. It had been that long since her beloved husband Colin had lost his life in a tragic plane crash, leaving her alone to raise their only son Gary, who was two years old. On many occasions, Mary had planned to go to England to see her dear parents and brother Adam. Several reasons had prevented her from making the trip. The main one was her fear of flying, and the thought that would not go away: what if something happened to her? It would leave their only son an orphan. This nightmare had been with her for years, but with the help of Aunt Lucy, Laura, and Colin's friends, plus the fact that airline travel was now much more reliable, and safe, in the last year she had felt more confident, and had announced that at last she was going to England.

Mary began making plans to make a new future for herself and her son. She would try to make the dream come true that Colin always wanted for his son. With her financial position she would make sure that her parents would have whatever they wanted. Having thought all this out, it was now time to tell Aunt Lucy.

Gary still had three more weeks before he would have to go back to boarding school. Mary decided to spend as much time with him as possible before leaving. Some years back, Colin had bought a property in Bear Valley. Mary had only visited it once. It was a large cabin with two bedrooms, two baths, a nice kitchen, large lounge with stone fireplace, and a large basement, and it had a wrap-around deck that was literally in the treetops. There were dozens of cabins, each set in a three-acre lot. There was a large clubhouse, pool, restaurant, horse riding, and tennis facilities. Mary decided it would be nice to take Gary, his friend Tony and Aunt Lucy. Tony's mother was grateful, she had five-year-old twins and found it hard to keep Tony occupied. 'It will be a nice break for me, and I know Tony will love it,' she said. 'Thank you very much.'

The next two weeks went by too quickly for everyone, especially Gary and Tony. They enjoyed every minute, filling their time with climbing trees, swimming, and all the things that boys at that age do. The time had also given Mary the chance to have a serious chat with Aunt Lucy regarding her visit. When Mary first mentioned that she would be buying a property in Oxford,

Aunt Lucy's face took on a worried look. 'Will you and Gary be moving to England permanently?' she asked. Mary took hold of Aunt Lucy hands.

'There is nothing in this world would make me leave you,' she replied. 'I am going because I want to see my parents and my dear brother, and to plan for Gary what Colin always talked about.' Then bringing her closer, she said, 'On my next visit I want you and Gary to come with me and meet all my family.' Aunt Lucy smiled; it was obvious that what Mary had said put her mind at rest.

On their return, Mary had the peace of mind that in her absence, Aunt Lucy, Laura and Mark would make sure that on visiting days at Gary's school, they would visit him. When she brought up the subject with Gary, he thought it was a wonderful idea; the thought of his mother being a little selfish never crossed his mind.

It was decided that Mary would make the trip by the new, magically fast, commercial airliner in April 1951. She visited Wendell's International Travel in San Francisco, which Colin had always used. The travel agent there figured out an itinerary that would have Mary leaving San Francisco early on Sunday 1 April and returning on a flight, leaving Heathrow on Saturday 12 May. She would fly both ways first-class on a Lockheed Constellation of Trans World Airlines (TWA), with a one-day stop over in New York recommended to ease the effects of eight one-hour time zones.

When the travel agent completed outlining what could be arranged, including the overnight stay at the Warwick Hotel, New York, Mary replied with a touch of determination in her voice, 'Wrap it up, I will take it.'

This will get me back over a month before school is out, she thought. Gary will be so occupied at school that he won't even miss me. However, he will. And I will miss him, too. I will just think of it all as part of growing up.

Mary was back in Carmel before 5 p.m. that afternoon. Before leaving San Francisco, she drove out to Pacific Heights to visit her best friend Laura, now Mrs Mark Edwards. Mark and Laura had married in 1947 after Laura had trained another college graduate with great promise but no legal experience to become the manager of the San Francisco office. Miss Cahill remained in the Los Angeles office of the law firm, and was so fit and trim it looked like she would be there for ever. Colin's estimate that she would never leave Southern California proved right.

Mary's visit with Laura was necessarily short. Because she wanted to get back to Carmel and spend a few hours with Gary after class let out for the day and before he would have to go back for dinner at the Fox Point Academy. She drove south on US 101 after her visit with Laura. She admitted to herself that while the arrangements could have been done over the telephone, she had wanted to meet Laura to assure herself that Laura was truly in favour of this trip. And would help Aunt Lucy to look after Gary during her absence, on the weekends which he always spent at Aunt Lucy's, Laura's enthusiasm for the whole idea was effusive. Mary now had a good feeling about the whole thing.

She drove into the Fox Point Academy car park exactly ten minutes before the last class of the day was over.

If all the timing during the next couple of months goes like today, it will be a fabulous trip, she thought.

That night Mary placed a long-distance overseas telephone call to Adam. In order to catch him at home at 8 a.m. in England, her call from California had to go through at midnight on the West Coast. In 1951, overseas long-distance calling was far different than it was later to become with the introduction of computers and mobile phones. At 11.15 that night, Mary called the overseas long distance operator at the telephone company in Salina. She gave her all the information required for placing a call. The phone in Adam's house rang as Rose was pouring Adam a cup of tea. It was 8 a.m.

Adam was, of course, thrilled when Mary told him of her travel plans. She could hear the enthusiasm in his voice.

'Oh yes, Adam', Mary added, 'an important thing the travel agent told me to suggest to you. My scheduled arrival time at Heathrow is more of an estimate than anything. Weather over the North Atlantic is unpredictable at this time of year, and he suggested that a delay was very possible after arriving at Shannon, Ireland, which is the last refuelling stop; passengers are put up in a good hotel then fly on to Heathrow the following morning. The agent said it would be better if only one person comes to meet me, so that if there is a delay only one person has to book in a hotel at Heathrow.'

'That makes good sense to me.'

'I thought you would say that!' I will leave it to you to convince the rest of the family that only you should make the trip to London. According to my ticket, I'm due to arrive on 4 April at 7.20 p.m.'

Adam said he would pack an overnight bag just in case, then they brought their long-distance call to an end.

Chapter Sixty-three

Mark, Laura and Aunt Lucy had just said their goodbyes to Mary and promised to look after Gary after dropping her off at the airport. Mary was about to start the first leg of her flight to England. Having booked in, she was enjoying a coffee in the first-class departure lounge. It was another forty-five minutes before boarding and there were several other passengers sitting there: a middle-aged couple, three younger men who all seemed to be travelling alone, and the last person to enter the lounge, who was a very well-dressed woman, Mary quickly put her age at thirty-something. She took the lounge chair next to Mary, and immediately introduced herself as Coleen McMann. She had been in America for several weeks, visiting relatives.

'I have enjoyed it but I'll be pleased to get back home to Ireland.'

Although she was a very talkative person, and a little loud, Mary knew she would like her.

'My name is Mary Johnson and I am travelling to England. It will be my first long flight.'

Coleen put her hand on Mary's shoulder.

'Don't worry, dear, I fly all the time. You will enjoy it.'

Just then, a smart young woman appeared in a blue and yellow uniform and announced, 'Ladies and gentlemen, it is now time to board.'

All the passengers were escorted across the concrete apron to where the Lockheed Constellation was waiting. Coleen may have requested it, or it may have just been coincidence, but Mary was shown to the seat next to Coleen.

The flight to New York would take seven hours, Once they had taken off and reached a cruising height of 27,000 feet, the stewardess came round with drinks. Both Mary and Coleen had a gin and tonic. They began to chat; anyone would have thought that they were old friends. Coleen willingly told how her grandfather had owned a big racehorse-training establishment in County Wicklow, Ireland.

'When he died my father took it over, and trained the winner of last year's Grand National, Shelia's Cottage, a seven-year-old mare. I have one brother who works for him and no doubt will one day take over. I love horses and like to ride but that is were it stops, I could never spend my whole life working with them. I did get married twelve years ago but it only lasted three years; my father warned me that he was a loser.

'I did a lot of the office work in the family business, and still do. I have my own house on the estate. Fortunately we have 500 acres and I am far enough away from the stables.'

Mary had to assume what benefit that was.

The first hour of the flight had gone and Mary was feeling a little sleepy as she had been up very early. Without sounding too rude she said, 'That's very interesting, Coleen. Do you mind if we continue our conversation later? I would like to close my eyes for a while.'

'Of course, dear, I know I go on a bit, but come to think of it, I feel a little sleepy, too. I will just have another gin and tonic, then I will have a little nap.'

Both ladies must have fallen asleep as the stewardess woke them both to say, 'We will be serving lunch shortly. We have a choice of fresh salmon salad, or chicken noodle salad. Desserts are choc mel muffins, and maple pears with cranberries.

Coleen spoke first.

'I feel so much better,' she said, then to the stewardess, 'I will have the salmon please.'

Mary nodded her approval.

'Yes, I will have the same please.'

After a quick freshen-up, they both settled in their really comfortable first-class seats. The steward put the little folding table in position and asked what they would like to drink with their meal. The stewardess was surprised to hear them both ask for water.

The meal was very nice and everyone aboard seemed to enjoy it. Coleen turned to Mary.

'Now, dear, tell me about yourself. How did you come to be in America?'

Normally, Mary would not have volunteered information like that to anyone other than close friends and family. However from the very first moment, she had that feeling that Coleen was a genuine person.

Mary, for whatever reason, felt really relaxed and wondered if she would have felt like that if she had not met Coleen.

She began, 'Well, unlike you, Coleen, I was born in the North of England, in very happy, but poor circumstances. I have one brother, whose name is Adam. My dear parents are still living and I am happy to say in much better circumstances, thanks to the good fortune of my brother and me. I always loved school, and worked very hard to educate myself as much as possible. When I was eighteen, the schoolmaster, Mr Amos Cooper, got me on a student exchange programme to America, along with three other girls –' she looked at Coleen – 'one of the girls came from Ireland, and yes, her name was Linda. Anyway, we were only supposed to be on a one-year student exchange, then as you know, the war started.'

There was a little pause, as though Mary was already getting a little emotional.

'We could not get back. I had a boyfriend in England who hoped we would marry on my return. All that and much more did not happen.' Mary explained how after a while she met Colin and they married. She omitted to mention that Colin had died, but continued, 'I have not seen my dear brother and parents for thirteen years.' At this point, Coleen noticed a little break in Mary's voice.

'If you don't feel like talking, don't go upsetting yourself. I understand.'

Mary composed herself, 'No, I am sorry. It's so long ago, but somehow I feel better telling you.'

She then told Coleen about how Colin had died, although this may have not been the place to say that, and very briefly the thought flashed into her mind, What if?

Suddenly Mary sat up straight in her seat. Neither Coleen or Mary realised how long they had been chatting. The stewardess informed them that they would be landing at New York International airport in one hour and asked if they would like another drink. Mary and Coleen asked for coffee.

On arrival in New York, they shared a cab to the Warwick Hotel, which was situated in Midtown, near the Rockefeller Center, an ideal position for seeing shows and upmarket shopping. Coleen and Mary were the only two people who would be flying on to Shannon, Ireland the following evening, which was how they came to be in the same hotel. After they had settled in their respective rooms, showered, and changed, they met in the bar. It was 8 p.m. They decided over a drink to walk the short distance to a little Chinese restaurant, the Tang Pavilion, two blocks away. The hotel was almost full, the barman informed them, the reason being the Broadway show *The King and I*, with Yul Brynner and Gertrude Lawrence. Also, the next night there was a big boxing match on at Madison Square Garden.

The ladies did not comment on the boxing match, but both were disappointed that they would not have the time to see *The King and I* because of their flight arrangements.

The evening was very enjoyable and they had a really nice meal. Then got into a conversation with a couple from Boston who had tickets for *The King and I* the following night, and were very excited. Back at the hotel they had a nightcap, then both decided that they would get some sleep. They said goodnight like old friends.

The next morning after an early breakfast, the airline taxi collected them and took them to the airport. It was 9.45 a.m. when they took off. Mary would spend another night at Shannon Airport before taking the short flight to Heathrow the next morning.

Seven hours later they arrived at Shannon airport after a very enjoyable flight. Mary had to admit, the company of Coleen had made it much more interesting than it otherwise would have been.

After collecting their luggage, Coleen had to go on to County Wicklow, which was a two-hour drive. Mary on the other hand would have to spend a night in the airport hotel. They had exchanged telephone contact numbers, and promised to keep in touch. Suddenly, Coleen said, 'Why don't you come home with me? We can have dinner with my parents, and Dad will get one of the lads to bring you back here tomorrow, in time for your afternoon flight. It will be better than spending a night here on your own.'

At first, Mary dismissed the idea, but then thought, Why not? This is the first time I have been to Ireland. Turning to Coleen, she said, 'If you're sure you don't mind, I would love to come.'

'Right, that's settled. You can leave your main luggage here – just bring your small bag. I will call my Mum to say we are on our way.'

Outside the airport, there were several taxis waiting in line for fares. Coleen went straight to the first one, 'Could you take us to McMann's Racing Stables?'

'I sure can, me darlings. It's a one-hour drive, but being such a powerful morning I'm sure you will enjoy every mile.'

The driver was a typical Irish cabbie full of the blarney. 'I'll take you the scenic route at no extra charge.'

Coleen winked at Mary and whispered, 'He will just expect a double tip.'

Within minutes the girls were on their way. Immediately Shaun, the driver, started giving the commentary that he had obviously made a hundred times.

County Wicklow is a place of spectacular valleys, like the Glenmature, Glencree, and the famous Glendalough, famed for its beautiful scenery and historic monuments. The majestic mountains completed the picture. Mary was awestruck; she had seen lovely places in America and had got used to mountains and valleys in California, but the bonus here was the greenery. Coleen pointed out the monastery which was founded by St Kevin in the sixth century. The settlement expanded and flourished for many years before being destroyed in the sixteenth century. The buildings that survived date from the eighth century, the main one being the superb round tower.

Another few miles and it became obvious that they were on the McMann's land; there were dozens of beautiful horses. Coleen pointed out that most of them were mares with their foals. She explained that, in two years' time the little ones would go into serious training, if they made the grade. Coleen tapped Shaun on the shoulder. This was it. They turned and went through massive wrought-iron gates with two full-size horse sculptures and the wording 'Patrick McMann's Racing Stables'.

After another half-mile or so, Mary saw one of the grandest houses she had ever seen. It was all built of stone and was, Coleen explained, part of the old brewery house. The stables used to be the workers' cottages. Her grandfather had bought it in 1912.

They both thanked Shaun and to his delight gave him a nice tip. Looking at his face it was probably the best tip he had every had. Mary was about to ask him to come for her tomorrow when Coleen said there was no need as it was all arranged.

The big door opened and a woman came out. She was about sixty, but really very good-looking, and one could see she had had a good life.

Coleen ran towards her.

'Oh, Mum, I enjoyed my trip but I am pleased to be back.' Turning to Mary, she said, 'This is my mother.'

Then said to her mother, 'This is my American friend, Mary,' quickly adding, 'Well, she is not really American but has lived there some time.'

Coleen's mother reached out and shook Mary's hand. 'You are very welcome, dear. My name is Claire. Come on, let's go inside.'

Inside Mary's surprises continued. The style and furnishings were in keeping with the grandeur of the house. Claire suggested to her daughter, 'Coleen, take Mary up to the guest room. When you have both freshened up, come down and we will have tea. Your father won't be back until six.'

Mary was wishing she had brought her camera with her; the room she had was unbelievable. She had a shower then changed into the wool suit that she had kept in her hand luggage, anticipating cooler weather. There was a tap on the door.

'Are you ready, Mary?'

It was Coleen. She too had made a quick change. They both went down into the kitchen. In one corner was a large Rayburn cooker with a magnificent array of pans and kitchenware. A long table stood in the centre that would seat a dozen people. The floor was made of slate and two old beams stretched across the ceiling.

The three ladies had tea and cakes. Mary was pleased that Claire took over the conversation. She was also very pleased that she was not inquisitive; the only thing she asked Mary was how long she could stay. When Mary said only that night as she had to get the flight to London tomorrow, Claire was obviously disappointed.

'Oh dear, can you not stop over the weekend?'

'No, I must go tomorrow. My family are expecting me.'

Claire looked a little puzzled. 'Why can't she stay a few days? It won't make much difference.'

As though reading her mother's thoughts, Coleen said, 'Mary has not seen her family for thirteen years.' That of course made Mary feel that she had to give some explanation. Coleen once again came to the rescue.

'I will tell you all about it later, Mam,' she said.

During the next hour Mary enjoyed a tour of the house, which was in no small terms very impressive. Claire announced that they would have drinks in the study at 7 and have dinner at 8.

At 7.15, Claire, Mary and Coleen were enjoying a class of wine in the study. Mary was admiring a large array of silver cups and gold medals. Among the many pictures, mostly of horses that had won big races, there was one which was obviously Patrick McMann. He was being presented with a large trophy by Her Majesty the Queen.

Suddenly the door opened and two men came in. The older one was Mr McMann. He was a very smart man and went straight to his wife.

'Sorry we are a little late, dear,' he said then he gave his daughter a big hug. 'How did you enjoy your trip? How was your Uncle Martin and Aunt Catherine?'

She answered, 'They're all fine. Dad, this is my friend, Mary.'

They shook hands, then Coleen said, 'This is my little brother, Brennan.' He was hardly little, standing a good six foot he and must have been all of 200 pounds. Everyone chatted and had another drink. Claire excused herself.

'I will just go and check with Angela and see how the dinner is going.' Mary had seen Angela just for a moment; she was obviously the cook. Claire returned after a couple of minutes and said that Angela wanted everyone in the dining room as dinner was ready.

Mary thought the whole evening was delightful, a very nice meal. Mary could not really make out what kind of meat it was but it was delicious. She found out later that it was wild roasted pheasant. In the very short time Mary was there, she got to know the family pretty well. Patrick and his brother, Martin, had been left the stables between them by their father, who had passed away fifteen years ago. On a visit to America seven years ago, Martin went to Ocala, Florida, which is big horse country. He fell in love with the place. Patrick bought him out, and Martin then bought a big spread in Ocala and bred quarter horses. He had two daughters and they all seemed very happy.

The next morning Patrick and Brennan had to go to the yearling sales in Kilcoole, County Wicklow. They had entered several yearlings in the sale. Mary was pleased to accept their offer of a ride to the airport. At 9 a.m., after hugs and promises to keep in touch, Mary got in the back of the Land Rover It was 10.15 a.m. when they dropped Mary off at the airport. Her flight to London was at noon. She made her way to the first-class lounge and relaxed. The last twenty-four hours had been unexpected, exciting and very, very enjoyable. Then she began to get more excited as she realised that in a very short time, she would be seeing her brother, Adam Roberts.

Chapter Sixty-four

During the first fifty or so miles of their journey home, their vigorous small talk continued, almost without pause. After passing Warwick, both fell silent, apparently preferring a little time to think things over on their own. From photographs Mary had sent from time to time, Adam had concluded that whatever Mary's concerns over the past several years may have been, money was not one of them. He also noticed that the five soft-leather suitcases that made up her luggage were of a quality he had only seen at the very upmarket stores in Liverpool – of which there were very few. Her clothes were obviously expensive by current British standards, but she was basically the same lovable Mary he remembered when she boarded the train with Amos Cooper back in 1938. Adam wasn't exactly expecting to meet a toffee-nose, but he was more than pleased that the only real change he noticed in his sister was that slight American accent.

Mary's thoughts of Adam were a bit more perceptive, as women's usually are. Aside from Adam clearly looking at least thirteen years older than when she had left, there was a certain maturity she found hard to define. He was obviously a good deal this side of being middle-aged, but in manner and speech, he was every inch a fully grown-up man. After all, in the time she had been away, he had got married, was now the father of three, and had begun to do well in business with Walter White. Now, of course, Walter and Lil were deceased, and Adam was carrying on on his own in some kind of business arrangement with a Mr Coleman of London, according to some mail she had received from Rose.

Adam is thirty-five, she thought, let's see: that's still three years younger than Colin was when we were married. Colin was no boy. Neither is Adam. In fact, I think Adam seems every bit as mature as Colin was at the time.

Mary made a mental note to ask Adam about his experiences at Dunkirk. But that should wait until later.

Rose had scripted the meeting sequence for when Adam and Mary arrived. As soon as they drove into the yard, she and everyone there, except John and Celia Roberts, would dash from the house to meet them in the driveway. The immediate greeting party would be Rose, her parents, Albert and Doris, her son Martyn, now fifteen, the twins, Carole and Gary (both fourteen), John's wife, May, and their son, Little Jack, fourteen. Brothers John and Tim simply couldn't get away from their building project at Burscough. The job there had a bonded completion date, and failure to meet that deadline would have been prohibitively expensive.[3] John would leave for Wrightington at the end of the working day, 5 p.m. Tim, on the other hand, had to drive their lorry from the job to the docks in Manchester to pick up some special building materials that had to be on the jobsite when work began the next morning. He wouldn't get back from Manchester until nearly midnight, so he wouldn't be able to see Mary until the next afternoon.

Rose had persuaded James and Celia to wait in Adam's study. 'I think you three should have your own private time together, after Mary has met the gang in the driveway.'

As anxious as James and Celia were to see their daughter, each saw the wisdom of Rose's suggestion. Mary's meeting 'the gang' shouldn't be all mixed in with what was bound to be a tearful reunion with her parents, even if all the tears were tears of joy. The younger set just wouldn't understand. Rose's suggestion eliminated any problems along that line.

Just before noon, Adam, Rose and her five handsome suitcases pulled into Adam's driveway. The gang poured out of the house, and, on Rose's signal, James and Celia went into Adam's study.

Mary sprang from Adam's car, and there were hugs and kisses all around in a sea of excitement. Mary tried to conceal her surprise at how tall Adam's children were. She had last seen them in 1938, and when Martyn was just beginning to walk and just learning to talk. The twins were still in nappies. Mary observed that Rose hadn't changed a great deal, except she had filled out a bit, and fifteen years of motherhood had had a noticeably maturing affect. Her parents were holding their age quite well. Albert had become a virtual teetotaller after learning the cruelty of spirits on the day Adam and Rose were married.

Mary had no sooner got through meeting and hugging everyone in the driveway, when the thought crossed her mind, My God. Where are Mum and Dad?

When she posed that question, Rose merely smiled, and gestured towards the side door of the house. Mary promptly said 'Excuse me' to everyone, and dashed into the house. Beyond the kitchen, she saw her parents standing in the doorway to Adam's study. She ran to embrace them, and the anticipated tears of joy quickly began.

Human happiness seldom exceeds the limits that were reached on this

---

[3] On construction projects where it was vital that the job be completed by a certain date, the building contractor often has to put up a bond to back up his promise to be done by that date. For every day over the limit, the bonding company is bound to pay the owner a fixed sum. If the bonding company has to pay, the bonded party is liable for full reimbursement.

occasion. In spite of her overwhelming delight, Mary couldn't help a slight feeling of apprehension about how her parents had aged. It was more than thirteen years. James still had a full head of hair, but it had turned to a very distinct grey. Celia's hair had not turned grey, but she looked about twenty pounds lighter than Mary last remembered.

Involuntarily, thoughts raced across Mary's mind. I don't know what it will be, you wonderful people, but before I leave I'm going to do something handsome for both of you. Oh, how could I have stayed away so long?

Of course, Mary wasn't looking at anything more than the fact that most people who have lived most of their lives facing tough times tend to age faster when they get into middle age. Their longevity records, too, reflect how fast life can proceed when the vigour and resilience of youth have disappeared.

Rose tried to keep everyone occupied in the driveway for about ten minutes, and then the party moved inside. Rose served tea and cake, and for the next three hours it was anyone's guess whether Mary answered more questions than she asked. Everyone was curious about life in America, and Mary was curious about what had happened locally since she left. Who had done what? Who had got married? How many children had they had? All the small talk that long-separate friends seem to find absolutely absorbing. Mary had some pictures of her Gary, which were passed around to many oohs and aahs.

John arrived around 6 p.m., whereupon Adam lit up his barbeque.

Mary's chatting with John brought her up to date on what had happened to Tim. A full-fledged adventure all by itself.

'One thing I don't understand about Tim is why he works so hard. I had a crew of five I kept busy most of the time before Tim come back. Good lads. All rounds. I paid 'em all a pound a week over average. Tim come back with no real special experience in construction. I gave 'im a job. He learned faster'n anyone I've ever seen. Now he outworks the lot.'

'What's so unusual about that?' asked Mary. 'My recollection of Tim was that he was always a hard worker.'

'What's so unusual about that, you ask?' said John. 'I'll tell you. He don't need to,' he said. 'Every month this mineral water company in Australia sends pots of money to him, direct to the Lloyds Bank in Wigan. I don't ask him how much, 'cos it's none of my business. But I know it's a lot more than these poor sods doing our kind of work earn.

'Like I say,' he concluded, 'Tim's well off, and I know it, and yet he works like someone's threatening to foreclose on his house. I mean Adam's house there towards Burscough. You remember that house on the first land Adam bought after he went in with Walter?'

'I remember his buying, what was it, 200 acres?' said Mary.

'That's it,' said John, 'and me and Tim fixed up the farmhouse on it. That was before you left, wasn't it?'

'I'm not sure,' answered Mary. 'No. I remember. Tim was still living at home when I left.'

'Well, no matter,' said John, 'we did fix it up and Tim lived in it till he went on that binge and ended up in the Fusiliers out in Burma. Ah, but that's another story.'

Mary knew that 'other story'. Rose had written that when Tim learned that she had married Colin, he had gone on a mind-numbing drunken binge that surely ended by the time he arrived in Burma.

The chatting went on until after 10 p.m. Albert and Doris had left around 8.30. James and Celia had gone to bed at 9.30. Little Jack fell asleep in sofa chair, and May was beginning to nod off when John noticed the hour. They were gone in five minutes. Rose and Adam were still wide awake when Rose said she was going to have to turn in, which they took to mean she wanted to go to bed.

By 10.30, the lights were all out in Adam's house, which was filled with very happy people, all fast asleep.

Chapter Sixty-five

As noted previously, one of the reasons for Mary's wanting to make this first trip back alone was to allow her the freedom of going about without any encumbrances. Inexplicably, she had given no thought as to how she would go here and go there, as she pleased. Had the importance of having a car at her disposal at all times crossed her mind before she arrived in Wrightington, she could have used a new resource which had only recently become available at Heathrow: a car rental firm. That didn't happen.

Through her travel agent in San Francisco, Mary had already opened a cheque account at Barclays Bank in Wigan via a cabled bank deposit of $20,000 and 'special delivery' air mailing of Mary's signature on all the other necessary signed papers two weeks before she arrived. Her opening balance was £7,142. To give the reader an idea of the purchasing power of such a sum of money at the time, it is noted that by the turn of the century – that is 1 January 2000 – it would take 100,000 American dollars to buy what $20,000 would have bought in 1951.

The morning after Mary's arrival, Rose was up before the others, and was putting the finishing touches to the breakfast for her husband, sister-in-law, in-laws and three children when Adam wondered into the kitchen. The others walked in a few minutes later. Their plates were filled and distributed. Shortly after finishing their breakfast, Martyn, Carole and Gary gave each of the adults a quick kiss and departed for school. Rose poured tea for the others, and began clearing the breakfast dishes from the table.

At that point Mary told Adam about her faux pas regarding her transportation needs on her first trip back home. She made it clear she wanted to buy a new car. She added that she was a new depositor at Barclays Bank in Wigan. All she needed was Adam's guidance as to what kind she should get, and where to buy it.

'No problem,' Adam had replied. 'We'll go to Timberlakes. It opens in less than an hour.'

Rose overheard this conversation and asked to come along, adding, 'And I could give May a call. I'm sure she would like to come too.'

Adam parked his car near Timberlakes, which had been Wigan's Ford dealership for ever and a day. Adam, Rose, Mary and May got out, and the four of them walked into the Timberlake's showroom where they were greeted by Timberlake's veteran salesman, Ron Barker. He knew Adam, Rose and May from prior dealings, and greeted them all warmly. Adam introduced his sister Mary, adding, 'She might be interested in buying a car.'

Ron, extended his right hand towards Mary, saying, 'I have heard a lot about you and I am very pleased to meet you.'

Mary shook his hand as she returned his affable smile.

My, isn't he a friendly fellow, she thought. But he doesn't seem as oily as most car salesmen I've encountered in the States.

Ron picked up immediately on Mary's sort-of American accent which was still undeniably English.

He led them over to a highly polished Ford Zephyr which was painted a light green, with a crisp white trim. It was strategically positioned in the centre of the circular showroom. The six other less expensive new Ford models were positioned around the periphery, seemingly 'aimed' toward the Zephyr. Ron proceeded to point out all of the features of their 'flagship offering'. After demonstrating how neatly all four doors opened and shut, Ron asked Mary to sit in the rear seat while he pointed out the car's superb interior upholstery. 'Merchant's puffing', aside, the 'flagship offering' was a class act by any measure. Even Mary, who had become accustomed to things being first rate, was very impressed; more so than she let on.

Next Ron directed everyone's attention to the movable little fan and, 'Something you'll probably use a good deal more than the fan, the interior heater.' Then came the panorama of items on the car's dashboard. Amperage. Oil pressure. Speedometer. The lot. Then Ron pointed to the dial of a radio! It was attached below the dashboard, just left of centre. It had two round operating knobs on either side of the dial. The one on the left was used to turn the radio on, and to control the volume; the knob on the left was for selecting radio stations. The present circumstances gave listeners their choice of BBC's regular broadcast, or its Third Programme, which broadcast classical music. Ron turned the car's ignition switch to the 'on' position, and then turned on the radio. After twenty seconds while the vacuum tubes warmed to a glow, a BBC announcer was heard reading the latest news. Ron concluded this tour of the Zephyr's interior by pointing out how the ceiling dome light automatically stayed on when any of the car's doors were even slightly ajar. Exiting the Zephyr, he made some favourable comments about the 'hard' paint on the exterior. Then he lifted the bonnet to reveal 'the best feature, which you seldom see and hardly hear': the spotless and powerful-looking 175-horsepower V-8 engine.

The 1951 Zephyr was a big car by British standards, but it looked small to Mary. On the other hand, she quivered at the thought of trying to drive an American-sized car, say, a Packard, through some of the narrow country lanes in England. Some of those lanes were too narrow for even this car.

'This is our biggest car,' said Ron, 'and I'd like to show you any of the rest you'd like to see.'

Mary gestured towards the other cars on the showroom floor, and Ron led the way, where he gave them a less detailed tour of the other new models on display.

As he was about to extol the virtues of the fourth other model, Mary indicated she would like to go back to the 'one we looked at the beginning'. Ron smiled as he led the way back to the Ford Zephyr.

'How much are you asking for this one?' she asked.

'Of course, my guv'nor would like to get all he can, but I know the lowest I can sell it for is 500 pounds. It's Ford's top of the line for this year.'

It seemed a fair price.

Mary nodded her head in agreement. She promptly withdrew her cheque book from her purse, and using the exalted Zephyr's bonnet as a makeshift desktop, she wrote out a cheque for £500. She handed the cheque to the young salesman, asking, 'How soon will it be ready to go?'

'I can have it road-ready for you tomorrow by dinner time,' Ron replied.

'That will be fine,' said Mary. 'Thank you, Ron. We'll be seeing you tomorrow at noon.'

'That will be fine,' said the very pleased-looking car salesman. 'Would you have time for a fifteen- to twenty-minute demonstration ride?' he added. 'I could point out some of the Zephyr's road-handling features you might find useful.'

'That's very kind of you,' replied Mary, 'but I don't think it will be necessary. I've driven one very similar in the States. The only thing I'm worried about is remembering to drive on the left – and I don't think you could help me a great deal with that!'

After completing all arrangements at Timberlake's, the four walked to the nearby wine lodge for a light lunch.

Mary gazed all about as they entered this long-established bistro. She had been there twice before in connection with Adam and Rose's wedding preparations, which was a long time ago. Nevertheless, she could see that everything inside had been changed. The wine bar was on the right; on the left of the entrance were different-sized wooden round tables that would accommodate two to six customers. The waitresses wore their trademark white blouses and black skirts.

Mary noticed that the business section of Wigan looked basically as she remembered it; not that she had spent much time noticing Wigan before she left for America. Fortunately the Germans never thought the little town was a worthy bombing target. Unfortunately the same could not be said for nearby Manchester and Liverpool. It was while she and Adam were passing through

Manchester the day before that she first saw any actual bomb damage.

After their lunch, the four walked back to Adam's car and were soon on their way to Wrightington. When they arrived back at Adam's home, it was obvious that everyone had been working hard preparing for the party planned for that evening.

James and Celia had been there when the children returned from school. Martyn had filled a regular water bucket with charcoal, which was standing next to the barbeque near Adam's garage. Carole handed her mother a note she had made from a telephone call.

'Uncle John called. He will get the chicken and the steaks in Parbold and expects to be here by 5.30.'

Carole had spread the tablecloths and laid out the cutlery. Everything seemed to be very well organised.

Celia told Adam that Gordon had called to say he and his wife would arrive about at 6 p.m.

Mary announced she was going to lie down for a little rest. She was still feeling the time difference from her transatlantic flight. Adam said he was going to do the same thing.

'We should get things going at about 6,' said Adam as he headed toward his bedroom for a little nap.

Chapter Sixty-six

Mary was awoken by voices outside the house. It was almost 6 p.m. She sat up and looked through the window. She could see several people outside, below her window. She didn't recognise most of them. Adam was talking to a very tall man, who looked to be in his fifties. The lady walking with Rose looked to Mary like she was probably the tall man's wife. Mary got up and quickly changed into her evening clothes. As she opened the bedroom door to go down the stairs, she heard Carole shout. 'Uncle Tim is here!'

Mary walked back to the window and looked towards the road. She saw a Land Rover coming up the drive. When it came to a stop, a little dog jumped out through an open window and raced as fast as he could to Carole. Tim stepped out of the vehicle and Mary realised she could not take her eyes off him. He seemed much bigger than she remembered. His hair was blonde and his face was very tanned. Mary admitted to herself the sight of Tim excited her.

She saw Tim speaking with Carole, and the two walked out of sight as if heading towards the back of the property.

Mary didn't know what that was all about, but it was time to join the party.

She stepped back from the window and proceeded downstairs. When she walked into the lounge area, she saw that about twenty-five people had gathered. She knew most of them.

Adam came over to her accompanied by a couple she had seen from the upstairs window.

'Mary, I want you to meet my partner, Gordon Coleman. This is his wife, Joyce. They live in London.'

Mary and the Colemans shook hands warmly, and an immediate friendly atmosphere was apparent. Then came the small talk. Joyce had never been to America and asked Mary dozens of questions about things there she had read about the States.

Generally, the least remembered conversations on earth are held at cocktail parties. The proceedings on this occasion were no exception.

'I've heard you've just bought a new car,' said Joyce.

'I bought it this morning,' said Mary, 'picking it up tomorrow.'

'How exciting,' replied Joyce, adding, 'I've seen some photos of your son; how old is he now?'

'He's nine years old,' answered Mary, obviously pleased to be discussing her boy. 'He's in the fifth grade at a very fine prep school near Monterey Bay, about 125 miles south of San Francisco. A school which his father attended as a boy. Otherwise, of course, I would have brought him with me. My husband's – I mean my deceased husband's – Aunt Lucy lives near the school and is looking after him. They are the greatest of friends.'

'Well, that's just grand,' answered Joyce. 'Yes, I knew your husband was deceased, I'm so sorry. I'm sure it takes a long to get over something like that.'

Mary swallowed very obviously, as these words clearly caused an emotional reaction. 'You've no idea,' she said, 'and I hope you never have any idea along those lines. It's been eight years now, and it's only been during the last two to three years where I could even discuss it without there being a very emotional scene. But I've got a son to raise and life can't be an endless veil of tears. I'm getting over it now. Anyway,' she said, as if intentionally changing the subject, 'I understand your husband is in furniture manufacturing and, though my big brother hasn't told me the particulars, the two are somehow in business together.'

'It's true,' said Joyce, 'they get on like two peas in a pod. It's a terrible thing to say, but I think it has a lot to do with each one thinking the other is the only completely honest businessman the other has met – well, that's not entirely what I wanted to say. There was Walter White, I'm sure you knew him.'

'I did,' replied Mary, 'a wonderful man. And his wife Lil. They were both just wonderful, particularly to Adam. I know they thought of him like he was their son.'

'I got to know them both,' said Joyce, 'and you're right. Walter was the second "only one-hundred-per-cent-honest man" Gordon says he ever met.'

They both had a good laugh at the way Joyce imitated her husband's manner of speaking.

'They met during the war, as I understand,' said Mary.

'True,' said Joyce, 'I never did learn the fine details, as Gordon isn't much of an extrovert, but I clearly recall the change that came over him once he struck some kind of deal with Walter White and your brother that solved some transport problems that seemed to be ageing him at an alarming rate.'

The ladies had been chinning for almost twenty minutes when Carole approached them and said, 'Auntie Mary, Mum told me to ask if you would please lend a hand with something in the kitchen.'

Mary asked to be excused, and Joyce turned to join in the conversation with Gordon, Adam and Adam's parents.

Chapter Sixty-seven

When Mary entered the kitchen a minute later, to her delight and surprise, in through the back door walked Tim, followed by Carole.

She and Tim just stood there and looked at each other for nearly half a minute. Carole looked a bit dumbstruck, not quite being able to figure out what was going on.

'I am sorry I didn't come in the house when I first arrived,' said Tim. 'Carole said you were resting, and asked me to check out a place for a stable. I got the idea from what she was saying that you are planning to talk Adam into buying her a pony.'

An unwitting smile crossed little Carole's face. She wisely decided her presence would be better appreciated elsewhere, and promptly took her leave.

Mary watched Carole go.

'Tell your mum I won't be long with the plates,' Mary called after her.

Mary then walked up to Tim. They were now the only ones in the kitchen and each had been hoping that would be the case for at least a few minutes.

'You look so different, but you also look great,' said Mary. Her face reflected her emotions at the moment: delight and desire.

Tim returned the compliment, 'You look fantastic.' His face and general manner beamed the same reaction. Although neither was about to burst out with any dialogue, each had missed the other for so long. Nothing needed saying along those lines. It was mutually felt and mutually understood. A long period of unspoken longing and loneliness was coming to an end. In this swirl of feelings, Mary realised that her earlier thoughts of wanting to make this trip alone was not just for the freedom she would have to go here and go there. It was Tim all along.

After staring into each other's soul for a few seconds, they fell into a grasping and passionate embrace. Mary could somehow feel her mind and body come alive. An awareness she hadn't experienced since she and Colin had done the same thing right after landing at Lake Tahoe on their honeymoon. That had been almost eleven years ago. Time and Mary had just stepped back from this magic moment when Rose opened the kitchen door.

Rose hadn't seen her brother and sister-in-law in each other's arms, but those uncanny perceptions unique to the fair sex told her that these two were more than incidental friends.

This is wonderful, crossed Rose's mind. These two are the loneliest, loveliest people in the world. I so hope they meld their lives together. Then she walked nonchalantly to a drawer, withdrew a handful of knives and forks and returned through the same door, almost as if she hadn't seen Tim and Mary. During the whole sortie, Rose didn't say a word. She merely smiled at both of them, as she hastened to get back to the living room with those badly need eating utensils.

'Well, isn't she just the "passing-through-hope-I-didn't-interrupt-anything" little lady,' said Tim.

'Oh, don't over-react,' said Mary. 'Rose probably understands a lot more about these things that we do.'

'Look,' said Tim, 'we've got so many things to talk over, and this nice party just isn't the time or place. Besides, John and I are working on a job at Burscough that will start costing us if we don't wind it up by Monday. That means we even get to work this Saturday and Sunday. And I know you're anxious to get reacquainted with your folks.'

The two continued to hold each other's elbows, as Mary nodded her agreement with what Tim was saying.

'You're all put back together? I mean, the amnesia is gone and everything?' she asked.

'Oh yes,' said Tim. 'I'll tell you all about it. Strangest thing I ever heard of. Several years of wondering who you were and what has happened. Then one day you blink in surprise, and everything is there. Like a big curtain was lifted by magic, and you remember everything, just like looking at your whole past life. Better yet, your brain has wired a new route into your old memory. That big curtain won't be coming down again.'

'Anyway,' he continued, speaking a bit more rapidly, 'we can get into all of that and you'll have to fill me in on everything since you left. Why don't we plan to meet at some out-of-the-way place next Tuesday? My mind won't be on that bloody Burscough business, and that will let you spend some time with your mum and dad, and things will all slow down a bit.'

'Sounds great,' said Mary. 'Let's talk by phone on the weekend, and work out the detail. Now we'd better join the party.'

Tim walked alone through the kitchen door, and joined into a conversation Adam and John were having. Mary let a minute pass before she came back into the living room and started chatting with May and Rose.

The party started breaking up with the first departures being John, May and Little Jack at about 10 p.m. After all, it was a week night, and John had to be on the job by 7 a.m., and Little Jack had to go to school.

James and Celia retired to their bedroom around 10.30.

By 11, the Birchalls left. Then Gordon and Joyce were off to the country hotel where they'd booked rooms in Wigan.

Shortly after that, Tim said he'd have to leave, 'To make sure John doesn't outwork me tomorrow.' That caused a ripple of laughter. Mary saw him to the door, and when no one seemed to be looking their way, they exchanged a quick peck of a kiss, and he was gone.

By 11.30, everyone staying at Adam's was in bed. All lights were out. An occasional snore could be heard, if anyone was listening. Fortunately, no one was.

Chapter Sixty-eight

Mary looked at the clock. It was 3.45.

'I will have to go; I promised Carole I would pick her up from school. She wants to take me to her friend's place and look at a pony.'

'That will be fine; the boys stay on today for football practice,' Rose replied.

When Carole came out of school and saw the new car, she came running over with her friend Sandra.

'Oh, Auntie Mary, it's fantastic! This is Sandra, my best friend. Can we sit in the front?'

The drive to Sandra's only took ten minutes. Driving up the farm lane, on the right was a large paddock. Carole asked Aunt Mary to stop, and the girls got out and went over to the gate. A frisky pony came trotting up, who obviously knew them.

'We will see you at the house,' called Carole. Both girls got on to Dancer's back, and he trotted up the field towards the top gate.

Mary shouted, 'Be careful!'

Sandra's parents, Ted and Julie, were very friendly people. They invited Mary in, but she could see that they were busy.

'Thank you but I won't interrupt your work. Maybe another time.' Mary said that no doubt she would be bringing Sandra home many times. Mary then called Carole and they left.

Back at the house, Rose told Mary that Laura had called, then added that it was good news; she wanted Mary to call her at the office. Mary looked at her watch. It was 5.30; that would be 9.30 a.m. in LA.

Rose suggested that Mary could make the call from the study, which she did. Laura answered. The first thing Mary asked was whether Gary was all right. Laura quickly assured her that everything was great, and that it was very good news.

'You remember the case we had in February, defending the Mexican restaurant, El Toro? The mother and son had a takeaway, they both became ill and the mother was taken to the emergency room, where three hours later she died? The husband claimed for death caused by sepsis. It caused severe infections of the bowel and that is what killed her. Apparently, the owners had been warned several times about tainted food, and evidence of rats. Needless to say the place has now been closed.'

Changing the subject. 'How is the old boyfriend?'

'Well, he looks great. He came with me to collect my new car, and we are arranging to spend time together next week. Tomorrow I am taking my mum and dad back to Lancaster, I will stay over and see old friends.'

Just before they ended their conversation, Mary said to Laura, 'Tell Aunt Lucy I will call her at the weekend. Bye for now. I love you all.'

Later that night, Mary got the chance to ask Rose and Adam if they would allow Carole to have her own pony.

'I want to get all the children something, and I would also like to get Mum and Dad a bungalow near here.'

Adam interrupted, 'I have asked them several times, but they love their little cottage and I don't think you will get them to move. If you managed to persuade them, the kids would love it, and we would feel much happier.'

Mary said, 'Right, leave it to me, I will work on it.'

The following morning, the children said their goodbyes to their grandparents before leaving for school. Rose was going to Warrington with Adam, Mary and her parents. They all sat on the bench seat in front of the Zephyr, all waving as they set off for Lancaster.

The weather was cloudy but at least it was dry. There was even a chance it might be sunny later on. Mary kept the speed down to forty miles per hour. James was very quiet; he was watching every move that Mary made, operating the car, obviously proud of his daughter's confidence. Celia was sitting with a rug over her knees. Mary got a very satisfied feeling, just knowing they were both enjoying the experience. She reached down and clicked the radio button and soft pleasant music filled the car. The surprised look on her dad's face almost made Mary laugh out loud.

As they where nearing Clitheroe, Mary pulled in at the Old Post House. It had been there forever and was operating in the days of horse-drawn carriages; in fact, the old stables were still there, where they changed horses, for the longhaul journeys. Of course, they were now converted into tea rooms.

They all went inside and had tea and toasted muffins. Celia thought it was wonderful. Mary bought several souvenirs from the little shop, including a silk scarf for her mother and a nice country cap for her dad.

Forty-five minutes later, they arrived at the cottage in Gateley.

Although Mary really tried not to get emotional, it was difficult.

When she got inside, it was so small. Celia had kept Adam's and her rooms the same except for the beds, which had been replaced.

Going up the little narrow staircase, Mary entered her room and sat on the bed, looking round at all the drawings and pictures that she had made with her brother all those years ago which were still on the wall.

Mary's eyes were filling with tears of happiness. She decided there and then that even if her parents did move, she would keep the cottage. It would always serve as a holiday cottage for all the family. And she would get a big kick from showing her son and Aunt Lucy where she was born. Mary then went downstairs and gave her mum and dad a big hug.

'I love you both so much.'

'We love you and are so pleased that both you and Adam have done so well. All we want now is to see our American grandson,' replied James.

'You will soon, I promise,' said Mary.

Celia then announced, 'I am cooking dinner tonight and I will make your favourite. If you want to visit some old friends in the village, be back here at 7 p.m.'

'That'll be nice. I think I will walk along the canal; it looks as though the sun has come out.'

As she walked slowly along the canal towpath, it was easy to remember all the times and places where she and Adam had played all those years ago. Further on she came across a couple of old gypsy caravans, long since abandoned. She walked over the bridge and on a little way to the Navigation pub. It was early afternoon, and there were only several people sitting outside. Mary did not recognise anyone, so she just said hello and walked to the paddock behind the pub. There in a corner, head towards the sun, eyes closed, dozing, was a donkey.

Mary thought, It can't be, it is impossible! She leaned on the fence and called, 'Edward,' then called again a little louder. The donkey lifted his head and came over to the fence very slowly. He put his head through the railings.

Mary heard a voice behind her. 'You will have to give him an apple now, Mary Roberts.' When Mary turned there was an old woman.

'How did you know my name?'

The old lady walk over and sat on the wooden bench.

'I should know your name – I delivered you and your brother into this world.'

Mary knew then.

'You're Mrs Barker.'

'I am, dear, I am.'

'But how did you recognise me?'

'I very often see your mother and dad, and your brother and his family. They always kept me and the other villagers up to date with your travels. We were all sorry to hear of your loss.'

Mary held the old lady's hand; she must have been in her eighties but she had a very kind face.

Then she said, 'Surely this can't be the same donkey?'

The old lady assured her it was; he had survived the war. 'Everyone in the village makes bets who will last longer, him or me!'

Mary sat on the bench with the old lady and they chatted. Mrs Barker asked how long she was staying.

'Maybe until Sunday but I will be visiting pretty often.'

'Amos Cooper was asking about you; I think he had an idea you would be visiting. He will be in church on Sunday.'

Mary promised she would be there and then stood up.

'It has been very nice meeting you, Mrs Barker, and I will see you on Sunday.'

As she walked away she got another apple out of the barrel and tossed it over to Edward. 'And I will see you too,' she added.

As Mary walked back she passed the old colliery buildings and the loading bays, all derelict. This made Mary start thinking back to her childhood again. Smiling to herself, she thought of how Adam would take her along the canal. Sometimes they would get a ride on a barge, up to the locks. On the walk back they would pick blackberries. All lovely and happy memories.

Going through the village she passed the school where she taught the small children, and then at the other end of the village, Dr Mason's surgery, where she had a part-time job. Mary's father had told her that the doctor had moved away several years ago to Grasmere in the Lakes.

As Mary walked up the garden path, she could smell the cooking and knew it would be Lancashire hot pot. It used to be her favourite meal. Maybe it was because at that time there was not a lot of money and families made cheap but wholesome, nourishing meals. Nevertheless, it was very nice and the three of them enjoyed being together. But secretly it was no longer Mary's favourite meal.

Mary helped her mother to clean up, then she went to the car and brought back a nice bottle of wine.

'I want us all to sit down. I have something to ask you. I want you to listen to what I have to say, and then think about it over the weekend. I have discussed this with Adam and Rose. Adam and I are in a good position financially. They have three children. I know that I am on my own but I have a great son. At this stage, I can't say that I will get married again.

'When Colin died, I could not get involved with the law firm directly. Colin had invested very wisely over the years and left me and Gary a very large amount of money, and property. His life insurance alone was five million dollars. Maurice, who looks after my investments, tells me I am worth in excess of fifty million US dollars.'

Celia almost fell off the chair. 'I don't understand dollars, but fifty million is a lot of anything!'

James got up poured himself another glass, then said very slowly, 'Mary, you could buy the whole village for that!'

Mary smiled. 'I don't think Mr Lloyd would appreciate me doing that. I intend to help all the family, and I want you to consider moving nearer to Adam, but you would be able to keep this place.' Looking at her dad, Mary said, 'I know you are at retirement age, but there is no reason why you can't learn to drive and have a little car.' On that score James did not reply. 'I will put up a trust fund for all the children, including Jack, John and May's boy. Carole wants to be a vet, so I can help her.

'Also I have plans to buy a house near Oxford before I go back to America. I want to give Gary the chance to study at Oxford if he makes the grade and I am confident that he will.' Then she put her arms around them. 'You did your best for me and Adam; now let us help you and all the family.'

The following morning Mary walked to the church with her parents. After the service, most of the villagers would congregate at the Navigation pub, still a regular, weekly event. It gave the people of Gateley a chance to exchange gossip and keep in touch with each other. This particular week, Mary was the main attraction. Adam had called the landlord, and told him that his sister would be visiting. He in turn had cleared the back room and arranged for most of Mary's old school friends to be there. It was a very nice surprise for Mary, as she met several girls she went to school with. Two of her best friends were there with their husbands and children. She got to know that a couple she asked about had gone to Australia. Another girl had married a Canadian army guy and was living in Canada.

Amos Cooper was also there. Mary asked him to come back to the cottage, Amos had a pre-arranged meeting but said he would love to see her the following morning for coffee.

'How about that little place where you first asked me to go to America?' Mary suggested.

They arranged to meet at 10.30. Mary enjoyed the couple of hours in the pub, and before leaving she thanked the owners, Kathy and Bob Halsall. She said that she would be visiting Gateley on regular basis.

James and Celia suggested they walk along the canal and through the woods, so James could check on the allotment.

Mary could not believe what he had done with that waste ground. It was all neatly planted out and he had a greenhouse. He collected some potatoes, a cabbage, and some salad from the greenhouse.

Celia told Mary how James loved the allotment. If they did move he would really miss it. Mary made a mental note of that, thinking, When I find them a place, it has got to have a piece of land.

They all had another nice evening together in the cottage, and Mary was up early and the weather looked good the next morning.

Celia, of course, insisted the Mary have a good breakfast and told her several times to be careful driving back to Wigan.

After saying goodbye to her mum and dad, Mary drove the short distance to the coffee shop, parked her car and went inside. Amos was already there. He stood as Mary entered, then he called the waitress and ordered coffee. Mary asked about Linda O'Brian. 'Well, she carried on teaching, then married a teacher. They got married and went back to Ireland. They have a six-year-old daughter.'

Amos asked about Laura.

'Does she still work at the law office?'

'Yes, she married one of the lawyers, Mark. They have no children but are very happy.'

They exchanged questions for the best part of an hour before Amos looked at his watch.

'Oh dear, I will have to go. I let my wife have the car, so I will have to get the bus, I don't want to be late and it is the other side of town.'

'No problem; I will drive you.'

They walked outside, and Mary had to smile at the look on Amos's face when he saw her car. He got inside, saying, 'The last time we met you came on your bike!'

After dropping him off, she gave him a little hug.

'Look after yourself and I will see you again before I go back to America.'

Mary turned onto the Lancaster Road heading south-west. The drive back was very pleasant. She switched the radio on, feeling very pleased with herself, just cruising along at forty miles per hour.

When she got back to Wrightington, she was surprised to find May in the house on her own.

'Did you have a good journey?'

'Oh yes, I love the car.'

Rose had gone with Adam and would only be back at 9 p.m. May had brought the kids back from school.

'I promised I would arrange the meal for us and be here when you got back. John and Tim will be over later.'

Carole insisted on serving both her aunts with a cup of tea, then sat down, listening to the conversation, which was not very interesting to Carole. Mary saw that she was getting bored, and winking at May, she said, 'If we are on our own, why don't we go to the fish and chip shop at Appley Bridge?' Then she added, 'But I don't think the boys would like that.' Carole beamed out, 'They will, they will! I will go and get them.'

All that arranged, Mary took her bags up to her room and made a call to Aunt Lucy in America. Everything was fine; she had visited Gary and he had received her letter. Before ending the call, Aunt Lucy reminded Mary, 'If you can find some happiness for yourself, take it. I love you; you and Gary are all I have.'

When Mary went downstairs, May noticed that she looked a little down. 'What's wrong? Bad news?'

'Oh no, I can have anything I want. It just feels like there is something missing.'

May replied, 'Come over here and sit down. You have been on your own a long time, and I think you need someone to share your life with.'

'I know .Aunt Lucy just told me the same thing.'

Just then, the boys came charging in. Everyone wanted to sit in the front. Mary gave the order: 'Ladies in front, boys and Skipper in the back.' Needless to say, the rest of the night was hectic but enjoyable. Later, when all the kids were in bed, May and Mary pored themselves a deserved glass of wine.

Mary must have slept very late. Rose came in the bedroom with a cup of tea.

'Carole wanted to bring it but I thought I would let you sleep. I must apologise for all of us being so late last night. Adam got involved and the time just flew.

'I believe our Tim promised to show you his house. Well, he called this morning, said he would be over at 10.30.'

Mary was hoping he would enlighten her on his business involvement.

After just a light breakfast, Mary was having her second cup of coffee when she saw Tim's Land Rover come up the drive.

He asked about her trip to Lancaster and how the car was. Her lovely smile answered both questions.

'I want to call in the village for some gas, sorry, petrol,' she told Tim.

The house was only thirty minutes away. He turned off the Southport Road at Cue Gardens, then up an unmade road. Tim pointed out, 'This is why I have a Land Rover. I intend to make the road wider and put tarmac down.'

When they got inside, Mary was really surprised at how big it was. It had a huge stone fireplace and old beams.

'I had lots of plans for this place, but now I'm not sure if I want to continue.'

Mary looked at him. 'Why ever not? I think it is a wonderful placc!'

Tim was quick to explain, 'Don't get me wrong – I will always keep it, I just don't think I could live here all the time. Now that I have another income, I want to try other things.'

Mary went towards him. 'There is something you are not telling me, Tim Birchall. Come on, what is it?'

Tim smiled, 'I will tell you tomorrow when I take you out for dinner.'

Suddenly, Mary cried out, 'Oh dear, I completely forgot to tell you! I can't have dinner with you tomorrow.'

The disappointment showed immediately in Tim's face, 'Why not? I've booked a table at the Grange.'

Mary explained, 'When I got back from Lancaster, Gordon had left a message to say there was a large house in Oxford going for auction the day after tomorrow. I was thinking of driving down early tomorrow morning. I don't think a late night would be a good thing for me. I don't suppose you would like to come with me?'

The immediate change in Tim was like switching a light on. 'I would love to drive you down,' he said.

'No, I want to drive. I will probably be doing the trip on a regular basis, so I will have to get used to it.'

Having made their plans, Tim suggested that they drive into Preston for lunch, have a look around then he could take her back.

'That way, you can have an early night, and we can have a nice afternoon together.'

Chapter Sixty-nine

It was 8 a.m. when they set off for the three-hour drive to Oxford. Mary felt so confident and happy, they chatted about everything except what, without doubt, was on both their minds.

The journey was very pleasant, and before long they arrived at the Regent Hotel, which was close to the south gate of the college. Mary went straight to the front desk.

'Mary Johnson. I booked a room by telephone for tonight.'

The clerk looked at the register.

'Yes, madam, here is your key.'

He summoned the porter to take her bags.

'Have you got another room free?' Mary asked.

'Yes, we have one across the hall from yours. Number thirty-two.'

Mary said, 'That will be fine. I will take that also.'

She saw the smile on Tim's face, so he said, 'I hope you did not think I was expecting to share your room?'

Feeling a little embarrassed, she said, 'No, I did not. I have come here to deal with business.' Then, feeling a little forward, she said, 'If things work out satisfactorily, we could be booking one room in the not-so-distant future.' They went up to their rooms and arranged to meet downstairs in the bar in an hour.

It was 1.30 when Gordon and his wife Joyce walked in.

They all had coffee. As the auction was to start at 3 p.m., Mary suggested that they all go in her car. If they left now, they would have time for a quick look before the sale started.

The house was approached by a long-curving drive. It was obvious that it had been neglected. The house was two-storey and double-fronted. They had a quick look at the roof, which Tim said was the main part, and he said that it looked in very good order. Inside there were four bedrooms, three bathrooms, a laundry room, a very large lounge, study, kitchen and a dining room. The entrance hall Mary thought was very impressive, with its wide staircase, but it would require lots of work. Tim had looked outside and he reported to Mary that the structure looked OK. The boundary walls were Cornish stone and there was about three acres of land.

There were about thirty people there. Gordon pointed out a middle age man.

'He owns most of the adjoining land and is very keen to buy this property. I think they will start the bidding off around 5,000 pounds.'

Very soon the bidding reached almost 6,000 pounds. Both Gordon and Tim thought that 7,000 would be the limit. But it kept up until it reached 7,500 pounds. At this stage only three people were still bidding, but the old boy seemed hellbent on getting it. Mary made the next bid, up to 8,000, then the old boy, after a long pause, nervously, went up another 200 pounds. At this stage Gordon said to Mary, 'I don't think you will outbid him.'

Mary just smiled. 'Want to bet?'

She then put her hand up and shouted, '10,000 pounds,' The old boy turned to Mary and said, 'You must be crazy! You can have it,' and marched out of the room.

Mary and Gordon went over to the auctioneer. She wrote out a cheque and instructed him to send all the paperwork to Adam's and Gordon's solicitors. Gordon produced a card with the correct addresses on, and after handshakes all round they left.

Mary felt very pleased, and turning to Gordon and Joyce, she said, 'I would like you to join Tim and me for dinner tonight. A little celebration, on me.' It was agreed they all meet in the bar at seven.

Back at the hotel, Mary said she would like to have a little rest. Tim agreed.

'I feel a little tired, I will do the same. It is 5 p.m. now – I will tap on your door at 6.30.'

Mary and Tim were already in the bar when Gordon and Joyce came in. The four of them had a pleasant night. The conversation, obviously, was mainly about the house. Joyce asked what she would call it. Without hesitation Mary said, 'It will be known as the Willows. I made my mind up on that even before I had bought it, when I saw those beautiful weeping willows. I said, that's the name.'

Another surprise for Mary was when Gordon said to Tim, 'Adam tells me that your water venture in Australia is paying off handsomely.'

Tim had to smile; he thought he owed Mary an explanation, so he explained briefly how he had come to get involved with the largest water company in Australia.

Mary listened with amazement then asked, 'Does it take much of your time?'

That was the cue for Tim to have a little joke. 'Yes, I may not be able to help you with the house.'

Mary was on the point of apologising for asking him to help.

'You see every month I have to check it out.'

Gordon, of course, knew he was winding Mary up. Mary looked completely puzzled. 'You mean you have to fly to Australia every month?'

'Oh, no! I have to see the bank manager at Barclays in Wigan and check on how my money is rolling in!'

Before Gordon and Joyce left, they made Mary promise that she would visit them before going back to America.

'We are delighted that you will be living close by,' they told her. Mary thanked them for showing interest.

'I am looking forward to moving in, but it will take some time to fix up.'

Mary and Tim spent another hour in the bar chatting, Mary wanting to know more about Tim's involvement with this water company, Tim made light of it.

'I was just lucky. Now I have a good independent income, I am looking forward to doing other things.'

It was midnight when they both went upstairs. They stopped outside Mary's room. Tim put his arms around her and told her how much he loved her. 'I will be miserable when you go back.'

Mary kissed him. 'It won't be long. Just give me a little more time.'

Before heading back to Wigan, they decided to have a look around Oxford. Mary was really impressed with the city and the college buildings. As they passed the south gate, Mary decided to call in the reception of the Mansfield College. A charming woman of about forty greeted her.

'Good morning. How can I be of help?'

After a brief explanation of what information she wanted, the lady gave Mary a stack of leaflets and a large thick book marked 'Application Requirements Guide', and mentioned to Mary, 'If you would like a tour of the college, you would have to fill this form in. The tours are held twice each month. She handed Mary another separate green form. Mary thanked the lady, and, with all the information in a large folder, Mary left.

When they arrived back at Wrightington, everyone wanted to know how things had gone. Mary told everyone the story.

'When the house is ready, on my next visit we will have a big party.'

Carole was quick to ask, 'What if it's not ready?'

Mary answered, 'Well, young lady, you will have to tell your Uncle Tim to make sure it is.'

'Adam, Rose and May were going to Liverpool the following day. Rose asked Mary if she would like to join them.

Adam has to attend a meeting, so I thought we would look around the shops.'

'It sounds wonderful but I have lots of things to do,' replied Mary. 'I want to make several calls to home and give some thought to what I want doing at the house. You enjoy your day, I will pick the kids up from school. You don't have to hurry back.'

The day after, when everyone had gone, Mary felt lost in such a big house on her own. She made a long-distance call speak to Aunt Lucy and Laura, told them all the news about the house, then spoke to Mark. She asked him to let Maurice know that she would be making several investments during the next couple of months.

When all the business side of the call was completed, Laura came back on the line. Mary confessed, 'I think I am warming a lot more towards Tim, but please do not say anything to Aunt Lucy. When I am sure, I want to tell her myself.' Laura was pleased for Mary.

'I'm sure it will work out for you and I know Aunt Lucy wants more than anything for you to be happy. We all do.' Then they concluded their call.

Over dinner the next day, Adam mentioned that there were two bungalows for sale, one in Dalton, and another in Roby Mill. He asked Mary, 'Would you like to get the keys from the agent so we can look at them tomorrow?'

Mary was very keen.

'Yes, that would be fine,' she said.

However, the one in Roby Mill had been sold two days ago, so they picked up the keys for the other and drove out to Dalton, which was three miles north-west of Wigan. It was obvious it had been standing empty for some considerable time. The entrance gates were broken and the drive and pathways overgrown with weeds and brambles. Inside there were three small bedrooms and just one bathroom as well as a fairly large kitchen and lounge that really required complete gutting.

The good points were that it was close to Adam and Rose, and that the property stood in a good acre of flat land. Adam pointed out that over the boundary at the back there was a large paddock with a small stream. The land would require a burning off of all the chick weed, harrowing, and re-seeding but that would be no problem for John and Tim. They both spent a good couple of hours there, then Mary asked her brother what he thought.

Adam sat down on the old wooden seat and did a quick estimate on what it would cost.

'Well, the work would not be a problem, but the price of £2,000 seems a little high. I suggest that we go back to the agent and offer the full price if we can have that field at the back. But if not, don't worry – there are always other places.'

They drove back to the agents and put in their offer.

Chapter Seventy

In the meantime, Tim had been busy organising the plans for the Willows in Oxford. He had got the outline plan, which was for all the outside work. He pointed out to Mary that this would require planning permission; all interior work on existing buildings did not. Tim, taking advantage of his knowledge on stone-wall building, had shown on the plan most of the work would be done in Cornish stone. Although it would put the cost up considerably, he knew the planning authorities would love it.

The Wigan architect Philip Holmes, who was a friend of Tim's, and well known for planning barn conversions, had done a marvellous job on the interior. Unknown to Mary, he had gone up to Oxford with Phil, who had taken dozens of pictures and measurements.

Tim wanted it to be a surprise for Mary.

Adam, Rose, Mary, and all the children were all sitting in the lounge. Mary had been telling them all about life in America, Mary suggested that they should all go over as they would love it. Carole immediately ran to her dad.

'Can we, oh please, Dad, can we all go?'

'Well, it will take some planning. I can't say when, but I promise we will all go, sometime.'

They heard a car pull up. It was Tim. Carole, of course, ran to meet him, shouting, 'We are all going to America!'

Tim, smiling, replied, 'Well, I hope I can come with you.'

Rose then asked her brother, 'Where have you been all week?'

'Oh, I have had a busy time.' He sat next to Mary and asked, 'What have you been up to?'

She explained that she and Adam had been looking for a place for their parents, and were waiting to find out if their offer had been accepted.

Tim said he was going home to freshen up then he asked Mary if she would like to go to the Fox & Hounds at Roby Mill for a meal?

Looking at Rose, she replied, 'Well, I promised I would help with the meal here tonight.'

'Well, don't worry, you two take off! Adam and I will catch up on the paperwork. I have a beef stew prepared for later,' Rose said, reminding Mary to take a key. 'We will probably have gone to bed. Have a nice time.'

The minute Tim and Mary left, both Rose and Adam started laughing. 'I think it is beginning to work out with those two,' said Adam.

Tim drove the couple of miles or so to the Fox & Hounds.

Jack Rowland, the landlord, stood behind the bar. He greeted Tim.

'Hello, nice to see you again!'

Tim introduced Mary. When they had got their drinks, they asked for the menu and sat down in the corner booth. Mary asked Tim, 'Have you known the boss a long time?'

Tim explained, 'I have known of him for many years. He played for Wigan RFC before the war and was capped several times for England. The war interrupted his career, and when it was over he was a little too old. That's when he took over this pub. He is very well known and very well liked.'

During their meal, Tim informed Mary that he had got all the outline plans from the architect. 'After our meal, if you want, we can call at my place before I take you back. Then you can have a look and see if you like them.' Mary thought that was a good idea.

The pub started to get busy. Just before Tim and Mary left, a man about forty came over to Tim.

'I'm so pleased I have seen you. I was going to call you tomorrow. That old stone wall around the boundary, I want it removing. Could you come up and give me an estimate?'

Tim said he would call in on Friday afternoon.

As they were leaving he told Mary, 'That's Jimmy Taylor, another former Wigan rugby player. He has a big house at Coppull; it used to be an old bakery. He has done a lot of work on it, but for some reason does not like the tall stone wall. He said it's like living in a bloody prison. Actually I think the stone is Yorkshire, and if I am right I will remove it for free. The stone is worth a fortune; I could use it at the cottage.'

As they walked across car park Mary linked her arm and his. 'You are a crafty one, Tim Birchall.'

When they got back to Tim's place, it was still only 9.45 p.m.

They went inside. In the stone fireplace the logs were still smouldering. Tim threw another one on. He got the plans from a drawer and spread them out on the coffee table. 'Look over those, I will get us a drink.'

The next hour was spent explaining the plans to Mary. She was thrilled to see how the gardens had been planned, and the space enlarged for the kitchen, as well as two extra bathrooms, and a large extension on the back, for entertaining.

'How long do you think it will take for all this work?'

Tim suggested that he take two very good construction workers, a carpenter and bricklayer.

'They would be happy to live in the place; in other words, they would be living on the job. I looked at the west side of the house; that requires the least amount of work. The guys that I have in mind would be willing and able to make themselves comfortable in that part. That, of course, is up to you. If you agree, I will arrange a meeting with them. They finish their present contract next week.'

Mary was pleased with the arrangements.

It was 1 a.m. when Tim drove into Adam's place. Apart from the porch light, everything was in darkness. He left his car near the gates, so as not to disturb anyone. They walked up to the house. Mary was relaxed and content and allowed Tim to kiss her several times.

Before he left, he said, 'I'm afraid I won't be able to see you for a few days. I have to go up to the Lakes.'

He did not explain for what, and Mary did not ask.

The day after, over breakfast, Adam informed her that the agent in Wigan had accepted the offer of £2,000 for the bungalow, and would include the extra land.

'That's great! I will go in this morning and pay for it.'

Adam did not like the way his sister rushed into paying for everything so quickly. However, he understood her point of view; she was only here for a limited time and was keen to finalise as much as possible. Adam asked, 'What if Mum and Dad don't like it?'

Without hesitation, Mary said, 'Well, it will come in for one of the kids.' Adam had no answer for that.

Then she called Tim.

'What time are you going up to the Lakes?'

'Oh, in about two hours. Why?'

'I will be going to Gateley later today and staying overnight. If we can combine our trips, we can use one car.'

Tim was all for that, but there were a couple of problems.

'Before I leave I have to do that deal with Jimmy Taylor; remember the stone wall? I don't want to miss out on that. The other thing, I will have to be at the Lakes at least two days. If you can work around that, it will be great. They agreed on that arrangement. Tim said he would pick her up at 10 a.m.

Mary told Adam and Rose her plan. 'I will probably be away a couple of days,' she said, she then asked Adam to call the agent in Wigan to tell him she was on her way and would sign for the bungalow.

Three hours later Tim and Mary were driving along the Preston Road. Mary was actually humming a little tune to herself.

She had signed for the bungalow and Tim had done a good deal with the Yorkshire stone. He would have it all stored at the cottage; already he had plans for its use. They decided that they would have lunch on the way, then Tim would drop Mary off at her parents' place. He would then hopefully complete his business, then pick her up back at her parents' cottage. The plans dovetailed, apart from his needing three days rather than two. However, Mary enjoyed spending time with her mum and dad. She had visited his allotment and taken her mum into Garstang on the local bus, which was a lovely and different experience for her. Tim called every night at 9 p.m. and chatted with Mary. On the third evening, Mary was having dinner with her parents. They had discussed the bungalow. Her parents said they would love to move nearer the grandchildren, but would like to keep the cottage. Mary explained that it would not be a problem, then the phone rang.

Mary jumped up to answer it. James and Celia didn't bother, knowing it would be Tim.

When she returned to the table the big smile said it all.

'Tim has finished all his business and will call for me tomorrow around 11 a.m.'

Mary was up bright and early, but even so, when she got downstairs, Celia was already cooking the eggs and bacon.

During breakfast, Celia asked her daughter, 'Do you think that you and Tim will get married?'

'Mum, at this stage I really don't know. We think a lot about each other, and I would like to think that we will get married.' She paused and put her arm around her mother. 'You and Dad will be the first to know,' she assured her.

Just before leaving, Mary asked her dad, 'Where would I find Fred?'

James thought for a moment. 'Well, for the last several years on a Wednesday afternoon, there's only one place he would be: the horse sales at Ben Fisher's farm. The Romanies from all over still gather there to buy and sell ponies, dogs and carts.'

'I think you took Adam and me once when we were little,' answered Mary.

She and Tim waved as they drove off.

Chapter Seventy-one

It was only a fifteen minute drive before they turned into a very large field. Tim parked near a group of cars. They walked over to the paddock, where a large crowd was gathered. Within a few minutes she spotted Fred. He was obviously much older, and bigger, but it was definitely Fred. As she approached him, he turned and immediately recognised her.

'Well, well, well!' he exclaimed, 'It's Mary! I heard you were visiting from America.'

Mary smiled then shook hands.

'You already know Tim.'

'Indeed I do.'

Mary came right to the point.

'I want to buy a nice quiet pony, suitable for riding and also used to harness. It's for my niece, who's thirteen years old.'

Fred took them over to his Land Rover, where he had tethered three ponies that he had bought that morning. He went straight to a brown colt.

'Now, this I bought from a friend, who I can trust. He broke him for riding and trap.'

Mary asked, 'Would you sell him to me?'

'Well,' said Fred, 'That's what I do for a living!'

'How much do you want?'

'Normally I would get thirty pounds for him but I owe Adam, so you can have him for twenty-five.'

'Could you deliver the pony to Adam's place? Next Saturday it is my niece's birthday.'

Mary then asked about a very nice trap that Fred had made.

'Yes, that's also for sale: fifty pounds.'

Mary then got right to the point.

'OK, Fred, I want the pony, the trap, a harness, and a saddle for riding, all delivered. Can you do that for me?'

'I sure can.'

'How much for the lot?'

It did not take Fred long to calculate the price.

'I will let you have a good deal. 160 pounds.'

Mary took a roll of notes out of her bag, counted out 200 and gave it to Fred. They shook hands and the deal was done.

'Just before Mary and Tim left, Fred shouted, 'You have given me too much!'

Mary replied, 'Treat that lovely wife of yours! Thank you, Fred.'

Back at Adam's house, Mary told her brother and sister-in-law, 'I have bought a pony for Carole. Fred is bringing it on Saturday. He will put it in the orchard before we get back. I thought I would take all the kids to Blackpool on Saturday, then it will be a nice surprise for Carole when we get back.'

Mary mentioned that she would like to do little something for everyone.

'There's no need to do that,' Adam told her. Mary insisted, 'I have missed them growing up and this is what I want to do. Adam knew better than to argue with his sister.

When Tim found out that Mary was taking all the children to Blackpool, he called her and said he would like to come.

'That would be fine. I am leaving at 8 a.m. and will be taking my car,' she told him.

The next morning, every one was up and ready to go, they were lucky with the weather. Martyn, Gary, Jack and Carole all got in the back, and Tim sat in the front with Mary. It was a really nice drive along the Blackpool Road. Round the next bend, the famous tower was in sight, and twenty minutes later Mary parked the car in the Winter Gardens car park.

They all walked across the road to the Promenade, where the children made a mad dash for the sands. Tim got two coffees from the nearby kiosk. They sat down and Tim pulled a photo out of his wallet.

'Do you remember this?'

'It was a picture of him and Mary walking along the Promenade. Mary started laughing.

'God, we looked older there than we do now! I suppose it was the way we were dressed.'

When the kids returned, they all wanted to go to the Pleasure Beach. This was a British Coney Island, two miles south of the Tower. They all got on the topless tram, and when they arrived, Mary gave each of them five shillings.

'Now, I want you all to come back here when you are ready. This is were Uncle Tim and I will be.'

As Tim and Mary walked around, they talked about the pony she had got for Carole.

'I'm afraid that I have created a big job for you.'

Tim assured her it was no problem.

Every time they saw the kids on a ride, they had to wave; they were obviously having a ball.

Like all good things, it passed too quickly and it was time to leave. But Tim suggested that they all go up the Tower before heading for home. This was greeted with yells of, 'Oh, yes, yes!' and turned out to be the big favourite of the day.

At a short stop on the way home at Walton-le-Dale near Preston, there was ice cream all round, and Mary got the chance to call Rose. She was happy to learn that Fred had kept his promise, and everything had been delivered.

Mary then asked Tim, 'When we get back, would you mind taking the boys into Wigan. I left 100 pounds with Tom Hughes.'

Tom owned the town's top bicycle shop.

'I gave instructions that when the boys call, they are to choose whichever bike they want.'

Tim did this on the pretence that he was picking something up for Adam, and wanted some help. Carole could not wait to tell her mother what a smashing time they had all had in Blackpool.

Rose then asked Carole, 'Can you go to the bottom orchard and get some apples? I will make a pie for tonight.' Carole was in such a happy mood, she grabbed a basket.

'Would you like to come with me, Auntie Mary?' she asked.

'I would love to.'

They both walked down the path and across the field towards the orchard. Mary was expecting to see the pony, but there was no sign of it. Mary was beginning to get a little worried. Had the pony escaped? Then, without warning, when they turned the corner, standing in the middle of the path was Bowler. Carole dropped the basket of apples and stood there with her mouth wide open.

She said, 'I wonder how he got here? We must get back to the house and call the police. He must have broken loose from somewhere.'

Mary thought it was time to explain. She took Carole's hand.

'Come and sit down here. They both sat on the old tree log. Bowler walked over and helped himself to an apple.

'Would you be happy if he was yours?' Mary asked.

'Oh, Auntie Mary, I would do anything, anything at all!' Mary put her arms around Carole.

'Well, his name is Bowler, and he is yours. I will be going back to America in a couple of weeks, but I will be coming back soon and Gary and Aunt Lucy will be with me.'

Carole was overcome with excitement. She hugged her aunt.

'I will miss you, but I will write every week. And I love you so much.'

Mary told her, 'I said I would get you a pony, and now you have one of your own. Promise me that you will look after him and keep me informed on how you get on.'

Carole wanted to make really sure she was not dreaming.

'You mean that he is really mine?'

Tears were streaming down her face as Bowler came over and pushed his nose into Carole's hands.

Mary got up. 'You stay here and get to know Bowler,' she said.

Chapter Seventy-two

When Mary got back in the house, she walked into the kitchen with the apples and told Rose that Carole was still down with Bowler.

Rose replied, 'It would not surprise me if she wanted to sleep in the barn tonight.' Rose thanked Mary for her generosity.

Tim had taken the boys to the cycle shop. They, like Carole, could not believe their eyes when they saw all the top bikes on show. Tim then told each one of them, 'Your Aunt Mary has treated you all. You can choose any bike you want.' They all decided on a Claud Butler model, hand-built with light-weight tubing. Martyn chose a red one, Gary had blue, and Little Jack had a black one with chrome forks. Tim loaded them all into the Land Rover, and when he got to the Adam's drive, he lifted them out, telling all the boys to wait five minutes then all come riding up the drive. Tim got everyone outside on the porch.

'I want you to see this,' he told them.

On cue, all the boys came racing up the drive. Rose could not help feeling that her sister-in-law really loved children and was a very special lady. When Rose said, 'You are spoiling them!' Mary looked at her and said, 'I intend on spoiling you all.'

When John and May arrived, Little Jack went running over to his parents.

'Come and look what Auntie Mary's bought me!'

He jumped on his bike and proudly showed how he could operate the gears.

May said to Mary, 'Before you go back to America, we would like you, Tim, Adam and Rose to come over to us for a meal.'

'That would be lovely, thanks.'

Rose had arranged a cold-meat buffet. All the food was in the kitchen but Adam had put the big tables on the terrace. Everyone filled their plates and sat outside.

It had been two hours since Mary had left Carole. She mentioned this to Adam.

'Oh, she will be OK. When she gets hungry, she will be here.'

Mary went inside for her movie camera. When she came out, everyone was leaning on the fence, looking down the field. Carole was cantering around the orchard on Bowler. She was riding bareback, just holding on to Bowler's mane; she was obviously a natural.

All the boys thought Bowler was fantastic. Carole's brother Martyn even said she could ride his new bike if he could ride Bowler. Tim said it would be better if they left that for another day.

Tim volunteered to take him down to the barn, and Carole went with him.

'He will be OK in here until I build a stable,' he told her.

Mary had arranged for her parents to come to Wigan on the train. She met them and took them straight to the bungalow. James and Celia had never seen anything like it. Although there was lots to do, it was habitable, and it would not take long to decorate.

Mary had arranged to take her parents shopping in Southport and she invited Rose along, who did not need asking a second time. Mary instructed them to be ready for 9am the following morning. As it was a very nice sunny morning, Mary decided to put the top down on her Zephyr Six. Her parents sat in the back, Rose next to Mary in the front. At 9:15 they pulled out of the drive. Mary drove the 28 miles via Rufford; it was a very enjoyable drive through beautiful countryside. An hour later Mary parked the car on the seafront, they all had coffee and then made their way along the famous Lord Street. Mary told them both, 'Whatever you want for your new home, if you see it, I want you to have it.'

James spotted a large garden store. He wasn't one for looking at curtains and such. Mary realised this and said, 'Look, Dad, why don't you go inside and pick out a few things? We won't be long.'

A broad smile appeared on his face.

'Oh you don't have to rush back, I will be fine here.'

Mary had chance to see the salesman. 'This is my father. Whatever he wants, he can have, just put it at one side until I come back.'

Mary and her mother went further along Lord Street. The looked in various shops, then they went into the Kardoma tea rooms. In the meantime James was enjoying looking at all the latest gardening gear and listening to the salesman explaining a rotary cultivator; this gadget certainly beat all the back-breaking spade work.

When Mary and her mum walked back into the shop, there was a pile of assorted gear that James had chosen near the door. James was at the far end of the store looking at a mini tractor with a neat half-tonne trailer and various attachments. James could not believe the things it could do. Mary asked him if he would like it.

'I sure would but it is 150 pounds,' he replied.

Mary gave the salesman the address of the bungalow at Dalton.

'I want you to deliver all the stuff that my father has picked out, and include the tractor he was looking at,' she said. Mary paid the man and they all left.

Back in Wrightington, Mary explained to her brother what she had done, arranging for all the stuff that James wanted to be delivered at the bungalow.

The following day was Saturday. In the afternoon, Rose, Celia and Mary went to Chorley market; they wanted to get new curtains and several rugs. Chorley Market was the place for such things. Carole had invited Sandra, her friend, for the day. They were going out with Bowler and the new trap. All the boys had gone to Parbold Gardens on their bikes.

Adam had taken James over to the bungalow to check on the decorators. Everyone had arranged to be back at the house at 6 p.m. The day at the market turned out to be a real bonanza shopping day. It was a good thing that Mary had a large car.

Apart from the curtains and rugs, Rose had bought a couple of tracksuits for the boys, and a thick blanket for Carole to keep her warm when she was out with Bowler and the trap. During the morning Mary had managed to go missing for half an hour. She came back with several small parcels, but did not comment to Rose or Celia about what she had got.

Adam was pleasantly surprised at the amount of work the decorators had done in four days; the place looked really homely.

As arranged everyone met up at Adam's house except Tim. It was only 6 p.m., Adam told them that the bungalow was looking good and the decorating would be finished in a couple of days.

Mary suggested, as all the stuff that they had bought was still in the car, 'Why don't I drive round there and put it in the bedroom? Then at least it is there.' Everyone thought that was a good idea. 'Come on, Mum, you come with me,' she suggested.

She drove them the short distance to Dalton.

Carole and her friend Sandra came in. They had spent a smashing afternoon trotting round the country lanes. All excited, she told everyone how good Bowler was pulling the trap, and how everyone they passed stopped to watch. Then she said, 'Where is Aunt Mary?' Rose told her she had taken her granny to the bungalow, but wouldn't be long.

Then Carole wanted to know how long it would be before they had dinner.

When she found out it would be another hour or so, she suggested that she and Sandra go down to the barn to make sure Bowler was OK. Looking round, she called Skipper, who bounded down the path in front of them.

The whole family had a marvellous week. Mary was delighted with what she had been able to achieve with the help of her brother and Tim. She was particularly happy, knowing that her mum and dad would be very close to Adam and Rose. She had got to know all the family again after so long, and met most of their friends.

On Monday morning Mary and Rose, like always, had a cup of tea in the kitchen after the kids had gone to school and Adam had gone to work. Rose loved having a chat with her sister-in-law. The conversation always came down to her brother, Tim.

'I have loved being here and thank you all very much for looking after me. I can't believe how quickly the time as gone. Next Saturday I will be leaving! I will be sorry to go, but I am longing to see my son.' Then she took Rose's hand, 'I will be back in six months,' she said. 'Gary and Aunt Lucy will be with me.' Suddenly, trying not to get too down, she said, 'I am going round to Mother's, to see how they are doing. Why don't you come with me? Then I can take you for lunch, then we can pick up the kids from school.'

Rose replied, 'You're on. I will be ready in two minutes.'

The last few days of Mary's visit were a mixture of joy and tears. Her parents had settled in the bungalow. Her mum had got it looking very nice with the new furniture and curtains, and her dad had got all his gear from Southport and had already started to clear the back with his little tractor. He promised his daughter, 'You won't recognise this place when you come back.'

Carole spent more time down at the barn with Bowler and Skipper than in the house. The boys Gary and Martyn and their cousin Jack had all joined the Wigan Wheelers Cycling Club.

Adam was expanding, buying land, and all in all the Roberts and Birchalls were doing OK.

Mary must have been miles away, sitting next to Tim, when she heard him say, 'Are you all right?'

They were on their way to Oxford. Tim had promised to drive her down, check on the house, and then, after a night in a hotel, Mary would fly out of Heathrow back to America.

Mary slid along the bench seat and got closer to Tim. 'Oh yes, I am fine.' They were using Mary's car. Tim would then take it back and store it in the barn until her next visit.

When they arrived at the Willows, Mary was very pleased to see three workmen there and even more pleased when she saw what they had already done. Bill Robinson, Greg Leyland and Allen Monks were the three builders that Tim had recommended. Bill seemed to be the one in charge. They had made themselves comfortable in the part of the house that required the least work.

Bill promised Mary that they would do a good job and that it would all be completed as per plan in six months. Feeling content and happy with that arrangement, they left for London.

Mary had booked two rooms at the Imperial, and after booking in they decided to go out for dinner rather than stay in the hotel.

Although it would be their last night together for some time, and everything had gone to plan, they both knew that the following morning, would be difficult.

At 6.30 Tim went to reception and booked a taxi. He had already booked a table at the Italian restaurant, Nino's. The desk clerk had recommended it. It turned out that he knew what he was talking about. Their meal consisted of risotto, fish, salad and a bottle of red wine, They both lingered over their last glass and it was after midnight when they got back to the hotel. The bar was still open. Tim took Mary's hand, 'Come on, let's have a nightcap.'

It was then that Mary started to feel herself getting emotional. The situation, and the wine, were beginning to take effect. Tim had never tried to force her into a romantic obligation; this was one of many things that Mary respected him for. They held hands across the table, the thought of sharing a room that night in both their minds.

Chapter Seventy-three

Mary heard the stewardess ask, 'Are you all right, Madam?

She must have been asking her something.

'Oh, I am sorry. I was miles away.'

The stewardess smiled.

'Would you like a drink?'

'Oh yes, please. I would love a black coffee. How long have we been travelling?'

'Three hours and ten minutes. You have been asleep for over two hours, we will be serving lunch shortly.'

Mary had been going over the previous night. Tim had not put any pressure on her to share a room. They had got the lift up to their rooms, holding hands. Mary, without saying a word walked into her room, leading Tim.

She closed the door and they kissed passionately.

It had been very hard saying goodbye. For the first time in ten years, she realised that she could love another man. Tim knew that she had to go back to America. He had always loved her and had told her many times, although it would be several months before they would be together again. As he drove back to Wigan he was singing, and felt happier than he had been for a very long time.

They had promised to call each other every day.

Aunt Lucy, Laura and Mark were all waiting in the arrival lounge at LA airport. There were lots of hugs all round, and they were all back at the house at 3 p.m. The first thing that Mary did was call the college and let Gary know she was back and would visit him on the following weekend.

The following Saturday, Tim had accepted an invitation from his sister to go over for dinner. He also wanted to get started on the stable for Carole's pony, Bowler.

After dinner Rose said to Tim, 'Come in the kitchen and help me with the dishes.'

Adam knew what she was up to and said, 'I will check on the children.'

Rose closed the door of the kitchen, turned to her brother and asked, 'Come on, what happened in Oxford? When did you last speak to her? Is it serious?'

'Hang on, slow down.' Tim, smiling, said, 'I spoke to her yesterday, and when I get home I will call her. Midnight here is afternoon in California.'

'I know all that,' said Rose, getting more impatient. 'But do you think—'

Tim put his hand on his sister's shoulder.

'We both feel a lot for each other and I would marry her tomorrow, but she has lots to sort out in America first. If I tell you something, I don't want you to mention it to anyone, especially Adam.'

Rose could not contain her excitement.

I know! I know! You spent the night together!'

The smile on Tim's face said it all. Rose flung her arms around him.

'I am so pleased. Adam and I did the same thing on the barge so you have made a good start.'

Mary had been busy catching up with all what had happened while she was away in England. Mark had been working very hard and had secured two more big insurance cases to defend. Colin always said that he would turn out to be a good lawyer. She walked over to his picture on the dresser, picked it up and with damp eyes whispered, 'You were always so right.'

She showered and put on a new dress she had bought in England, then went downstairs. She was looking forward to picking Gary up and bringing him home for the weekend. Mary had asked Aunt Lucy to come with her. They had already talked about her involvement with Tim, but she still felt a little guilty. Aunt Lucy had assured her that it was perfectly normal; she should make a new life for herself.

Mary confessed, 'I am nervous how I should tell Gary.'

Aunt Lucy suggested, 'Why don't we both tell him tonight? Remember, Gary never knew his father, and I am sure he will look forward to meeting Tim. I have not even met him yet, I have spoken to him on several occasions, and with what you say he sounds like a very charming man. Stop worrying, look forward to a happy life. That's what Colin would have wanted for you and Gary.'

'Oh, Aunty, I love you so much.'

'I love you too. Now, let's go and collect that handsome son of yours.'

Over the weekend, Gary wanted to know all about England and looked at the films several times that Mary had made on her cine camera. He thought all his cousins looked great, and Carole's pony and trap were fantastic.

'When can I go and visit?' he asked.

Mary told him that next summer break she would like to take him and Aunt Lucy. Mary suggested that he should start calling his cousins more often and write to them.

Adam had been interested in a good stretch of land that that was situated along the canal and included some old buildings that were no longer used. He decided to go up to Lancaster and take a closer look. He asked John and Tim to go with him. The three of them set off in Tim's Land Rover at 8 a.m. They made a stop ten miles north of Lancaster for breakfast, at a place called the May Field transport café, and they all had a big fry up.

When they got to Gateley, Tim parked near the old derelict loading bay and Adam had to mention, 'This is where I worked as a twelve-year-old.'

Most of the morning was spent walking the towpaths and making notes. Later they drove down to the Navigation pub for a pint and a sandwich. The whole parcel of land was in the region of twenty-five acres. The attraction to Adam was the 500 yards of canal frontage the old footbridge, and locks.

The three men discussed the development of a marina. Adam spotted a couple of old guys in the corner. He recognised them as Bill Morgan and Ted Leyland. Adam bought them both a pint and reminisced a little. They asked about his parents.

'Yes, Dad loves his new allotment and Mum loves being near the kids,' he told them. He then asked them if they would be interested in a part-time job. If the deal he was working on came off, they were both interested.

Adam then suggested that they should pop in the planning department in Lancaster were the land in question was registered.

It was early afternoon, when they walked into the high-street planning office. Adam asked could they speak to the planning officer. The girl went into a back office came out and told Adam, 'Mr Spencer will see you, if it won't take too long. He has another appointment in one hour.'

All three went into the back office. Adam introduced himself, then John and Tim. Adam began, 'Thank you for seeing us at such a short notice; I know you are a busy person. I will come straight to the point. We are interested in the land near the old colliery, down by the canal.'

The officer went over to a large cupboard, took out a roll of plans and spread them out on the desk.

'Now show me which part you are referring to,' he said.

Adam explained the area, then added, 'We would like all this, providing it is a reasonable price.'

'Well, the going rate for that particular area is £30 per acre.'

After several minutes with pencil and paper, Andrew Spencer, trying to look very businesslike, said, 'That will be £900 for the freehold. But I must warn you that price is subject to several conditions.'

Adam asked what they were.

'You would have to clean the whole place up, replace the old bridge, repair or replace the locks, and all the old buildings would have to be made safe. Also you would have to employ a pre-eminent watchman. Adam quickly assessed what it would mean, although he expected to do all that and lots more.

'Well, Mr Spencer, my firm can promise you and your councillors that if we take this on it will be transferred into something that will benefit the whole town. Providing we can have planning permission for a marina.'

'That's our offer,' said Mr Spencer. They all shook hands, and Mr Spencer told them, 'I cannot give the final decision, but I am confident the council will agree on those terms. I will let you know within two weeks.'

At that, Adam, John and Tim left.

He then asked Tim to drive back into the village, so he could call on Fred. When they arrived at Fred's place, Marion, his wife, was hanging out the washing when she saw Adam.

'Good heavens, Adam Roberts! What are you doing here?'

'We have been attending to a little business. I would like to have a chat with Fred; is he about?'

'Oh he's where he always is: down in the barn, working. If you are going down there, bring him back. I will put the kettle on.'

They found Fred putting the finishing touches to a colourful design on the side of a cart he had built. Fred was as surprised to see Adam and his brothers-in-law, as Marion had been. He warmly greeted them. Tim was really impressed with the workmanship of the cart and complimented Fred.

'I have to get it ready for this customer. He will use it in the Kendal show next week.'

Adam told him briefly about the land deal.

'Marion wants you to come back up to your van with us. I can explain in more detail to you both.'

They all strolled back. Marion had made tea and brought out a variety of home-made cakes which they all enjoyed. Adam got right to the point.

'I am hoping to buy the freehold on the old loading site, plus the acreage adjoining it and I would like you to help me develop it. You could move your van up near the old blacksmith shop, which I want to enlarge into an operational centre for the whole project.

'There are several conditions: the bridge has to be replaced, locks repaired, and so on, but nothing that your skills can't handle. I will pay you well, and you can still do your own work.'

Fred was really all for it. Before they left Adam said he would come up again in a couple of weeks.

'I am hoping to have all the final permissions by then.' As they were driving away, Marion shouted, 'Bring Rose with you, and that lovely daughter of yours.' Adam shouted back, 'I will.'

When they got back to Wrightington, all three went into the house. Rose mentioned to Tim that Mary had been on the phone.

'She said to tell you that she would call you tonight at 6.30 p.m. our time.'

Tim looked at his watch. It was almost 6 p.m. He finished his beer and left.

He had only been in the house a few minutes when the phone rang, Tim picked it up on the first ring.

'Hi, how are you?'

Mary could not believe it. 'How did you know it was me?'

'My sister told me. I have only just got back.'

Mary did not waste any time. 'I would like you to come over for a couple of weeks; can you manage that?'

'Well, I don't really know. I will have a word with Adam.'

Mary interrupted, 'Tim, just tell that brother of mine he has got to give you time off to come. I have made up my mind on several things and I want you and I to discuss them.'

'OK, I will see him tomorrow and call you,' replied Tim.

Chapter Seventy-four

Tim mentioned to Adam that he would like to take a couple of weeks off. Adam had no problem with that as things were running pretty smoothly.

Tim went ahead and booked a flight, leaving from London and changing planes in New York. His plans were to go down to Oxford, take more pictures of the Willows, stay overnight, and fly out the following morning.

On the day Tim was due to arrive, Mary checked that the plane was on time and had left New York; it would be seven hours before it would arrive at the Los Angeles International Airport. With the help of Aunt Lucy, Mary got the guest room ready, realising that after such a long journey Tim would be tired and would feel better after a little rest. She had arranged a dinner party for that evening, so Tim could meet some of her friends; caterers would prepare it all. Before leaving for the airport, she reminded Aunt Lucy that the caterers would arrive early. 'They will do everything; just show them the kitchen,' she told her.

Mary arrived at the airport a good hour before the plane was due to land. She went into the airport lounge, ordered a coffee and picked up a magazine. The next hour seemed to go so quickly, and after checking her make-up in the ladies' room, she made her way to the arrival gate. Tim had never visited America before. As all the passengers started to come through, Mary was looking out for him. When it seemed everyone had come through and there was no sign of Tim, Mary started to get concerned. Had he missed the plane? She was just about to ask when there he was.

Mary almost burst out laughing. Tim was wearing a heavy tweed jacket with thick shirt and tie, carrying two small bags. He looked as though he would collapse any moment.

After Mary had hugged and kissed him, she said, 'Take that coat and tie off! You are in LA now. Outside the airport it is eighty degrees.'

Tim asked if he could have a cool beer. Mary took him to the bar, got him a beer and let him cool down. They then went to Mary's car. When Tim saw it he said, 'You don't go for anything small, do you?'

Tim put his bags into the boot and got in the car. On the way back, Mary stopped at an outfitter's.

'We will go in here and get you some sensible clothes to wear.' He looked a little embarrassed. 'Take your time – I will look next door in the ladies' department.'

Forty-five minutes later Tim looked a completely different person. He was wearing a lightweight pair of blue trousers with matching shirt and white boating shoes. Mary had told Andrea, the manager of the clothes outfitters where Mary took Tim, to make up an extra outfit, including shorts and swimwear. All this was done and loaded into the trunk of Mary's car. On the ride to the house, Mary could see that he was impressed with the surroundings. Although he had seen lots of pictures of the house, when they turned into the drive he could not believe his eyes. The house was enormous.

Mary could see that Tim was fading fast and his eyes were closing.

'Come on, I will take you up to your room.'

The bedroom was twice the size of his at home, and had a great view of the pool with the mountains in the distance. Mary kissed him.

'I am so pleased that you are here! Now have a shower and a rest; I don't want you to go to sleep on me tonight.'

Mary went downstairs and called England. Rose answered.

'I just wanted to let you know that Tim has arrived and is having a little nap. I did not want him falling asleep on me tonight.'

Rose could not help the asking, 'Will you be sharing a room?'

Mary replied, 'Of course not!' Then gave a little chuckle, 'Well, not here anyway. I will be taking him on several trips so maybe when we are on our own.'

Rose wanted to know more but Mary asked to speak to her brother. 'I will call you again in a day or so,' she promised.

Adam came on. Mary thanked him for letting Tim come over.

'No problem! How are things going?'

'I have decided to put everything on the line. I am taking him on a couple of trips and tonight I am giving a dinner party so he will meet some of my friends. I want to find out if he would like America, because if we do get married we would have to live here at least six months out of the year.'

Mary ended the call saying, 'I will let you know how it works out. Give my love to the children.'

As Mary put the phone down, the doorbell rang. It was the caterers. She took the couple through to the kitchen, then showed them the dining room and reminded them that she would like dinner served at 8 p.m.

Mary looked across the street. She could see Aunt Lucy in her garden. Mary walked across.

'What are you doing, working in this heat?'

'I thought I would cut some of these lovely flowers and bring them over. I notice that Tim has arrived; did he have a good flight?'

'Yes, everything went OK. He was shattered, so I told him to have a rest. I would like you to come over before the others arrive, as I don't want to swamp him, meeting every one at the same time.' Mary took the flowers, then asked her aunt to come over at 6 p.m. before going to check on Tim.

When she tapped on the bedroom door, there was no sound. Mary decided to let him have another half-hour. She went into her own room and put on a different dress and fresh make-up, then she heard the shower going in Tim's room. She knocked on the door and went in. Tim had just walked out of the shower with a towel around him and a big smile on his face.

'How do you feel? You certainly look all right.'

'I feel great,' he said and went over to put his arms around her and give her a hug.

Mary, not quiet trusting herself with the situation, quickly said, 'It is 5.45. The guests will start arriving at 6.30. I have brought you these new clothes; everyone will be dressed casually. When you're ready come downstairs. I want you to meet Aunt Lucy properly first.'

Twenty minutes later, Tim walked into the study, Mary and her aunt were standing near the window. Tim walked straight to Aunt Lucy and gave her a big hug.

'I am so pleased to meet you at last,' he said.

Mary left them and went to check on the caterers. This gave them time to get to know each other.

During the evening Tim met all Mary's friends and to her delight he seemed to take it all in his stride. He got on particularly well with Maurice, looking relaxed with them all, and mixing freely.

Mark and Laura were a very interesting couple. He could understand why Laura was Mary's best friend. It was almost midnight when the last guest left. Lucy came over to Tim.

'I have loved being with you and am looking forward to visiting England,' she said.

Tim promised to show her around London. Lucy was delighted when he said he would walk her home. After making sure that she was OK, he went back to the house and he and Mary were on their own. Mary poured them both a nightcap, then said, 'You haven't seen my room, have you?' They walked up the stairs went into Mary's room and closed the door.

Mary was up bright and early, prepared breakfast then called Tim. They had their coffee at the poolside.

'How did you enjoy your first night in America?'

'It was a very nice evening. You have some very nice people around you. The whole evening was very enjoyable,' then with his cheeky smile, he added, 'Especially the last couple of hours.' He took hold of her hand. 'I do hope we can work things out.'

Mary poured more coffee. 'That's what we have to do during your visit.' Mary went on to explain what she wanted to show and tell him. 'Gary is the most important person in the world to me and whatever I do, he must feel part of it. You already know that the business is a very large concern, although I don't have any control over it directly. It provides me with a very good lifestyle. If we did get married, we would have to be here at least six months every year.'

Tim stretched his arms across the table, taking hold of Mary's hands.

'Now, I want you to listen to me. I loved you when neither of us had anything. Remember the time we went to Blackpool? The fact that you are now a very wealthy woman makes no difference to how I feel about you. You know a little about my Australian investment. Well, it is providing me with more than enough income, and can only improve. I also have other things going on with your brother, plus I have started to create the stone wall business. What I am really trying to say is, all your wealth is for that son of yours; I don't have to rely on any of it.'

After two exhausting days showing Tim around all the offices and the buildings that were being turned into further offices, the waterfront apartment, as well as the general local amenities, it was time to meet Gary; school was out for the holiday week. Mary pulled into the campus, parked and walked into the side entrance where lots of other parents were waiting.

It wasn't long before dozens of boys came charging out. Gary was one of the first. He ran straight to his mother and they hugged each other, then Gary looked at Tim. 'Hello, you are Mum's boyfriend. I am Gary. Pleased to meet you; you look a lot bigger than your photograph.' Gary then introduced a friend. 'This is Richard, he lives in Boston and does not go home on short-term visits. Could he come home with us?'

Mary, of course, said yes but said she would have to see the principal first. Tim shook hands with both boys. When Mary had sorted it out with the school's principal, Richard got his bag, and all four got into the car.

Gary asked Tim non-stop questions: 'How long are you here for? Do you like sailing and fishing? Can you swim?'

In the end Mary had to stop him. 'You will find out all those things later,' she said. The boys chatted with excitement. It was a regular thing that Mary always stopped at Mario's ice-cream parlour. The boys had a large strawberry cone and Tim and Mary had a rum raisin each.

The first thing that Gary did when they got to the house, was to take his friend over to his grandmother's, give her a big hug, and introduce his friend.

'We are having a BBQ tonight and Mum wants you to join us,' he told her, then Gary shouted, 'See you later, Grandma.'

They could not wait to get in the pool. Tim had already changed into his swimwear and was waiting for the boys. He had promised them $5 each if they beat him in a two-length pool race. Mary would be the starter. Tim had to give them five seconds' start.

They lined up and Mary said, 'On your marks, set, go!'

The boys were off and very good. Mary then counted, 'Five, four, three, two, one, go!'

Tim dived in. Mary had never seen him swim and was amazed how powerful he was. Without making it too obvious, he let the boys win, then spent had half an hour fooling around with them.

After Tim had showered and changed into casual slacks and a shirt, he got himself a beer and sat next to Mary. They watched the boys for a few more minutes, who were still in the pool. Then Mary shouted, 'Come on, you two. Go and get ready. We have to get organised for tonight.'

Tim offered to go to the store and take the boys with him. It was only a short drive down to the harbour. When they had put all the shopping in the cool box, Gary grabbed Tim's hand. 'Come on, I will show you a boat. Mum will get me one like it when I have graduated.'

He took Tim along the boardwalk. Anchored at the far end was a thirty-footer with inboard engine. The name *Sea Dancer* was painted across the stern. Tim had noticed a picture in Aunt Lucy's lounge showing Colin and Mary on the boat. Colin was holding Gary up against the wheel, with a captain's cap on.

The evening was very relaxing for Mary, Tim and Aunt Lucy. When the boys had gone to bed, Tim escorted Lucy across the road to her house. Then he and Mary sat on the terrace, just discussing various plans.

The following week was a real eye-opener for Tim. In such a short time he felt he belonged in America. He had enjoyed being with Gary and already felt he could be a father to him. However, all good things come to an end, and it was time for Gary and Richard to go back to school. Then Tim had only two days before he would have to fly back to England. He wanted to take Laura and Mark out for dinner; he did invite Lucy too but she politely refused, knowing she would be the odd one out.

Mary booked a room at the Hilton near the airport for the last night. The four of them enjoyed their dinner together and Tim told Mark how much he had enjoyed meeting him and Laura. Early next morning, before they left, they went over to Lucy's. Tim gave her a big hug. 'It won't be long before you will all be in England, and I promise I will take you to Windsor Castle, and Gary can watch the changing of the guards.'

Mary drove them to the hotel. Both he and Mary were satisfied with what they had achieved regarding their plans for the future. That last night they dined alone. Parting was difficult, but because their future together seemed settled, it was also a happy time.

Chapter Seventy-five

During Tim's absence, his brother and Adam had decided on the land at Ormskirk. They would try once more to improve the soil, by adding one hundred tonnes of seaweed which they would transport from near by Southport. They also put in for planning permission for development as an alterative. Everything seemed to be going well, but lately Adam had been complained about always feeling tired. This particular morning, he did not feel very well, so Rose insisted he go back to bed, and she called the doctor. A quick examination revealed that he had appendicitis. The doctor called the ambulance and got him into Wigan Infirmary.

The doctor assured Rose, 'Having your appendix out is a minor operation. He will be as good as new in a week.'

When Carole came in, having seen the ambulance driving out of the drive, she ran to her mother.

'Mum, what's wrong?'

'Your dad is to have a little operation,' Rose replied.

Carole had always thought of her dad as invincible and started to cry. Rose consoled her.

'Now, come on. Help me get a few things together and we will take them to the hospital.'

When they got there Adam had already been prepared for his operation. Rose was told, 'You will be able to see him tomorrow. Call after 7 p.m. tonight and we can then let you know how he is, but don't worry: he will be fine.'

Mary spent most of the day telephoning the family and cancelling Adam's appointments. She decided not to call Mary until it was all over.

Rose called the hospital at 7, and she was told that Adam had been operated on and there was no problem. 'He is sleeping but you can visit him tomorrow afternoon.'

Rose felt much better with the good news.

All the kids got out of school early so Rose picked them up and they all went to the hospital. When they entered the ward, Adam was looking a little pale but was sitting up in bed. All the kids were delighted and when they tried to give their dad a hug, he joked, 'Don't squeeze too hard.'

The ward sister told Rose, 'He will be home at the weekend, but will have to rest for a couple of weeks.'

Rose promptly said, 'I will see to that.' That evening she called Mary and told her about Adam, but told her not to worry as he would be home at the weekend.

Mary sounded a little angry. 'Rose, you should have told me, he his my brother,' she said.

'I did not want to worry you; it wasn't serious.'

After the shock, Mary settled down. 'I will call on Sunday,' she said. 'Give him my love.'

Mary had a long conversation with her brother, who told her that he was expecting to be back to normal in a couple of weeks. In the past Adam had always been the one to advise Mary. Now Mary was telling her brother, 'You don't be too eager to get back working. We are not in our teens any more, so slow down.'

Knowing it would please his little sister, Adam assured her he would take things easy.

Sure enough four weeks to the day after his operation Adam was feeling great. He arranged a visit to Lancaster on the Saturday, and took Rose and Carole. Of course Carole asked if she could she invite Sandra. On the Saturday morning, all four set off on the two-hour drive, arriving at the little cottage at 11 a.m. He was very happy with the progress. Carole had a lovely time with Fred's daughter. Rose enjoyed some time with Fred's wife, Marion. When Adam had discussed further plans with Fred, he treated all of them to lunch at the Navigation Pub. On the way back, Rose suggested that they call on Aunt Elizabeth in Standish, who was very pleased to see them. After having tea with her, Rose reminded her, 'Whenever you want to visit, just call me and I will come for you.' Elizabeth said she would love that, and suggested they meet in another few weeks when it was warmer.

Several weeks later, Carole was down in the barn, busy grooming Bowler. Skipper was sitting on a bale of straw, watching every move. The apple blossom was in full bloom. Carole had just started her school break and was looking forward to her Aunt Mary visiting with her cousin Gary and Aunt Lucy. Uncle Tim had gone to meet them at Heathrow. They would all spend three days at the Willows then come up to Wrightington. Mary's parents, James and Celia, were so excited. James had worked hard on the garden at Dalton; he had completed the water feature and it was all looking really nice.

Tim met Mary, Lucy and Gary at the airport and drove them to the Willows. Mary was very pleased with all the work that had been done. The new hallway was very spacious and the oak staircase gave a warm and welcoming impression. The kitchen had been fitted out with American-style appliances. Gary was already running around, asking, 'Which is my room?'

Tim shouted, 'Yours is the one at the end of the landing.'

Gary replied, 'What's a landing?'

There was there was still a lot of furniture required for the large lounge and study so Tim had arranged to meet Gordon.

'He will introduce you to the right person for furniture! Then we can all go down to the pub tonight for a meal. They do very good food.'

Tim carried all the luggage upstairs. Aunt Lucy had the room opposite Gary's. Mary's was at the other end. It had a dressing room and bathroom. The other rooms had not been furnished, with the exception of a bed that Tim had been using.

The following day they all drove into London and met Gordon as arranged. Mary was introduced to a man called Darren Wilson. He was the owner of the furniture store. When Mary saw the size of the place, she realised it would be a long job choosing all the things she wanted. Tim suggested he could take Aunt Lucy and Gary into town for two or three hours and show them the Palace. He knew Mary would not want to rush. That settled, Darren gave Mary a book of stickers.

'Just wander around, take your time. Whatever you see that you like, just put a sticker on it. If you want any help I will be in my office.'

Mary spent several hours before making a final decision. Darren promised to deliver everything that afternoon.

'I will send three men. You just tell them where you want it putting.' She then had a coffee with him and paid for everything.

Tim arrived back after spending almost three hours in the city. Lucy and Gary could not believe their eyes when they saw Buckingham Palace, the Tower and the Houses of Parliament. Tim promised to take them on a more extended tour before they went back to America. Gary wanted to see the changing of the guards. The next couple of days were hectic. All the furniture had been installed and Tim had hung several more pictures in the hall. The whole place was looking more like a home. Mary called her brother and said they would all arrive around lunch time the next day. Adam suggested that if the weather was still fine, they could have a BBQ with all the family.

Adam had arranged for Aunt Lucy to stay with them. The weather was good, everyone was there to greet them and it was quite an emotional occasion.

The boys wanted to take Gary to the den and show him some of the medals they had won cycling. When they invited Gary to join them on the weekend ride, he admitted that he had not done much cycling and was afraid that he may not be able to keep up. Martyn thought it would be better if they just took him on a short ride to begin with.

During the evening everyone got to know Gary and Aunt Lucy pretty well. Celia and Lucy chatted together most of the night. As Carole's twin brother and Mary's son were both named Gary, Mary performed a mock christening on her son, pouring a cup of water over his head.

'From this moment, you will be known as GJ,' she said, not realising it would stick for a very long time.

'Everyone cheered and shouted, 'Welcome to England, GJ!' It was the end of a great night.

Before GJ went to bed, he gave his grandparents a big hug, and said how lucky and happy he was having such great grandparents, then he went round to all his relatives and thanked them for a super night.

Tim's parents were staying with their son John and his wife May. Tim and Mary drove her mum and dad home to Dalton, then went back to Tim's cottage. It was the first time they had been on their own for some time. They sat on the sofa holding each other and discussing what they would like to do.

During the weekend the boys all went to the rugby match in Wigan then had a short ride on their bikes. Carole felt a little left out. Rose realised this and asked, 'Would you like to come with us tomorrow? We are going to Southport shopping.'

Carole said she would take the trap out. The boys were off again on their bikes but GJ decided not to go.

Then she started laughing, 'Don't tell him, but Aunt Mary told me, he said his butt was sore. I think he meant his bum!'

Before the boys left Carole asked them where they were going, and Martyn replied they were only going as far as Rufford.

When everyone had left, Carole went down to the stable, harnessed Bowler to the trap and set off up the road towards the house. She was surprised to see GJ.

'Hello! I thought you had gone to Southport with your mum,' she said.

'No, I felt a little tired.'

Carole said she was going for a ride around the country lanes, and asked if he wanted to come.

GJ thought that would be much more fun. 'I would love to!'

'Come on then, jump up here,' she said, patting the seat next to her.

GJ was very impressed at the way she handled the rig. Carole called on her friend Sandra, who lived on a farm not far from Wrightington. As they were driving up the lane towards the farmhouse, Carole spotted Sandra. She was in the paddock with her pony. Carole pulled up and waved to her and Sandra came over to the fence.

'I am just going back to the house. Come on up – I have something for you. When Sandra saw GJ on the trap she knew it was Carole's cousin and was eager to meet him. Sandra's parents came out and Carole introduced GJ to them all. When Sandra's brother found out that GJ came from America, he asked him, 'Do you know Roy Rogers, the cowboy?'

Sandra asked Carole, 'Would you like to come to the village dance on Saturday?'

'Oh yes, that would be fine,' she replied.

Before they left, Sandra shouted making sure GJ heard, 'See you at the dance on Saturday!'

On the way back GJ remarked what a pretty girl Sandra was.

Both families enjoyed the remaining weeks being together. Adam arranged a trip to Lancaster. Mary took Aunt Lucy and GJ to the little cottage where she was brought up. They could not believe how small it was. They also visited the Navigation pub and the little school that Mary attended, then walked to the doctor's were she got her first job. At the end of the day both Lucy and GJ had a better picture of how Mary and Adam had spent their early lives. Most important, the two families seemed to be much closer.

Mary was pleased she had got her house, the Willows, all completed. She had come to a decision with Tim. Gary had got really attached to all his cousins and had a special friendship with Sandra. However, like all good things, it was getting near to the time when they would have to leave for America. Mary had decided that they would spend the last few days at Wrightington, then have their last day at the Willows. Adam came up with an alterative, 'You and Tim go down to Oxford, leave Aunt Lucy and GJ here. I will bring them down later.'

At first Mary thought that was a good idea but in the end decided against it. The day before they all left, Mary and Tim went on their own to Southport, just for the day. All the kids had a day in Wigan. That evening, Adam, and Rose had arranged a family party, which concluded with Tim making the announcement that he and Mary had got engaged. Tim had purchased a three-carat diamond ring from Baker's jewellers in Wigan two weeks before, and they had decided to get married in America during the Christmas holidays. The whole family was invited. Of course, all the family was delighted.

Chapter Seventy-six

GJ had been at Oxford one year and during that time he had visited Wigan several times and always enjoyed seeing his aunties, uncles, and cousins. He had not seen much of Carole as she was, like him, at university, in her case at Liverpool. Sandra was also studying to become a teacher. Tim was a good step-father to GJ, and they spent as much time as possible together.

It was coming up to the Easter break, and GJ was talking to one of his college friends, Mike Smith, whose father owned a well-known nightclub in Blackpool, called the Windmill. Mike had invited him to Blackpool.

'That would be great. I am going to Wigan for a couple of nights then I will join you, thank you.'

GJ called his Aunt Rose. 'Would it be OK if I come up during the holidays?'

Rose told him to come for as long as he liked, and to drive carefully.

Soon after GJ got to Wigan, Carole arrived. She had not seen much of her family in recent months, but now she had a full week at home. Seeing everyone made her feel very happy. She asked GJ how things were going at Oxford, and they chatted for some time, telling each other about their respective studies.

Then Rose shouted from the kitchen, 'Carole, I think Sandra has arrived.'

Carole went out to meet her. When GJ saw her, he could not help feeling a little excited. She was a little taller than Carole, and was now a very attractive blonde young lady, very smartly dressed. It was obvious that Sandra thought the same about GJ. He had filled out since she last saw him. He looked, and acted, like a confident young man. After the meal, all the younger ones went outside. It was a little chilly but they did not seem to mind. Sandra told GJ, 'I love teaching but I would like to travel and teach. I believe your mother went out to America before the war.'

Martyn was working in the family business, but still carried on his business course at Wigan College. Carole told GJ she thought her brother would announce his engagement to Ann before long. Little Jack, although he was not that little any more, came roaring up the drive on his motorbike with his girlfriend clinging to him on the back. Adam asked them, 'Where have you been? We expected you at 6.'

'We went to Bellevue, and watched the speedway finals,' Little Jack replied.

'Do you want anything to eat?' asked Rose.

'Oh yes, we are starving!'

Rose told them to go in the kitchen and help themselves. Jack did not need telling twice. He and Julie made for the kitchen.

The phone rang and Adam shouted to GJ. 'There is a Mike on the phone asking for you.'

GJ knew who it was.

Mike asked him, 'Can you come on Saturday night?'

GJ said he was with all his cousins and their girlfriends and there may be nine of them.

'No problem, bring them along. I hope the odd one is a very attractive, sexy-looking unattached girl.'

'As a matter of fact, yes, she is. And before you ask why am I not with her, she happens to be my cousin. Her name is Carole.'

Mike gave GJ instructions how to find his parents' place in Lytham-St-Annes. It was an hour's drive. He had his mother's Zephyr car and they could all go together. Martyn was very familiar with the area and they arrived without any problem. It was a very large house, and when they pulled up on the drive Mike came bouncing out, wearing his shorts, followed by two Labradors that jumped all over everyone.

After the introductions Mike took them all inside, pointed out where the bathrooms were and mentioned that there was lots of rooms if they decided to stay the night. His parents were in Scotland for the week. The first impression that Carole had of Mike was that he was a little over the top. He was a big guy with massive legs, which was probably why he was wearing shorts, because it wasn't that warm. She did not think he was good-looking; he had a rather large nose. Then she felt a little ashamed, thinking all that about a person who she had only just met. The plan was for everyone to go to the Pleasure Beach and have a little fun, come back to the house, freshen up and go to the Windmill Club. Everyone was in favour.

At the Pleasure Beach, before Carole could realise what was happening, Mike grabbed her hand. 'Come on, I will take you on the big dipper,' he said.

Sandra confessed to GJ that she wasn't to keen on any of the so-called thrill rides. GJ admitted that he would like to have a coffee, so they had a couple of hours before meeting up with the rest of them. GJ and Sandra walked along the south promenade and found a little coffee shop. He was very content to sit and chat with her. 'Would you really like to go to America?' he asked her. 'What time of the year would be best for you to visit?'

Sandra replied, 'In the summer,' and without hesitation GJ said, 'I don't want you to go in the summer.'

Puzzled, Sandra asked, 'Why not?'

'Well, I will be here all summer. My parents will be here. I want to visit

Italy. I would like you to come with me. Driving would be the best way to do it. Then in the Christmas break you could come back with the rest of the family.'

Sandra felt herself blushing.

'Could you put up with me for two weeks?'

GJ took her hand.

'I could put up with you for much longer than that.'

After they had finished their coffee, they walked back to the Pleasure Beach and found a couple of nice slow rides. Everyone met as agreed and drove back to Mike's home. Debra complained that she was cold. Gary had insisted on taking her on the water ride. Poor Debra had got soaked. Mike announced, 'I am going in the sauna with a beer. Anyone want to join me?'

Martyn and Gary went with him. All the rest showered and changed, then as Mike had told them, GJ went to the little bar and got everyone a drink. Gary and Martyn had left Mike still in the sauna. GJ went and reminded him they were ready to leave. He had obviously had several beers.

'I am sorry. I felt so relaxed,' he said. 'I won't be long.'

It was 7.15 when they entered the foyer of the Windmill. Don Lacey, who had worked for Mike's father for ten years, greeted them.

'Good evening, your table is ready for you and your friends.'

When they entered the club's cabaret room, a young girl came rushing over to Mike.

'How are you? Your mum and dad said you were home for a couple of weeks. I hope we can spend some time together.'

Mike tried to make little of the comment, and walked over to the big round table which was positioned on the edge of the small dance floor.

Mike offered Carole a chair, then sat next to her. A waitress brought the wine over, and apparently deliberately started a conversation with Mike.

Mike cut her short and asked her to bring a bottle of champagne.

'It is my girlfriend's birthday. She is twenty tomorrow!'

He looked at Carole and gave her a cheeky wink. Although Carole did not care much for him, he had a great sense of humour.

They all enjoyed a nice meal which Mike had obviously arranged. Sid, the bandleader, came over and shook hands with Mike.

Mike introduced his friends then Sid went back on the stage. At 9 p.m. the cabaret started. The very popular singer Thelma Jones was introduced by Sid Gatley, then he sat down at the piano and played the introduction for Thelma. She sang several popular ballads during the first half.

By this time Mike was feeling the effects of the wine. He gave Carole a little squeeze. Unbeknownst to GJ, he had told Sid that GJ could sing, and just for a bit of fun, when the cabaret had finished, Sid was to announce him. This little plot was agreed on, and when Thelma had finished her show, Sid announced, 'Ladies and gentlemen, tonight we have a little surprise. In the audience we have a young man from America who will give you a song.'

Normally this would not have bothered GJ. He loved to sing, and had a very nice voice, but he realised that Mike had set him up. Thelma came over to the table and went straight to GJ.

'I believe you're on,' she said. GJ, without any sign of nerves, gave Thelma his chair and poured her a glass of wine. He then walked up to the stage. Even Sid was a surprised at his calmness. GJ told Sid a couple of songs that he knew, and while Sid was looking up the music, GJ introduced himself.

'I have a couple of songs that I like to sing, I hope you enjoy them.' He nodded to Sid.

At this point everyone was quiet, then taking the mic, he began to sing. After the first few notes, the audience knew he could sing. He embarrassed Sandra by walking over to the table as he sang 'My Kind of Girl'.

Thelma later complimented him, 'You have a really nice voice. Have you ever thought of making a career of it?'

'Oh no, I am studying to join my family firm in America. I just like to sing as a hobby.'

Before they left the club, lots of customers wanted to shake hands with GJ and asked if he would be coming back.

On the way back, Mike was not feeling that great. At the house Martyn and Gary had to carry him to bed. The others had a coffee, remarked on how they had all enjoyed it, then went to bed. GJ used the settee in the lounge. 'I will be OK here. See you in the morning,' he told them.

At 7.30 GJ could hear voices in the kitchen. Thinking it was the girls, he had a shock when he saw Mike cooking piles bacon and eggs.

'Go and tell everyone breakfast in twenty minutes,' Mike announced. GJ went upstairs, had a shower and shouted, 'Breakfast is ready!'

Once again it was Mike who suggested a walk along the beach, which they all enjoyed. Then they got a tram at central pier and booked a return trip to Fleetwood. Mike invited Carole to stay, at which she made some excuse. Then he started to come on heavy.

'What about next weekend? Would you like to come to the Lakes?'

Carole was pleased when they got to the car park. She thanked Mike and gave him a quick kiss on the cheek. This did not upset Mike as he tried this on with all the girls. GJ shook hands with him, and said, 'See you back at college.'

It was 3.30 p.m. when they all arrived at Wrightington, Rose was outside planting out a border of Busy Lizzies along the deck. She got up off her knees.

'Thank goodness that's done. My back is killing me. Did you all have a good time?' Everyone answered that it was great. Rose invited them all inside. 'We can have a cup of tea and you can tell me all about it.' Sandra said that she would have to go home, as she had several things to do. Carole asked her if she would see her later?

Rose noticed Sandra kissing GJ, and asked Carole what was going on.

'Oh, she has been in the clouds since she heard him sing last night.'

Martyn took Ann home and said to his mother, 'I may stay at their place tonight.'

Little Jack also left with Julie. Her father had a motorbike shop in Standish. Julie still thought he was more interested in the motorbikes than her. Rose gave Carole a beer and said, 'Take this to your dad. He is in the lounge.'

Carole walked in, kissed her dad and sat on the arm of the chair.

'How are you feeling? You are working too hard, and Mum looks tired. Why don't you both go over to Auntie Mary's for a break?'

'Oh, I'm all right. I have had a lot on my mind recently, but things are settling down now,' Adam said. 'I may take your mum down to the marina for a couple of days—'

Carole interrupted, 'That's no good; you always get involved. You want a complete change and rest.'

Carole said she would go and help her mum with the dinner. 'You have a little nap.'

In the kitchen, GJ was chatting to Rose, who was teasing him about Sandra. Carole also mentioned that Sandra was very found of GJ.

He said, 'I'm off. You are both getting at me. I will have a shower and then call my parents.'

Rose remarked, 'Whoever gets that young man will have a good one.'

Carole asked her mum, 'Did Uncle Tim always like Aunty Mary?'

Rose turned towards her daughter. 'I have never known a man to be so much in love with a woman.' Then, smiling, she said, 'with the exception of your dad.'

There was only the four of them for dinner: Rose, Adam, Carole and GJ. Rose had cooked a nice roast chicken. Adam was asking GJ all about his studies at Oxford, then they all started talking about America. When Adam asked GJ would he ever want to leave the States, his reply was positive.

'No, I would never leave permanently, and when and if I qualify and become a lawyer, I would be committed to living in America.'

The next hour was spent with the four of them having a pleasant conversation, chatting about almost everything.

Carole then said, 'I will have to go down to the barn and check on Bowler.' GJ thanked his aunt for a lovely meal and offered to walk down to the barn with Carole. Skipper heard the word 'barn' and was already at the door. Carole picked up a couple of apples from the kitchen, as Bowler always liked a treat. Sure enough, Bowler had his head sticking out over the stable door.

Carole gave him one of the apples. GJ watched her. 'You really think a lot of him, don't you?'

Stroking his head, Carole said, 'When your mother bought him for me, it was the happiest day of my entire life.'

After making sure that Bowler was bedded down for the night, they walked down by the little steam and sat on the seat that Uncle Tim had made for her years ago.

Then Carole asked GJ, 'Do you think you could get serious with Sandra? She is my best friend, and if you were, it would be nice. I remember on your first visit, she told me that she liked you.'

When they got back to the house, Rose said, 'Sandra's been on the phone.'

Carole called her back. Sandra invited them both over for a drink. It was only a short drive to the Rawlins Farm. Sandra's parents, Ted and Julie, worked thirty acres of mainly root crops, but also had two acres of glasshouses. Sandra said to her father, 'You remember GJ?'

'Of course I do. It is nice to see you again. How are you enjoying Oxford?'

'It is very nice. I like it very much, thank you.'

After a short time Julie got the message. 'Sandra, you go in the other room. Your dad can help me clean up.'

Sandra took Carole and GJ into the very large lounge. The building was very old, dating back to the seventeenth century. It had a large stone fireplace and massive beams. GJ had never seen anything like it.

During the rest of the evening several plans were made. The girls were both horse riding the following day, and GJ was having a day with Martyn.

GJ had asked both girls would they like to have a tour of Oxford University. Sandra was all for it, and being very tactful, Carole said that she had promised to help out at the Ormskirk Clinic. Before they left, Ted shook hands with GJ, but he got a kiss on the cheek from Julie. He asked them both if it would be all right if he took Sandra to Oxford and arranged a tour of the university.

Ted put his hand on GJ's shoulder.

'Our Sandra is old enough to make her own mind up, and we are sure you will treat her right and with respect.'

Sandra just had time to say to Carole, 'Carole Roberts, you told me it was Wednesday you worked at the clinic!'

Carole smiled, 'That's right but I thought you would have more fun without me.' Then she whispered, 'It looks like it will be more fun than I thought. Sandra Rawlins, you have gone all red!'

Chapter Seventy-seven

It was the usual sunny morning in California. Mary was about to leave for downtown. She had some things to pick up at the cleaners. Tim had spent the night on the boat down at the marina. He had been working on varnishing the deck. He had worked pretty late and decided to sleep on the boat so he could complete the work. The arrangement was for Mary to come down at lunchtime. However, when Mary picked up the phone, it was Aunt Lucy. She had fallen in the garden.

Mary ran across the road and found Lucy lying on the terrace, holding her arm. She helped her on to a chair and made her comfortable. Mary then went for the car and got her aunty to hospital. After examination, it was discovered that she had a dislocated shoulder.

The doctor explained, 'I have sedated her and put the shoulder back. However I think it wise if she spends the night here.'

Mary agreed with the doctor, went into the room and told her aunt, 'You have a little nap. Tim and I will come to see you later.'

Mary went straight to the marina and told Tim what had happened. Later that night they both went to the hospital. Lucy was sitting up in bed with her arm in a sling, but looked comfortable. It was going to take three weeks before Lucy would be back to normal. Before leaving, Tim and Mary agreed that Lucy would be better off staying with them until she was OK. Giving her a little kiss they promised to collect her the following morning.

Laura called Mary and invited them over for dinner. It had been several weeks since they had spent any time together. Aunt Lucy was fully recovered and had moved back into her own place. The invite would be a nice break for them. During the evening Laura mentioned that she would like to visit her mother, who lived in Ireland and was ninety years old.

'I would like her to meet Mark before it is too late. Then Mark wants me to go to Canada for a few days.'

'Well, I am sure that won't be a problem,' said Mary.

Chapter Seventy-eight

The past year had brought a mixed bag of achievements, mostly good. But they were marred by a couple of very sad events.

Adam and Mary's father James, died a couple of months after seeing his granddaughter qualify as a vet. James was seventy-six years old. He died peacefully at home. Mary and Adam were grateful that they had been able to make the last years enjoyable for their parents. Celia wanted to stay in the bungalow. Adam agreed, so he got one of his men, Bob Moore, who lived in Roby Mill, to do the garden and generally look after things.

Martyn was now married to Ann Taylor, and Carole was working as an assistant vet in the Ormskirk surgery. Her best friend Sandra was engaged to GJ, who had another year to do at Oxford. Gary was taking more responsibility at the marina and the relationship between him and Fred's daughter was getting serious. Jack, John and May's son, had persuaded Julie's parents to open another bike shop in Preston.

Adam and Rose had just spent a week at Sagamore. It was Adam's pride and joy; every time he walked over the large lawn he had a little chuckle. Rose could never understand why every time Adam went for a little walk, he always came back with a twinkle in his eye.

Carole was enjoying enlarging her experience with working at the surgery, and had now been there six months. Her boss asked her if she would like to go to the Lake District. The annual sheep dog trials were in two weeks and they were asking for volunteers to man the mobile veterinary stations. Carole was very keen to go, knowing it would be practical experience. When everything was arranged, Carole left Wigan on Thursday afternoon. The drive to Keswick took just over an hour. A room at the Keswick Hotel had been reserved for her. Carole soon got acquainted with several other vets. There were two young men from Scotland, and an elderly lady who was local. She had been practicing in the same area for twenty years. Her name was Mildred Roper. Her clinic was in Kendal. Carole really liked her and was pleased when she found out that they would share the same mobile unit.

After the first day, the only injuries were cut paws. The next day was very hot and could have been a problem for some of the dogs, but they seemed to cope with the heat very well. The exception was one old farmer, who came up to Carole and asked, 'Have you got anything for old Shep? He keeps stopping every few yards.'

Mildred interrupted, 'How old is he?'

'Well, I really don't know but he has competed in nine of these events and won four.'

Carole wanted to assure Mildred that, although she was new to the profession, she had worked with mostly dogs.

Without hesitation Carole looked into the dog's eyes, then felt his hind legs.

'I would think he is ten or eleven years old. He has a little arthritis in his back legs.'

She went into the trailer and brought out a small box of pills.

'Give him one a day and don't let him lie in a damp place.'

The old boy thanked Carole and turned to his dog.

'Come on. From now on you sleep with me.'

Mildred then mentioned that Carole had done exactly what she would have done.

Things went very well after that and their services were really not required. At the end of all the events, everyone congregated around the centre of the field for the prize-giving. In the confusion of vehicles and tractors driving around, at the far corner of the field there was a crowd gathering. Someone called to Mildred and Carole. 'You'd better get over here. There is a dog hurt.' Apparently a border collie puppy had been snoozing under a truck and the driver had unintentionally run over the dog's back paw. Fortunately in that spot the ground was very soft. Mildred gave the puppy an injection and examined the leg. Nothing seemed to be broken. When they asked who owned the dog, a small boy came running up. He started to cry.

'I have only had him three days. I haven't thought of a name yet,' he said.

Carole carried the puppy to her car and the boy got in with her. Carole took the boy home. Everything turned out OK and before Carole left, after making sure he was home and explaining the situation to his mother, said, 'I think you should call your puppy Lucky.'

As Carole was driving back along the farm road she came across a Land Rover with a horse box in tow, but no driver and no horse. It was completely blocking the road. Carole got out but there was no one in sight. She was about to go back to the cottage when a young man appeared. He was a big guy with two collies walking behind him.

'I am so sorry, I did not expect anyone to be using this road.'

He quickly moved his Land Rover then went over to Carole. They looked at each other then started to laugh. It was Bob Leyland; they had first met at the horse trials in Blackpool ten years ago.

'Your horse was called Bouncer,' he said.

Carole laughed, and corrected him. 'It was Bowler. He is getting on a bit now, but he still likes to pull the trap.'

Carole told him that she was now a vet and had been working at the trials. 'I will be going to the dinner tonight and will go back home tomorrow.'

Bob was delighted. 'I always attend the dinner, so I will look forward to seeing you there.'

When Carole arrived at the old England Hotel in Windermere, it was already crowded and looked like being a grand occasion.

Carole sat with Mildred during the dinner, and afterwards she mingled with the locals. It was obvious that all the farmers in the lakes knew Mildred. Bob mentioned that as a small boy he remembered her coming to his father's farm. Bob told Carole, 'I think she will retire soon. Why don't you buy the business from her?'

When Carole first met Bob all those years ago he was a good looking seventeen-year-old, but now he was overweight and smoked and drank far too much. Carole was pleased when at 10 p.m. Mildred asked Carole if she was ready to go back to the hotel. Bob was so involved with a crowd of young farmers at the bar, he did not even notice Carole had left. Mildred gave Carole some sound advice and she explained that she had spent twenty-five years of being called out usually in the middle of the night, trudging over the Dales in wellington boots, then having her arm inside some filthy cow, up to her knees in muck.

'You get yourself a little practice in a city looking after old ladies' cats and dogs. Let them bring their animals to you. Get regular contracts with all the top shows. You will make more money, and find it a lot easier.'

As Carole was driving home, she was thinking about what Mildred had said. Carole had always loved living in Wrightington. It was handy for most places. She was twenty-five years old and decided it was time to make a move. She had also mentioned her wishes to her mum and dad. The year had gone by so quickly. The extra time she had worked at the Ormskirk surgery had given her valuable experience.

During a day out in Southport with her best friend Sandra, she spotted a sign in a shop window. It read, 'For sale, property with flat above. Suitable for any business. Large parking facilities.'

Sandra persuaded Carole to go in. The lady explained that it was the far side of Church Town, near the marshes. The keys were available. Although Carole hesitated a little, Sandra said, 'Thank you,' and took the keys. 'We would love to view it.'

They drove the full length of Lord Street. The properties started to thin out a little and after another half-mile, there was very little development. Then on the right-hand side they saw the sign 'For Sale'. It was a couple of old Victorian houses. All the lower rooms had been opened up, the top rooms had obviously been used for accommodation and there were great views looking over the marshes. Outside were several small buildings, and about a half-acre of land.

Rose was in the kitchen as usual when the girls got back.

'Have you had a nice time in Southport?'

'Oh yes, we did all our shopping then had lunch in the Kardoma.'

'Then what did you do?'

Carole tried to sound casual. 'Oh, we went to look at a flat in Church Town.'

After taking almost half an hour to explain, Carole said, 'Mum, it would make a great place for me to live and start up on my own.'

Later that night Adam joined his daughter and her friend Sandra in the living room.

'Your mum tells me that you have found a place in Southport.'

'Yes, I have, Dad. It would be a great spot if it were cheaper. It is £8,000 pounds.'

Adam remarked that it was a lot of money, but promised to get all the information during the next couple of days.

Carole looked a little disappointed, as it may have been sold by then. Adam reassured his daughter.

'The first lesson is, don't be too keen. Call and make an appointment to view, then cancel at the last minute. Try again in a week's time. If it is still for sale, I will guarantee you will get it cheaper.'

The next day Adam and Rose drove out to the property, without Carole knowing. Adam just wanted to find out the location. On the north side of the house there were about fifteen acres with easy access to the marshes. When Adam got back to Wigan he asked his solicitor to find out who owned the land.

The following weekend Sandra went down to Oxford. GJ had called her.

'I have had my nose stuck into books all week and I feel like a break.' They spent a quiet couple of days, just walking along the river. GJ discovered another of Sandra's talents; she was a marvellous cook.

Sandra had gone down on the train. On the return trip she sat near the window, feeling happier than she had ever felt.

John and May had just returned from France. May had been suffering from a severe bout of influenza. They invited Adam and Rose over for dinner, and during the meal John mentioned that he had noticed British trucks on the French roads.

'Maybe we should start thinking of acquiring contracts there.'

Adam agreed, 'We don't want to miss out. We will have a little meeting next week and investigate the possibilities.'

Adam then mentioned the house and land in Church Town.

'I can get the lot for £10,000 but I have to let them know tomorrow. Could you ride out there tomorrow with me?'

John agreed, and the ladies, hearing the conversation, said, 'I hope that means us! We can do a bit of shopping.' The four of them made a day of it. Adam agreed to buy the house and land; the girls enjoyed an afternoon of shopping.

Two weeks later it was Carole's birthday. Rose had promised her a party. GJ was coming up, which made Sandra happy, and all the family would be there. Rose pointed out, 'We are not doing anything special; just a family get-together, and of course special friends.'

A good time was had by all. Then Adam called for everyone's attention.

'I would like to make a toast to our daughter, Carole. Wish her happy birthday, and the best of luck when she starts her own practice.'

Adam then handed his daughter a large package. When Carole opened it, she was overcome with joy. Inside were the deeds to the property. She read the line at the top several times: 'Freehold owned by Miss Carole Roberts.' Carole had to go to her room and redo her make-up, Sandra followed her.

'You have a great chance. All you need now is a great guy.'

Both girls hugged each other. They were two happy young ladies.

Chapter Seventy-nine

Carole continued to work for Morris Belshaw and his wife Pat at the Ormskirk Clinic. Adam had organised workmen to do all the necessary work at the Southport property. Mr Belshaw gave his expert help in suggesting the layout of the clinic. Sandra helped her with the flat above. They had made a two-bed, two-bath accommodation, with a large lounge and a very nice kitchen.

When it came time for Carole to leave, Morris and Pat wished her all the best and told her to keep in touch. On the day that Carole moved, Adam and Rose drove over as well. Rose was worried.

'I don't like you being out here on your own, in what seems such a desolate place.'

'Mum, I am twenty-six years old and Sandra is moving in with me, so don't fuss,' replied Carole.

She had placed a couple of advertisements in the local Southport papers, that read, 'Come and meet Carole, your new veterinary surgeon. Bring your pets for a free examination.' She wandered around her new surgery, and felt really proud and excited. Sandra was coming to stay a couple of weeks and would help her with the registration of the anticipated new customers. She went upstairs and sat on the new settee. Sandra would be arriving soon, and they had planned to have a meal together, and relax. When Sandra arrived they had a simple meal and a glass of wine, then spent the rest of the evening planning how they would deal with the grand opening.

On the Monday morning when Carole opened the doors of the clinic, she was pleasantly surprised. There was about thirty people in line, mostly with dogs of all breeds, although she spotted a few with cats and little girl with a rabbit. Carole explained, 'First you must register, over there,' pointing to where Sandra was, 'then come into this room and see me.'

It turned out to be a very busy day, with a steady stream of people arriving. At the end of the day, Sandra had done a good job with the files and Carole now, at least, had an organised filing system with lots of information. They both realised that they had not even had a break since 9 a.m., and it was now 4.45 p.m. Carole dealt with the last person, a little old woman who had a cat that could not walk. The cat's problem was that it was way overweight.

At 5 p.m. Carole said, 'Right, that's enough. I am dying for a coffee.'

Sandra replied, 'Me too. You go up, call your mum, and make the coffee. I will lock up.'

When Rose heard the good news, she was delighted.

'Your dad is not in yet, but I will tell him the good news when he gets back,' she promised.

When Carole put the phone down she heard Sandra talking to someone, then she came upstairs.

'There's a guy with a black Labrador. I think you should see him.'

Carole, being really shattered, said, 'Tell him to come tomorrow.'

Sandra almost insisted, 'I really think you should see him now.'

Looking puzzled, Carole asked, 'Why, is the dog badly injured?'

With a broad smile, Sandra said, 'I mean you should see the man, not the dog.'

Reluctantly Carole went back down. Standing in the doorway was a man with a very well-trained dog. Carole asked, 'What is the problem?'

Then in a very cultured voice the man said, 'I am very sorry to disturb you after hours, but I think Molly –' pointing to the dog – 'has scratched her eye running in the reeds. I would really appreciate you having a look. By the way my name is Tony, Tony Holland.'

Carole took the dog into the surgery.

'Could you lift her on the table?'

Tony just gave the command and Molly jumped up and sat. The dog's eye was indeed badly scratched, but it wasn't serious. Carole put some drops in to stop any infection, and then told Tony to bring her in tomorrow. Tony explained that he could only come at 5.30, and could see on the sign that Carole closed at 5. Carole by this time had to admit Sandra was right; this man was something.

She looked at the dog and said, 'Well, Molly, we will have to make allowances! See you tomorrow at 5.30.'

Back upstairs Sandra's first question was, 'Well, what did you think?'

'Oh, it was only a little scratch on her eye.'

Sandra shrieked, 'Carole Roberts, I mean the guy! Is he coming back?'

Now it was Carole's turn.

'Oh yes, I will have to see Molly at least five times!'

They both started laughing.

The next few weeks Carole and Sandra got to know lots of people. More customers were beginning to come in, but Carole always looked forward to when Tony brought Molly. It was during one of these visits that Carole was telling him that Molly was OK, and would not require any further treatment. Sandra, still playing the matchmaker, called downstairs. 'I have just made some coffee.' Carole felt obliged to ask Tony if he would like to join them. He accepted, telling Molly to stay, and went with Carole. Over coffee they found out that Tony was an artist. He spent lots of time on the marshes sketching and taking photographs, mostly of wildlife, but he also liked to do landscapes.

He mentioned that he would choose the best, then paint them in his studio which was on the edge of the marshes. When the girls showed interest, he invited them to his studio. Realising Carole worked, he suggested Sunday afternoon. Sandra said that she would love to go but on Sunday she had to be in Birmingham for the day. Tony looked at Carole and said, 'Perhaps you would like to come?'

Sandra answered for her. 'Yes, Carole, it would be a little break for you. Don't worry about me, I won't be back until late.'

They heard a little solitary bark from Molly. Tony said she was hungry. He thanked them for the coffee and said he would come for Carole at 11 a.m. Sunday morning, then he left.

The following week was very busy at the clinic. Carole realised that although Sandra was staying with her, she had her own job and could only help at weekends and school holidays. She would have to get permanent help.

Her parents called and she mentioned this to her dad, who advised her to advertise and when she decided on someone to take them on trial first. Carole took his advice and put several adverts in various papers and veterinary magazines. On the Saturday, Tony called.

'I know that I arranged to come for you tomorrow, but a friend of mine called. He lives on the moors at Uppermill. He spotted a couple of ospreys, which as you will know are very rare. Well, I would like to go and hopefully get a picture. I wondered if you would like to come, then we can have a pub meal on the way back.'

Carole was pleased to accept. The drive from Southport was very pleasant and it was obvious that Molly went everywhere with Tony; she sat in the back, all contented, just looking through the window. Tony's friends Harry Parkinson and his wife Shelia lived in the village of Uppermill in Saddleworth. It was a small cottage but fitted well in the little village. Carole immediately liked them both. Inside the cottage they had a superb collection of sketches and paintings. Carole assumed that Harry was also an artist or his wife was. However, she found out later that it was all Tony's work.

The site where Harry had seen the birds was only a mile or so away. When they got there, it was an old quarry that had filled up years ago, which made it a haven for wild life. Tony set up his powerful camera on the tripod, then they all sat down and waited. It seemed like hours but in fact was only about an hour. Tony, looking through his binoculars, spotted the makings of a nest on the granite wall of the quarry. Several minutes later, a big bird with a six-foot wingspan glided across the water and settled on the ledge near the nest. Tony was taking pictures all the time and was a very happy man when they returned to Harry's cottage.

Carole had been chatting to Shelia all the time and felt that she had known her forever. Shelia and Harry had been married five years. Shelia worked in the village post office. Harry was a print setter and worked in Preston. Tony had met them six years ago when they had bought one of his paintings at an art show in Grasmere. Shelia was surprised when she found out that Carole had only recently met Tony.

Inside the cottage the large painting over the fireplace was a country scene, and looked very real. When Carole asked who painted it, Shelia gave her a magnifying glass.

'Look in the bottom right corner,' she said.

Carole saw the name Tony Holland.

The men suggested that they all walk down to the Fox and Hounds pub. It turned out to be a very nice evening. Shelia told Carole that Tony was brought up by his grandparents. At the time they owned Holland Transport in Southport. The old boy sold out and they bought a big house near the marshes. Unfortunately his grandfather died, but he continued to live with his grandmother. She put him through art college, and about nine years ago she died and left the house to Tony. He turned part of it into a studio and lived there with his dog Molly.

'Anyway, I don't think it is fair for me to go on like this,' she concluded. 'I am sure that if he wants you to know, he will tell you.'

Chapter Eighty

Adam and Rose visited Carole a couple of times each week just to make sure she was all right. Her brothers also visited and were very impressed at what she had achieved.

After another busy day, Carole decided to have a night on her own; she wanted some time to think a couple of things out. Although she had not known Tony long, she felt that she could get serious with him, but at the same time she did not know if he felt the same. Also, there was the decision on choosing the right person to help her. She had interviewed five girls and had got down to the final two, both girls and both lived locally. Carole had a strong feeling that the older of the two, Linda, was the best choice. She would call her tomorrow.

Sandra had just spent the weekend with GJ in Oxford, so Carole decided to call her at her parents' home. They chatted and Sandra wanted to know if there had been any further developments regarding her and Tony. When Carole told her that she felt that she could get serious, Sandra was really pleased.

'What are you waiting for?'

'I don't want him to think I am running after him,' replied Carole.

Sandra asked, 'When are you seeing him again?'·

'I don't know. He may call me tomorrow.'

'Why don't you call him and invite him to Wrightington?'

Before they finished their conversation, Sandra said that she would stay at her parents' place during the week.

'I will come over to you when I leave work on Friday.'

Carole took Sandra's advice and called Tony.

He answered, 'I was just going to call you. How are you?'

'I'm fine, thank you.'

Tony asked if she would like to go out for a ride on Saturday afternoon?

'I would love to but I am going over to my parents' place, I have to look after Bowler, my horse. Why don't you come with me?'

Tony thought that was a nice idea and Carole was pleased that he didn't even have to think about it.

Tony had never been to Wrightington. He found the area very interesting, and was surprised to see that there was a very large lake. Carole introduced him to her parents and Rose asked them if they would be staying for dinner.

'That would be lovely, Mum, thank you,' replied Carole.

They knew that she was dating but had never met Tony up to now. Carole said that she would take the trap, as they would be calling at Sandra's, then on the way back she planned to call in and see her grandma.

Rose told her to be careful, and that dinner would be at 7.30.

Tony and Carole walked down to the barn. Bowler came up to the fence but Skipper decided to stay in the sun until he saw Molly, then he came running over. Carole opened the gate and Bowler seemed to know he was going out. Tony helped with the harness and they started off, the two dogs in the back. As they went past the house, Rose waved to them, then said to Adam, 'He seems a nice young man. Do you think they will get serious?'

Adam's reply was a little disappointing.

'They have only just met.' Then, teasing, her husband said, 'Well, I had only just met you but you wanted me.'

She gave him a little kiss.

'You always said that Carole was like me.'

Trotting along at an easy pace, Carole put a rug over her knees. I should have put my trousers on instead of a skirt, she thought.

'Are you warm enough?' Tony asked.

'I am fine, thank you,' she replied.

The two dogs were watching for any movement in the hedgerows. They drove along the narrow lanes on into Pepper Lane then into Coppull, where she turned into the cross-country lane; this was a short cut to Dalton, where her grandma lived.

At the bottom of the slope, Carole pulled in.

'I always stop here to give Skipper a run and Bowler has his apple.'

Carole asked Tony to get the hamper. She had a flask of hot coffee and two pieces of her mum's cake. Skipper, knowing where he was, jumped down and was off across the field. He turned and looked at Molly as though saying, 'Are you coming or not? I know the way.' Molly bounded after him.

It was a little chilly but a very peaceful setting. Tony, as always, got his camera out and took several pictures.

Carole told him, 'I always come here ever since my Aunt Mary bought me Bowler.' After half an hour Carole got a little concerned. Skipper had not come back. Tony said, 'Don't worry, I will get them back.'

Taking a small whistle out of his pocket, he gave two sharp whistles. Carole heard a bark from the other side of the field, and Molly came at full speed with Skipper trailing behind. Both dogs were covered in mud after drinking from the stream but, getting a treat, they jumped into the back of the trap.

During the afternoon they visited Sandra, then called on Carole's grandma. Tony was impressed with the bungalow and he asked Grandma if he could come back some time and sketch it. Celia was so thrilled she told him to come whenever he liked. Before they left Celia gave Carole three jars of homemade jam, and one of the cakes she had just baked. Carole gave her a hug, and said, 'Thank you, we will come to see you again soon.'

Celia said, 'I think your boyfriend is a nice man.'

When they had unhitched Bowler, they let him in the field and both walked up to the house, Skipper and Molly running ahead.

When they went inside the house, Adam and John were in the lounge. Carole took Tony to join them then went into the kitchen. Rose and May were busy preparing the food. When Adam and John found out that Tony was an artist, Adam brought out a painting that one of the gypsies had done fifty years ago. Old Walter had given it to Adam. It was a painting of a horse-drawn gypsy caravan. Tony examined it in great detail and was very impressed. He mentioned that he would like the chance to paint one, but he didn't suppose that there were many like that about today.

'No, you're right on that, but I have a special barge that I would like you to paint, the *Mary Rose*.'

As usual the meal was excellent and conversation was interesting. Carole and Tony left after dinner, and Rose, Adam, May, and John all agreed that Tony was a very nice guy. Adam remarked that he was also obviously talented. Then Rose said, 'And very smitten with our Carole.'

The weather was beginning to warm up; it was early May, all the spring flowers were showing. Rose was at home on her own. She heard the phone ringing and picked it up. It was Laura.

'I am calling you from Ireland,' she said. 'Mark and I have been here several days with my mother and sister. In three days we are leaving for Canada. I want to meet Mark's family, then we will get back home on the twenty-eighth. Mary would like Mark and I to see GJ for a couple of days in Oxford; do you think you and Adam can manage it?'

Rose thought it would be OK.

'I will have a word with Adam and call you back later.'

After confirming it with Adam, as promised Rose called Laura and said they would get there late afternoon on the Thursday. Mary had already been in touch with GJ and instructed him to make sure that everything was OK, to call Mrs Longhurst and ask her to get the rooms ready, and if he wanted to invite Sandra, she could come down with his Uncle Adam.

GJ did not waste any time. He called Sandra and invited her down for the weekend, then he called his cousin Carole. She said she could come on the Saturday just for one night. Then he said, 'I believe you have a boyfriend – bring him along.'

Having everything in place, GJ was looking forward to a good weekend. It had been some time since he had seen Laura and Mark. Considering they only had a weekend together, Laura and Mark enjoyed meeting up with GJ and the other family members, and of course Tony, who had not had much family life, found it all really exciting. Mark and Laura were the last to leave; they were flying back to America on the Monday afternoon. GJ managed to show them a little of the university, and they were impressed with the university and GJ's achievements.

Chapter Eighty-one

Six Years On

Although the winter had not really started – it was only early September – it was bitterly cold. Adam had been up to the marina; the cold weather had almost closed the place down. Cruising on a canal boat wasn't the ideal way to spend a vacation in this freezing weather.

Rose heard Adam's car, and went to greet him.

'You're early!'

He kissed her and Rose shrieked, 'You're freezing!' Go in the lounge; I have a fire going. I will bring you a hot drink.'

After a short time in front of the fire and a hot cup of tea, Adam felt much better. Rose asked if he had called to see Debra, Gary's wife. They had been married two years and had a little girl, one year old, called Kathleen. Adam said that he did not call but had spent a couple of hours with Gary and Fred, and they both said the baby was fine.

'I told them that we would go down next week.'

Rose got up and sat on Adam's knee.

'You look tired. Are you OK?'

'Oh, I feel all right really. Just getting old. Driving home today I was thinking it is five years since Carole started her own clinic. She and Tony have been married two years.'

Martyn, their eldest, had been married to Ann for four years and they had two boys: Paul who was three, and Robert who was eighteen months. Martyn had worked hard for several years at business college and with the knowledge accumulated by his father, he was a very shrewd businessman.

Rose continued, 'Now that all the kids are grown up, we should spend more time together. Sandra's mum and dad are going to America next spring. They've never been; it must be a couple of years since GJ and Sandra got married.'

The doorbell rang. It was John and May.

'We have just been to the Standish shop to see our Jack and Julie. She had made a lovely hot pot; just the thing for this cold weather.' Then May gave a little sigh. 'I wish they would get married; she is such a nice girl. Our Jack was full of grease. He insisted that his dad look at the motorbike he was working on; he even tried to sell him one.'

Adam started laughing. 'I was just like that.'

Then John replied, 'Not when you were twenty-seven.'

Later on the four of them were having drinks sitting by the fire when the conversation got to discussing cruises.

Carole had been at the clinic all day. She was pleased when it was time to close. Tony had been in his studio and, like Carole, was ready for a rest. He had been commissioned to paint a landscape of the tarns in the Lake District. The client wanted the painting for his niece who lived in the south of France. Carole had just had a shower when she heard Tony's car. Looking through the window, she saw Molly jump out of the car. Tony looked up, smiled and waved to his wife. He told her that he was very pleased with the work he had done.

'I will go and get cleaned up; can you feed Molly?'

The dog seemed to understand and followed Carole into the kitchen. She had become very found of Molly.

It had been six months since that awful day when she went down to the stable. Bowler did not come to the door as usual. Inside Skipper was curled up on a bale of straw; she knew that her little pet was dead. Bowler also knew. He hung his head over the little dog. Although she was a vet, every time she looked at the picture on the fridge door of Bowler and Skipper she got upset.

Looking at Molly she said, 'Think on, I want you to live until you are one hundred years old.' When Tony appeared, he could see what had happened.

'Come here,' he said, putting his arms around her.

Carole had to admit she was a big softie, but she couldn't help it.

Tony kissed her. 'Go and fix your make-up. I am taking you out tonight. I've told your mum and dad we will meet them in the Red Lion. We can call for your grandma on the way.'

It was a special treat for Celia and such a surprise, having a night out with her son and his wife, her grandchild and husband. Adam told them that Aunt Mary had been on the phone and they were coming on the twenty-fifth, then, all excited, Celia announced that Aunt Lucy would be staying with her. Carole was disappointed that Sandra and GJ could not come with them. Before leaving the pub, Carole told her mum that she would come over tomorrow.

'I may ride Bowler over to Sandra's parents, if the weather is dry,' she said. 'Tony won't be able to come as he has to finish a painting, and will be at the studio most of the day.'

Carole was surprised when she arrived with Molly at her mum's. Her brother Martyn and her sister-in-law with their two children, Paul and Robert were there. Martyn had an appointment in Wigan; the idea was for Rose to look after the young one. Then she suggested that Carole take Ann and Paul with her as it would be hours before Martyn got back. When Carole had

Bowler all harnessed, Paul sat between his mum and aunty and Molly jumped in the back. Carole enjoyed the ride with Ann. She always liked her, but somehow they never seemed to spend much time together.

Adam and Rose had been giving a lot of thought to where they might live after their retirement. Sagamore was a magnificent house in beautiful grounds. They could let Tony and Carole have Sagamore. Rose mentioned selling Sagamore and building a new bungalow for themselves. Carole and Tony could still move in there and it would be nice to be close. Adam did not even like hearing the words 'selling Sagamore'. He made Rose promise that even if she were left on her own, he never wanted Sagamore to be sold. Rose could see that the conversation was upsetting Adam.

'Don't be serious. I have never seen you like this before. Come on, we will have a cup of tea. In any case, I have no intentions of being left on my own. We are going to live until we are a hundred!'

Tony had completed the painting. He brought it home as he wanted Carole to see it before Major Harris called to collect it. Carole thought it was one of best works.

Tony's said, 'That's very nice of you to say that, I hope the Major thinks the same.'

Tony hung the painting on the far wall in the lounge where the best light was. It would be another hour before the Major would arrive. Both Carole and Tony changed and waited. Exactly on 7 p.m. the doorbell rang. Tony went down and greeted the Major. Carole was in the living room and Tony introduced her. Carole put his age around sixty. He was smartly dressed with a cultured voice, which one would expect of a retired army major. The three of them chatted for a few minutes over a glass of wine. The Major said how much he was looking forward to seeing his niece and spending some time exploring the area. He mentioned that she had a very nice villa in a place called Antibes, a town south of Nice. Carole offered him another glass of wine but he refused, saying that he would be making a very early start in the morning.

Tony said, 'Well, Major, would you like to see what you are paying me for?'

All three walked into the lounge. The Major stood for a moment then walked over to the painting. He must have been gazing at it for what seemed ages. Tony was getting a little worried that he may not like it when suddenly he turned around.

'Magnificent! Bloody magnificent,' he exclaimed. 'The water in the tarns looks so real. I feel like if I touched it, I would get wet.' He went over to Tony, 'I really want to thank you for doing this. You can be assured that it will be appreciated where it is going, and will be displayed in a fitting position. I also have a feeling that when some certain people see this, you will be hearing from them.'

Tony packed the painting in the special crate then carried it down to the Major's car. When he came back upstairs, he was all smiles and rushed over to his wife, gave her a big hug and waved the cheque for 2,000 pounds.

'You are a very talented, handsome man, Tony Holland! What are you buying me?'

They both had another glass of wine. Molly jumped up on the settee between them.

GJ drove his parents and Aunt Lucy to the airport for their trip to England. They spent a night in New York, and got the flight to Heathrow the following morning. It was a seven-hour flight but very comfortable. When they arrived at Heathrow, Tony hired a car and drove them to Oxford. The Willows looked really fantastic; all the new trees that had been planted years ago were well and truly established. At the back the huge willow trees still stood on the far bank. They had given the house its name. Mary had got really attached to it. It was so different to living in America.

The next couple of days were spent resting up at the Willows. Mary called her brother and said that they would all come up to Wrightington on the Friday afternoon. Rose had arranged for all the family to be there for dinner. It was always nice to have a family gatherings as it gave everyone a chance to catch up with what had been happening.

Tony, Mary and Aunt Lucy made a very early start arriving at Wrightington by midday. Fortunately, the weather was warm. Adam and Rose were the only ones there; all the rest would arrived later. Celia was there and warmly greeted Lucy. As it was very early, Mary asked her brother if they could visit their father's grave in Standish, which was only ten minutes away.

He mentioned to Rose what he was doing. 'We will slip away, and won't be long.'

Sister and brother stood by the grave in the little churchyard in silent thought. Mary shed a few tears and whispered, 'I do miss you.' Adam took her hand. 'Come on, at least he had a few happy years, and was able to see the grandkids. We can make sure that Mum enjoys the rest of her life.'

They decided not to rush back and they both walked around the little village, reminiscing about when they were kids.

When they did get back, Celia, Rose and Lucy were sitting in the garden having tea. Tim had gone to his house, as he wanted to get Mary's car out of the barn where it had been stored. Mary joined the ladies for tea, then said she would have a little rest. Adam was in the study making endless phone calls, checking on various contracts. At 6 p.m., Carole and Tony arrived, then Martyn, his wife Ann, and the two children. Julie and Ted Rawlins, Sandra's parents, arrived and of course bombarded Mary with questions about their daughter and GJ. Tim had been talking to his brother most of the time; they had a lot to catch up on. Carole was so pleased to see her Aunt Mary and Uncle Tim. Mary was amazed when she saw Carole and Tony.

'You both look so well! How are things going at the clinic?'

Carole told her, 'I am doing pretty well, and Tony is beginning to get known in the art world.'

Celia and Lucy were in deep conversation, no doubt planning a few outings.

Everyone was about to go in for dinner, when a motorbike and sidecar came roaring up the drive. Julie was in the open sidecar with a dog on her lap. Now that everyone was together, it had the atmosphere of a good family night. Celia was insistent that she and Lucy spend time together in her bungalow. Adam arranged for a local taxi firm to take them wherever they wanted to go. He gave Celia a number.

'When you want a driver, call this number.'

At the end of another great night with the family, Mary and Tim were using Tim's place as a base before they left. Mary mentioned that the next family get-together, it would be nice to hold it at the Willows.

'I thought if Mother and Lucy have a couple of weeks and do their own thing then you could all come down to the Willows, and I could organise a few outings.'

On the Monday, Mary asked Tim if he would like to go to Lancaster for the day.

'I would love to,' he said, 'but your brother wants me to go with him and Martyn. I think I should; after all, I still draw a salary from the firm, and being honest, I don't do a great deal for it.'

Tim told his wife, 'You go and visit friends, drive carefully, and call me when you get back.'

It never ceased to excite Mary driving up to Lancaster; she had so many pleasant memories of the area. She had called ahead to Gary, who was living in the cottage where she was brought up. When she arrived, Debra was there with her daughter, Kathleen. It was a surprise to see that the little girl was already walking. Mary suggested that she drive them down to the marina and then they could come back with Gary.

'I will see a couple of friends then come back here.'

Debra thought that was a great idea.

'I can see Mum and Dad and my sisters.'

Gary and Fred were in the office. Fred was obviously very proud of his first grandchild and he insisted that they go down to his bungalow, which was situated at the other end of the marina. Fred's wife, Marion, made them all tea, then took the opportunity to fuss over her little grandchild. Mary explained that it was only a quick visit but she would come again with Tim and stay a couple of days. Gary said that would be fine; they could take one of the barges and have a trip down the canal. When Gary and Debra decided to stay for dinner, Marion was delighted.

'I will ask your sisters to come over,' she said.

Mary left at 2.30 and drove down the main street in Gateley. The little coffee shop was still there where it had all started, when Amos had got her the teaching job. Amos lived in Lancaster. Mary had his address and decided to call on him. It was only a twenty-minute drive. When she arrived at the old Victorian house, she had a shock. Mary remembered it as a very tidy and neat place, but now she was looking at a property that looked a mess with peeling paint and broken windows, and a small garden that was overgrown with weeds.

After ringing the bell a couple of times and getting no response, she walked around the back. At the bottom of the garden in the greenhouse, Mary could see someone inside. She called out, 'Hello? Is that you, Mr Cooper?'

The old gentleman came out, looking very old and wearing an old, battered hat.

'It's me, Mary Roberts.'

The old man smiled.

'Mary, my dear, how are you? What a pleasant surprise!'

They went inside the house. It was obvious that the place wanted decorating and numerous repairs. There were several photographs on the sideboard. Mary recognised a couple that were taken on the *Queen Mary* all those years ago. Amos admitted that the big old house was too much for him. He had kept in touch for a long time with the other two girls. Tina Williams worked a London embassy for several years then married and went abroad. He was afraid that he didn't know where Linda O'Brian was living in Dublin.

'It would be very nice if we could all meet up,' he said, looking at Mary, 'but I don't think it will really happen.'

Mary put her arm on the old man's shoulder. 'I don't see why not,' she replied.

Chapter Eighty-two

As Mary was driving, she could not help feeling sorry for Amos. He had been an inspiration to her and was the reason she was what she was today. Since he lost his wife and got older, it was obvious the house was far too much for him. Mary decided that she would ask Adam the best way to help him. When she mentioned it, Adam promised he would have a word with Fred. One of his men could go and sort it out, he assured his sister. 'Don't worry, leave it to me,' he promised.

Celia and Lucy, after having had a good day at Chorley Market, got Bob Willis to drive them over to Adam's place. Mary was so pleased to see her mother laughing; since her dad died, it had not been easy for her.

'You two look like you have had a good day?'

'We have, and tomorrow we are going to the Ideal Home Exhibition in Preston.'

Then she asked Mary, 'Would you like to join me and Lucy for a sherry?'

'Mother, it is only 4 p.m!' she replied, then started laughing.

Tim arrived back and Mary reminded him, 'We are going over to Southport tonight. We promised Carole and Tony that we would have dinner with them.'

Kissing her mum and Aunt Lucy, she said, 'We will see you tomorrow,' and she and Tim left for his place. They would have time to change before they went to Southport.

At the cottage, she called America and spoke to GJ and Sandra. Everything was OK, and they were looking forward to their visit. The drive to Southport was just forty-five minutes and they arrived 6.30. Mary and Tim were surprised to see how spacious the flat was upstairs. Carole got them a drink.

'Tony called and said he would be a little late,' she told them. 'You relax while I go and change.'

Mary was looking at several paintings that were hanging on the far wall in the lounge. She mentioned to Tim, 'I would like Tony to paint the Willows and the old cottage in Lancaster. He is very good.'

Tony arrived and apologised for being late. Carole came in, dressed in a red trouser suit. She looked great. Tony apologised again to his wife. 'Sorry, I am late, darling.' She gave him a little kiss. 'No problem. You get yourself ready and I will feed Molly.'

Tony had booked a table at the Balmoral in Church Town for the evening. The conversation switched from one country to the other. Carole wanted to know all about Sandra and GJ. She said how much she was looking forward to their visit. Mary mentioned to Tony that she would like him to do a painting of the Willows. Then, when Tim suggested they come down for a weekend Tony was very keen to do that. 'I can do some sketches along the River Thames.'

Mary added, 'And bring your camera.'

'Oh, I will! I never go anywhere with out it.'

The four of them had a very interesting evening. When Tim and Mary got back to Tim's place, they remarked what a nice couple they made.

GJ got home very late, he had been in court all day with Mark. He walked into the house and sank into the big easy chair. Sandra got him a cold beer.

'You look shattered. Relax for a while; we can have dinner later.'

GJ never made it a rule to discuss work at home, but the trial he was working on had been going for some considerable time. Both GJ and Mark were almost certain that they would reach a settlement during the next few days, so he made an exception and told Sandra. He had promised to take her to England when it was over.

'I think you can safely go and book our flights tomorrow. Book them for two weeks from today.' Sandra could not contain her excitement and gave him a big kiss.

'I can't wait to see my mum, dad and my little brother, Ben,' she said.

Mary got the good news that GJ and Sandra would be coming over in two weeks. Mary suggested that they do something special.

'If the weather is kind we could have a really good American BBQ.'

Tim teased, 'What's wrong with a good English BBQ?'

When Adam knew about the upcoming arrangements, he suggested that it would be ideal to have it at Sagamore, so they could all go out on the river. Adam asked them to come up for the weekend. He also invited John and May.

On the following Saturday morning after a short drive Mary and Tim arrived at Sagamore. May and John had come down with Adam and Rose the previous day. They sat on the large terrace, watching the boats go by.

Mary commented, 'You certainly got the right spot for this house, but what made you build it at the very end of the land?' Rose said that she had asked him the same question.

'Oh, I had a very good reason,' replied Adam. Everyone together said, 'Well?'

'It's a long story. I will tell you about it sometime.'

Adam did what he loved to do: at 5 p.m. he went into the boathouse with Tim and John. He loved showing off the *Mary Rose*. It had been beautifully restored and was now only taken out on special occasions. Adam skilfully manoeuvred the barge alongside the house and everyone got on board. Adam put on his captain's cap, which was always hanging on the galley door. They sailed up river to Henley, where Rose had booked a table at Mario's. Everyone had a good time. It was unanimous that the party should be at Sagamore when GJ and Sandra arrived.

Carole and Tony were expected at the Willows, just to stay one night. Carole managed to get away early. Linda, her assistant, had become a very good help. Tony wanted to make some sketches of the Willows and take lots of photos. They made good time driving up to Oxford and arrived in the early afternoon. As they were only staying a short time, it was decided to go to the local pub which was only a short walk away. The four of them chatted, then walked in the garden. Tim explained what they had improved on. Tony of course was taking pictures all the time. They went back in the house and Mary took Carole up to the guest room.

'If we all freshen up we can have a drink together before we leave,' she said.

Tony promised that he would paint the Willows. 'I am pretty busy so it may take some time,' he said, but Mary was delighted.

Tony then excused himself, walked out to the car and returned with a large package, which he handed to Mary.

'This is for you,' he said.

Mary opened it and immediately her eyes filled with tears. She just stared at the painting. Tim asked, 'What's wrong, dear?'

'There's nothing wrong. It's wonderful!'

Tim looked over her shoulder at the painting. Tony had spent several months on the picture. It was a picture of her parents sitting outside their bungalow in Dalton, the surrounding garden ablaze with colour. What Mary found incredible was the fact that Tony had never met James, her father. He had died before Carole met Tony, but somehow he had painted them together on the little seat in front of the bungalow. Carole said he had done it from a photo and included them on the painting. It looked so natural. Mary gave Tony a big hug.

'It's wonderful. I will always treasure it. Thank you.'

Chapter Eighty-three

GJ and Sandra had gone into Pasadena very early. They had finished their second cup of coffee and it was still only a little after 9 a.m. when they entered the upmarket Italian store with all the latest fashions. The manager greeted them. He had known GJ's father for many years. GJ explained that they were going to England and wanted a couple of outfits each suitable for the trip. The manager called to the female assistant. 'Please show Mrs Johnson our collection.'

GJ said he would look around himself. 'If I require any help, I will call you.'

Three hours later a couple of assistants carried several large boxes to their car.

Back home they both relaxed. GJ called his mother and mentioned that he would like to take Sandra to France for a few days during their visit. Sandra spoke to her parents and promised to bring them a big surprise. They wanted to know what it was but Sandra would not tell them. When she put the phone down, GJ had heard the conversation.

'What's this about a surprise?'

'I have one for you, too, but you will have to wait until we get to England.'

GJ could not help laughing. 'I hope you haven't bought me a horse!'

In the meantime Carole had offered to help Mildred, her veterinary friend who lived in the Lakes. Mildred was getting on a bit, but had offered to operate on a pedigree Devonshire bull. Although Carole had never done anything like that, Mildred said it would be good experience. Carole said it would have to be at the weekend, and Tony agreed he would go with her.

'We can have a night at the Coniston Hotel; I can do some sketches around the lake until you have finished.'

The operation was a success, and Tony invited Mildred back to the hotel for dinner. They also invited her to visit them in Southport.

'That would be great. I would love to see your clinic,' Mildred said.

Carole and Tony had to call at her mother's to collect Molly. Jack, her cousin, was there with Julie. They were on the lawn with Molly and a little golden retriever puppy. Carole picked the puppy up.

'When did you get him?'

'We called at the Boar's Head. The landlord's dog had five puppies but only one left. I want him but Jack's not sure.'

He then asked Carole to check the pup out, then making one of his corny jokes, said, 'The landlord, big Jim Mason, wants five pounds for him. I don't want to be sold a pup!'

Only Jack laughed.

Carole said, 'He is worth a lot more than that,' winking at Julie. They took the pup home. As Jack drove away he shouted, 'We will call him Mistake!'

The night before GJ and Sandra were due to arrive at Heathrow, Mary invited Sandra's parents down to the Willows; she thought it would be nice for the six of them to have a few days together. It was arranged that Julie and Ted would stay at the house. When they heard the car they would go into their room and make a surprise appearance. Mary and Tim were waiting in the arrival lounge at Heathrow. The plane was on time and as the passengers were coming through, Tim spotted them.

'There they are!'

Mary looked and saw this six-foot, handsome young man with a broad smile on his face. Sandra was at his side. She looked stunning. When GJ got up to them he put the small bag down and almost lifted his mother off the ground. Mary then gave Sandra a big hug. After they had got their luggage loaded in the car, they headed back to Oxford.

On the way Mary explained that she had told everyone in Wigan that they would rest up here for a couple of days, then they could all go to Wigan. Sandra said she did not mind but did not want to stay any longer; she was dying to see my parents.

Ted and Julie heard the car and retreated to their room Sandra wanted to call her mum as soon as she got into the house but somehow Mary talked her out of it.

'We will all have a nice pot of tea then you can go into the study and make your call.'

Mary managed to slip away for a minute and tell Ted and Julie to go in the study.

'Sandra will be going in to call you in a minute or so,' she told them.

After ten minutes, Sandra said, 'I will go in the study and call my parents.'

They waited a few seconds, then heard this shrieking. When GJ heard his mother-in-law's voice, he realised what had happened. After the surprise everyone was trying to talk at the same time. GJ and Sandra were falling asleep with the time change. Julie said, 'OK, you two had better get some sleep, we are all going out tonight.'

It was four hours later when GJ and Sandra appeared on the terrace. After a few hours' sleep and a change of clothes, they felt and looked ready for anything. Mary and Julie were chatting and GJ asked where were Ted and

Tim. When he found out that Tim was showing Ted the new summer house, he decided to join them.

Mary had ordered a taxi to take them the short distance to the Eagle and Child pub, but before they left, Mary told Tim to get the wine out, so they could have a drink to welcome them back. Both parents congratulated GJ on his success, and he in turn thanked his mother for all her help. He also thanked Sandra's parents for providing him with such a wonderful wife.

Then Sandra stood up, glass in hand.

'I would like to make a toast,' she said.

This was very unlike Sandra, and she got their attention immediately.

'I would like to make a special toast to your first grandchild.'

Julie almost dropped her glass.

Mary told Tim, 'You'd better get the champagne.'

GJ went over to his wife and gave her a kiss. 'You never told me.'

'I wanted to be sure, I only knew myself two weeks ago and I wanted to surprise everyone.' Sandra told them that she was three months pregnant and felt great. Needless to say, the night out was a real celebration all round.

Two days later, they all arrived at Adam's place in Wigan. Carole and Tony were there, although the month that GJ had planned slipped by so quickly. He did manage to take Sandra to Paris for a couple of days. It was fortunate that both families were financially able to visit each other and spend regular time together.

Martyn was now running more of the business and Adam allowed him to get more help and let him make some decisions. Gary had done extremely well with the marina. He had mentioned to his father that a derelict pub was for sale along the canal, not far from the marina. He had suggested that they buy it. Adam encouraged his son to investigate the possibility further. Carole was also doing very well now that she had permanent staff.

It was one of the rare weekends that Adam and Rose spent at Sagamore. They loved to remind themselves of how fortunate they had been. All their children were happily married, and they had five lovely grandchildren. They sat together like a young courting couple, had another drink and discussed going on a cruise. They went to bed two very happy and contented people neither of them knowing that in a short time all the success and happiness was going to be shattered by a chain of events that nothing could stop.

Chapter Eighty-four

Mary was looking down at the grave in Standish churchyard, reading the inscription on the headstone to herself. 'James Roberts, Celia Roberts.' It had been ten years since her father had died. Her mother had joined him three years ago. She was eighty-seven years old. During the last few years, Aunt Lucy and her mother spent all their time together, either in America or England. Mary always thought that her mother's death contributed to Lucy's death two years later. Mary must have been in deep thought, as a young lady walked by and asked, 'Are you all right, dear?'

Mary turned around.

'Yes, I was just thinking.'

The girl could see tears in Mary's eyes.

'I understand.' She walked a few steps. 'This is my husband's grave. He was only thirty-two years old. We had been married six years. He died of cancer. I have a little boy who is five. My mum keeps saying I should get married again, but I don't think I will.'

They chatted for a while and she said her name was Sally and she lived in Coppull.

'I will have to go now and catch the bus. It drops me off at the nursery school where I pick my little boy up.'

Mary offered to drive her home. Sally was surprised but accepted. They picked the little boy up from nursery and drove to the little terraced house in Coppull. Sally apologised.

'I am afraid it is in a bit of a state. I have a part-time job and I am trying to buy this house.'

Mary spent a good half-hour with Sally and her son, Simon. On the way back she called at Jack's cycle shop in Standish.

'Have you got any little bikes suitable for a five-year-old boy?' she asked.

'I have bikes for all ages.'

Mary picked a red one and gave Jack Sally's address.

'Can you deliver this today?'

Jack smiled. He knew his aunt was helping someone out again. When he looked at the address, he said, 'I will drop it off myself. It is only five minutes away.'

Meeting Sally had put Mary in a good mood. It reminded her of when she was a little girl.

GJ and Sandra with their two children had moved into Mary's house. They had more room and eight-year-old Elaine loved the pool. Six-year-old Colin preferred the treehouse that Tim had built. Mary and Tim had moved across the street to Aunt Lucy's place; it was big enough for the little time they spent there. The bungalow in Dalton had been empty for some time. After discussing it with her brother they offered it to Carole and Tony. They accepted but Tony insisted that they buy it. Just to make it legal Mary charged them £200 for the freehold. There was a good bit of land with it. Mary had no doubt that Tony would extend the property and make use of the land.

Adam was a little worried about Carole. She was working too hard and looked tired. He had a word with Tony.

'Why don't you and Carole have a weekend at Sagamore? We can look after the kids.' Tony was in full agreement; it had been some time since they had taken a break.

When they arrived at Sagamore, Mrs Williams, the housekeeper, had prepared everything and the place was nice and warm. She had also filled the fridge with essentials. She had left a little note, 'Hope you find everything in order, I will come over tomorrow.' It was signed, 'Nora.'

Tony and Carole had decided they would do no cooking; just relax and take walks along the river. Carole gave Tony strict orders not to work but she knew that he could not resist doing a few sketches.

After the weekend they both agreed that they felt much better and should do it more often.

Carole was pleased that Susan had not been too busy at the clinic, Mrs Ellington's cat, Rusty, had died; it was twelve years old and had always been overweight. Tony called Adam from the bungalow to say he would come and collect the kids. Adam persuaded him to leave it until tomorrow as they were all having a good time. Rose has promised them fish and chips that night. Tony thanked him for the weekend and said he'd be over tomorrow.

Mary and Tim were spending several days in New York at the Warwick Hotel. It was during breakfast that Tim passed the paper to Mary.

'What do you think of this?' It concerned a young couple. The victim was a girl from the North of England. She had been seriously wounded in a shooting and one of her daughters had been killed. All this had happened some considerable time ago. Mrs Wilson was out of hospital but would be confined to a wheelchair for the rest of her life.

Mary commented, 'I have never practised law, but have heard lots of cases discussed, and to me it sounds like a cover-up. I think I will call GJ.'

He told her that the office was aware of the case, which was famous and known as the Elevator Shooting. 'When the police are involved it could take years,' he told her.

Mary poured another coffee.

'I feel so sorry for this young couple. I think we will go and see them.'

Tim looked at her in amazement.

'Do you think that would be wise, getting involved?'

'Well, it won't do any harm, and we are close to were they live.'

One hour later Mary was speaking to the young lady. Her name was Lillian, and she had been born in Ashton near Wigan. When Mary heard that information, she definitely wanted to meet her, and they arranged to call the following day.

The couple lived in a little town called Greenport which was a four-hour drive. Mary told Tim that she had been there with the girls, when she first came to America. 'I remember Laura and I riding on the famous antique carousel in Mitchell Park. The place was discovered by a guy named Barnabas Horton. He was an adventurer who crossed the Atlantic in 1640 and set foot in Southold, which now holds the village of Greenport.'

Tim smiled. 'You seem to know the history of the place.'

'I do know a little. It's such a beautiful place. You will see when we get there.'

The drive was a very pleasant experience and when they arrived finding the Park view address was easy. Tim spotted the number 127. They pulled on the drive and Mary rang the doorbell.

A young good-looking man opened the door and invited them inside. 'My name is Greg,' he said.

'Pleased to meet you. I am Mary Johnson and this is my husband Tim.'

Greg took them through the lounge and into the garden. He went over to his wife, Lillian, and Mary took her hand. 'I am so pleased to meet you,' she said.

Greg went back into the house to make some coffee.

Tim could see that Mary wanted to talk to Lillian.

'I will go and give Greg a hand with the coffee,' he announced.

Lillian said that she was trying very hard to come to terms with what had happened on that awful morning.

'Greg has been marvellous. We worry about all the medical expenses, and his boss helps us, but there seems no end to the mounting costs.' Then, getting upset, she sobbed, 'And my sweet little daughter is gone.'

At this point Lillian could not control her emotions. Mary tried to console her.

Greg looked through the window; he could see what had happened. 'We will stay here a little longer.'

Tim said he was sorry that they had upset her. Greg explained that his wife cried every single day.

'I think if Mandy had not been killed we somehow could have coped.'

When Lillian had regained control of her emotions, Greg and Tim came out with the coffee. Mary, not wanting to dwell on the subject, started to tell them how she came to be in America.

'Like you I came from the North of England, and married an American.'

She went on to say that she had one son who was a lawyer, and that Tim was her second husband. During the afternoon, the four of them chatted and got on really well. As Tim and Mary were about to leave, a young woman came into the garden with a little girl. It was Greg's sister. She had been looking after the little girl, whose name was Tracy. Immediately she ran over to her mother and gave her a big hug. It was difficult for her to understand that her sister had gone. Mary asked Greg how the case was going and the name of the lawyers that were dealing with it.

From what Greg said it did not seem that much progress had been made. Lillian was due for more surgery and Greg would have to take more time off. Mary left a couple of phone numbers and asked him to type out exactly what happened and send it to her. She told him to include every little thing, and Greg promised he would do that. Mary also got the address of the hospital that was treating Lillian.

Mary and Tim had been back in Los Angeles two weeks when she received a large envelope that had been mailed in New York. Mary knew it was from Greg Wilson. Mary read the letter first. In it, Greg said the police had not got any further, and he had included a copy of the statement that Lillian had given when she was well enough to do so. Lillian had already told Mary that she met Greg in England, they had got married and moved to America. The first six years had been fantastic. They had a nice house, two lovely little girls and her parents came over twice each year.

For the reader's benefit this is an account of what happened on that terrible day in the lives of Greg Wilson's family.

Greg Wilson was a twenty-five-year-old sergeant in the American Air Force. He was stationed in the North of England at the Burtonwood Base in Lancashire. During his stay he had met and fallen in love with a pretty, dark-haired girl, Lillian Morrison, who was twenty-two years old and worked as a secretary in Wigan. Greg had only two more months of service to do. He was a qualified engineer and had a good job waiting for him back home. They married and Lillian was excited at going to live in America. In six years they had a nice little house and two daughters. Lillian had her own car and was very confident driving around. She had no need to work, as Greg had a good position and a salary to match, However Lillian did a part-time job at the local school that Mandy attended. She would drop Tracy off at the nursery then take Mandy to school. Everything was perfect, and Lillian was a very happy woman.

The school break was three weeks away and her parents had booked for a month's visit. The following week, Greg gave his wife $200 to take the kids shopping and buy herself a new dress. He joked, 'I don't want your mum and dad thinking I neglect you.'

At 9 a.m. the following morning Lillian parked her car at Bellmount's, the big department store. It had only been open a few minutes. She was greeted with a cheerful, 'Good morning, you are bright and early,' and a compliment on her two lovely little girls.

The ground floor was mainly gents wear. Lillian knew that what she wanted was on the third floor, so she made for the elevator. Making sure the children were safely inside she pressed the button and the doors closed. At that precise moment, two young guys came in the store's main entrance. One pulled a gun and the other told the manager to fill the bag with cash. One of the staff had already pressed the alarm, and within two minutes a couple of police officers came rushing in with drawn guns. They saw that one of the men had a gun, so told him, 'Drop the gun now and get down on the floor.'

The young man turned, still holding the gun, so the officers fired several shots, wounding the man in the leg. Both men then lay on the floor and the officers handcuffed them. It turned out that the gun the men had was a toy, but of course the police did not know that.

Two more police cars arrived and the men were taken away. Everybody gave a sigh of relief. They were thankful no one was seriously hurt. Then they heard banging and screaming coming from the elevator. The police had to use the axe from the nearby fire point to open the elevator door. What they saw was like a scene from a movie. There was blood everywhere. A woman and one child were motionless, the other little girl was hysterical. 911 was immediately called. The officers established that the woman was still alive, but the little girl was dead. It turned out that the two guys had botched everything. They had intended cutting the alarms, but had cut the power supply to the lift and trapped the people inside.

Mary let GJ read the whole report and statements. He had to tell his mother. 'I know you get upset and want to help everyone. It is very sad, but we can't just jump in and take over. What I will do first, is make sure that all this is correct, then find out what the lawyers dealing with it have got. Then, and only then, I would have to get Mr Wilson's permission if he wanted our help. If it would make you feel any better, I will send someone to check it out, but remember we just can't jump in.' Mary was grateful, and felt much better.

Carole had received a call at the clinic from her mother.

'I think you'd better come over here.'

'What's wrong? Is it Dad?'

'No, your father is fine. He is in Preston. I went down to the orchard; the small pony was in the field but I could not see Bowler. I looked in the stable and he was lying down breathing very hard.'

Carole said she would be there in half an hour. She put the phone down, grabbed her bag and explained to Susan she had to go to Wrightington. Carole was expecting the worst. Bowler was after all twenty-seven years old.

She drove at full speed and when she arrived went straight down to the stable. Her mother followed her. Carole knelt down and put her hand on Bowler's head. He was having difficulty breathing as his lungs were filling up with fluid. She gave him an injection and turned to her mother.

'He will be OK for a couple of hours. I want to call Mildred.'

She explained what had happened. Mildred had been a vet for twenty-five years in the Lake District and dealt mostly with farm animals. She told Carole, 'I will leave now.'

Carole went back down to the stable and told her mother, 'When Mildred arrives, send her down.'

Bowler was breathing much better, but Carole knew it was the end. The injection had worked but would not last long. Carole knelt down, cradling Bowler's head. His big eyes looked up at her. She was thinking of all the good times they had spent together. It was only when she heard voices that she looked up to see her mother and Mildred standing there.

Mildred put her hand on Carole's shoulder.

'You know what we have to do. Say goodbye and I will deal with it.'

Carole walked back with her mother, tears flowing freely. Twenty minutes later Mildred came in the house. She assured Carole that he just went to sleep.

'Do you want me to arrange for him to be collected?'

'Oh no, I want him buried here, near Skipper.'

Carole apologised for not being able to handle it.

Mildred told her, 'I have seen big strong farmers cry when I have had to put one of their cows down.'

Carol's reply was, 'Yes, but I am a vet.'

Mildred admitted, 'It does not make any difference. I had a collie for eleven years, followed me everywhere. When he died I cried for ages. I still think about him when I walk past his grave.'

Chapter Eighty-five

Rose was busy packing the bags for their trip to Sagamore. Ann and Martyn and their two sons had decided to drive down later. Mary and Tim had left America but had gone directly to Paris, and would be at Sagamore in a couple of days, in time for the bank holiday. Adam was hoping that all the family would be able to meet up. He loved taking them on the *Mary Rose* along the river.

Carole and Tony's place was looking really good now they had completed all the extensions. The new studio was finished and Tony found it much better. Carole had taken more help on at the clinic and she was able to spend a little more time with their son, Larry, who was now fourteen. They were hopeful he would get into college.

GJ was in the middle of the Elevator Shooting case, which had been going on for a very long time. GJ was confident on getting the Wilson's a good settlement.

'When I get that out of the way I will bring Sandra and the kids to England,' he told his mother.

The Sunday of the bank holiday weekend, most of the family were at Sagamore. Adam took everyone on the *Mary Rose* to Henley. He loved putting on his captain's cap that he had bought for two shillings all those years ago. Rose told him come and sit down and let Martyn take the tiller. Adam explained that it was very crowed and would be tricky manoeuvring through the locks.

'Come on, you know that Martyn is very good; after all he had a good teacher!'

Martyn did handle the *Mary Rose* perfectly. Docking in a difficult berth at Henley, Adam shouted so everyone could hear. 'You were right, Rose, Martyn did have a good teacher!'

The day after Tony fancied a couple of hours' fishing. He asked Carole if she wanted to come.

'No, dear, you go. I have a few things to do. See you later.'

Adam had gone down to the greenhouse and Rose and Mary were sitting in the summer house. Rose said, 'I feel shattered after all these late nights, I think I will go inside and take a nap.'

Mary said she was OK but would take her brother a cup of tea down to the greenhouse. Adam was examining his plants when he saw Mary and asked what she was doing to there.

'I have brought you a nice cup of tea,' she said.

They sat down on the seat and Mary looked around at all the young plants.

'You have a nice collection here.'

'Yes, they are for the hanging baskets later.'

They started talking about their childhood in Lancaster. Then, without warning Mary said, 'We always promised there would be no secrets between us.'

Adam looked at his sister.

'I hope that's still true.'

This was the chance Mary had waited for.

'OK, big brother, what's all this mystery about Sagamore? Is there a ghost?'

Adam started laughing.

'No, there is no ghost. At least, not that I know about. But it has a great secret and it's no fairy tale.'

Mary was getting very excited.

'Come on then, tell me!'

'Oh, it is a very long story.'

He would not enlighten her any further.

'You always said that we would not have any secrets,' she pleaded.

Adam looked at her very seriously.

'I promise I will tell you when the time is right,' he said earnestly.

When it came time for Mary and Tim to leave Sagamore, they decided to have a couple of days in London before going back to the Willows. They thanked Adam and Rose for a super weekend. 'We will get together again soon,' Tim promised. It was 10 a.m. when they left.

Mary drove first hundred miles then after a short coffee break Tim took over, and they arrived at the Mayfair Hotel at 3 p.m. Settled in their room, Mary said that she would have a rest. Tim was feeling OK and said he would have a short walk. When he returned a couple of hours later, Mary had showered and changed, so Tim did likewise and they had a drink before going down to dinner. Although they had spent weekends in London many times, Mary always found it exciting and enjoyable.

This particular weekend turned out to be more exciting. It was after dinner. They had returned to their room and were relaxing, watching the TV. It was on the late BBC news that they heard the announcement: an American lawyer had won a record settlement for a British woman who had been badly wounded and one of her children killed. It did not give any more detailed reports.

Mary looked at the time. It was just after 11 p.m. which would be afternoon in Los Angeles. Mary, very excited, put a call through. Sandra answered that GJ was in Boston wouldn't be back until Wednesday.

Mary told her that they had just seen the news regarding the settlement.

'We are in London, and just by chance heard a brief report on the TV.'

Sandra explained, 'I wanted to call you but GJ said he wanted to tell you himself.' After a minute or so, Sandra said, 'There is someone here who wants to speak to you.'

It was Elaine, her granddaughter.

'Hi, Grandma, we will all be coming to England soon.'

'I know, and I have a lovely surprise for you! I will see you soon, now let me speak to your mum again.'

They chatted for some time then, when Mary finally put the phone down, she turned to Tim.

'That is wonderful news. I am so proud of him. We must plan something special when they come over.'

The following day, back at the Willows, Rose called.

'Did you see GJ on TV last night?'

Mary said that they only caught the short report. Rose told her that on the 9 p.m. news, GJ was interviewed outside the Boston courthouse.

'He was so confident; you must be very proud of him.'

The next two weeks saw Mary organising a surprise for when GJ and the family would be here. They could only come for a short stay but Mary intended on making it a wonderful time for all the family. It turned out to be just that.

Chapter Eighty-six

AS GJ drove down the busy highway to his office, it was hard to believe that he had spent a very enjoyable time in England with his family: the time had gone so quickly. Sandra had taken Elaine to school and dropped Robert off at the pre-school centre. Driving back home she felt so happy that she started singing. She never dreamed that she would have two lovely children, a nice house and be sharing it all with a handsome, talented husband.

Carole now only went into the clinic three days every week. She had taken on another qualified vet, whose name was Una. Her husband was a policeman. The flat above had been empty so Carole let Una and her husband have it. The bonus was that when Carole and Tony went away, the business was in good hands.

Mary and Tim were in New York. They intended visiting Greg and Lillian Wilson but Mary noticed that Tim looked a little down. She thought, Perhaps he does not want to visit them.

As they were drinking their coffee in Ramsey's coffee shop. Mary asked, 'If you do not feel like visiting the Wilsons, we don't have to.'

Tim was quick to reply, 'No, it's not that, but you are right. I have something that will be difficult to explain. Drink your coffee and we will go back to the hotel and I will tell you the whole story.'

Mary, looking worried, said, 'I don't want my coffee. Let's go.'

Tony was on his way back from Whalley; he had been up there for the past three days. The commission he had taken was for the famous Pilkington family. He wanted to complete it before leaving for America. Lord Pilkington had seen several of Tony's works and had commissioned him to do a sketch of Pilkington Manor. He had called Carole at the clinic and arranged to meet her there. When he did arrive he was surprised. Una and Carole had been called out, so Susan the assistant told him Mrs Holland said she would be home at about 6 p.m.

Tony had a cup of tea with Susan. It was 3 p.m.

'If I leave now, I can pick the kids up from school then call at my in-laws'. Martyn and Gary had been investigating the possibilities of buying a large barge dredger. The old Bolton and Bury canal had a disused loop basin which had been neglected for years. Cleaned out, it would make a drop-off station for leisure cruises. Gary had approached the authorities, and was offered it if he would maintain it.

When they consulted Adam, he told them, 'If you can buy it for less than two thousand, and get permission for an office-come-bungalow, go ahead, I will leave you to deal with it.'

When Carole arrived home, Tony was in the garden with Larry. Elaine was in the house; although she was still at school, she was a good little cook and loved preparing a surprise meal for her parents and brother, although Larry was never keen on her cooking.

Chapter Eighty-seven

Mary and Tim arrived back at their hotel and went directly to their room. Mary placed her handbag on the small desk and walked to the closet to hang up her sweater. As she did so, Tim withdrew a large manila envelope from his travel bag. He placed it on the nightstand by the bed. As Mary turned from the closet, he turned towards her with a very serious expression on his face.

'I have had that for a week,' he said, pointing toward the envelope, 'and it's about something we must discuss. I'm sorry I didn't tell you sooner, but I just felt it would be better if we took it up when we were just by ourselves. That's why I wanted to come here.'

He walked over beside his Mary and took her hands.

'I'll go out on the terrace, so you can read what this is all about on your own,' he said, pointing toward the nightstand.

'When you've read it, call out and we can have out talk.'

He walked from the room to the third-floor balcony terrace outside their room.

Mary just stood there for a few seconds, trying to grasp what was going on. Then she walked to the nightstand and opened the envelope.

She sat on the edge of the bed and withdrew the contents: a letter, two photographs, and a handwritten page that appeared carefully torn from a diary.

Mary first studied the faded photograph on top. It showed a middle-aged couple seated at a picnic table in front of two young men standing on either side of a very pretty young girl who appeared in her late teens, or early twenties. They were all smiling for the camera. From the background, Mary surmised the picture had been taken in a small park near a small town. There was no indication of where the picture had been taken, but Mary saw mountains in the background that clearly ruled out any place in England.

Mary recognised one of the young men. It was Tim, looking more as he did when she had left for America.

Then she read the letter.

Dear Mr Birchall,

This letter will no doubt come as a bit of a shock, after such a long time. I was twenty years old before I was told that I had been adopted when I was a three-month old baby. I won't bore you with the details of the long search I have made (all outside of my regular working hours) over the past sixteen years, but all the effort will have been worth it if your reply to this letter can confirm what I now have good reason to believe are the facts.

The enclosed photograph shows my real mother when she was working as one of the maids for a well to do farmer named Wilson near the small town of Katherine in the Northern Territory back in 1945. I have learned that the young man standing to my mother's right is Alex Wilson and his parents are seated at the table. I have good reason to believe that the young man standing to my mother's left is my father, and very possibly could be you.

Mary paused to study the faded photo.

Oh, that's Tim all right, she thought. No doubt about that. Then she continued reading.

I'm also enclosing a recent picture of me, all decked out in my uniform. I am now thirty-six years of age, and have made a career in the Australian Navy.

I have never married, but I have had a very good life. Under the Navy rules, I am eligible to retire in a few years with a very good pension.

Mary gazed at the other photograph. A full length picture of a very attractive young woman dressed in a junior field-grade naval officer's uniform. Near the bottom of the picture was written, 'Jean Lewis'.

I have also included a page which I removed from my mother's diary.

Mary switched to that and read:

It breaks my heart to give my little baby away, but the doctor says I don't have a long time to live, and I feel so horrible. I believe he's only telling me the sad truth. I just pray to God my darling little girl will be loved and have a good and happy life.

Jean's letter concluded:

Please don't think I am trying to upset your life. You are probably by now a settled married man with a family of your own. However, if you are my dad, I want to meet you.

Jean

On the back of the large envelope there was a return address:
Lt JG Jean Lewis
Naval Headquarters, 1st Naval District
Royal Australian Navy
3915 Marine Drive
Brisbane, NSW PC 2584
Australia

Then Mary read the next entry on the enclosed diary page several times:

I have decided not to tell Tim I became pregnant. I know he never felt the same towards me as I did for him. I really didn't know him for very long, but he was a kind and gentle man, and I'm sure he would have been a good husband and father. I realise it just was not to be.

Mary could not hold back the tears.

Perhaps, she thought, it was just as much my fault as anyone's.

Mary put everything back in the envelope. She freshened up, making sure her tears had dried. After a light go with a powder puff on both cheeks, she called out to Tim.

When he walked into the room, Mary was standing near the bed. They looked at each other, a bit nonplussed, without either saying a word. After a few seconds, which seemed an eternity, Mary walked over to Tim and put her arms around him. He responded quite emotionally; his voice was barely audible.

'I am so sorry, Mary,' he uttered.

She took his hand. 'Come over here,' she said, leading him towards the sofa, 'and sit down.'

They both sat. It was a very comfortable sofa. Mary was no sooner seated than she promptly stood and proceeded to pour two drinks from the decanter filled with sherry on the dresser. She handed Tim one glass and sat down beside him.

In a very firm and positive voice, Mary said, 'I want you to listen to me,' she began. 'I have read that letter over several times, and I feel so sorry for this young woman. As a very young girl, she obviously had the character to pick up her life and make a good career for herself. The entire tone of her letter conveys that she is a very nice person. And I feel as much to blame as you. The war just happened, and circumstances just parted us and unpredictable things just happened. Quite frankly, I believe fate has brought us back together.'

Mary's words and manner caused Tim to feel an immediate resurgence of vitality.

'What do you think I should do?' he asked.

'I will tell you, Tim Birchall, exactly what we are going to do,' she replied. 'We are going to be off shortly to Australia to meet that lovely daughter of ours!'

Tim put down his drink and with a face almost showing glee, he gave his wife a strong hug, and a kiss that lasted several seconds.

My God, what a wonderful woman! I've got to be the luckiest man alive!

Tim felt both relief and exuberance.

'After we've gone down for dinner,' said Mary, 'I am going to call my brother and tell him we are about to begin a little tour. First thing tomorrow morning we'll book a flight to Brisbane.'

At dinner Tim felt much better and Mary could see he was now totally relaxed. Over dinner, Mary said, 'We have a whole new chapter in our lives about to unfold. Let's go for it!'

A smile broke out on Tim's face. 'You are something else!' he exclaimed.

Dinner completed, they walked back to their room holding hands. Their mood and manner reflected both affection and contentment.

The next morning the concierge referred them to a travel agent in the lobby. After a few minutes with the travel agent, they learned that they would best get to Brisbane by a non-stop to Sidney, and a 'local' to Brisbane, which was almost 500 miles north of Australia's largest metropolis. The travel tickets were promptly ordered.

Chapter Eighty-eight

After a long and tiring thirteen-hour flight to Sidney, they changed planes and after ninety more minutes in the air, they were at Brisbane. Tim picked up the hire car at the airport and an hour later he and Mary arrived at the car park of the Embassy Hotel. When they got to their room, they decided to shower and get a couple of hours' sleep. Mary was the first to waken. She looked at the bedside clock. It was 4.15 p.m. Tim was still fast asleep. Mary quietly slipped out of the queen-sized bed. She promptly took another shower, dressed and then made coffee.

The percolator had only stopped gurgling when Tim awoke. After one glance at the clock, he could not believe he had slept so long. As he sat up in that comfortable bed, Mary handed him a coffee.

'Drink this and we'll get ready and go down and find out where the good restaurants are,' she said cheerfully.

Mary had never been in Australia before, and Tim had only been in the far north in Queensland years ago.

They got in the bar at 6 p.m. It was very pleasant, with a cascading waterfall at the far end. Mary and Tim sat on the bar stools and ordered their drinks.

Two other couples were also seated at the bar, and several people sat at the smaller tables near the waterfall. The young good-looking barman came over.

'Hi,' he said, 'welcome to the Embassy, and what would you like to drink?'

Now that's a charming accent, thought Mary. I remember someone once saying that an Australian was a Brit with a bad accent.

Tim ordered two chardonnays, adding, 'Make sure it's Australian.'

'For sure,' replied the barman. 'We serve nothing but New South Wales's finest,' he added, as he reached for the glasses.

When the young man served the drinks, he said, 'My name is Mike. If you want any help, just ask.'

Mary looked at Tim and smiled, then said, 'Can you recommend a good place to eat?'

Mike reeled out the names and the 'minutes away' of several restaurants.

'What about seafood?' asked Tim.

'Neptune's,' answered Mike. 'Best in the city, and only ten minutes away by cab.'

Then Mary inquired if he had any suggestions on getting to the Naval Headquarters in Brisbane.

'When you're ready,' answered Mike, 'just go to the concierge in the lobby. Name's June. Tell her where you want to drive, and she'll mark a local map for you and it will be a cup o' tea.' He smiled. 'Not far, actually,' he added, and walked to his left to wait on a newly arrived customer.

The main Naval Headquarters building was visible from miles away. Once the base came into view, Tim had no difficulty whatever in driving right to the entrance gate. There he told the sentry what he wanted. They were handed a visitor's pass each and given good directions to the civilian parking area next to the headquarters.

Once they entered the headquarters, a senior cadet, earning extra credits for volunteering as a guide, directed them to the personnel office where they could make their enquiry as to Lieutenant Jean Lewis.

In Personnel, and without delay, they were offered a seat. As the officer to whom they had been directed picked up a phone he remarked that he had known Jean for years. 'She's a very good officer, I might add!'

It was then determined that Jean was on a temporary leave, and was at her little place in Placid Springs, some 128 miles north-west.

'I'd say in the bush, but it's in the mountains – beautiful, actually.'

Then a now-comes-the-dawn look came over the officer's face.

'You've a bit of luck, if you don't mind flying in our mail plane that's leaving here in about an hour. Of course, you understand, I couldn't be offering this if you weren't Jean's parents having come all this way from America.'

Both Tim and Jean nodded in complete understanding.

'I am curious,' said Tim. 'Why would a Navy mail plane be going to an out of the way place like Placid Springs?'

'Because of the fuelling needs and limitations involved,' replied the officer. 'Our pilot goes every day from here, first to Placid Springs so he can leave there with his tanks topped, and then he's on to a naval base near Darwin. Problem is, leaving here topped off won't quite do it with the plane assigned to us, so we have to do it this other way.'

Everyone smiled broadly.

'There's plenty of room, if you want to go that way. Otherwise, I can give you directions, but it's a very windy road, and frankly, the scenery doesn't quite justify the inconvenience. Of driving, I mean.'

Both Tim and Mary thought all of this was getting to sound very exciting, and they warmed to the offer accordingly. Within twenty minutes, they had their hire car safely locked in the car park, and their luggage safely strapped in the cargo bay of the Navy's mail plane.

On the short flight the young pilot pointed out various interesting ground locations along the way. After about an hour in the air, they spotted a small village outside of which there was a small airport consisting of an asphalt airstrip, and some small wooden buildings.

'Placid Springs,' the pilot hollered over the roar of the engine, as he pointed repeatedly at the village ahead and below.

The Navy pilot made a smooth landing on the airstrip and taxied to a fuelling area near the wooden hangar. A big guy in overalls came out of the hangar. He had 'aeroplane mechanic' written all over his hands, face and clothes. He and the pilot were obviously long-time acquaintances.

'Hi, Reggie,' said the pilot. 'Brought you some guests. Told them you'd rent them that old Holden I know you keep out back to rent out. Did I tell them the truth?'

Reggie smiled. 'Well, if one of them has a driver's licence and they've got at least twenty dollars between them, I might.'

Within thirty minutes, the Navy plane cleared the runway heading north, and the Holden cleared the airport heading south. Reggie had helped them transfer their luggage, filled the car's tank and given them instructions on getting into Placid Creek and its finest (albeit only) hotel.

'One thing,' said Reggie, as Tim was about to engage the clutch.

'Folks around here don't travel much, and in your elegant clothes, you're going to sort of stick out like sore thumbs. Well, I mean look kinda funny. You might want to stop in at Cooper's Clothing if you feel like it. All up to you, of course. I just thought I'd keep our Good Advice Department in operation.'

Everyone exhaled a brief but involuntary laugh, and the Holden moved off the airport.

Chapter Eighty-nine

Tim looked every inch the spiv in his new electric-blue, long-sleeve shirt. Mary stood there in her in her new light-weight cotton frock, a starburst of autumnal reds and browns. 'Now wouldn't we be the pair back home in these get-ups?' said Mary.

'Oh, ah!' said Tim. 'I'd end up in the nick and when I got out, I'd be visiting you in the local loony bin.'

They burst out laughing.

'Not to worry,' said Tim. 'Here we'll slip into the landscape like two salamanders.'

Tim and Mary cleared off the bill at Cooper's Clothing, and walked out to the pavement. The same people on the street visibly turned at the sight of these strangers in their new clothes. Now they really did stand out. Tim and Mary decided to ignore the stares, and let their new impression set in as they ambled back to the hotel.

They entered the lobby. Meg was back behind the registration desk. Her eyes involuntarily flared a bit on seeing her new guests' idea of going native. They both saw her reaction, and decided not to react.

'Tell me,' said Mary, 'Uh, two questions. Would you happen to know if the old Lewis place has a phone? Secondly, if so, how would I get the number?'

Meg answered, 'Yes to your first question. Jean has all the modern conveniences out there.' Then she pointed towards a small table in the centre of the lobby. 'You can find the number in that little phone book on that cadenza at the back of the sofa.'

As Mary scanned the phone book, Meg called out, 'You can use the phone here in the office,' pointing to the small glass-enclosed office behind the registration desk.

Mary dialled the number. After three rings, the voice of a younger woman answered. 'Jean Lewis here.'

Mary said, 'Well, Jean, all this may come as a bit of a surprise, but I'm Mary Johnson Birchall and we – that is, Tim Birchall and I – are here. That is, in Placid Springs, all the way from England. And, I mean –' Jean's mental circuitry was beginning to jam a bit – 'well, I think I may be your stepmother, and we're here in Placid Creek to meet with you. And, I know this must sound a bit mixed up, but, well, we're at the Leighton, and, could you possibly—'

Jean felt momentarily overwhelmed and she sat down to steady herself.

'You're here? Oh my gosh, that's so wonderful. I, I don't know what to say. Uh, uh… Just stay right there. I'll be there within fifteen minutes. Oh, I'm so delighted. And my fath— uh, you say Tim Birchall is there with you?'

'Yes, yes,' replied Mary, 'we're here. Oh, please come as quickly as you can. We'll be right here waiting.'

Jean sprang to her closet, where she quickly replaced her work shirt and jeans with a nice white print dress covered with small yellow flowers. A brief stop before the mirror to give her hair three fast swipes with a brush, and she was out the door. Her heart was leaping for joy. She could feel her heartbeat pounding. Had her blood pressure stayed at its current level, she would never pass her next Navy medical. Jean was about as happy as any one human can get. She raced to the Jeep she kept there. Within five minutes after speaking with Mary, Jean and Jeep were leaving a trail of dust in the direction of Placid Springs.

Mary returned to the lobby.

'She's on her way!' she said to Tim.

It is not within the author's capacity to describe the emotions that surged through Tim Birchall at that moment. He was simply overcome. Mary could see his response.

'Tim,' she said, taking his hand. 'Jean will be here shortly, and I think it best we step into the bar and get your nerves calmed down with a, uh, why not a double sherry?'

'That sound's great to me,' answered Tim.

Overhearing all this, but not really knowing what it was all about, Meg piped up, 'Just the two of you sit right down there, and I'll bring your sherries. And, they're on the house as the Americans say.'

In a matter of moments, Mary and Tim were seated on the sofa, sipping their sherries, and Meg was back at her perch behind the registration desk. They were all awaiting the grand entrance of Jean Lewis.

While it was only fifteen minutes later, to Tim it seemed like an eternity before the girl in the photograph came racing through the front entrance to the Leighton. Tim blinked in disbelief. The girl coming into the lobby looked almost exactly like a photograph of his mother taken at Blackpool when she was about the same age. It was astounding. Tim knew nothing about genetic inheritance, but he could easily see the obvious physical and facial resemblances. This was nothing less than awesome. How could it be?

Not to worry about a lot of things I don't understand, he told himself. I'm looking at a Birchall, and I'd have to be blind not to recognise it. Adam and Rose won't believe their eyes when they meet this girl. And all these years. It doesn't seem possible!

Daughter saw father. Father saw daughter. Whether it was genetic recognition or some other exotic phenomenon, the verification stage of their relation was history. They both ran to embrace.

By any measure, it was a very emotional moment. No one cried, but there wasn't a dry eye in the house – or at least in the lobby. Even Meg sensed she was witnessing a most unusual event – and right here in the lobby of Placid Creek's best and only hotel, too.

Mary joined the embrace and then said, 'Let's go up to our room where we can talk.'

'May I make a suggestion?' said Jean.

Tim and Mary turned and Mary nodded in the affirmative.

'Wouldn't it all work out better if you were to check out of here and put your luggage in my Jeep? We could have an early dinner here at the Leighton and then drive out to my place, where we can talk all evening. I've got a load of photographs I'm sure you will enjoy, and we can discuss a lot of things out there.'

'Sounds great to me,' said Tim. Mary eagerly nodded her concurrence.

Meg, of course, heard it all, and said, 'You've got a plan, and there'll be no charge. Get your things together, and I'll back all this off your Visa card. Then you can decide on dinner.'

Tim and Mary excused themselves briefly to go to their room to get out of their 'native' attire. Both Jean and Meg couldn't help smiling as the man in the electric-blue suit jacket and the woman in the bright red and brown dress disappeared down the hall.

At dinner, Tim waved off the menu. 'Something we'd only get in Australia,' he said to Meg.

'Would you like chiko rolls?' asked Meg. 'Believe me, we make the best such rolls you're likely to get in this country.'

'What's that?' asked Mary.

'Well,' said Meg, 'I have this mutton just boned, and you take that, add some celery, cabbage, barley, rice, carrots, tube of egg—'

Tim interrupted. 'No. No. No. Meg, don't tell us. I'm sure to forget something. Same as if I were to tell you all the things that go into Lancashire hotpot. Just go ahead. I know we'll like it.'

'She's right,' chimed in Jean, 'the chiko rolls you get here are better than you'll get anywhere else.'

'I'll let you prepare your taste buds for this local gourmet delight with some nice chilled chardonnay,' said Meg. She hurried off to the wine cabinet cooler.

While their dinner was being prepared, Mary turned the conversation towards Jean's Navy career. She said they wanted to hear about the various things Jean had done during her career in the Navy, and they were especially interested how a girl got to be an officer in the Navy. She knew in England and in the US it was 'This Man's Navy', and you hardly ever heard about women in any naval service.

Jean assured her it wasn't all that difficult, at least since elected officials figured out that promoting career programmes that benefited females was a good way to get re-elected.

'Same as in the States,' observed Mary. 'Only we seem to have a lot of sometimes very aggressive "women's rights" groups that make a business of harassing politicians suspected of favouring "the old ways".

'Anyway,' Mary continued, 'I don't want to labour the point, but we are both very interested hearing about your going in the Navy and your career.'

'Well,' said Jean, 'it's a long story, and I wouldn't bore you with an autobiography, but I can sort of fill you in on how it all came about.'

Tim and Mary's very interested looks encouraged Jean to try, at least, to give them the big picture of her career. She recounted that before she completed her matriculation, the Australian equivalent of finishing high school, she still had not decided what she wanted to do with her life.

'That was back in 1963, about a month before I graduated. And there was one wonderful teacher in my life who fairly hypnotised me, Miss Ellen Darby. God rest her soul. She was great. Anyway, Miss Darby came up to me after class shortly before I was about to graduate and asked me what I was going to do after graduation. I told her I was wondering the same thing. Somehow, I think she had guessed I was one of those full-of-get-up-and-go types, but hadn't decided where I wanted to go. Anyway, she began telling me about her sister who was in the WRANS. "The what?" I said. WRANS, she told me stood for Women's Royal Australian Naval Service.

' "Well," I said, "I really never planned on becoming a sailor." '

' "Oh, nothing like that, exactly," Miss Darby said. "It's actually a service within a service, made up all of girls, or ladies, who do all kinds of jobs in the Navy, but they can't be assigned to sea duty." '

As Jean was talking, Meg began bringing the various courses of their dinner at the Leighton. They proceeded to eat at a rather leisurely pace as Jean continued telling about the beginning.

Jean went on to relate how Miss Darby's sister had become the commanding officer of a cryptology division in Naval Intelligence. She had just received the most interesting letter from her about the messages they were intercepting from Indonesia about how that awful President Sukarno was trying to do a lot of things she couldn't tell even her own sister, but that Miss Darby should watch for some "big happenings" in Malaysia. Actually Sukarno was still the President when I went to a language school in Indonesia starting later that same year. Sure enough, although it didn't happen until 1967, I vividly remember that was the year that awful man was thrown out of office by one of his own generals, a General Suharto who made himself their next president.'

Jean told them that the half-hour she spent listening to Miss Darby that afternoon telling her about her sister's career in the Navy truly changed her life. The next day after school she had gone to a nearby Naval recruiting station where she was given 'a whole ream' of written material describing the career opportunities for 'truly qualified' young women serving in the WRANS. 'The truly qualified,' she explained, meant those who scored high on a battery of aptitude and intelligence tests which were given to all applicants.

Jean had taken those tests during the week after graduation. One week to the day after that, she received a telephone call at home from a very mature-sounding woman with a very friendly voice. The lady told Jean she was the chief of WRANS recruitment, calling from Brisbane. While all that was sinking in, the lady told her she had scored in the highest two per cent.

'Then I heard her say "Jean, I'll make it short and sweet: we want you." I was eighteen years old, and I can't tell you how really good all that made me feel. "Yes! Yes!" I heard myself saying, and the very next day I joined the WRANS. Oh, those were exciting days,' she reminisced.

She went on to describe how she was first stationed at the RAN training facility called HMAS *Nirimba* at Quakers Hill, west of Sydney in New South Wales for her basic training.

'That lasted twelve weeks,' she said, as Meg placed their dessert on the table. 'Look,' said Jean, 'it is getting a bit late, and you want to get checked out of here so we can go out to my place where we can look at some old photos and talk before bedtime. Why don't I stop talking about the Navy for now, and tomorrow on the trip back to Bribie Island I can fill you in on some of the more interesting unclassified things I've been involved in?'

'Unclassified?' asked Mary, looking a bit surprised.

'Well, yes,' explained Jean, 'I took Ms Darby's advice and after basic training I went into Naval Intelligence, in which there were any number of those "you are sworn never to discuss with unauthorised persons" and "need to know" things,' she said, with her voice sounding very stern.

'There are also a lot of things I think you'll find interesting.'

'Such as?' asked Mary, now looking very interested.

'Oh, the somewhat subterfuge language schools in Indonesia and Malay, the I-spy exercises, and any number of the declassified events,' Jean replied.

'Sounds like a plan to me,' chimed in Tim. 'Mary,' he went on, 'why don't you and Jean go up and sort of put our things together? I'll get the bill paid and get us cleared to leave this lovely place.'

Very shortly thereafter, Tim was handing Meg a cheque, and the ladies were up in the room with the packing nearly completed.

When they arrived at Jean's place, the headlights of the Jeep lit up the front of the house when she drove into the fenced yard. It wasn't a large place, but to Tim's estimate it was a good deal larger than the lock-keeper's cottage he grew up in near Rufford.

Jean suggested they stay put until she got some lights turned on. Then Tim lugged their suitcases through the front door.

Jean directed Mary to her room.

At first, Jean started to put a kettle over a gas burner, and then she had a second thought. 'It's too late for tea,' said Jean, 'we'd lay awake all night. I'll break out a bottle of merlot, and we can just relax.'

As the ladies went about their tasks, Tim busied himself walking about the stone fireplace scanning the numerous framed photographs hung on the walls on either side. They were obviously not recent photos. To his considerable surprise, he spotted himself in three of the pictures. As he studied them, he felt a faint familiarity with several persons in the photos, but he tried in vain to remember their names. Except for Jean's mother, her uncle and grandmother, he couldn't call up one other name.

As they sat with their wine glasses, Tim asked questions about the family history after he had left for England.

Jean's mother had never married. While Jean's 'version' of a great deal had to be what she had learned from others, her real mother had clung to life for several months after the adoption. Her adopted mother had a life very much in character with what would have transpired among the family to which he had become so endeared during his three years Down Under.

When Jean's mother found that she was with child, after Tim had left, she was a very frightened young girl. She never hesitated to tell her mother what had happened, but she had been very apprehensive about her father finding out. Apparently both her parents proved to be very understanding and had fully faced up to the social stigma, which didn't last long. Her infant daughter had turned out to be a delightful child who endeared herself early on to virtually all of the family's acquaintances.

'No,' said Jean, her real mother had a brief and not very happy life starting with her pregnancy, and as Jean grew up, she somehow felt responsible for that.

Tim was simply nonplussed with that statement. He felt he ought to say something, but what? If he were to say that had he known, he would have hastened back to Australia to do the right thing, he might sound like a phony, as he wasn't at all certain that was what he would have done. Truth be told, he didn't know what he would have done. Had he known then that doing 'the right thing' would have prevented his later having Mary for his wife, he felt it a serious question whether he would have been quite so honourable. On the other hand, by that time in his life, he knew that Mary had married in America and was having a family of her own. So he might well have come back to Australia. Probably would have. Maybe not. Oh, it would have been such a tangled web, he decided that now he was not sure what he would have done. Maybe I ought to try to change the subject, he thought.

'How long have you had this lovely place?' asked Mary.

Thank God, thought Tim. Mary changed the subject for me.

'I can't remember when it was otherwise,' said Jean. 'It's been in the family since my dad acquired it when I was just a little girl.

'I've had it all to myself since my mum – actually, my aunt, as you know – passed away. But I've always loved it, and I've decided never to sell it. I think that, somehow, it's just become a part of me.'

'That's sweet,' said Mary. 'I suspect there's a generation in this country that's long gone from America and, I suspect, from England, too.

'Look,' said Mary, 'we want you to meet the rest of your family in America and in England, and if you knew them you'd be eager to meet them, too.

'I recall reading something about your not being too far away from some kind of retirement, or eligibility for retirement, and you mentioned during dinner something about your "next tour of sea duty". Could you give us some idea of your schedule during the next couple of years, and let's see what we can work out?'

'I'm almost eligible for what the WRAN calls a form of early retirement. My twenty years of basic service will be completed in just under three years. I'll be thirty-six then, which is only nineteen years short of the minimum retirement age of fifty-five. But, after twenty years of active service, at least those of us who started serving before 1970, can transfer to the standby reserve, and begin receiving retirement pay when we reach age fifty-five.'

'The what reserve?' asked Tim.

'Standby,' said Jean, 'it means you're subject to being called up in case of an emergency, but otherwise, you're only expected to keep up on what your rank is expected to know at a minimum if you were suddenly recalled to active duty. They just mail the up-to-date materials periodically, and you're expected to read them till you know them by heart.'

'Well,' said Mary, 'do you want to remain as you say on active duty after you could take this early retirement?'

'Or,' added Tim, 'might you need to continue on active duty after you could transfer to the reserve?'

'Well, I certainly wouldn't need to, as you put it. I've saved over half of what I've earned on active duty, and I've inherited all that my parents and my uncle had. I wouldn't describe myself as exactly wealthy by some people's standards, but I'd sure be neurotic if I ever caught myself worrying about money.

'The direct answer to your question is that I very much enjoy serving in the Royal Navy, but I'd not hesitate to do something I fancy I'd enjoy more.'

At this point, Mary thought the familiarity factors were sufficient for her to ask a very personal question that had been a bit on her mind.

'Tell me, Jean,' Mary said, 'if I'm not being too presumptuous, have you every considered marriage?'

Jean didn't bat an eye.

'Oh,' she said, 'I was practically a bride once, when I was just twenty-three. A wonderful young man, Bill Plancton. He was a pilot in the Royal Australian Air Force. We met when I was serving my first and he was flying heavy transport aircraft in an air lift group known as No. 38 Squadron. He was stationed at the Royal Australian Air Force base at Amberly, some fifty kilometres southwest of Brisbane. Bill and his mates were caught one night trying to land in a typhoon about three months before our wedding date. Oh, it was so terrible, I can't even talk about it.'

Jean's eyes became moist, but somehow she managed not to break down. This was the second show of deep emotions Mary had seen by this lovely young girl.

'I don't think I ever really got over it,' she added, regaining her composure. 'And since,' she continued, 'I've even gone steady with a number of young men, mostly in the Navy, but I suspect a part of me died with Bill. I don't know. It's just a chapter in my life that has been tender and painful ever since it happened. Since then, I think I've been unfair with some of the other chaps I've grown quite fond of, and who've shown a real interest in me. I've caught myself measuring them against Bill, and I know that's not right, but, none of them have really measured up, either – for one reason or another.'

'What about if you tried the early retirement, and decided you'd like to come back into the Navy?' asked Tim, intending to get on to less sensitive subjects.

'No problem,' said Jean. 'There's always room for experienced personnel in the Royal Australian Navy.'

'Well,' said Mary, 'that gives us some time frames to work in.'

'Tell me,' she added, 'do you have anything like six to eight weeks' leave coming up in the next year?'

'I'm eligible to apply for that kind of leave any time, as long as I do so at least six months in advance.'

'Wonderful,' said Tim. 'We can plan for a big trip early next year. How does that sound?'

Everything had actually gone beyond Jean's fondest dreams. She showed her happy satisfaction with a big smile. 'I think I would enjoy that about as much or more than anything I've ever done.'

Tim and Mary were equally pleased.

'Great,' said Tim. 'Just great! Now,' he added, looking at his wrist watch, 'why don't we get a good night's sleep and strike out early in the morning for the base on Bribie Island. Our car's parked outside your commanding officer's headquarters and—'

'And,' chimed in Jean, 'that's just where I have to check in to tell them where they could reach me in an emergency during the seven days left on my current leave.'

It had been a long and eventful day and everyone was beginning to feel the effects of all that had happened. Tim couldn't avoid a yawn. Power of suggestion. Mary put her hand over her mouth and attempted to swallow a yawn.

'That's it,' said Jean. 'Let's all get to bed. We have a big day ahead of us tomorrow.'

It was lights out within five minutes.

Chapter Ninety

Tim drove from the Naval base at Bribie Island to the Hotel Embassy in Brisbane. Jean sat in the front seat, Mary sat in the back.

The conversation remained lively, with Tim and Mary asking most of the questions, and Jean mostly answering. Jean told them how surprised she had been to be offered the opportunity of going to naval officer's school shortly after she entered the Navy. When asked how that all came about, all she was told was that she hadn't 'exactly failed the IQ and aptitude tests'.

'I'll never forget thinking that the personnel officer who told me acted as if I well knew what their testing had shown. I was tempted to ask for more details, but, then I thought the better of it. In checking, they might find they made a mistake, so why not quit while I was winning, so to speak.'

Everything she's discussed so far sure suggests she's not short on brains, Tim thought. As so often occurs between married people, Mary was entertaining exactly the same thought at the same time.

Jean also told them about her various station assignments and her three tours of sea duty that had taken her to Calcutta, Tokyo and Montevideo. It all sounded very exciting, and almost before they knew it, Tim was driving into the Hotel Embassy's guests' car park, just off Turbot street.

He killed the engine at exactly 7.30 p.m. and breathed a sigh of relief. It had been a full day indeed.

At the reception desk, they got Jean checked into a room on the same floor as theirs, just four doors down the hall on the right.

Tim, Mary and Jean, accompanied by a bellman with all of their luggage on a trolley, took the lift to the seventh floor. As the party approached Tim and Mary's room, Tim spoke up.

'Jean, why don't you get a bit settled and then ring our room? We've all had a long day, and I personally don't feel like dressing up to go to the hotel's dining room for dinner. We can order it off of the room service menu and let them bring it to us.'

'Will do,' replied Jean, as she followed the bellman to her room.

Mary walked into their room, and simply flopped on the bed. Tim opened the door to the small refrigerator and withdrew a bottle of Pinot Noir labelled 'New South Wales's Finest'.

Jean rang about thirty minutes later, and Tim told her to come on over. After

Jean joined them, the three perused the room service menu.

'It's like looking at a menu in England,' said Tim, 'except here everything is priced in dollars, not pounds.'

After everyone had decided, Tim called room service and ordered their dinners.

Their dinner order arrived promptly and picked them all up considerably.

As they were nearing the end of their meal, Mary said, 'I've got an idea, and we won't have to get all dressed up to do it.'

'What's that?' asked Tim.

'Lets drop down to the bar and have a nightcap.' Turning to face Jean, she said, 'There's a perfectly delightful bartender down there, and I think you'll enjoy him and his potions…'

Within five minutes, they were descending the lift, en route to the hotel bar to introduce their daughter to Mike.

They sat at the bar, with Jean in the middle. Mike recognised them – rather, two of them – and walked up immediately.

'Mike,' said Tim, 'we'd like you to meet our daughter, Jean.'

Mike's answer pleased both Tim and Mary.

'You have got to be kidding!'

Then Mike studied the faces of all three.

'She does look a lot like you in some ways, Tim,' he uttered, 'but that lovely hair is just like her mum's.'

All three smiled, but Jean was the only one to speak.

'I'm very glad to meet you, Mike,' she said, extending her right hand.

'I'm pleased, too,' Mike replied, as he shook her extended hand.

'When your parents were here a few days ago, they didn't mention having a stunning girl like you at home,' he added.

'Well,' replied Jean, 'I'm not exactly at home. I'm actually finishing my seventeenth year in the WRAN.'

'The Navy!' said Mike, looking quite surprised. 'I did two hitches myself. I was a mechanic, first on HMAS *Melbourne*, and I wound up on the carrier *Invincible*.'

'Well,' replied Jean, 'it's a small world indeed. I was once engaged to a Navy pilot whose squadron used to practise landings on the *Invincible*.'

'What do you know about that,' Mike exclaimed. 'It's been almost ten years since I left the Navy, and several times since, I've thought that giving all that up wasn't the smartest thing I ever did.'

'Tell you what,' interjected Tim, 'before you two semi-old salts get too engrossed in your memoirs, Mike, why don't you pick up that bottle of brandy there, and pour us a night-cap?'

'Ah,' said Mike, 'that's exactly what I'm here for.'

Surprisingly, at first, he put the nearby bottle of brandy on the back bar and opened the cabinet below. From there he withdrew an impressively shaped bottle which bore the label, 'Australian Blended Brandy', immediately below which were the boldly printed words in black: *VERY OLD – MINIMUM TEN YEARS'.*

'Now these, my good friends, are on the house, as the Americans say.'

Mary and Jean burst out laughing. Tim didn't know the joke, but he knew good brandy when he saw it, and he couldn't have looked more pleased.

Mike poured them each about four fingers of brandy in what seemed like large snifters.

'I'd join you,' he said, 'but that would be against the rules of the house.' This noble statement was followed by a practised quick glance to first right, then left, and then about two fingers of that prize brandy went into a small glass that just seemed to be perfectly positioned for ready use should there be an emergency, or some other unusual occasion requiring such equipment.

'To us all,' said Tim, raising his brandy snifter to propose the toast.

'To us all,' echoed the voices of Mary, Mike and Jean.

The author will not tempt any reader by describing how this splendid beverage assuaged the parched throats of these hardy travellers and the amiable purveyor of such fine liquor. Suffice it to say that the satisfaction of relief was quite visible, even on the countenance of the purveyor, who didn't even have a parched throat.

Shortly after what almost turned out to be a ceremony, Tim and the ladies thanked Mike and made their way to the lift and a most wonderful night's sleep.

The next morning a real English breakfast (bacon, eggs, beans, and sausage) was enjoyed by all, and they boarded the hotel's 'guest van' to spend most of the day on nearby Brisbane Beach.

Tim felt the need for exercise, and spent several hours swimming. Tim had a good memory of the rocky beaches around England, which made him appreciate the fine grain sand that was lapped with gentle breakers. He took full advantage of his opportunity, and swam in about thirty-minute bursts, and took a few catnaps. Jean and Mary were more occupied in enjoying the sunshine and chinning. Mary described her family history, including the indescribable exultation when the family learned that Tim had survived the war. She could almost quote verbatim Rose's letter to her in America, telling her that Tim was alive.

That night, they took a cab to the Neptune restaurant and stopped by Mike's bar when they returned. The amiability persisted and this time, Tim ordered three Australian Blended Brandies, 'and one for the bartender, should he feel so inclined'.

Mike brought out three brandy snifters. As he poured, he told Tim he would have to decline the generous offer, and went on to describe two close friends that had unwisely failed to recognise the industrial hazards of bartending, who were no longer among us.

'I learned to limit my indulgence to one drink every other day,' he concluded, 'and I find that to be a happy medium, as far as me and my liver are concerned.'

The next two days followed much the same pattern. Lots of good food, good conversation, daytime exercising, and the hotel's offerings in the libation department weren't exactly overlooked, but never abused.

Unfortunately the time went so quickly and it was soon the last day before Jean would be joining her ship. Tim and Mary would fly back to New York then on to LA. Jean knew the ship would be spending time in Hawaii and Honolulu. She had their number and would get in touch every time she was in port. Jean took a couple more photographs. Tim gave his daughter a really big hug and said, 'I will send you lots of family pictures.' Then Jean got into her car and drove away.

On the flight back to New York, Tim never stopped talking about all the plans he had for Jean. Mary had to remind him, 'She is not a little girl. Jean is a mature woman, with a good career. We will see a lot of her, and should be thankful it has turned out so well.' Then Mary took Tim's hand. 'We now have a daughter and a son.'

Then she asked the air hostess to bring two large vodka tonics.

When Mary and Tim arrived back in New York, the first thing that Mary did was to call GJ from the hotel. He informed his mother that all the family had arrived and wanted to know their flight details so he could meet hem in LA. Mary told him that they would have a night in New York, then fly out the following afternoon. Tim and Mary, after the exhausting twenty-four hours, decided to rest and have dinner in the hotel. When Tim unpacked his small bag, he took out a package that Jean had given him just before she left. Inside was a picture of Jean in her Navy uniform. It was signed, 'To my new parents, with love.' The picture was in a beautiful gold frame. Mary looked at it.

'I know just the place for this when we get home,' she said.

The following morning they got a cab to the airport and got the 11 a.m. flight to LA. They would arrive late afternoon. Mary had already given GJ the flight details. He was there to meet them.

Sandra and Rose, with the help of the girls, had been working all day, preparing the evening dinner for all the family. The main topic of conversation was the news that Tim had found out he had a daughter. All the family were pleased and looked forward to the time when they would meet her. During the stay in America GJ had really gone to town on the organisation. They had several days in Mexico, visited Las Vegas, and also had a couple of trips on GJ's new boat.

Poor Larry had spent too much time in the sun and suffered sunburn, but Carole treated him and he was OK after a couple of days, but had learned his lesson.

Like all good things the weeks went by so quickly. During the last week of their vacation, they had all just finished dinner and the phone rang.

GJ said, 'I will get it in the study.'

The voice on the other end asked to speak to Tim or Mary Johnson and GJ asked who was calling.

'This is Jean. I am his daughter.'

GJ explained who he was and said, 'We have heard all about you. The family are all looking forward to meeting you.'

Jean said she was calling from Hawaii.

'I have a land line in my cabin; we are here for twenty-four hours.'

GJ shouted for Tim to pick the other phone up. Tim chatted with his daughter, then one by one all the family said hi, which made Jean feel that she really belonged.

Jean promised that when she had completed this tour, she would visit. When she put the phone down, despite being alone in her cabin, she was a very happy woman.

Chapter Ninety-one

Life, as always, was good for all the families and continued like that for the next couple of years. Sandra and GJ were very pleased with their two children, who were both doing well at school. Robert was attending GJ's old school. Elaine was at the all-girls school in Pasadena.

Adam and Rose did not travel very much now. Adam had suffered a couple of minor heart attacks, and naturally his doctor advised him to slow down, so they spent more of their time at Sagamore. Adam loved taking his old barge, *Mary Rose*, on the river. Their two sons visited on a regular basis. Carole and Tony came down every other weekend, and of course when the grandchildren were there it was a bonus. Rose and May seemed to have got closer and when possible they would go shopping together. Rose always did the driving, because May had a slight problem with her eyes. Occasionally they would plan a trip to Lancaster and visit Gary at the marina. Debra would always provide afternoon tea. Kathleen, who was now a teenager, would help out at the marina during school holidays.

Adam did not mind Rose travelling without him; he would always say that he was busy. The truth was he did not want to worry Rose, but he seemed to feel tired all the time. Without Adam knowing, Rose had discussed Adam's health with Dr Pearson, who had been looking after the family for years. He told Rose that Adam had a condition of the heart, but with medication and rest, he could go on for years. It was entirely up to him.

Rose and May had to admit, they are all getting older.

'We can afford it, so let's the four of us go on a cruise. We can organise it and surprise them,' suggested Rose.

It was a warm Sunday morning and Carole and Tony were sitting on the porch of their bungalow in Dalton. It had been ten years since her grandma had died and they had moved in. Since then they had done lots of alterations inside and out. They were admiring the big water feature that Carol's granddad had built. Tony had also done several projects, including a paddock and stable for Larry's pony, although at the present time it was kept at Wrightington with the other two ponies. Tony looked down at Molly. She was sixteen years old and despite Carole giving her all her attention, she would not last much longer.

Tony patted her head. 'You don't want to leave here, do you, old girl?' he said affectionately.

Tony heard the phone ring so he went inside. When he answered, it was the police from Southport.

'Can we speak to Mrs Carole Holland?'

'I am Mr Holland, what's happened?'

'Well, sir, we've got a report of smoke coming from behind the clinic. We called the fire station and they are there now dealing with it.'

Tony put the phone down and called to Carole. 'Come on, dear, we have to go to the clinic. There's a fire.'

Carole's immediate response was, 'Oh my god, are Una and Bob OK?'

Tony drove to Southport in forty minutes. Fortunately, it being Sunday there was very little traffic.

When they pulled up, it did not look good. Apparently the fire had started at the back and spread quickly down one side, destroying the surgery and the recovery kennels, but again being Sunday the kennels were empty. The business van was destroyed, but Carole noticed that Bob's car wasn't there. Usually on a Sunday Bob and Una went to his parents' place for tea. Two hours later, when it was safer to get a closer look, it was obvious that the place would not be able to operate for a long time.

It was almost dark when Una and Bob returned. Una ran over to Carole.

'Oh, whatever has happened? We only left at 11.30!'

Carole calmed her down, saying, 'The main thing is that you are both OK. I want you to book in the Scarisbrick Hotel.'

Bob quickly said, 'We can stay at my parents' place.'

Tony had a word with the police and firemen. He was assured that a couple of men would be there all night. Carole was worried regarding all the drugs on the premises. The police again assured them that no one would be allowed inside until it was completely safe.

'We would like you back here tomorrow morning early, so you can inspect the damage,' she was told.

Carole called her parents and told them what had happened.

'The clinic is badly damaged but the main thing is that no one was hurt. I will let you know more later. Tony and I have to be there early tomorrow morning.'

It was 9 a.m. when they arrived and they were very surprised to see Una and Bob already there. The police took statements from Una and, of course, with Bob being a policeman, Una understood all this had to be done. On further inspection, the flat had escaped most of the damage, but was completely flooded with the water that the firemen had to use, and there was obviously smoke damage. Carole supervised all the drugs and medical equipment were stored separately; they would have to be kept for insurance purposes. It was a very hard day for everyone.

Martyn had turned up with a large van and he took what he could back to Wrightington. Rose suggested fish and chips, which went down very well after such a long day with nothing to eat. Adam comforted his daughter; he was so organised.

He told Carole, 'Tomorrow, call the *Southport Gazette* and tell your customers that you will be open in three days' time.'

'Dad, that is not possible.'

'Yes, it is. I have already ordered a couple of mobile units. They will be there tomorrow afternoon.' Martyn arranged for several men to go and help out with the clean-up. Carole got in touch with her past employer in Ormskirk, who offered to help out with any emergencies. When Aunt Mary in America got the news, she offered any necessary financial help. Carole thanked her but said she would be OK and everything was insured.

Within one week two mobile units were fitted out, and business was carrying on pretty well. All the family rallied round with help and organisation.

Tony had been in touch with an architect friend of his. During the last few years new technology had improved veterinary techniques, but it required lots of specialised and very expensive equipment. The insurance obviously would not go to that, but Carole owned the land and both her father and her husband said to go for it; she had the opportunity to have the best clinic in the north-west.

Jean had just completed her tour of duty and was due for several weeks' leave so she called her father, Tim.

'I am in Brisbane at the moment; I have just started my leave. If it is OK I would like to visit you and Mother.'

Tim was delighted. 'You know that you can visit any time for as long as you want.'

Jean said she could get a flight the day after, so it was arranged that Tim and Mary would meet her.

Sandra and Mary had secretly been discussing the possibility of getting Jean a boyfriend. Jean had already told them on a previous visit that her first boyfriend's name was Richard Robinson. They had gone to the same school, but she had not seen him for twenty years. It was this information that Mary and Sandra decided to pursue. On the second night Tim was outside fiddling with the pool filter. The three women went into Pasadena shopping, and during a coffee break Sandra asked Jean, 'Have you any idea were that first boyfriend of yours is?'

They were surprised to hear Jean say, 'Oh yes, I know were he is. At least, where he was.'

Sandra said, 'That's great! When we get back home, why don't we try to locate him?'

Jean gave a little giggle. 'Well, it would be nice to know what he his doing.'

During happy hour that evening, they managed to get a phone number that could just be Richard's. By this time, the ladies were feeling the effects of the wine. Tim was a little puzzled with all the giggling, and when they told him he just smiled.

'I will have a beer outside and leave you to it.'

They persuaded Jean to call the number and pretend she was someone just doing a survey. Jean did this, and Richard answered the phone.

'Richard Robinson here, who's calling?'

Jean went on automatic.

'Oh, hello. Sorry to bother you, we are doing a survey on people living alone. Would you mind answering a few questions?'

'Well, I have nothing better to do at the moment. Why not? What do you want to know?'

'How long have you lived on your own?'

'Much too long.'

'Have you ever been married?'

'Well, if being married for ten months qualifies me, yes.'

Jean went on to ask several more stupid questions; his answers were full of humour. Jean thanked him for his time and cooperation. Before she was about to hang up, he said, 'OK, now it is my turn. What's your name and where do you come from?'

'My name is Jean and I live in Brisbane.'

Richard then said he used to live in Brisbane and knew a lady named Jean. She interrupted, 'What happened to her?'

There was a long pause. 'Well, I don't know were she is at the moment, but I have a feeling I am speaking to her right now.'

Jean could not help herself, 'You knew all the time!'

Richard said, 'I did not know at first, then when you said your name was Jean and you lived in Brisbane, I knew I was being taken. But I would love to meet you.'

Jean told him that she was in Los Angeles, but would be back in Brisbane at the weekend and would call him. When Jean put the phone down, Mary and Sandra wanted to know everything.

'I promise I will let you know when I have met him. It was such a long time ago.'

Back in England Martyn was up early and ready for what he hoped would be a good day. The first thing he did was call his father.

'Dad, I want to see you this morning. It is very important.'

Adam and Rose had planned on going to Southport to see Carole but he agreed to meet Martyn in the Bowling Green pub for lunch.

'Bring Ann along; we will call there on the way back.'

Carole was a little worried when she saw her father; he did not look very well. She confided in her mother.

'Dad looks so tired, has he seen the doctor?

Rose said, 'You know what he is like; he keeps putting it off.'

Carole gave her dad a good talking to.

'I want you to promise me that you will see the doctor tomorrow.'

Under protest, he promised he would, but added, 'Don't worry, I am OK. I just haven't been sleeping well.'

Rose drove back and when they got to the Bowling Green, Martyn was there with his wife, Ann. Martyn ordered the lunch, Adam only wanted a sandwich.

After their light meal, Martyn started to explain what had happened at the meeting. They want to buy the property and turn it into luxury flats. 'What do you think we should do? They talked big money, and I think we should sell.'

Adam looked at his son.

'You are in charge. If you and your brother think selling is good for the business, then sell.'

'Come on, Dad, you have always made the right move. Tell me honestly, what would you do?'

Although Adam was not feeling that great, being asked to make the final decision perked him up. He leaned over.

'Son, you go back to them tell them you want a million and five per cent of the sales. Also, you want the pick of a flat when they are completed.'

Martyn was quiet for some time, then said, 'I don't think they will go for that.' Adam stood up. 'Well, son, if they don't, we don't sell.'

He gave a little smile to his son, kissed Ann, then said to Rose, 'I am ready for my nap.'

Before they left, Rose made Ann promise that they would come over at the weekend; Carole and Tony would be there. Then all four walked out to the car park and drove off.

As Adam had predicted, Frazier and Brooks had requested another meeting in London. Adam advised his son to call them back and say he couldn't make it Friday, but would meet them in their Liverpool office. That will give them all weekend to discuss it.

On Monday morning Martyn picked his dad up and they drove to Liverpool, had an early lunch and went to the office. Two smart young men arrived at 2 p.m. Martyn did not recognise them, but assumed they were two of the main directors. When they introduced themselves as Jeremy Frazier and

Vincent Brooks, Martyn's assumption proved correct. The men got down to business, and ideas and suggestions were thrown around, but after four hours and endless cups of coffee no agreement was reached.

Vincent Brooks suggested that they all go back to their hotel, have a meal then resume. Adam had a strong feeling that the main obstacle was the percentage; the two men would not accept any form of percentage deal. Adam requested fifteen minutes with his son, and promised they would come back with their final decision.

Adam and Martyn went into the hotel lounge.

'We will withdraw our percentage deal, and ask for another £20,000, plus one of the apartments.'

When they returned and put that to them, it did not take long for the deal to be completed. The two directors of Frazier and Brooks stretched out their hands to confirm deal. They all went into the bar.

Chapter Ninety-two

During the flight home, Jean was beginning to have second thoughts about meeting Richard. However, in the end she convinced herself that she would at least meet him. She had left her car at the hotel, and decided to stay one night before driving home. Jean showered and changed, then went down to the bar. Mike recognised her immediately and greeted her.

'Hi, did you have a good time in California?'

'Yes, thank you. It was great!'

The hotel was very quiet, and Mike was due to finish in another hour. He invited Jean out to dinner, but she said that she was tired and would eat in the hotel.

'I want to be away early tomorrow morning; I have a long drive.'

Mike was quick to say, 'Why eat here on your own? I am only asking you out for a meal; I don't want to spend the night with you.'

In the end she accepted. It turned out to be a nice night. Mike took her to a little Chinese café just a short distance from the hotel, which was busy with young people. Everyone seemed to know Mike; he was obviously very popular. Jean could not remember when she laughed as much. She found out that Mike was an orphan and had done a spell in the Forces.

'I have been at the hotel for three years and love the work,' he told her.

He was a very laid-back guy. At the end of the night he told Jean, 'I have really enjoyed your company. Have a safe journey tomorrow and when you are back in town, pop in for a drink.'

On the way to the lodge, Jean stopped at Molly's just to let her know she was back, then picked up some supplies from the village shop. The first thing Jean did was call her father to say she was back home, then she had a chat with Mary. When she said that she would be seeing Richard at the weekend, Mary reminded her to let her know how it went. Jean then made herself a drink and some salad and switched on the TV. It was nice to be back in her own place, happy and contented.

The following Friday, Jean set off for Dawson Creek. The instructions that Richard had given her were spot on. Driving through the entrance to the trailer park, she went straight to the office. The young girl told her that Richard was in number seven; he always booked that one because it was down by the creek. Jean was directed down the track. At the bottom she was to leave her car near the tackle shop, then walk down to the creek.

Richard's trailer was on the right. It was dark green with an Aborigine design on the side. Jean knocked on the door, but there was no answer. She walked around the side and shouted hello. Still no response. The place was all set out: table, chairs and BBQ. She sat down and waited. It was very hot and humid, and after some considerable time she was contemplating going back to the office. Suddenly a large wet Labrador came bounding out of the mangroves. It made straight for a large bowl of water and almost emptied it. Then it came over to Jean, wagging her tail. A couple of minutes later, the dog heard someone coming and ran back into the mangroves. Jean probably didn't do a good job of hiding the look of shock on her face. Richard was over six feet tall, way overweight, wearing shorts and a big Australian bush hat. When he saw Jean, he went over to her and shook hands, then apologised for not being there.

'Come on, let's get inside. The air conditioning will make you feel much better,' he said.

For the next hour they both asked each other questions about what had happened since college days. Richard was very impressed when he learned that Jean had been in the Navy over twenty years. He admitted that he had made a bad start with his life.

'My marriage only lasted a very short time. It was a mistake from the start. Probably my own fault; I always put work first. That's why I like doing what I'm doing: I can take off for a while any time I feel like it.

'I come here several times each year. Pointing to his dog, Lucky, he said, 'She loves it.' He had found her wandering in the desert. She had been dumped and was near to staving.

'I carried her into the RV and put ice on her to bring her temperature down. Another day out there she would have been dead.' It was obvious that Richard was really found of the dog. He said she even went to work with him.

Jean remarked, 'I understand why you call her Lucky.'

Richard refilled the coffee cups. 'Would you like something to eat?'

'No, thank you, I had a big breakfast.'

Richard asked, 'How long will you be in Dawson Creek?'

'I don't really know, I have nothing to rush back for.'

'That's great! Why don't we spend some time together and catch up on the last few years?'

Jean reminded him it had been well over twenty years. That news seemed to stun him. 'I must be lot older than I thought!' Richard knew the area very well and he suggested that he would like to take her out for dinner. He arranged to pick her up at 7 p.m. back at the motel. Jean suddenly thought, Surely he won't come in that forty-foot RV.

The motel was a single-storey building. Jean's unit was on the corner. At

6 p.m. someone knocked on the door, when she opened it, she almost started laughing. Richard was standing there, dressed in the most odd-looking outfit she had ever seen. He had cowboy boots on, and a red and black shirt with a matching bandana. He stood with a big smile, his white teeth looking even whiter through his black beard.

Jean said, 'You are early: I'm not really ready.'

'Oh, come on, you look fine! I know a little place twenty miles from here; if we leave now we can catch the sunset.'

When Jean walked outside, she got another shock. There was a huge gold and black Harley Davidson motorbike. He told her to jump on the pillion. Jean had never been on a motorbike in her life.

'You can hang on to the side handles, or hang on to me.'

When he started the engine and let out the clutch, Jean felt this enormous power. Letting go of the handles, she flung her arms around Richard.

The next twenty minutes Jean clung on for dear life, as they travelled at what seemed like a hundred miles an hour. When, to Jean's relief, they arrived at the lakeside venue, there were at least twenty bikes parked, mostly Harley Davidsons. Jean's fist impression was that it was a rough place. Richard introduced her to several of his friends and their women; they seemed a fun-loving lot. They were just in time to get a drink and watch the sunset from the deck. One of the women who arrived later, whose name was Nancy Williams, came over to Jean.

'I don't recall seeing you here before.'

Jean introduced herself. 'This is my first time; Richard brought me.'

Nancy, without hesitation, said, 'Make sure he takes you back. He usually goes missing later on. I have had to take his friends home on many occasions.'

Nancy invited Jean to join her and three more women. 'I will get you a beer.' Jean declined the beer.

'I will have a glass of wine, please.'

The food was a mix-up; everything was just laid out and you helped yourself. Chicken, steak, fish; you name it, they had it. All in all it was a lively place, and Jean got on well with the other women, but she had already made her mind up that it really wasn't her scene. Richard spent most of the time with another guy at the pool table. The beers he consumed didn't seem to have any effect on him. This was obviously the normal way: the men drank, played pool and discussed motorbikes: the women were content just to chat and have a beer.

At 9.30 Jean asked Richard if he would take her back to the motel.

'Oh, it is only early. Have another drink then I will take you back. I will just give Bob another game.'

An hour later Jean could see Richard was not for leaving. Nancy could see that Jean had had enough.

'If you want to go, I will take you. I will be honest with you. Richard will play another game and then another; he is always the last to leave.'

Jean asked about getting a cab.

'No, honey, I am the official get-you-home service.'

They walked outside. Nancy had a much smaller bike and did not speed. Jean enjoyed the ride back to the motel. Nancy lived another ten miles further on. Jean thanked her for the ride, and asked her if she wanted to come in for a coffee. The two women sat in the small room drinking coffee.

Nancy asked, 'How long have you known Richard?'

When Jean said it was about thirty years, Nancy almost fell off the chair. He'd never said a word. Jean quickly explained the situation.

'I was really shocked when I saw him after all this time. I know we are all getting older but...' She hesitated. 'He is a slob!'

It was interesting what Nancy had to say. She had known Richard for fifteen years and watched him go downhill. Jean asked, 'Was it drinking that ruined his marriage?'

'No, that had nothing to do with the break-up.'

Nancy went on to explain it was what Richard's wife did and the way she did it. Just as Jean was getting really interested, Nancy looked at her watch.

'Oh my, look at the time, I must go!'

Jean really wanted to know more, so she suggested that they meet up in town and have a day together. Nancy was all for that. 'I will look forward to it,' she said. Then she left.

The next morning, Jean parked her car and went to meet Nancy. She was really surprised. Nancy had come in on the bus and was dressed very smartly. She looked like a completely different person, without all the motorbike gear. Dressed in a pale-blue suit and expertly applied make-up, she was really attractive.

Jean invited Nancy back to her place. It was only a couple of hours' drive and they could have lunch on the way. During the trip the conversation soon got back to Richard's wedding.

'Before I tell you anything more, I want you to promise that you won't tell Richard. If he wants you to know, I am sure he will tell you.'

When they arrived at the lodge, it was 5 p.m. Nancy could not believe what she saw.

'Is all this really yours?'

Jean smiled, 'Yes, every bit of it.'

'Well, I won't ever be able to invite you to my one-bed apartment.'

'I want you to make yourself at home. I have to make several phone calls;

you feel free to look around.'

After Jean had made all her calls she went back into the lounge. Nancy was looking at all the photographs on the dresser.

'I see you are in the Navy. Who are all these people with you?'

During the next hour, Jean tried to give Nancy a quick run through of her life.

'Gosh, you have had a fantastic life! The highlight for me was when I got my new motorbike. I have never been out of Australia.'

Jean suddenly realised that it was getting dark outside. 'I did intend taking you to Molly's bar for dinner, but I can fix something here, then why don't you stay the night?'

'I would love to but I did not bring anything with me.'

'That's no problem; there is a closet full of stuff in the guest room. Find something comfortable to wear. I will go in the kitchen and organise a meal.'

Half hour later Nancy joined Jean in the kitchen wearing dark slacks and a red sweater. They had a chicken salad and white wine, then went back into the lounge.

Jean came straight to the point.

'I would like to know more about what happened to Richard,' she said.

'Richard's wife, Thelma, from the start always wanted to party. She objected to the long hours that Richard worked. She got bored and started drinking more. Richard found out that she had also been seeing other guys. I don't know the full story; apparently she got married again then got into drugs, and moved to New Zealand. Richard decided to sell out, got an RV and began to travel around, servicing all the engines for a large trucking company. He is very good at it and well-known for his expertise.'

Nancy asked Jean, 'Do you think you will see him again?'

'Well, before you told me all this, I had made my mind up that I would not bother. However, when I take you home tomorrow, I will call on him.' Nancy smiled her approval.

'I think he would like that,' she said.

After dropping Nancy off and promising to keep in touch, Jean drove on to Dawson Creek. It was noon as she approached the RV site. She could hear loud music. Lucky came towards her, tail wagging. When Richard saw her, he switched off the radio.

'What a nice surprise! I did not expect to see you again. I am very sorry for the other night.'

Jean made light of it. 'Don't worry, I could see that you were enjoying the game.'

'They sat outside with a cold drink.

'I hope you won't judge me on our first outing. I would love another chance to take you out.'

Jean had already made her plan, which in turn would decide if she would want to continue seeing him. 'I have a couple of things to attend to, but I will come back for you at 6 p.m. and take you out for dinner.' Richard could not believe what she had said.

'That's the first time I have been invited out by a woman.'

'Well, you be ready. Don't expect too much; I am just inviting you for dinner.'

On the way into Dawson, she had noticed a what looked like a nice place about eight miles north. She had booked in again at the same motel. When she described the restaurant to the desk lady, it turned out that it was a very upmarket place. Jean got the number and booked a table for 7.30. After a visit to the hair salon, at 5.15 she left the motel dressed in pink trouser suit with stylish black shoes. As she got into the car she felt good and very much in charge.

When Richard opened the door to his RV, Jean was pleasantly surprised. He was wearing a light grey suit with blue shirt and tie. He had obviously had it tailor-made.

'Have we time for a drink?' Jean accepted.

'Just a small one please.'

Before they left, Richard excused himself.

'I will make sure Lucky is OK for water.'

Jean had a closer look at the photos on the wall. One was of Richard with two other guys. They were standing outside some office buildings. Richard was a lot slimmer and did not have a beard. Jean recognised him with his dark hair and white teeth. He was also much taller than the other two guys. Then she heard Richard shout, 'OK, I am ready when you are!' They got in the car and drove off.

During the evening Jean began to warm towards him. He was so different; not only his appearance, but the way he conducted himself. He was the perfect gentleman. Jean decided to stay in Dawson Creek a little longer. They spent the days walking along the trails with Lucky and Jean really got to know him. When it came time for Jean to leave, Richard plucked up courage, 'Do you think we could make something out of us meeting up again?' Then before she had time to answer, he added, 'I want you to be really honest with me.'

'Very well, I will. I have enjoyed spending time with you. However, I want you to understand that I spend time in America and will visit England too. Also, what I am about to say I don't want you to take the wrong way. I don't like the beard and I would like you to lose considerable weight.' Jean, noticing the look on his face, said, 'You asked me to be honest.'

Richard stroked the beard. 'This is no problem.' Then looking at his waist, he said, 'This I will work on.'

Before Jean left the following day, they had lunch together. Jean had to go to Brisbane then report back for duty. It would be two months before they would see each other. Although only having spent a week with her, he knew that he would miss her. He walked her to the car. Jean gave him a big hug but she did not attempt to kiss him with all that fuzz on his face.

'I will call you tonight,' she said and she drove off.

Chapter Ninety-three

In London, England, the old factory had been demolished and the new luxury apartments had been completed.

Adam and Rose had just returned from America; they had spent three weeks with Mary and Tim. Adam was looking much older and his health had not improved. On their return, he confided in Rose that he didn't want to make any more long trips abroad. Rose, although a little younger than Adam, agreed.

They sat together, reminiscing on the wonderful life they had experienced. Their three children had done exceptionally well. Martyn was running the business; he had two managers looking after the hauling and property sides, and he was always like his dad, travelling around looking for good deals. Gary had extended the marina in Lancaster and started another one in Rufford, making use of the acreage along the side of the Rufford canal, which was part of the farm that his dad had bought all those years ago.

Carole now had the best veterinary clinic in the north-west, and, on the advice of her daughter Tina, had opened a grooming section which was proving to be a very good business investment. Tina had qualified as vet, but with a staff of eight, like Martyn, she was fully occupied managing. This left Carole more time to travel with Tony, who loved to spend time in their villa in the south of France painting.

It had been almost a year since Jean had retired from the Navy and married Richard. Tim and Mary had spent two weeks in Brisbane with them after the wedding. Then Richard and his new wife took off. Tim was so pleased that his new-found daughter had found a good guy and got married.

Both families, the Robertses and Birchalls, had done extremely well from their humble beginnings. Adam Roberts was well known and liked, not only in the north of England, but in London business circles. During the last ten years he had made substantial donations to certain charities. He always insisted on the family getting together at least once a month at Sagamore. However, the younger members of the family were not always able to do this. Adam and Rose were spending more time at Sagamore. Adam would sit in the river room, watching the boats go by, something which he never tired of. In the evenings he and Rose would sit in the study, mostly discussing their children. All around the big house there were reminders of their life together. Rose would get the family album to look at photographs of her parents. One that always brought tears was her dad pictured working the locks at Rufford. Another was of her two brothers and her on the old tractor. Over the stone fireplace was a large painting of Sagamore house with the *Mary Rose* tied in front of the house. Its title was 'Excellence on Water and Land'. Tony had given it to them on their fiftieth wedding anniversary.

Adam, Rose, John, May, Tim and Mary all decided to have a day going down memory lane before Tim and Mary went back to the Willows. First they visited Rufford. They parked the car at the Rufford Arms pub, then walked slowly along the canal towpath to the locks that Rose's father had operated for most of his life. The farmhouse was still there, as were the fields where Tim and John had worked. The farmhouse had been extended and several stable blocks built; it was now an equestrian centre.

John teased Rose. 'I remember you used to make the excuse of taking the dog for a walk when you really wanted to meet Adam!'

Coming up to the locks, they let their minds drift back almost sixty years.

Later they met Gary in Lancaster. Adam got the keys to Grandma's cottage. Inside they looked at the little room, where their mother cooked all the meals on an open fire. The room was so small, it was difficult for all six of them to be together.

Leaving Adam and Mary inside, all the others went into the garden. Adam and Mary stood gazing at the cast-iron fireplace. From the mantleshelf, Adam picked up an Oxo tin box. Inside there were several sixpences, four pennies and a couple of shillings. They talked about how Adam would bring the money he earned as a boy and would give it all to his mother. Celia would smile and give him a small amount back, which went into the tin box. Mary remembered always wanting to count it. They both got quiet emotional. Mary opened her purse, took out a twenty-dollar note and put it in the box. They dried their eyes and went outside to join the others.

They all had lunch in the Navigation, then drove home.

Chapter Ninety-four

It was the millennium year, 2000. Martyn, now fifty years old, and his wife, Ann, had been living in the house at Wrightington ever since he had received that phone call from his mother eight years ago with the terrible news that his father had suffered a massive heart attack. He had been rushed to Reading Heart Centre and was in intensive care. Martyn recalled how he and Ann drove down at high speed to Henley. Despite getting there in record time, sadly it was too late. His father had passed away without regaining consciousness. Martyn insisted that his mother came back to Wrightington. Spending time with her children, and grandchildren helped, as did the fact that she could still drive and take May, her sister-in-law, out shopping. All this kept her active and occasionally she would go down to Sagamore with members of the family.

Adam had left certain clauses in his will but had treated all the family very fairly. Martyn would become the managing director of Roberts enterprises. Gary would be a director, and although Carole had her own business, she also would have her place on the board. Rose would still have her yearly income of fifty thousand pounds, and retain the ownership of Sagamore. It was also stated that Sagamore must never be sold but passed on to the family.

Martyn always had visions of improving the business. He had great initiative, and was a natural leader. The last few years he had expanded at every opportunity. He had been thinking for some time of having a lasting memorial to his father, so he made up his mind to meet with his brother and sister. After throwing ideas around, it was decided that the memorial would be in Lancaster, near the canal where he was born. The marina would now be registered as the Adam Roberts Marina.

Martyn, his sister and their brother Gary, after careful thought unanimously agreed to build a new footbridge over the stretch of canal near the marina. This would replace the old wooden bridge that Adam and his sister Mary used almost daily to cross the canal on their way to school. It would be known as the Mary Rose Bridge.

It was almost a year later and Martyn had got permission from the council in Gateley, so he had commissioned the engineers Wilcock & Keres of Preston to build and erect it. The work had been kept a secret from his mother and Aunt Mary to coincide with Aunt Mary's and Uncle Tim's visit. He had arranged for the opening to be on the 25 July 2001. Martyn had taken them up to Lancaster to see the new big sign to the entrance of the marina. The weather could not have been kinder: beautiful blue sky and seventy-four degrees. The marina was busy when they arrived. Mary, Tim and Rose were thrilled at the very large new sign which had been put up over the stone entrance. It had two-foot wrought-iron letters, painted gold.

Although it was a very happy day, when Mary and Rose looked up at the sign, they hugged each other; seeing the name 'Adam Roberts', a dear brother and husband, was too much for them. Tim and Martyn consoled them, and Gary invited them for a coffee in the new marina café. Martyn then announced that he wanted them all at the far end of the marina in thirty minutes.

'I have something special to show you,' he said.

He had previously organised a little ceremonial gathering down at the new bridge, for midday. When they got there, the bridge had a blue sheet covering the middle. Thomas Bailey, the manager of the waterways, with several of his staff, were all standing in the middle of the bridge. Martyn led his mother and Aunt Mary over to where several seats had been placed and they all sat down.

By this time a small crowd had gathered, anticipating that something was going to happen. Martyn gave the signal to Thomas, who picked up the microphone and got the attention of everyone.

'Good morning, ladies and gentlemen.'

He went on to describe how this lovely marina not too long before was just wasteland, but now as they could all see was the best recreational facility in the North.

'This was a dream of a young man who was born in the village and at the age of twelve started work on this very stretch of the canal. Throughout his life he created many opportunities for young men all over the country. Today I want you to witness the opening of this footbridge, in memory of that man. The bridge will give easy access to the beautiful countryside and be a lasting memorial to the man that made all this possible.' He then called on Martyn who declared the bridge open by pulling the cord and exposing the name.

Mary Rose Footbridge, in Memory of Adam Roberts.

Tim, and Mary, John and his wife, May, had all retired. They were reasonably healthy despite their age, and kept up an active lifestyle. Rose was always invited when the four of them went on a trip, although she did not like the long-haul flights. Mary suggested that they should all go on a world cruise. Tim and John thought three months was too long. Although Mary, and indeed all the family, could easily afford whatever they wanted, but not one single member of the family had ever experienced flying supersonic. Mary reminded Tim of the lecture that they had attended during their cruise in the Caribbean a few months earlier. It was given by a Captain Dick Routledge who had flown

Concorde for the past ten years. During the last week of the cruise, Mary and Tim got really friendly with the captain, and his charming wife Karen. They had drinks together. Mary discovered that Karen, before getting married, had been a Cunard Line cruise director for twenty years. Before they left the ship they exchanged contact numbers. After further discussions, it was agreed that they would fly Concorde to New York, then join the *Queen Elizabeth II* in San Francisco.

All arrangements taken care of and Martyn, Ann, Carole and Tony all drove down to the Willows to spend a nice evening together. The following morning the limo arrived to take all nine of them to Heathrow airport. The Concorde representative met them and escorted them into the VIP lounge. It would be another hour before boarding time. All the family had a glass of complementary champagne while they waited.

When the time came to board, Martyn and Carole hugged their mother and told her not to worry. The goodbyes over, the stewardess escorted the passengers down the walkway to the waiting Concorde. It looked so sleek and beautiful, just like a big bird. Once aboard and settled in their seats, the anticipation and excitement took over. The captain announce that the flying time to New York would be two hours and fifty-eight minutes, this news was greeted with total amazement from the one hundred passengers. The captain went on to say it would be a little noisy taking off, but once they were clear of London and reached their altitude of 62,000 feet, their speed would be mach 2.2, which was twice the speed of sound, 1,450 miles per hour. They would be able to hear a pin drop. During the short flight, two stewardesses served whatever the passengers required. The menu was equal to any top London restaurants, all served with silverware and china. At the end of the flight every passenger was given a leather toiletry case and a Concorde souvenir pen.

The weather in New York was a little chilly but sunny. Feeling really refreshed after the fantastic flight, they transferred to the British Airways desk and caught their connecting flight to San Francisco. The flight time was six hours. Although not up to the standards of Concorde, it was a enjoyable flight, very smooth, to the delight of Rose.

GJ had to go to the San Francisco office. He had arranged to meet his mother, aunts and uncles in the Four Seasons Hotel where he and Sandra were staying. He had booked three rooms for them, and they would have two days before embarking on the Cunard QE II. The Four Seasons Hotel was one of the finest in San Francisco. It was situated in the Yerba Buena district, not far from the firm's offices.

It was a really good couple of days. John and May had never been to San Francisco and decided to go on a lightning tour of the city and waterfront.

Mary, Tim and Rose were content to relax. Mary told GJ about the Concorde. 'You must use it on your next visit!' Believe me, it is wonderful and so much quicker,' she told her son.

GJ took his mother and Tim to the office. Mary had not seen the new one. When they entered the reception hall, behind the big desk on the wall were pictures of all twenty lawyers who worked there. Mary noticed the portrait of Colin. It bore the inscription, 'Colin Johnson, founder and president of the Johnson & Johnson Law Firm', then under the inscription it read, 'Gary F Johnson, President, 1991'.

Tim looked at his wife, 'You certainly have something to be proud of,' he said.

Mary was thinking to herself, Well, Colin you got your wish: our son did make it.

GJ gave them a quick tour of the numerous offices, then he took them for lunch at the Fisherman's Wharf.

GJ and Sandra went down to see the family safely aboard the *QE II*. They were allowed to go aboard with them. Everyone was impressed with the elegant lines of the interior and the three-tier lobby, with its elegant chandeliers. The first-class cabins all had their own balconies. Mary again thought of the time she had boarded the old *Queen Mary* before the war and sailed to America. How different it would be now. The ship's siren blasted three times indicating that all people aboard not sailing must now disembark. The whole family walked out on to the middle deck. GJ and Sandra wished them all bon voyage, and Mary said she would ring them from every port of call.

As the great liner pulled away, all the passengers waved to their friends and families on the quayside.

Chapter Ninety-five

The next three days were spent cruising, the weather getting warmer every day. The first port of call was Lahaina in Hawaii. After dropping anchor, and awaiting the tenders to take then to the port, they were treated to a magnificent display of whales swimming around the ship. Once ashore, they explored the main street of Lahaina with its array of fine stores and restaurants. They also visited the two museums.

When John spotted a funny-looking tree, he asked, 'Whatever is that?' Mary, taking a little pride in her knowledge, with every confidence, explained. 'That is a banyan tree. As you can see, it drops its roots from the branches, and they become trunks. I would say this is well over a hundred years old.'

Mary omitted to tell them that on her first visit with Colin she had asked the very same question, and he had told her all about them.

Back on board they all enjoyed the deck party. Before arriving in Honolulu, John and Tim went on a tour to the Pearl Harbor memorial, where over a thousand men had died in the 1941 attack. Life onboard was a non-stop party; the Robertses all found out that they were not as young as they thought. Afternoon naps became a way of surviving.

The next port was the beautiful island of Pago Pago, which is the capital of American Samoa. It is eighteen miles long. The harbour is a drowned volcanic crater one mile wide and three miles long. The scenery was breathtaking, and the people were charming.

Life on board was very enjoyable and there were many activities to keep them pleasantly occupied, although the Roberts family went ashore at each port. Fiji is one of the largest islands; the main export is sugar. The island also has a magnificent backdrop of mountains and orchid gardens. They then sailed on to Auckland, New Zealand, the largest city in the country. The harbour was a very impressive sight accommodating hundreds of yachts; it is where the famous American Cup is sometimes held. Another highlight was their tour of the city Christchurch. Of course, they had a tram ride and visited the museum. John and Tim went to watch a sheep-shearing competition; the ladies carried on with their endless shopping.

The next day they were in Wellington, the capital, which of course housed their parliament building and government departments. Two more days cruising and they arrived in Sydney, Australia, cruising into the famous harbour and seeing the Opera House and the Sydney Harbour Bridge. The whole voyage had been a real pick-me-up. This was most evident with Rose; she had smiled more in the last few weeks than she had done for a very long time.

It was time for them to disembark and they all booked into the Waterfront Hotel. It had been some time since Mary and Tim were there last. Mary, Rose and May all made calls to England and reported to their families where they were staying, and assured them that everything was OK. It had been decided that it would be a change to do the journey to Brisbane by car. Having four drivers, the six-hour drive would not be a problem. Tim had been in touch with his daughter Jean and her husband Richard; they were staying at Jean's lodge in Placid Creek.

They made an early start. Tim had hired a people carrier with eight comfortable seats and a large boot. Tim was driving and Mary was pointing out all the places along the coast. They made several stops along the way, which helped to make the long journey quite pleasant.

It was late afternoon when they pulled into Placid Creek, and booked into the one and only hotel. Meg was still behind the desk. When she saw Mary and Tim she rushed forward and gave them a hug.

'Jean told me you were on a cruise but would make a side trip to see her! She talks about you all the time.'

Meg was introduced to the others, and then took them to their rooms. The first thing Tim did was to call Jean and although she was expecting them, she was surprised that they had made such good time.

'I want you all to come here for dinner; it is all arranged,' she said. Tim put Mary on, who had a little chat, then said, 'We will all have a little rest and freshen up. See you both at 7.'

The week in Placid Creek passed very quickly. Tim and Mary were very pleased as they could see that their daughter and son-in-law Richard were very happy. Richard had a big contract in New Zealand, so they had a house there but came to Placid Creek at every opportunity.

Rose, John and May really enjoyed the local trips. It was all new territory to them.

When Richard told Tim that he would be bringing Jean to England next spring, this news seemed to make it much easier for him when it was time to leave. It was now time for the Roberts family to decide which way they would go back home: by sea or fly in stages. After discussing it, they decided to have a couple of weeks in Brisbane, then fly to Singapore, which was a seven-hour flight, and from there sail back to Southampton, England. Rose was not as enthusiastic as the rest about the flying part but decided she would go for it.

The whole trip was a success for the family. It had given them a chance to travel together and see places that from their humble beginnings would never have seemed possible. The memories they had would last a lifetime and indeed they did. Mary Roberts must have been dreaming about all this, dozing in the summer house at Sagamore. It was 15 July 2010. Mary was ninety-four years old.

Martyn had been living at Sagamore for years. Carole and Tony had moved into Wrightington. GJ had maintained and looked after the Willows. All the children looked after Mary. Despite her age she still knew what was going on and loved the family gatherings.

This was such an occasion. Martyn had the *Mary Rose* all ready to take the whole family along the river into Henley. This was always something that his father Adam had always enjoyed. GJ with the help of Martyn, got his mother aboard the *Mary Rose*. They helped her into the big chair near the tiller, which had been specially elevated to give her a better view of the river. All safely aboard, they set of for Henley. GJ thanked his cousin Martyn for letting his mother sit in his father's chair. They both looked at Mary sitting there with a wistful but contented look her face. She was staring at the old tattered captain's cap hanging just inside the hatch, no doubt remembering her brother Adam buying it in Liverpool so long, long, ago.

They made a short stop at the marina in Henley. GJ and Sandra stayed onboard with his mother. All the rest went into the little town and bought several items. An hour or so later they returned, Carole, Mary's eldest niece, with a large bunch of flowers. She never forgot how her aunt Mary had bought her first pony, Bowler. After a slow cruise back to Sagamore, Carole and Sandra went inside and made tea, which every one enjoyed on the terrace.

Mary asked GJ to thank everyone for giving her such a nice day.

'I am feeling a little tired now. I would like to go up to my room.'

Sandra helped her upstairs and got her into bed. GJ came into the room and the three of them chatted for a few minutes, then Sandra kissed her mother-in-law and left GJ with his mother. He sat on the side of the bed and fixed the pillows so she could look out of the window. All the grandchildren were running around on the great lawn with the dogs. Martyn and his brother were admiring the sunflowers, which seemed to get more golden every year.

GJ asked his mother, 'Do you really think there is gold buried?'

'Well, your Uncle Adam knew something. He always said that if it was never disturbed, it would always be a happy place.' She paused. 'Look at that,' she said, pointing to the window. 'If that's not a happy picture, I don't know what is. I wish my dear brother and your father could have seen it.'

GJ held his mother's hand.

'Maybe they are looking at it right now.' He kissed her. 'Have a good night's sleep,' he said, and he walked out of the room.

Mary Ann Roberts Johnson, glanced towards the window one more time, then lay back and closed her eyes for the last time.

Three years later Martyn picked up the phone to a man claiming to be the grandson of Derek Barnett.

'I believe my grandfather and your father did some business during the war. I would like to meet you.'